JOAN AND PETER

JOAN AND PETER

THE STORY OF AN EDUCATION

H.G. WELLS

WILDSIDE PRESS

www.wildsidebooks.com

CONTENTS

JOAN AND PETER

THE STORY OF AN EDUCATION

CHAPTER THE FIRST

PETER'S PARENTAGE

§ 1

EARLY one summer morning in England, in the year 1893 in the reign—which seemed in those days to have been going on for ever and to be likely to go on for evermore—of Queen Victoria, there was born a little boy named Peter. Peter was a novel name then; he was before the great crop of Peters who derived their name from Peter Pan. He was born with some difficulty. His father, who had not been to bed all night, for the trouble of the birth had begun overnight at about nine o'clock, was walking about in the garden in a dewy dawn, thinking the world very dreadful and beautiful, when he first heard Peter cry. Peter, he thought, made a noise like a little frightened hen that something big had caught. . . . Peter's mother had been moaning but now she moaned no more, and Peter's father stood outside and whispered "Oh, God! Oh! Damn them and *damn* them! why don't they *tell* me?"

Then the nurse put her head out of the window; it was a casement window with white roses about it; said "Everything's all right. I'll tell you when to come in," and vanished again.

Peter's father turned about very sharply so that she should not see he was fool enough to weep, and went along the flagged path to the end of the garden, where was the little summer-house that looked over the Weald. But he could not see the Weald because his tears blinded him. All night Peter's father had been thinking what an imperfect

1

husband he had always been and how he had never really
told his wife how much he loved her, and how indeed until
now he had never understood how very much he loved her,
and he had been making good resolutions for the future in
great abundance, in enormous abundance, the most remarkable good resolutions, and one waking nightmare after another had been chasing across his mind nightmares of a
dreadful dark-grey world in which there would be no Dolly,
no Dolly at all anywhere, even if you went out into the
garden and whistled your utmost, and he would be a widower
with only one little lonely child to console him. He could
not imagine any other woman for him but Dolly.

The last trailing vestige of those twilight distresses vanished when presently he saw Dolly looking tired indeed but
pink and healthy, with her hair almost roguishly astray, and
the room full of warm daylight from the dawn-flushed sky,
full of fresh south-west air from the Sussex downs, full of
the sense of invincible life, and young master Peter, very
puckered and ugly and red and pitiful, in a blanket in the
nurse's arms, and Dr. Fremisson smirking behind her, entirely satisfied with himself and the universe and every detail of it.

When Dolly had been kissed and whispered to they gave
Peter to his father to hold.

Peter's father had never understood before that a baby is
an exquisite thing.

§ 2

The parents of Peter were modern young people, and
Peter was no accidental intruder. Their heads were full of
new ideas, new that is in the days when Queen Victoria
seemed immortal and the world settled for ever. They put
Peter in their two sunniest rooms; rarely were the windows
shut; his nursery was white and green, bright with pretty
pictures and never without flowers. It had a cork carpet
and a rug displaying amusing black cats on pink, and he was
weighed carefully first once a week and then once a month
until he was four years old.

His father, whom everybody called Stubbo, came of an old Quaker stock. Quakerism in its beginnings was a very fine and wonderful religion indeed, a real research for the Kingdom of Heaven on earth, a new way of thinking and living, but weaknesses of the mind and spirit brought it back very soon to a commoner texture. The Stubland family was among those which had been most influenced by the evangelical wave of the Wesleyan time. Peter's great-grand-father, old Stubland, the West-of-England cloth manufac-turer, was an emotional person with pietistic inclinations that nearly carried him over at different times to the Ply-mouth Brethren, to the Wesleyan Methodists, and to the Countess of Huntingdon's connexion. Religion was his only social recreation, most other things he held to be sinful, and his surplus energies went all into the business. He had an aptitude for mechanical organization and started the York-shire factory; his son, still more evangelical and still more successful, left a business worth well over two hundred thou-sand pounds among thirteen children, of whom Peter's father was the youngest. "Stublands" became a limited company with uncles Rigby and John as directors, and the rest of the family was let loose, each one with a nice little secure six hundred a year or thereabouts from Stubland de-bentures and Stubland ordinary shares, to do what it liked in the world.

It wasn't, of course, told that it could do what it liked in the world. That it found out for itself—in the teeth of much early teaching to the contrary. That early teaching had been predominantly prohibitive, there had been no end of "thou shalt not" and very little of "thou shalt," an irk-some teaching for young people destined to leisure. Man-kind was presented waiting about for the Judgment Day, with Satan as busy as a pickpocket in a crowd. Also he offered roundabouts and cocoanut-shies. . . . This family doctrine tallied so little with the manifest circumstances and natural activity of the young Stublands that it just fell off their young minds. The keynote of Stubbo's upbringing had been a persistent unanswered "Why *not?*" to all the things he was told not to do. "Why *not* dance? Why *not* go to theatres and music-halls? Why *not* make love? Why

not read and quote this exciting new poetry of Swinburne's?'' . . .

The early 'nineties were a period of careless diastole in
British affairs. There seemed to be enough and to spare for
every one, given only a little generosity. Peace dwelt on the
earth for ever. It was difficult to prove the proprietorship
of Satan in the roundabouts and the cocoanut-shies. There
was a general belief that one's parents and grandparents had
taken life far too grimly and suspiciously, a belief which,
indeed, took possession of Stubbo before he was in trousers.

His emancipation was greatly aided by his elder sister
Phyllis, a girl with an abnormal sense of humour. It was
Phyllis who brightened the Sunday afternoons, when she and
her sister Phœbe and her brothers were supposed to be com-
mitting passages of scripture to memory in the attic, by the
invention of increasingly irreligious Limericks. Phœbe
would sometimes be dreadfully shocked and sometimes join
in with great vigour and glory. Phyllis was also an artist
in misquotation. She began by taking a facetious view of
the ark and Jonah's whale, and as her courage grew she
went on to the Resurrection. She had a genius for asking
seemingly respectful but really destructive questions about
religious matters, that made her parents shy of instruction.
The Stubland parents had learnt their faith with more reverence than intelligence from *their* parents, who had had it in
a similar spirit from their parents, who had had it from their
parents; so that nobody had looked into it closely for some
generations, and something vital had evaporated unsuspected. It had evaporated so completely that when Peter's
father and Peter's aunts and uncles came in their turn as
children to examine the precious casket, they not only perceived that there was nothing in it, but they could very readily jump to the rash conclusion that there never had been
anything in it. It seemed just an odd blend of empty
resonant phrases and comical and sometimes slightly improper stories, that lent themselves very pleasantly to facetious illustration.

Stubbo, as he grew up under these circumstances, had not
so much taken on the burthen of life as thrown it off. He
decided he would not go into business—business struck him

as a purely avaricious occupation—and after a pleasant year at Cambridge he became quite clear that the need of the world and his temperament was Art. The world was not beautiful enough. This was more particularly true of the human contribution. So he went into Art to make the world more beautiful, and came up to London to study and to wear a highly decorative blue linen blouse in private and to collect posters—people then were just beginning to collect posters.

From the last stage of Quakerism to the last extremity of decoration is but a step. Quite an important section of the art world in Britain owes itself to the Quakers and Plymouth Brethren, and to the drab and grey disposition of the sterner evangelicals. It is as if that elect strain in the race had shut its eyes for a generation or so, merely in order to open them again and see brighter. The reaction of the revolting generation has always been toward colour; the pyrotechnic display of the Omega workshops in London is but the last violent outbreak of the Quaker spirit. Young Stubland, a quarter of a century before the Omega enterprise, was already slaking a thirst for chromatic richness behind the lead of William Morris and the Pre-Raphaelites. It took a year or so and several teachers and much friendly frankness to persuade him he could neither draw nor paint, and then he relapsed into decoration and craftsmanship. He beat out copper into great weals of pattern and he bound books grossly. He spent some time upon lettering, and learnt how to make the simplest inscription beautifully illegible. He decided to be an architect. In the meantime he made the acquaintance of a large circle of artistic and literary people, became a Fabian socialist, abandoned Stubland tweeds for fluffy artistically dyed garments, bicycled about a lot—those were the early days of the bicycle, before the automobile robbed it of its glory—talked endlessly, and had a very good time. He met his wife and married her, and he built his own house as a sample of what he could do as an architect.

It was, with one exception, the only house he ever built. It was quite original in design and almost indistinguishable from the houses of a round dozen contemporaries of Mr. Charles Voysey. It was a little low-browed, white house, with an enormous and very expensive roof of green slates; it had wide, low mullioned casement windows, its rooms were eight feet high and its doors five foot seven, and all about it were enormous buttresses fit to sustain a castle. It had sun-traps and verandahs and a terrace, and it snuggled into the ruddy hillside and stared fatly out across the Weald from beyond Limpsfield, and it was quite a jolly little house to live in when you had learnt to be shorter than five feet seven inches and to dodge the low bits of ceiling and the beam over the ingle-nook.

And therein, to crown the work of the builder, Peter was born.

§ 3

Peter's mother came from quite a different strand in the complicated web of British life. Her "people"—she was brought up to call them that—were county people, but old-fashioned and prolific, and her father had been the sixth son of a third son and very lucky to get a living. He was the Vicar of Long Downport and an early widower; his two sons had gone to Oxford with scholarships, and Dolly had stayed at home, a leggy, dark-eyed girl with a sceptical manner, much given to reading history. One of her brothers passed from Oxford into the higher division of the Civil Service and went to India; the other took to scornful, reactionary journalism, dramatic criticism, musical comedy lyrics, parody, and drink—which indeed is almost a necessity if a man is to stick to reactionary journalism; this story will presently inherit Joan from him; she had a galaxy of cousins who were parsons, missionaries, schoolmasters, and soldiers; one was an explorer; not one was in business. Her father was a bookish inattentive man who had just missed a fellowship because of a general discursiveness; if he could have afforded it he would have been very liberal indeed in his theology; and, like grains of pepper amidst milder nourishment, there were all sorts of sceptical books about the house: Renan's *Life of Christ*, Strauss's *Life of Christ*, Gibbon, various eighteenth century memoirs, Huxley's Essays, much Victor Hugo, and a "collected" Shelley, books that his daughter read with a resolute frown, sitting for the most part with one leg tucked up under her in the chair, her chin on her fists, and her elbows on either side of the volume undergoing assimilation.

Her reading was historical, and her tendency romantic. Her private daydream through some years of girlhood was that she was Cæsar's wife. She was present at all his battles, and sometimes, when he had had another of his never altogether fatal wounds, she led the army. Also, which was a happy thought, she stabbed Brutus first, and so her Cæsar, contrariwise to history, reigned happily with her for many, many years. She would go to sleep of a night dreaming of Mr. and Mrs. Imperator driving in triumph through the gates of Rome after some little warlike jaunt. Sometimes she drove. And also they came to Britain to drive out the Picts and Scots, and were quartered with her father in Long Downport, conquering Picts, Scots, Danes, and the most terrific anachronisms with an equal stoutness and courage. The private title she bestowed upon herself (and never told to any human being) was "The Imperatrix."

As she grew up she became desirous of more freedom and education. After much argument with her father she came up to an aunt in London, and went to study science in the Huxley days as a free student at the Royal College of Science. She saw her future husband at an art students' soirée, he looked tall and bright and masterful; he had a fine profile, and his blond hair poured nobly off his forehead; she did not dream that Peter's impatience for incarnation put ideas into her head, she forgot her duty to Cæsar and imagined a devotion to art and beauty. They made a pretty couple, and she married amidst universal approval—after a slight dispute whether it was to be a religious or a civil marriage. She was married in her father's church.

In the excitement of meeting, appreciating and marrying Stubbo, she forgot that she had had a great pity and tenderness and admiration for her shy and impulsive cousin, Oswald Sydenham, with the glass eye and cruelly scarred face, who had won the V.C. before he was twenty at the bombardment of Alexandria, and who had since done the most remarkable things in Nyasaland. It had been quite typical

heroism that had won him the V.C.   He had thrown a shell
overboard, and it had burst in the air as he threw it and
pulped one side of his face.   But when she married, she had
temporarily forgotten Cousin Oswald.   She was just carried
away by Arthur Stubland's profile, and the wave in his hair,
and—life.

Arthur was Stubbo's Christian name because he had been
born under the spell of "The Idylls of the King."

Afterwards when Oswald came home again, she thought
the good side of his face, the side of his face that hadn't been
so seriously damaged by the Egyptian shell, looked at her
rather queerly.   But the wounded side remained a Sphinx-
like mask.

"Congratulations!" said Oswald, fumbling with the word.
"Congratulations!   I hope you'll be happy, Dolly." . . .

She was far gone in rationalism before she met Arthur,
and he completed her emancipation.   Their ideas ran closely
together.   They projected some years of travel before they
settled down.   He wanted to see mediaeval Italy "thoroughly," and she longed for Imperial Rome.   They took just
a couple of rooms in South Kensington and spent all the rest
of their income in long stretches of holiday.   They honey-
mooned in pleasant inns in South Germany; they did some
climbing in the Tyrol and the Dolomites—she had a good
head—they had a summer holiday on the Adriatic coast, and
she learnt to swim and dive well, and they did one long knapsack tramp round and along the Swiss Italian frontier and
then another through the Apennines to Florence.

It was a perfectly lovely time.   Everything was bright
and happy, and they got on wonderfully together, except
that——   There was a shadow for her.   She found it difficult to say exactly what the shadow was, and it is still more
difficult for the historian to define it.   She dismissed the
idea that it had anything to do with Cousin Oswald's one
reproachful eye.   She sometimes had a faint suspicion that
it was her jilted Cæsar asking for at least a Rubicon to
cross, but it is doubtful if she ever had any suspicion of
Peter, waiting outside the doors of life.   Yet the feeling of
something forgotten, of something left out, grew throughout
those sunny days.   It was in some sweet meadows high up

on the great hill above Fiesole, that she tried to tell Arthur of this vexatious feeling of deficiency.

Manifestly she puzzled him, which was not to be wondered at since the feeling puzzled her. But it also had a queer effect of irritating him.

"Arthur, if you always say I don't love you," she said, "when I tell you anything, then how can I tell you anything at all?"

"Aren't we having the loveliest times?" he asked.

"Yes," she said without complete conviction. "It isn't that."

"You admit you love me. You admit you're having the loveliest time!"

She sat up with her elbows on her knees and her knuckles pressing her round, firm chin.

"It's just all one holiday," she said.

"I did some work last month."

He had planned three impossible houses and made a most amusing cardboard model of one of them. She disregarded this plea.

"When we came up here people were working in the fields. Even that pretty little girl among the bushes was looking after sheep."

"By Jove! I wish I could paint her—and those Holman Hunt-faced sheep of hers. It's tantalizing to be able to see —and yet not to have the—the expressive gift. . . ."

"Things are going on now, Arthur. Down there in the valley along that white road, people are going and coming. . . . There is a busy little train now. . . . Things are happening. Things are going to happen. And the work that goes on! The hard work! Today—there are thousands and thousands of men in mines. Out of this sunshine. . . ."

There was an interval. Arthur rolled over on his face to look at the minute railway and road and river bed far below at the bottom of a deep lake of pellucid blue air.

"I don't agree with you," he said at last.

"Too much is happening," he said. "Noisy, vulgar fuss. Commercialism, competition, factory production. Does it make people happy? Look at that horrid little railway disturbing all this beautiful simple Tuscan life. . . ."

Another long pause.

She made a further step. "But if something beautiful is being destroyed," she tried, "we ought not to be here."

That also took a little time to soak in.

Then he stirred impatiently.

"Don't we," he asked, "protest? By the mere act of living our own lives? Don't I, in my small way, try to do my share in the Restoration of Craftsmanship? Aren't people of our sort doing something—something a little too unpretending to be obvious—to develop the conception of a fairer and better, a less hurried, less greedy life?"

He raised an appealing face to her.

She sat with knitted brows. She did not assent, but it was difficult to argue her disaccord.

He took advantage of her pause.

"Confess," he said, "you would like to have me a business manager—of some big concern. Or a politician. You want me to be in the scrimmage. No!—lording it over the scrimmage. The real things aren't *done* like that, Dolly. The real things aren't done like that!"

She put her next thought out in its stark simplicity.

"Are we doing any real thing in the world at all?"

He did not answer for some seconds.

Then he astonished her by losing his temper. It was exactly as if her question had probed down to some secret soreness deep within him. "Oh, *damn!*" he shouted. "And on this lovely morning! It's too bad of you, Dolly!" It was as if he had bit upon a tender tooth. Perhaps a fragment of the stopping had come out of his Nonconformist conscience.

He knelt up and stared at her. "You don't love *this,* anyhow—whether you love me or not."

He tried to alter his tone from a note of sheer quarrelsomeness to badinage. "You Blue Conscience, you! You Gnawing Question! Are we doing anything real at all, you say. Is no one, then, to stand up and meet the sunlight for its own sake, when God sends it to us? No! You can't unsay it now." (Though she was not unsaying it. She was only trying for some more acceptable way of saying it over again.) "My day is spoilt! You've stuck a fever into me!"

He looked about him. He wanted some vivid gesture. "Oh, come on!" he cried.

He sprang up. He gesticulated over her. He banished the view with a sweep of rejection. "Let us go back to the inn. Let us take our traps back to stuffy old Florence. Let us see three churches and two picture-galleries before sunset! And take our tickets for home. We aren't rushing and we ought to rush. Life is rush. This holiday has lasted too long, Dolly."

> " 'Life is real! Life is earnest!'
> Simple joys are not its goal."

"Own, my Dolly! If only this afternoon we could find some solid serious lecture down there! Or an election. You'd love an election. . . . And anyhow, it's nearly lunch time."

She knelt, took his hand, and stood up.

"You mock," she said. "But you know that what I want to say—isn't that. . . ."

§ 4

He did know. But all the way back to England he was a man with an irritating dart sticking in his mind. And the discussion she had released that day worried him for months.

He wanted it to be clear that their lives were on a very high level indeed. No mere idlers were they. Hitherto he said they had been keeping honeymoon, but that was only before they began life in earnest. Now they were really going to begin. They were going to take hold of life.

House and Peter followed quite logically upon that.

How easy was life in those days—at least, for countless thousands of independent people! It was the age of freedom—for the independent. They went where they listed; the world was full of good hotels, and every country had its Baedeker well up to date. Every cultivated home had its little corner of weather-worn guide books, a nest of memories, an *Orario*, an *Indicateur*, or a *Continental Bradshaw*. The happy multitude of the free travelled out to beautiful places

and returned to comfortable homes.   The chief anxiety in
life was to get good servants—and there were plenty of good
servants.   Politics went on, at home and abroad, a traditional
game between the Ins and Outs.   The world was like a spinning top that seems to be quite still and stable. . . . Yet
youth was apt to feel as Dolly felt, that there was something
lacking.

Arthur was quite ready to fall in with this idea that something was lacking.   He was inclined to think that one got to
the root of it by recognizing that there was not enough
Craftsmanship and too much cheap material, too much machine production, and, more especially, too much aniline dye.
He was particularly strong against aniline dyes.   All Britain was strong against aniline dyes,—and so that trade went
to Germany.   He reached socialism by way of æsthetic criticism.   Individual competition was making the world hideous.
It was destroying individuality.   What the world needed
was a non-competitive communism for the collective discouragement of machinery.   (Meanwhile he bought a bicycle.)
He decided that his modest six hundred a year was all that
he and Dolly needed to live upon; he would never work for
money—that would be ''sordid''—but for the joy of work,
and on his income they would lead a simple working-man's
existence, free from the vulgarities of competition, politics
and commercialism.

Dolly was fascinated, delighted, terrified and assuaged by
Peter, and Peter and a simple house free also from the
vulgarities of modern mechanism kept her so busy with
only one servant to help her, that it was only in odd times,
in the late evening when the sky grew solemn or after some
book had stirred her mind, that she recalled that once oppressive feeling of something wanting, something that was still
wanting. . . .

CHAPTER THE SECOND

STUBLANDS IN COUNCIL

§ 1

BUT although Dolly did not pursue her husband with
any sustained criticism, he seemed now to feel always
that her attitude was critical and needed an answer.
The feeling made him something of a thinker and something
of a talker. Sometimes the thinker was uppermost, and then
he would sit silent and rather in profile (his profile, it has
already been stated, was a good one, and much enhanced by
a romantic bang of warm golden hair that hung down over
one eye), very picturesque in his beautiful blue linen blouse,
listening to whatever was said; and sometimes he would turn
upon the company and talk with a sort of experimental dog-
matism, as is the way with men a little insecure in their
convictions, but quite good talk. He would talk of education, and work, and Peter, and of love and beauty, and the
finer purposes of life, and things like that.

A lot of talk came the way of Peter's father.

Along the Limpsfield ridge and away east and west and
north, there was a scattered community of congenial intel-
lectuals. It spread along the ridge beyond Dorking, and
resumed again at Haslemere and Hindhead, where Grant
Allen and Richard Le Gallienne were established. They
were mostly people of the same detached and independent
class as the Stublands; they were the children of careful
people who had created considerable businesses, or the children of the more successful of middle Victorian celebrities,
or dons, or writers themselves, or they came from Hampstead, which was in those days a nest of considerable people's
children, inheritors of reputations and writers of memoirs, an
hour's 'bus drive from London and outside the cab radius.

A thin flavour of Hampstead spread out, indeed, over all Surrey. Some of these newcomers lived in old adapted cottages; some of them had built little houses after the fashion of the Stublands; some had got into the real old houses that already existed. There was much Sunday walking and "dropping in" and long evenings and suppers. Safety bicycles were coming into use and greatly increasing intercourse. And there was a coming and going of Stubland aunts and uncles and of Sydenhams and Dolly's "people." Nearly all were youngish folk; it was a new generation and a new sort of population for the countryside. They were dotted among the farms and the estates and preserves and "places" of the old county family pattern. The "county" wondered a little at them, kept busy with horse and dog and gun, and, except for an occasional stiff call, left them alone. The church lamented their neglected Sabbaths. The doctors were not unfriendly.

One of the frequent visitors, indeed, at The Ingle-Nook— that was the name of Peter's birthplace—was Doctor Fremisson, the local general practitioner. He was a man, he said, who liked "Ideas." The aborigines lacked Ideas, it seemed; but Stubland was a continual feast of them. The doctor's diagnosis of the difference between these new English and the older English of the country rested entirely on the presence or absence of Ideas. But there he was wrong. The established people were people of fixed ideas; the immigrants had abandoned fixed ideas for discussion. So far from their having no ideas, those occasional callers who came dropping in so soon as the Stublands were settled in The Ingle-Nook before Peter was born, struck the Stublands as having ideas like monstrous and insurmountable cliffs. To fling your own ideas at them was like trying to lob stones into Zermatt from Macugnana.

One day when Mrs. Darcy, old Lady Darcy's daughter-in-law, had driven over, some devil prompted Arthur to shock her. He talked his extremest Fabianism. He would have the government control all railways, land, natural products; nobody should have a wage of less than two pounds a week; the whole country should be administered for the universal benefit; everybody should be educated.

"I'm sure the dear old Queen does all she can," said Mrs. Darcy.

"I'm a democratic republican," said Arthur.

He might as well have called himself a Christadelphian for any idea he conveyed.

Presently, seized by a gust of unreasonable irritation, he went out of the room.

"Mr. Stubland talks," said Mrs. Darcy; *"really——"* She paused. She hesitated. She spoke with a little disarming titter lest what she said should seem too dreadful. "He says such things. I really believe he's more than half a Liberal. *There!* You mustn't mind what I say, Mrs. Stubland. . . ."

Dolly, by virtue of her vicarage training, understood these people better than Peter's father. She had read herself out of the great Anglican culture, but she remembered things from the inside. She was still in close touch with numerous relations who were quite completely inside. Before the little green gate had clicked behind their departing backs, Arthur would protest to her and heaven that these visitors were impossible, that such visitors could not be, they were phantoms or bad practical jokes, undergraduates dressed up to pull his leg.

"They know nothing," he said.

"They know all sorts of things you don't know," she corrected.

"What *do* they know? There isn't a topic one can start on which they are not just blank."

"You start the wrong topics. They can tell you all sorts of things about the dear Queen's grandchildren. They know things about horses. And about regiments and barracks. Tell me, Arthur, how is the charming young Prince of Bulgaria, who is just getting married, related to the late Prince Consort."

"Damn their Royal Marriages!"

"If you say that, then they have an equal right to say, 'damn your Wildes and Beardsleys and William Morrises and Swinburnes.'"

"They read nothing."

"They read Mrs. Henry Wood. They read lots of authors

you have never heard of, *nice* authors.   They read so many
of them that for the most part they forget their names.
The bold ones read Ouida—who isn't half bad.   They read
every scrap they can find about the marriage of the Princess
Marie to the Crown Prince of Roumania.   Mrs. Bagshot-
Fawcett talked about it yesterday.   It seems he's really a
rarer and better sort of Hohenzollern than the young German Emperor, our sailor grandson that is.   She isn't very
clear about it, but she seems to think that the Prince of
Hohenzollern ought rightfully to be German Emperor."

"Oh, what *rot!*"

"But perhaps she's right.   How do you know?   *I* don't.
She takes an almost voluptuous delight in the two marriage
ceremonies.   You know, I suppose, dear, that there were two
ceremonies, a Protestant one and a Catholic one, because the
Roumanian Hohenzollerns are Catholic Hohenzollerns.   Of
course, the dear princess would become a Catholic——"

"Oh, *don't!*" cried Peter's father; "don't!"

"I had to listen to three-quarters of an hour of it yesterday.   Such a happy and convenient occurrence, the princess's conversion, but—archly—of course, my dear, I suppose
there's sometimes just a little *persuasion* in these cases."

"Dolly, you go too far!"

"But that isn't, of course, the great interest just at present.   The great interest just at present is George and May.
You know they're going to be married."

Arthur lifted a protesting profile.   "My dear!   *Who* is
May?" he tenored.

"Affected ignorance!   She is the Princess May who was
engaged to the late Duke of Clarence, the Princess Mary of
Teck.   And now he's dead, she's going to marry the Duke of
York.   Surely you understand about that.   He is your
Future Sovereign.   Mrs. Bagshot-Fawcett gets positively
lush about him.   It was George she always lurved, Mrs. Bagshot-Fawcett says, but she accepted his brother for Reasons
of State.   So after all it's rather nice and romantic that the
elder brother——"

Arthur roared and tore his hair and walked up and down
the low room.   "What are these people to me?" he shouted.
"What are these people to me?"

"But there is twenty times as much about that sort of thing in the papers as there is about *our* sort of things.''

There was no disputing it.

"We're in a foreign country,'' cried Arthur, going off at a tangent. "We're in a foreign country. We English are a subject people. . . . Talk of Home Rule for Ireland! . . . Why are there no *English* Nationalists? One of these days I will hoist the cross of St. George outside this cottage. But I doubt if any one on this countryside will know it for the English flag.''

§ 2

Whatever is seems right, and it is only now, after five and twenty years of change, that we do begin to see as a remarkable thing the detached life that great masses of the English were leading beneath the canopy of the Hanoverian monarchy. For in those days the court thought in German; Teutonized Anglicans, sentimental, materialistic and resolutely "loyal,'' dominated society; Gladstone was notoriously disliked by them for his anti-German policy and his Irish and Russian sympathies, and the old Queen's selection of bishops guided feeling in the way it ought to go. But there was a leakage none the less. More and more people were drifting out of relationship to church and state, exactly as Peter's parents had drifted out. The Court dominated, but it did not dominate intelligently; it controlled the church to no effect, its influence upon universities and schools and art and literature was merely deadening; it responded to flattery but it failed to direct; it was the court of an alien-spirited old lady, making much of the pathos of her widowhood and trading still on the gallantry and generosity that had welcomed her as a "girl queen.'' The real England separated itself more and more from that superficial England of the genteel that looked to Osborne and Balmoral. To the real England, dissentient England, court taste was a joke, court art was a scandal; of English literature and science notoriously the court knew nothing. In the huge pacific industrial individualism of Great Britain it did not seem a serious matter that the army and navy and the Indian administra-

tion were orientated to the court. Peter's parents and the
large class of detached people to which they belonged, were
out of politics, out of the system, scornful, or facetious and
aloof. Just as they were out of religion. These things did
not concern them.

The great form of the empire contained these indifferents,
the great roof of church and state hung over them. Royal
visits, diplomatic exchanges and the like passed to and fro,
alien, uninteresting proceedings; Heligoland was given to
the young Emperor William the Second by Lord Salisbury,
the old Queen's favourite prime minister, English politicians
jostled the French in Africa as roughly as possible to "larn
them to be" republicans, and resisted the Home Rule aspira-
tions and the ill-concealed republicanism of the "Keltic
fringe"; one's Anglican neighbours of the "ruling class"
went off to rule India and the empire with manners that
would have maddened Job; they stood for Parliament and
played the game of politics upon factitious issues. Sir
Charles Dilke, the last of the English Republicans, and
Charles Stewart Parnell, the uncrowned King of Ireland,
had both been extinguished by opportune divorce cases.
(Liberal opinion, it was felt, must choose between the private and the public life. You could not have it both ways.)
It did not seem to be a state of affairs to make a fuss about.
The general life went on comfortably enough. We built our
pretty rough-cast houses, taught Shirley poppies to spring
artlessly between the paving-stones in our garden paths, be-
got the happy children who were to grow up under that roof
of a dynastic system that was never going to fall in. (Because it never had fallen in.)

Never before had nurseries been so pretty as they were in
that glowing pause at the end of the nineteenth century.

Peter's nursery was a perfect room in which to hatch the
soul of a little boy. Its walls were done in a warm cream-
coloured paint, and upon them Peter's father had put the
most lovely pattern of trotting and jumping horses and dancing cats and dogs and leaping lambs, a carnival of beasts.
He had copied these figures from books, enlarging them as he
did so; he had cut them out in paper, stuck them on the wall,
and then flicked bright blue paint at them until they were all

outlined in a penumbra of stippled blue. Then he unpinned
the paper and took it on to another part of the wall and so
made his pattern. There was a big brass fireguard in Peter's
nursery that hooked on to the jambs of the fireplace, and all
the tables had smoothly rounded corners against the days
when Peter would run about. The floor was of cork carpet
on which Peter would put his toys, and there was a crimson
hearthrug on which Peter was destined to crawl. And a
number of stuffed dogs and elephants, whose bead eyes had
been carefully removed by Dolly and replaced with eyes of
black cloth that Peter would be less likely to worry off and
swallow, awaited his maturing clutch. (But there were no
Teddy Bears yet; Teddy Bears had still to come into the
world. America had still to discover the charm of its
Teddy.) There were scales in Peter's nursery to weigh
Peter every week, and tables to show how much he ought to
weigh and when one should begin to feel anxious. There
was nothing casual about the early years of Peter.

Peter began well, a remarkably fine child, Dr. Fremisson
said, of nine pounds. Although he was born in warm summer weather we never went back upon that. He favoured
his mother perhaps more than an impartial child should, but
that was at any rate a source of satisfaction to Cousin Oswald
(of the artificial eye).

Cousin Oswald was doing his best to behave nicely and
persuade himself that all this show had been got up by
Dolly and was Dolly's show—and that Arthur just happened to be about.

"Look at him," said Cousin Oswald as Peter regarded the
world with unwinking intelligence from behind an appreciated bottle; "the Luck of him. He's the Heir of the Ages.
Look at this room and this house and every one about him."

Dolly remarked foolishly that Peter was a "nittle darum.
'E dizzerves-i-tall. Nevything."

"The very sunshine on the wall looks as though it had
been got for him specially," said Cousin Oswald.

"It *was* got for him specially," said Dolly, with a light of
amusement in her eyes that reminded him of former times.

This visit was a great occasion. It was the first time
Cousin Oswald had seen either Arthur or Peter. Almost

directly after he had learnt about Dolly's engagement and jerked out his congratulations, he had cut short his holiday in England and gone back to Central Africa. Now he was in England again, looked baked and hard, and his hair, which had always been stubby, more stubby than ever. The scarred half of him had lost its harsh redness and become brown. He was staying with his aunt, Dolly's second cousin by marriage, Lady Charlotte Sydenham, not ten miles away towards Tonbridge, and he took to bicycling over to The Ingle-Nook every other day or so and gossiping.

"These bicycles," he said, "are most useful things. Wonderful things. As soon as they get cheap—bound to get cheap—they will play a wonderful part in Central Africa."

"But there are no roads in Central Africa!" said Arthur.

"Better. Foot tracks padded by bare feet for generations. You could ride for hundreds of miles without dismounting. . . ."

"Compared with our little black babies," said Cousin Oswald, "Peter seems immobile. He's like a baby on a lotus flower meditating existence. Those others are like young black indiarubber kittens—all acrawl. But then they've got to look sharp and run for themselves as soon as possible, and he hasn't. . . . Things happen there."

"I wonder," said Arthur in his lifting tenor, "how far all this opening up of Africa to civilization and gin and Bibles is justifiable."

The one living eye glared at him. "It isn't exactly like that," said Oswald stiffly, and offered no occasion for further controversy at the moment.

The conversation hung for a little while. Dolly wanted to say to her cousin: "He isn't thinking of you. It's just his way of generalizing about things. . . ."

"Anyhow this young man has a tremendous future," said Oswald, going back to the original topic. "Think of what lies before him. Never has the world been so safe and settled—most of it that is—as it is now. I suppose really the world's hardly begun to *touch* education. In this house everything seems educational—pictures, toys, everything. When one sees how small niggers can be moulded and changed even in a missionary school, it makes one think. I wish I knew more about education.   I lie awake at nights thinking of the man I might be, if I knew all I don't know, and of all I could do if I did.   And it's the same with others.   Every one who seems worth anything seems regretting his education wasn't better.   Hitherto of course there's always been wars, interruptions, religious rows; the world's been confused and poor, a thorough muddle; there's never been a real planned education for people.   Just scraps and hints. But we're changing all that.   Here's a big safe world at last.   No wars in Europe since '71 and no likelihood in our time of any more big wars.   Things settle down.   And *he* comes in for it all.''

''I hope all this settling down won't make the world too monotonous,'' said Arthur.

''You artists and writers have got to see to that.   No, I don't see it getting monotonous.   There's always differences of climate and colour.   Temperament.   All sorts of differences.''

''And Nature,'' said Arthur profoundly.   ''Old Mother Nature.''

''Have you christened Peter yet?'' Oswald asked abruptly.

''He's not going to be christened,'' said Dolly.   ''Not until he asks to be.   We've just registered him.   He's a registered baby.''

''So he won't have two godfathers and a godmother to be damned for him.''

''We've weighed the risk,'' said Arthur.

''He might have a godfather just—*pour rire*,'' said Oswald.

''That's different,'' Dolly encouraged promptly.   ''We must get him one.''

''I'd like to be Peter's godfather,'' said Oswald.

''I will deny him no advantage,'' said Arthur.   ''The ceremony—— The ceremony shall be a simple one.   Godfather, Peter; Peter, godfather.   Peter, my son, salute your godfather.''

Oswald seemed trying to remember a formula.   ''I promise and vow three things in his name; first a beautiful mug; secondly that he shall be duly instructed in chemistry, biology, mathematics, the French and German tongues and

all that sort of thing; and thirdly, that—what is thirdly?
That he shall renounce the devil and all his works. But
there isn't a devil nowadays.''

Peter having consumed his bottle to the dregs and dreamt
over it for a space, now thrust it from him and turning towards Oswald, regurgitated—but within the limits of nursery good manners. Then he smiled a toothless, slightly
derisive smile.

''Intelligent 'e is!'' crooned Dolly. ''Unstand evlyfling
'e does. . . .''

§ 3

This conversation about Peter's future, once it had been
started, rambled on for the next three weeks, and then
Oswald very abruptly saw fit to be called away to Africa
again. . . .

Various interlocutors dropped in while that talk was in
progress. Arthur felt his way to his real opinions through
a series of experimental dogmas.

Arthur's disposition was towards an extreme Rousseauism.
It is the tendency of the interrogative class in all settled
communities. He thought that a boy or girl ought to run
wild until twelve and not be bothered by lessons, ought to eat
little else but fruit and nuts, go bareheaded and barefooted.
Why not? Oswald's disposition would have been to oppose
Arthur anyhow, but against these views all his circle of
ideas fought by necessity. If Arthur was Ruskinite and
Morrisite, Oswald was as completely Huxleyite. If Arthur
thought the world perishing for need of Art and Nature,
Oswald stood as strongly for the saving power of Science.
In this matter of bare feet——

''There's thorns, pins, snakes, tetanus,'' reflected Oswald.

''The foot hardens.''

''Only the sole,'' said Oswald. ''And not enough.''

''Shielded from all the corruptions of town and society,''
said Arthur presently.

''There's no such corruptor as that old Mother Nature of

yours. You daren't leave that bottle of milk to her for half an hour but what she turns it sour or poisons it with one of her beastly germs.''

"I never approved of the bottle," said Arthur, bringing a flash of hot resentment into Dolly's eyes. . . .

Oswald regretted his illustration.

"Old Mother Nature is a half-wit," he said. "She's distraught. You overrate the jade. She's thinking of everything at once. All her affairs got into a hopeless mess from the very start. Most of her world is desert with water running to waste. A tropical forest is three-quarters death and decay, and what is alive is either murdering or being murdered. It's only when you come to artificial things, such as a ploughed field, for example, that you get space and health and every blade doing its best.''

"I don't call a ploughed field an artificial thing," said Arthur.

"But it is," said Oswald.

Dr. Fremisson was dragged into this dispute. "A ploughed field," he maintained, "is part of the natural life of man.''

"Like boots and reading.''

"I wouldn't say that," said Dr. Fremisson warily. He had the usual general practitioner's belief that any education whatever is a terrible strain on the young, and he was quite on the side of Rousseau and Arthur in that matter. Moreover, as a result of his professional endeavours he had been forced to a belief that Nature's remedies are the best.

"I'd like to know just what does belong to the natural life of man and what is artificial," said Oswald. "If a ploughed field belongs then a plough belongs. And if a plough belongs a foundry belongs—and a coal mine. And you wouldn't plough in bare feet—not in those Weald Clays down there? You want good stout boots for those. And you'd let your ploughman read at least a calendar? Boots and books come in, you see.''

"You're a perfect lawyer, Mr. Sydenham," said the doctor, and pretended the discussion had become fanciful. . . .

"But you'll not leave him to go unlettered until he is half

grown up!'' said Oswald to Dolly in real distress. ''It's so easy to teach 'em to read early and so hard later. I remember my little brother. . . .''

''I am the mother and I muth,'' said Dolly. ''When Peter displays the slightest interest in the alphabet, the alphabet it shall be.''

Oswald felt reassured. He had a curious confidence that Dolly could be trusted to protect his godchild.

§ 4

One day Aunt Phyllis and Aunt Phœbe came down.

Both sisters participated in the Stubland break back to colour, but while Aunt Phyllis was a wit and her hats a spree Aunt Phœbe was fantastically serious and her hats went beyond a joke. They got their stuffs apparently from the shop of William Morris and Co., they had their dresses built upon Pre-Raphaelite lines, they did their hair plainly and simply but very carelessly, and their hats were noble brimmers or extravagant toques. Their profiles were as fine almost as Arthur's, a type of profile not so suitable for young women as for golden youth. They were bright-eyed and a little convulsive in their movements. Beneath these extravagances and a certain conversational wildness they lived nervously austere lives. They were greatly delighted with Peter, but they did not know what to do with him. Phyllis held him rather better than Phœbe, but Phœbe with her chatelaine amused him rather more than Phyllis.

''How happy a tinker's baby must be,'' said Aunt Phœbe, rattling her trinkets: ''Or a tin-smith's.''

''I begin to see some use in a Hindoo woman's bangles,'' said Aunt Phyllis, ''or in that clatter machine of yours, Phœbe. Every young mother should rattle. Make a note of it, Phœbe dear, for your book. . . .''

''Whatever you do with him, Dolly,'' said Aunt Phœbe, ''teach him anyhow to respect women and treat them as his equals. From the Very First.''

''Meaning votes,'' said Aunt Phyllis. ''Didums *want* give um's mummy a *Vote* den.''

"Never let him touch butcher's meat in any shape or form," said Aunt Phœbe. "Once a human child tastes blood the mischief is done."

"Avoid patriotic songs and symbols," prompted Aunt Phyllis, who had heard these ideas already in the train coming down.

"And never buy him toy soldiers, drums, guns, trumpets. These things soak deeper into the mind than people suppose. They make wickedness domestic. . . . Surround him with beautiful things. Accustom him——"

She winced that Arthur should hear her, but she spoke as one having a duty to perform.

"Accustom him to the nude, Dolly, from his early years. Associate it with innocent amusements. Retrieve the fall. Never let him wear a hat upon his head nor boots upon his feet. As soon tie him up into a papoose. As soon tight-lace. A child's first years should be one long dream of loveliness and spontaneous activity."

But at this point Peter betrayed signs that he found his aunts overstimulating. He released his grip upon the thimble-case of the chatelaine. His face puckered, ridges and waves and puckers of pink fatness ran distractedly over it, and he threw his head back and opened a large square toothless mouth.

"Mary," cried Dolly, and a comfortable presence that had been hovering mistrustfully outside the door ever since the aunts appeared, entered with alacrity and bore Peter protectingly away.

"He must be almost entirely lungs," said Aunt Phœbe, when her voice could be heard through the receding bawl. "Other internal organs no doubt develop later."

"Come out to the stone table under the roses," said Dolly. "We argue there about Peter's upbringing almost every afternoon."

"Argue, I grant you," said Aunt Phœbe, following her hostess and dangling her chatelaine from one hand as if to illustrate her remarks, "but argue rightly."

When Oswald came over in the afternoon he was disposed to regard the two aunts as serious reinforcements to Arthur's educational heresies. Phyllis and Phœbe were a little in-

clined to be shy with him as a strange man, and he and
Arthur did most of the talking, but they made their positions plain by occasional interpolations. Arthur, supported
by their presence, was all for letting Peter grow up a wild
untrammelled child of nature. Oswald became genuinely
distressed.

"But education," he protested, "is as natural to a human
being as nests to birds."

"Then why force it?" said Phyllis with dexterity.

"Even a cat boxes its kittens' ears!"

"A domesticated cat," said Phœbe. "A *civilized* cat."

"But I've seen a wild lioness——"

"Are we to learn how to manage our young from lions and
hyenas!" cried Phœbe.

They were too good for Oswald. He saw Peter already
ruined, a fat, foolish, undisciplined cub.

Dolly with sympathetic amusement watched his distress,
which his living half face betrayed in the oddest contrast to
his left hand calm.

Arthur had been thinking gracefully while his sisters
tackled their adversary. Now he decided to sum up the discussion. His authoritative manner on these occasions was
always slightly irritating to Oswald. Like so many who read
only occasionally and take thought as a special exercise,
Arthur had a fixed persuasion that nobody else ever read or
thought at all. So that he did not so much discuss as
adjudicate.

"Of course," he said, "we have to be reasonable in these
things. For men a certain artificiality is undoubtedly natural. That is, so to speak, the human paradox. But artificiality is the last resort. Instinct is our basis. For the
larger part the boy has just to grow. But We watch his
growth. Education is really watching—keeping the course.
The human error is to do too much, to distrust instinct too
much, to over-teach, over-legislate, over-manage, over-
decorate——"

"No, you *don't*, my gentleman," came the voice of Mary
from the shadow under the old pear tree.

"Now I wonder——" said Arthur, craning his neck to
look over the rose bushes.

"Diddums then," said Mary. "Woun't they lettim put'tt in's mouf? *Oooh!*"

"Trust her instinct," said Dolly, and Arthur was re-strained.

Oswald took advantage of the interruption to take the word from Arthur.

"We joke and sharpen our wits in this sort of talk," he said, "but education, you know, isn't a joke. It might be the greatest power in the world. If I didn't think I was a sort of school-master in Africa. . . . That's the only decent excuse a white man has for going there. . . . I'm getting to be a fanatic about education. Give me the schools of the world and I would make a Millennium in half a century. . . . You don't mean to let Peter drift. You say it, but you can't mean it. Drift is waste. We don't make half of what we *could* make of our children. We don't make a quarter—not a tenth. They could know ever so much more, think ever so much better. We're all at sixes and sevens."

He realized he wasn't good at expressing his ideas. He had intended something very clear and compelling, a sort of ultimatum about Peter.

"I believe in Sir Francis Galton," Aunt Phœbe remarked in his pause; saying with stern resolution things that she felt had to be said. They made her a little breathless, and she fixed her eye on the view until they were said. "Eugenics. It is a new idea. A revival. Plato had it. Men ought to be bred like horses. No marriage or any nonsense of that kind. Just a simple scientific blending of points. Then Everything would be different."

"Almost too different," Arthur reflected. . . .

"When I consider Peter and think of all one could do for him——" said Oswald, still floundering for some clenching way of putting it. . . .

§ 5

One evening Dolly caught her cousin looking at her husband with an expression that stuck in her memory. It was Oswald's habit to sit if he could in such a position that he could rest the obliterated cheek of his face upon a shadowing hand, his fingers on his forehead. Then one saw what a pleasant-faced man he would have been if only he had left that Egyptian shell alone. So he was sitting on this occasion, his elbow on the arm of the settle. His brow was knit, his one eye keen and steady. He was listening to his host discoursing upon the many superiorities of the artisan in the middle ages to his successor of today. And he seemed to be weighing and estimating Arthur with some little difficulty.

Then, as if it was a part of the calculation he was making, he turned to look at Dolly. Their eyes met; for a moment he could not mask himself.

Then he turned to Arthur again with his expression restored to polite interest.

It was the most trivial of incidents, but it stayed, a mental burr.

§ 6

A little accident which happened a few weeks after Oswald's departure put the idea of making a will into Arthur's head. Dolly had wanted to ride a bicycle, but he had some theory that she would not need to ride alone or that it would over-exert her to ride alone, and so he had got a tandem bicycle instead, on which they could ride together. Those were the days when all England echoed to the strains of

> "*Disy, Disy*, tell me your answer true;
> I'm arf *crizy*
> All fer the love of you-oo . . .
>
> Yew'd look sweet
> Upon the seat
> Of-a-bicycle-mide-fer-two."

A wandering thrush of a cockney whistled it on their first expedition. Dolly went out a little resentfully with Arthur's broad back obscuring most of her landscape, and her third ride ended in a destructive spill down Ipinghanger Hill. The bicycle brake was still in a primitive stage in those days; one steadied one's progress down a hill by the art, since lost to mankind again, of "back-pedalling," and Dolly's feet were carried over and thrown off the pedals and the machine got away. Arthur's nerve was a good one. He fought the gathering pace and steered with skill down to the very last bend of that downland descent. The last corner got them. They took the bank and hedge sideways and the crumpled tandem remained on one side of the bank and Arthur and Dolly found themselves torn and sprained but essentially unbroken in a hollow of wet moss and marsh-mallows beyond the hedge.

The sense of adventure helped them through an afternoon of toilsome return. . . .

"But we might both have been killed that time," said Arthur with a certain gusto.

"If we had," said Arthur presently, expanding that idea, "what would have become of Peter?" . . .

They had both made simple wills copied out of *Whitaker's Almanack,* leaving everything to each other; it had not occurred to them before that two young parents who cross glaciers together, go cycling together, travel in the same trains, cross the seas in the same boats, might very easily get into the same smash. In that case the law, it appeared, presumed that the wife, being the weaker vessel, would expire first, and so Uncle Rigby, who had relapsed more and more stuffily into evangelical narrowness since his marriage, would extend a dark protection over Peter's life. "Lucy wouldn't even feed him properly," said Dolly. "She's so close and childlessly inhuman. I can't bear to think of it."

On the other hand, if by any chance Dolly should show a flicker of life after the extinction of Arthur, Peter and all his possessions would fall under the hand of Dolly's shady brother, the failure of the family, a being of incalculable misdemeanours, a gross, white-faced literary man, an artist in parody (itself a vice), who smelt of tobacco always, and already at thirty-eight, it was but too evident, preferred port and old brandy to his self-respect.

"We ought to remake our wills and each appoint the same guardian," said Arthur.

It was not very easy to find the perfect guardian.

Then as Arthur sat at lunch one day the sunshine made a glory of the little silver tankard that adorned the Welsh dresser at the end of the room.

"Dolly," he said, "old Oswald would like this job."

She'd known that by instinct from the first, but she had never expected Arthur to discover it.

"He's got a sort of fancy for Peter," he said.

"I think we could trust him," said Dolly temperately.

"Poor old Oswald," said Arthur; "he's a tragic figure. That mask of his cuts him off from so much. He idolizes you and Peter, Dolly. You don't suspect it, but he does. He's our man."

CHAPTER THE THIRD

ARTHUR OR OSWALD?

§ 1

DESTINY is at times a slashing sculptor. At first Destiny seemed to have intended Oswald Sydenham to be a specimen of the school-boy hero; he made record scores in the school matches, climbed trees higher than any one else did, and was moreover a good all-round boy at his work; he was healthy, very tall but strong, dark, pleasant-looking, and popular with men and women and—he was quite aware of these facts. He shone with equal brightness as a midshipman; he dared, he could lead. Several women of thirty or thereabouts adored him—before it is good for youth to be adored. He had a knack of success, he achieved a number of things; he judged himself and found that this he had done "pretty decently," and that "passing well." Then Destiny decided apparently that he was not thinking as freshly or as abundantly as he ought to do—a healthy, successful life does not leave much time for original thinking—and smashed off the right side of his face. In a manner indeed quite creditable to him. It was given to few men in those pacific days to get the V.C. before the age of twenty-one.

He lay in hospital for a long spell, painful but self-satisfied. The nature of his injuries was not yet clear to him. Presently he would get all right again. "V.C.," he whispered. "At twenty. Pretty decent."

He saw himself in the looking-glass with half his face bandaged, and there was nothing very shocking in that. Then one day came his first glimpse of his unbandaged self. . . .

"One must take it decently," he said to himself again and again through a night of bottomless dismay.

31

And, "How can I look a woman in the face again?"

He stuck to his bandages as long as possible.

He learnt soon enough that some women could not look him in the face anyhow, and among them was one who should have hidden her inability from him at any cost.

And he was not only disfigured; he was crippled and unserviceable; so the Navy decided. Something had gone out of his eyesight; he could no longer jump safely nor hit a ball with certainty. He could not play tennis at all; he had ten minutes of humiliation with one of the nurses, protesting all the time. "Give me another chance and I'll begin to get into it. Let me get my eye in—my only eye in. Oh, the devil! give a chap a chance! . . . Sorry, nurse. Now! . . . *Damn!* It's no good. Oh God! it's no good. What shall I do?" Even his walk had now a little flavour of precaution. But he could still shoot straight up to two or three hundred yards. . . . These facts formed the basis for much thinking on the part of a young man who had taken it for granted that he was destined to a bright and leading rôle in the world.

When first he realized that he was crippled and disabled for life, he thought of suicide. But in an entirely detached and theoretical spirit. Suicide had no real attraction for him. He meant to live anyhow. The only question therefore was the question of what he was to do. He would lie awake at nights sketching out careers that did not require athleticism or a good presence. "I suppose it's got to be chiefly using my brains," he decided. "The great trouble will be not to get fat and stuffy. I've never liked indoors. . . ."

He did his best to ignore the fact that an honourable life before him meant a life of celibacy. But he could not do so. For many reasons arising out of his temperament and the experiences those women friendships had thrust upon him, that limitation had an effect of dismaying cruelty upon his mind. "Perhaps some day I shall find a blind girl," he said, and felt his face doubtfully. "Oh, damn!" He perceived that the sewing up of his face was a mere prelude to the sewing up of his life. It distressed him beyond measure. It was the persuasion that the deprivation was final that obsessed him with erotic imaginations. For a time he was obsessed almost to the verge of madness.

He had moods of raving anger on account of this extravagant and uncontrollable preoccupation. He would indulge secretly in storms of cursing, torrents of foulness and foul blasphemies that left him strangely relieved. But he had an unquenchable sense of the need of a fight.

"I'll get square with this damned world somehow," he said. "I won't be beaten."

There were some ugly and dismal aspects in his attempt not to be beaten, plunges into strange mires with remorse at the far side. They need not deflect our present story.

"What's the whole beastly game about anyhow?" he asked. "Why are we made like this?"

Meanwhile his pride kept up a valiant front. No one should suspect he was not cheerful. No one should suspect he felt himself to be a thing apart. He hid his vicious strain —or made a jest of it. He developed a style of humour that turned largely on his disfigurement. His internal stresses reflected a dry bitterness upon the world.

It was a great comfort presently to get hints that here and there other souls had had to learn lessons as hard as his own. One day he chanced upon the paralyzed Heine's farewell to beauty. "Perhaps," he said, "I've only got by a short cut to where a lot of people must come out sooner or later. Every one who lives on must get bald and old—anyhow." He took a hint from an article he found in some monthly review upon Richard Crookback. "A crippled body makes a crippled mind," he read. "Is that going to happen to me?"

Thence he got to: "If I think about myself now," he asked, "what else can happen? I'll go bitter."

"Something I can do well, but something in which I can forget myself." That, he realized, was his recipe.

"Let's find out what the whole beastly game is about," he decided—a large proposition. "And stop thinking of my personal set-back altogether."

But that is easier said than done.

§ 2

He would, he decided, "go in for science."

He had read about science in the magazines, and about its remorseless way with things. Science had always had a temperamental call upon his mind. The idea of a pitiless acceptance of fact had now a greater fascination than ever for him. Art was always getting sentimental and sensuous —this was in the early 'eighties; religion was mystical and puritanical; science just looked at facts squarely, and would see a cancer or a liver fluke or a healing scar as beautiful as Venus. Moreover it told you coldly and correctly of the skin glands of Venus. It neither stimulated nor condemned. It would steady the mind. He had an income of four hundred a year, and fairly good expectations of another twelve hundred. There was nothing to prevent him going in altogether for scientific work.

Those were the great days when Huxley lectured on zoology at South Kensington, and to him Oswald went. Oswald did indeed find science consoling and inspiring. Scientific studies were at once rarer and more touched by enthusiasm a quarter of a century ago than they are now, and he was soon a passionate naturalist, consumed by the insatiable craving to know how. That little, long upper laboratory in the Normal School of Science, as the place was then called, with the preparations and diagrams along one side, the sinks and windows along the other, the row of small tables down the windows, and the ever-present vague mixed smell of methylated spirit, Canada balsam, and a sweetish decay, opened vast new horizons to him. To the world of the eighteen-eighties the story of life, of the origin and branching out of species, of the making of continents, was still the most inspiring of new romances. Comparative anatomy in particular was then a great and philosophical "new learning," a mighty training of the mind; the drift of biological teaching towards specialization was still to come.

For a time Oswald thought of giving his life to biology. But biology unhappily had little need of Oswald. He was a clumsy dissector because of his injury, and unhandy at most of the practical work, he had to work with his head on one

side and rather close to what he was doing, but it dawned
upon him one day as a remarkable discovery that neither
personal beauty nor great agility are demanded from an explorer or collector. It was a picture he saw in an illustrated
paper of H. M. Stanley traversing an African forest in a
litter, with a great retinue of porters, that first put this
precious idea into his head. "One wants pluck and a certain toughness," he said. "I'm tough enough. And then I
shall be out of reach of—Piccadilly."

He had excellent reasons for disliking the West End. It
lured him, it exasperated him, it demoralized him and made
him ashamed. He got and read every book of African travel
he could hear of. In 1885 he snatched at an opportunity
and went with an expedition through Portuguese East
Africa to Nyasa and Tanganyika. He found fatigue and illness and hardship there—and peace of nerve and imagination. He remained in that region of Africa for three years.

But biology and Africa were merely the fields of human
interest in which Oswald's mind was most active in those
days. Such inquiries were only a part of his valiant all-
round struggle to reconstruct the life that it had become impossible to carry on as a drama of the noble and picturesque
loves and adventures of Oswald Sydenham. His questions
led him into philosophy; he tried over religion, which had
hitherto in his romantic phase simply furnished suitable
church scenery for meetings and repentances. He read
many books, listened to preachers, hunted out any teacher
who seemed to promise help in the mending of his life, considered this "movement" and that "question." His resolve to find what "the whole beastly game was about," was
no passing ejaculation. He followed the trend of his time
towards a religious scepticism and an entire neglect of current politics. Religion was then at the nadir of formalism;
current politics was an outwardly idiotic, inwardly dishonest, party duel between the followers of Gladstone and
Disraeli. Social and economic questions he was inclined to
leave to the professors. Those were the early days of socialist thought in England, the days before Fabianism, and he
did not take to the new teachings very kindly. He was a
moderate man in æsthetic matters, William Morris left him

tepid, he had no sense of grievance against machinery and aniline dyes, he did not grasp the workers' demand because it was outside his traditions and experiences. Science seemed to him more and more plainly to be the big regenerative thing in human life, and the mission immediately before men of energy was the spreading of civilization, that is to say of knowledge, apparatus, clear thought, and release from instinct and superstition, about the world.

In those days science was at its maximum of aggressive hopefulness. With the idea of scientific progress there was also bound up in many British minds the idea of a racial mission. The long Napoleonic wars had cut off British thought from the thought of the continent of Europe, and this separation was never completely healed throughout the nineteenth century. In spite of their world-empire the British remained remarkably self-centred and self-satisfied. They were a world-people, and no other people were. They were at once insular and world-wide. During the nineteenth century until its last quarter there was no real challenge to their extra-European ascendancy. A man like Sydenham did not so much come to the conclusion that the subjugation and civilization of the world by science and the Anglican culture was the mission of the British Empire, as find that conclusion ready-made by tradition and circumstances in his mind. He did not even trouble to express it; it seemed to him self-evident. When Kipling wrote of the White Man's Burthen, Briton was understood. Everywhere the British went about the world, working often very disinterestedly and ably, quite unaware of the amazement and exasperation created in French and German and American minds by the discovery of these tranquil assumptions.

So it was with Oswald Sydenham for many years. For three years he was in the district between Bangweolo and Lake Nyasa, making his headquarters at Blantyre, collecting specimens and learning much about mankind and womankind in that chaos of Arab slavers, Scotch missionaries, traders, prospectors, native tribes, Zulu raiders, Indian store-keepers, and black "Portuguese"; then, discovering that Blantyre had picked up a nick-name from the natives of "Half Face" for him, he took a temporary dislike to Blantyre, and decided to go by way of Tanganyika either to Uganda or Zanzibar, first sending home a considerable collection of specimens by way of Mozambique. He got through at last to Uganda, after some ugly days and hours, only to learn of a very good reason why he should return at once to the southern lakes. He heard that a new British consul was going up the Zambesi to Nyasaland with a British protectorate up his sleeve, and he became passionately anxious to secure a position near the ear of this official. There were many things the man ought to know at once that neither traders nor mission men would tell him.

To get any official position it was necessary for Oswald to return to London and use the influence of various allied Sydenhams. He winced at the thought of coming back to England and meeting the eyes of people who had known him before his disfigurement, but the need to have some sort of official recognition if he was to explain himself properly in Nyasaland made it necessary that he should come. That was in the summer of 1889.

He went down to visit his uncle at Long Downport while the ''influences'' brewed, and here it was he first met Dolly. He did not know it, but now his face was no longer a shock to the observer. The injured side which had been at first mostly a harsh, reddish blank scar with a glass eye, had not only been baked and weatherworn by Africa, but it had in some indefinable way been assimilated by the unmutilated half. It had been taken up into his individuality; his renascent character possessed it now; it had been humanized and become a part of him; it had acquired dignity. Muscles and nerves had reconstructed some of their relations and partially resumed abandoned duties. If only he had known it, there was nothing repulsive about him to Dolly. Though he was not a pretty man, he had the look of a strong one. The touch of imagination in her composition made her see behind this half vizor of immobilized countenance the young hero who had risked giving his life for his fellows; his disfigurement did but witness the price he had paid. In those days at home in England one forgot that most men were brave. No one had much occasion nor excuse for bravery. A brave man seemed a wonderful man.

He loved Dolly with a love in which a passion of gratitude
was added to the commoner ingredients. Her smiling eyes
restored his self-respect. He felt he was no longer a horror
to women. But could it be love she felt for him? Was not
that to presume too far? She gave him friendliness. He
guessed she gave him pity. She gave him the infinite reassurance of her frank eyes. Would it not be an ill return to
demand more than these gracious gifts?

The possibility of humiliation—and of humiliating Dolly
—touched a vein of abject cowardice in his composition. He
could not bring himself to the test. He tried some vague
signalling that she did not seem to understand. His time
ran out and he went—awkwardly. When he returned for a
second time, he returned to find that Arthur's fine profile
had eclipsed his memory.

§ 3

After the visit that made him a godfather, Oswald did not
return again to England until his godson had attained the
ripe age of four years. And when Oswald came again he
had changed very greatly. He was now almost completely
his new self; the original good-looking midshipman, that
sunny "type," was buried deep in a highly individualized
person, who had in England something of the effect of a
block of seasoned ship's timber among new-cut blocks of
white deal. He had been used and tested. He had been
scarred, and survived. His obsession had lifted. He had
got himself well under control.

He was now acquiring a considerable knowledge of things
African, and more particularly of those mysterious processes
of change and adventure that were presented to the British
consciousness in those days as "empire building."

He had seen this part of Africa change dramatically under
his eyes. When first he had gone out it was but a dozen
years from the death of Livingstone, who had been the first
white man in this land. In Livingstone's wake had come
rifles, missionaries, and the big game hunter. The people of
the Shire Highlands were now mostly under the rule of
chiefs who had come into the country with Livingstone as

Basuto porters, and whom he had armed with rifles. The town of Blantyre had been established by Scotch missionaries to preserve Livingstone's memory and his work. Things had gone badly for a time. A certain number of lay helpers to the Church of Scotland Mission had set up as quasi-independent sovereigns, with powers of life and death, about their mission stations; many of them had got completely out of hand and were guilty of much extortion and cruelty. One of them, Fennick, murdered a chief in a drunken bout, got himself killed, and nearly provoked a native war only a year or so before Oswald's arrival. Arab adventurers from Zanzibar and black Portuguese from the Zambesi were also pushing into this country. The Yao to the north and the Angoni-Zulus to the south, tribes of a highly militant spirit, added their quota to a kaleidoscope of murder, rape, robbery and incalculable chances, which were further complicated by the annexational propaganda of more or less vaguely accredited German, Belgian, Portuguese and British agents.

Oswald reached Tanganyika in the company of a steamboat (in portable pieces) which had been sent by the Scotch missionaries by way of the Zambesi and Lake Nyasa; he helped with its reconstruction, and took a considerable share in fighting the Arab slavers between Nyasa and Tanganyika. One of his earliest impressions of African warfare was the figure of a blistered and wounded negro standing painfully to tell his story of the fight from which he had escaped. "You see," the Scotch trader who was translating, explained, "he's saying they had just spears and the Arabs had guns, and they got driven back on the lagoon into the reeds. The reeds were dry, and the Arabs set them on fire. That's how he's got his arm and leg burns, he says. Nasty places. But they'll heal all right; he's a vegetarian and a teetotaller—usually. Those reeds burn like thatch, and if the poor devils ran out they got stabbed or shot, and if they went into the water the crocodiles would be getting them. I know that end of the lake. It's fairly alive with crocodiles. A perfect bank holiday for the crocodiles. Poor devils! Poor devils!"

The whole of Africa, seen in those days from the viewpoint of Blantyre, was the most desolating spectacle of human indiscipline it is possible to conceive. Everywhere was the adventurer and violence and cruelty and fever, nowhere law and discipline. The mission men turned robbers, the traders became drunkards, the porters betrayed their masters. Mission intrigued against mission, disobeyed the consuls, and got at hopeless loggerheads with the traders and early planters. Where there is no control, there is no self-control. Thirst and lust racked every human being; even some of the missionaries deemed it better to marry native women than to burn. In his own person Oswald played microcosm to human society. He had his falls and bitter moments, but his faith in science and civilization, human will and self-control, stumbled to its feet again. "We'll get things straight here presently," he said. Of himself as of Nyasaland. "Never say damned till you're dead."

His first return to England not only gave him a futile dream of Dolly to keep him clean and fastidious in Africa, but restored his waning belief in an orderly world. Seen from that distant point, the conflicts in Africa fell into a proper perspective as the froth and confusion before the launching of a new and unprecedented peace. Africa had been a black stew of lust, bloodshed and disease since the beginnings of history. These latter days were but the last flare-up of an ancient disorder before the net of the law and the roads and railways, the net of the hospitals and microscopes and anthropologists, caught and tamed and studied and mastered the black continent. He got his official recognition and went back to join this new British agent, Mr. Harry Johnston, in Nyasaland and see a kind of order establish itself and grow more orderly and secure, over the human confusion round and about the Shire Highlands. He found in his chief, who presently became Commissioner and Administrator (with a uniform rather like an Admiral's for state occasions), a man after his own heart, with the same unquenchable faith in the new learning of science and the same belief in the better future that opened before mankind. The Commissioner, a little animated, talkative man of tireless interest and countless interests, reciprocated Oswald's liking. In Central Africa one is either too busy or too tired and ill to do much talking, but there were one or two evenings when Oswald was alone with his chief and they could exchange views. Johnston had a modern religious philosophy that saw God chiefly through the valiant hearts of men; he made Oswald read Winwood Reade's *Martyrdom of Man*, which had become, so to speak, his own theological point of departure. It was a book of sombre optimism productive of a kind of dark hopefulness—"provided we stick it"—that accorded well with the midday twilight of the Congo forests into which Oswald was presently sent. It marched with much that Oswald had been thinking out for himself. It did not so much tell him new things as crystallize his own thoughts.

Two ideas were becoming the guiding lights of Oswald Sydenham's thought and life. One was the idea of self-devotion to British Imperial expansion. The British Empire was to be the instrument of world civilization, the protectress and vehicle of science; the critical examination of Imperialism in the light of these pretensions had still to come. He had still to discover that science could be talked in other languages than English, and thought go on behind brown and yellow foreheads. His second idea was that the civilizing process was essentially an educational process, a training in toleration and devotion, the tempering of egotism by wide ideas. Thereby "we shall get things straighter presently. We shall get them very straight in the long run." . . .

Directly after Oswald's second visit to England, the one in which he became Peter's godfather, a series of campaigns against the slave-raiding Arab chiefs, who still remained practically independent in the Protectorate, began. Oswald commanded in a very "near thing" in the Highlands, during which he held a small stockade against the Yao with six Sikhs and a few Atonga for three days, and was finally rescued when his ammunition had almost given out; and after that he was entrusted with a force of over three hundred men in the expedition that ended in the capture and hanging of old Mlozi. He fought in steamy heat and pouring rain, his head aching and his body shivering, and he ended his campaigning with a first experience of blackwater fever. It

struck him as an unutterably beastly experience, although
the doctor assured him he had been let down lightly. However, this was almost the end of the clearing-up fighting in
the Protectorate, and Oswald could take things easily for a
time. Thereafter the work of pacification, road-making,
and postal and telegraphic organization went on swiftly and
steadily.

But these days of peaceful organization were ended by a
disagreeable emotional situation. Oswald found himself
amused and attracted by a pretty woman he despised thoroughly and disliked a good deal. She was the wife of a
planter near Blantyre. So far from thinking him an ugly
and disfigured being, she made it plain to him that his ugliness was an unprecedented excitement for her. Always imprisoned in his mind was the desire to have a woman of his
very own; at times he envied even the Yao warriors their
black slave mistresses; and he was more than half disposed
to snatch this craving creature in spite of the lies and tricks
and an incessant chattering vanity that disfigured her soul,
and end all his work in Africa, to gratify, if only for some
lurid months, his hunger for a human possession. The situation took him by surprise in a negligent phase; he pulled up
sharply when he was already looking down a slippery slope
of indignity and dishonour. If he had as yet done no foolish
things he had thought and said them. The memory of Dolly
came to him in the night. He declared to himself, and he
tried to declare it without reservation, that it was better to
sit for a time within a yard of Dolly's inaccessible goodness
than paint a Protectorate already British enough to be scan-
dal-loving, with the very brightest hues of passion's flame-
colour. He ran away from this woman.

So he came back—by no means single-mindedly. There
were lapses indeed on the slow steamer journey to Egypt
into almost unendurable torments of regret. Of which,
however, no traces appeared when he came into the presence
of Dolly and his godson at The Ingle-Nook.

§ 4

Peter took to Oswald and Oswald took to Peter from the
beginning.

Peter, by this time, had Joan for a foster-sister. And also he had Nobby. Nobby was a beloved Dutch doll, armless and legless, but adored and trusted as no other doll has ever been in the whole history of dolls since the world began. He had been Peter's first doll. One day when he was playing tunes with Nobby on the nursery fender, one exceptionally accented note splintered off a side of Nobby's smooth but already much obliterated countenance. Peter was not so much grieved as dismayed, and Arthur was very sympa‚ thetic and did his best to put things right with a fine brush and some black paint. But when Peter saw Oswald he met him with a cry of delight and recognition.

"It's Nobby!" he cried.

"But who's Nobby?" asked Oswald.

"*You*—Nobby," Peter insisted with a squeak, and turned about just in time to prevent Arthur from hiding the fetish away. "Gimme my Nobby!" he said.

"Nobby is his private god," Dolly hastened to explain. "It is his dearest possession. It is the most beautiful thing in the world to him. Every night he must have Nobby under his pillow. . . ."

Oswald stood with his wooden double in his hand for a moment, recognized himself at a glance, thought it over, and smiled his grim, one-sided smile.

"I'm Nobby right enough," he said. "Big Nobby, Peter. He takes you off to Dreamland. Some day I'll take you to the Mountains of the Moon."

So far Joan, a black-headed, black-eyed doll, had been coyly on the edge of the conversation, a little disposed to take refuge in the skirts of Mary. Now she made a great effort on her own account. "Nobby," she screamed; "big, *Big* Nobby!" And, realizing she had made a success, hid her face.

"Nobby to you," said Oswald. "Does *that* want a god-father too? It's my rôle. . . ."

§ 5

The changes in the Stubland nursery, though they were the most apparent, were certainly not the greatest in the little home that looked over the Weald. Arthur had been unfaithful to Dolly—on principle it would seem. That did not reach Oswald's perceptions all at once, though even on his first visit he felt a difference between them.

The later 'nineties were the "Sex Problem" period in Great Britain. Not that sex has been anything else than a perplexity in all ages, but it was just about this time that that unanswerable "Why not?"—that bacterium of social decay, spreading out from the dark corners of unventilated religious dogmas into a moribund system of morals, reached, in the case of the children of the serious middle-classes of Great Britain, this important field of conduct. The manner of the question and the answer remained still serious. Those were the days of "The Woman Who Did" and the "Keynote Series," of adultery without fun and fornication for conscience' sake. Arthur, with ample leisure, a high-grade bicycle, the consciousness of the artistic temperament and a gnawing secret realization, which had never left him since those early days in Florence, that Dolly did not really consider him as an important person in the world's affairs, was all too receptive of the new suggestions. After some discursive liberal conversations with various people he found the complication he sought in the youngest of three plain but passionate sisters, who lived a decorative life in a pretty little modern cottage on the edge of a wood beyond Limpsfield. The new gale of emancipation sent a fire through her veins. Her soul within her was like a flame. She wrote poetry with a peculiar wistful charm, and her decorative methods were so similar to Arthur's that it seemed natural to conclude they might be the precursors of an entirely new school. They put a new interest and life into each other's work. It became a sort of collaboration. . . .

The affair was not all priggishness on Arthur's part. The woman was honestly in love; and for most men love makes love; there is a pride and fascination for them in a new love adventure, in the hesitation, the dash, the soft capture, the triumph and kindness, that can manage with very poor excuses. And such a beautiful absence of mutual criticism always, such a kindly accepting blindness in passionate eyes!

At first Dolly did not realize how Arthur was rounding off his life. She was busy now with her niece, her disreputable elder brother's love child, as well as Peter; she did not miss Arthur very much during his increasing absences. Then Arthur, who wished to savour all the aspects of the new situation, revealed it to her one August evening in general terms by a discourse upon polygamy.

Dolly's quick mind seized the situation long before Arthur could state it.

She did not guess who her successful rival was. She did not know it was the younger Miss Blend, that familiar dark squat figure, quick and almost crowded in speech, and with a peculiar avidity about her manner and bearing. She assumed it must be some person of transcendant and humiliating merit; that much her romantic standards demanded. She was also a little disgusted, as though Arthur had discovered himself to be physically unclean. Her immediate impulse was to arrest a specific confession.

"You forget instinct, Arthur dear," she said, colouring brightly. "What you say is perfectly reasonable, wonderfully so. Only—it would make me feel sick—I *mean* sick—if, for example, I thought *you*——"

She turned away and looked at the view.

"Are you so sure that is instinct? Or convention?" he asked, after a pause of half comprehension.

"Instinct—for certain. . . . Lovers are one. Whither you go, *I* go—in the spirit. You can't go alone with another woman while I—while I—— In those things. . . . Oh, it's inconceivable!"

"That's a primitive point of view."

"Love—lust for the matter of that. . . . They *are* primitive things," said Dolly, undisguisedly wretched.

"There's reason in the control of them."

"Polygamy!" she cried scornfully.

Arthur was immensely disconcerted.

He lit a cigarette, and his movements were slow and clumsy.

"Ideas may differ," he said lamely. . . .

He did not make his personal confession after all.

In the middle of the night Arthur was lying awake

thinking with unusual violence, and for the first time for a
long while seeing a question from a standpoint other than his
own.   Also he fancied he had heard a sound of great significance at bedtime.   That uncertain memory worried him
more and more.   He got up now with excessive precautions
against noise and crept with extreme slowness and care to
the little door between his room and Dolly's.   It was locked.
Then she had understood!
A solemn, an almost awe-stricken Arthur paddled back
to his own bed through a pool of moonlight on the floor.   A
pair of pallid, blue-veined feet and bright pyjama legs and
a perplexed, vague continuation upward was all the moon
could see.

§ 6

It was, it seemed to Arthur, a very hard, resolute and
unapproachable Dolly who met him at the breakfast-table
on the brick terrace outside the little kitchen window.   He
reflected that the ultimate injury a wife can do to a husband
is ruthless humiliation, and she was certainly making him
feel most abominably ashamed of himself.   She had always,
he reflected, made him feel that she didn't very greatly believe in him.   There was just a touch of the spitfire in
Dolly. . . .
But, indeed, within Dolly was a stormy cavern of dismay
and indignation and bitter understanding.   She had wept
a great deal in the night and thought interminably; she
knew already that there was much more in this thing than a
simple romantic issue.
Her first impulses had been quite in the romantic tradition: "Never again!" and "Now we part!" and "Henceforth we are as strangers!"
She had already got ten thousand miles beyond that.
She did not even know whether she hated him or loved
him.   She doubted if she had ever known.
Her state of mind was an extraordinary patchwork.
Every possibility in her being was in a state of intense excitement.   She was swayed by a violently excited passion
for him that was only restrained by a still more violent re-

solve to punish and prevail over him. He had never seemed so good-looking, so pleasant-faced, so much "old Arthur"— or such a fatuous being. And he was watching her, watching her, watching her, obliquely, furtively, while he pretended awkwardly to be at his ease. What a scared *comic* thing Arthur could be! There were moments when she could have screamed with laughter at his solicitous face.

Meanwhile some serviceable part of her mind devoted itself to the table needs of Joan and Peter.

Peter was disposed to incite Joan to a porridge-eating race. You just looked at Joan and began to eat fast very quietly, and then Joan would catch on and begin to eat fast too. Her spoon would go quicker and quicker, and make a noise—whack, whack, whack! And as it was necessary that she should keep her wicked black eyes fixed on your plate all the time to see how you were getting on, she would sometimes get an empty spoon up, sometimes miss her mouth, sometimes splash. But Mummy took a strong hand that morning. There was an argument, but Mummy was unusually firm. She turned breakfast into a drill. "Fill spoon. 'Tention! Mouf. Withdraw spoon." Not bad fun, really, though Mummy looked much too stern for any liberties. And Daddy wasn't game for a diversion. Wouldn't look at a little boy. . . .

After breakfast Arthur decided that he was not going to be bullied. He got out his bicycle and announced in a dry, off-hand tone that he was going out for the day.

"So long, Guv'nor," said Dolly, as off-handedly, and stood at the door in an expressionless way until he was beyond the green road gate.

Then she strolled back through the house into the garden, and stood for a time considering the situation.

"So I am to bring up two babies—and grow old, while *this* goes on!" she whispered.

She went to clear the things off the breakfast-table, and stood motionless again.

"My God!" she said; "why wasn't I born a man?"

And that, or some image that followed it, let her thoughts out to Africa and a sturdy, teak-complexioned figure with a one-sided face under its big sun-helmet. . . .

"Why didn't I marry a man?" she said. "Why didn't I get me a mate?"

§ 7

These were the primary factors of the situation that Oswald, arriving six weeks later, was slowly to discover and comprehend.   As he did so he felt the self-imposed restraints of his relations to Arthur and Dolly slip from him.   Arthur was now abundantly absent.   Never before had Oswald and Dolly been so much alone together.   Peter and Joan in the foreground were a small restraint upon speech and understanding.

But now this story falls away from romance.   Romance requires that a woman should love a man or not love a man; that she should love one man only and go with the man of her choice, that no other consideration, unless it be duty or virtue, should matter.   But Dolly found with infinite dismay that she was divided.

She loved certain things in Oswald and certain things in Arthur.   The romantic tradition which ruled in these matters, provided no instructions in such a case.   The two men were not sufficiently contrasted.   One was not black enough; the other not white enough.   Oswald was a strong man and brave, but Arthur, though he lived a tame and indolent life, seemed almost insensible to danger.   She had never seen him afraid or rattled.   He was a magnificent rock climber, for example; his physical nerve was perfect.   Everything would have been so much simpler if he had been a "soft."   She was sensitive to physical quality.   It was good to watch Arthur move; Oswald's injuries made him clumsy and a little cautious in his movements.   But Oswald was growing into a politician; he had already taken great responsibilities in Africa; he talked like a prince and like a lover about his Atonga and his Sikhs, and about the whiteclad kingdom of Uganda and about the fantastic gallant Masai, who must be saved from extermination.   That princely way of thinking was the fine thing about him; there he outshone Arthur.   He was wonderful to her when he talked of those Central African kingdoms that were rotting into chaos under the

influence of the Arab and European invasions, chaos from
which a few honest Englishmen might yet rescue a group of
splendid peoples.

He could be loyal all through; it was his nature. And he
loved her—as Arthur had never loved her. With a gleam
of fierceness. As though there was a streak of anger in his
love.

"Why do you endure it?" he fretted. "Why do you
endure it?"

But he was irritable, absurd about many little things. He
could lose his temper over games; particularly if Arthur
played too.

Yet there was a power about Oswald. It was a quality
that made her fear him and herself. She feared for the
freedom of her spirit. If ever she became Oswald's she
would become his much more than she had ever been Arthur's. There was something about him that was real and
commanding, in a sense in which nothing was real about
Arthur.

She had a dread, which made her very wary, that one day
Oswald would seize upon her, that he would take her in his
arms and kiss her. This possibility accumulated. She had
a feeling that it would be something very dreadful, painful
and enormous; that it would be like being branded, that there-
with Arthur would be abolished for her. . . . At the thought
she realized that she did not want Arthur to be abolished.
She had an enormous kindliness for Arthur that would have
been impossible without a little streak of humorous superiority. If Oswald threatened her with his latent mastery, Arthur had the appeal of much dependence.

And apart from Oswald or Arthur, something else in her
protested, an instinct or a deeply-rooted tradition. The
thought of a second man was like thinking of the dislocation
of her soul. It involved a nightmare of overlapping, of
partial obliteration, of contrast and replacement, in things
that she felt could have no honour or dignity unless they are
as simple and natural as inadvertent actions. . . .

The thing that swayed her most towards Oswald, oddly
enough, was his mutilated face. That held her back from
any decision against him. "If I do not go with him," she

thought, "he will think it is that." She could not endure that he should be so wounded.

Then, least personal and selfish thought of all, was the question of Joan and Peter. What would happen to them? In any case, Dolly knew they would come to her. There was no bitter vindictiveness in Arthur, and he shirked every responsibility he could. She could leave him and go to Uganda and return to them. She knew there would be no attempt to deprive her of Peter. Oswald would be as good a father as Arthur. The children weighed on neither side.

Dolly's mind had become discontinuous as it had never been discontinuous before. None of these things were in her mind all the time; sometimes one aspect was uppermost and sometimes another. Sometimes she was ruled by nothing but vindictive pride which urged her to put herself on a level with Arthur. At times again her pride was white and tight-lipped, exhorting her above all things not to put herself on a level with Arthur. When Oswald pressed her, her every impulse was to resist; when he was away and she felt her loneliness—and his—her heart went out to him.

She had given herself to Arthur, that seemed conclusive. But Arthur had dishonoured the gift. She had a great sense of obligation to Oswald. She had loved Oswald before she had ever seen Arthur; years ago she had given her cousin the hope and claim that burnt accusingly in his eye today.

"Come with me, Dolly," he said. "Come with me. Share my life. This isn't life here."

"But could I come with you?"

"If you dared. Not to Blantyre, perhaps. That's—respectable. Church and women and chatter. Blantyre's over. But there's Uganda. Baker took a wife there. It's still a land of wild romance. And I must go soon. I must get to Uganda. So much is happening. Muir says this Soudanese trouble won't wait. . . . But I hang on here, day after day. I can't leave you to it, Dolly. I can't endure that."

"You *have* to leave me," she said.

"No. Come with me. This soft grey-green countryside is no place for you. I want you in a royal leopard skin with a rifle in your hand. You are pale for want of the sun.

And while we were out there *he* could divorce you. He would divorce you—and marry some other copper puncher. Some Craftswoman. And stencil like hell. Then we could marry."

He gripped her wrists across the stone table. "Dolly, my darling!" he said; "don't let me go back alone."

"But what of Peter and Joan?"

"Leave them to nurses for a year or so and then bring them out to the sun. If the boy stays here, he will grow up—some sort of fiddling artist. He will punch copper and play about with book-binding."

She struggled suddenly to free her wrists, and he gripped them tighter until he saw that she was looking towards the house. At last he realized that Arthur approached.

"Oh, *damn!*" said Oswald. . . .

§ 8

Dolly cut this knot she could not untie, and as soon as she had cut it she began to repent.

Indecision may become an unendurable torment. On the one hand that dark strong life in the African sunblaze with this man she feared in spite of his unconcealed worship, called to a long-suppressed vein of courage in her being; on the other hand was her sense of duty, her fastidious cleanness, this English home with its thousand gentle associations and Arthur, Arthur who had suddenly abandoned neglect, become attentive, mutely apologetic, but who had said not a word, since he had put himself out of court, about Oswald.

He had said nothing, but he had become grave in his manner. Once or twice she had watched him when he had not known she watched him, and she had tried to fathom what was now in his mind. Did he want her?

This and that pulled her.

One night in the middle of the night she lay awake, unable to sleep, unable to decide. She went to her window and pressed her forehead against the pane and stared at the garden in a mist of moonlight. "I must end it," she said. "I must end it."

She went to the door that separated her room from Ar-

thur's, and unlocked it noisily. She walked across the room
and stood by the window. Arthur was awake too. He leant
up upon his elbow and regarded her without a word.

"Arthur," she said, "am I to go to Africa or am I to stay
with you?"

Arthur answered after a little while. "I want you to
stay with me."

"On my conditions?"

"I have been a fool, Dolly. It's over. . . ."

They were both trembling, and their voices were unsteady.

"Can I believe you, Arthur?" she asked weakly. . . .

He came across the moonlight to her, and as he spoke his
tears came. Old, tender, well-remembered phrases were on
his lips. "Dolly! Little sweet Dolly," he said, and took her
hungrily into his arms. . . .

There remained nothing now of the knot but to tell Oswald
that she had made her irrevocable decision.

§ 9

Arthur was eloquent about their reconciliation. What became of her rival Dolly never learnt, nor greatly cared; she
was turned out of Arthur's heart, it would seem, rather as
one turns a superfluous cat out of doors. Arthur alluded to
the emotional situation generally as "this mess." "If I'd had
proper work to do and some outlet for my energy this mess
wouldn't have happened," he said. He announced in phrases
only too obviously derivative that he must find something
real to do. "Something that will take me and use me."

But Dolly was manifestly unhappy. He decided that the
crisis had overtaxed her. Oswald must have worried her
tremendously. (He thought it was splendid of her that
she never blamed Oswald.) The garden, the place, was full
now of painful associations—and moreover the rejected cat
was well within the range of a chance meeting. Travel
among beautiful scenery seemed the remedy indicated.
Their income happened to be a little overspent, but it only
added to his sense of rising to a great emotional emergency
that he should have to draw upon his capital. They started
upon a sort of recrudescence of their honeymoon, beginning
with Rome.

Aunt Phyllis and Aunt Phœbe came to mind the house and Joan and Peter. Aunt Phœbe was writing a little wise poetical book about education, mostly out of her inner consciousness, and she seized the opportunity of this experience very gladly. . . .

Dolly was a thing of moods for all that journey.

At times she was extravagantly hilarious, she was wild, as she had never been before. She would start out to scamper about a twilit town after a long day's travel, so that it was hard for Arthur to keep pace with her flitting energy; she would pretend to be Tarantula-bitten in some chestnut grove and dance love dances and flee like a dryad to be pursued and caught. And at other times she sat white and still as though she had a broken heart. Never did an entirely virtuous decision give a woman so much heartache. They went up Vesuvius by night on mules from Pompeii, and as they stood on the black edge of the crater, the guide called her attention to the vast steely extent of the moonlit southward sea.

She heard herself whisper ''Africa,'' and wondered if Arthur too had heard.

And at Capri Arthur had a dispute with a boatman. The boat was taken at the Marina Grande. The boatman proposed the tour of the island and all the grottos, and from the Marina Grande the project seemed reasonable enough. The sea, though not glassy smooth, was quite a practicable sea. But a point had to be explained very carefully. The boatman put it in slow and simple Italian with much helpful gesture. If the wind rose to a storm so that they would have to return before completing this ''giro,'' they would still pay the same fee.

''Oh quite,'' said Arthur carelessly in English, and the bargain was made.

They worked round the corner of the island, under the Salto di Tiberio, that towering cliff down which the legend says Tiberius flung his victims, and as soon as they came out from under the lee of the island Arthur dscovered a cheat. The gathering wind beyond the shelter of the cliffs was cutting up the blue water into a disorderly system of tumbling white-capped waves. The boat headed straight into a storm. It lifted and fell and swayed and staggered; the boatman at his oar dramatically exaggerated his difficulties. "He knew of this," said Arthur savagely. "He thinks we shall want to give in. Well, let's see who gives in first. Let's put him through his program and see how he likes it."

Arthur had taken off his hat, and clutched it to save it from the wind. He looked very fine with his hair blowing back. "Buona aria," he said, grinning cheerfully to the boatman. "Bellissima!"

The boatman was understood to say that the wind was rising and that it was going to be worse presently.

"Bellissima!" said Arthur, patting Dolly's back.

The boatman was seized with solicitude for the lady.

Dolly surveyed the great cliffs that towered overhead and the frothy crests against which the boat smacked and lifted. "Bellissima," she agreed, smiling at the boatman's consternation. "Avanti!"

The boat plunged and ploughed its way for a little while in silence. The boatman suggested that things were getting dangerous. Could the signora swim?

Arthur assured him that she could swim like a fish.

And the capitano?

Arthur accepted his promotion cheerfully and assured the boatman that his swimming was only second to Dolly's.

The boatman informed them that he himself could scarcely swim at all. He was not properly a seafaring man. He had come to Capri for his health; his lungs were weak. He had been a stonemason at Alessandria, but the dust had been bad for his lungs. He could not swim. He could not manage a boat very well in stormy weather. And he was an orphan.

"*Io* Orfano!" cried Arthur, greatly delighted, and stabbing himself with an elucidatory forefinger. "Io Orfano anche."

The boatman lapsed into gloom. In a little while they had beaten round the headland into view of the Faraglione, that big outstanding rock which is pierced by a great arch, upon the south-eastern side of the island. The passage through this Arco Naturale was in the boatman's agreement. They could see the swirl of the waters now through that natural gateway, rising, pouring almost to the top of the arch and then swirling down to the trough of the wave. The west wind whipped the orphan's blue-black curls about his ears. He began to cry off his bargain.

"We go through that arch," said Arthur, "or my name is not Stubland."

The boatman argued his case. The wind was rising; the further they went the more they came into the weather. He had not the skill of a man born to the sea.

"You made the bargain," said Arthur.

"Let us return while we are still safe," the boatman protested.

"Go through the arch," said Arthur. The boatman looked at the arch, the sky, the endless onslaught of advancing waves to seaward and Arthur, and then with a gesture of despair turned the boat towards the arch.

"He's frightened, Arthur," said Dolly.

"Serve him right. He won't try this game again in a hurry," said Arthur, and then relenting: "Go through the arch and we will return. . . ."

The boatman baulked at the arch twice. It was evident they must go through just behind the crest of a wave. He headed in just a moment or so too soon, got through on the very crest, bent double to save his head, made a clumsy lunge with his oar that struck the rock and threw him sideways. Then they were rushing with incredible swiftness out of the arch down a blue-green slope of water, and the Faraglione rose again before Dolly's eyes like a thing relieved after a moment of intense concentration. But suddenly everything was sideways. Everything was askew. The boat was half overturned and the boatman was sitting unsteadily on the gunwale, clutching at the opposite side which was rising, rising. The man, she realized, was going overboard, and Arthur's swift grab at him did but complete the capsize. The side of the boat was below her where the floor should be, and that gave way to streaming bubbling water into which one man plunged on the top of the other. . . .

Dolly leapt clear of the overturned boat, went under and came up. . . .

She tossed the wet hair from her head and looked about her. The Faraglione was already thirty yards or more away and receding fast. The boat was keel upward and rolling away towards the cliff. There were no signs of Arthur or the boatman.

What must she do? Just before the accident she had noted the Piccola Marina away to the north-west. That would mean a hard swim against the waves, but it would be the best thing to do. It could not be half a mile away. And Arthur? Arthur would look after himself. He would do that all right. She would only encumber him by swimming around. Perhaps he would get the man on to the boat. Perhaps people had seen them from the Piccola Marina. If so boats would come out to them.

She struck out shoreward.

How light one's clothes made one feel! But presently they would drag. (Never meet trouble half-way.) It was going to be a long swim. Even if there should be no current. . . .

She swam. . . .

Then she had doubts. Ought she to go back and look for Arthur? She could not be much good to him even if she found him. It was her first duty to save herself. Peter was not old enough to be left. No one would care for Joan and him as she could care for them. It was a long enough swim without looking for Arthur. It was going to be a very long swim. . . .

She wished she could get a glimpse of Arthur. She looked this way and that. It would be easier to swim side by side. But in this choppy sea he might be quite close and still be hidden. . . . Best not to bother about things—just swim.

For a long time she swam like a machine. . . .

After a time she began to think of her clothes again. The waves now seemed to be trying to get them off. She was being tugged back by her clothes. Could she get some of them off? Not in this rough water. It would be more exhausting than helpful. Clothes ought to be easier to get off; not so much tying and pinning. . . .

The waves were coming faster now. The wind must be freshening. They were more numerous and less regular.

Splash! That last wave was a trencherous beast—no!—

treacherous beast. . . . Phew, ugh! Salt in the mouth. Salt in the eyes. And here was another, too soon! . . . Oh *fight!*

It was hard to see the Piccola Marina. Wait for the lift of the next wave. . . . She was going too much to the left, ever so much too much to the left. . . .

One must exert oneself for Peter's sake.

What was Arthur doing?

It seemed a long time now since she had got into the water, and the shore was still a long way off. There was nobody there at all that she could see. . . . Boats drawn high and dry. Plenty of boats. Extraordinary people these Italians —they let stonemasons take charge of boats. Extortionate stonemasons. . . . She was horribly tired. Not in good fettle. . . . She looked at the Faraglione over her shoulder. It was still disgustingly near and big. She had hardly swum a third of the way yet. Or else there was a current. Better not think of currents. She had to stick to it. Perhaps it was the worst third of the way she had done. But what infinite joy and relief it would be just to stop swimming and spread one's arms and feet!

She had to stick to it for little Peter's sake. For little Peter's sake. Peter too young to be left. . . .

Arthur? Best not to think about Arthur just yet. It had been silly to insist on the Arco Naturale. . . .

What a burthen and bother dress was to a woman! What a leaden burthen! . . .

She must not think. She must not think. She must swim like a machine. Like a machine. One. . . . Two. . . . One. . . . Two. . . . Slow and even.

She fell asleep. For some moments she was fast asleep. She woke up with the water rising over her head and struck out again.

There was a sound of many waters in her ears and an enormous indolence in her limbs against which she struggled in vain. She did struggle, and the thought that spurred her to struggle was still the thought of Peter.

"Peter is too young to be left yet," sang like a refrain in her head as she roused herself for her last fight with the water. Peter was too young to be left yet. Peter, her little

son. But the salt blinded her now; she was altogether out
of step with the slow and resolute rhythm of the waves.
They broke foaming upon her and beat upon her, and presently turned her about and over like a leaf in an eddy.

CHAPTER THE FOURTH

§ 1

PETER could not remember a time when Joan was not in his world, and from the beginning it seemed to him that the chief fact was Mary. "Nanny," you called her, or "Mare-*wi*," or you simply howled and she came. She was omnipresent; if she was not visible then she was just round the corner, by night or day. Other figures were more intermittent, "Daddy," a large, loud, exciting, almost terrific thing; "Mummy," who was soft and made gentle noises but was, in comparison with Mary, rather a fool about one's bottle; "Pussy," and then the transitory smiling propitiatory human stuff that was difficult to remember and name correctly. "Aunties," "Mannies" and suchlike. But also there were inanimate persons. There were the brass-headed sentinels about one's cot and the great brown round-headed newel post. His name was Bungo-Peter; he was a king and knew everything, he watched the stairs, but you did not tell people this because they would not understand. Also there was the brass-eyed monster with the triple belly who was called Chester-Drawers; he shammed dead and watched you, and in the night he creaked about the room. And there was Gope the stove, imprisoned in the fender with hell burning inside him, and there was Nobby. Nobby was the protector of little boys against Chester-Drawers, stray bears, the Thing on the Landing, spider scratchings and many such discomforts of nursery life. Of course you could also draw a deep breath and yell for "Mare-*wi*," but she was apt not to understand one's explanation and to scold. It was better to hold tight to Nobby. And also Nobby was lovely and went whack.

Moreover if you called "Mare-*wi*," then when the lights

came Joan would sit up in her cot and stare sleepily while
you were being scolded. She would say that she *knew* there
weren't such things. And you would be filled with an indefinable sense of foolishness. Behind an impenetrable veil of
darkness with an intervening floor space acrawl with bears
and "burdlars" she could say such things with impunity.
In the morning one forgot. Joan in the daytime was a fairly
amusing companion, except that she sometimes tried to touch
Nobby. Once Peter caught her playing with Nobby and
pretending that Nobby was a baby. One hand took Nobby
by the head, and the other took Joan by the hair. That was
the time when Peter had his first spanking, but Joan was
careful not to touch Nobby again.

Generally Joan was passable. Of course she was an intrusion and in the way, but if one wanted to march round
and round shouting "Tara-ra-ra, ra-ra, ra-ra, Tara *boom* de
ay," banging something, a pan or a drum, with Nobby, she
could be trusted to join in very effectively. She was good
for noise-marches always, and they would not have been any
fun without her. She had the processional sense, and knew
that her place was second. She talked also in a sort of way,
but it was not necessary to listen. She could be managed.
If, for example, she touched Peter's bricks he yelled in a
soul-destroying way and went for her with a brick in each
hand. She was quick to take a hint of that sort.

It was Arthur's theory that little children should not be
solitary. Mutual aid is the basis of social life, and from
their earliest years children must be accustomed to co-operation. They had to be trained for the co-operative commonwealth as set forth in the writings of Prince Kropotkin.
Mary thought differently. So Arthur used to go in his beautiful blue blouse and sit in the sunny nursery amidst the
toys and the children, inciting them to premature co-opera-
tions.

"Now Peter put a brick," he used to say.

"Now Joan put a brick."

"Now Dadda put a brick."

Mary used to watch proceedings with a cynical and irritating expression.

"Peter's tower," Peter would propose.

"*Our* tower," Arthur used to say.

"Peter knock it over."

"No. No one knock it over."

"Peter put *two* bricks."

"Very well."

"Dadda not put any more bricks. No. Peter finish it."

"Na-ow!" from Joan in a voice like a little cat. "*Me* finish it."

Arthur wanted to preserve against this original sin of individualism. He got quite cross at last imposing joyful and willing co-operation upon two highly resistant minds.

Mary's way was altogether different. She greatly appreciated the fact that Dolly and Arthur had had the floor of the nursery covered with cork carpet, and that Arthur at the suggestion of Aunt Phœbe had got a blackboard and chalks in order to instil a free gesture in drawing from the earliest years. With a piece of chalk Mary would draw a line across the floor of the nursery, fairly dividing the warmth of the stove and the light of the window.

"That's your bit, Peter," she would say, "and that's your bit, Joan. Them's your share of bricks and them's yours. Now don't you think of going outside your bit, either of you, whatever you do. Nohow. Nor touch so much as a brick that isn't yours."

Whereupon both children would settle down to play with infinite contentment.

Yet these individualists were not indifferent to each other. If Joan wanted to draw on the blackboard with chalk, then always Peter wanted to draw on the blackboard with chalk at the same time, and here again it was necessary for Mary to mark a boundary between them; and if Peter wanted to build with bricks then Joan did also. Each was uneasy if the other was not in sight. And they would each do the same thing on different sides of their chalk boundary, with a wary eye on the other's proceedings and with an endless stream of explanation of what they were doing.

"Peter's building a love-i-lay house."

"Joan's building, oh!—a lovelay-er house. Wiv a cross on it."

"Why not build one lovely house for both of you?" said

Arthur, still with the Co-operative Commonwealth in mind.

Neither child considered that his proposal called for argument. It went over their heads and vanished. They continued building individually as before, but in silence lest Arthur should be tempted to intervene again.

§ 2

Joan was a dancer from the age of three.

Perhaps she got some hint from Dolly, there is no telling; but anyhow she frisked and capered rhythmically by a kind of instinct whenever Dolly played the piano. So Dolly showed her steps and then more steps. Peter did not take to dancing so readily as Joan and his disposition was towards burlesque. Joan danced for the love of dancing, but Peter was inventive and turned his dances into expression. He invented the Fat Dance, with a pillow under his pinafore, the Thin Dance, with a concave stomach and a meagre expression, the One Leg dance and the Bird Dance, this latter like the birds about the crumbs in winter time. Also the Tipsy Dance, bacchic, which Arthur thought vulgar and discouraged. Dolly taught Joan the Flower Dance, with a very red cap like a pistil, and white silk skirt petals upheld by her arms. These she opened slowly, and at last dropped and then drooped. This needed a day of preparation. Peter produced his first remembered æsthetic judgment on a human being on this occasion.

"*Pritty* Joan," he said with conviction, as she stood flushed and bright-eyed after the dance, and with that he went and kissed her.

"He's beginning young," said Arthur.

It is what all parents say, and it is true of all children. But parents keep on saying it. . . .

Before he was fully four Peter was conducting an æsthetic analysis of his world. He liked some of the tunes Dolly played and disapproved of others. He distributed "pritty" lavishly but by no means indiscriminately over the things of the world. "Oh pritty fo'wers," was the primordial form of these expanding decisions. But he knew that Nobby was not pretty.

Arthur did his best to encourage and assist these budding appreciations.

One evening there was a beautiful still sunset. The sun went down, a great flattening sphere of reddening gold sinking into vast levels of blue over the remoter hills. Joan had already been carried off to bed, but Arthur seized upon Peter and stood him in the window seat. "Look," said Arthur. Peter looked intently, and both his parents sat beside him, watching his nice little round head and the downy edge of his intent profile.

"Look," said Arthur, "it goes. It goes. It's going . . . going . . . going. . . ."

The sun became a crescent, a red scimitar, a streak of fire.

"Ah!" said Arthur, "it's gone."

Came an immense pause.

"Do it *adain*, Dadda," said Peter with immense approval. "Do it adain. . . ."

§ 3

The theory of Ideals played almost as important a part in the early philosophy of Peter as it did in the philosophy of Plato. But Peter did not call them "Ideals," he called them "toys." Toys were the simplified essences of things, pure, perfect and manageable; Real Things were troublesome, uncontrollable, over complicated and largely irrelevant. A Real Train, for example, was a poor, big, clumsy, limited thing that was obliged to go to Red Hill or Croydon or London, that was full of stuffy unnecessary strangers, usually sitting firmly in the window seats, that you could do nothing satisfactory with at all. A Toy Train was your very own; it took you wherever you wanted, to Fairyland or Russia or anywhere, at whatever pace you chose. Then there was a beautiful rag doll named "Pleeceman," who had a comic, almost luminous red nose, and smiled perpetually; you could hit Joan with him and make her squawk and yet be sure of not hurting her within the meaning of the law; how inferior was the great formless lump of a thing, with a pale uneventful visitor's sort of face we saw out of the train at Caterham!

Nobody could have lifted him by a leg and waved him about; and if you had shied him into a corner, instead of all going just anyhow and still smiling, he would probably have been cross and revengeful. How inferior again was the Real Cow, with its chewing habits, its threatening stare and moo and its essential rudeness, to Suzannah, the cow on the green board. Perhaps the best real things in the world were young pigs. . . .

But this much is simply to explain how it was that Peter was grateful but not overwhelmed to find that there was also a real Nobby in existence as well as his beloved fetish. And this Nobby was, as real things went, much better than one could have expected him to be. Peter's heart went out to him from the very first encounter, and never found reason to relinquish him again.

Nobby wasted a good lot of time that might have been better employed in play, by talking to Mummy; and when a little boy set himself to rescue his friend from so tepid an occupation, Mary showed a peculiar disposition to thwart one. "Oh! *leave* them alone," she said, with the tart note in her voice. "I'm sure they don't want either of you."

Still Mummy didn't always get Nobby, and a little boy and girl could hear him talk and play about with him. When he told really truly things it was better than any one else telling stories. He had had all sorts of experiences; he had been a sailor; *he knew what was inside a ship.* That had been a growing need in Peter's life. All Peter's ships had been solid hitherto. And Nobby had been in the same field, practically speaking, with lions ever so many times. Lions, of course, are not nearly so dreadful as bears in a little boy's world; bears are the most dreadful things in the world (especially is this true of the black, under-bed bear, *Ursus Pedivorus*) but lions are dreadful enough. If one saw one in a field one would instantly get back over the stile again and go home, Mary or no Mary. But one day near Nairobi, Nobby had come upon a lion in broad daylight right in the middle of the path. Nobby had nothing but a stick. "I was in a hurry and I felt annoyed," said Nobby. "So I just walked towards him and waved my stick at him, and shouted to him to get out of my way."

"*Yes?*" breathless.

"And he went. Most lions will get away from a man if they can. Not always though."

A pause. There was evidently another story to that. "Tell us," said Mummy, more interested even than the children.

Big Nobby made model African villages out of twigs and such-like nothings in the garden, and he brought down Joan and Peter boxes of Zulu warriors from London to inhabit them. Also he bought two boxes of "Egyptian camel corps." One wet day he "made Africa" on the nursery floor. He made mountains out of books and wood blocks, and put a gold-mine of gold paper therein; he got in a lot of twigs of box from the garden and made the most lovely forest you can imagine; he built villages of bricks for the Zulus; he put out the animals of Peter's Noah's ark in the woods. "Here's the lion," he said, propping up the lion against the tree because of its broken leg.

"Gurr Woooooah!" said Joan.

"Exactly," said Nobby, encouraging her.

"Waar-oooh. Waaaa!" said Joan, presuming on it.

"Bang!" said Peter. "You're *dead*, Joan," and stopped any more of that.

§ 4

Then one day an extraordinary thing happened. It was towards lunch-time, and Mary was bringing Joan and Peter home from a walk in the woods. Joan was tired, but Peter had been enterprising and had run on far ahead; he was trotting his fat legs down the rusty lane that ran through the bushes close to the garden fence when he saw Nobby's lank form coming towards him from the house, walking slowly and as if he couldn't see where he was going. Peter was for slipping into the bushes and jumping out at him and saying "Boo." Then he saw Nobby stop and stand still and stare back at the house, and then, most wonderful and dreadful! this great big grown-up began to sob and cry. He said "Ooo-er!" just as Peter did sometimes when he felt unendurably ill-used. And he kept raising his clenched fists as if he was going to shake them—and not doing so.

"I will go to Hell," said Nobby. "I will go to Hell." In a passion!

(Peter was shocked and ashamed for Nobby.)

Then Nobby turned and saw Peter before Peter could hide away from him. He stopped crying at once, but there was his funny face all red and shiny on one side.

"Hullo, old Peter boy," said Nobby. "I'm off. I'm going right away. Been fooled."

So that was it. But hadn't he Africa and lions and elephants and black men to go to, a great Real Play Nursery instead of a Nursery of Toys? Why make a fuss of it?

He came to Peter and lifted him up in his arms. "Goodbye, old Peter," he said. "Good-bye, Peter. Keep off the copper punching." He kissed his godson—how wet his face was!—and put him down, and was going off along the path and Peter hadn't said a word.

He wanted to cry too, to think that Nobby was going. He stared and then ran a little way after his friend.

"Nobby," he shouted; "good-bye!"

"Good-bye, old man," Nobby cried back to him.

"Good-bye. Gooood-bye-er."

Then Peter trotted back to the house to be first with the sad but exciting news that Nobby had gone. But as he came down from the green wicket to the house he looked up and saw his father at the upstairs window, gazing after Nobby with an unusual expression that perplexed him, and in the little hall he found his mother, and she had been crying too, though she was pretending she hadn't. They knew about Nobby. Something strange was in the air, perceptible to a little boy but utterly beyond his understanding. Perhaps Nobby had been naughty. So he thought it best to change the subject, and began talking at once about a wonderful long bicycle with no less than three men on it—not two, Mummy, but three—that he had seen upon the highroad. They had thin white silk shirts without sleeves, and rode furiously with their heads down. Their shirts were blown out funnily behind them in the middles of their backs. They went like *that!* . . .

All through the midday meal nobody said a word about Nobby. . . .

Nobody ever did say anything about Nobby again.   When on a few occasions Peter himself talked appreciatively of Nobby nobody, unless it was Joan now and then, seemed the least bit interested. . . .

One side consequence of Oswald's visit had been the dethronement of the original Nobby.   The real Nobby had somehow thrust the toy Nobby into the background.   Perhaps he drifted into the recesses of some box or cupboard. At any rate when Peter thought of him one day he was nowhere to be found.   That did not matter so much as it would have done a couple of months before.   Now if the bears and "burdlars" got busy in the night-nursery Peter used to pretend that the pillow was the real Nobby, the Nobby who wasn't even afraid of lions and had driven off one with a stick.   A prowling bear hadn't much chance against a little boy who snuggled up to *that* Nobby.

§ 5

Mummy was rather dull in those days, and Daddy seemed always to be looking at her.   Daddy had a sort of inelasticity in his manner too.   Suddenly Aunt Phyllis and Aunt Phœbe appeared, and it was announced that Daddy and Mummy were going off to Italy.   It was too far for them to take little boys and girls, they said, and besides there were, oh! *horrid* spiders.   And Peter must stay to mind the house and Joan and his aunts; it wasn't right not to have some man about. He was to have a sailor suit with trousers also, great responsibilities altogether for a boy not much over four.   So there was a great kissing and going off, and Joan and Peter settled down to the rule of the aunts and only missed Mummy and Daddy now and then.

Then one day something happened over the children's heads.   Mary had red eyes and wouldn't say why; the aunts had told her not to do so.

Phyllis and Phœbe decided not to darken the children's lives by wearing mourning, but Mary said that anyhow she would go into black.   But neither Joan nor Peter took much notice of the black dress.

"Why don't Mummy and Daddy come back?" asked Peter one day of Aunt Phœbe.

"They've travelled to such wonderful places," said Aunt Phœbe with a catch in her voice. "They may not be back for ever so long. No. Not till Peter is ever so big."

"Then why don't they send us cull'd poce-cards like they did't first?" said Peter.

Aunt Phœbe was so taken aback she could answer nothing.

"They just forgotten us," said Peter and reflected. "They gone on and on."

"Isn't Nobby ever coming back either?" he asked, abruptly, displaying a devastating acceptance of the new situation.

"But who's Nobby?"

"That's Mr. Oswald Sydenham," said Mary.

"He's coming back quite soon," said Aunt Phœbe. "He's on his way now."

" 'Cos he *promised* me a lion skin," said Peter.

§ 6

Aunts Phyllis and Phœbe found themselves two of the four guardians appointed under Arthur's will.

It had been one of Arthur's occasional lapses into deceit that he destroyed the will which made Oswald the sole guardian of Joan—so far as he could dispose of Joan—and Peter, without saying a word about it to Dolly. He had vacillated between various substitutes for Oswald up to the very moment when he named the four upon whom he decided finally, to his solicitor. Some streak of jealousy or pride, combined with a doubt whether Oswald would now consent to act, had first prompted the alteration. Instead he had decided to shift the responsibility to his sisters. Then a twinge of compunction had made him replace Oswald. Then feeling that Oswald might still be out talked or out voted by his sisters, he had stuck in the name of Dolly's wealthy and important cousin, Lady Charlotte Sydenham. He had only seen her twice, but she had seemed a lady of considerable importance and strength of character. Anyhow it made things fairer to the Sydenham side.

But Phyllis and Phœbe at once assumed, not without

secret gladness, that the burthen of this responsibility would fall upon them. Oswald Sydenham was away in the heart of Africa; Lady Charlotte Sydenham was also abroad. She had telegraphed, ''Unwell impossible to return to England six weeks continue children's life as hitherto.'' That seemed to promise a second sleeping partner in the business.

The sisters decided to continue The Ingle-Nook as the children's home, and made the necessary arrangements with Mr. Sycamore, the family solicitor, to that end.

They discussed their charges very carefully and fully. Phyllis was for a meticulous observance of Arthur's known or assumed ''wishes,'' but Phœbe took a broader view. Mary too pointed out the dangers of too literal an adhesion to precedent.

''We want everything to go on exactly as it did when *they* were alive,'' said Phyllis to Mary.

''Things 'ave got to be different,'' said Mary.

''Not if we can help it,'' said Aunt Phyllis.

''They'll *grow*,'' said Mary after reflection.

Phœbe became eloquent in the evening.

''We are to have the advantages of maternity, Phyllis, without—without the degradation. It is a solemn trust. Blessed are we among women, Phyllis. I feel a Madonna. We *are* Madonnas, Phyllis. Modern Madonnas. Just Touched by the Wings of the Dove. . . . These little souls dropped from heaven upon our knees. . . . Poor Arthur! It is our task to guide his offspring to that high destiny he might have attained. *Look*, Phyllis!''

With her flat hand she indicated the long garden path that Dolly had planned.

Phyllis peered forward without intelligence. ''What is it?'' she asked.

Phyllis perceived that Phœbe was flushed with poetical excitement. And Phœbe's voice dropped mystically to a deep whisper. ''Don't you see? *White lilies!* A coincidence, of course. But—Beautiful.''

''For a child with a high destiny, I doubt if Peter is careful enough with his clothes,'' said Phyllis, trying to sound a less Pre-Raphaelite note. ''He was a perfect little Disgrace this afternoon.''

"The darling! But I understand. . . . Joan too has much before her, Phyllis. As yet their minds are blank, *tabula rasa;* of either of them there is still to be made—*anything.* Peter—upon this Rock I set—a New Age. When women shall come to their own. Joan again. Joan of Arc. Coincidences no doubt. But leave me my fancies. Fancies —if you will. For me they are no fancies. Before the worlds, Phyllis, we were made for this."

She rested her chin on her hand, and stared out into the blue twilight, a brooding prophetess.

"Only a woman can understand a woman," she said presently. "Not a Word of this, Phyllis, to Others."

"I wish we had bought some cigarettes this afternoon," said Phyllis.

"The little red glow," reflected Phœbe indulgently. "It helps. But I don't want to smoke tonight. It would spoil it. Smoke! Let the Flame burn clear awhile. . . . We will get in cigarettes tomorrow."

§ 7

Joan and Peter remained unaware of the great destinies before them. More observant persons than they were might have guessed there were deep meanings in the way in which Aunt Phœbe smoothed back their hair from their foreheads and said "Ah," and bade them "Mark it well" whenever she imparted any general statement, but they took these things merely as her particular way of manifesting the irrational quality common to all grown-up people. Also she would say "Dignity! Your mission!" when they howled or fought. It was to the manuscript that grew into a bigger and bigger pile upon what had been Arthur's writing-desk in Arthur's workroom, that she restricted her most stirring ideas. She wrote there daily, going singing to it as healthy young men go singing to their bathrooms. She splashed her mind about and refreshed herself greatly. She wrote in a large hand, punctuating chiefly with dashes. She had conceived her book rather in the manner of the prophetic works of the admired Mr. Ruskin—with Carlylean lapses. It was to be called *Hail Bambino and the Grain of Mustard Seed.* It was all about the tremendousness of children.

The conscientious valiance of Aunt Phœbe was very manifest in the opening. "Cæsar," the book began, "and the son of Semele burst strangely into this world, but Jesus, Mohammed, Confucius, Newton, Darwin, Robert Burns, were born as peacefully as you or I. Nathless they came for such ends—if indeed one can think of any ending thereto!—as blot out the stars. Yesterday a puling babe—for Jesus puled, Mohammed puled, let us not spare ourselves, Newton, a delicate child, puled most offensively—Herod here and bacteria there, infantile colic, tuberculosis and what not, searched for each little life, in vain, and so to-day behold springing victoriously from each vital granule a tree of Teaching, of Consequence, that buds and burgeons and shoots and for ever spreads so that the Gates of Hell may not prevail against it! Here it is the Tree of Spirituality, here the Tree of Thought, predestined intertwiner with the Tree of Asgard, here in our last instance a chanting Beauty, a heartening lyrical Yawp and Whirlaboo. And forget it not, whatever else be forgotten, the Word of the Wise, '*as the twig is bent the tree inclines.*' So it is and utterly that we realize the importance of education, the pregnant intensity of the least urgency, the hint, the gleam, the offering of service, to these First Tender Years."

Here Aunt Phœbe had drawn breath for a moment, before she embarked upon her second paragraph; and here we will leave Aunt Phœbe glowing amidst her empurpled prose.

Joan and Peter took the substitution of Aunt Phœbe muttering like a Sibyl overhead and Aunt Phyllis, who was really amusing with odd drawings and twisted paper toys and much dancing and running about, in the place of Daddy and Mummy, with the stoical acceptance of the very young. About Daddy and Mummy there hung a faint flavour of departure but no sense of conclusive loss. No clear image and expectation of a return had been formed. No day of definite disappointment ever came. After all the essential habitual person, Mary, was still there, and all the little important routines of child-life continued very much as they had always done.

Yet there was already the dawn of further apprehensions in Peter's mind at least. One day Peter picked up a dead bird in the garden, a bird dead with no injuries manifest. He tried to make it stand up and peck.

"It ain't no good, Master Peter; it's dead," said Mary.

"What's dead?" said Peter.

"*That* is."

"*Gone* dead," said Peter.

"And won't ever go anything else now—except smell," said Mary.

Peter reflected. Later he re-visited the dead bird and was seen in profound meditation over it. Then he repaired to Aunt Phyllis and confided his intention of immortality.

"Peter," he said, "not go dead—nohow."

"Of course not," said Aunt Phyllis. "He's got too much sense. The idea!"

This was reassuring. But alone it was not enough.

"Joan not go dead," he said. "No."

"Certainly she shan't," said Aunt Phyllis and awaited further decisions.

"Pussy not go dead."

"Not until ninety times nine."

"Aunt Phyllis not go dead. Marewi not go dead."

He reflected further. He tried, "Mummy and Daddy not go dead. . . ."

Then after thought, "When are Daddy and Mummy coming back again?"

Aunt Phyllis told a wise lie. "Some day. Not for a long time. They've gone—oh, ever so far."

"Farther than ever so," said Peter.

He reflected. "When they come back Peter will be a Big Boy. Mummy and Daddy 'ardly know 'im."

And from that time, Daddy and Mummy ceased to be thought of further as immediate presences, and became hero and heroine in a dream of tomorrow, a dream of returning happiness when life was dull, of release and vindication when life was hard, a pleasant dream, a hope, a basis for imaginative anticipations and pillow fairy tales, sleeping Parents like those sleeping Kings who figure in the childhood of nations, like King Arthur or Barbarossa. Sometimes it was one parent and sometimes it was the other that dominated the thought, "When Mummy comes back. . . . When Daddy comes back."

Joan learnt very soon to say it too.

§ 8

Death was too big a thing for Peter to comprehend. He had hardly begun yet with life. And he had made not even a beginning with religion. He had never been baptized; he had learnt no prayers at his mother's knee. The priceless Mary had come to the Stublands warranted a churchwoman, but as with so many of her class, her orthodoxy had been only a professional uniform to cloak a very keen hostility and contempt for the clergy, and she dropped quite readily into the ways of a household in which religion was entirely ignored. The first Peter heard of religion was at the age of four and a half, and that was from a serious friend of Mary's, a Particular Baptist, who came for a week's visit to The Ingle-Nook. The visitor was really distressed at the spiritual outlook of the two children. She borrowed Peter for a "little walk." She thought she would begin with him and try Joan afterwards. Then as plainly and impressively as possible she imparted the elements of her faith to Peter and taught him a brief, simple prayer. "He's a Love," she told Mary, "and so Quick! It's a *shime* to keep him such a little heathen. I didn't say that prayer over twice before he had it Pat."

Mary was rather moved by her friend's feelings. She felt that she was going behind the back of the aunts, but nevertheless she saw no great harm in what had happened. The deaths of Arthur and Dolly had shaken Mary's innate scepticism; she had a vague feeling that there might be grave risks, well worth consideration, beyond the further edge of life.

Aunt Phyllis was the first of the responsible people overhead to discover what had happened. Peter loved his prayer; it was full of the most beautiful phrases; no words had ever so filled his mouth and mind. There was for example, "For Jesus Krice sake Amen." Like a song. You could use it anywhere. Aunt Phyllis found him playing trains with his bricks in the nursery one afternoon. *"Hoo!* Chuff-Chuff. Chuff-Chuff. Change for Reigate, change for London. For Jesus Krice sake Amen."

Aunt Phyllis sat down in the little chair. "Peter," she said, "who is this Jesus Krice?"

Peter was reluctant to give information. "I know all about 'im," he said, and would at first throw no other light on the matter.

Then he relented and told a wonder. He turned his back on his brick train and drew close to Aunt Phyllis. His manner was solemn and impressive exactly as Mary's friend's had been; his words were as slow and deliberate. "Jesus Krice could go dead and come alive again," he said, "over and over, whenever He wanted to."

And having paused a moment to complete the effect of this marvel, Peter turned about again, squatted down like a little brown holland mushroom with a busy little knob on the top, and resumed his shouting. *"Hoo!* Chuff-Chuff. Chuff-Chuff. Chuff."

§ 9

One day Mary with an unaccustomed urgency in her manner hurried Joan and Peter out of the garden and into the nursery, and there tidied them up with emphasis. Joan showed fight a bit but not much; Peter was thinking of something else and was just limp. Then Mary took them down to the living-room, the big low room with the inglenook and the dining-table in the far bay beside the second fireplace. There they beheld a large female Visitor of the worst sort. They approached her with extreme reluctance, impelled by Mary's gentle but persistent hand. The Visitor was sitting in the window-seat with Aunt Phyllis beside her. And Aunt Phœbe was standing before the little fireplace. But these were incidental observations; the great fact was the Visitor.

She was the largest lady that Peter had ever seen; she had a plumed hat with black chiffon and large purple bows and a brim of soft black stuff and suchlike things, and she wore a large cape in three tiers and a large black feather boa that hissed when she moved and disseminated feathers. Her shoulders were enormously exaggerated by a kind of vast epaulette, and after the custom of all loyal Anglicans in those days her neck was tightly swathed about and adorned with a big purple bow. Everything she wore had been decorated and sewn upon, and her chequered skirts below were cut out by panels and revelations of flounced purple. In the midst of this costume, beneath the hat and a pale blonde fuss of hair, was set a large, pale, freckled, square-featured face with two hard blue eyes and a fascinating little tussock of sandy hair growing out of one cheek that instantly captured the eye of the little boy. And out of the face proceeded a harsh voice, slow, loud, and pitched in that note of arrogance which was the method of the ruling class in those days. "So *these* are our little Wards," said the voice, and as she spoke her lips wrinkled and her teeth showed.

She turned to Phyllis with a confidential air, but spoke still in the same clear tones. "Which is the By-blow, my dear, the Boy or the Gel?"

"Lady Charlotte!" exclaimed Phyllis, and then spoke inaudibly, explaining something.

But Peter made a note of "By-blow." It was a lovely word.

"Not even in Black. They ought to wear Black," he heard the big lady say.

Then he found himself being scrutinized.

"Haugh!" said the big lady, making a noise like the casual sounds emitted by large wading birds. "They both take after the Sydenhams, anyhow. They might be brother and sister!"

"Practically they are," said Aunt Phœbe.

Lady Charlotte confuted her with an unreal smile. "Practically *not*," she said decisively.

There was a little pause. "Well, Master Stubland," said the Visitor abruptly and quite terrifyingly. "What have *you* got to say for yourself?"

As Peter had not yet learnt to swear freely, he had nothing to say for himself just at that moment.

"Not very Bright yet," said Lady Charlotte goadingly. "I suppose they have run wild hitherto."

"It was poor Arthur's wish——" began Aunt Phyllis.

"We must alter all that now," Lady Charlotte interrupted. "Tell me your name, little boy."

"Peter Picktoe," said Peter with invention. "You going to stop here long?"

"So you've found your tongue at last," said Lady Charlotte. "That's only your nickname. What's your proper name?"

"Can we go out in the garden now, Auntie?" said Peter; "and play at By-blows?"

"Garden now," said Joan.

"He's Brighter than you seem to think," said Aunt Phœbe with gentle sarcasm.

"Commina *Garden,*" said Joan, tugging at Peter's pinafore.

"But I must ask him his name first," said Lady Charlotte. "and," with growing firmness, "he must tell it me. Come! What is your name, my dear?"

"Peter," prompted Mary.

"Peter," said Peter, satisfied that it was a silly game and anxious to get it over and away from this horror as soon as possible.

"And who gave you that name?"

"Nobody; it's mine," said Peter.

"Isn't the poor child even *beginning* to learn his Catechism?" asked Lady Charlotte.

"Yes, the garden," said Aunt Phœbe to Mary, and the scene began to close upon the children as they moved gardenward. Joan danced ahead. Peter followed thoughtfully before Mary's gentle urgency. What was that last word?"

"Cattymism?" Then a fresh thought occurred to him.

"Mary," said Peter, in an impassioned and all too audible undertone; "look. She's got a Whisker. *Here!* Troof!"

"It was my brother's *wish,*" Phyllis was explaining as the children disappeared through the door. . . .

"It isn't the modern way to begin so early with rote-learning," said Aunt Phœbe; "the little fellow's still not five."

"He's a pretty good size."

"Because we haven't worried his mind yet. Milk, light, play, like a happy little animal."

"We must change all that now," said Lady Charlotte Sydenham with conviction.

CHAPTER THE FIFTH

THE CHRISTENING

§ 1

LADY CHARLOTTE SYDENHAM was one of those large, ignorant, ruthless, low-church, wealthy, and well-born ladies who did so much to make England what it was in the days before the Great War. She was educated with the utmost care by totally illiterate governesses who were ladies by birth, chiefly on the importance and privileges of her social position, the Anglican faith and Mrs. Strickland's "Queens of England"; she had French from a guaranteed Protestant teacher and German from a North German instructress (Lutheran Protestant), who also taught her to play the piano with the force and precision of a crack regiment of cavalry. Subsequently she had improved her mind by reading memoirs and biographies of noble and distinguished people and by travel amidst obvious scenery and good foreign hotels. She had married at two-and-thirty when things were beginning to look rather doubtful for her.

Old Mr. Sydenham, who had made his money and undermined his health in India in the John Company days, had been fifty-four, and from the very outset she had been ever so much too much for him. At sixty-five he had petered out like an exhausted lode. She had already got an abject confidential maid into thorough training, and was fully prepared for widowhood. She hung out big black bonnets and expensive black clothes upon her projections, so as to look larger than ever, and took her place and even more than her place, very resolutely, among the leaders of the county Anglicans.

She had early mastered the simple arts of county family intercourse. Her style in contradiction was very good, her insults were frequently witty, she could pretend to love horses, there was no need for her to pretend to despise and

78

hate tradesmen and working people, and she kept herself well-informed upon the domestic details of the large and spreading family of the "Dear Queen." She was very good at taking down impertinent people, and most people struck her as impertinent; she could make a young man or a plain girl or a social inferior "feel small" quicker (and smaller) than almost any one in that part of Surrey. She was a woman without vices; her chief pleasure was to feel all right and important and the centre of things, and to that her maid as a sort of grand Vizieress, her well-disciplined little household and her choice of friends ministered. The early fear of "Romanists" in which she had been trained had been a little dispelled by the wider charities of maturity, but she held secularists and socialists in an ever-deepening abhorrence. They planned, she knew, to disturb the minds of the lower classes, upset her investments, behead the Dear Queen, and plunge the whole world into vice and rapine and Sabbath-breaking. She interested herself in such leisure as the care of her own health and comfort left her, in movements designed to circumvent and defeat the aims of these enemies of God and (all that was worth considering in) Man. She even countenanced quite indulgent charities if they seemed designed to take the wind out of the sails of socialism. She drove about the district in a one-horse carriage and delivered devastating calls.

Such was the lady whom Arthur had made one of the four guardians of his little son and niece. He had seen her twice; he had rather liked a short speech of five sentences she made at a Flower Show, and he had heard her being extremely rude to a curate. He believed her to be wealthy and trustworthy and very well suited to act as a counter influence to any extravagant tendencies there might be in Aunt Phœbe. Also she was Dolly's cousin, and appointing her had seemed a sort of compensation for altering his will without Dolly's knowledge. Besides, it had been very unlikely that she would ever act. And he had been in a hurry when he altered his will, and could not think of any one else.

Now Lady Charlotte was not by any means satisfied by her visit to The Ingle-Nook. The children looked unusually big for their years and disrespectful and out of hand. It

was clear they had not taken to her. The nurse, too, had a
sort of unbroken look in her eye that was unbecoming in a
menial position. The aunts were odd persons; Phyllis was
much too disposed to accentuate the father's wishes, and
Lady Charlotte had a most extraordinary and indecent feeling all the time she was talking to her that Aunt Phœbe
wasn't wearing stays. (Could the woman have forgotten
them, or was it deliberate? It was like pretending to be
clothed when you were really naked.)

Their conversation had been queer, most queer. They did
not seem to realize that she was by way of being a leader in
the county and accustomed to being listened to with deference. Nearly everything she said they had quietly contradicted or ignored. The way in which the children were
whisked away from her presence was distinctly disrespectful. She had a right, it was her duty, to look at them well
and question them clearly about their treatment, to see that
they had proper treatment, and it was necessary that they
should fully understand her importance in their lives. But
those two oddly-dressed young women—youngish women,
rather, for probably they were both over thirty—did not
themselves seem to understand that she was naturally the
Principal Guardian.

Phyllis had been constantly referring to the wishes of this
Stubland person who had married George Sydenham's Dolly.
Apparently the woman supposed that those wishes were to
override every rational consideration for the children's welfare. After all, the boy was as much Dolly's child as a
Stubland, and as for the girl, except that the Stublands had
been allowed to keep her, she wasn't a Stubland at all. She
wasn't anything at all. She was pure Charity. There was
not the slightest obligation upon Any one to do Anything
for her. Making her out to be an equal with a legitimate
child was just the subversive, wrong-headed sort of thing
these glorified shoddy-makers, the Stublands, would do. But
like to like. Their own genealogy probably wouldn't bear
scrutiny for six generations. She ought to be trained as a
Maid. There were none too many trained Maids nowadays.
But Arthur Stubland had actually settled money on her.

There was much to put right in this situation, a great occa-

sion for a large, important lady to impress herself tremendously on a little group of people insultingly disposed to be
unaware of her.   The more she thought the matter over the
more plainly she saw her duty before her.   She did not talk
to servants; no lady talks to servants; but it was her habit
to think aloud during the ministrations of Unwin, her maid,
and often Unwin would overhear and reply quite helpfully.

"It's an odd job I've got with these two new Wards of
mine," she said.

"They put too much on you, m'lady," said Unwin, pinning.

"I shall do what is Right.   I shall see that what is Right
is done."

"You don't spare yourself enough, m'lady."

"I must go over again and again.   Those women don't like
me.   I disturb them.   They're up to no good."

"It won't be the first Dark Place, m'lady, you've thrown
light into."

The lady surveyed her reflection in the glass with a knowing expression.   She knitted her brows, partly closed one
eye, and nodded slowly as she spoke.

"There's something queer about the boy's religious instruction.   It's being kept back.   Now why did they get embarrassed when I asked *who* were the godparents?   I ought
to have followed that up."

"My godfathers and godmothers wherein I was made,"
murmured Unwin, with the quiet satisfaction of the well-in-
structed.

"Properly it's the business of the godparents.   I have a
right to know."

"I suppose the poor boy *has* godparents, m'lady," said
Unwin, coming up from obscure duties with the skirt.

"But of *course* he has godparents!"

"Pardon me, m'lady, but not *of course.*"

"But what do you mean, Unwin?"

"I hardly like to say it, m'lady, of relations, 'owever distant, of ours.   Still, m'lady——"

"Don't Chew it about, Unwin."

"Then I out with it, m'lady.   'Ave they been baptized,
m'lady, either of them?   'Ave they been baptized?"

§ 2

Before a fortnight was out Lady Charlotte had made two more visits to The Ingle-Nook, she had had an acrimonious dispute upon religious questions with Phœbe, and she was well on her way to the terrible realization that these two apparently imbecile ladies in the shapeless "arty" dresses were really socialists and secularists—of course, like all other socialists and secularists, "of the worst type." It was impossible that those two unfortunate children should be left in their aunts' "clutches," and she prepared herself with a steadily increasing determination and grandeur to seize upon and take over and rescue these two innocent souls from the moral and spiritual destruction that threatened them. Once in her hands, Lady Charlotte was convinced it would not be too late to teach the little fellow a proper respect for those in authority over him and to bring home to the girl an adequate sense of that taint upon her life of which she was still so shockingly unaware. The boy must be taught not to call attention to people's physical peculiarities, and to answer properly when spoken to; a certain sharpness would not be lost upon him; and it was but false kindness to the girl to let her grow up in ignorance of her disadvantage. Sooner or later it would have to be brought home to her, and the later it was the more difficult would it be for her to accept her proper position with a becoming humility. And a thing of immediate urgency was, of course, the baptism of both these little lost souls.

In pursuit of these entirely praiseworthy aims Lady Charlotte was subjected to a series of very irritating rebuffs that did but rouse her to a greater firmness. On her fourth visit she was not even allowed to see the children; the specious excuse was made that they were "out for a walk," and when she passed that over forgivingly and said: "It does not matter very much. What I want to arrange today is the business of the Christening," both aunts began to answer at once and in almost identical words. Phœbe gave way to her sister. "If their parents had wanted them Christened," said Aunt Phyllis, "there was ample time for them to have had it done."

"*We* are the parents now," said Lady Charlotte.

"And two of us are quite of the parents' mind."

"You forget that I also speak for my nephew Oswald," said Lady Charlotte.

"But *do* you?" said Aunt Phyllis, with almost obtruded incredulity.

"Certainly," said Lady Charlotte, with a sweeping, triumphant gesture, a conclusive waving of the head.

"You know he is on his way back from Uganda?" Aunt Phyllis remarked with an unreal innocence.

Lady Charlotte had not known. But she stood up gallantly to the blow. "I know he will support me by insisting upon the proper treatment of these poor children."

"What can a man know about the little souls of children?" cried Phœbe.

But Aunt Phyllis restrained her. "I have no doubt Mr. Sydenham will have his own views in the matter," said Phyllis.

"I have no doubt he will," said Lady Charlotte imposingly. . . .

Even Mary showed the same disposition to insolence. As Lady Charlotte was returning along the little path through the bushes that ran up to the high road where her carriage with the white horse waited, she saw Mary and the children approaching. Peter saw Lady Charlotte first and flew back. "Lady wiv de Whisker!" he said earnestly and breathlessly, and dodged off into the bushes. Joan hesitated, and fled after him. By a detour the fluttering little figures outflanked the great lady and escaped homeward.

"Come *here*, children!" she cried. "I want you."

Spurt on the part of the children.

"They are really most distressingly Rude," she said to Mary. "It's inexcusable. Tell them to come back. I have something to say to them."

"They won't, Mum," said Mary—though surely aware of the title.

"But I tell you to."

"It's no good, Mum. It's shyness. If they won't come, they won't."

"But, my good woman, have you *no* control?"

"They always race 'ome like that," said Mary.

"Then you aren't fit to control them. As one of the children's guardians, I—— But we shall see."

She went her way, a stately figure of passion.

"Orty old Ag," said Mary, and dismissed the encounter from her mind.

§ 3

"You got your rights like anybody, m'lady," said Unwin.

It was that phrase put it into Lady Charlotte's head to consult her solicitor. He opened new vistas to her imagination.

Lady Charlotte's solicitor was a lean, long, faded blond of forty-five or so. He was the descendant of five generations of Lincoln's Inn solicitors, a Low Churchman, a man of notoriously pure life, and very artful indeed. He talked in a thin, high tenor voice, and was given to nibbling his thumbnail and wincing with his eyes as he talked. His thumbnail produced gaps of indistinctness in his speech.

"Powers of a guardian, m'lady. Defends upon whafower want exercise over thinfant."

"I do *wish* you'd keep your thumb out of your mouth," said Lady Charlotte.

"Sorry," said Mr. Grimes, wincing and trying painfully to rearrange his arm. "Still, I'd like to know—position."

"There are three other guardians."

"Generous allowance," said Mr. Grimes. "Do you all act?"

"One of us is lost in the Wilds of Africa. The others I want to consult you about. They do not seem to me to be fit and proper persons to be entrusted with the care of young children, and they do not seem disposed to afford me a proper share in the direction of affairs."

"Ah!" said Mr. Grimes, replacing his thumb. "Sees t'point t'Chacery."

Lady Charlotte disregarded this comment. She wished to describe Aunts Phyllis and Phœbe in her own words.

"They are quite extraordinary young women—not by any stretch of language to be called Ladies. They dress in that way—like the pictures in the Grosvenor Gallery.''

''Æsthetic?''

''I could find a harsher word for it. They smoke. Not a nice thing for children to see. I suspect them strongly of vegetarianism. From something one of them said. In which case the children will not be properly nourished. And they speak quite openly of socialism in front of their charges. Neither of the poor little creatures had been bought a scrap of mourning. Not a scrap. I doubt if they have even been made to understand that their parents are dead. But that is only the beginning. I am totally unable to ascertain whether either of the poor mites has been christened. Apparently they have not. . . .''

Mr. Grimes withdrew his thumb for a moment. ''You are perfectly within yer rights—insisting—knowing''—thumb replaced—''all these things.''

''Exactly. And in having my say in their general upbringing.''

''How far do they prevent that?''

''Oh; they get in my way. They send the children out whenever they feel I am coming. They do not listen to me and accept any suggestions I make. Oh!—sniff at it.''

''And you want to make 'em?''

''I want to do my duty by those two children, Mr. Grimes. It is a charge that has been laid upon me.''

Mr. Grimes reflected, rubbing his thumb thoughtfully along the front of his teeth.

''They are getting no religious instruction whatever,'' said Lady Charlotte. ''None.''

''Hot was the 'ligion father?'' said Mr. Grimes suddenly.

Lady Charlotte was not to be deterred by a silly and inopportune question. She just paused for an instant and reddened. ''He was a member of the Church of England,'' she said.

''Even if he wasn't,'' said Mr. Grimes understandingly, but with thumb still in place, ''Ligion necessary t'welfare. Case of Besant Chil'n zample. Thlis is Klistian country.''

''I sometimes doubt it,'' said Lady Charlotte.

''Legally,'' said Mr. Grimes.

''If the law did its duty!''

"You don't wanner goatallaw fewcan 'void it?" asked Mr.
Grimes, grasping his job.

Lady Charlotte assumed an expression of pained protest,
and lifted one black-gloved hand. Mr. Grimes hastily withdrew his thumbnail from his mouth. "I am saying, Lady
Charlotte, that what you want to do is to assert your authority, if possible, without legal proceedings."

He was trying to get the whole situation clear in his mind
before he tendered any exact advice. Most children who
are quarrelled over in this way gravitate very rapidly into
the care of the Lord Chancellor; to that no doubt these
children would come; but Lady Charlotte was a prosperous
lady with a lot of fight in her and a knack of illegality, and
before these children became Wards in Chancery she might,
under suitable provocation, run up a very considerable little
bill for expenses and special advice in extracting her from
such holes as she got herself into. It is an unjust libel upon
solicitors that they tempt their clients into litigation. So
far is this unjust that the great majority will spare neither
time nor expense in getting a case settled out of court.

Nor did Lady Charlotte want to litigate. Courts are uncertain, irritating places. She just wanted to get hold of
her two wards, and to deal with them in such a way as to
inflict the maximum of annoyance and humiliation upon
those queer Stubland aunts. And to save the children
from socialism, secularism, Catholicism, and all the wandering wolves of opinion that lie in wait for the improperly
trained.

But also she went in fear of Oswald. Oswald was one of
the few human beings of whom she went in awe. He was
always rude and overbearing with her. From the very first
moment when he had seen her as his uncle's new wife, he
had realized in a flash of boyish intuition that if he did
not get in with an insult first, he would be her victim. So
his first words to her had been an apparently involuntary
"O God!" Then he had pretended to dissemble his contempt with a cold politeness. Those were the days of his
good looks; he was as tall and big as he was ever to be, and
she had expected a "little midshipmite," whom she would

treat like a child, and possibly even send early to bed. From the first she was at a disadvantage. He had a material hold on her too, now. He was his uncle's heir and her Trustee; and she had the belief of all Victorian women in the unlimited power of Trustees to abuse their trust unless they are abjectly propitiated. He used to come and stay in her house as if it was already his own; the servants would take their orders from him. She was assuring Grimes as she had assured the Stubland aunts that he was on her side; "The Sydenhams are all sound churchmen." But even as she said this she saw his grim, one-sided face and its one hard intent eye pinning her. "Acting without authority again, my good aunt," he would say. "You'll get yourself into trouble yet."

That was one of his invariable stabs whenever he came to see her. Always he would ask, sooner or later, in that first meeting:

"Any one bagged you for libel yet? *No!* Or insulting behaviour? Some one will get you sooner or later."

"Anything that *I* say about people," she would reply with dignity, "is True, Oswald."

"They'll double the damages if you stick *that* out." . . .

And she saw him now standing beside the irritating, necessary Grimes, sardonically ready to take part against her, prepared even to give those abominable aunts an unendurable triumph over her. . . .

"I want no vulgar litigation," she said. "Everything ought to be done as quietly as possible. There is no need to ventilate the family affairs of the Sydenhams, and particularly when I tell you that one of the children is——" She hesitated. "Irregular."

The thumb went back, and Mr. Grimes' face assumed a diplomatic innocence. "Whascalled a love-shild?"

"Exactly," said Lady Charlotte, with a nod that forbade all research for paternity. If Joan were assumed to be of Stubland origin, so much the better for Lady Charlotte's case. "Everything must be done quietly and privately," she said.

"Sactly," said Mr. Grimes, and was reminded of his

thumb by her eye. He coughed, put his arm down, and sat up in his chair. *"They* have possession of the children?" he said.

"Should I be here?" she appealed.

"Ah! That gives the key of the situation. . . . Would *they* litigate?"

"Why should they?"

"If by chance you got possession?"

"That would be difficult."

"But not impossible? Perhaps something could be managed. With my assistance. Once or twice before I have had cases that turned on the custody of minors. Custody, like possession, is nine points of the law. Then *they* would have to come into court."

"We want nobody to come into court."

"Exactly, m'lady. I am pointing out to you how improbable it is that they will do so. I am gauging their disinclination."

The attitude of Mr. Grimes relaxed unconsciously until once more the teeth and thumbnail were at their little play again.

He continued with thoughtful eyes upon his client's expression. "Possibly *they* wouldn't li'e 'nquiry into character."

"Oh, *do* take that thumb away!" cried Lady Charlotte. "And *don't* lounge."

"I'm sorry, m'lady," said Mr. Grimes, sitting up. "I was saying, practically, do we know of any little irregularities, anything—I won't say actually immoral, but *indiscreet,* in these two ladies' lives? Anything they wouldn't like to have publicly discussed. In the case of most people there's a Something. Few people will readily and cheerfully face a discussion of Character. Even quite innocent people."

"They're certainly very lax—very. They smoke. Inordinately. I saw the cigarette stains on their fingers. And unless I am very much mistaken, one of them—well"— Lady Charlotte leant forward towards him with an air of scandalous condescension—"she wears no stays at all, Mr. Grimes—none at all! No! She's a very queer young woman indeed in my opinion."

"M'm! . . . No visitors to the house—no *gentlemen,* for example—who might seem a little dubious?"

Lady Charlotte did not know. "I will get my maid to make enquiries—discreetly. We certainly ought to know that."

"The elder one writes poetry," she threw out.

"We must see to that, too. If we can procure some of that. Nowadays there is quite a quantity—of *very* indiscreet poetry. Many people do not realize the use that might be made of it against them. And even if the poetry is not indiscreet, it creates a prejudice. . . ."

He proceeded to unfold his suggestions. Lady Charlotte must subdue herself for a while to a reassuring demeanour towards the aunts at The Ingle-Nook. She must gain the confidence of the children. "And of the children's maid!" he said acutely. "She's rather an important factor."

"She's a very impertinent young woman," said Lady Charlotte.

"But you must reassure her for a time, Lady Charlotte, if the children are to come to you—ultimately."

"I can make the sacrifice," the lady said; "if you think it is my duty."

Meanwhile Mr. Grimes would write a letter, a temperate letter, yet "just a little stiff in tone," pointing out the legal and enforceable right of his client to see and have free communication with the children, and to be consulted about their affairs, and trusting that the Misses Stubland would see their way to accord these privileges without further evasion.

§ 4

The Stubland aunts were not the ladies to receive a solicitor's letter calmly. They were thrown into a state of extreme trepidation. A solicitor's letter had for them the powers of an injunction. It was clear that Lady Charlotte must be afforded that reasonable access, that consultative importance to which she was entitled. Phyllis became extremely reasonable. Perhaps they had been a little disposed to monopolize the children. They were not the only Madonnas upon the tree. That was Phyllis's response to this threat. Phœbe was less disposed to make concessions. "Those children are a sacred charge to us," she said. "What can a woman of that sort know or care for children? Lapdogs are *her* children. Let us make such concessions as we must, but let us *guard essentials*, Phyllis. . . . As the apples of our eyes. . . ."

In the wake of this letter came Lady Charlotte herself, closely supported by the faithful Unwin, no longer combative, no longer actively self-assertive, but terribly suave. Her movements were accompanied by unaccustomed gestures of urbanity, done chiefly by throwing out the open hand sideways, and she made large, kind tenor noises as reassuring as anything Mr. Grimes could have wished. She astonished Aunt Phyllis with "Ha'ow are the dear little things today?"

Mary was very mistrustful, and Aunt Phyllis had to expostulate with her. "You see, Mary, it seems she's the children's guardian just as we are. They *must* see a little of her. . . ."

"And *ha-ow's* Peter?" said Lady Charlotte.

"Very well, thank you, Lady Charlotte," said Mary.

"Very well, thank you lazy Cha'lot," said Peter.

"That's right. We shall soon get along Famously. And how's my little Joan?"

Joan took refuge behind Mary.

"Pee-Bo!" said Lady Charlotte tremendously, and craned her head.

Peter regarded the lady incredulously. He wanted to ask a question about the whisker. But something in Mary's grip upon his wrist warned him not to do that. In this world, he remembered suddenly, there are Unspeakable Things. Perhaps this was one of them. . . . That made it all the more fascinating, of course.

Lady Charlotte was shown the nursery; she stayed to nursery tea. She admired everything loudly.

"And so these are your Toys, lucky Peter. Do you play with them all?"

"Joan's toys too," said Joan.

"Such a Pretty Room!" said Lady Charlotte with gestures of approval. "Such a Pretty Outlook. I wonder you didn't make it the Drawing-Room. Isn't it a pretty room, Unwin?"

"Very pritty, m'lady."

Very skilfully she made her first tentative towards the coup she had in mind.

"One day, Mary, you must bring them over to Tea with *me*," she said. . . .

"I do so want the dear children to come over to me," she said presently in the garden to aunts Phyllis and Phœbe. "If they would come over quite informally—with their Mary. Just to Tea and scamper about the shrubbery. . . ."

Mary and Unwin surveyed the garden conversation from the nursery window, and talked sourly and distrustfully.

"Been with 'er long?" asked Mary.

"Seven years," said Unwin.

"Purgat'ry?" said Mary.

"She 'as to be managed," said Unwin.

§ 5

The day of the great coup of Lady Charlotte was tragic and painful from the beginning. Peter got up wicked. It was his custom, and a very bad one, to bang with his spoon upon the bottom of his little porringer as he ate his porridge. It had grown out of his appreciation of the noise the spoon made as he dug up his food. Now, as Mary said, he *"d'librately 'ammered."* How frequently had not Mary told him he would do it "once too often!" This was the once too often. The porridge plate cracked and broke, and the porridge and the milk and sugar escaped in horrid hot gouts and lumps over tablecloth and floor and Peter's knees. It was a fearful mess. It was enough to cow the stoutest heart. Peter, a great boy of five, lifted up his voice and wept.

So this dire day began.

Then there was a new thin summer blouse, a glaring white silk thing, for Peter, and in those days all new things meant trouble with him. It was put on after a hot fight with Mary; his head came through flushed and crumpled. But Joan accepted her new blouse as good as gold. Then for some reason the higher powers would not let us go and look at the kittens, the dear little blind kittens in the out-house. There were six of them, all different, for the Ingle-Nook cat was a generous, large-minded creature. Only after a dispute in which Joan threatened to go the way of Peter was "just a glimpse" conceded. And they were softer and squealier and warmer than anything one had ever imagined. We wanted to linger. Mary talked of a miracle. "Any time," she said, "one of them kitties may eat up all the others. Any time. Kitties often do that. But it's always the best one does it."

We wanted to stay and see if this would happen. No! We were dragged reluctantly to our walk.

Was it Peter's fault that when we got to the edge of the common the fence of Master's paddock had been freshly tarred? Must a little boy test the freshness of the paint on every fence before he wriggles half under it and stares at Wonderland on the other side? If so, this was a new law.

But anyhow here we were in trouble once more, this beastly new white blouse "completely spoilt," Mary said, and Mary in an awful stew. The walk was to be given up and we were to go home in dire disgrace and change. . . .

Even Aunt Phyllis turned against Peter. She looked at him and said, "O *Peter! What* a mess!"

Then it was that sorrow and the knowledge of death came upon Joan.

She was left downstairs while Peter was hauled rather than taken upstairs to change, and in that atmosphere of unrest and disaster it seemed a sweet and comforting thing to do to go and look at the kittens again. But beyond the corner of the house she saw old Groombridge, the Occasional Gard-ener, digging a hole, and beside him in a pitiful heap lay five wet little objects and close at hand was a pail. Dark ap-prehension came upon Joan's soul, but she went up to him nevertheless. "What you been doing to my kittays?" she asked.

"I drownded five," said old Groombridge in a warm and kindly voice. "But I kep' the best un. 'E's a beauty 'E is."

"But why you drownded 'em?" asked Joan.

"Eh! you got to drown kittens, little Missie," said old Groombridge. "Else ud be too many of um. But ollays there's one or so kep'. Callum Jubilee I reckon. 'Tis all the go this year agin."

Joan had to tell some one. She turned about towards the house, but long before she could find a hearer her sorrowful news burst through her. Aunt Phœbe writing Ruskinian about the marvellous purity of childish intuitions was suddenly disturbed by the bitter cry of Niobe Joan going past beneath the window. Joan had a voluminous voice when she was fully roused.

"They been 'n dwouwnded my kittays, Petah. They been 'n dwouwnded my kittays."

§ 6

It seemed to Mary that Lady Charlotte's invitation came as a "perfect godsend." It was at once used to its utmost value to distract the two little flushed and tearful things from their distresses. Great expectations were aroused. That very afternoon they were to go out to tea to Chastlands, a lovely place; they were to have a real ride in a real carriage, not a cab like the station-cab that smells of straw, but a carriage; and Mary was coming too, she was going to wear her best hat with the red flower and enjoy herself "no end," and there would be cake and all sorts of things and a big shrubbery to play in and a flower garden—oh! miles bigger than our garden. "Only you mustn't go picking the flowers," said Mary. "Lady Charlotte won't like that."

Was Auntie Phyllis coming too?

No, Auntie wasn't coming too; she'd *love* to come, but she couldn't. . . .

It all began very much as Mary had promised. The carriage with the white horse was waiting punctually at two o'clock on the high road above the house. There was a real carpet, green with a yellow coat-of-arms, on the floor of the carriage, and the same coat-of-arms on the panel of the door; the brass door-handle was so bright and attractive that Mary had to tell Joan to keep her greedy little hands off it or she would fall out. They drove through pine woods for a time and then across a great common with geese on it, and then up a deep-hedged, winding, uphill road and so to an open road that lay over a great cornfield, and then by a snug downland village of thatched white cottages very gay with flowers. And so to a real lodge with a garden round it and a white-aproned gate-keeper, which impressed Mary very favourably.

"It's a sort of park she has," said Mary.

As they drew near the house they were met by a very gay and smiling and obviously pretty lady, in a dress of blue cotton stuff and flowers in her hat. She had round blue eyes and glowing cheeks and a rejoicing sort of voice.

"Here they are!" she cried. "Hullo, old Peter! Hullo, old Joan! Would you like to get out?"

They would.

"Would they like to see the garden?"

They would.

And a little bit of "chockky" each?

Glances for approval at Mary and encouraging nods from Mary. They would. They got quite big pieces of chocolate and pouched them solemnly, and went on with grave, unsymmetrical faces. And the bright lady took them each by a hand and began to talk of flowers and birds and all the things they were going to see, a summerhouse, a croquet-poky lawn, a little old pony stable, a churchy-perchy, and all sorts of things. Particularly the churchy-perchy.

Mary dropped behind amicably.

So accompanied it was not very dreadful to meet the great whisker-woman herself in a white and mauve patterned dress of innumerable flounces and a sunshade with a deep valance to it, to match. She didn't come very near to the children, but waved her hand to them and crowed in what was manifestly a friendly spirit. And across the lawn they saw a marvel, a lawn-mower pushed by a man and drawn by a little piebald pony in boots.

"He puts on his booty-pootys when little boys have to take them off, to walk over the grassy green carpet," said the .blue cotton lady.

Peter was emboldened to address Lady Charlotte.

"Puts on 'is booty-pootys," he said impressively.
"*Wise* little pony," said Lady Charlotte.
They saw all sorts of things, the stables, the summerhouse, a little pond with a swan upon it, a lane through dark
bushes, and so they came to the church.

§ 7

Lady Charlotte had decided to christen both the children.
She was not sure whether she wanted to take possession
of them altogether, in spite of Mr. Grimes' suggestion. Her
health was uncertain, at any time she might have to go
abroad; she was liable to nervous headaches to which the
proximity of captive and possibly insurgent children would
be unhelpful, and her two pet dogs were past that first
happy fever of youth which makes the presence of children
acceptable. And also there was Oswald—that woman had
said he was coming home. But christened Lady Charlotte
was resolved those children should be, at whatever cost. It
was her duty. It would be an act of the completest self-
vindication, and the completest vindication of sound Anglican
ideas. And once it was done it would be done, let the
Ingle-Nook aunts rage ever so wildly.
Within a quarter of a mile of Chastlands stood a little
church among evergreen trees, Otfield Church, so near to
Chastlands and so far from Otfield that Lady Charlotte
used to point out, "It's practically my Chapel of Ease."
Her outer shrubbery ran to the churchyard wall, and she had
a gate of her own and went to church through a respectful
avenue of her own rhododendrons and in by a convenient
door. Wiscott, the curate in charge, was an agreeable, easily
trodden-on young man with a wife of obscure origins—Lady
Charlotte suspected a childhood behind some retail shop—
and abject social ambitions. It was Wiscott whose bullying
Arthur had overheard when he conceived his admiration for
Lady Charlotte. Lady Charlotte had no social prejudices;
she liked these neighbours in her own way and would entertain them to tea and even occasionally to lunch. The organ
in Otfield church was played in those days by a terrified
National schoolmistress, a sound, nice churchwoman of the

very lowest educational qualifications permissible, and the sexton, a most respectful worthy old fellow, eked out his income as an extra hand in Lady Charlotte's garden and was the father of one of her housemaids. Moreover he was the husband of a richly grateful wife in whose rheumatism Lady Charlotte took quite a kindly interest. All these things gave Lady Charlotte a nice homelike feeling in God's little house in Otfield; God seemed to come nearer to her there and to be more aware of her importance in His world than anywhere else; and it was there that she proposed to hold the simple ceremony that should snatch Peter and Joan like brands from the burning.

Her plans were made very carefully. Mrs. Wiscott had a wide and winning way with children, and she was to capture their young hearts from the outset and lead them to the church. Mary, whom Lady Charlotte regarded as doubtfully friendly, was to be detached by Unwin and got away for a talk. At the church would be the curate and the organist and the sexton and his daughter and Cashel, the butler, a very fine type of the more serious variety of Anglican butlers, slender and very active and earnest and a teetotaler. And to the children it would all seem like a little game.

Mr. Wiscott had been in some doubt about the ceremony. He had baptized infants, he had baptized "those of riper years," but he had never yet had to deal with children of four or five. The rubric provides that for such the form for the Public Baptism of Infants is available with the change of the word "infant" to "child" where occasion requires it, but the rubric says nothing of the handling of the children concerned. He consulted Lady Charlotte. Should he lift up Peter and Joan in succession to the font when the moment of the actual sprinkling came, or should he deal with them as if they were adults? Lady Charlotte decided that he had better lift. "They are only little mites," said Lady Charlotte.

Now up to that point the ceremony went marvellously according to plan. It is true that Mary wasn't quite got out of the way; she was obliged to follow at a distance because the children in spite of every hospitality would every now and then look round for her to nod reassuringly to them; but when she saw the rest of the party going into the little church she shied away with the instinctive avoidance of the reluctant church woman, and remained remotely visible through the open doorway afar off in the rhododendron walk conversing deeply with Unwin. They were conversing about the unreasonableness of Unwin's sister-in-law in not minding what she ate in spite of her indigestion.

The children, poor little heathens! had never been in church before and everything was a wonder. They saw a gentleman standing in the midst of the church and clad in a manner strange to them, in a surplice and cassock, and under it you saw his trousers and boots—it was as if he wore night clothes over his day clothes—and immediately he began to read very fast but yet in a strangely impressive manner out of a book. They had great confidence now in Mrs. Wiscott, and accompanied her into a pew and sat up neatly on hassocks beside her. The gentleman in the white robe kept on reading, and every now and then the others, who had also got hold of books, answered him. At first Peter wanted to laugh, then he got very solemn, and then he began to want to answer too: "wow wow wow," when the others did. But he knew he had best do it very softly. There was reverence in the air. Then everybody got up and went and stood, and Mrs. Wiscott made Joan and Peter stand, round about the font. She stood close beside Joan and Peter with her hands very reassuringly behind them. From this point Peter could see the curate's Adam's apple moving in a very fascinating way. So things went on quite successfully until the fatal moment when Mr. Wiscott took Peter up in his arms.

"Come along," he said very pleasantly—not realizing that Peter did not like his Adam's apple.

"He's going to show you the pretty water," said Mrs. Wiscott.

"*Naw!*" said Peter sharply and backed as the curate gripped his arm, and then everything seemed to go wrong.

Mr. Wiscott had never handled a sturdy little boy of five before. Peter would have got away if Mrs. Wiscott, abandoning Joan, had not picked him up and handed him neatly to

her husband. Then came a breathless struggle on the edge
of the font, and upon every one, even upon Lady Charlotte,
came a strange sense as though they were engaged in some
deed of darkness. The water splashed loudly. It splashed
on Peter's face and Peter's abundant voice sent out its
S. O. S. call: "Mare-*wi!*"

Mr. Wiscott compressed his lips and held Peter firmly,
hushing resolutely, and presently struggled on above a tremendous din towards the sign of the cross. . . .

But Joan had formed her own rash judgments.

She bolted down the aisle and out through the open door,
and her voice filled the universe. "They dwounding Petah.
They dwounding Petah—like they did the kittays!"

Far away was Mary, but turning towards her amazed.

Joan rushed headlong to her for sanctuary, wild with
terror.

"I wanna be *kep,* Marewi," she bawled. "I wanna be
kep!"

§ 8

But here Mary was to astonish Lady Charlotte. "Why
couldn't they tell *me?*" she asked Unwin when she grasped
the situation.

"It's all right, Joan," she said. "Nobody ain't killing
Peter. You come alongo me and see."

And it was Mary who stilled the hideous bawling of
Peter, and Mary who induced Joan to brave the horrors of
this great experience and to desist from her reiterated assertion: "Done *wan'* nergenelman t'wash me!"

And it was Mary who said in the carriage going back:

"Don't you say nothing about being naughty to yer Aunt
Phyllis and I won't neether."

And so she did her best to avoid any further discussion of
the matter.

But in this pacific intention she was thwarted by Lady
Charlotte, who presently drove over to The Ingle-Nook to
see her "two little Christians" and how Aunt Phœbe was
taking it. She had the pleasure of explaining what had happened herself.

"We had them christened," she said. "It all passed off very well."

"It is an outrage," cried Aunt Phœbe, "on my brother's memory. It must be undone."

"That I fear can *never* be," said Lady Charlotte serenely. folding her hands before her and smiling loftily.

"Their Little White Souls!" exclaimed Aunt Phœbe, and then seizing a weapon from the enemy's armoury: "*I shall write to our solicitor.*"

§ 9

Even Lady Charlotte quailed a little before a strange solicitor; she knew that even Grimes held the secret of many tremendous powers; and when Mr. Sycamore introduced himself as having "had the pleasure of meeting your nephew, Mr. Oswald Sydenham, on one or two occasions," she prepared to be civil, wary, and evasive to the best of her ability. Mr. Sycamore was a very good-looking, rosy little man with silvery hair, twinkling gold spectacles, a soft voice and a manner of imperturbable urbanity. "I felt sure your ladyship would be willing to talk about this little business," he said. "So often a little explanation between reasonable people prevents, oh! the most disagreeable experiences. Nowadays when courts are so very prone to stand upon their dignity and inflict quite excessive penalties upon infractions —such as this."

Lady Charlotte said she was quite prepared to defend all that she had done—anywhere.

Mr. Sycamore hoped she would never be put to that inconvenience. He did not wish to discuss the legal aspects of the case at all, still—there was such a thing as Contempt. He thought that Lady Charlotte would understand that already she had gone rather far.

"Mr. Sycamore," said Lady Charlotte, heavily and impressively, "at the present time I am ill, seriously ill. I ought to have been at Bordighera a month ago. But law or no law I could not think of those poor innocent children remaining unbaptized. I stayed—to do my duty."

"I doubt if any court would sustain the plea that it *was*

your duty, single-handed, without authorization, in defiance it is alleged of the expressed wishes of the parents.''

''But *you*, Mr. Sycamore, know that it was my duty.''

''That depends, Lady Charlotte, on one's opinions upon the efficacy of infant baptism. Opinions, you know, vary widely. I have read very few books upon the subject, and what I have read confused me rather than otherwise.''

And Mr. Sycamore put his hands together before him and sat with his head a little on one side regarding Lady Charlotte attentively through the gold-rimmed spectacles.

''Well, anyhow you wouldn't let children grow up socialists and secularists without *some* attempt to prevent it!''

''Within the law,'' said Mr. Sycamore gently, and coughed behind his hand and continued to beam through his glasses. . . .

They talked in this entirely inconsecutive way for some time with a tremendous air of discussing things deeply. Lady Charlotte expressed a great number of opinions very forcibly, and Mr. Sycamore listened with the manner of a man who had at last after many years of intellectual destitution met a profoundly interesting talker. Only now and then did he seem to question her view. But yet he succeeded in betraying a genuine anxiety about the possible penalties that might fall upon Lady Charlotte. Presently, she never knew quite how, she found herself accusing Joan of her illegitimacy.

''But my dear Lady Charlotte, the poor child is scarcely responsible.''

''If we made no penalties on account of illegitimacy the whole world would dissolve away in immorality.''

Mr. Sycamore looked quite arch. ''My dear lady, surely there would be one or *two* exceptions!'' . . .

Finally, with a tremendous effect of having really got to the bottom of the matter, he said: ''Then I conclude, Lady Charlotte, that now that the children are baptized and their spiritual welfare is assured, all you wish is for things to go on quietly and smoothly without the Miss Stublands annoying you further.''

''Exactly,'' said Lady Charlotte. ''My one desire is to go abroad—now that my task is done.''

"You have every reason to be satisfied, Lady Charlotte, with things as they are. I take it that what I have to do now is to talk over the Miss Stublands and prevent any vindictive litigation arising out of the informality of your proceedings. I think—yes, I think and hope that I can do it."

And this being agreed upon Mr. Sycamore lunched comfortably and departed to The Ingle-Nook, where he showed the same receptive intelligence to Aunt Phœbe. There was the same air of taking soundings in the deep places of opinion.

"I understand," he said at last, "that your one desire is to be free from further raids and invasions from Lady Charlotte. I can quite understand it. Practically she will agree to that. I can secure that. I think I can induce her to waive what she considers to be her rights. You can't unbaptize the children, but I should think that under your care the effect, whatever the effect may be, can be trusted to wear off. . . ."

And having secured a similar promise of inaction from the Miss Stublands, Mr. Sycamore returned to London, twinkling pleasantly about the spectacles as he speculated exactly what it was that he had so evidently quite satisfactorily settled.

CHAPTER THE SIXTH

THE FOURTH GUARDIAN

§ 1

IT was just a quarter of a year after the death of Dolly and Arthur before Oswald Sydenham heard of the event and of Arthur's will and of the disputes of his three fellow guardians in England. For when the stone-mason boatman staggered and fell and the boat turned over beneath the Arco Naturale, Oswald was already marching with a long string of porters and armed men beyond the reach of letters and telegrams into the wilderness.

He was in pursuit of a detachment of the Sudanese mutineers who, with a following of wives, children and captives, were making their way round through the wet forest country north of Lake Kioga towards the Nile province. With Sydenham was an able young subaltern, Muir, the only other white man of the party. In that net of rivers, marsh and forest they were destined to spend some feverish months. They pushed too far eastward and went too fast, and they found themselves presently not the pursuers but the pursued, cut off from their supports to the south. They built a stockade near Lake Salisbury, and were loosely besieged. For a time both sides in the conflict were regarded with an impartial unfriendliness by the naked blacks who then cultivated that primitive region, and it was only the looting and violence of the Sudanese that finally turned the scale in favour of Sydenham's little force. Sydenham was able to attack in his turn with the help of a local levy; he took the Sudanese camp, killed twenty or thirty of the mutineers, captured most of their women and gear, and made five prisoners with very little loss to his own party. He led the attack, a tall, lean, dreadful figure with half a face that stared fiercely and half a red, tight-skinned, blind mask. Two Sudanese upon whom his one-sided visage came suddenly, yelled with dismay, dropped their rifles and started a stampede. Black men they knew and white men, but this was a horrible red and white man. A remnant of the enemy got away to the north and eluded his pursuit until it became dangerous to push on further. They were getting towards the district in which was the rebel chief Kabarega, and a union of his forces with the Sudanese fugitives would have been more than Sydenham and Muir could have tackled.

The government force turned southward again. Oswald had been suffering from fatigue and a recurrence of blackwater fever, a short, sharp spell that passed off as suddenly as it came; but it left him weak and nervously shaken; for some painful days before he gave in he ruled his force with an iron discipline that was at once irrational and terrifying, and afterwards he was carried in a litter, and Muir took over the details of command. It was only when Oswald was within two days' journey of Luba Fort upon Lake Victoria Nyanza that his letters reached him.

§ 2

During all this time until he heard of Dolly's death, Oswald's heart was bitter against her and womankind. He had left England in a fever of thwarted loneliness. He did his best to "go to Hell" even as he had vowed in the first ecstasy of rage, humiliation and loss. He found himself incapable of a self-destructive depravity. He tried drinking heavily and he could never be sure that he was completely drunk; some toughness in his fibre defeated this overrated consolation. He attempted other forms of dissipation, and he could not even achieve remorse, nothing but exasperation with that fiddling pettiness of sexual misbehaviour which we call Vice. He desired a gigantic sense of desolation and black damnation, and he got only shame for a sort of childish nastiness. "If this is Sin!" cried Oswald at last, "then God help the Devil!"

"There's nothing like Work," said Oswald, "nothing like Work for forgetfulness. And getting hurt. And being shot at. I've done with this sort of thing for good and all. . . ."

"What a fool I was to come here! . . ."

And he went on his way to Uganda.

The toil of his expedition kept his mind from any clear thinking about Dolly. But if he thought little he felt much. His mind stuck and raged at one intolerable thought, and could not get beyond it. Dolly had come towards him and then had broken faith with the promise in her eyes, and fled back to Arthur's arms. And now she was with Arthur. Arthur was with her, Arthur had got her. And it was intolerably stupid of her. And yet she wasn't stupid. There she was in that affected little white cottage with its idiotic big roof, waiting about while that fool punched copper or tenored about æsthetics. (Oswald's objection to copper repoussé had long since passed the limits of sanity.) Always Dolly was at Arthur's command now. Until the end of things. And she might be here beside her mate, with the flash in her eyes, with her invincible spirit, sharing danger, fever and achievement; empire building, mankind saving. . . .

Now and then indeed his mind generalized his bitter personal disappointment with a fine air of getting beyond it. The Blantyre woman and that older woman of his first experiences who had screamed at the sight of his disfigured face, were then brought into the case to establish a universal misogyny. Women were just things of sex, child-bearers, dressed up to look like human beings. They promised companionship as the bait on the hook promises food. They were the cheap lures of that reproductive maniac, herself feminine, old Mother Nature; sham souls blind to their own worthless quality through an inordinate vanity and self-importance. Ruthless they were in their distribution of disappointment. Sterile themselves, life nested in them. They were the crowning torment in the Martyrdom of Man.

Thus Oswald in the moments when thought overtook him. And when it came to any dispute about women among the men, and particularly to the disposal of the women after the defeat of the mutineers near Lake Salisbury, it suited his humour to treat them as chattels and to note how ready they were to be treated as chattels, how easy in the transfer of their affections and services from their defeated masters to their new owners. This, he said, was the natural way with women. In Europe life was artificial; women were out of hand; we were making an inferior into a superior as the Egyptian made a god of the cat. Like cat worship it was a phase in development that would pass in its turn.

The camp at which his letters met him was in the Busoga country, and all day long the expedition had been tramping between high banks of big-leaved plants, blue flowering salvias, dracenas and the like, and under huge flowering trees. Captain Wilkinson from Luba Fort had sent runners and porters to meet them, and at the halting-place, an open space near the banana fields of a village, they found tea already set. for them. Oswald was ill and tired, and Muir took over the bothers of supervision while Oswald sat in a deck chair, drank tea, and opened his letters. The first that came to hand was from Sycamore, the Stubland solicitor. Its news astonished him.

Dear Sir, wrote Mr. Sycamore.

I regret to have to inform you of the death of my two clients, your friends Mr. and Mrs. Arthur Stubland. They were drowned by a boat accident at Capri on the third of this month, and they probably died within a few minutes of each other. They had been in Italy upon a walking tour together. There were no witnesses of the accident—the boatman was drowned with them—and the presumption in such cases is that the husband survived the wife. This is important because by the will of Mrs. Stubland you are nominated as the sole guardian both of the son and the adopted daughter, while by the will of Mr. Stubland you are one of four such guardians. In all other respects the wills are in identical terms. . . .

At this point Oswald ceased to read.

He was realizing that these words meant that Dolly was dead.

§ 3

Oswald felt very little grief at the first instant of this realization. We grieve acutely for what we have lost, whether it be a reality or a dream, but Dolly had become for Oswald neither a possession nor a hope. In his mind she was established as an intense quarrel. Whatever he had to learn about her further had necessarily to begin in terms of that. The first blow of this news made him furious. He could not think of any act or happening of Dolly's except in terms of it being aimed at him. And he was irrationally angry with her for dying in such a way. That she had gone back to Arthur and resumed his embraces was, he felt, bad enough; but that she should start out to travel with Arthur alone, to walk by Arthur's side exactly as Oswald had desired her to walk by his side—he had dreamt of her radiant companionship, it had seemed within his grasp—and at last to get drowned with Arthur, that was the thing to strike him first. He did not read the rest of the letter attentively. He threw it down on the folding table before him and hit it with his fist, and gave his soul up to a storm of rage and jealousy.

"To let that fool drown here!" he cried. "She'd do anything for him. . . .

"And I might go to *Hell!* . . .

"Oh, *damn* all women! . . ."

It was not a pretty way of taking this blow. But such are the instinctive emotions of the thwarted male. His first reception of the news of Dolly's death was to curse her and all her sex. . . .

And then suddenly he had a gleam of imagination and saw Dolly white and wet and pitiful. Without any intermediate stage his mind leapt straight from storming anger to that. . . .

For a time he stared at that vision—reproached and stunned. . . .

Something that had darkened his thoughts was dispelled. His mind was illuminated by understanding. He saw Dolly again very clearly as she had talked to him in the garden. It was as if he had never seen her before. For the first time he realized her indecision. He understood now why it was she had snatched herself back from him and taken what she knew would be an irrevocable step, and he knew now that it was his own jealous pride that had made that step irrevocable. The Dolly who had told him of that decision next morning

was a Dolly already half penitent and altogether dismayed.
And if indeed he had loved her better than his pride, even
then he might have held on still and won her. He remembered how she had winced when she made her hinting confession to him. No proud, cold-hearted woman had she been
when she had whispered, "Oswald, now you must certainly
go."

It was as plain as daylight, and never before had he seen
it plain.

He had left her, weak thing that she was, because she was
weak, for this fellow to waste and drown. And it was over
now and irrevocable.

"Men and women, poor fools together," he said. "Poor
fools. Poor fools," and then at the thought of Dolly, broken
and shrinking, ashamed of the thing she had done, at the
thought of the insults he had slashed at her, knowing how
much she was ashamed and thinking nevertheless only of his
own indignity, and at the thought of how all this was now
stilled forever in death, an overwhelming sense of the pitifulness of human pride and hatred, passion and desire came upon
him. How we hated! how we hurt one another! and how
fate mocked all our spites and hopes! God sold us a bargain
in life. Dolly was sold. Arthur the golden-crested victor
was sold. He himself was sold. The story had ended in this
pitiless smacking of every one of the three poor tiresome
bits of self-assertion who had acted in it. It was a joke,
really, just a joke. He began to laugh as a dog barks, and
then burst into bitter weeping. . . .

He wept noisily for a time. He blubbered with his
elbows on the table.

His Swahili attendant watched him with an undiminished
respect, for Africa weeps and laughs freely and knows well
that great chiefs also may weep.

Presently his tears gave out; he became very still and
controlled, feeling as if in all his life he would never weep
again.

He took up Mr. Sycamore's letter and went on reading it.

"In all other respects the wills are in identical terms,"
the letter ran. *"In both I am appointed sole executor, a*

*confidence I appreciate as a tribute to my lifelong friendship
with Mr. Stubland and his parents.   The other guardians
are Miss Phyllis and Miss Phœbe Stubland and your aunt-
in-law, Lady Charlotte Sydenham.''*

''Good heavens!'' cried Oswald wearily, as one hears a
hopelessly weak jest.   ''But *why?*''

*''I do not know if you will remember me, but I have had
the pleasure of meeting you on one or two occasions, notably
after your admirable paper read to the Royal Geographical
Society.   This fact and the opinion our chance meetings have
enabled me to form of you, emboldens me to add something
here that I should not I think have stated to a perfect
stranger, and that is my impression that Mr. Stubland was
particularly anxious that you should become a guardian under his will.   I knew Mr. Stubland from quite a little boy;
his character was a curious one, there was a streak of distrust
and secretiveness in it, due I think to a Keltic strain that
came in from his mother's side.   He altered his will a couple
of days before he started for Italy, and from his manner and
from the fact that Mrs. Stubland's will was not also altered,
I conclude that he did so without consulting her.   He did so
because for some reason he had taken it into his head that
you would not act, and he did so for no other reason that I
can fathom.   Otherwise he would have left the former will
alone.   Under the circumstances I feel bound to tell you this
because it may materially affect your decision to undertake
this responsibility.   I think it will be greatly to the advantage of the children if you do.   I may add that I know
the two Miss Stublands as well as I knew their brother, and
that I have a certain knowledge of Lady Charlotte, having
been consulted on one occasion by a client in relation to her.
The Misses Stubland were taking care of The Ingle-Nook and
children—there is a trustworthy nurse—in the absence of the
parents up to the time of the parents' decease, and it will
be easy to prolong this convenient arrangement for the present.   The children are still of tender age and for the next
few years they could scarcely be better off.   I trust that in
the children's interest you will see your way to accept this
duty to your friend.   My hope is enhanced by the thought*

*that so I may be able later to meet again a man for whose
courage and abilities and achievements I have a very great
admiration indeed.*

I am, dear Sir,

Very truly yours,

George Sycamore."

"Yes," said Oswald, "but I can't, you know."

He turned over Sycamore's letter again, and it seemed no
longer a jest and an insult that Arthur had made him Peter's
guardian. Sycamore's phrases did somehow convey the hesitating Arthur, penitent of the advantages that had restored
him Dolly and still fatuously confident of Oswald's good
faith.

"But I can't do it, my man," said Oswald. "It's too
much for human nature. Your own people must see to your
own breed."

He sat quite still for a long time thinking of another child
that now could never be born.

"Why didn't I stick to her?" he whispered. "Why didn't
I hold out for her?"

He took up Sycamore's letter again.

"But why the devil did he shove in old Charlotte?" he
exclaimed. "The man was no better than an idiot. And
underhand at that."

His eye went to a pile of still unopened letters. "Ah! here
we are!" he said, selecting one in a bulky stone-grey envelope.

He opened it and extracted a number of sheets of stone-grey
paper covered with a vast, loose handwriting, for which
previous experience had given Oswald a strong distaste.

My dear Nephew, her letter began.

*I suppose you have already heard the unhappy end of that
Stubland marriage. I have always said that it was bound
to end in a tragedy. . . .*

"Oh Lord!" said Oswald, and pitched the letter aside and
fell into deep thought. . . .

He became aware of Muir standing and staring down at
him. One of the boys must have gone off to Muir and told
him of Oswald's emotion.

"Hullo," said Muir. "All right?"

"I've been crying," said Oswald drily. "I've had bad news. This fever leaves one rotten."

"Old Wilkinson has sent us up a bottle of champagne," said Muir. "He's thought of everything. The cook's got curry powder again and there's a basket of fish. We shall dine to-night. It's what you want."

"Perhaps it is," said Oswald.

§ 4

After dinner, the best dinner they had had for many weeks, a dinner beautifully suggestive to a sick man of getting back once more to a world in which there is enough and comfort, Oswald's tongue was loosened and he told his story. He was not usually a communicative man but this was a brimming occasion; Muir he knew for a model of discretion, Muir had been his colleague, his nurse and his intimate friend to the exclusion of all others, for three eventful months, and Muir had already made his confidences. So Oswald told about Dolly and how his scar and his scruples had come between them, and what he thought and felt about Arthur, and so to much experimental wisdom about love and the bitterness of life. He mentioned the children, and presently Muir, who had the firm conscientiousness of the Scotch, brought him back to Peter.

"He was a decent little chap," said Oswald. "He was tremendously like Dolly."

"And not like that other man?" said Muir sympathetically.

"No. Not a bit."

"I'm thinking you ought to stand by him for all you're worth."

Oswald thought.

"I will," he said. . . .

The next morning life did not seem nearly so rounded and kindly as it had been after his emotional storm of the evening before; he was angry and jealous about Dolly and Arthur again, and again disposed to regard his guardianship as an imposition, but he felt he had given his word overnight and that he was bound now to stand by Joan and Peter as well as he could.   Moreover neither Lady Charlotte nor the sisters Stubland were really, he thought, people to whom children should be entrusted.   His party reached Luba's the next evening, and he at once arranged to send a cable to Mr. Sycamore accepting his responsibility and adding: "Prefer children should go on as much as possible mother's ideas until my return."

CHAPTER THE SEVENTH

THE SCHOOL OF ST. GEORGE AND THE VENERABLE BEDE

§ 1

SO for a time this contest of the newer England of free thought, sentimental socialism, and invested profits (so far as it was embodied in the Stubland sisters) and the traditional land-owning, church-going Tory England (so far that is as Lady Charlotte Sydenham was able to represent it), for the upbringing of Joan and Peter was suspended, and the Stubland sisters remained in control of these fortunate heirs of the ages. The two ladies determined to make the most of their opportunity to train the children to.be, as Aunt Phœbe put it, "free and simple, but fearlessly advanced, unbiassed and yet exquisitely cultivated, inheritors of the treasure of the past purged of all ancient defilement, sensuous, passionate, determined, forerunners of a super-humanity"—for already the phrases at least of Nietzsche were trickling into the restricted but turbid current of British thought.

In their design the Stubland sisters were greatly aided by the sudden appearance of Miss Murgatroyd in the neighbourhood, and the rapid and emphatic establishment of the School of Saint George and the Venerable Bede within two miles of The Ingle-Nook door.

Miss Murgatroyd was a sturdy, rufous lady with a resentful manner, as though she felt that everything and everybody were deliberately getting in her way, and an effort of tension that passed very readily from anger to enthusiasm and from enthusiasm to anger. Her place was in the van. She did not mind very much where the van was going so long as she was in it. She was a born teacher, too, and so overpoweringly moved to teach that what she taught was a

112

secondary consideration. She wanted to do something for mankind—it hardly mattered what. In America she would have been altogether advanced and new, but it was a peculiarity of middle-class British liberalism at the end of the nineteenth century just as it was of middle-class French liberalism a hundred years before, that it was strongly reactionary in colour. In the place of Rousseau and his demand for a return to the age of innocence, we English had Ruskin and Morris, who demanded a return to the Middle Ages. And in Miss Murgatroyd there was Rousseau as well as Ruskin; she wanted, she said, the best of everything; she was very comprehensive; she epitomized the movements of her time.

A love disappointment—the man had fled inexplicably to the ends of the earth and vanished—had exacerbated in Miss Murgatroyd a passion for the plastic affections of children; she had resolved to give herself wholly to the creation of a new sort of school embodying all the best ideals of the time. She saw herself a richly-robed, creative prophetess among the clustering and adoring young.

She had had a certain amount of capital available, and this she had expended upon the adaptation of a pleasant, many-roomed, modern house that looked out bravely over the valley of the Weald about a mile and three-quarters from The Ingle-Nook, to the necessities of a boarding-school, and here she presently accumulated her scholars. She furnished it very brightly in art colours and Morris patterns; wherever possible the woodwork was stained a pleasing green and perforated with heart-shaped holes; there were big, flat, obscurely symbolical colour-prints by Walter Crane, reproductions in bright colours of the works of Rossetti and Burne Jones and Botticelli, and a full-size cast of the Venus of Milo. The name was Ruskinian in spirit with a touch of J. R. Green's *Short History of the English People*.

Miss Murgatroyd was indiscriminately receptive of new educational ideas; she meant to miss nothing; and some of these ideas were quite good and some were quite silly; and nearly every holiday she went off with a large notebook and much enthusiasm to educational congresses and conferences and summer schools and got some more. One that she acquired quite early, soon after the battle of Omdurman, was

to put all her girls and most of her boys into Djibbahs—
loose, pretty garments that were imitated from and named
after the Dervish form of shirt.   Hers was one of the first of
those numerous ''djibbah schools'' that still flourish in England.

Also she had a natural proclivity towards bare legs and
sandals and hatlessness, and only a certain respect for the
parents kept the school from waves of pure vegetarianism.
And she did all she could to carry her classes out of the
classrooms and into the open air. . . .

The end of the nineteenth century was a happy and beautiful time for the bodies of the children of the more prosperous classes.   Children had become precious.   Among such
people as the Stublands one never heard of such a thing as
the death of a child; all their children lived and grew up.
It was a point upon which Arthur had never tired of insisting.   Whenever he had felt bored and wanting a brief holiday he had been accustomed to go off with a knapsack to study
church architecture, and he had never failed to note the lists
of children on the monuments.   ''There you are again,''
he would say.   ''Look at that one: 'and of Susan his wife
by whom he had issue eleven children of whom three survived him.'   That's the universal story of a woman's life
in the sixteenth and seventeenth century.   Nowadays it
would read, 'by whom he had issue three children who all survived him.'   And you see here, she died first, worn out,
and he married again.   And here are five more children, and
three die in infancy and childhood.   There was a frightful
boom in dying in those days; dying was a career in itself for
two-thirds of the children born.   They made an art of early
death.   They were trained to die in an edifying manner.
Parents wrote books about their little lost saints.   Instead
of rearing them——'' . . . .

Miss Murgatroyd's school was indeed healthy and pretty
and full of physical happiness, but the teaching and mental
training that went on in it was of a lower quality.   Mental
strength and mental balance do not show in quite the same
way as their physical equivalents.   Minds do not grow as
bodies do, through leaving the windows open and singing in
the sun.

§ 2

Aunt Phœbe was an old acquaintance of Miss Murgatroyd. They had met at Adelboden during one of the early Fabian excursions in Switzerland. Afterwards Miss Murgatroyd had been charmed by Aunt Phœbe's first book, a little thin volume of bold ideas in grey covers and a white back, called, *By-thoughts of a Stitchwoman*. In it Aunt Phœbe represented herself rather after the fashion of one of those richly conceived women who sit and stitch in the background of Sir Frederick Leighton's great wall paintings at South Kensington, "The Industrial Arts applied to Peace" and "The Industrial Arts Applied to War" (her needlework was really very bad indeed) and while she stitched she thought. She thought outrageously; that was the idea; and she represented all the quiet stitching sex as thinking as outrageously. Miss Murgatroyd had a kindred craving for outrageous thinking, and the book became the link of a great intellectual friendship. They vied with one another in the extremity of their opinions and the mystical extravagance of their expressions. They maintained a tumescent flow of thought that was mostly feeling and feeling that was mostly imitation, far over the heads of the nice little children, who ran about the bright and airy school premises free from most of the current infections of body and spirit, and grew as children do grow under favourable circumstances, after the manner of Nature in her better moods, that is to say after the manner of Nature ploughed and weeded and given light and air.

So far as Aunt Phœbe was concerned, the great thoughts were confined to one or two intimates and—a rather hypothetical circle—her readers. Her mental galumphings were a thing apart. A kind of shyness prevented her with strangers and children. But Miss Murgatroyd was impelled by a sense of duty to build up the character of her children by discourse, more particularly on Sundays. On Sunday mornings the whole school went to church; in the afternoon it had a decorous walk, or it read or talked, and Miss Mills, the junior assistant, read aloud to the little ones; in the evening it read or it drew and painted, except for a special half hour when Miss Murgatroyd built its character up. That was her time. Thus, for example, she built it up about Truth.

"Girls," she began, "I want to talk to you a little this evening about Truth. I want you to think about Truth, to concentrate your minds upon it and see just all it means and can mean to us. You know we must all tell the Truth, but has it ever occurred to you to ask *why* we must tell the Truth? I want you to ask that. I want you to be aware of why you have to be good in this way and that. I do not want you to be unthinkingly good. I want you to be

'Not like dumb, driven cattle!
Be a hero in the strife!'

or a heroine as the case may be. And so, why do we tell the Truth? Is it because if we did not do so people would be deceived and things go wrong? Partly. Is it because if we did not do so, people would not trust us? Also yes, partly. But the real reason, girls and boys, is this, the real reason is that Lying Lips are an Abomination to the Lord, they are disgusting to Him, and so they ought to be disgusting to us. That is the real reason why we should tell the truth. Because it is a thing offensive and disgraceful, and if we did not do so, then we should tell a Lie.

("Doris, *do* stop plaiting your sister's hair, please. There is a time for all things.)

"I hope there is no one here who can bear to think calmly of telling a Lie; and yet every time you do not tell the Truth manfully and bravely you do that. It is an offence so dreadful that we are told in Scripture that whosoever calleth his brother a liar—no doubt without sufficient evidence— is in danger of Hell Fire. I hope you will think of that if ever you should be tempted at any time to tell a Lie.

"But now I want you to think a little of what is Truth. It is clear you cannot tell the truth unless you know what truth is. Well, what is truth? One thing, I think, will occur to you all at once as part at least of the answer. Truth is straightness. When we say a ruler is true we mean that it is straight, and when we say a wall or a corner is out of truth we mean that it isn't straight. And, in vulgar parlance, when we say a man is a straight man we mean one

whose acts and words are true.   And another thing of which
our great teacher Ruskin so often reminds us is, that Truth
is Simplicity.   True people are always simple, and simple
people are usually too simple to be anything but true.
Truth never explains.   It never argues.   When I have to
ask a girl—and sometimes I have to ask a girl—did she or did
she not do this or that, then if she answers me simply and
straightly Yes or No, I feel I am getting the truth, but if
she answers back, 'that depends,' or 'Please, Miss Murgatroyd, may I explain just how it was?' then I know that there
is something coming—something else coming, and not the
straight and simple, the homespun, simple, valiant English
Truth at all.   Yes and No are the true words, because as
Plato and Aristotle and the Greek philosophers generally
taught us in the Science of Logic long ago, and taught it to
us for all time, a thing either is or else it is not; it is no
good explaining or trying to explain, nothing can ever alter
that now for ever.   Either you *did* do the thing or you
didn't do the thing.   There is no other choice.   That is the
very essence of Logic; it would be impossible to have Logic
without it.'' . . .

So Miss Murgatroyd building up in her pupils' minds by
precept and example, the wonderful art and practice of
English ratiocination.

§ 3

At first Joan and Peter did not see very much of Miss
Murgatroyd.   She moved about at the back of things, very
dignified and remote, decorative and vaguely terrible.   Their
business lay chiefly with Miss Mills.

Miss Mills was also an educational enthusiast, but of a
milder, gentler type than Miss Murgatroyd; she lacked
Miss Murgatroyd's confidence and boldness; she sometimes
doubted whether everything wasn't almost too difficult to
teach.   She was no blind disciple of her employer.   She had
a suppressed sense of academic humour that she had acquired by staying with an aunt who kept a small Berlin-
wool shop in Oxford, and once or twice she had thought
of the most dreadful witticisms about Miss Murgatroyd.

Though she had told them to no one, they had kept her ears
hot for days.   Often she wanted quite badly to titter at the
school; it was so different from an ordinary school.   Yet
she liked wearing a djibbah and sandals.   That was fun.
She had no educational qualifications, but year by year she
was slowly taking the diploma of Associate of the London
College of Preceptors.   It is a kindly college; the examinations for the diploma may be taken subject by subject over
a long term of years.   She used to enjoy going up to London
for her diploma at Christmas and Midsummer.   Her great
difficulty was the arithmetic.   The sums never came right.

Miss Murgatroyd was usually very severe upon what she
called the Fetish of Examinations; she herself had neither
degree nor diploma, it was a moral incapacity, and she admitted that she could as soon steal as pass an examination;
but it was understood that Miss Mills pursued this qualifica-
tion with no idea whatever of passing but merely ''for the
sake of the stimulus.''   She made a point of never preparing
at all (''cramming'' that is) for any of the papers she
''took.''   This put the thing on a higher level altogether.

She had already done the Theory and Practice of Education part of the diploma.   For that she had read parts of
Leonard and Gertrude, and she had attended five lectures upon Froebel.   Those were days long before the Mon-
tessori System, which is now so popular with our Miss
Millses; the prevalent educational vogues in the 'nineties
were Kindergarten and Swedish drill (the Ling System).
Miss Mills was an enthusiast for the Kindergarten.   She
began teaching Joan and Peter queer little practices with
paper mats and paper-pattern folding, and the stringing of
beads.   As Joan and Peter had been doing such things for a
year or so at home as ''play,'' their ready teachability impressed her very favourably.   All the children who fell under Miss Mills got a lot of Kindergarten, even though some
of them were as old as nine or ten.   They had lots of little
songs that she made them sing with appropriate action.   All
these little songs dealt with the familiar daily life—as it
was lived in South Germany four score years ago.   The children pretended to be shoemakers, foresters, and woodcut-
ters and hunters and cowherds and masons and students

wandering about the country, and they imitated the hammering of shoes, the sawing of stone or the chopping down of trees, and so forth. It had never dawned upon Miss Mills that such types as these were rare objects upon the Surrey countryside. In the country about her there were no masons because there was no stone, no cowherds because there were no cows on the hills and the cows below grazed in enclosed fields, trees and wood were handled wholesale by machinery, and people's boots came from Northampton or America, and were repaired in London. If any one had suggested songs about golf caddies, jobbing gardeners, or traction-engines, or steam-ploughs, or sawmills, or rate-collectors, or grocers' boys, or season-ticket holders, or stockbrokers from London stealing rights-of-way, or carpenters putting up fences and trespass-notice boards, she would have thought it a very vulgar suggestion indeed.

Kindergarten did not occupy all the time-table of Miss Mills. She regarded kindergarten as a special subject. She also taught her class to read, she taught them to write, she imparted the elements of history and geography, she did not so much lay the foundations of mathematics as accumulate a sort of rubble on which Mr. Beldame, the visiting mathematical master (Tuesdays and Thursdays), was afterwards to build. Here again Joan and Peter were fortunate. Peter had learnt his alphabet before he was two; Joan had not been much later with it, and both of them could read easy little stories already before they came under Miss Mills' guidance. That English spelling was entirely illogical, had not troubled them in the least. Insistence upon logical consistency comes later in life. Miss Mills never discovered their previous knowledge. She had heard of a method of teaching to read which was called the "Look and Say Method," and the essence of it was that you *never* learnt your letters. It was devised for the use of those older children who go to elementary schools from illiterate homes, and who are beginning to think for themselves a little. From the first by this method the pupils learnt the letters in combination.

"Now, Peter," Miss Mills would say, "this is 'to.' Look and say—to."

"To," said Peter.

"Now I put this little squiggle to it."

("P," said Peter privately).

"And it is 'top'."

"Top," said Peter.

"And now *this* is 'co.' What is this? Look and say."

Peter regarded "cop" for a moment. He knew c-o-p was the signal for "cop," just as S.O.S. is the signal for "help urgently needed," but he knew also it was forbidden to read out the letters of the signal.

"Cop," said Peter, after going through the necessary process of thought.

His inmost feeling about the matter was that Miss Mills did not know her letters, but had some queer roundabout way of reading of her own, and that he was taking an agreeable advantage of her. . . .

Then Miss Mills taught Peter to add and subtract and multiply and divide. She had once heard some lectures upon teaching arithmetic by graphic methods that had pleased her very much. They had seemed so clear. The lecturer had suggested that for a time easy sums might be shown in the concrete as well as in figures. You would first of all draw your operation or express it by wood blocks, and then you would present it in figures. You would draw an addition of 3 to 4, thus:

And then when your pupil had counted it and verified it you would write it down:

$$3 \quad + \quad 4 \quad = \quad 7$$

But Miss Mills, when she made her notes, had had no time to draw all the parallelograms; she had just put down one and a number over it in each case, and then her memory had muddled the idea. So she taught Joan and Peter thus: "See," she said, "I will make it perfectly plain to you. Perfectly plain. You take three—so," and she drew

3 .

"and then you take four—so," and she drew

4

"and then you see three plus four makes seven—so:

3   +   4   =   7

"Do you see now how it *must* be so, Peter?"

Peter tried to feel that he did.

Peter quite agreed that it was nice to draw frames about the figures in this way. Afterwards he tried a variation that looked like the face of old Chester Drawers:

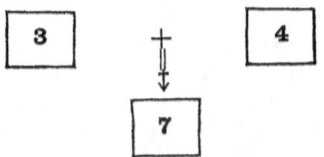

But for some reason Miss Mills would not see the beauty of that. Instead of laughing, she said: "Oh, no, that's *quite* wrong!" which seemed to Peter just selfishly insisting on her own way.

Well, one had to let her have her own way. She was a grown-up. If it had been Joan, Peter would have had his way. . . .

Both Joan and Peter were much addicted to drawing when they went to the School of St. George and the Vener-

able Bede. They had picked it up from Dolly. They produced sketches that were something between a scribble and
an inspired sketch. They drew three-legged horses that
really kicked and men who really struck hard with arms
longer than themselves, terrific blows. If Peter wanted to
make a soldier looking very fierce in profile, he drew an
extra eye aglare beyond the tip of the man's nose. If Joan
wanted to do a pussy-cat curled up, she curled it up into
long spirals like a snake. Any intelligent person could be
amused by the sketches of Joan and Peter. But Miss Mills
discovered they were all "out of proportion," and Miss
Murgatroyd said that this sort of thing was "mere scrib-
bling." She called Peter's attention to the strong, firm outlines of various drawings by Walter Crane. She said that
what the hands of Joan and Peter wanted was discipline.
She said that a drawing wasn't a drawing until it was "lined
in." She set the two children drawing pages and pages
of firm, straight lines. She related a wonderful fable of
how Giotto's one aim in life was to draw a perfect free-
hand circle. She held out hopes that some day they might
draw "from models," cones and cubes and such-like stirring
objects. But she did not think they would ever draw well
enough to draw human beings. Neither Miss Mills nor Miss
Murgatroyd thought it was possible for any one, not being
a professional artist, to draw a human being in motion.
They knew it took years and years of training. Even then
it was very exhausting to the model. They thought it was
impertinent for any one young to attempt it.

So Joan and Peter got through their "drawing lessons"
by being as inattentive as possible, and in secret they practised drawing human beings as a vice, as something forbidden and detrimental and delightful. They drew them
kicking about and doing all sorts of things. They drew
them with squinting eyes and frightful noses. Sometimes
they would sort of come like people they knew. They made
each other laugh. Peter would draw nonsense things to
amuse the older girls. When he found difficulties with hands
or feet or horses' legs he would look secretly at pictures to
see how they were done. He thought it was wrong to do this,
but he did it. He wanted to make his pictures alive-er and

liker every time; he was unscrupulous how he did it.   So
gradually the two children became caricaturists.   But in
their school reports there was never anything about their
drawing except ''Untidy,'' or, in the case of Joan, ''Could
do better if she would try.''

Peter was rather good at arithmetic, in spite of Miss
Mills' instruction. He got sums right. It was held to be
a gift. Joan was less fortunate. Like most people who
have been badly taught, Miss Mills had one or two foggy
places in her own arithmetical equipment. She was not
clear about seven sevens and eight eights; she had a confused, irregular tendency to think that they might amount
in either case to fifty-six, and also she had a trick of adding
seven to nine as fifteen, although she always got from nine
to seven correctly as sixteen. Every learner of arithmetic
has a tendency to start little local flaws of this sort, standing sources of error, and every good, trained teacher looks out
for them, knows how to test for them and set them right.
Once they have been faced in a clear-headed way, such
flaws can be cured in an hour or so. But few teachers in
upper and middle-class schools in England, in those days,
knew even the elements of their business; and it was the
custom to let the baffling influence of such flaws develop
into the persuasion that the pupil had not ''the gift for
mathematics.'' Very few women indeed of the English
''educated'' classes to this day can understand a fraction
or do an ordinary multiplication sum. They think compu-
tation is a sort of fudging—in which some people are
persistently lucky enough to guess right—''the gift for
mathematics''—or impudent enough to carry their points.
That was Miss Mills' secret and unformulated conviction, a
conviction with which she was infecting a large proportion of
the youngsters committed to her care. Joan became a mathematical gambler of the wildest description. But there was
a guiding light in Peter's little head that made him grip
at last upon the conviction that seven sevens make always
forty-nine, and eight eights always sixty-four, and that
when this haunting fifty-six flapped about in the sums it
was because Miss Mills, grown-up teacher though she was,
was wrong.

Mr. Robert Mond, who has done admirable things for the organized study and organized rearing of infants, once told me that a baby was the hardest thing in the world to kill. If it were not, he said, there would be no grown-up people at all.   "But a lot," he added, " get their digestions spoilt, mind you, or grow up rickety." . . . Still harder is it to kill a child's intelligence.   There is something heroic about the fight that every infant mind has to make against the bad explanations, the misleading suggestions, the sheer foolishness in which we adults entangle it.   The dawning intelligence of Peter, like a young Hercules, fought with the serpentine muddle-headedness of Miss Mills in its cradle, and escaped—remarkably undamaged. . . . Joan's, too, fought and escaped, except perhaps for a slight serpentine infection.   She was feminine and flexible; she lacked a certain brutality of conviction that Peter possessed.

§ 4

But the regular teaching was the least important thing in the life of the School of St. George and the Venerable Bede. It existed largely in order to be put on one side.

Miss Murgatroyd had the temperament of a sensational editor.   Her school was a vehicle for Booms.   Every term there was at least one fundamental change.

The year when Joan and Peter joined the school was the year of the Diamond Jubilee, and Miss Murgatroyd had a season of loyalty.   The "Empire" and a remarkable work called *Sixty Years a Queen* dominated the school; Victoria, that poor little old panting German widow, was represented as building up a great fabric of liberty and order, as reconciling nations, as showing what a woman's heart, a mother's instinct, could do for mankind.   She was, Miss Murgatroyd conveyed, the instigator of such inventions as the electric light and the telephone; she spread railways over the world as one spreads bread with butter; she inspired Tennyson and Dickens, Carlyle and William Morris to their remarkable efforts.   The whole world revered her. All this glow of personal loyalty vanished from the school before the year was out; the Queen ceased to be mentioned and the theme of Hand Industry replaced her.   Everything was to be taught by hand and no books were to be used. Education had become too bookish. "Rote learning" was forbidden throughout the establishment and "text-books" were to be replaced by simple note-books made by the children themselves. Then two bright girls came to the school whose father was French, and, by a happy accident, a little boy also joined up who had been very well trained by a French governess. All three spoke French extremely well. Miss Murgatroyd was inspired to put the school French on a colloquial footing, and the time-table was reconstructed with a view to the production of *Le Bourgeois Gentilhomme* on St. George's Day, the anniversary day of the school.

A parent who could paint was requisitioned as a scene-painter, the stage was put up in the main schoolroom, and those who could take no other part were set to help make the costumes and distribute programs at the performance. . . .

These things happened over the heads of Joan and Peter very much as the things in the newspaper used to happen over our heads before the Great War got hold of us. They went about their small lives amidst these things and with a vast indifference to all such things. They played their little parts in them—the realities of life were not there.

To begin with, Mary used to take them to school; but after a year and a half of that it occurred to Aunt Phyllis that it would cultivate self-reliance if they went alone. So Mary only went to fetch them when there was need of an umbrella or some such serious occasion. The path ran up through the bushes to the high road past the fence of Master's paddock where Peter had once covered himself with tar. Then they had to go along the high road with a pine-wood to the right—a winding path amidst the trees ran parallel to the road—and presently with a pine-wood to the left, which hid the hollow in which the parents of young Cuspard had made their abode and out of which young Cuspard would sometimes appear, a ginger-haired, hard-breathing youngster, bare-headed and bare-footed and altogether very advanced, and so to the little common where there would be geese or a tethered pony. Joan and Peter crossed this obliquely by the path, which was often boggy in wet weather, and went along by the Sheldrick's holly hedge to the open crest of heather from which one could run down to the school. One could see the playground and games going on long before one could get down to them. And if it were not too stormy the school flag with its red St. George and the Dragon on white would be flying. There were no indications of the Venerable Bede on the Flag, but Joan had concluded privately that he was represented by the red knob at the top of the flagstaff. For a year and more Joan thought that the Venerable Bede was really a large old bead of profound mystical significance.

Joan and Peter varied with the seasons, but except when Joan wore a djibbah they were dressed almost alike; in high summer with bare legs and brown smocks and Heidelberg sandals, and in winter like rolls of green wool stuck on leather gaiters. When they grew beyond the smock stage, then they both wore art green blouses with the school emblem of St. George on the pockets, but Joan wore a dark blue gym skirt and Peter had dark blue knickerbockers simply. The walk altered a little every day. Now the trees were dark and the brambles by the roadside wet and wilted, now all the world was shooting green buds except for the pines, now the pines were taking up the spring brightness, now all the world was hot and dusty and full of the smell of resin, and now again it was wet and misty and with a thousand sorts of brightly coloured fungus among the pine stems. Joan and Peter learnt by experience that throwing pine-cones hurts, and reserved them for the Cuspard boy who had never mastered this lesson. Peter started a "Mooseum" of fungi in the playroom, and made a great display of specimens that presently dried up or deliquesced and stank. When the snow came in the winter the Cuspard boy waylaid them at the corner with a prepared heap of snowballs and fell upon them with shrieks of excitement, throwing so fast and wildly and playing the giddy windmill so completely that it was quite easy for Joan and Peter to close in and capture his heap. Whereupon he fled toward the school weeping loudly that it was *his* heap and refusing to be comforted.

But afterwards all three of them made common cause

against a treacherous ambuscade behind the Sheldrick holly hedge.

It was on these journeyings that Joan began to hear first of the marvellous adventures of Uncle Nobby and Bungo Peter. She most liked Bungo Peter because he had such a satisfying name; Peter never told her he was really the newel knob at home, but she always understood him to be something very large and round and humorous and richly coloured. Sometimes he was as big as the world and sometimes he was a suitable playmate for little children. He was the one constant link in a wandering interminable Saga that came like a spider's thread endlessly out of Peter's busy brain. It was a story of quests and wanderings, experiments and tasks and feuds and wars; Nobby was almost always in it, kind and dreadfully brave and always having narrow escapes and being rescued by Bungo Peter. Daddy and Mummy came in and went out again, Peter and Joan joined in. For a time Bungo Peter had a Wonderful Cat that would have shamed Puss-in-boots. Sometimes the story would get funny, so funny that the two children would roll along the road, drunken with laughter. As for example when Bungo Peter had hiccups and couldn't say anything else whatever you asked him.

After a time Joan learned the trick of the Saga and would go on with it in her own mind as a day-dream. She invented that really and truly Bungo Peter loved her desperately and that she loved Bungo Peter; but she knew, though she knew not why nor wherefore, that this was a thing Peter must never be told.

Sometimes she would try to cut in and make some of the saga herself. "Lemme tell *you*, Petah," she used to squeal. "You just lemme tell *you.*" But it was a rare thing for Peter to give way to her; sometimes he would not listen at all to what she had to say about Bungo Peter; he would smite her down with "No, he didn't do nuffin of the sort, not reely," and sometimes when she had thought of a really good thing to tell about him, Peter would take it away from her and go on telling about it himself, as for instance when she thought of "Lightning-slick," that Bungo Peter used to put on his heels.

Peter listened to her poor speeding-up with "Lightning-slick" for a while.

Then he said: "And after that, Joan, after that——"

"Oh! *lemme* go on, Petah. *Do* lemme go on. The fird time he was runned after by anyfing it was this."

"He put it on his bicycle wheels," said Peter, getting bored by her, "instead of oil."

"He put it on his bicycle wheels instead of oil," said Joan, accepting the idea, "and along came a Tiger." (She had already done a Mad Dog and a Bear.)

But after that Peter took over altogether while she was waving about rather helplessly and breathlessly with "the *Forf* time Bungo Peter used Lightning-slick, the forf time——" and hesitating whether to make it a snake or an elephant, Peter could stand it no longer.

"But you don't know what Bungo Peter did the *Forf* time, Joan—you don't *reely* and I do. Bungo Peter told me. Bungo Peter wanted the holidays to come, so Bungo Peter went and put Lightning-slick on the axles of the Erf."

"What good was that?"

"It went fast. It went faster and faster. The Erf. It regular spun round. And the sun rose and the sun set jest in an hour or so. 'Cos it *would*, Joan. It *would*. Yes, it *would*. There wasn't any time for anyfing. People got up and had their breckfus—and it was bedtime. People went out for walks and got b'nighted. Then when the holidays came Bungo Peter just put a stick in the place and stopped it going fast any more."

"Put a stick in *what* place?"

"Where the Erf goes round. And then, *then* the days were as long as long. They lasted—oo, 'undreds of 'ours, heaps."

"Didn't they get 'ungry?" said Joan, overcome by this magnificent invention.

"They 'ad *free* dinners every day, sometimes four, and 's many teas as they wanted. Out-of-doors. Only you see they didn't 'ave to go to bed, 'ardly ever. See, Joan? . . ."

There had to be a pause of blissful contemplation before their minds could go on to any further invention.

"I believe if I had the fings I could make Lightning-slick," said Peter with a rising inflection of the voice.

He *did* believe. As soon as it was really said he believed it. Joan, round-eyed with admiration, believed too. . . .

This Saga of Bungo Peter did not so much end as die out, when Aunt Phyllis got little bicycles for her charges after Joan's seventh birthday, and they began to ride to school. You cannot tell legends on a bicycle.

§ 5

Mr. Sheldrick was a large, loose painter man held together by a very hairy tweed suit, and the Sheldricks were a large, loose family not so much born and brought up as negligently let loose into the world at the slightest provocation by a small facetious mother. It was Mr. Sheldrick who painted the scenery for the school play productions, and it was the Sheldricks who first put it into Miss Murgatroyd's head that children could be reasonably expected to act. The elder Sheldricks were so to speak the camels and giraffes of Miss Murgatroyd's school, but the younger ones came down to dimensions that made them practicable playmates for Joan and Peter. Every now and then there would be a Sheldrick birthday (and once Mr. Sheldrick sold a picture) and then there would be a children's tea-party. It was always a dressing-up tea-party at the Sheldricks. The Sheldrick household possessed a big chest full of pieces of coloured stuff, cloaks, fragmentary wigs, tinsel, wooden swords and the like; this chest stood on the big landing outside the studio and it was called the "dressing-up box." It was an inexhaustible source of joy and a liberal education to the Sheldricks and their friends.

There were grades of experience in these dressing-up parties. At the lowest, when you were just a "little darling" fit only for gusty embraces—Joan was that to begin with and Peter by dint of a resolute angularity was but battling his way out of it—you put on a preposterous hat or something and ran about yelling, "Look at meeeeee!" Then you rose—Peter rose almost at once and saw to it that Joan rose too, to Dumb Crambo.

In Dumb Crambo one half of the party, the bored half, is "in." It chooses a word, such as "sleep," it tells the "outs" that it rhymes with "sneep," and the "outs" then prepare and act as rapidly as possible, "deep," "creep," "sheep," and so on until they hit upon the right word. There was always much rushing about upon the landing, a great fermentation of ideas, a perpetual "I say, let's——," imagination, contrivance, co-operation. So rapidly, joyfully and abundantly, with a disarming effect of confusion, the Sheldricks at their tea-parties did exactly what Miss Mills believed she was doing in her slow, elaborate, remote-spirited Kindergarten lessons, in which she was perpetually saying, "No; no, dear, that isn't right!" or "Now let us all do it over again just once more and get it perfect." It was Peter who discovered that these strange ritual-exercises of Miss Mills' were really a rigid version of the Sheldrick entertainments, and tried to introduce novelties of gesture and facial play and slight but pleasing variations in the verses. He got a laugh or so. But Miss Mills soon put a stop to these experiments.

From Dumb Crambo the Sheldrick dressing-up games rose to scenes from history and charades. Then Mrs. Sheldrick was moved to write a children's play about fairies and bluebells and butterflies and an angel-child who had died untimely, a play that broke out into a wild burlesque of itself even at its first rehearsals. Then came a wave of Shakespearian enthusiasm that was started by the two elder Sheldricks and skilfully fostered by Daddy Sheldrick, who was getting bored by Dumb Crambo and charades. After a little resistance the younger ones fell in with the new movement and an auspicious beginning was made with selections from *A Midsummer Night's Dream*. Miss Murgatroyd was first made aware of this new development by a case of discipline. The second Sheldrick girl was charged with furtively learning passages of Shakespeare by heart instead of pretending to attend to Miss Mills' display of a total inability to explain the method used in the extraction of the square root. Had it been any other playwright than

Shakespeare, things might have gone hard with the Sheldrick girl, but "Shakespeare is different."

Miss Murgatroyd, perceiving there was more in this than a mere question of discipline, came to see one of the Sheldrick performances, was converted, and annexed the whole thing. The next term of school life she made a Shakespeare Boom, and she astonished the world and herself by an altogether charming production of *A Midsummer Night's Dream*. In those days the histrionic possibilities of young children were unsuspected by the parents and schoolmasters who walked over them. Romeo was still played in England by elderly men with time-worn jowls and reverberating voices, and Juliet by dear old actresses for whom the theatre-going public had a genuine filial affection. England had forgotten how young she was in the days of good Queen Elizabeth.

Both Joan and Peter took a prominent part in Miss Murgatroyd's production because, in spite of nearly four years of Miss Mills, they still had wonderfully good memories. Peter made a dignified Oberon and also a delightfully quaint Thisbe, and Joan was Puck. She danced a dance. She danced in front of the Queen Titania after the Fairy song. It was a dance in which she ceased to be human and became a little brown imp with flashing snake's eyes and hair like a thunder-cloud. It had been invented years ago by poor dead and drowned Dolly, and the Sheldricks had picked it up again from Joan and developed and improved it for her.

§ 6

But the Sheldricks were not always acting Shakespeare. There were phases in those tea-parties when a kind of wildness came into their blood and the blood of those they entertained that called for something more violent than dressing-up or acting. Then in summertime they had a great scampering and hiding in the garden, it was the sort of garden where you can run across the beds and charge through the shrubs, and in winter they played "Ogre" or "Darkness Ogre" indoors. In Ogre some one—it was usually Mr. Sheldrick—was Ogre, and the little corner room out of the hall was his Den. And you hid. In the Sheldrick's house you could hide anywhere except in the studio or the pantry and china closet; you could hide in Mrs. Sheldrick's wardrobe or in the linen cupboard over the hot-water pipes (until it got too hot for you) or under any-body's bed in anybody's room. And the Ogre came after you and caught you—often by the foot you had left out carelessly beyond the counterpane—and took you to his Den, and there you were a prisoner until some brave soul came careering across the hall to touch your hand and rescue you and set you free again. The Ogre was never safe against rescues until every one was caught, and everybody never was caught; sooner or later came a gaol delivery, and so the game began all over again and went on until a meal or something released the Ogre or the Ogre struck work. Nobody was so good an Ogre as Mr. Sheldrick; there was such a nice terribleness about him, and he had a way of chanting "Yumpty-Ow. Yumpty-Ow," as he came after you.

Of course every house is not suitable for Ogre. Intelligent children who understand the delights of Ogre classify homes into two sorts. There are the commonplace homes we most of us inhabit with one staircase, and there are the glorious homes with two, so that you can sneak down one while the Ogre hunts for you up the other. The Sheldrick home had two entirely separate staircases and a long passage between them, and a sort of loop-line arrangement of communicating bedrooms. And also, though this has nothing to do with Ogre, it was easy to get out upon the Sheldrick roof.

"Darkness Ogre" was more exciting in a dreadful kind of way than Ogre. It was only played in winter, and all the blinds and curtains were drawn and all the lights put out. You didn't need to hide. You just got into a corner and stood still, holding your breath. And the Ogre took off his boots and put on felt slippers, and all the noise he made was a rustle and a creak, and you were never sure that it was him—unless he betrayed himself by whispering "Yumpty-Ow." He creaked rather more than most, but that was a matter for delicate perceptions. There were frightful moments when you could hear him moving about and feeling about in the very room where you stood frozen, getting nearer and nearer to you. You had to bite your knuckles not to scream.

Once when they were playing Darkness Ogre, Peter was in a corner of Mrs. Sheldrick's room with Sydney Sheldrick, the third of the Sheldrick sisters, and they were crowding up very close together. And suddenly Sydney put her arms round Peter and began to kiss his ears and cheek. Peter resisted, pushed her away from him. "Ssh," said Sydney. "You be my little sweetheart." Peter resisted this proposal with vigour. Then they heard the Ogre creaking down the passage. Sydney drew Peter closer to her, but Peter struggled away from her and made a dash for the further door. He was almost caught. He escaped because somebody else started into flight from the corner of the landing outside the studio and drew the Ogre off the scent.

Afterwards Peter avoided secluded corners when Sydney was about.

But somehow he could not forget what had happened. He kept on thinking of Sydney for a time, and after that she seemed always to be a little more important than the rest of his older schoolmates. Perhaps it was because she took more notice of him. She wanted to help his work, and she would ruffle his hair or pinch his ear as she went past him. She wore a peculiar long jersey so that you could distinguish her from the others quite a long way off. She had level brows and a radiant smile, her shoulders were strong and her legs and feet were very pretty. He noted how well she walked. She always seemed to be looking at Peter. When he shut his eyes and thought of her he could remember her better than he could other people. He did not know whether he liked her or disliked her more than the others; but he perceived that she had in some way become exceptional.

§ 7

Young Winterbaum was another of Miss Murgatroyd's pupils who made a lasting impression on Peter. He was dark-eyed and fuzzy-haired, the contour of his face had a curious resemblance to that of a sheep, and his head was fixed on in a different way so that he looked more skyward and down his face at you. His expression was one of placid self-satisfaction; his hands twisted about, and ever and again he pranced as he walked. He had a superfluity of gesture, and his voice was a fat voice with the remotest possible hint of a lisp. He had two little round, jolly, frizzy, knock-about sisters who ousted Joan and Peter from their position as the little darlings of the school. The only boy in the school who at all resembled him was young Cuspard, but young Cuspard had not the same bold lines either in his face or conduct; he was red-haired, his nose was a snout instead of a hook, and instead of rather full, well-modelled lips he had that sort of loose mouth that blows. Young Winterbaum said his nose had the Norman arch, and that it showed he was aristocratic and one of the conquerors of England. He was second cousin to a peer, Lord Contango. It was only slowly that Peter came to apprehend the full peculiarity of young Winterbaum.

The differences in form and gesture of the two boys were only the outward and visible signs of profound differences between their imaginations. For example, the heroes of Peter's romancings were wonderful humorous persons, Nobbys and Bungo Peters, and his themes adventures, struggles, quests that left them neither richer nor poorer than before in a limitless, undisciplined, delightful world, but young Winterbaum's hero was himself, and he thought in terms of achievement and acquisition. He was a King and the strongest and bravest and richest of all Kings. He had wonderful horses, wonderful bicycles, wonderful catapults and an astonishing army. He counted these things. He walked from the other direction to school, and though no one knew it but himself, he walked in procession. Guards went before him and behind him, and ancient councillors walked beside him. And always he was going on to fresh triumphs and possessions.

He had a diplomatic side to him. He was prepared to negotiate upon the matter of kingship. One day he reached the crest above the school while it was still early, and found Joan and Peter sitting and surveying the playground, waiting for the first bell before they ran down. He stood beside Peter.

"All this is my Kingdom," he said, waving both his arms about over the Weald. "I am King of all this, I have a great army."

"Not over this part," said Peter modestly but firmly.

"You be King up to here," said young Winterbaum. "You have an army too."

"*I* want a kingdom too," said Joan.

Young Winterbaum proposed a fair division of Peter's kingdom between Joan and Peter.

Peter let Joan have what young Winterbaum gave her. It took some moments to grasp this new situation. "My kingdom," he said suddenly, "goes right over to those ponds there and up to the church."

"You can't," said young Winterbaum. "*I've* claimed that."

Peter grunted. It did not seem worth while to have a kingdom unless those ponds were included.

"But if you like I'll give your people permission to go over all that country whenever they like."

Peter still felt there was a catch in it somewhere.

"I've got a hundred and seven soldiers," said young Winterbaum. "And six guns that shoot."

Joan was surprised and shocked to hear that Peter had five hundred soldiers.

"Each of my soldiers, each one, counts as a thousand men," said young Winterbaum, getting ahead again.

Then the first bell rang and suspended the dispute. But Peter went down to the school with a worried feeling. He wished he had thought of claiming all Surrey as his kingdom first. It was a lamentable oversight. He was disposed to ask the eldest Sheldrick girl whether young Winterbaum really had a *right* to claim all the Weald. There was a reason in these things. . . .

Young Winterbaum had an extraordinary knack of accentuating possessions. Joan and Peter were very pleased and proud to have bicycles; the first time they arrived upon them at the school young Winterbaum took possession of them and examined them thoroughly. They were really good bicycles, excellent bicycles, he explained, and new, not second-hand; but they were not absolutely the best sort.

The best sort nowadays had wood rims. He was going to
have a bicycle with wood rims. And there ought to be a
Bowden brake in front as well as behind; the one in front
was only a spoon brake. It was a pity to have a spoon
brake; it would injure the tyre. He doubted if the tubing
was helical tubing. And the bell wasn't a "King of the
Road." It was no good for Peter to pretend it had a good
sound, "the King of the Road" had a better sound. When
young Winterbaum got his bicycle *his* bell was going to be
a "King of the Road, 1902 pattern." . . .

Young Winterbaum was always doing this with things,
bringing them up into the foreground of life, grading them,
making them competitive and irritating. There was no getting ahead of him. He made Peter feel that the very dust
in the Winterbaum dustbin was Grade A. Standard I. while
The Ingle-Nook was satisfied with any old makeshift stuff.

Young Winterbaum's clothes were made by Samuelson's,
the best boys' tailor in London; there was no disputing it
because there was an advertisement in *The Daily Telegraph*
that said as much; he was in trousers and Peter had knickerbockers; he wore sock suspenders, and he had his name in
gold letters inside his straw hat. Also he had a pencil-
case like no other pencil-case in the school. He was always
proposing a comparison of pencil-cases.

His imagination turned precociously and easily to romance and love and the beauty of women. He read a
number of novelettes that he had borrowed from his sister's
nurse. He imparted to Peter the idea of a selective pairing
off of the species, an idea for which *A Midsummer Night's
Dream* had already prepared a favourable soil. It was
after he had seen Joan dance her dance when that play was
performed and heard the unstinted applause that greeted her,
that he decided to honour her above all the school with his
affections. Previously he had wavered between the eldest
Sheldrick girl because she was the biggest, tallest and heav-
iest girl in the school (though a formidable person to approach) and little Minnie Restharrow who was top in so many
classes. But now he knew that Joan was "it," and that he
was in love with her.

But some instinct told him that Peter had to be dealt with. He approached Peter in this manner.

"Who's your girl, Peter?" said young Winterbaum. "Who is your own true love? You've got to have some one."

Peter drew a bow at a venture, and subconscious processes guided the answer. "Sydney Sheldrick," he said.

Young Winterbaum seemed to snatch even before Peter had done speaking. "I'm going to have Joan," he said. "She dances better than any one. She's going to be, oh! —a lovely woman."

Peter was dimly aware of an error. He had forgotten Joan. "I'm going to have Joan too," he said.

"You can't have two sweethearts," said young Winterbaum.

"I *can*. I'm going to. I'm different."

"But Joan's mine already."

"Get out," said Peter indignantly. "You can't have her."

"But she's mine."

"Shut it," said Peter vulgarly.

"I'll fight you a duel for her. We will fight a real duel for her."

"You hadn't better begin," said Peter.

"But I mean—you know—a duel, Peter."

"Let's fight one now," said Peter, " 'f you think you're going to have Joan for *your* girl."

"We will fight with swords."

"Sticks."

"Yes, but *call* them swords. And we shall have to have seconds and a doctor."

"Joan's my second."

"You can't have Joan. *My* second's the Grand Duke of Surrey-Sussex."

"Then mine's Bungo-Peter."

"But we've got no sticks."

"I know where there's two sticks," said Peter. "Under the stairs. And we can fight in the shrubbery over by the fence."

The sticks were convenient little canes. "They ought to have hilts," said young Winterbaum. "You ever fenced?"

"Not much," said Peter guardedly.

"I've often fenced with my cousin, the honourable Ralph—you know. Like this—guard. One. Two. You've got to have a wrist."

They repaired to the field of battle. "We stand aside while the seconds pace out the ground," explained young Winterbaum. "Now we shake hands. Now we take our places."

They proceeded to strike fencer-like attitudes. Young Winterbaum suddenly became one of the master swordsmen of the world, but Peter was chiefly intent on where he should hit young Winterbaum. He had got to hit him and hurt him a lot, or else he would get Joan. They crossed swords. Then young Winterbaum feinted and Peter hit him hard on the arm. Then young Winterbaum thrust Peter in the chest, and began to explain at once volubly that Peter was now defeated and dead and everything conclusively settled.

But nobody was going to take away Peter's Joan on such easy terms. Peter, giving his antagonist no time to complete his explanation, slashed him painfully on the knuckles. "I'm *not* dead," said Peter, slashing again. "I'm not dead. See? Come on!"

Whereupon young Winterbaum cried out, as it were with a trumpet, in a loud and grief-stricken voice. "Now I shall *hurt* you. That's too much," and swiped viciously at Peter's face and raised a weal on Peter's cheek. Whereupon Peter, feeling that Joan was slipping from him, began to rain blows upon young Winterbaum wherever young Winterbaum might be supposed to be tender, and young Winterbaum began to dance about obliquely and cry out, "Mustn't hit my legs. Mustn't hit my legs. Not fair. Oo-oh! my knuckles!" And after one or two revengeful slashes at Peter's head which Peter—who had had his experiences with Joan in a rage—parried with an uplifted arm, young Winterbaum turned and ran—ran into the arms of Miss Murgatroyd, who had been attracted to the shrubbery by his cries. . . .

It was the first fight that had ever happened in the school of St. George and the Venerable Bede since its foundation.

"He said I couldn't fight him," said Peter.

"He went on fighting after I'd pinked him," said young Winterbaum.

Neither of them said a word about Joan.

So Miss Murgatroyd made a great session of the school, and the two combatants, flushed and a little heroic, sat on either side of her discourse. She said that this was the first time she had ever had to reprove any of her pupils for fighting. She hoped that never again would it be necessary for her to do so. She said that nothing we could do was quite so wicked as fighting because nothing was so flatly contradictory to our Lord's commandment that we should love one another. The only fight we might fight with a good conscience was the good fight. In that sense we were all warriors. We were fighters for righteousness. In a sense every one was a knight and a fighter, every girl as well as every boy. Because there was no more reason why girls should not fight as well as boys. Some day she hoped this would be recognized, and girls would be given knighthoods and wear their spurs as proudly as the opposite sex. Earth was a battlefield, and none of us must be dumb driven cattle or submit to injustice or cruelty. We must not think that life was made for silken ease or self-indulgence. Let us think rather of the Red Indian perpetually in training for conflict, lean and vigorous and breathing only through his nose. No one who breathed through his or her open mouth would ever be a fighter.

At this point Miss Murgatroyd seemed to hesitate for a time. Breathing was a very attractive topic to her, and it was drawing her away from her main theme. She was, so to speak, dredging for her lost thread in the swift undertow of hygienic doctrine as one might dredge for a lost cable. She got it presently, and concluded by hoping that this would be a lesson to Philip and Peter and that henceforth they would learn that great lesson of Prince Kropotkin's that co-operation is better than conflict.

Neither of the two combatants listened very closely to this discourse. Peter was wrestling with the question whether a hot red weal across one's cheek is compatible with victory, and young Winterbaum with the still more subtle difficulty of whether he had been actually running away or merely stepping back when he had collided with Miss Murgatroyd, and what impression this apparently retrograde movement had made on her mind and upon the mind of Peter. Did they understand that sometimes a swordsman *had* to go back and could go back without the slightest discredit? . . .

§ 8

After this incident the disposal of Joan ceased to be a topic for conversation between young Winterbaum and Peter, and presently young Winterbaum conveyed to Peter in an offhand manner that he adored Minnie Restharrow as the cleverest and most charming girl in the school. She was indeed absolutely the best thing to be got in that way. She was, he opined, cleverer even than Miss Murgatroyd. He was therefore, he intimated, in love with Minnie Restharrow. It was a great passion.

So far as Peter was concerned, he gathered, it might be.

All the canons of romance required that Peter, having fought for and won Joan, should thereupon love Joan and her only until he was of an age to marry her. As a matter of fact, having disposed of this invader of his private ascendancy over Joan, he thought no more of her in that relationship. He decided, however, that if young Winterbaum was going to have a sweetheart he must have one too, and mysterious processes of his mind indicated Sydney Sheldrick as the only possible person. It was not that Peter particularly wanted a sweetheart, but he was not going to let young Winterbaum come it over him—any more than he was going to let young Winterbaum be King of more than half of Surrey. He was profoundly bored by all this competitiveness, but obscure instincts urged him to keep his end up.

One day Miss Murgatroyd was expatiating to the mother of a prospective pupil upon the wonderful effects of coeducation in calming the passions. "The boys and girls grow up together, get used to each other, and there's never any nonsense between them."

"And don't they—well, take an interest in each other?"

"Not in that way. Not in any *undesirable* way. Such as they would if they had been morbidly separated."

"But it seems almost unnatural for them not to take an interest."

"Experience, I can assure you, shows otherwise," said Miss Murgatroyd conclusively.

At that moment two figures, gravely conversing together, passed across the lawn in the middle distance; one was a well-grown girl of thirteen in a short-skirted gymnasium dress, the other a nice-looking boy of ten, knickerbockered, bare-legged, sandalled, and wearing the art green blouse of the school. They looked the most open-air and unsophisticated children of modernity it was possible to conceive. This is what they were saying:

"Sydney, when I grow up I'm going to marry you. You got to be my sweetheart. See?"

"You darling! Is that what you have to tell me? I didn't think you loved me a little bit."

"I'm going to marry you," said Peter, sticking to the facts of the case.

"I'd hug you. Only old Muggy is looking out of the window. But the very first chance I get I'll kiss you. And you'll have to kiss me back, mind, Peter."

"Where some one can't see us," Peter stipulated.

"Oh! I *love* spooning," said the ardent Sydney. " 'Member when I kissed you before? . . ."

"The girls refine the boys and the whole atmosphere is just a *family* atmosphere," Miss Murgatroyd was explaining at the window.

CHAPTER THE EIGHTH

THE HIGH CROSS PREPARATORY SCHOOL

§ 1

FROM the time when he was christened until he was ten, Lady Charlotte Sydenham remained only a figure in the remotest background of Peter's life. Once or twice he saw her in the downstairs room at The Ingle-Nook with his aunts bristling defensively beside her, and once she came to the school, and each time she looked at him with a large, hard, hostile smile and said: "And ha-ow's Peter?" and then with a deepening disapproval: "Ha-ow's Joan?" But that did not mean that Lady Charlotte had done with Joan and Peter, nor that she had relinquished in the slightest degree her claims to dominate their upbringing. She was just letting them grow up a little "according to their mother's ideas, poor woman," and biding her time. She wrote every now and then to Aunts Phyllis and Phœbe, just to remind them of her authority, and she wrote two long and serious letters to Oswald about what was to be done. He answered her briefly in such terms as: "Let well alone. Religion comes later." Oswald had never returned to England. He had been in Uganda now for five long years, and her fear of him was dying down. She was beginning to think that perhaps he did not care very much for Joan and Peter. He had had blackwater fever again. Perhaps he would never come home any more.

Then in the years 1901 and 1902 she had been much occupied by a special campaign against various London socialists that had ended in a libel case. She was quite convinced that all socialists were extremely immoral people, she was greatly alarmed at the spread of socialism, and so she wrote and employed a secretary to write letters to a number of

142

people marked "private and confidential," warning them against this or that prominent socialist. In these she made various definite statements which, as her counsel vainly tried to argue, were not to be regarded as statements of fact so much as illustrations of the tendency of socialist teaching. She was tackled by a gentleman in a red necktie named Bamshot, of impregnable virtue, in whom her free gift of "numerous illegitimate children" had evoked no gratitude. Her efforts to have him "thoroughly cross-examined" produced no sympathy in either judge or jury. All men, she realized, are wicked and anxious to shield each other. She left the court with a passionate and almost uncontrollable desire to write more letters about Bamshot and more, worse than ever, and with much nastier charges. And it was perhaps a subconscious effort to shift the pressure of this dangerous impulse that turned her mind to the state of spiritual neglect in which Joan and Peter were growing out of childhood.

A number of other minor causes moved her in the same direction. She had had a violent quarrel about the bill with the widow of an Anglican clergyman who kept her favourite pension at Bordighera; and she could still not forgive the establishment at Pallanza that, two years before, had refused to dismiss its head-waiter for saying "Vivent les Boers!" in her hearing. She had been taking advice about a suitable and thoroughly comfortable substitute for these resorts, and meanwhile she had stayed on in England—until there were oysters on the table. Lady Charlotte Sydenham had an unrefined appetite for oysters, and with oysters came a still less refined craving for Dublin stout. It was an odd secret weakness understood only by her domestics, and noted only by a small circle of intimate friends.

"I don't seem to fancy anything very much to-day, Unwin," Lady Charlotte used to say.

"I don't know if you'd be tempted by a nice oyster or two, m'lady. They're very pick-me-up things," the faithful attendant would suggest. "It's September now, and there's an R in the month, so it's safe to venture."

"Mm."

"And if I might make so bold as to add a 'arf bottle of

good Guinness, m'lady. It's a tonic. Run down as you
are.''

Without oysters neither Lady Charlotte nor Unwin would
have considered stout a proper drink for a lady. And indeed it was not a proper drink for Lady Charlotte. A very
little stout sufficed to derange her naturally delicate internal
chemistry. Upon the internal chemistry of Lady Charlotte
her equanimity ultimately depended. There is wrath in
stout. . . .

Then Mr. Grimes, who had never ceased to hope that considerable out-of-court activities might still be developed
around these two little wards, had taken great pains to bring
Aunt Phœbe's *Collected Papers of a Stitchwoman (Second Series)* and her little precious volume *Carmen Naturæ*
before his client's notice.

These books certainly made startling reading for Lady
Charlotte. She had never seen the first ''Stitchwoman''
papers, she knew nothing of Swinburne, Ruskin, Carlyle, the
decadents, nothing of the rich inspirations of the later Victorian period, and so the almost luscious richness of Aunt
Phœbe's imagination, her florid verbiage, her note of sensuous defiance, burst almost devastatingly upon a mind that
was habituated to the ordered passions and pearly greys of
Mrs. Henry Wood's novels *More Leaves, Good Words,* and
The Quiver.

'' 'With what measure ye mete,' '' she read, '' 'so shall it be
meted unto you again,' and the Standard that Man has fixed
for woman recoils now upon his head. Which standard is
it to be,—His or Hers? No longer can we fight under two
flags. Wild oats, or the Immaculate Banner? Question to
be answered shrewdly, and according to whether we deem
it is Experience or Escape we live for, now that we are out of
Eden footing it among the sturdy, exhilarating thistles.
What will ye, my masters?—pallid man unstained, or seasoned woman? Judgment hesitates. Judgment may indeed
hesitate. I, who sit here stitching, mark her hesitation, myself—observant. Is it too bold a speculation that presently
golden lassies as well as golden lads will sow their wild oats
bravely on the slopes of life? Is it too much to dream of
that grave mother of a greater world, the Woman of the

Future, glancing back from the glowing harvest of her life to some tall premonition by the wayside?—her One Wild Oat! the crown and seal of her education!''

"Either she means nothing by that," said Lady Charlotte, "or she means just sheer depravity. Wild Oat, indeed! Really! To call it *that!* With Joan on her hands already!''

And here again is a little poem from *Carmen Naturæ,* which also impressed Lady Charlotte very unfavourably:

THE MATERIALIST SINGS

Put by your tangled Trinities
And let the atoms swing,
The merry magic atoms
That trace out everything.

These ancient gods are fantasies,
Mere Metaphors and Names;
But I can feel the Vortex Ring
Go singing through my veins.

No casket of a pallid ghost,
But all compact of thrills,
My body beats and throbs and lives,
My Mighty Atom wills.

"I *don't* know what the world is coming to," said Lady Charlotte. "In other times a woman who ventured to write such blasphemy would have been Struck Dead. . . .''

"Thrills again!" said Lady Charlotte, turning over the offending pages. "In a book that any one may read. Exposing her thrills to any Bagman who chooses to put down three and sixpence for the pleasure. Imagine it, Unwin!''

Unwin did her best, assuming an earnest expression. . . .

Other contributory influences upon Lady Charlotte's state of mind were her secret anxiety for the moral welfare of the realm now that Queen Victoria had given place to the notoriously lax Edward VII., and the renascence of sectarian controversies in connexion with Mr. Balfour's Education Act. Anglicanism was rousing itself for a new struggle to keep hold of the nation's children, the Cecils and Lord Halifax were ranging wide and free with the educational dragnet, and Lady Charlotte was a part of the great system of

Anglicanism. The gale that blows the ships home, lifts the leaves. . . . But far more powerful than any of these causes was the death of a certain Mr. Pybus, who was Unwin's brother-in-law; he died through an operation undertaken by a plucky rather than highly educated general practitioner, to remove a neglected tumour. This left Unwin's sister in want of subsidies, and while Unwin lay in bed one night puzzling over this family problem, it occurred to her that if her sister could get some little girl to mind——. . .

§ 2

Mr. Grimes was very helpful and sympathetic when Lady Charlotte consulted him. He repeated the advice he had given five years ago, that Lady Charlotte should not litigate but act, and so thrust upon the other parties the onus of litigation. She should obtain possession of the two children, put them into suitable schools—"I don't see how we can put that By-blow into a school," Lady Charlotte interpolated—and refuse to let the aunts know where they were until they consented to reasonable terms, to the proper religious education of the children, to their proper clothing, and to their separation. "Directly we have the engagement of the Misses Stubland not to disturb the new arrangement," said Mr. Grimes, "we shall have gained our point. I see no harm in letting the children rejoin their aunts for their holidays."

"That woman may corrupt them at any time," said Lady Charlotte.

"On that point we can watch and enquire. Of course, the boy might stay at the school for the holiday times. There is a class of school which caters for that sort of thing. That we can see to later." . . .

Mr. Grimes arranged all the details of the abduction of Joan and Peter with much tact and imagination. As a preliminary step he made Lady Charlotte write to Aunt Phœbe expressing her opinion that the time was now ripe to put the education of the children upon a rational footing. They were no longer little children, and it was no longer possible for them to go on as they were going. Peter was born an

English gentleman, and he ought to go to a good preparatory school for boys forthwith; Joan's destinies in life were different, but they were certainly destinies for which play-acting, running about with bare feet, and dressing like a little savage could be no sort of training. Lady Charlotte (Mr. Grimes made her say) had been hoping against hope that some suggestion for a change would come from the Misses Stubland. She could not hope against hope for ever. She must therefore request a conference, at which Mr. Grimes could be present, for a discussion of the new arrangements that were now urgently necessary. To this the Misses Stubland replied evasively and carelessly. In their reply Mr. Grimes, without resentment, detected the hand of Mr. Sycamore. They were willing to take part in a conference as soon as Mr. Oswald Sydenham returned. They had reason to believe he was on his way to England now.

Lady Charlotte, still guided by Mr. Grimes, then assumed a more peremptory tone. She declared that in the interests of both children it was impossible for things to go on any longer as they had been going. Already the boy was ten. The plea that nothing could be done until Mr. Sydenham returned was a mere delaying device. The boy ought to go to school forthwith. Lady Charlotte was extremely sorry that the Misses Stubland would not come to any agreement upon this urgent matter. She could not rest content with things in this state, and she would be obliged to consider what her course of action—for the time had come for her to take action—must be.

With the way thus cleared, Mr. Grimes set his forces in motion. "Leave it to me, Lady Charlotte," he said. "Leave it to me." A polite young man appeared one morning seated in a chariot of fire outside the road gate of the School of St. George and the Venerable Bede. He was in one of those strange and novel portents, a "motor-car." This alone made him interesting and attractive, and it greatly impressed young Winterbaum to discover that the visitor had come about Joan and Peter. Young Winterbaum went out to scrutinize the motor-car and its driver, and see if there was anything wrong about it. But it was difficult to underestimate.

"It's a petrol car," he said. "Belsize. . . . Those are fine lamps."

Miss Murgatroyd gathered that the guardians of Joan and Peter found it necessary to interview the children, and had sent the car to fetch them.

"Miss Stubland said nothing of this when I saw her the day before yesterday," said Miss Murgatroyd. "We do not care for interruptions in the children's work."

The young man explained that the case was urgent. "Lady Charlotte has been called away. And she must see the children before she goes out of England."

There was something very reassuring about the motor-car. They departed cheerfully to the ill-concealed envy and admiration of young Winterbaum.

The young man had red hair, a white, freckled face, and a costly and remarkable made-up necktie of green plush. The expression of his pale blue eyes was apprehensive, and ever and again he blew. His efforts at conversation were fragmentary and unilluminating. "I got to take you for a long ride," he said, seating himself between Peter and Joan. "A lovely long ride."

"Where?" said Joan.

"You'll see in a bit," said the young man.

"We going to Chastlands?" asked Peter.

"No," said the young man.

"Then where are we going?" said Peter.

"These here cars'll do forty—fifty miles an hour," said the young man, changing the subject.

In a little while they had passed beyond the limits of Peter's knowledge altogether, and were upon an unknown road. It was astonishing how the car devoured the road. You saw a corner a long way off and then immediately you were turning this corner. The car went as swiftly up the hills as down. It said "honk." The trees and hedges flew by as if one was in a train, and behind we trailed a marvellous cloud of dust. The driver sat before us with his head sunken between his hunched-up shoulders; he never seemed to move; he was quite different from the swaying, noble coachman with the sun-red face, wearing a top hat with a waist and a broad brim, who sat erect and poised his whip and drove Lady Charlotte's white horse.

§ 3

For a time the road ran undulating between high hedges and tall trees and through villages, and all along to the right of it were the steep, round-headed Downs. Then came a little town, and the automobile turned off into a valley that cut the Downs across and opened out more and more, and then came heathery common and a town, and then lanes and many villages, flat meadows and flatter, poplars, and then another town with a bridge, and then across long levels of green a glimpse of the big tower of Windsor Castle. "This is Runnymede, where Magna Carta was signed," said the young man suddenly. "And that's Windsor, where the King lives—when he isn't living somewhere else, as he usually does. . . . He's a *'ot* un is the King. . . . See the chap there sailing a boat?"

They went right into Windsor and had a glimpse of the great gates of the Castle and the round tower very near to them, and then they turned down a steep, narrow, paved street and so came into a district of little mean villas in rows and rows. And outside one of these the car stopped.

"Here we are," said the young man.

"Where are we?" asked Peter.

"Where we get out," said the young man. "Time we had a feed."

"Dinnah," said Joan, with a bright expression, and prepared to descend.

A small, white-faced, anxious woman appeared at the door. She was wearing amiability as one wears a Sabbath garment. Moreover, she had a greyish-black dress that ended in a dingy, stiff buff frilling at the neck and wrists.

"You Mrs. Pybus?" asked the young man.

"I been expecting you a nour," said Mrs. Pybus, acquiescing in the name. "Is this the young lady and gentleman?"

That again was a question that needed no answer. The group halted awkwardly on the doorstep for a few seconds. "And this is Miss Joan?" said Mrs. Pybus, with a joyless smile. "I didn't expect you to be 'arf yr' size. And what a short dress they put you in! You must 'ave regular shot up. Makes you what I call leggy. . . ."

This again was poor as a conversational opening.

" 'Ow old might you be, dearie?" asked Mrs. Pybus.

"I'm eight," said Joan. "But I'll be nine soon."

The young man for inscrutable reasons found this funny. He guffawed. "She's eight," he said to the world at large; "but she'll be nine soon. That's good, that is!"

"If you're spared, you shud say," said Mrs. Pybus. "You're a big eight, any'ow. 'Ow old are *you*, dear?"

Peter was disliking her quietly with his hands in his pockets. He paused for a moment, doubting whether he would answer to the name of "dear." "Ten," he said.

"Just ten?" asked the young man as if alert for humour.

Peter nodded, and the young man was thwarted.

"I suppose you'll be ready for something to eat," said Mrs. Pybus. " 'Adn't you better come in?"

They went in.

The room they entered was, perhaps, the most ordinary sort of room in England at that time, but it struck upon the observant minds of Joan and Peter as being strange and remarkable. They had never been before in an ordinary English living-room. It was a small, oblong room with a faint projection towards the street, as if it had attempted to develop a bow window and had lacked the strength to do so. On one side was a fireplace surmounted by a mantelshelf and an "overmantel," an affair of walnut-wood with a number of patches of looking-glass and small brackets and niches on which were displayed an array of worthless objects made to suggest ornaments, small sham bronzes, shepherdesses, sham Japanese fans, a disjointed German pipe and the like. In the midst of the mantelshelf stood a black marble clock insisting fixedly that the time was half-past seven, and the mantelshelf itself and the fireplace were "draped" with a very cheap figured muslin that one might well have supposed had never been to the wash except for the fact that its pattern was so manifestly washed out. The walls were papered with a florid pink wallpaper, and all the woodwork was painted a dirty brownish-yellow colour and "grained"

so as to render the detection of dirt impossible.   Small as this
room was there had been a strenuous and successful attempt
to obliterate such floor space as it contained by an accumulation of useless furniture; there were flimsy things called
whatnots in two of its corners, there was a bulky veneered
mahogany chiffonier opposite the fireplace, and in the window two ferns and a rubber plant in wool-adorned pots died
slowly upon a rickety table of bamboo.   The walls had
been a basis for much decorative activity, partly it would
seem to conceal or minimize a mysterious skin disease that
affected the wallpaper, but partly also for a mere perverse
impulse towards litter.   There were weak fret work brackets
stuck up for their own sakes and more or less askew, and
stouter brackets entrusted with the support of more "ornaments," small bowls and a tea-pot that valiantly pretended
they were things of beauty; there were crossed palm fans,
there was a steel engraving of Queen Victoria giving the
Bible to a dusky potentate as the secret of England's greatness; there was "The Soul's Awakening," two portraits of
George and May, and a large but faded photograph of the
sea front at Scarborough in an Oxford frame.   A gas "chan-
delier" descended into the midst of this apartment, betraying a confused ornate disposition in its lines, and the obliteration of the floor space was completed by a number of black
horsehair chairs and a large table, now "laid" with a worn
and greyish-white cloth for a meal.   Such were the homes
that the Victorian age had evolved by the million in England,
and to such nests did the common mind of the British resort
when it wished to meditate upon the problems of its Imperial
destiny.   Joan and Peter surveyed it open-mouthed.

The table was laid about a cruet as its central fact, a large,
metallic edifice surmounted by a ring and bearing weary
mustard, spiritless pepper, faded cayenne pepper, vinegar
and mysteries in bottles.   Joan and Peter were interested
in this strange object and at the same time vaguely aware
of something missing.   What they missed were flowers; on
this table there were no flowers.   There was a cold joint, a
white jug of beer and a glass jug of water, and pickles.   "I
got cold meat," said Mrs. Pybus, "not being sure when you
were coming."   She arranged her guests.   But she did not

immediately begin. She had had an idea. She regarded Peter.

"Now, Peter," she said, "let me 'ear you say Grice."

Peter wondered.

"Say Grice, dearie."

"Grice," said Peter.

The young man with the red hair was convulsed with merriment. "That's good," he said. "That's reely Good. Kids *are* amusing."

"But I tole you to say Grice," said Mrs. Pybus, ruffled. "I said it."

The young man's voice squeaked as he explained. "He doesn't know *'ow* to say Grace," he said. "Never 'eard of it."

"Is it a catch?" asked Peter.

The young man caught and restrained a fresh outburst of merriment with the back of his hand, and then explained again to Mrs. Pybus.

" 'E's a perfec' little 'eathen," said Mrs. Pybus. "I *never* did. They'll teach you to say grice all right, my boy, before you're very much older. Mark my words." And with a sort of businesslike reverence Mrs. Pybus gabbled her formula. Then she proceeded to carve. As she carved she pursed her lips and frowned.

The cold meat was not bad, but the children ate fastidiously, and Joan, after her fashion, left all her fat. This attracted the attention of Mrs. Pybus. "Eat it up, dearie," said Mrs. Pybus. "Wiste not, want not."

"I don't eat fat."

"But you *must* eat fat," said Mrs. Pybus.

Joan shook her head.

"We'll 'ave to teach you to eat fat," said Mrs. Pybus with a dangerous gentleness. For the time, however, the teaching was not insisted upon. "Lovely bits! Enough to feed a little dog," said Mrs. Pybus, as she removed Joan's plate to make way for apple tart.

The conversation was intermittent. It was as if they waited for some further event. The young man with the red hair spoke of the great world of London and the funeral of Lord Salisbury.

" 'E was a great statesman, say what you like," said the young man with red hair.

He also spoke of Holbein's attempt to swim the channel.

"They say 'e oils 'imself all over," said the young man.

"Lor'!" said Mrs. Pybus.

"It can't be comfortable," said the young man; "say what you like."

Presently the young man broke a silence by saying: "These here Balkans seem to be giving trouble again."

"Troublesome lot they are," said Mrs. Pybus.

"Greeks and Macedonians and Turks and Bulgarians and such. It fair makes my head spin, the lot of them. Servians there are too, and Montenegroes. Too many of 'em altogether. Cat and dog."

"Are them the same Greeks that used to be so clever?" asked Mrs. Pybus.

"*Used* to be," said the young man with a kind of dark scorn, and suddenly began to pick his teeth with a pin.

"They can't even speak their own language now—not properly. Fair rotten," the young man added.

He fascinated Joan. She had never watched anything like him. But Peter just hated him.

§ 4

Upon this scene there presently appeared a new actor. He was preluded by a knocking at the door, he was ushered in by Mrs. Pybus who was opening and shutting her mouth in a state of breathless respect; he was received with the utmost deference by the young man with red hair. Indeed, from the moment when his knocking was heard without, the manner and bearing of the red-haired young man underwent the most marvellous change. An agitated alacrity appeared in his manner; he stood up and moved nervously; by weak, neckward movements of his head he seemed to indicate he now regretted wearing such a bright green tie. The newcomer appeared in the doorway. He was a tall, grey-clad, fair gentleman, with a face that twitched and a hand that dandled in front of him. He grinned his teeth at the room. "So thassem," he said, touching his teeth with his thumbnail.

He nodded confidentially to the red-haired young man without removing his eyes from Joan and Peter. He showed still more of his teeth and rattled his thumbnail along them. Then he waved his hand over the table. "Clear all this away," he said, and sat down in the young man's chair. Mrs. Pybus cleared away rapidly, assisted abjectly by the young man.

Mr. Grimes seemed to check off the two children. "You're Joan," he said. "I needn't bother about you. You're provided for. Peter. Peter's our business."

He got out a pocket-book and pencil. "Let's look at you, Peter. Just come out here, will you?"

Peter obeyed reluctantly and suspiciously.

"No stockings. Don't they wear stockings at that school of yours?"

"Not when we don't want them," said Peter. "No."

" 'Mazes me you wear anything," said Mr. Grimes. "S'pose it'll come to that. Let's see your hat."

"Haven't got a hat," said Peter. "Wouldn't wear it if I had."

"*Wouldn't* you!" said Mr. Grimes. "H'm!"

"Nice little handful," said Mr. Grimes, and hummed. He produced a paper from the pocket-book and read it, rubbing his teeth with the point of his pencil.

"Lersee whassor outfit we wan'," said Mr. Grimes. "H'm. . . . H'm. . . . H'm. . . ."

He stood up briskly. "Well, young man, we must go out and get you some clothes and things. What's called a school outfit. We'll have to go in that motor-car again. Quickest way. Get your hat. But you haven't got a hat."

"Me come too," said Joan.

"No. You can't come to a tailor's, and that's where we're going. Little girls can't come to tailors, you know," said Mr. Grimes.

Peter thought privately that Mr. Grimes was just the sort of beast who would take you to a tailor's. Well, he would stick it out. This couldn't go on for ever. He allowed himself to be guided by Mr. Grimes to the door. He restrained an impulse to ask to be allowed to sit beside the driver. One doesn't ask favours of beasts like Grimes.

Joan went to the window to watch the car and Mr. Grimes' proceedings mistrustfully.

"I got a nice picture-book for you to look at," said Mrs. Pybus, coming behind her. "Don't go standing and staring out of the window, dearie. It's an idle thing to stare out of windows."

Joan had an unpleasant feeling that she had to comply with this. Under the initiative of Mrs. Pybus she sat up to the table and permitted a large book to be opened in front of her, feigning attention. She kept her eye as much as possible on the window. She was aware of Peter getting into the car with Mr. Grimes. There was a sudden buzzing of machinery, the slam of a door, and the automobile moved and vanished.

She gave a divided attention to the picture-book before her, which was really not properly a picture-book at all but an old bound volume of the *Illustrated London News* full of wood engravings of royal processions and suchlike desiccated matter. It was a dusty, frowsty volume, damp-stained at the edges. She tried to be amused. But it was very grey and dull, and she felt strangely uneasy. Every few minutes she would look up expecting to see the car back outside, but it did not return. . . .

She heard the red-haired young man in the passage saying he thought he'd have to be getting round to the railway-station, and there was some point explained by Mrs. Pybus at great length and over and over again about the difference between the Great Western and the South Western Railway. The front door slammed after him at last, and Mrs. Pybus was audible returning to her kitchen.

Presently she came and looked at Joan with a thin, unreal smile on her white face.

"Getting on all right with the pretty pictures, dearie?" she asked.

"When's Peter coming back?" asked Joan.

"Oh, not for a longish bit," said Mrs. Pybus. "You see, he's going to school."

"Can I go to school?"

"Not *'is* school. He's going to a boy school."

"Oh!" said Joan, learning for the first time that schools have sexes. "Can I go out in the garden?"

"It isn't much of a garden," said Mrs. Pybus. "But what there is you're welcome."

It wasn't much of a garden. Rather it was a yard, into which a lean-to scullery, a coal shed, and a dustbin bit deeply. Along one side was a high fence cutting it off from a similar yard, and against this high fence a few nasturtiums gingered the colour scheme. A clothes-line stretched diagonally across this space and bore a depressed pair of black stockings, and in the corner at the far end a lilac bush was slowly but steadily and successfully wishing itself dead. The opposite corner was devoted to a collection of bottles, the ribs of an umbrella, and a dust-pan that had lost its handle. From beneath this curious rather than pleasing accumulation peeped the skeleton of a "rockery" built of brick clinkers and free from vegetation of any sort. An unseen baby a garden or two away deplored its existence loudly. At intervals a voice that sounded like the voice of an embittered little girl cut across these lamentations:

"Well, you shouldn't 'ave *broke* yer bottle," said the voice, with a note of moral demonstration. . . .

Joan stayed in this garden for exactly three minutes. Then she returned to Mrs. Pybus, who was engaged in some dim operations with a kettle in the kitchen. "Drat this old kitchener!" said Mrs. Pybus, rattling at a damper.

"Want to go 'ome," Joan said, in a voice that betrayed emotion.

Mrs. Pybus turned her meagre face and surveyed Joan without excessive tenderness.

"This *is* your 'ome, dearie," she said.

"I live at Ingle-Nook," said Joan.

Mrs. Pybus shook her head. "All that's been done away with," she said. "Your aunts 'ave give you up, and you're going to live 'ere for good—'long o' me."

§ 5

Meanwhile Mr. Grimes, with a cheerful kindliness that Peter perceived to be assumed, conveyed that young gentle-

man first to an outfitter, where he was subjected to nameless
indignities with a tape, and finally sent behind a screen
and told to change out of his nice, comfortable old clothes
and Heidelberg sandals into a shirt and a collar and a grey
flannel suit, and hard black shoes. All of which he did in a
mute, helpless rage, because he did not consider himself equal
to Mr. Grimes and the outfitter and his staff (with possibly
the chauffeur thrown in) in open combat. He was then
taken to a hairdresser and severely clipped, which struck him
as a more sensible proceeding; the stuff they put on his head
was indeed pleasingly aromatic; and then he was bought
some foolery of towels and things, and finally a Bible and
a prayer-book and a box. With this box he returned to the
outfitter's, and was quite interested in discovering that a
pile of things had accumulated on the counter, ties, collars
and things, and were to be packed in the box for him forthwith. A junior assistant was doing up his Limpsfield clothes
in a separate parcel. So do we put off childish things. That
parcel was to go via Mr. Grimes to The Ingle-Nook.

A memory of certain beloved sea stories came into Peter's
head. "This my kit?" he asked Mr. Grimes abruptly.

"You might call it your kit," said Mr. Grimes.

"Am I going on a battleship?" asked Peter.

Mr. Grimes—and the two outfitting assistants in sympathy
—were loudly amused.

"You're going to High Cross School," said Mr. Grimes,
emerging from his mirth. "Firm treatment. Sound
Church training. Unruly boys not objected to."

"I didn't know," said Peter.

They returned to the automobile, and after a mile or so of
roads and turnings stopped outside a gaunt brace of drab-
coloured semi-detached villas standing back behind a patch
of lawn, and having a walled enclosure to the left and an
overgrown laurel shrubbery to the right. "Here's High
Cross School," said Mr. Grimes, a statement that was rendered unnecessary by a conspicuous black and gold board
that rose above the walled enclosure. They descended.

"Wonther which ithe houth," mused Mr. Grimes, consulting his teeth, and then suddenly decided and led Peter towards the right hand of the two associated doors. "This,"

said Mr. Grimes, as they waited on the doorstep, ''is a *real* school. . . . No nonsense about it,'' said Mr. Grimes.

Peter nodded with affected intelligence.

They were ushered by a slatternly maid-servant into the presence of a baldish man with a white, puffy face and pale grey eyes, who was wearing a university gown and seemed to be expecting them. He was standing before the fireplace in the front parlour, which had a general air of being a study. There were an untidy desk facing the window and bookshelves in the recess on either side of the fireplace. Over the mantel was a tobacco-jar bearing the arms of some college, and reminders of Mr. Mainwearing's university achievements in the form of a college shield and Cambridge photographs.

''Well,'' said Mr. Grimes, ''here's your young man,'' and thrust Peter forward.

''So you've come to join us?'' said Mr. Mainwearing with a sort of clouded amiability.

''Join what?'' said Peter.

Mr. Mainwearing raised his eyebrows. ''High Cross School,'' he said.

''I'm at the School of St. George and the Venerable Bede,'' said Peter. ''So how can I?''

''No,'' said Mr. Grimes; ''you're joining here now.''

''But I can't go to *two* schools.''

''Consequently you're coming to *this* one,'' said Mr. Grimes.

''It's very sudden,'' said Peter.

''What's this about the School of Saint What's-his-name?'' asked Mr. Mainwearing of Mr. Grimes.

''It's just a sort of fad school they've been sending him to,'' Mr. Grimes explained. ''We're altering all that. It's a girls' school, and he's a growing boy. It's a school where socialism and play-acting are school subjects, and everybody runs about with next to nothing on. So his proper guardians have decided that's got to stop. And here we are.''

Mr. Mainwearing regarded Peter heavily while this was going on.

''Done any square root yet?'' he asked suddenly.

Peter had not.

"Know the date of Magna Carta?"

Peter did not. "It was under John," he said.

"I wanted the date," said Mr. Mainwearing. "What's the capital of Bulgaria?"

Peter did not know.

"Know any French irregular verbs?"

Peter said he didn't.

"Got to begin at the beginning," said Mr. Mainwearing. "Got your outfit?"

"We've just seen to that," said Mr. Grimes. "There's one or two things I'd like to say to you—"

He glanced at Peter.

Mr. Mainwearing comprehended. He came and laid one hand on Peter. "Time you saw some of your schoolfellows," he said.

Under his guiding pressure Peter was impelled along a passage, through an archway, across an empty but frowsty schoolroom in which one solitary small boy sat and sobbed grievously, and so by way of another passage to a kind of glass back-door from which steps went down to a large gravelled space, behind the high wall that carried the black and gold board. In the corner were parallel bars. A group of nine or ten boys were standing round these bars; they were all clad in the same sort of grey flannels that Peter was wearing, and they had all started round at the sound of the opening of the door. One shock-headed boy, perhaps a head taller than any of the rest, had a great red mouth beneath a red nose.

"Boys!" shouted Mr. Mainwearing; "here's a new chum. See that he learns his way about a bit, Probyn."

"Yessir!" said the shock-headed boy in a loud adult kind of voice.

Mr. Mainwearing gave Peter a shove that started him down the steps towards the playground, and slammed the door behind him.

Most of these boys were bigger than any boys that Peter had ever known before. They looked enormous. He reckoned some must be fifteen or sixteen—quite. They were as big as the biggest Sheldrick girl. Probyn seemed indeed as big as a man; Peter could see right across the playground

that he had a black smear of moustache.   His neck and wrists
and elbows stuck out of his clothes.

Peter with his hands in his new-found pockets walked
slowly towards these formidable creatures across the stony
playground.   They regarded him enigmatically.   So explorers must feel, who land on a strange beach in the presence
of an unknown race of men.

§ 6

"Come on, fathead!" said Probyn as he drew near.

Peter had expected that tone.   He affected indifference.

"What's your name?" asked Probyn.

"Stubland," said Peter.   "You Probyn?"

"Stubland," said Probyn.   "Stubland.   What's your
Christian name?"

"Peter.   What's yours?"

Probyn disregarded this counter question markedly.
"Simon Peter, eh!   Your father got you out of the Bible,
I expect.   Know anything of cricket, Simon Peter?"

"Not much," said Simon Peter.

"Can you swim?"

"No."

"Can you fight?"

"I don't know."

"What's your father?"

Peter didn't answer.   Instead, he fixed his attention upon
a fair-haired boy of about his own size who was standing
at the end of the parallel bars.   "What's *your* name?" he
asked.

The fair boy looked at Probyn.

"Damn it!" said Probyn.   "I asked *you* a question, Mr.
Simon Peter."

Peter continued disregardful.   "Hasn't this school got
a flagstaff?" he asked generally.

Probyn came closer to him and gripped him by the shoulder.   "I asked you a question, Mr. Simon Peter.   What is
your father?"

It was a question Peter could not answer because for some
obscure reason he could not bring himself to say that his

father was dead. If ever he said that, he knew his father would be dead. But what else could he say of his father? So he seemed to shrink a little and remained mute. "We'll have to cross-examine you," said Probyn, and shook him.

The fair boy came in front of Peter. It was clear he had great confidence in Probyn. He had a fat, smooth, round face that Peter disliked.

"Simon Peter," he said. "Answer up."

"What is your father?" said Probyn.

"What's your father?" repeated the fair boy, and then suddenly flicked Peter under the nose with his finger.

But this did at least enable Peter to change the subject. He smote at the fat-faced boy with great vigour and missed him. The fat-faced boy dodged back quickly.

"Hullo!" said Probyn. "Ginger!"

"That chap's not going to touch my nose," said Peter. "Anyhow."

"Touch it when I like," said the fat-faced boy.

"You won't."

"You want to *fight?*" asked the fat-faced boy, conscious of popular support.

Peter said he wasn't going to have his nose flicked anyhow.

"Flick it again, Newton," said Probyn, "and see."

"I'll show you in no time," said Newton.

"Why!—I'd lick you with one hand," continued Newton.

Peter said nothing. But he regarded his antagonist very intently.

"Skinny little snipe," said Newton. "Whaddyou think you'd do to me?"

"Hit him, Newton," said a cadaverous boy with freckles.

"Hit him, Newton. He's too cocky," said another. "Flick his silly nose again and see."

"I'll hit him 'f 'e wants it," said Newton, and buttoned up his jacket in a preparatory way.

"Hit him, Newton," other voices urged.

"Let him put up his fists," said Newton.

"Do that when I please," said Peter rather faintly.

Newton had seemed at first just about Peter's size. Now he seemed very much larger. All the boys seemed to have grown larger. They were gathering in a vast circle of doom round a minute and friendless Peter. Probyn loomed over him like a figure of fate. Peter wondered whether he need have hit at Newton. It seemed now a very unwise thing indeed to have done. Newton was alternately swaying towards him and swaying away from him, and repeating his demand for Peter to put his hands up. He seemed on the verge of flicking again. He was going to flick. Probyn watched them both critically. Then with a rapid movement of the mind Peter realized that Newton's face was swaying now well within his range; the moment had come, and desperately, with a great effort and a wide and sweeping movement of the arm, he smote hard at Newton's cheek. Smack. A good blow. Newton recoiled with an expression of astonishment. "You—swine!" he said.

Two other boys came running across the playground, and voices explained, "New boy. . . . Fight. . . ."

But curiously enough the fight did not go on. Newton at a slightly greater distance continued to loom threateningly, but did no more than loom. His cheek was very red. "I'll break your jaw, cutting at me like that," he said. "You swine!" He used foul and novel terms expressive of rage. He looked at Probyn as if for approval, but Probyn offered none. He continued to threaten, but he did not come within arm's length again.

"Hit him back, Newton," several voices urged, but with no success.

"Wait till I start on him," said Newton.

"Buck up, young Newton," said Probyn suddenly, "and stop jawing. You began it. *I'm* not going to help you. Make a ring, you chaps. It's a fair fight."

Peter found himself facing Newton in the centre of an interested circle.

Newton was walking crab fashion athwart the circle, swaying with his fists and elbows high. He was now acting a dangerous intentness. "Come on," he said terribly.

"Hit him, Newton," said the cadaverous boy. "Don't wait for him."

"You started it, Newton," Probyn insisted. "And he's hit you fair."

A loud familiar sound, the clamorous ringing of a bell,

struck across the suspended drama. "That's tea," said Newton eagerly, dropping his fists. "It's no good starting on him now."

"You'll have to fight him later," said Probyn. "Now he's hit you."

"It's up to you, Newton," said the cadaverous boy, evidently following Probyn's lead.

"Cavé. It's Noser," said a voice.

There was a little pause.

"Toke!" cried Probyn.

"Toke, Simon Peter," said the cadaverous boy informingly. . . .

Peter found himself no longer in focus. Every one was moving towards the door whence Peter had descended to the playground, and at this door there now stood a middle-aged man with a large nose and a sly expression, surveying the boys.

Impelled by gregarious instincts, Peter followed the crowd.

He did not like these hostile boys. He did not like this shabby-looking place. He was quite ready to believe that presently he would have to go on fighting Newton. He was not particularly afraid of Newton, but he perceived that Probyn stood behind him. He detested Probyn already. He was afraid of Probyn. Probyn was like a golliwog. He knew by instinct that Probyn was full of disagreeable possibilities for him, and that it would be very hard to get away from Probyn. And what did it all mean? Was he never going back to Limpsfield again?

The bell had had exactly the tone of the tea bell at Miss Murgatroyd's school. It might have been the same bell. And it had made his heart homesick for the colour and brightness of the School of St. George and the Venerable Bede, and for the friendly garden and familiar rooms of Ingle-Nook. For the first time he realized that he had fallen into this school as an animal falls into a trap, that his world had changed, that home was very far away. . . .

And what had they done to Joan? . . .

Had he to live here always? . . .

It struck Mr. Noakley, the assistant master with the large nose, as he watched the boys at tea, that the new boy had a face like a doll, but really that face with its set, shining, expressionless eyes was only the mask, the very thin mask, that covered a violent disposition to blubber. . . .

Well, no one was going to see Peter blub. No one was going to hear him blub. . . .

Tonight perhaps in bed.

He had still to realize the publicity of a school dormitory. . . .

He knew he couldn't box, but he had seen something in Newton's eyes that made him feel that Newton was not invincible. He would grip his fists in a very knobby way and hit Newton as hard as he could in the face. Oh!—*frightfully* hard. . . .

Peter was not eating very much. "Bags I your slice of Toke," said the cadaverous boy.

"Take the beastly stuff," said Peter.

"Little spoilt mammy coddle," thought old Nosey Noakley. "We aren't good enough for him."

§ 7

So it was that Mr. Grimes, acting for Lady Charlotte, set about the rescue of Joan and Peter from, as she put it, "the freaks, faddists and Hill-Top philosophies of the Surrey hills," and their restoration to the established sobrieties and decorums of English life. Very naturally this sudden action came as an astonishing blow to the two advanced aunts. At nine o'clock that evening Miss Murgatroyd was called down to see Miss Phyllis Stubland, who had ridden over on her bicycle. "Where are the children?" asked Aunt Phyllis.

"You sent for them," said Miss Murgatroyd.

"Sent for them!"

"Yes. I remember now. The young man said it was Lady Charlotte Sydenham. Didn't you know? She is going abroad tomorrow or the next day."

"Sent for them!" Aunt Phyllis repeated. . . .

Two hours later Aunt Phyllis was telling the terrible news to Mary. Aunt Phœbe was in London for the night to see Mr. Tree play *Richard II*, and there were no means of communicating with her until the morning. The Ingle-Nook was much too Pre-Raphaelite to possess a telephone, and Aunt Phœbe was sleeping at the flat of a friend in Church Row, Hampstead.   Next morning a telegram found her still in bed.

"Children kidnapped by Lady Charlotte consult Sycamore Phyllis"

said the telegram.

"*No!*" cried Aunt Phœbe sharply.

Then as the little servant-maid was on the point of closing the door, "Tell Miss Jepson," Aunt Phœbe commanded. . . .

Miss Jepson found Aunt Phœbe out of bed and dressing with a rapid casualness.   It was manifest that some great crisis had happened.   "An outrage upon all women," said Aunt Phœbe.   "I have been outraged."

"My dear!" said Miss Jepson.

"Read that telegram!" cried Aunt Phœbe, pointing to a small ball of pink paper in the corner of the room.

Miss Jepson went over to the corner with a perplexed expression, and smoothed out the telegram and read it.

"A *Bradshaw* and a hansom!" Aunt Phœbe was demanding as she moved rapidly about the room from one scattered garment to another.   "No breakfast.   I can eat nothing.   Nothing.   I am a tigress.   A maddened tigress. Maddened.   Beyond endurance.   Oh!   Can you reach these buttons, dear?"

Miss Jepson hovered about her guest readjusting her costume in accordance with commonplace standards while Aunt Phœbe expressed herself in Sibylline utterances.

"Children dedicated to the future. . . . Reek of ancient corruptions. . . . Abomination of desolation. . . . The nine fifty-three. . . . Say half an hour. . . . Remonstrance. . . . An avenging sword. . . . The sword of the Lord and of Gideon."

"Are you going to this Mr. Sycamore?" asked Miss Jepson suddenly.

Aunt Phœbe seemed lost for a time and emerged with, "Good God!—*No!*   This is an occasion when a woman must show she can act as a man.   This tries us, Amanda.   I will have no man in this.   No man at all!   Are women to loll in hareems for ever while men act and fight?   When little children are assailed? . . ."

"Chastlands," said Aunt Phœbe to the cabman, waving Miss Jepson's *Bradshaw* in her hand.

The man looked stupid.

"Oh! Charing Cross," she cried scornfully. "The rest is beyond you."

And in the train she startled her sole fellow-traveller and made him get out at the next station by saying suddenly twice over in her loud, clear contralto voice the one word *"Action."* She left Miss Jepson's *Bradshaw* in the compartment when she got out.

She found Chastlands far gone in packing for Lady Charlotte's flight abroad. "I demand Lady Charlotte," she said. She followed up old Cashel as he went to announce her. He heard her coming behind him, but his impression of her was so vivid that he deemed it wiser not to notice this informality. And besides in his dry, thin way he wanted to hear why she demanded Lady Charlotte. He perceived the possibilities of a memorable clash. He was a quiet, contemplative man who hid his humour like a miser's treasure and lived much upon his memories. Weeks after a thing had happened he would suddenly titter, in bed, or in church, or while he was cleaning his plate. And none were told why he tittered.

For a moment Aunt Phœbe hovered on the landing outside the Chastlands drawing-room.

"I can't see her," she heard Lady Charlotte say, with something like a note of terror. "It is impossible."

"Leave her to me, me Lady," said a man's voice.

"Tell her to wait, Cashel," said Lady Charlotte.

Aunt Phœbe entered, trailing her artistic robes. Before her by the writing-table in the big window stood Lady Charlotte, flounced, bonneted, dressed as if for instant flight. A slender, fair, wincing man in grey stood nearer, his expression agitated but formidable. They had evidently both risen to their feet as Aunt Phœbe entered. Cashel made insincere demonstrations of intervention, but Aunt Phœbe disposed of him with a gesture. A haughty and terrible politeness was in her manner, but she sobbed slightly as she spoke.

"Lady Charlotte," she said, "where are my wards?"

"They are *my* wards," said Lady Charlotte no less haughtily.

"Excuse me, Lady Charlotte. Permit me," said Mr. Grimes, with soothing gestures of his lean white hands.

"Please do not intervene," said Aunt Phœbe.

"Mr. Grimes, madam, is my solicitor," said Lady Charlotte. "You may go, Cashel."

Cashel went reluctantly.

Mr. Grimes advanced a step and dandled his hands and smiled ingratiatingly. Italian and Spanish women will stab, he had heard, and fishwives are a violent class. Otherwise he believed all women, however terrible in appearance, to be harmless. This gave him courage.

"Miss Stubland, I believe," he said. "These young people, young Stubland and his foster-sister to wit, are at present in my charge—under instructions from Lady Charlotte."

"Where?" asked Aunt Phœbe.

"Our case, Miss Stubland, is that they were not being properly educated in your charge. That is our case. They were receiving no sound moral and religious training, and they were being brought up in—to say the least of it—an eccentric fashion. Our aim in taking them out of your charge is to secure for them a proper ordinary English bringing up."

"Every word an insult," panted Aunt Phœbe. "Every word. What have you done with them?"

"Until we are satisfied that you will consent to continue their training on proper lines, Miss Stubland, you can scarcely expect us to put it in your power to annoy these poor children further."

Mr. Grimes' face was wincing much more than usual, and these involuntary grimaces affected Aunt Phœbe in her present mood as though they were deliberate insults. He did not allow for this added exasperation.

"Annoy!" cried Aunt Phœbe.

"That is the usual expression. We are perfectly within our rights in refusing you access. Having regard to your manifest determination to upset any proper arrangement."

"You refuse to let me know where those children are?"

"Unless you can get an order against us."

"You mean—go to some old judge?"

Mr. Grimes gesticulated assent. If she chose to phrase it in that way, so much the worse for her application.

"You won't—— You will go on with this kidnapping?"

"Miss Stubland, we are entirely satisfied with our present course and our present position."

Lady Charlotte endorsed him with three great nods.

Aunt Phœbe stood aghast.

Mr. Grimes remained quietly triumphant. Lady Charlotte stood quietly triumphant behind him. For a moment it seemed as if Aunt Phœbe had no reply of any sort to make.

Then suddenly she advanced three steps and seized upon Mr. Grimes. One hand gripped his nice grey coat below the collar behind, the other, the looseness of his waistcoat just below the tie. And lifting him up upon his toes Aunt Phœbe shook him.

Mr. Grimes was a lean, spare, ironical man. Aunt Phœbe was a well-developed woman. Yet only by an enormous effort did she break the instinctive barriers that make a man sacred from feminine assault. It was an effort so enormous that when at last it broke down the dam of self-restraint, it came through a boiling flood of physical power. It came through with a sort of instantaneousness. At one moment Mr. Grimes stood before Lady Charlotte's eyes dominating the scene; at the next he was, as materialists say of the universe, "all vibrations." He was a rag, he was a scrap of carpet in Aunt Phœbe's hands. The appetite for shaking seemed to grow in Aunt Phœbe as she shook.

From the moment when Aunt Phœbe gripped him until she had done shaking him nobody except Lady Charlotte made an articulate sound. And all that Lady Charlotte said, before astonishment overcame her, was one loud "Haw!" The face of Mr. Grimes remained set, except for a certain mechanical rattling of the teeth in a wild stare at Aunt Phœbe; Aunt Phœbe's features bore that earnest calm one may see upon the face of a good woman who washes clothes or kneads bread. Then suddenly it was as if Aunt Phœbe woke up out of a trance.

"You make—you make me forget myself!" said Aunt

Phœbe with a low sob, and after one last shake relinquished him.

Mr. Grimes gyrated for a moment and came to rest against a massive table. He was still staring at Aunt Phœbe.

For a moment the three people remained breathing heavily and contemplating the outrage. At last Mr. Grimes was able to raise a wavering, pointing finger to gasp, "You have—you have—yes—indeed—forgotten yourself!"

Then, as if he struggled to apprehend the position, "You—you have assaulted me."

"Let it be—let it be a warning to you," said Aunt Phœbe.

"That is a threat."

"Agreed," panted Aunt Phœbe with spirit, though she had not meant to threaten him at all.

"If you think, madam, that you can assault me with impunity——"

"I shouldn't have thought it—before I took hold of you. A bag of bones. . . . Man indeed!" And then very earnestly—"*Yes.*"

She paused. The pause held all three of them still.

"But why—oh, why!—should I bandy words with such a thing as you?" she asked with a sudden belated recovery of her dignity. "*You*—"

She sought her word carefully.

"Flibber-gib!"

And forgetting altogether the mission upon which she had come, Aunt Phœbe turned about to make her exit from the scene. It seemed to her, perhaps justly, that it was impossible to continue the parley further. "Legalized scoundrel!" she said over her shoulder, and moved towards the door. In that first tremendous clash of the New Woman and the Terrific Old Lady, it must be admitted that the New Woman carried off, so to speak, the physical honours. Lady Charlotte stood against the fireplace visibly appalled. Only when Aunt Phœbe was already at the door did it occur to Lady Charlotte to ring the bell to have her visitor "shown out." Her shaking hand could scarcely find the bell handle. For the rest she was ineffective, wasting great opportunities for scorn and dignity. She despised herself for not having a larger, fiercer solicitor. She doubted herself. For the first time in her life Lady Charlotte Sydenham doubted herself, and quailed before a new birth of time.

Upon the landing appeared old Cashel, mutely respectful. He showed out Aunt Phœbe in profound silence. He watched her retreating form with affectionate respect, stroking his cheek slowly with two fingers. He closed the door.

He stood as one who seeks to remember. "Flibber-jib," he said at last very softly, without exultation or disapproval. He simply wanted to have it exactly right. Then he went upstairs to have a long, mild, respectful look at Mr. Grimes, and to ask if he could do anything for him. . . .

§ 8

Aunt Phœbe's return to The Ingle-Nook blended triumph and perplexity.

"I could never have imagined a man so flimsy," she said.

"But where are the children?" asked Aunt Phyllis.

"If all men are like him—then masculine ascendancy is an imposture."

("Yes, but where are the children?")

"So a baulked tigress might feel."

Aunt Phyllis decided to write to Mr. Sycamore.

§ 9

Mr. Mainwearing was the proprietor of a private school for young gentlemen, not by choice but by reason of the weaknesses of his character. It was card-playing more than anything else that had made him an educator. And it was vanity and the want of any sense of proportion that had led to the card-playing.

Mr. Mainwearing's father had been a severe parent, severe to the pitch of hostility. He had lost his wife early, and he had taken a grudge against his only son, whose looks he did not like. He had sent him to Cambridge with a bitter assurance that he would do no good there; had kept him too short of money to be comfortable, spent most of his property—he was a retired tea-broker—in disappointing and embittering jaunts into vice, and died suddenly, leaving—unwillingly, but he had to leave it—about three thousand pounds to his heir. Young Mainwearing had always been short of pocket-money, and for a time he regarded this legacy as limitless wealth; he flashed from dingy obscurity into splendour, got himself coloured shirts and remarkable ties, sought the acquaintance of horses, slipped down to London for music-halls and "life." When it dawned upon him that even three thousand pounds was not a limitless ocean of money, he attempted to maintain its level by winning more from his fellow undergraduates. Nap and poker were the particular forms of sport he affected. He reckoned that he was, in a quiet way, rather cleverer than most fellows, and that he would win. But he was out in his reckoning. He left Cambridge with a Junior Optime in the Mathematical Tripos and a residuum of about seven hundred pounds. He was a careful cricketer, and he had liked football at school in his concluding years when he was big enough to barge into the other chaps. Surveying the prospect before him, he decided that a school was the best place for him, he advertised himself as "of gentlemanly appearance" and "good at games," and he found his billet in a preparatory school at Brighton. Thence he went to a big grammar school, and thence came to the High Cross School to remain first as assistant, then as son-in-law and partner, and now as sole proprietor. Mrs. Mainwearing was not very useful as a helpmeet, as she was slightly but not offensively defective in her mind; still one must take life as one finds it. She was, at any rate, regular in her habits, and did not interfere with the housekeeper, a worthy, confidence-creating woman, much tipped by the tenderer sort of parent.

Of course Mr. Mainwearing had no special training as a teacher. He had no ideas about education at all. He had no social philosophy. He had never asked why he was alive or what he was up to. Instinct, perhaps, warned him that the answer might be disagreeable. Much less did he inquire what his boys were likely to be up to. And it did not occur to him, it did not occur to any one in those days, to consider that these deficiencies barred him in any way from the preparation of the genteel young for life. He taught as he had been taught; his teachers had done the same; he was

the last link of a long chain of tradition that had perhaps
in the beginning had some element of intention in it as
to what was to be made of the pupil.   Schools, like religions,
tend perpetually to forget what they are for.   High Cross
School, like numberless schools in Great Britain in those days,
had forgotten completely; it was a mysterious fated routine;
the underlying idea seemed to be that boys must go to
school as puppies have the mange.   Certain school books
existed, God alone knew why, and the classes were taken
through them.   It was like reading prayers.   Certain examination boards checked this process in a way that Mr.
Mainwearing felt reflected upon his honour, and like all
fundamentally dishonest people he was inclined to be touchy
about his honour.   But parents wanted examination results
and he had to give in.   Preparation for examinations dominated the school; no work was done in the school that did
not lead towards an examination paper; if there had been
no examinations, no work would have been done at all.   But
these examinations might have been worse than they were.
The examiners were experienced teachers and considerate
for their kind.   They respected the great routine.   The examiners in classics had, at best, Babu Latin and less Greek,
and so they knew quite well how to set a paper that would
enable the intelligent candidate to conceal an entire incapacity for reading, writing, or speaking a classical language;
the examiners in mathematics knew nothing of practical calculations, and treated the subject as a sort of Patience game;
the foreign language examiners stuck loyally to the grammar; in drawing the examiners asked you to copy "copies,"
they did not, at any rate, require you to draw things; and
altogether the "curse of examinations" might have pressed
on Mr. Mainwearing harder than it did.   Suppose the language papers had been just long passages to translate into
and out of English, and that the mathematical test had been
all problems, and the drawing test had been a test of drawing anything!   What school could have stood the strain?
     To assist him in the work of his school Mr. Mainwearing
had gathered about him a staff of three.   He had found a
young man rather of his own social quality, but very timid,
a B.A. Cantab. by way of the botanical special; then there

was Noakley, a rather older, sly creature, with a large over-balancing nose, who had failed to qualify years ago as an elementary assistant school-master and so had strayed into the uncharted and uncertificated ways of a private school; and finally there was Kahn, an Alsatian, who taught languages and the piano. With these three and the active assistance of Mrs. Rich, the housekeeper, the school maintained its sluggish routines.

The boys slept in two long rooms that had been made by knocking through partitions in the two upper floors, and converted into dormitories by the simple expedient of crowding them with iron bedsteads and small chests of drawers. It was the business of Noakley—who had a separate room on the top floor—to arouse the boys at seven with cries and violence for the business of the day. But there was a tacit understanding between him and the boys not to molest each other until about twenty minutes past.

It was a rule, established by Mr. Mainwearing in a phase of hygienic enthusiasm some years before, that on fine mornings throughout the year the boys should go for a sharp run before breakfast. It was a modern and impressive thing to do and it cost him nothing. It was Noakley's duty to accompany them on this run. He was unable to imagine any more loathsome duty. So that he had invented a method of supplementing the rains of heaven by means of a private watering-pot. His room was directly above Mr. Mainwearing's, and Mr. Mainwearing slept with his window shut and his blinds down, and about seven-fifteen or so every morning the curious passer-by might have seen a lean, sly man with an enormous nose, his mouth wide open and his tongue out with effort, leaning far out of an upper bedroom of High Cross School and industriously and carefully watering the window and window-sill of the room two storeys below him. Later, perhaps, a patient observer might have been rewarded by the raising of Mr. Mainwearing's blind and a glimpse of Mr. Mainwearing, unshaven and in a white cotton nightgown, glancing out at the weather. . . .

So generally the morning began with a tedious, sticky, still sleepy hour called Early Prep. in the schoolroom on the ground floor. It was only during Kahn's alternate week of morning duty that the run ever occurred. Then it wasn't a run. It began as a run and settled down as soon as it was out of sight of the school to a sulky walk and a muttered monologue by Kahn in German—he never spoke any language but German before breakfast—about his "magen."

Noakley's method in early prep. was to sit as near to the fire as possible in the winter and at the high desk in summer, and to leave the boys alone so long as they left him alone. They conversed in undertones, made and threw paper darts at one another, read forbidden fiction, and so forth. Breakfast at half-past eight released them, and there was a spell of playground before morning school at half-past nine. At half-past nine Mr. Mainwearing and Mr. Smithers, the botanical Cantab, appeared in the world, gowned and a little irritable, and prayers and scripture inaugurated the official day. Mr. Mainwearing's connexion was a sound Church connexion, and he opened the day with an abbreviated Matins and the collect and lessons for the day. Then the junior half of the school went upstairs to the second class-room with Mr. Smithers, while Mr. Mainwearing dealt tediously with Chronicles or Kings. Meanwhile Kahn and Noakley corrected exercise-books in the third class-room, and waited their time to take up their part in the great task of building up the British imperial mind. By eleven o'clock each of the four class-rooms was thoroughly stuffy and the school was in full swing; Mr. Mainwearing, who could not have translated a new satire by Juvenal to save his life, was "teaching" Greek or Latin or history, Mr. Smithers was setting or explaining exercises on the way to quadratic equations or Euclid Book II., which were the culminating points of High Cross mathematics; Kahn, hoarse with loud anger, was making a personal quarrel of the French class; and Noakley was gently setting the feet of the younger boys astray in geography or arithmetic or parsing. This was the high-water mark of the day's effort.

After the midday dinner, which was greasy and with much too much potato in it, came a visible decline. In the afternoon Mr. Mainwearing would start a class upon some sort of exercises, delegate Probyn to keep order, and retire to slumber in his study; Smithers and Kahn, who both suffered from indigestion, would quarrel bitterly with boys they disliked and inflict punishments; Noakley would sleep quietly through a drawing class on the tacit understanding that there was no audible misbehaviour, and that the boys would awaken him if they heard Mr. Mainwearing coming.

Mr. Mainwearing, when he came, usually came viciously. He would awaken in an evil temper and sit cursing his life for some time before he could rouse himself to a return to duty. He would suddenly become filled with suspicions, about the behaviour of the boys or the worthiness of his assistants. He would take his cane and return with a heavy scowl on his face through the archway to his abandoned class.

He would hear a murmur of disorder, a squeak of "cavé!" and a hush.

Or he would hear Probyn's loud bellow: "Shut up, young Pyecroft. Shut it, I say!—or I'll report you!"

He would appear threateningly in the doorway.

"What's he doing, Probyn?" he would ask. "What's he doing?"

"Humbugging about, Sir. He's *always* humbugging about."

The diffused wrath of Mr. Mainwearing would gather to a focus. If there were no little beasts like young Pyecroft he wouldn't be in this infernal, dull, dreary hole of a school.

"*I'll* teach you to humbug about, Pyecroft," he would say. "Come out, Sir!"

"Please, Sir!"

Roar. "Don't *bandy* words with me, you little Hound! Come out, I say!"

"Please——!" Young Pyecroft would come out slowly and weeping. Mr. Mainwearing would grip him hungrily.

"I'll teach you to humbug about. (Cut.) I'll teach you! (Cut.) I can't leave this class-room for a moment but half a dozen of you must go turning it upside down." (Cut.)

"Wow!"

"Don't answer *me*, Sir!" (Cut.) "Don't answer me." (Cut.) "*Now*, Sir?"

Pyecroft completely subdued. Pyecroft relinquished.

"Now, are there any more of you?" asked Mr. Mainwearing, feeling a little better.

Then he would hesitate. Should he take the set work at once, or should he steal upstairs on tiptoe to catch out one of the assistants? His practice varied. He always suspected Noakley of his afternoon sleep, and was never able to catch him. Noakley slept with the class-room door slightly open. His boys could hear the opening of the class-room door downstairs. When they did they would smack down a book upon the desk close beside him, and Noakley would start teaching instantly like an automaton that has just been released. He didn't take a second to awaken, so that he was very hard indeed to catch.

The school remained a scene of jaded activities until four, when a bell rang for afternoon prayers under Mr. Mainwearing in the main schoolroom. Then the boys would sing a hymn while Kahn accompanied on a small harmonium that stood in the corner of the room. While prayers were going on a certain scattered minority of the boys were speculating whether Kahn or Smithers would remember this or that task that had been imposed in a moment of passion, weighing whether it was safer to obey or forget. Kahn and Smithers would return to the class-rooms reluctantly to gather in the harvest of their own wrath, but now for a little time Noakley was free to do nothing. Noakley hardly ever imposed punishments. When he was spoken to upon the subject he would put his nose down in a thoughtful manner and reply in a tone of mild observation: "The boys, they seem to *mind* me somehow."

Meanwhile the released boys dispersed to loaf about the playground and the outhouses and playing-field until tea at five. Sometimes there was a hectic attempt at cricket or football in the field in which Mr. Mainwearing participated, and then tea was at half-past five. When Mr. Mainwearing participated he liked to bat, and he did not like to be bowled out. Noakley was vaguely supposed to superintend tea and evening prep., and the boys, after a supper of milk and biscuits, were packed off to bed at half-past eight. It was much too early to send the bigger boys to bed, but "Good God!" said Mr. Mainwearing; "am I to have *no* peace in my day?" And he tried to ease his conscience about what might go on in the dormitories after bedtime by directing

Noakley to "exercise a general supervision," and by occasionally stealing upstairs in his socks.

Wednesday and Saturday were half-holidays, and in the afternoon the boys wore flannels or shorts, according to the season, and played pick-up cricket or football or hockey in a well-worn field at the back of the school, or they went for a walk with Noakley or Smithers. On Sundays they wore top hats and pseudo-Eton jackets, and went to church in the morning and the evening. In the afternoon Smithers took Scripture wearily for an hour, and then went for a walk with Noakley. And on Sunday evening they wrote home carefully supervised letters saying how happy they were and how they were all in the best of health and about "examinational prospects," and how they hoped they were making satisfactory progress and suchlike topics. But they never gave any account of the talk that went on during the playground loafing, nor of the strange games and ceremonies over which Probyn presided in the dormitories, nor of the exercises of Mr. Mainwearing's cane. There was no library, and the boys never read anything except school books and such printed matter as they themselves introduced into the school. They never read nor drew nor painted nor made verses to please themselves. They never dreamt of acting or singing. Their only training in the use of their hands was at cricket, and they never looked at a newspaper. Occasionally Smithers gave a lesson in botany, but there was no other science teaching. Science teaching requires apparatus and apparatus costs money, and so far as the prospectus went it was quite easy to call the botany "science." . . .

§ 10

In this manner did High Cross School grind and polish its little batch of boys for their participation in the affairs of the greatest, most civilized and most civilizing empire the world has ever seen.

It was, perhaps, a bad specimen of an English private school, but it was a specimen. There were worse as well as better among the schools of England. There were no

doubt many newer and larger, many cleaner, many better
classified. Some had visiting drill-sergeants, some had chemistry cupboards, some had specially built gymnasia, some
even had school libraries of a hundred volumes or so. . . .
Most of them had better housing and better arranged dormitories.   And most of them were consistently "preparatory,"
stuck to an upward age-limit, and turned out a boy as soon
as he became a youth to go on to business or medicine or the
public schools.   Mr. Mainwearing's school was exceptional in
this, that it had to hold on to all it could get.   He had a
connexion with one or two solicitors, an understanding—
Mr. Grimes was one of his friends—and his school contained
in addition to Peter several other samples of that unfortunate
type of boy whose school is found for him by a solicitor.
Some stayed at Windsor with Mr. Mainwearing during the
holidays.   In that matter High Cross School was exceptional.
But the want of any intellectual interest, of any spontaneous activities of the mind at all in High Cross School,
was no exceptional thing.

Life never stands altogether still, but it has a queer
tendency to form stationary eddies, and very much of the
education of middle-class and upper-class youth in England
had been an eddy for a century.   The still exquisite and
impressionable brains of the new generation came tumbling
down the stream, curious, active, greedy, and the eddying
schools caught them with a grip of iron and spun them
round and round for six or seven precious years and at last
flung them out. . . .

§ 11

Into this vicious eddy about Mr. Mainwearing's life and
school came the developing brain of Master Peter Stubland,
and resented it extremely.   At first he had been too much
astonished by his transfer from Limpsfield to entertain any
other emotion; it was only after some days at High Cross
School that he began to realize that the experience was not
simply astonishing but uncongenial, and indeed hateful.

He discovered he hated the whole place.   Comprehended
within this general hatred were particular ones.   He hated

Newton. The fight remained in suspense, neither boy knew anything of scientific fisticuffs, neither had ever worn a boxing-glove, and both were disposed to evade the hard, clear issue of the ring. But Newton continued to threaten and grimace at him, and once as he was passing Peter on the staircase he turned about and punched him in the back.

For Newton Peter's hatred was uncomplicated; for Probyn and a second boy nearly as big, a fair, sleepy boy named Ames, Peter had a feeling that differed from a clear, clean hatred; it had an element of disgust and dread in it. Probyn, with Ames as an accessory and Newton as his pet toady, dominated the school. It is an unnatural and an unwholesome thing for boys and youths of various ages to be herded as closely together as they were in High Cross School; the natural instinct of the young is against such an association. In a good, big school whose atmosphere is wholesome, boys will classify themselves out in the completest way; they will not associate, they will scarcely speak with boys outside their own year. There is a foolish way of disposing of this fact by saying that boys are "such Snobs." But indeed they are kept apart by the fiercest instinct of self-preservation. All life and all its questions are stirring and unfolding in the young boy; in every sort of young creature a natural discretion fights against forced and premature developments. "Keep to your phase," says nature. The older boys, perplexed by novel urgencies and curiosities, are embarrassed by their younger fellows; younger boys are naturally afraid of older ones and a little disposed to cringe. But what were such considerations as these to a man like Mainwearing? He had never thought over, he had long since forgotten, his own development. Any boy, old or young, whose parents could pay the bill, was got into the school and kept in the school as long as possible. None of the school work was interesting; there were constant gaps in the routine when there was nothing to do but loaf. It was inevitable that the older boys should become mischievous louts; they bullied and tormented and corrupted the younger boys because there was nothing else to do; if there had been anything else to do they would have absolutely disregarded the younger boys; and the younger boys did what they could

to propitiate these powerful and unaccountable giants. The
younger boys "sucked up" to the bigger boys; they became,
as it were, clients; they were annexed by patrons. They
professed unlimited obedience in exchange for protection.
Newton, for instance, called himself Probyn's "monkey";
Pyecroft was Ames's. Probyn would help Newton with his
sums, amuse himself by putting him to the torture (when
Newton was expected to display a doglike submission) or
make him jealous by professing an affection for other small
boys.

Peter came into this stuffy atmosphere of forced and
undignified relationships instinct, though he knew it not,
with a passionate sense of honour. From the very beginning he knew there was something in these boys and in their
atmosphere that made them different from himself, something from which he had to keep himself aloof. There was
a word missing from his vocabulary that would have expressed it, and that word was "Cad." But at the School
of St. George and the Venerable Bede they were not taught
to call any people "cads."

He was a boy capable of considerable reserve. He did not,
like young Winterbaum, press his every thought and idea
upon those about him. He could be frank where he was
confident, but this sense of difference smote him dumb. Several of his schoolfellows, old Noakley, and Mr. Mainwearing,
became uncomfortably aware of an effect of unspoken comment in Peter. He would receive a sudden phrase of abuse
with a thoughtful expression, as though he weighed it and
compared it with some exterior standard. This irritated a
school staff accustomed to use abusive language. Probyn,
after Peter had hit Newton, took a fancy to him that did not
in the least modify Peter's instinctive detestation of the red
nostrils and the sloppy mouth and the voluminous bellow.
Peter became rapidly skilful in avoiding Probyn's conversation, and this monstrously enhanced his attraction for Probyn. Probyn's attention varied between deliberate attempts
to vex and deliberate attempts to propitiate. He kept alive
the promise of a fight with Newton, and frankly declared
that Peter could lick Newton any day. Newton was as distressed as a cast mistress.

One evening the cadaverous boy discovered Peter drawing warriors on horseback. He reported this strange gift to Ames. Ames came demanding performances, and Peter obliged.

"He *can* draw," said Ames. "George and the Dragon, eh? It's *good.*"

Probyn was shouted to, and joined in the admiration.

Peter drew this and that by request.

"Draw a woman," said Ames, and then, as the nimble pencil obeyed, "No—not an old woman. Draw—you know. Draw a savage woman."

"Draw a girl bathing—like they are in *Ally Sloper's Half-Holiday,*" said Probyn. "Just with light things on."

"Draw a heathen goddess," said Ames. "With nothing on at all."

Peter said he couldn't draw goddesses.

"Go on," said Ames. "Draw a savage woman."

Peter, being pressed, tried a negress. They hung over him insisting upon details.

"Get *out,* young Newton!" cried Probyn. "Don't come hanging round here. He's drawing things."

Ames pressed further requests.

"Shan't draw any more," said Peter with a sudden disinclination.

"Go it, Simon Peter," said Ames, "don't be a mammy-good."

"Gaw! if I could draw!" said Probyn.

But Peter had finished drawing.

§ 12

No further questions were asked Peter about his father, but on Sunday night, when home-letter time came round, any doubt about the soundness of his social position was set at rest by Mr. Mainwearing himself. Home-letters from High Cross School involved so many delicate considerations that the proprietor made it his custom to supervise them himself. He distributed sheets of paper with the school heading, and afterwards he collected them and addressed them himself in his study. "You, Stubland, must write a letter to your aunt," he said loudly across the room, "and tell her how you are getting on."

"Aunt Phyllis?" said Peter.

"No, no!" Mr. Mainwearing answered in clear tones. "Your aunt, Lady Charlotte Sydenham."

Respectful glances at Peter, and a stare of admiration from Probyn.

After a season of reflection Peter held up his hand. "Please, Sir, I don't write letters to Lady Charlotte."

"You must begin."

Still further reflection. "I want to write to my Aunt Phyllis."

"Nonsense! Do as I tell you."

Peter reflected again for some minutes. He was deeply moved. He controlled a disposition to weep. (No one was going to see Peter blub in this school—ever.) Then Mr. Mainwearing saw him begin to write, with intervals of deep thought. But the letter was an unsatisfactory one.

"Dear Aunt Phyllis," it began—in spite of instructions.

"This is a very nice school and I like it very much. I have no pocket-money. We eat Toke. Please come and take me away now. Your affectionate nephew

"PETER."

Then Peter rubbed his eyes and it made his finger wet, and there was a drop of eye wet fell on the paper, but he did not blub. He did not blub, he knew, because he had made up his mind not to blub, but his face was flushed almost like that of a boy who has been blubbing.

Mr. Mainwearing came and read the letter. "Come, come," he said, "this won't do," which was just what Peter had expected. "This is obstinacy," said Mr. Mainwearing.

He got Peter a fresh sheet of paper and stood over him. "Write as I tell you," said Mr. Mainwearing.

The other boys listened as this letter was dictated to a quiet but obedient Peter:

"Dear Lady Charlotte,
"I arrived safely on Wednesday at High Cross School,

*which I like very much.   I had a long ride in an automo-
bile. Mr. Grimes bought me a splendid bat. Mr. Mainwearing has examined me upon my attainments, and believes
that with effort I shall make satisfactory progress here.   We
play cricket here and do modern science as well as our classical studies.   I hope you may never be disappointed by my
efforts after all your kindness to me.*

"Your affectionate nephew,
*"*PETER STUBLAND.*"*

In the night Peter woke up out of an ugly and miserable
dream, and his eyes were wet with tears.   He believed he
was caught at High Cross School for good and all.   He believed that all the things he hated and dreaded were about
him now for ever.

§ 13

From the first Mr. Mainwearing had been prepared for
Peter's antagonism.   He had been warned by Mr. Grimes
that Peter might prove "a little difficult."   The letter to
Aunt Phyllis confirmed this impression he had already formed
of a fund of stiff resistance in his new pupil.   "I shall have
to talk to that young man," he said.

The occasion was not long in coming.

It came next morning in the general Scripture lesson.   The
boys were reading the Gospel of St. Matthew verse by verse,
and in order to check inattention Mr. Mainwearing, instead
of allowing the boys to read in rotation, was dodging the
next verse irregularly from boy to boy.   "Now, Pyecroft,"
he would say; "Now—Rivers."

He was always ready to pick up a nickname and improve
upon it for the general amusement.   "Now, Simonides," he
said.

No answer.

"Simonides!"

Peter, with his New Testament open before him, was studying the map of Africa on the end wall.   That was Egypt
and that was the Nile, and down that you went to Uganda,
where all the people dressed in white and Nobby walked
fearlessly among lions.

Peter became aware of a loud shout of "Sim-on-i-des!"

It was apparently being addressed to him by Mr. Main-wearing. He returned at a jump to Europe and High Cross School.

"Wool-gathering again," said Mr. Mainwearing. "Think-ing of the dear old Agapemone, eh? We can't have that here, young man. We can't allow that here. We must quicken that proud but sluggish spirit of yours. With the usual stimulus. Come out, sir."

He moved towards the cane, which hung from a nail beside the high desk.

Obliging schoolfellows explained to Peter. "He spoke to you three times." "He's going to swish you." "You'll get it."

Peter went very white and sat very tight.

"Now, young man," said Mr. Mainwearing, flicking the cane. "Step out, please. . . .

"Come out here, sir."

No answer from Peter.

"Stubland," roared Mr. Mainwearing. "Come out at once."

There came a break in the traditions of High Cross School.

Peter rose to his feet. It seemed he was going to obey. And then he said in a voice, faint and small but perfectly clear, "I ain't going to be caned. No."

There was a great pause. There was as it were silence in Heaven. And then, his footsteps echoing through that im-mensity of awe, Mr. Mainwearing advanced upon Peter. Peter with a loud undignified cry fled along the wall under the map of Palestine towards the door.

"Stop him there, Ames!" cried Mr. Mainwearing.

Ames was slow to understand.

Mr. Mainwearing put down the cane on the mantelshelf and became very active; he leapt a desk clumsily, upset an inkpot, and collided with Ames at the door a moment after Peter had vanished. On the landing outside Peter hesitated, and then doubled downstairs to the boot-hole. For a moment Mr. Mainwearing was at fault. "Hell!" he said. All the class-room heard him say "Hell!" All the school treasured that cry in its heart for future use. "Young—," said Mr. Mainwearing. It was long a matter for secret disputation in the school what particularly choice sort of young thing Mr. Mainwearing had called Peter. Then he heard a crash in the boot-hole and was downstairs in a moment. Peter was out in the area, up the area steps as quick as a scared grey mouse, and then he made his mistake.. He struck out across the open in front of the house. In a dozen strides Mr. Mainwearing had him.

"I'll thrash you, Sir," said Mr. Mainwearing, swinging the little body by the collar, and shaking him as a dog might shake a rat. "I'll thrash you. I'll thrash you before the whole school."

But two people had their blood up now.

"I'll tell my uncle Nobby," yelled Peter. "I'll tell my uncle Nobby. He's a soldier."

Thus disputing they presently reappeared in the lower class-room. Peter was tremendously dishevelled and still kicking, and Mr. Mainwearing was holding him by the general slack of his garments.

"Silence, Sir, while I thrash you," said Mr. Mainwearing, and he was red and moist.

"My uncle, he's a soldier. He's a V.C. You thrash me and he'll kill you. He'll kill you. He'll *kill* you."

"Gimme my cane, some one," said Mr. Mainwearing.

"He'll *kill* you."

Nobody got the cane. "Probyn," cried Mr. Mainwearing, "give me my cane."

Probyn hesitated, and then said to young Newton, "You get it." Young Newton had been standing up, half offering himself for this service. He handed the cane to Mr. Mainwearing.

"You touch me!" threatened Peter, "you *touch* me. He'll kill you," and taking advantage of the moment when Mr. Mainwearing's hand was extended for the cane he scored a sound kick on the master's knee. Then by an inspired wriggle he sought to involve himself with Mr. Mainwearing's gown in such a manner as to protect his more vulnerable area.

But now Mr. Mainwearing was in a position to score. He stuck his cane between his teeth in an impressive and terrible manner, and then got his gown loose and altered his grip on his small victim. Now for it! The school hung breathless. *Cut*. Peter became as lively as an eel. *Cut*.

There were tears in his voice, but his voice was full and clear.

"He'll kill you. He'll come here and kill you. I'll burn down the school."

"You will, will you?"

Cut. A kick. *Cut*. Silent wriggles.

"Five. Six. Seven. Eight. Nine. Ten," counted Mr. Mainwearing and stopped, and let go his hold with a shove. "Now go to your place," he said. He was secretly grateful to Peter that he went. Peter had a way at times of looking a very small boy, and he did so now. He was tearful, red and amazingly dishevelled, but still not broken down to technical blubbing. His face was streaked with emotion; it was only too manifest that the routines of High Cross had reduced his private ablutions to a minimum. He glanced over his shoulder to see if he was still pursued. He could still sob, "My uncle."

But Mr. Mainwearing did not mean this to be the close of the encounter. He had thought out the problems of discipline according to his lights; a boy must give in. Peter had still to give in.

"And now Stubland," he proclaimed, "stay in after afternoon school, stay in all tomorrow, and write me out five hundred times, '*I must not sulk. I must obey.*' Five hundred times, Sir."

Something muffled was audible from Peter, something suggestive of a refusal.

"Bring them to me on Wednesday evening at latest. That will keep you busy—and no time to spare. You hear me, Sir? '*I must not sulk*' and '*I must obey.*' And if they are not ready, Sir, twelve strokes good and full. And every morning until they *are* ready, twelve strokes. That's how we do things here. No shirking. Play the fool with me and you pay for it—up to the hilt. This, at any rate, is a school, a school where discipline is respected, whatever queer Socialist Agapemone you may have frequented before. And now I've taken you in hand, young man, I mean to go through with you—if you have a hundred uncles Nobchick armed to the teeth. If you have a thousand uncles Nobchick, they won't help you, if you air your stubborn temper at High Cross School. . . .''

Perhaps Peter would have written the lines, but young Newton, in the company of two friends, came up to him in the playground before dinner. ''Going to write those lines, Simon Peter?'' asked young Newton.

What could a chap do but say, ''No fear.''

''You'll write 'em all right,'' said Newton, and turned scornfully. So Peter sat in the stuffy schoolroom during detention time, and drew pictures of soldiers and battles and adventures and mused and made his plans.

He was going to run away. He was going to run right out of this disgusting place into the world. He would run away tomorrow after the midday meal. It would be the Wednesday half-holiday, and to go off then gave him his very best chance of a start; he might not be missed by any one in particular throughout the afternoon. The gap of time until tea-time seemed to him to be a limitless gap. ''Abscond,'' said Peter, a beautiful, newly-acquired word. Just exactly whither he wanted to go, he did not know. Vaguely he supposed he would have to go to his Limpsfield aunts, but what he wanted to think he was doing was running away to sea. He was going to run away to sea and meet Nobby very soon; he was going to run against Nobby by the happiest chance, Nobby alone, or perhaps even (this was still dreamier) Daddy and Mummy. Then they would go on explorations together, and he and Nobby would sleep side by side at camp fires amidst the howling of lions. Somewhere upon that expedition he would come upon Mainwearing and Probyn and Newton, captives perhaps in the hands of savages.

What would he and Nobby and Mummy and Daddy and Bungo Peter and Joan do to such miscreants? . . .

This kept Peter thinking a long time. Because it was beyond the limits of Peter's generosity just now to spare Mr. Mainwearing. Probyn perhaps. Probyn, penitent to the pitch of tears, might be reduced to the status of a humble fag; even Newton might go on living in some very menial capacity—there could be a dog with the party of which New-ton would always go in fear—but Mr. Mainwearing had exceeded the limits of mercy. . . .

A man like that was capable of any treason. . . .

Peter had it!—a beautiful scene. Mr. Mainwearing detected in a hideous conspiracy with a sinister Arab trader to murder the entire expedition, would be captured redhanded by Peter (armed with a revolver and a cutlass) and brought before Nobby and Bungo Peter. "The man must die," Nobby would say. "And quickly," Bungo Peter would echo, "seeing how perilous is our present situation."

Then Peter would step forward. Mr. Mainwearing in a state of abject terror would fling himself down before him, cling to his knees, pray for forgiveness, pray Peter to intercede.

Yes. On the whole—yes. Peter would intercede.

Peter began to see the scene as a very beautiful one indeed. . . .

But Nobby would be made of sterner stuff. "You are too noble, Peter. In such a country as this we cannot be cumbered with traitor carrion. We have killed the Arab. Is it just to spare this thousand times more perjured wretch, this blot upon the fair name of Englishman? Mainwearing, if such indeed be your true name, down on your knees and make your peace with God." . . .

At this moment the reverie was interrupted by Mr. Mainwearing in cricketing flannels traversing the schoolroom. He was going to have a whack before tea. He just stood at the wickets and made the bigger boys bowl to him.

Little he knew!

Peter affected to write industriously. . . .

§ 14

After the midday meal on Wednesday Peter loafed for a little time in the playground.

"Coming to play cricket, Simon Peter?" said Probyn.

"Got to stay in the schoolroom," said Peter.

"He's going to write his five hundred lines," said young Newton. "I said he would."

(Young Newton would know better later.)

Peter went back unobtrusively to the schoolroom. In his desk were two slices of bread-and-butter secreted from the breakfast table and wrapped in clean pages from an exercise-book. These were his simple provisions. With these, a pencil, and a good serviceable catapult he proposed to set out into the wide, wide world. He had no money.

He "scouted" Mr. Mainwearing into his study, marked that he shut the door, and heard him pull down the blind. The armchair creaked as the schoolmaster sat down for the afternoon's repose. That would make a retreat from the front door of the school house possible. The back of the house meant a risk of being seen by the servants, the playground door or the cricket-field might attract the attention of some sneak. But from the front door to the road and the shelter of the playground wall was but ten seconds dash. Still Peter, from the moment he crept out of the main class-room into the passage to the moment when he was out of sight of the windows was as tightly strung as a fiddle-string. Never before in all his little life had he lived at such a pitch of nervous intensity. Once in the road he ran, and continued to run until he turned into the road to Clewer. Then he dropped into a good smart walk. The world was all before him.

The world was a warm October afternoon and a straight road, poplars and red roofs ahead. Whither the road ran he had no idea, but in the back of his mind, obscured but by no means hidden by a cloud of dreams, was the necessity of getting to Ingle-Nook. After he had walked perhaps half a mile upon the road to Clewer it occurred to Peter that he would ask his way.

The first person he asked was a nice little old lady with a kind face, and she did not know where the road went nor whence it came. "That way it goes to Pescod Street," she said, "if you take the right turning, and that way it goes past the racecourse. But you have to turn off, you know. That's Clewer Church."

No, she didn't know which was the way to Limpsfield. Perhaps if Peter asked the postman *he'd* know.

No postman was visible. . . .

The next person Peter asked was as excessive as the old lady was deficient. He was a large, smiling, self-satisfied man, with a hearty laugh.

"Where does the road go, my boy?" he repeated. "Why! it goes to Maidenhead and Cookham. Cookham! Have you hear the story? This is the way the man told the waiter to take the underdone potatoes. Because it's the way to Cookham. See? Good, eh? But not so good as telling him to take peas *that* was. Through Windsor, you know. Because it's the way to Turnham Green. Ha, ha!

"How far is Maidenhead? Oh! a tidy bit—a *tidy* bit. Say four miles. *Put* it at four miles."

When Peter asked for Limpsfield the large man at once jumped to the conclusion he meant Winchfield. "That's a bit on your left," he said, "just a bit on your left. How far? Oh! a tidy bit. Say five miles—five miles and a 'arf, say."

When he had gone on a little way the genial man shouted back to Peter: "Might be six miles, perhaps," he said. "Not more."

Which was comforting news. So Peter went on his way with his back to Limpsfield—which was a good thirty miles and more away from him—and a pleasant illusion that Aunts Phyllis and Phœbe were quite conveniently just round the corner. . . .

About four o'clock he had discovered Maidenhead bridge, and thereafter the river held him to the end. He had never had a good look at a river before. It was a glowing October afternoon, and the river life was enjoying its Indian summer. High Cross School was an infinite distance away, and all its shadows were dismissed from his mind. Boats are wonderful things to a small boy who has lived among hills. He wandered slowly along the towing-path, and watched several boats and barges through the lock. In each boat he hoped to see Uncle Nobby. But it just happened that Uncle Nobby wasn't there. Near the lock some people were feeding two swans. When they had gone through the lock Peter went close down to the swans. They came to him in a manner so friendly that he gave them the better part of his provisions. After that he watched the operations of a man repairing a Canadian canoe beside a

boat-letting place.   Then he became interested in the shoaling
fish in the shallows.   After that he walked for a time, on
past some little islands.   At last, as he was now a little
foot-sore, he sat down on the bank in the lush grass above
some clumps of sweet rush.

He was just opposite the autumnal fires of the Cleveden
woods, amidst which he could catch glimpses of Italian
balustrading.   The water was a dark mirror over which
hung a bloom of mist.   Now and then an infrequent boat
would glide noiselessly or with a measured beat of rowlocks, through the brown water.   Afar off was a swan. . . .

Presently he would go on to Ingle-Nook.   But not just yet.
When his feet and legs were a little rested he would go on.
He would ask first for Limpsfield and then for Ingle-Nook.
It would be three or four miles.   He would get there in time
for supper.

He was struck by a thought that should have enlightened
him.   He wondered no one had ever brought him before
from Ingle-Nook to this beautiful place.   It was funny they
did not know of it. . . .

Above that balustrading among the trees over there, must
be a palace, and in that palace lived a beautiful princess who
loved Peter. . . .

§ 15

It seemed at the first blush the most delightful accident
in the world that the man with the ample face should ask
Peter to mind his boat.

He rowed up to the wooden steps close by where Peter was
sitting.   He seemed to argue a little with the lady who was
steering and had to back away again, but at last he got
the steps and shipped his oars and held on with a boat hook
and got out.   He helped the lady to land.

"Here, Tommy!" he shouted, tying up the boat to the
rail of the steps.   "Just look after this boat a bit.   We're
going to have some tea."

"We shall have to walk miles," said the lady.

"Damn!" said the man.

Something seemed to tell Peter that the man was cross.

Peter doubted whether he was properly Tommy.   Then he saw that there was something attractive in looking after a boat.

"Don't let any one steal it," said the man with the ample face, with an unreal geniality.   "And I'll give you a tanner."

Peter arose and came to the steps.   The lady and the gentleman stood for a time on the top of the bank, disputing fiercely—she wanted to go one way and he another—and finally disappeared, still disputing, in the lady's direction. Or rather, the lady made off in the direction of Cookham and the gentleman followed protesting.   "Any way it's miles," she said. . . .

Slowly the afternoon quiet healed again.   Peter was left in solitude with the boat, the silvery river, the overhanging woods, the distant swan.

At first he just sat and looked at the boat.

It had crimson cushions in it, and the lady had left a Japanese sunshade.   The name of the boat was the *Princess May*.   The lining wood of the boat was pale and the outer wood and the wood of the rowlocks darker with just one exquisite gold line.   The oars were very wonderful, but the boat-hook with its paddle was much more wonderful.   It would be lovely to touch that boat-hook.   It was a thing you could paddle with or you could catch hold with the hook or poke with the spike.

In a minute or so the call of the boat-hook had become irresistible, and Peter had got it out of the boat.   He held it up like a spear, he waved it about.   He poked the boat out with it and tried to paddle with it in the water between the boat and the bank, but the boat swung back too soon.

Presently he got into the boat very carefully so as to paddle with the boat-hook in the water beyond the boat.   In wielding the paddle he almost knocked off his hat, so he took it off and laid it in the bottom of the boat.   Then he became deeply interested in his paddling.

When he paddled in a certain way the whole boat, he found, began to swing out and round, and when he stopped paddling it went back against the bank.   But it could not go completely round because of the tight way in which the ample-faced man had tied it to the rail of the steps. If the rope were tied quite at its end the boat could be paddled completely round. It would be beautiful to paddle it completely round with the waggling rudder up-stream instead of down.

That thought did not lead to immediate action. But within two minutes Peter was untying the boat and retying it in accordance with his ambitions.

In those days the Boy Scout movement was already in existence, but it had still to disseminate sound views about knot-tying among the rising generation. Peter's knot was not so much a knot as a knot-like gesture. How bad it was he only discovered when he was back in the boat and had paddled it nearly half-way round. Then he saw that the end of the rope was slipping off the rail to which he had tied it as a weary snake might slink off into the grass. The stem of the boat was perhaps a yard from shore.

Peter acted with promptitude. He dropped his paddle, ran to the bows, and jumped. Except for his left leg he landed safely. His left leg he recovered from the water. But there was no catching the rope. It trailed submerged after the boat, and the boat with an exasperating leisureliness, with a movement that was barely perceptible, widened its distance from the bank.

For a time Peter's mind wrestled with this problem. Should he try and find a stick that would reach the boat? Should he throw stones so as to bring it back in shore?

Or perhaps if he told some one that the boat was adrift?

He went up the steps to the towing-path. There was no one who looked at all helpful within sight. He watched the boat drift slowly for a time towards the middle of the stream. Then it seemed to be struck with an idea of going down to Maidenhead. He watched it recede and followed it slowly. When he saw some people afar off he tried to look as though he did not belong to the boat. He decided that presently somebody would appear rowing—whom he would ask to catch his boat for him. Then he would tow it back to its old position.

Presently Peter came to the white gate of a bungalow and considered the advisability of telling a busy gardener who was mowing a lawn, about the boat. But it was difficult to frame a suitable form of address.

Still further on a pleasant middle-aged woman who was trimming a privet hedge very carefully with garden shears, seemed a less terrible person to accost. Peter said to her modestly and self-forgetfully; "I *think* there's a boat adrift down there."

The middle-aged woman peered through her spectacles.

"Some one couldn't have tied it up," she said, and having looked at the boat with a quiet intelligence for some time she resumed her clipping.

Her behaviour did much to dispel Peter's idea of calling in adult help.

When he looked again the boat had turned round. It had drifted out into the middle of the stream, and it seemed now to be travelling rather faster and to be rocking slightly. It was not going down towards the lock but away towards where a board said "Danger." Danger. It was as if a cold hand was laid on Peter's heart. He no longer wanted to find the man with the ample face and tell him that his boat was adrift. The sun had set, the light seemed to have gone out of things, and Peter had a feeling that it was long past tea-time. He wished now he had never seen the man with the ample face. Would he have to pay for the boat? Could he say he had never promised to mind it?

But if that was so why had he got into the boat and played about with it?

His left shoe and his left trouser-leg were very wet and getting cold.

A great craving for tea and home comforts generally arose in Peter's wayward mind. Home comforts and forgetfulness. It seemed to him high time that he asked some one the way to Limpsfield. . . .

§ 16

When Noakley and Probyn arrived at Maidenhead bridge in the late afternoon it seemed to them that they had done all that reasonable searchers could do, and that the best thing now was to take the train back to Windsor. They were tired and they felt futile. And then, when hope was exhausted, they struck the trail of Peter. The policeman at the foot of the bridge had actually noted him. " 'Ovvered about the bridge for a bit," said the policeman, "and then went along the towing path. A little grave chap in grey flannel. Funny thing, but I thought 'E might be a runaway. . . . Something about 'im. . . ."

So it was that Noakley and Probyn came upon the ample-faced man at the lock, in the full tide of his distress.

He was vociferous to get across to the weir. "The boat ought to have come down long ago," he was saying, "unless it's caught up in something. If he was in the boat the kid's drowned for certain. . . ."

Noakley had some difficulty in getting him to explain *what* kid. It was difficult to secure the attention of the ample-faced man. In fact before this could be done he twice pushed back Noakley's face with his hand as though it was some sort of inanimate obstacle.

It was a great and tragic experience for Probyn. They both went across by the lock to the island behind the lead of the lockkeeper and the ample-faced man. They came out in sight of the weir; the river was still full from the late September rains and the weir was a frothing cascade, and at the crest of it they saw an upturned boat jammed by the current against the timbers. A Japanese umbrella circled open in a foamy eddy below, stick upward. The sun was down now; a chill was in the air; a sense of coming winter.

And then close at hand, caught in some weedy willow stems that dipped in the rushing water Probyn discovered a little soddened straw hat, a little half-submerged hat, bobbing with the swift current, entangled in the willow stems.

It was unmistakable. It bore the white and black ribbon of High Cross School.

"Oh, my God!" cried Probyn at the sight of the hat, and burst into tears.

"Poor *little* Peter. I'd have done anything for him!"

He sobbed, and as he sobbed he talked. He became so remorseful and so grossly sentimental that even Noakley was surprised. . . .

§ 17

When next morning Mr. Grimes learnt by a long and
expensive telegram from Mr. Mainwearing, followed almost
immediately by a long explanatory letter, that Peter had run
away from school and had been drowned near Boulter's Lock,
he was overcome with terror. He had visions of Aunt
Phœbe—*doubled,* for he imagined Aunt Phyllis to be just
such another—as an avenger of blood. At the bare thought
he became again a storm of vibrations. His clerks in the
office outside could hear his nails running along his teeth all
the morning, like the wind among the reeds. His imagination threw up wild and hasty schemes for a long holiday in
some inaccessible place, in Norway or Switzerland, but the
further he fled from civilization the more unbridled the
vengeance, when it did overtake him, might be. Lady Charlotte was still in England. On the day appointed and for
two days after, the Channel sea was reported stormy. All
her plans were shattered and she had stayed on. She was
still staying on. In a spasm of spite he telegraphed the
dire news to her. Then he went down to Windsor, all
a-quiver, to see that Mr. Mainwearing did not make a fool
of himself, and to help him with the inquest on Peter as soon
as the body was recovered.

His telegram did have a very considerable effect upon
Lady Charlotte, the more so as it arrived within an hour or
so of a letter from Mrs. Pybus containing some very disconcerting news about Joan. At midday came Mr. Mainwearing's story—pitched to a high note of Anglican piety.
The body, he said, was still not found, "but we must hope
for the best." When Mr. Sycamore arrived at Chastlands
in the afternoon he found Lady Charlotte immensely spread
out in her drawing-room as an invalid, with Unwin on guard
behind her. She lay, a large bundle of ribbon, lace, and distresses, upon a sofa; she had hoisted an enormous beribboned
lace cap with black-and-gold bows. On a table close at hand
were a scent-bottle, smelling-salts, camphor, menthol, and
suchlike aids. There were also a few choice black grapes
and a tonic. She meant to make a brave fight for it.

Mr. Sycamore was not aware how very dead Peter was at

Chastlands and Windsor, seeing that he was now also at The Ingle-Nook in a state of considerable vitality. It was some moments before he realized this localized demise. Indeed it was upon an entirely different aspect of this War of the Guardians that he was now visiting the enemy camp.

At first there was a little difficulty made about admitting him. Cashel explained that Lady Charlotte was "much upset. Terribly upset." Finally he found himself in her large presence.

She gave him no time to speak.

"I am ill, Mr. Sycamore. I am in a wretched state. Properly I should be in bed now. I have been unable to travel abroad to rest. I have been totally unable to attend to affairs. And now comes this last blow. Terrible! A judgment."

"I was not aware, Lady Charlotte, that you knew," Mr. Sycamore began.

"Of course I know. Telegrams, letters. No attempt to break it to me. The brutal truth. I cannot tell you how I deplore my supineness that has led to this catastrophe."

"Hardly supine," Mr. Sycamore ventured.

"Yes, supine. If I had taken up my responsibilities years ago—when these poor children were christened, none of this might have happened. Nothing."

Mr. Sycamore perceived that he was in the presence of something more than mere fuss about Peter's running away. A wary gleam came into his spectacles.

"Perhaps, Lady Charlotte, if I could see your telegram," he said.

"Give it him, Unwin," she said.

"Stole a boat—carried over a weir," he read. "But this is terrible! I had no idea."

"Give him the letter. No—not that one. The other."

"Body not yet recovered," he read, and commented with confidence, "It will turn up later, I feel sure. Of course, all this is—news to me; boat—weir—everything. Yes."

"And I was ill already!" said Lady Charlotte. "There is reason to suppose my heart is weak. I use myself too hard. I am too concerned about many things. I cannot live for myself alone. It is not my nature. The doctor had commanded a quiet month here before I even *thought* of travel—literally *commanded*. And then comes this blow. The wretched child could not have chosen a worse time.''

She gave a gesture of despair. She fell back upon her piled pillows with a gesture of furious exhaustion.

''In the last twenty-four hours,'' she said, ''I have eaten one egg, Mr. Sycamore. . . . And some of that I left.''

Mr. Sycamore's note of sympathy was perhaps a little insincere. ''Of course,'' he said, ''in taking the children away from their school—where they were at least safe and happy—you undertook a considerable responsibility.''

Lady Charlotte took him up with emphasis. ''I admit no responsibility—none whatever. Understand, Mr. Sycamore, once for all, I am not responsible for—whatever has happened to this wretched little boy. Sorry for him—yes, but I have nothing to regret. I took him away from—undesirable surroundings—and sent him to a school, by no means a cheap school, that was recommended very highly, very highly indeed, by Mr. Grimes. It was my plain duty to do as much. There my responsibility ends.''

Mr. Sycamore had drifted quietly into a chair, and was sitting obliquely to her in an attitude more becoming a family doctor than a hostile lawyer. He regarded the cornice in the far corner of the room as she spoke, and replied without looking at her, softly and almost as if in soliloquy: ''Legally—*no.*''

''I am not responsible,'' the lady repeated. ''If any one is responsible, it is Mr. Grimes.''

''I came to ask you to produce your two wards,'' said Mr. Sycamore abruptly, ''because Mr. Oswald Sydenham lands at Southampton tonight.''

''He has always been coming.''

''This time he has come.''

''If he had come earlier all this would not have happened. Has he really come?''

''He is here—in England, that is.''

Lady Charlotte gasped and lay back. Unwin handed her the bottle of smelling-salts. ''I have done nothing more than my duty,'' she said.

Mr. Sycamore became more gentle in his manner than ever. "As the person finally responsible—"

"*No!*"

"Haven't you been just a little careless?"

"Mr. Sycamore, it was this boy who was careless. I am sorry to say it now that he— I can only hope that at the last— But he was not a good boy. Anything but a good boy. He had been altogether demoralized by those mad, violent creatures. He ran away from this school, an excellent school, highly recommended. And you must remember, Mr. Sycamore, that I was paying for it. The abnormal position of the property, the way in which apparently all the income is to be paid over to these women—without consulting me. Well, I won't complain of that now. I was prepared to pay. I paid. But the boy was already thoroughly corrupted. His character was undermined. He ran away. I wash my hands of the consequences."

Mr. Sycamore was on the point of saying something and thought better of it.

"At any rate," he said, "I have to ask you on behalf of Mr. Oswald Sydenham to produce the other child—the girl."

"She *can't* be produced," said Lady Charlotte desperately.

"That really *does* make things serious."

"Oh, don't misunderstand me! The child is in excellent hands—excellent hands. But there are—neighbours. She was told to keep indoors, carefully told. What must she do but rush out at the first chance! She had had fair warning that there were measles about, she had had measles explained to her carefully, yet she must needs go and make friends with a lot of dirty little wretches!"

"And catch measles."

"Exactly."

"That's why—?"

"That's why—"

"There again, Lady Charlotte, and again with all due respect, haven't you been just a little careless? At that nice, airy school in Surrey there was never any contagion—of any sort."

"There was no proper religious teaching."

"Was there any where you placed these children?"

"I was led to believe—"

She left it at that.

Mr. Sycamore allowed himself to point the moral. "It is a very remarkable thing to me, Lady Charlotte, most remarkable, that Catholic people and Church of England people— you must forgive me for saying it—and religious bodies generally should be so very anxious and energetic to get control of the education of children and so careless—indeed they are dreadfully careless—of the tone, the wholesomeness and the quality of the education they supply. And of the homes they permit. It's almost as if they cared more for getting the children branded than whether they lived or died."

"The school was an excellent school," said Lady Charlotte; "an excellent school. Your remarks are cruel and painful."

Mr. Sycamore again restrained some retort. Then he said, "I think it would be well for Mr. Oswald Sydenham to have the address of the little girl."

Lady Charlotte considered. "There is nothing to conceal," she said, and gave the address of Mrs. Pybus, "a most trustworthy woman." Mr. Sycamore took it down very carefully in a little note-book that came out of his vest pocket. Then he seemed to consider whether he should become more offensive or not, and to decide upon the former alternative.

"I suppose," he said reflectively as he replaced the little book, "that the demand for religious observances and religious orthodoxy as a first condition in schools is productive of more hypocrisy and rottenness in education than any other single cause. It is a matter of common observation. A school is generally about as inefficient as its religious stripe is marked. I suppose it is because if you put the weight on one thing you cannot put it on another. Or perhaps it is because no test is so easy for a thoroughly mean and dishonest person to satisfy as a religious test. Schools which have no claims to any other merit can always pass themselves off as severely religious. Perhaps the truth is that all bad schools profess orthodoxy rather than that orthodoxy makes bad schools. Nowadays it is religion that is the last refuge of a scoundrel."

"If you have nothing further to say than this Secularist

lecturing," said Lady Charlotte with great dignity, "I should be obliged if you would find somewhere—some Hall of Science—. . . Considering what my feelings must be. , . Scarcely in the mood for—blasphemies."

"Lady Charlotte," said Mr. Sycamore, betraying a note of indignation in his voice; "this school into which you flung your little ward was a very badly conducted school indeed."

"It was nothing of the sort," said Lady Charlotte. "How dare you reproach me ?"

Mr. Sycamore went on as though she had not spoken. "There was a lot of bullying and nasty behaviour among the boys, and the masters inflicted punishments without rhyme or reason."

"How can you know anything of the sort ?"

"On the best authority—the boy's."

"But how could he—"

"He was thrashed absurdly and set an impossible task for not answering to a silly nickname. There was no one to whom he could complain. He ran away. He had an idea of reaching Limpsfield, but when he realized that night was coming on, being really a very sensible little boy, he selected a kindly-looking house, asked to see the lady of the house, and told her he had run away from home and wanted to go back. He gave his aunt's address at The Ingle-Nook, and he was sent home in the morning. He arrived home this morning."

Lady Charlotte made a strange noise, but Mr. Sycamore hurried on. "How this delusion about a boat and a weir got into the story I don't know. He says nothing about them. Indeed, he says very little about anything. He's a reserved little boy. We have to get what we can out of him."

"You mean to say that the boy is still alive !" cried Lady Charlotte.

"Happily !"

"In face of these telegrams !"

"I saw him not two hours ago."

"But how do you account for these telegrams and letters ?"

Mr. Sycamore positively tittered. "That's for Mr. Grimes to explain."

"And he is alive—and unhurt ?"

"As fresh as paint; and quite happy."

"Then if ever a little boy deserved a whipping, a thoroughly good whipping," cried Lady Charlotte, "it is Master Peter Stubland! Safe, indeed! It's outrageous! After all I have gone through! Unwin!"

Unwin handed the salts.

Mr. Sycamore stood up. He still had the essence of his business to communicate, but there was something in the great lady's blue eyes that made him want to stand up. And that little tussock of fair hair on her cheek—in some indescribable way it had become fierce.

"To think," said Lady Charlotte, "that I have been put to all this unutterable worry and distress—"

She was at a loss for words. Mr. Sycamore appreciated the fact that if he had anything more to say to her he must communicate it before the storm burst. He stroked his chin thoughtfully, and began to deliver his message with just the faintest quality of hurry in his delivery.

"The real business upon which I came to you today, Lady Charlotte, has really nothing to do with this—escapade at all. It is something else. Things have arisen that alter the outlook for those children very considerably. There is every reason to suppose that neither you nor the Misses Stubland are properly guardians of Joan and Peter at all. No. One moment more, Lady Charlotte; let me explain. Two young Germans, it would appear, witnessed the accident to the boat from the top of the Capri headland. They saw Mr. Stubland apparently wrestling with the boatman, then the boat overset and the two men never reappeared. They must have dragged each other down. The witnesses are quite certain about that. But Mrs. Stubland, poor young lady, could be seen swimming for quite a long time; she swam nearly halfway to land before she gave in, although the water was very choppy indeed. I made enquiries when I was in Naples this spring, and I do not think there would be much trouble in producing those witnesses still. They were part of the—what shall I call it?—social circle of that man Krupp, the gunmaker. He lived at Capri. If we accept this story, then, Lady Charlotte, Mrs. Stubland's will holds good, and her husband's does not, and Mr. Oswald Sydenham becomes the sole guardian of the children. . . .''

He paused.   The lady's square face slowly assumed an expression of dignified satisfaction.

"So long as those poor children are rescued from those *women*," said Lady Charlotte, "my task is done.   I do not grudge any exertion, any sacrifice I have made, so long as that end is secured.   I do not look for thanks.   Much less repayment.   Perhaps some day these children may come to understand—"

Unwin made a sound like the responses in church.

"I would go through it all again," said Lady Charlotte— "willingly. . . Now that my nephew has returned I have no more anxiety."   She made an elegant early-Georgian movement with the smelling-salts.   "I am completely justified.   I have been slighted, tricked, threatened, insulted, made ill . . . but I am justified."

She resorted again to the salts.

CHAPTER THE NINTH

OSWALD TAKES CONTROL

§ 1

WHILE Mr. Sycamore was regaling himself with the discomfiture of Lady Charlotte, Oswald Sydenham was already walking about the West End of London.

He had come upon a fresh crisis in his life. He was doing his best to accept some thoroughly disagreeable limitations. His London specialist had but confirmed his own conviction. It was no longer possible for him to continue in Africa. He had reached the maximum of blackwater fever permitted to normal men. The next bout—if there was a next bout—would kill him. In addition to this very valid reason for a return, certain small fragments of that Egyptian shell long dormant in his arm had awakened to mischief, and had to be removed under the more favourable conditions to be found in England. He had come back therefore to a land where he had now no close friends and no special occupations, and once more he had to begin life afresh.

He had returned with extreme reluctance. He could not see anything ahead of him in England that gripped his imagination at all. He was strongly tempted to have his arm patched up, and return to Africa for a last spell of work and a last conclusive dose of the fever germ. But in England he might be of use for a longer period, and a kind of godless conscience in him insisted that there must be no deliberate waste in his disposal of his life.

For some time he had been distressed by the general ignorance in England of the realities of things African, and by the general coarsening and deterioration, as he held it to be, of the Imperial idea. There was much over here that needed looking into, he felt, and when it was looked into then the indications for further work might appear. Why not, so far as his powers permitted, do something in helping English people to realize all that Africa was and might be. That was work he might do, and live. In Africa there was little more for him to do but die.

That was all very well in theory. It did not alter his persuasion that he was going to be intolerably lonely if he stayed on in England. Out there were the Chief Commissioner and Muir and half a dozen other people for whom he had developed a strong affection; he was used to his native servants and he liked them; he had his round of intensely interesting activities, he was accustomed to the life. Out there, too, there was sunshine. Such sunshine as the temperate zone can never reproduce. This English world was a grey, draughty, cloudy, lonely world, and one could not always be working. That sunshine alone meant a vast deprivation.

This sort of work he thought of doing and which seemed the only thing now that he could possibly do, wasn't, he reflected uncomfortably, by any means the work that he could do best. He knew he was bad-tempered. Ill-health intensified a natural irritability. He knew his brain was now a very uncertain instrument, sometimes quite good, sometimes a weary fount of half-formed ideas and indecisions. As an advocate of the right way in Africa, he would do some good no doubt; but he would certainly get into some tiresome squabbles, he would bark his knuckles and bruise his shins. Nevertheless—cheerless though the outlook was—it was, he felt, the work he ought to do.

"Pump up enthusiasm," said Oswald. "Begin again. What else *can* I do?"

But what he was pumping up that afternoon in London was really far more like anger. Rage and swearing were the natural secretions of Oswald's mind at every season of perplexity; he became angry when other types would be despondent. Where melancholic men abandon effort, men of the choleric type take to kicking and smashing. Where the former contract, the latter beat about and spread themselves. Oswald, beneath his superficial resignation, was working up for a quarrel with something. His instinct was to convert the distress of his developing physical insufficiencies into hostility to some external antagonist.

He knew of, and he was doing his best to control, this black urgency to violent thoughts and conclusions. He wanted to kick and he knew he must not yet waste energy in kicking. He was not justified in kicking. He must not allow his sense of personal grievance against fate to disturb his mind. He must behave with a studied calm and aloofness.

"Damn!" said Oswald, no doubt by way of endorsing this decision.

Pursuant to these virtuous resolutions this tall, lean, thwarted man, full of jealous solicitude for the empire he had helped enlarge, this disfigured man whose face was in two halves like those partially treated portraits one sees outside the shops of picture-cleaners, was engaged in comporting himself as much as possible like some pleasant, leisurely man of the world with no obligation or concern but to make himself comfortable and find amusement in things about him. He was doing his best to feel that there was no hurry about anything, and no reason whatever for getting into a state of mind. Just a calm quiet onlooker he had to be. He was, he told himself, taking a look round London as a preliminary to settling down there. Perhaps he was going to settle down in London. Or perhaps in the country somewhere. It did not matter which—whichever was the most pleasant. It was all very pleasant. Very pleasant indeed. A life now of wise lounging and judicious, temperate activities it had to be. He must not fuss.

He had arrived in England the day before, but as yet, except for a brief note to Mr. Sycamore, he had notified no one of his return. He had put up at the Climax Club in Piccadilly, a proprietary club that was half hotel, where one could get a sitting-room as well as a bedroom; and after a visit to his doctor—a visit that confirmed all his worst apprehensions of the need of abandoning Africa for ever—he had spent the evening in the club trying to be calm over the newspapers and magazines. But when one is ill and tired as Oswald was, all that one reads in the newspapers and magazines is wrong and exasperating.

It was 1903; the time when Mr. Joseph Chamberlain returned from South Africa to launch his Tariff Reform agitation—and Oswald was temperamentally a Free Trader. The whole press, daily, weekly, monthly, was full of the noises of the controversy. It impressed him as a controversy almost intolerably mean. His Imperialism was essentially a romantic and generous imagination, a dream of service, of himself, serving the Empire and of the Empire serving mankind. The tacit assumption underlying this most sordid of political campaigns that the Empire was really nothing of the kind, that it was an adventure of exploitation, a national enterprise in the higher piracy, borrowing a faded picturesqueness from the scoundrelism of the Elizabethan and Jacobean buccaneers, the men who started the British slave trade and the Ulster trouble and founded no Empire at all except the plantations of Virginia and Barbados, distressed and perplexed his mind almost unendurably. It was so maddeningly plausible. It was so manifestly the pathway of destruction.

After throwing *The National Review* into a distant armchair and then, when he met the startled eye of a fellow member, trying to look as though that was his usual way with a magazine, he sought distraction in Southey's "Doctor," which happened to be in the club library. After dinner he went out for a stroll in the West End, and visited the Alhambra. He found that more soothing than the papers. The old excitement of the human moth at the candles of vice he no longer felt. He wondered why these flitting allurements had ever stirred him. But he liked the stir and the lights and the pleasant inconsecutive imbecility of the entertainment.

He slept fairly well. In the morning a clerk of Mr. Sycamore's telephoned to say that that gentleman was out of town, he had been called down to see Lady Charlotte Sydenham, but that he would be back, and would probably try to "get" Oswald about eleven in the evening. He had something important to tell Oswald. The day began cloudy, and repented and became fine. By midday it was, for London, a golden day. Yet to Oswald it seemed but a weak solution of sunshine. If you stood bareheaded in such sunshine you would catch a chill. But he made the best of it.

"October mild and boon," he quoted. He assured himself
that it would be entertaining to stroll about the West End
and look at the shops and mark the changes in things. He
breakfasted late at one of the windows overlooking the
Green Park, visited the club barber, walked along to his
tailor, bought three new hats and a stout gold-banded cane
with an agate top in Bond Street, a pair of boots, gloves and
other sundries. Then he went into his second club, the Plantain, in Pall Mall, to read the papers—until he discovered
that he was beginning to worry about Tariff Reform again.
He saw no one he knew, and lunched alone. In the afternoon
he strolled out into London once more.

He was, he found, no longer uncomfortable and self-conscious in the streets of London. His one-sided, blank-sided
face did not make him self-conscious now as it used to do,
he had reconciled himself to his disfigurement. If at first
he had exaggerated its effect, he now inclined to forget it
altogether. He wore hats nowadays with a good broad brim,
and cocked them to over-shadow the missing eye; his dark
moustache had grown and was thick and symmetrical; he
had acquired the habit of looking at himself in glasses so as
to minimize his defaced half. It seemed to him a natural
thing now that the casual passer-by should pull up for the
fraction of a second at the sight of his tall figure, or look
back at him as if to verify a first impression. Didn't people
do that to everybody?

He went along Pall Mall, whose high gentility was still in
those days untroubled by the Royal Automobile Club and
scarcely ruffled by a discreet shop or so; he turned up through
St. James's Street to Piccadilly with a reminiscent glance by
the way down Jermyn Street, where he had had his first experiences of restaurants and suchlike dissipations in his early
midshipman days. How far away those follies seemed now!
The shops of Bond Street drew him northward; the Doré
Gallery of his childhood, he noted, was still going on; he
prowled along Oxford Street as far as the Marble Arch—
Gillows was still Gillows in those days, and Selfridge had yet
to dawn on the London world—and beat back by way of
Seymour Street to Regent Street. He nodded to Verrey's,
where long ago he had lunched in a short plaid frock and

white socks under the auspices of his godmother, old Lady
Percival Pelham. It was all very much as he had left it in
'97. That fever of rebuilding and rearrangement which was
already wrecking the old Strand and sweeping away Book-
sellers' Row and the Drury Lane slums and a score of ancient
landmarks, had not yet reached the West End. There was
the same abundance of smart hansom cabs crawling in the
streets or neatly ranked on the stands; the same populous
horse omnibuses, the same brightly dressed people, and, in
Regent Street and Piccadilly, the same too-brightly-dressed
women loiterers, only now most of them were visibly coarse
and painted; there were the same mendicants and sandwich-
men at the pavement edge. Perhaps there were more omnibuses crowding upon one another at Piccadilly and Oxford
Circuses, and more people everywhere. Or perhaps that was
only the effect of returning from a less crowded world.

Now and then he saw automobiles, queer, clumsy carriages
without horses they seemed to be, or else low, heavy-looking
vehicles with a flavour of battleship about them. Several
emitted bluish smoke and trailed an evil smell. In Regent
Street outside Liberty's art shop one of these mechanical
novelties was in trouble. Everybody seemed pleased. The
passing cabmen were openly derisive. Oswald joined the little group of people at the pavement edge who were watching
the heated and bothered driver engaged in some obscure
struggle beneath his car.

An old gentleman in a white waistcoat stood beside Oswald,
and presently turned to him.

"Silly things," he said. "Noisy, dangerous, *stinking*
things. They ought to be forbidden."

"Perhaps they will improve," said Oswald.

"How could *that* thing improve?" asked the old gentleman. "Lotto dirty ironmongery."

He turned away with the air of a man for whom a question
had been settled. Oswald followed him thoughtfully. . .

He resumed his identifications. Piccadilly Circus! Here
was the good old Café Monico; yonder the Criterion. . .

But everything seemed smaller.

That was the thing that struck him most forcibly; London
revisited he discovered to be an intense *little* place.

It was extraordinary that this should be the head of the
Empire. It seemed, when one came back to it, so entirely
indifferent to the Empire, so entirely self-absorbed. When
one was out beyond there, in Uganda, East Africa, Sudan,
Egypt, in all those vast regions where the British were doing
the best work they had ever done in pacification and civilization, one thought of London as if it were a great head that
watched one from afar, that could hear a cry for help, that
could send support. Yet here were these people in these
narrow, brightly served streets, very busy about their own
affairs, almost as busy and self-absorbed as the white-robed
crowd in the big market-place in Mengo, and conspicuously,
remarkably not thinking of Africa—or anything of the sort.
He compared Bond Street and its crowded, inconvenient
side-walks with one of the great garden vistas of the Uganda
capital, much to the advantage of the latter. He descended
by the Duke of York's steps, past the old milk stall with its
cow, into the Mall. Buckingham Palace, far away, was much
less impressive than the fort at Kampala on its commanding
hill; the vegetation of St. James's Park and its iron fencing
were a poor substitute for the rich-patterned reed palisades
and the wealth of fronds that bordered the wide prospects of
the Uganda capital. All English trees looked stunted to
Oswald's eyes.

Towards the palace, tree-felling was in progress, the felling
of trees that could never be replaced; and an ugly hoarding
veiled the erection of King Edward's pious memorial to
Queen Victoria, the memorial which later her grandson, the
Kaiser, was to unveil.

He went on into Whitehall—there was no Admiralty Arch
in those days, and one came out of the Mall by way of Spring
Gardens round the corner of an obtrusive bank. Oswald
paused for a minute to survey the squat buildings and high
column of Trafalgar Square, pale amber in the October sunshine, and then strolled down towards Westminster. He
became more and more consciously the loitering home-comer.
He smiled at the mounted soldiers in their boxes outside the
Horse Guards, paused at and approved of the architectural
intentions of the new War Office, and nodded to his old
friends, the Admiralty and the Colonial Office. Here they

brewed the destinies of the Old World outside Europe and kept the Seven Seas. He played his part with increased self-approval. He made his way to Westminster Bridge and spent some time surveying the down river prospect. It was, after all, a little ditch of a river. St. Paul's was fairly visible, and the red, rusty shed of Charing Cross station and its brutal iron bridge, fit monument of the clumsy looting by "private enterprise" that characterized the Victorian age, had never looked uglier.

He crossed from one side of the bridge to the other, leant over the parapet and regarded the Houses of Parliament. The flag was flying, and a number of little groups of silk-hatted men and gaily dressed ladies were having tea on the terrace.

"I wonder why we rule our Empire from a sham Gothic building," thought Oswald. "If anything, it ought to be Roman. . . ."

He turned his attention to the traffic and the passers-by. "They don't realize," he said. "Suppose suddenly they were to have a mirage here of some of the lands and cities this old Parliament House controls?"

A little stout man driving a pony-trap caught his attention. It was a smart new pony-trap, and there was a look of new clothes about its driver; he smoked a cigar that stuck upward from the corner of his mouth, and in his button-hole was a red chrysanthemum; his whole bearing suggested absolute contentment with himself and acquiescence in the universe; he handled his reins and drew his whip across the flanks of his shining cob as delicately as if he was fly-fishing. "What does he think he is up to?" asked Oswald. A thousand times he had seen that Sphinx of perfect self-contentment on passing negro faces.

"The Empire doesn't worry *him*," said Oswald.

§ 2

It was worrying Oswald a lot. Everything was worrying Oswald just then. It is a subtle question to answer of such cases whether the physical depression shapes the despondent thought, or whether the gnawing doubt prepares the nervous illness. His confidence in his work and the system to which he belonged had vanished by imperceptible degrees.

For some years he had gone about his work with very few doubts. He had been too busy. But now ill-health had conspired with external circumstances to expose him to questionings about things he had never questioned before. They were very fundamental doubts. They cut at the roots of his life. He was beginning to doubt whether the Empire was indeed as good a thing and as great a thing as he had assumed it to be. . . . The Empire to which his life had been given.

This did not make him any less an Imperialist than he had been, but it sharpened his imperialism with a sense of urgency that cut into his mind.

Altogether Oswald had now given nearly eighteen years to East and Central Africa. His illness had called a halt in a very busy life. For two years and more after his last visit to England, he had been occupied chiefly in operations in and beyond the Lango country against Kabarega and the remnant of the rebel Sudanese. He had assisted in the rounding-up of King Mwanga, the rebel king of Uganda, and in setting up the child king and the regency that replaced him. At the end of 1899 his former chief, Sir Harry Johnston, had come up from British Central Africa as Special Commissioner to Uganda, and the work of land settlement, of provincial organization, of railways and postal development had gone on apace. Next year indeed war had come again, but it was the last war in this part of the world for some time. It was caused by the obstinate disposition of the Nandi people to steal the copper wire from the telegraph poles that had been set up in their country. Hitherto their chief use for copper wire had been to make bracelets and anklets for their married women. They were shocked by this endless stretching out of attenuated feminine adornment. They did their best to restore it to what they considered was its proper use. It was a homely misunderstanding rather than a war. Oswald had led that expedition to a successful explanation. Thereafter the leading fact in the history of Uganda until the sleeping sickness came had been the construction of the railway from the coast to Lake Victoria Nyanza.

In Uganda as in Nyasaland Oswald Sydenham had found himself part of a rapid and busy process of tidying up the world. For some years it had carried him along and determined all his views.

The tidying-up of Africa during the closing years of the nineteenth century was indeed one of the most rapid and effective tidyings up in history. In the late 'eighties the whole of Africa from the frontiers of lower Egypt down to Rhodesia had been a world of chaotic adventure and misery; a black world of insecure barbarism invaded by the rifle, and the Arab and European adventurers who brought it. There had been no such thing as a school from Nubia to Rhodesia, and everywhere there had been constant aimless bloodshed. Long ages of conflict, arbitrary cruelty and instinctive fierceness seemed to have reached a culmination of destructive disorder. The increasing light that fell on Africa did but illuminate a scene of collapse. The new forces that were coming into the country appeared at first as hopelessly blind and cruel as the old; the only difference was that they were better armed. The Arab was frankly a slaver, European enterprise was deeply interested in forced labour. The first-fruits of Christianity had been civil war, and one of Oswald's earliest experiences of Uganda had been the attack of Mwanga and his Roman Catholic adherents upon the Anglicans in Mengo, who held out in Lugard's little fort and ultimately established the soundness of the Elizabethan compromise by means of a Maxim gun It was never a confident outlook for many years anywhere between the Zambesi and the Nile cataracts. Probably no honest man ever worked in west and central Africa between 1880 and 1900 who escaped altogether from phases of absolute despair; who did not face with a sinking heart, lust, hatred, cunning and treachery, black intolerance and ruthless aggression. And behind all the perversities of man worked the wickedness of tropical Nature, uncertain in her moods, frightful in her storms, fruitful of strange troubles through weed and parasite, insect and pestilence. Yet civilization had in the long run won an astonishing victory. In a score of years, so endless then, so brief in retrospect, roads that had been decaying tracks or non-existent were made safe and open everywhere, the railway and the post and telegraph came to stay, vast regions of Africa which since the beginning of things had known no rule but the whim and arbitrary power of transitory chiefs and kings, awoke to the conception of impartial law; war canoes vanished from the lakes and robber tribes learnt to tend their own cattle and cultivate their gardens. And now there were schools. There were hospitals. Perhaps a quarter of a million young people in Uganda alone could read and write; the percentage of literacy in Uganda was rapidly overtaking that in India and Russia.

On the face of it this was enough to set one thinking of the whole world as if it were sweeping forward to universal civilization and happiness. For some years that had been Oswald's habit of mind. It had been his sustaining faith. He had gone from task to task until this last attack of blackwater fever had arrested his activities. And then these doubts displayed themselves.

From South Africa, that land of destiny for western civilization, had come the first germ of his doubting. Sir Harry Johnston, Oswald's chief, a frank and bitter critic of the New Imperialism that had thrust up from the Cape to Nyasaland under the leadership of Cecil Rhodes, helped to shape and point his scepticism. The older tradition of the Empire was one of administration regardless of profit, Johnston declared; the new seemed inspired by conceptions of violent and hasty gain. The Rhodes example had set all Africa dancing to the tune of crude exploitation. It had fired the competitive greed of the King of the Belgians and unleashed blood and torture in the Congo Free State. The Congo State had begun as a noble experiment, a real attempt at international compromise; it had been given over to an unworthy trustee and wrecked hideously by his ruthless profit-hunting. All over the Empire, honest administrators and colonial politicians, friendly explorers and the missionaries of civilization, were becoming more and more acutely aware of a heavy acquisitive thrust behind the New Imperialism. Usually they felt it first in the treatment of the natives. The earlier ill-treatment of the native came from the local

trader, the local planter, the white rough; now as that sort
of thing was got in hand and men could begin to hope for a
new and better order, came extensive schemes from Europe
for the wholesale detachment of the native from his land, for
the wholesale working and sweating of the native population. . . .

Had we defeated the little robbers only to clear the way
for organized imperial robbery?

Such things were already troubling Oswald's mind before
the shock of the South African war. But before the war
they amounted to criticisms of this administration or that,
they were still untouched by any doubts of the general Imperial purpose or of the Empire as a whole. The South
African war laid bare an amazing and terrifying amount of
national incompetence. The Empire was not only hustled
into a war for which there was no occasion, but that war was
planned with a lack of intelligent foresight and conducted with a lack of soundness that dismayed every
thoughtful Englishman. After a monstrous wasteful struggle the national resources dragged it at last to a not very
decisive victory. The outstanding fact became evident that
the British army tradition was far gone in decay, that the
army was feebly organized and equipped, and that a large
proportion of its officers were under-educated men, narrow
and conventional, inferior in imagination and initiative to
the farmers, lawyers, cattle-drovers, and suchlike leaders
against whom their wits were pitted. Behind the rejoicings
that hailed the belated peace was a real and unprecedented
national humiliation. For the first time the educated British
were enquiring whether all was well with the national system
if so small a conquest seemed so great a task. Upon minds
thus sensitized came the realization of an ever more vigorous and ever more successful industrial and trade competition from Germany and the United States; Great Britain
was losing her metallurgical ascendancy, dropping far behind in the chemical industries and no longer supreme upon
the seas. For the first time a threat was apparent in the
methods of Germany. Germany was launching liner after
liner to challenge the British mercantile ascendancy, and she
was increasing her navy with a passionate vigour. What

did it mean? All over the world the British were discovering the German. And the German, it seemed, had got this New Imperialism that was in the British mind in a still harsher, still less scrupulous and still more vulgar form. "Wake up, England," said the Prince of Wales returning from a visit to Canada, and Oswald heard the phrase reverberating in Uganda and talked about it and thought it over continually.

(And Lord Rosebery spoke of "efficiency.")

But now when Oswald sought in the newspapers for signs of this waking up that he desired, he found instead this tremendous reiteration of the ideas of the New Imperialism, acquisitive, mercenary, and altogether selfish and national, which he already so profoundly disliked. The awakening he desired was an awakening of the spirit, an awakening to broader ideas and nobler conceptions of the nation's rôle in the world's affairs. He had hoped to find men talking of great schemes of national education, of new schools of ethnology, of tropical botany and oriental languages that would put the Imperial adventure on a broad basis of understanding and competent direction. Instead, he found England full of wild talk about "taxing the foreigner." A hasty search for national profit he refused to recognize as an awakening. For him indeed it had far more of the quality of a nightmare.

§ 3

It is remarkable how much our deeper convictions are at the mercy of physiological jolts.

Before the renewed attacks of fever had lowered his vitality, Oswald had felt doubtful of this and that, but he had never doubted of the ultimate human triumph; he had never even doubted that the great Empire he served would survive, achieve its mission triumphantly, and incorporate itself in some way with a unified mankind. He himself might blunder or fail, there might be all sorts of set-backs, but in the end what he called Anglo-Saxonism would prevail, the tradition of justice and free speech would be justified by victory, and the darkest phase of the Martyrdom of Man end. But now the fever had so wrought on his nerves and tissues that he no longer enjoyed this ultimate confidence. He could think that anything might fail. He could even doubt the stability of the Victorian world.

One night during this last illness that had brought him home he fell thinking of Zimbabwe and the lost cities of Africa, and then presently of the dead cities of Yucatan, and then of all the lost and vanished civilizations of the world, of the long succession of human failures to secure any abiding order and security. With this he mingled the suggestion of a recent anthropological essay he had read. Two races of men with big brains and subtle minds, the Neanderthal race and the Cro-Magnon race, it was argued very convincingly, had been entirely exterminated before the beginnings of our present humanity. Our own race too might fail and perish and pass away. In the night with a mounting temperature these were very grisly and horrible thoughts indeed. And when at last he passed from such weary and dismal speculations to sleep, there came a dream to crown and perpetuate his mood, a dream that was to return again and again.

It was one of those dreams that will sometimes give a nightmare reality of form and shape to the merest implications of the waking life, one of those dreams that run before and anticipate and perhaps direct one's daylight decisions. That black artist of delirium who throws his dark creations upon our quivering mental screens, had seized and utilized all Oswald's germinating misgivings and added queer suggestions of his own. Through a thousand irrelevant and transitory horrors one persistent idea ran through Oswald's distresses. It was the idea of a dark forest. And of an endless effort to escape from it. He was one of the captains of a vaguely conceived expedition that was lost in an interminable wilderness of shadows; sometimes it was an expedition of limitless millions, and the black trees and creepers about him went up as high as the sky, and sometimes he alone seemed to be the entire expedition, and the darkness rested on his eyes, and the thorns wounded him, and the great ropes of the creepers slashed his face. He was always struggling to get through this forest to some unknown hope,

to some place where there was light, where there was air and
freedom, where one could look with brotherly security upon
the stars; and this forest which was Life, held him back;
it held him with its darkness, it snared him with slime and
marshy pitfalls, it entangled him amidst pools and channels
of black and blood-red stinking water, it tripped him and
bound him with its creepers; evil beasts snared his followers,
great serpents put them to flight, inexplicable panics and
madnesses threw the long straggling columns into internecine
warfare, incredible imbecilities threatened the welfare of the
entire expedition. He would find himself examining the
loads of an endless string of porters, and this man had flung
away bread and loaded his pack with poisonous fungi, and
that one had replaced ammunition by rust and rubbish and
filth. He would find himself in frantic remonstrance with
porters who had flung aside their loads, who were sullenly
preparing to desert; or again, the whole multitude would be
stricken with some strange disease with the most foul and
horrible symptoms, and refuse the doubtful medicines he
tendered in his despair; or the ground would suddenly breed
an innumerable multitude of white thin voracious leeches
that turned red-black as they fed. . . .

Then far off through the straight bars of the tree stems
a light shone, and a great hope sprang up in him. And
then the light became red, a wavering red, a sudden hot
breeze brought a sound of crackling wood and the soughing
of falling trees, spires and flags and agonized phantoms of
flame rushed up to the zenith; through the undergrowth a
thousand black beasts stampeded, the air was thick with
wild flights of moths and humming-birds, and he realized
that the forest had caught fire. . . .

That forest fire was always a climax. With it came a
burning sensation in loins and back. It made him shout and
struggle and fight amidst the black fugitives and the black
thickets. Until the twigs and leaves about him were bursting
into flames like a Christmas tree that is being lit up. He
would awaken in a sweating agony.

Then presently he would be back again in the midst of
that vague innumerable expedition in the steamy deep grey
aisles of the forest, under the same gathering sense of urgent

necessity, amidst the same inextricable thickening tangle of confusions and cross-purposes.

In his waking moments Oswald, if he could, would have dismissed that dream altogether from his mind. He could argue that it was the creation of some purely pathological despondency, that it had no resemblance, no parallelism, no sort of relation to reality. Yet something of its dark hues was reflected in his waking thoughts. Sometimes this reflection was so faint as to be scarcely perceptible, but always it was there.

§ 4

The Plantain, to which Oswald drifted back to dine, was a club gathered from the ends of the earth and very proud of the fact; it was made up of explorers, travellers, colonial officials, K.C.M.G.'s and C.M.G.'s. It was understood to be a great exchange of imperial ideas, and except for a group or so of members who lived in and about London, it had no conversation because, living for the most part at different ends of the earth, its members did not get to know each other very well. Occasionally there was sporting gossip. Shy, sunburnt men drifted in at intervals of three or four years, and dined and departed. Once a member with a sunstroke from India gave way to religious mania, and tried to preach theosophy from the great staircase to three lonely gentlemen who were reading the telegrams in the hall. He was removed with difficulty. The great red-papered, white-painted silences of the club are copiously adorned with rather old yellow maps of remote regions, and in the hall big terrestrial and celestial globes are available for any members who wish to refresh their minds upon the broad facts of our position in space. But the great glory of the club is its wealth of ethnological and sporting trophies. Scarcely is there a variety of spear, stabbing or disembowelling knife, blowing tube, bow, crossbow, or matchlock, that is not at the disposal of any member nimble enough to pluck it from the wall. In addition there is a vast collection of the heads of beasts; everywhere they project from walls and pillars; heads of bison, gazelles and wart-hogs cheer the souls of the members even in the humblest recesses. In the dining-room, above each table, a hippopotamus or a rhinoceros or a tiger or a lion glares out with glassy eyes upon the world, showing every item in its dentition. Below these monsters sits an occasional empire-builder, in the careful evening dress of the occasional visitant to civilization, seeming by contrast a very pallid, little, nicely behaved thing indeed.

To the Plantain came Oswald, proposing to dine alone, and in this dining-room he discovered Slingsby Darton, the fiscal expert, a little Cockney with scarcely any nose at all, sitting with the utmost impudence under the largest moose. Oswald was so pleased to discover any one he knew that he only remembered that he detested Slingsby Darton as he prepared to sit down with him. There was nothing for it then but to make the best of him.

Oswald chose his dinner and his wine with care. Red wines were forbidden him, but the wine waiter had good authority, authority from India and gastrically very sensitive, for the Moselle he recommended. And in answer to Slingsby Darton's enquiries, Oswald spread out his theory that he was an amiable, pleased sort of person obliged to come home from Uganda, sorry to leave Uganda, but glad to be back in the dear old country and "at the centre of things," and ready to take up anything——

"Politics?" said Slingsby Darton. "We want a few voices that have got out of sight of the parish pump."

Politics—well, it might be. But it was a little hard to join on to things at first. "Fearful lot of squabbling—not very much doing. Not nearly as much as one had hoped."

That seemed a restrained, reasonable sort of thing to say. Nor was it extravagant to throw out, "I thought it was 'Wake up, England'; but she seems just to be talking in her sleep."

Out flares the New Imperialism at once in Oswald's face. "But have you read Chamberlain's great speeches?" Slingsby Darton protests.

"I had those in mind," said Oswald grimly.

Both gentlemen were in the early phase of encounter. It was not yet time to join issue. Slingsby Darton heard, but made no retort. Oswald was free to develop his discontents.

Nothing seemed to be getting done, he complained. The army had been proved inefficient, incapable even of a colonial war, but what were we doing?

"Exactly," said Slingsby Darton. "You dare not even whisper 'conscription.' "

Oswald had not been thinking of that but of a technical reorganization, more science, more equipment. But all that he could see in the way of a change were "these beastly new caps." (Those were the days of the hated 'Brodrick.') Then economic reorganization hung fire. "Unemployed" processions grew bigger every winter. ("Tariff," whispered Darton. "Intelligent organization," said Oswald.) Then education——

"Education," said Oswald, "is at the heart of the whole business."

"I wouldn't say *that* altogether," said Slingsby Darton.

"At the heart of the whole business," Oswald repeated as though Slingsby Darton had not spoken. "The people do not know. Our people do not understand." The Boer war had shown how horribly backward our education was—our higher education, our scientific and technical education, the education of our officials and generals in particular. "We have an empire as big as the world and an imagination as small as a parish." But it would be a troublesome job to change that. Much too troublesome. Oswald became bitter and accusatory. His living side sneered. It would bother a lot of Balfour's friends quite uncomfortably. The dear old Church couldn't keep its grip on an education of that sort, and of course the dear old Church must have its grip on education. So after a few large-minded flourishes, the politicians had swamped the whole question of educational reform in this row about church schools and the Passive Resistance movement, both sides only too glad to get away from reality. Oswald was as bitter against the Passive Resister as he was against the Church.

"I don't know whether I should give quite the primary place to education," said Slingsby Darton, battling against this tirade. "I don't know whether I should quite say that. Mr. Chamberlain——"

The fat, as the vulgar say, was in the fire.

October, 1903, was a feverish and impassioned time in
English affairs. From Birmingham that month the storm
had burst. With a great splash Mr. Joseph Chamberlain
had flung the issue of Protection into the sea of political
affairs; huge waves of disturbance were sweeping out to the
uttermost boundaries of the empire. Instead of paying
taxes we were to "tax the foreigner." To that our fine imperial dream had come. Over dinner-tables, in trains and
smoking-rooms, men were quarrelling with their oldest
friends. To Oswald the conversion of Imperialism into a
scheme for world exploitation in the interests of Birmingham seemed the most atrocious swamping of real issues by
private interests that it was possible to conceive. The
Sydenham strain was an uncommercial strain. Slingsby
Darton was manifestly in the full swirl of the new movement,
the man looked cunning and eager, he put his pert little
face on one side and raised his voice to argue. A gathering
quarrelsomeness took possession of Oswald. He began to
speak very rapidly and pungently. He assumed an exasperating and unjustifiable detachment in order to quarrel
better. He came into these things from the outside, he declared, quite unbiased, oh! quite unbiased. And this "nail-
trust organizer's campaign" shocked him—shocked him unspeakably. Here was England confessedly in a phase of inefficiency and deterioration, needing a careful all-round effort, in education, in business organization, in military preparation. And suddenly drowning everything else in his noise
came "this demagogue ironmonger with his panacea!"

Slingsby Darton was indignant. "My dear Sir! I cannot hear you speak of Mr. Chamberlain in such terms as
that!"

"But consider the situation," said Oswald. "Consider the
situation! When of all things we want steady and har-
monious constructive work, comes all the uproar, all the
cheap, mean thinking and dishonest spouting, the music-hall
tricks and poster arguments, of a Campaign."

Slingsby Darton argued. "But, my dear Sir, it is a *constructive* campaign! It is based on urgent economic needs."

Oswald would have none of that. Tariff Reform was a
quack remedy. "A Zollverein. Think of it! With an em-

pire in great detached patches all over the world. Each patch with different characteristics and different needs. A child could see that a Zollverein is absurd. A child could see it. Yet to read the speeches of Chamberlain you'd think a tariff could work geographical miracles and turn the empire into a compact continent, locked fast against the foreigner. How can a scattered host become a band of robbers? The mere attempt takes us straight towards disaster.''

"Straight away from it!" Slingsby Darton contradicted.

Oswald went on regardlessly. "An empire—scattered like ours—run on selfish and exclusive lines *must* bring us into conflict with every other people under the sun," he asserted. "It must do. Apart from the utter and wanton unrighteousness, apart from the treason to humanity. Oh! I *hate* this New Imperialism. I hate it and dread it. It spoils my sleep at nights. It worries me and worries me. . . .''

Slingsby Darton thought he would do better to worry about this free trade of ours which was bleeding us to death.

"I do not speak as one ignorant of the empire," said Oswald. "I have been watching it——"

Slingsby Darton, disregarded, maintained that he, too, had been watching.

But Oswald was now at the "I tell you, Sir," stage.

He declared that the New Imperialism came from Germany. It was invented by professors of Weltpolitik. Milner had grafted it upon us at Balliol. But German conditions were altogether different from ours, Germany was a geographical unity, all drawn together, unified by natural necessity, like a fist. Germany was indeed a fist—by geographical necessity. The British empire was like an open hand. Must be like an open hand. We were an open people—or we were nothing. We were a liberalizing power or we were the most pretentious sham in history. But we seemed to be forgetting that liberal idea for which we stood. We swaggered now like owners, forgetting that we were only trustees. Trustees for mankind. We were becoming a boastful and a sprawling people. The idea of grabbing half the world—and then shutting other peoples out with tariffs, was—Oswald was losing self-control—"a shoving tradesman's dream." And we were doing it—as one might expect "a trust-organizing nail-maker"—phrase rubbed in with needless emphasis—to do it. We were shoving about, treading on everybody's toes—and failing to educate, failing to arm Yes—shoving. It was a good word. He did not mind how many times he used it. "This dream of defying the world without an army, and dominating it without education!" The Germans were at least logical in their swagger. If they shoved about they also armed. And they educated. Anyhow they trained. But we trod on everybody's toes and tried to keep friends all round. . . .

So Oswald—under the moose—while Slingsby Darton did what he could by stabbing an objection at him now and again. It became clearer and clearer to Slingsby Darton that the only possibility before him of holding his own, short of throwing knives and glasses at Oswald, was to capture the offensive.

"You complain of a panacea," he said, poking out two arresting fingers at Oswald. "That Tariff Reform is a panacea. But what of education? What of this education of yours? That also is a panacea."

And just then apt to his aid came Walsall and the Bishop of Pinner from their table under the big, black, clerical-looking hippopotamus. Walsall was a naturalist, and had met Oswald in the days of his biological enthusiasm; the Bishop of Pinner had formerly been the Bishop of Tanganyika and knew Oswald by repute. So they came over to greet him and were at once seized upon as auxiliaries by Slingsby Darton.

"We're getting heated over politics," said Slingsby Darton, indicating that at least Oswald was.

"Every one is getting heated over politics," said the bishop. "It's as bad as the Home Rule split."

"Sydenham's panacea is to save the world by education. He won't hear of economic organization."

The bishop opened eyes and mouth at Oswald until he looked like the full moon. . . .

On that assertion of Slingsby Darton's they drifted past the paying-desk to the small smoking-room, and there they had a great dispute about education beneath a gallery audience, so to speak, composed of antelope, Barbary sheep, gnu, yaks, and a sea lion. Oswald had never realized before how passionately he believed in education. It was a revelation. He discovered himself. He wanted to tell these men they were uneducated. He did succeed in saying that Mr. Chamberlain was "essentially an uneducated man."

Walsall was a very trying opponent for a disputant of swift and passionate convictions. He had a judicial affectation, a Socratic pose. He was a grey, fluffy-headed man with large tortoiseshell spectacles and a general resemblance to a kind wise owl. He liked to waggle his head slowly from side to side and smile. He liked to begin sentences with "But have you thought——?" or "I think you have overlooked——" or "So far from believing that, I hold the exact converse." He said these things in a very suave voice as though each remark was carefully dressed in oil before serving.

He expressed grave doubts whether there was "any benefit in education—any benefit whatever."

But the argument that formed that evening's entertainment for the sea lion and those assorted ruminating artiodactyls was too prolonged and heated and discursive to interest any but the most sedulous reader. Every possible sort of heresy about education seemed loose that night for the affliction of Oswald. Slingsby Darton said, "Make men prosperous and education will come of its own accord." Walsall thought that the sort of people who benefited by education "would get on anyhow." He thought knowledge was of value according to the difficulty one experienced in attaining it. (Could any sane man really believe that?) "I would persecute science," said Walsall, "and then it would be taken care of by enthusiasts."

"But do you know," said Oswald, with an immense quiet in his manner, "that there is a—a British Empire? An empire with rather urgent needs?"

(Suppressed murmur from Slingsby Darton: "Then I don't see what your position is at all!")

Walsall disputed these "needs." Weren't we all too much disposed to make the empire a thing of plan and will? An empire was a growth. It was like a man, it grew without taking thought. Presently it aged and decayed. We were not going to save the empire by taking thought.

(Slingsby Darton, disregarded, now disagreeing with Walsall.)

"Germany takes thought," Oswald interjected.

"To its own undoing, perhaps," said Walsall. . . .

The bishop's method of annoyance was even blander than Walsall's, and more exasperating to the fevered victim. He talked of the evils of an "educated proletariat." For a stable community only a certain proportion of educated people was advisable. You could upset the social balance by over-educating the masses. "We destroy good, honest, simple-souled workers in order to make discontented clerks." Oswald spluttered, "You *must* make a citizen in a modern population understand something of the State he belongs to!"

"Better, Faith," said the bishop. "Far better, Faith. Teach them a simple Catechism."

He had visited Russia. He had been to the coronation of the Tzar, a beautiful ceremony, only a little marred by a quite accidental massacre of some of the spectators. Those were the days before the Russo-Japanese war and the coming of the Duma. There was much to admire in Russia, the good bishop declared; much to learn. Russia was the land of Mary, great-souled and blessed; ours alas! was the land of bustling Martha. Nothing more enviable than the political solidarity of Russia—"after our warring voices. . . . Time after time I asked myself, 'Aren't we Westerns on the wrong track? Here is something—Great. And growing greater. Something simple. Here is obedience and a sort of primitive contentment. Trust in the Little White Father, belief in God. Here Christianity *lives indeed.*'"

About eleven o'clock Walsall was propounding a paradox. "All this talk of education," he said, "reminds me of the man who tried to lift himself by his own ears. How, I ask myself, can a democracy such as ours take an intelligent interest in its destiny unless it is educated, and how can it educate itself unless it takes an intelligent interest in its destiny? How escape that dilemma?"

"A community," said Oswald, grappling with this after a moment, "a community isn't one mind, it's a number of minds, some more intelligent, some less. It's a perpetual flow of new minds——"

Then something gave way within him.

"We sit here," he said in a voice so full of fury that the mouth of the bishop fell open, "and while we talk this half-witted, half-clever *muck* to excuse ourselves from getting the nation into order, the sands run out of the glass. The time draws near when the empire will be challenged——"

He stood up abruptly.

"Have you any idea," he said, "what the empire might be? Have you thought of these hundreds of millions to whom we might give light—*had* we light? Are we to be a possessing and profit-hunting people because we have not the education to be a leaderly people? Are we to do no better than Rome and Carthage—and loot the provinces of the world? Loot or education, that is the choice of every imperial opportunity. All England, I find, is echoing with screams for loot. Have none of us vision? None?"

The bishop shook his head sadly. The man, he thought, was raving.

"What *is* this vision of yours?" sneered Walsall. "Ten thousand professors?"

"After all," said Slingsby Darton with a weary insidiousness, "we do not differ about our fundamental idea. You must have funds. You must endow your schools. Without Tariff Reform to give you revenue——"

But Oswald was not going to begin over again.

"I ought to be in bed," he said, looking at his watch. "My doctor sends me to bed at ten. . . ."

"My God!" he whispered as he put on his coat under the benevolent supervision of an exceptionally fine Indian buffalo.

"What is to happen to the empire," he cried, going out into the night and addressing himself to the moon, to the monument which commemorates the heroic incompetence of the Duke of York, and to an interested hansom cabby, "what is to happen to the empire—when these are its educated opinions?"

§ 5

But it is high time that Joan and Peter came back into this narrative. For this is their story, it bears their names on its covers and on its back and on its title-page and at the head of each left-hand page. It has been necessary to show the state of mind, the mental condition, the outlook, of their sole guardian when their affairs came into his hands. This done they now return by telephone. Oswald had not been back in the comfortable sitting-room at the Climax Club for ten minutes before he was rung up by Mr. Sycamore and reminded of his duty to his young charges. A club page called Mr. Sydenham to the receiver in his bedroom.

In those days the telephone was still far from perfection. It had not been in general use for a decade. . . . Mr. Sycamore was audible as a still small voice.

"Mr. Sydenham? Sycamore speaking."

"No need to be," said Oswald. "You haven't been speaking to me."

"Who am I speaking to? I want Mr. Sydenham. Sycamore speaking."

"I'm Mr. Sydenham. Who are you? No need to be sick of your speaking so far as I'm concerned. I've only just been called to the telephone——"

"Your solicitor, Sycamore. S.Y.C.A.M.O.R.E."

"Oh! Right O. How are you, Mr. Sycamore? I'm Sydenham. How are those children?"

"Hope you're well, Mr. Sydenham?"

"Gaudy—in a way. How are you?"

"I've been with Lady Charlotte today. I don't know if you've heard anything of——"

Whop! Whop. Bunnik. *Silence.*

After a little difficulty communication with Mr. Sycamore was partially restored. I say partially because his voice had now become very small and remote indeed. "I was saying, I don't know if you understand anything of the present state of affairs."

"Nothing," said Oswald. "Fire ahead."

"Can you hear me distinctly? I find you almost inaudible."

Remonstrances with the exchange led after a time to slightly improved communications.

"You were saying something about a fire?" said Mr. Sycamore.

"I said nothing about a fire. You were saying something about the children?"

"Well, well. Things are in a very confused state, Mr. Sydenham. I hope you mean to take hold of their education. These children are not being educated, they are being fought over."

"Who's thinking over them?"

"No one. But the Misses Stubland and Lady Charlotte are fighting over them. . . . F.I.G.H.T.I.N.G. I want *you* to think over them. . . . You—yes. . . . Think, yes. Both clever children. Great waste if they are not properly educated. . . . Matters are really urgent. I have been with Lady Charlotte today. You know she kidnapped them?"

"Kidnapped?"

A bright girlish voice, an essentially happy voice, cut into the conversation at this point. "Three minutes *up*," it said.

Empire-building language fell from Oswald. In some obscure way this feminine intervention was swept aside, and talk was resumed with Mr. Sycamore.

It continued to be a fragmentary talk, and for a time the burthen of some unknown lady complaining to an unknown friend about the behaviour of a third unknown named George, stated to lack "gumption," interwove with the main theme. But Mr. Sycamore did succeed in conveying to Oswald a sense of urgency about the welfare of his two charges. Immediate attention was demanded. They were being neglected. The girl was ill. "I would like to talk it over with you as soon as possible," said Mr. Sycamore.

"Can you come and breakfast here at eight?" said the man from the tropics.

"Half past nine," said the Londoner, and the talk closed.

The talk ended, but for a time the bell of Oswald's telephone remained in an agitated state, giving little nervous rings at intervals. When he answered these the exchange said "Number please," and when he said, "You rang *me*," the exchange said, "Oh, no! we didn't. . . ."

"An empire," whispered Oswald, sitting on the edge of his bed, "which cannot even run a telephone service efficiently. . . ."

"Education. . . ."

He tried to recall his last speech at the club. Had he ranted? What had they thought of it? What precisely had he said? While they sat and talked *muck*—his memory was unpleasantly insistent upon that *"muck"*—the sands ran out of the hour-glass, a new generation grew up.

Had he said that? That was the point of it all—about the new generation. A new generation was growing up and we were doing nothing to make it wiser, more efficient, to give it a broader outlook than the generation that had blundered into and blundered through the Boer war. Had he said that? That was what he ought to have said.

§ 6

For a long time he sat on his bed, blank-minded and too tired to finish undressing. He got to bed at last. But not to sleep. He found that the talk in the club had disturbed his mind almost unendurably. It had pointed and endorsed everything that he had been trying not to think about the old country. Now, too weary and too excited to sleep, he turned over and over again, unprofitably and unprogressively, the tangled impressions of his return to England.

How many millions of such hours of restless questioning must have been spent by wakeful Englishmen in the dozen years between the Boer war and the Great war; how many nocturnally scheming brains must have explored the complicated maze of national dangers, national ambitions, and national ineptitude! If "Wake up, England," sowed no great harvest of change in the daylight, it did at any rate produce large phantom crops at night. He argued with Walsall over and over again, sometimes wide awake and close to the point, sometimes drowsily with the discussion becoming vague and strangely misshapen and incoherent. Was Walsall right? Was it impossible to change the nature and quality of a people? Must we English always be laggards in peace and blunderers in war? Were our achievements accidents, and

our failures essential? Was slackness in our blood? Surely
a great effort might accomplish much, a great effort to reor-
ganize political life, to improve national education, to make
the press a better instrument of public thought and criticism.
To which Walsall answered again with, "How can a democratic community take an intelligent interest in its destinies
unless it is educated, and how can it educate itself unless it
takes an intelligent interest in its destinies?"

Oswald groaned and turned over in bed.

Thought passed by insensible degrees into dreaming and
dreaming shallowed again to wakefulness. Always he seemed
to be arguing with Walsall and the bishop for education and
effort; nevertheless, now vaguely apprehended as an atmos-
pheric background, now real and close, the black forest of his
African nightmare was about him. Always he was struggling on and always he was hoping to see down some vista the
warm gleam of daylight, the promise of the open. And Walsall, a vast forest owl with enormous spectacles, kept getting
in the way, flapping hands that were really great wings at
him and assuring him that there was no way out. None.
"This forest is life. This forest will always be life. There
is no other life. After all it isn't such a very bad forest."
Other figures, too, came and went; a gigantic bishop sitting
back in an easy chair blocked one hopeful vista, declaring
that book-learning only made the lower classes discontented
and mischievous, and then a stupidly contented fat man
smoking a fat cigar drove in a gig athwart the line of march.
He said nothing; he just drove his gig. Then somehow an
automobile came in, a most hopeful means of escape, except
that it had broken down; and Oswald was trying to repair it
in spite of the jeering of an elderly gentleman in a white
waistcoat. Suddenly the whole forest swarmed with children. There were countless children; there were just two
children. Instead of a multitudinous expedition Oswald
found himself alone in the black jungle with just two children, two white and stunted children who were dying for the
air and light. No one had cared for them. One was ill, seriously ill. Unless the way out was found they could not live.
They were Dolly's children, his wards. But what was he to
do for them? . . .

Then far ahead he saw that light of the great conflagration, that light that promised to be daylight and became a
fire. . . .

"Black coffee," said Oswald during one of the wide-awake
intervals. "Cigars. Talk. Over-excited. . . . I ought to
be more careful. . . . I forget how flimsy I am still. . . .

"I must get my mind off these things. I'll talk to old
Sycamore tomorrow and see about this little master Peter
Stubland and his foster-sister. I'll go into the matter thor-
oughly. I haven't thought of them before.

"I wonder if the boy still takes after Dolly. . . .

"After all," he said, rolling over, "it's true. Education
is the big neglected duty of the time. It's fundamental.
And what am I doing? It's just England—England all
over— to let that boy be dragged up. I ought to see about
him—now. I'll go down there. . . .

"I'll go and stay with Aunt Charlotte for a day or so.
I'll send her a wire tomorrow.

§ 7

The quiet but observant life of old Cashel at Chastlands
was greatly enlivened by the advent of Oswald.

Signs of a grave and increasing agitation in the mind of
Cashel's mistress became evident immediately after the departure of Mr. Sycamore. Manifestly whatever that gentleman had said or done—old Cashel had been able to catch very
little—had been of a highly stimulating nature. So soon as
he was out of the house, Lady Charlotte abandoned her sofa
and table, upsetting her tonic as she did so, and still wearing
her dressing-gown and cap, proceeded to direct a hasty packing for Italy. Unwin became much agitated, and a house-
maid being addressed as a "perfect fool" became a sniffing
fount of tears. There was a running to and fro with trunks
and tea-baskets, a ringing of bells, and minor orders were
issued and countermanded; the carriage was summoned twice
for an afternoon drive and twice dismissed. When at last
the lace peignoir was changed for a more suitable costume in
which to take tea, Lady Charlotte came so near to actual
physical violence that Unwin abruptly abandoned her quest

of a perfect pose for wig and cap, and her ladyship surprised and delighted Cashel with a blond curl cocked waggishly over one eye. She did not have tea until half-past five.

She talked to herself with her hard blue eyes fixed on vacancy. "I will not stay here to be insulted," she said.

"Rampageous," whispered Cashel on the landing. "Rumbustious. What's it all about?"

"Cashel!" she said sharply as he was taking away the tea-things.

"M'lady."

"Telephone to Mr. Grimes and ask him to take tickets as usual for myself and Unwin to Pallanza—for tomorrow."

It was terrible but pleasing to have to tell her that Mr. Grimes would now certainly have gone home from his office.

"See that it is done tomorrow. Tomorrow I must catch the eleven forty-seven for Charing Cross. I shall take lunch with me in the train. A wing of chicken. A drop of claret. Perhaps a sandwich. Gentleman's Relish or shrimp paste. And a grape or so. A mere mouthful. I shall expect you to be in attendance to help with the luggage as far as Charing Cross. . . ."

So she was going after all.

"Like a flight," mused Cashel. "What's after the Old Girl?" . . .

He grasped the situation a little more firmly next day.

The preparations for assembling Lady Charlotte in the hall before departure were well forward at eleven o'clock, although there was no need to start for the station until the half hour. A brief telegram from Oswald received about half-past ten had greatly stimulated these activities. . . .

Unwin, very white in the face—she always had a bilious headache when travelling was forward—and dressed in the peculiar speckled black dress and black hat that she considered most deterrent to foreign depravity, was already sitting stiffly in the hall with Lady Charlotte's purple-coloured dressing-bag beside her, and Cashel having seen to the roll of rugs was now just glancing through the tea-basket to make sure that it was in order, when suddenly there was the flapping, rustling sound of a large woman in rapid movement upon the landing above, and Lady Charlotte appeared at the

head of the stairs, all hatted, veiled and wrapped for travelling. Her face was bright white with excitement. "Unwin,
I want you," she cried. "Cashel, say I'm in bed. Say I'm
ill and must not be disturbed. Say I've been taken ill."

She vanished with the agility of a girl of twenty—except
that the landing was of a different opinion.

The two servants heard her scuttle into her room and slam
the door. There was a great moment of silence.

"Oh, *Lor'!*" Unwin rose with the sigh of a martyr, and
taking the dressing-bag with her—the fittings alone were
worth forty pounds—and pressing her handkerchief to her
aching brow, marched upstairs.

Cashel, agape, was roused by the ringing of the front door
bell. He opened to discover Mr. Oswald Sydenham with one
arm in a sling and a rug upon the other.

"Hullo, Cashel," he said. "I suppose my room isn't occupied? My telegram here? How's Lady Charlotte?"

"Very poorly, sir," said Cashel. "She's had to take in
her bed, sir."

"Pity. Anything serious?"

"A sudden attact, sir."

"H'm. Well, tell her I'm going to inflict myself upon
her for a day or so. Just take my traps in and I'll go on
with this fly to Limpsfield. Say I'll be back to dinner."

"Certainly, sir."

The old man bustled out to get in the valise and Gladstone
bag that constituted Oswald's luggage. When he came into
the hall again he found the visitor scrutinizing the tea-
basket and the roll of rugs with his one penetrating eye in
a manner that made him dread a question. But Oswald
never questioned servants; on this occasion only he winked
at one.

"Nothing wrong with the arm, sir?" asked old Cashel.

"Nothing," said Oswald, still looking markedly at the
symptoms of imminent travel. "H'm."

He went out to the fly, stood ready to enter it, and then
swivelled round very quickly and looked up at his aunt's
bedroom window in time to catch an instant impression of
a large, anxious face regarding him.

"Ah!" said Oswald, and returned smiling grimly into the hall.

"Cashel," he called.

"Sir?"

"Her ladyship is up. Tell her I have a few words to say to her before she goes."

"Beg pardon, sir——"

"Look here, Cashel, you do what I tell you."

"I'll tell Miss Unwin, sir."

He went upstairs, leaving Oswald still thinking over the rugs. Yes, she was *off!* She had got everything; pointed Alpine sticks, tea-basket, travelling campstool. It must be Switzerland or Italy for the winter at least. A great yearning to see his aunt with his own eye came upon Oswald. He followed Cashel upstairs quietly but swiftly, and found him in a hasty whispered consultation with Unwin on the second landing. "Oh my 'ed'll burst *bang*," Unwin was saying.

" 'Er ladyship, sir," she began at the sight of Oswald.

"Ssh!" he said to her, and held her and Cashel silent with an uplifted forefinger while he listened to the sounds of a large powerful woman going to bed swiftly and violently in her clothes.

"I must go in to her, sir," said Unwin breaking the silence. "Poor dear! It's a *very* sudden attact."

The door opened and closed upon Unwin.

"Lock the door on him, you—you *Idiot!*" they heard Lady Charlotte shout—too late.

The hated and dreaded visage of Oswald appeared looking round the corner of the door into the great lady's bedroom. Her hat had been flung aside, she was tying on an unconvincing night cap over her great blond travelling wig; her hastily assumed nightgown betrayed the agate brooch at her neck.

"How dare you, sir!" she cried at the sight of him.

"You're not ill. You're going to cut off to Italy this afternoon. What have you done to my Wards?"

"A lady's sick room! Sacred, Sir! Have you no sense of decency?"

"Is it measles, Auntie?"

"Go *away!*"

"I daren't. If I leave you alone in this country for a year or two you're bound to get into trouble. What am I to *do* with you?"

"Unbecoming intrusion!"

"You ought to be stopped by the Foreign Office. You'll lead to a war with Italy."

"Go for a doctor, Cashel," she cried aloud in her great voice. "Go for the doctor."

"M'lady," very faintly from the landing.

"And countermand the station cab, Cashel," said Oswald.

"If you do anything of the sort, Cashel!" she cried, and sitting up in bed clutched the sheets with such violence that a large spring-sided boot became visible at the foot of the bed. The great lady had gone to bed in her boots. Aunt and nephew both glared at this revelation in an astonished silence.

"How *can* you, Auntie," said Oswald.

"If I choose," said Lady Charlotte. "If I choose—— Oh! *Go away!*"

"Back to dinner," said Oswald sweetly, and withdrew.

He was still pensive upon the landing when Unwin appeared to make sure that the station cab was not countermanded. . . .

Under the circumstances he was not surprised to find on his return from The Ingle-Nook that he was now the only occupant of Chastlands. Aunt Charlotte had fled, leaving behind a note that had evidently been written before his arrival.

My dear Nephew,—I am sorry that my arrangements for going abroad this winter, already made, prevent my welcoming you home for this uninvited and totally unexpected visit. I am sure Cashel and the other servants will take good care of you. You seem to know the way to their good graces. There are many things I should have liked to talk over with you if you had given me due and proper notice of your return as you ought to have done, instead of leaving it to a solicitor to break the glad tidings to me, followed by a sixpenny telegram. As it is, I shall just miss you. I have to go, and I

*cannot wait. All my arrangements are made. I suppose it
is idle to expect civility from you ever or the slightest attention to the convenances. The Sydenhams have never shone
in manners. Well, I hope you will take those two poor children quite out of the hands of those smoking, blaspheming,
nightgown-wearing Limpsfield women. They are utterly un-
fit for such a responsibility. Utterly. I would not trust a
pauper brat in their hands. The children require firm treatment, the girl especially, or they will be utterly spoilt. She
is deceitful and dishonest, as one might expect; she gave
Mrs. Pybus a very trying time indeed, catching measles deliberately and so converting the poor woman's house into a
regular hospital. I fear for her later. I have done my best
for them both. No doubt you will find it all spun into a
fine tale, but I trust your penetration to see through a tissue
of lies, however plausible it may seem at the first blush. I
am glad to think you are now to relieve me of a serious responsibility, though how a single man not related to her in
the slightest degree can possibly bring up a young girl, even
though illegitimate, without grave scandal, passes my poor
comprehension. No doubt I am an old-fashioned old fool
nowadays! Thank God! I beg to be excused!*
Your affectionate Aunt
CHARLOTTE.

Towards the end of this note her ladyship's highly angular
handwriting betrayed by an enhanced size and considerable
irregularity, a deflection from her customary calm.

§ 8

Oswald knocked for some time at the open green door of
The Ingle-Nook before attracting any one's attention. Then
a small but apparently only servant appeared, a little round-
faced creature who looked up hard into Oswald's living eye
—as though she didn't quite like the other. She explained
that "Miss Phyllis" was not at home, and that "Miss Phœbe
mustn't be disturved." Miss Phœbe was working. Miss
Phyllis had gone away with Mary——

"Who's Mary?" said Oswald.

"Well, Sir, it's Mary who always *as* been 'ere, Sir,"— to Windsor to be with Miss Joan. "And it's orders no one's 'llowed to upset Miss Phœbe when she's writing. Not even Lady Charlotte Sydenham, Sir. I dursn't give your name, Sir, even. I dursn't."

"Except," she added reverentially, "it's Death or a Fire."

"You aren't the Piano, per'aps?" she asked.

Oswald had to confess he wasn't.

The little servant looked sorry for him.

And that was in truth the inexorable law now of The Ingle-Nook. Aunt Phœbe was taking herself very seriously —as became a Thinker whose *Stitchwoman* papers, deep, high, and occasionally broad in thought, were running into a sale of tens of thousands. So she sat hard and close at her writing-table from half-past nine to twelve every morning, secluded and defended from all the world, correcting, musing deeply over, and occasionally reading aloud the proofs of the third series of *Stitchwoman* papers. (Old Groombridge, the occasional gardener, used to listen outside in awe and admiration. "My word, but she do give it 'em!" old Groombridge used to say.) Oswald perceived that there was nothing to do but wait. "I'll wait," he said, "downstairs."

"I suppose I ought to let you in," said the little servant, evidently seeking advice.

"Oh, decidedly," said Oswald, and entered the room in which he had parted from Dolly six years ago.

The door closed behind the little servant, and Oswald found himself in a house far more heavily charged with memories than he could have expected. The furniture had been but little altered; it was the morning time again, the shadow masses fell in the same places, it had just the same atmosphere of quiet expectation it had had on that memorable day before the door beyond had opened and Dolly had appeared, subdued and ashamed, to tell him of the act that severed them for ever. How living she seemed here by virtue of those inanimate things! Had that door opened now he would have expected to see her standing there again. And he was alive still, strong and active, altered just a little by a touch of fever and six short years of experience, but the same thing of impulse and desire and anger, and she had gone beyond time and space, beyond hunger or desire. He had walked between this window and this fireplace on these same bricks on which he was pacing now, spitting abuse at her, a man mad with shame and thwarted desire. Never had he forgiven her, or stayed his mind to think what life had been for her, until she was dead. That outbreak, with gesticulating hands and an angry, grimacing face, had been her last memory of him. What a broken image he had made of himself in her mind! And now he could never set things right with her, never tell her of his belated understanding and pity. "I was a weak thing, confused and torn between my motives. Why did you—you who were my lover—why did you not help me after I had stumbled?" So the still phantom in that room reproached him, a phantom of his own creation, for Dolly had never reproached him; to the end she had had no reproaches in her heart for any one but herself because of their disaster.

"Hold tight to love, little people," he whispered. "Hold tight to love. . . . But we don't, we don't. . . ."

Never before had Oswald so felt the tremendous pitifulness of life. He felt that if he stayed longer in this room he must cry out. He walked to the garden door and stood looking at the empty flagstone path between the dahlias and sunflowers.

It was all as if he had but left it yesterday, except for the heartache that now mingled with the sunshine.

"Pat—whack—pat—whack"; he scarcely heeded that rhythmic noise.

Peter had gone out of his head altogether. He walked slowly along the pathway towards the little arbour that overhung the Weald. Then, turning, he discovered Peter with a bat in his hand, regarding him. . . .

Directly Oswald saw Peter he marvelled that he had not been eager to see him before. The boy was absurdly like Dolly; he had exactly the same smile; and directly he saw the gaunt figure of his one-eyed guardian he cried out, "It's Nobby!" with a voice that might have been hers. There was a squeak of genuine delight in his voice. He wasn't at all the sturdy little thing in a pinafore that Oswald remembered. He seemed indeed at the first glance just a thin, flat-chested little Dolly in grey flannel trousers.

He had obviously been bored before this happy arrival of Oswald. He had been banging a rubber ball against the scullery with a cricket-bat and counting hits and misses. It is a poor entertainment. Oswald did not realize how green his memory had been kept by the Bungo-Peter saga, and Peter's prompt recognition after six years flattered him.

The two approached one another slowly, taking each other in.

"You remember me?" said Oswald superfluously.

"Don't I just! You promised me a lion's skin."

"So I did."

He could not bear to begin this new relationship as a defaulter. "It's on its way to you," he equivocated, making secret plans.

Peter, tucking his bat under his arm and burying his hands in his trouser pockets, drew still nearer. At a distance of four feet or thereabouts he stopped short and Oswald stopped short. Peter regarded this still incredible homecomer with his head a little on one side.

"It was you, used to tell me stories."

"You don't remember my telling you stories?"

"I do. About the Ba-ganda who live in U-ganda. Don't you remember how you used to put out my Zulus and my elephants and lions on the floor and say it was Africa. You taught us roaring like lions—Joan and me. Don't you remember?"

Oswald remembered. He remembered himself on all fours with the children on the floor of the sunny play-room upstairs, and some one sometimes standing, sometimes sitting above the game, some one who listened as keenly as the children, some one at whom he talked about that world of lakes as large as seas, and of trackless, sunless forests and of park-like glades and wildernesses of flowers, and about strings of loaded porters and of encounters with marvelling people who had never before set eyes on a European. . . .

§ 9

The idea that the guardianship of Peter was just a little duty to be seen to, vanished at the sight of him in favour of the realization of a living relationship. There are moments when small boys of ten in perfect health and condition can look the smallest, flimsiest, and most pathetic of created things—and at the same time preternaturally valiant and intelligent. They take on a likeness to sacred flames that may at any moment flicker out. More particularly does this unconscious camouflage of delicacy occur in the presence of parents and guardians already in a state of self-reproach and emotional disorder. Mr. Grimes with an eye to growth had procured a grey flannel suit a little too large for Peter, but it never occurred to Oswald that the misfit could be due to anything but a swift and ominous shrinkage of the boy. He wanted to carry him off forthwith to beer and cream and sea-bathing.

But these were feelings he knew he must not betray.

"I must tell you some more stories," he said. "I've come back to England to live."

"*Here?*"—brightly.

"Well, near here. But I shall see a lot of you now, Peter."

"I'll like that," said Peter. "I've often thought of you. . . ."

A pause.

"You broken your arm?" said Peter

"Not so bad as that. I've got to have some bits of shell taken out."

"That Egyptian shell? When you got the V.C.?"

"I never told you of the Egyptian shell?" asked Oswald.

"Mummy did. Once. Long ago."

Another pause.

"This garden's not so greatly altered, Peter," said Oswald.

"There's a Friendship's Garden up that end," said Peter, indicating the end by a movement of his head. "But it isn't much. Aunt Phœbe started it and forgot it. Every one who came was to plant something. And me and Joan have gardens, but they've got all weedy now."

"Let's have a look at it all," said Oswald, and guardian and ward strolled towards the steep.

"The Dahlias are splendid this year," Oswald remarked, "and these Japanese roses are covered with berries. Splendid, aren't they? One can make a jelly of them Quite a good jelly. And let me see, wasn't there a little summer-house at the end of this path where one looked over the Weald? Ah! here it is. Hardly changed at all."

He sat down. Here he had talked with Dolly and taken her hand. . . .

He bestirred himself to talk.

"And exactly how old are you now, Peter?"

"Ten years and two months," said Peter.

"We'll have to find a school for you."

"Have you been in Africa since I saw you?" Peter asked, avoiding the topic.

"Since you saw me going off," said Oswald, and the man glanced at the boy and the boy glanced at the man, and each was wondering what the other remembered. "I've been in Uganda all the time. There's been fighting and working. Some day you must go to Uganda and see all that has been done. We've made a good railway and good roads and tele-graphs. We've put down robbers and cruelty."

"And shot a lot of lions?"

"Plenty. The lions were pretty awful for a bit. About Nairobi and along the line."

"Shot 'em when they were coming at you?"

"One was coming straight at me."

"That's my skin," said Peter.

Oswald make no answer.

"I'd like to go to Africa," said Peter.

"You shall."

He decided to begin at once upon his neglected task of making an Imperial citizen according to the ideas that pre-vailed before the advent of the New Imperialism. "That sort of thing," he said, "is what we Englishmen are for, you know, Peter. What our sort of Englishman is for any-how. We have to go about the world and make roads and keep the peace and see fair play. We've got to kill big beasts and climb hard mountains. That's the job of the

Englishman. He's a sort of policeman. A sort of working guardian Not a nosy slave-driver trying to get rich. He chases off slave-drivers. All the world's his beat. India, Africa, China, and the East, all the seas of the world. This little fat green country, all trim and tidy and set with houses and gardens, isn't much of a land for a man, you know— unless he's an invalid. It's a good land to grow up in and come back to die in. Or rest in. But in between, no!''

"No," said Peter.

"No."

"But you haven't come back to die, Uncle Nobby?''

"No fear. But I've had to come back. I'm resting. This old arm, you know, and all that sort of thing. Just for a time. . . . And besides I want to see a lot of you."

"Yes."

"You have to grow up here and learn all you can, science and all sorts of things, so that you can be a useful man— wherever you have to go."

"Africa," said Peter.

"Africa, perhaps. And that's why one has to go to school and college—and learn all about it."

"They haven't taught me much about it yet," said Peter.

"Well, you haven't been to much in the way of schools," said Oswald.

"Are there better schools?''

"No end. We're going to find one," said Oswald.

"I wish school was over," said Peter.

"Why? You've got no end to learn yet."

"I want to begin," said Peter, looking out across the tumbled gentleness of the Weald.

"Begin school?''

"No, begin—Africa, India—doing things."

"School first," said Oswald.

"Are there schools where you learn about guns and animals and mountains and foreign people?'' said Peter.

"There must be," said Oswald. "We'll find something."

"Where you don't do Latin and parsing and 'straction of the square root."

"Oh! those things have their place."

"Did you have to do them, Uncle Nobby?''

"Rather."

"Were they useful to you?"

"At times—in a way. Of course those things are good as training, you know—awfully good. Harden up the mental muscles, Peter."

Peter made no reply to that.

Presently Peter said, "Shall I learn about machines?"

"When you've done some mathematics, Peter."

"I'd like to fly," said Peter.

"That's far away yet."

"There was a boy at that school, his father was an engineer; and he said that flying machines were coming quite soon."

This was beyond Oswald's range.

"The French have got a balloon that steers about," he said. "That's as near as we are likely to come to flying for a long time yet."

"This boy said that he meant a real flying machine, not a balloon. It was to be heavier than air. It would fly like a kite or a bird."

"I doubt if we'll see that in my lifetime," said Oswald; "or yours," blind to the fate that had marked Peter for its own.

"H'm," said Peter, with a shadow falling upon one of his brightest dreams. (Nobby ought to know these things. His word ought surely to be final. Still, after all, this chap's father was an engineer.) "I'd love to fly," said Peter.

§ 10

Something with the decorative effect of a broad processional banner in a very High Church indeed, appeared upon the flagstone path. It was Aunt Phœbe.

She had come out into the garden half an hour before her usual time. But indeed from the moment when she had heard Oswald and Peter talking in the garden below she had been unable to write more. After some futile attempts to pick up the lost thread of her discourse, she had gone to her bedroom and revised her toilet, which was often careless in the morning, so as to be more expressive of her personality.

She was wearing a long djibbah-like garment with a richly embroidered yoke, she had sandals over her brown stockings, and rather by way of symbol of authorship than for any immediate use she bore a big leather portfolio. There was moreover now a gold-mounted fountain pen amidst the other ingredients of the cheerful chatelaine that had once delighted Peter's babyhood.

She seemed a fuller, more confident person than Oswald remembered. She came eloquent with apologies. "I have to make an inexorable rule," she said, "against disturbances. As if I were a man writer instead of a mere woman. Between nine and one I am a woman enclosed—cloistered—refused. Sacred hours of self-completeness. Unspeakably precious to me. Visitors are not even announced. It is a law—inflexible."

"We must all respect our work," said Oswald.

"It's over now," said Aunt Phœbe, smiling like the sun after clouds. "It's over now for the day. I am just human —until tomorrow again."

"You are writing a book?" Oswald asked rather ineptly.

"The Stitchwoman; Series Three. Much is expected; much must be given. I am the slave now of a Following."

Aunt Phœbe went to the wall and stood with her fine profile raised up over the view. She was a little breathless and twitching slightly, but very magnificent. Most of her hair was tidy. "Our old Weald, does it look the same?" she asked.

"Quite the same," said Oswald, standing up beside her.

"But not to me," she said. Indeed not to me. To me every day it is different. Always wide, always wonderful, but different, always different. I know it so well."

Oswald felt she had worked a "catch" on him. He was faintly nettled.

"Still," he said, "fundamentally one must recognize that it's the same Weald."

"I wonder," said Aunt Phœbe suddenly, looking at him very intently, and then, as if she tasted the word, "Fundamentally?"

"I don't know," she added.

Oswald was too much annoyed to reply.

"And what do you think of your new charge?" she asked. "I don't know whether Peter quite understands that yet. The young squire goes to the men. He casts aside childish things, and rides out in his little Caparison to join the ranks. Do you know that, Peter? Mr. Sydenham is now your sole guardian."

Peter looked at Oswald and smiled shyly, and his cheeks flushed.

"I think we shall get on together," said Oswald.

"Would that it ended there! You take the girl too?"

"It is not my doing," said Oswald.

Aunt Phœbe addressed the Weald.

"Poor Dolly! So it is that the mother soul cheats itself. Through the ages—always self-abnegation for the woman." She turned to Oswald. "If she had had time to think I am certain she would not have excluded women from this trust. Certain. What have men to do with education? With the education of a woman more particularly. The Greater from the Less. But the thing is done. It has been a great experiment, a wonderful experiment; teaching, I learnt—but I doubt if you will understand that."

There was a slight pause. "What exactly was the nature of the experiment?" asked Oswald modestly.

"Feminine influence. Dominant."

Oswald considered. "I don't know if you include Lady Charlotte," he threw out.

"Oh!" said Aunt Phœbe.

"But she has played her part, I gather."

"Feminine! No! She is completely a Man-made Woman. Quintessentially the Pampered Squaw. Holding her position by her former charms. A Sex Residuum. Relict. This last outrage. An incident—merely. Her course of action was dictated for her. A Man. A mere solicitor. One Grimes. The flimsiest creature! An aspen leaf—but Male. Male."

Stern thoughts kept Aunt Phœbe silent for a time. Then she remarked very quietly, "I shook him. I shook him *well*."

"I hope still to have the benefit of your advice," said Oswald gravely.

"Nay," she said. But she was pleased. "A shy comment, perhaps. But the difference will be essential. Don't expect me to guide you as you would wish to be guided. That phase is over between men and women. We hand the children over—since the law will have it so. Take them!''

And then addressing the Weald, Aunt Phœbe, in vibrating accents, uttered a word that was to be the keynote of a decade of feminine activities.

''The Vote,'' said Aunt Phœbe, getting a wonderful emotional buzz into her voice. ''The Vo-o-o-o-o-te.''

§ 11

So it was that Oswald found himself fully invested with his responsibilities.

There was a terrifying suggestion in Aunt Phœbe's manner that he would presently have to clap Peter's hat on, make up a small bundle of Peter's possessions, and fare forth with him into the wide world, picking up the convalescent at Windsor on the way, but that was a misapprehension of Aunt Phœbe's intentions. And, after all, it was Peter's house and garden if it came to that. For a time at least things could go on as they were. But the task of direction was now fully his. Whether these two young people were properly educated or not, whether they too became slackers and inadequate or worthy citizens of this great empire, rested now entirely in his hands.

''They must have the best,'' he said. . . .

The best was not immediately apparent.

From Chastlands and his two rooms at the Climax Club Oswald conducted his opening researches for the educational best, and whenever he was at Chastlands he came over nearly every day to The Ingle-Nook on his bicycle It was a well-remembered road. Scarcely was there a turn in it that did not recall some thought of the former time when he had ridden over daily for a sight of Dolly; he would leave his bicycle in a clump of gorse by the high road that was surely an outgrown fragment of the old bush in which he had been wont to leave it six years before; he would walk down the same rusty path, and his heart would quicken as it used to quicken at the thought of seeing Dolly. But presently Peter

began to oust Dolly from his thoughts. Sometimes Peter
would be standing waiting for him by the high road. Sometimes Peter, mounted on a little outgrown bicycle, would
meet him on the purple common half way.

A man and a boy of ten are perhaps better company than
a man and a boy of fifteen. There's so much less egotism between them. At any rate Peter and Oswald talked of education and travel and politics and philosophy with unembar-
rassed freedom. Oswald, like most childless people, had had
no suspicion of what the grey matter of a bright little boy's
brain can hold. He was amazed at Peter's views and curiosities. It was Oswald's instinct never to talk ''down'' to
man, woman or child. He had never thought about it, but
if you had questioned him he would have told you that that
was the sort of thing one didn't do. And this instinct gave
him a wide range of available companionship. Peter had
never conceived such good company as Oswald. You could
listen to Oswald for hours. They discoursed upon every
topic out of dreamland. And sometimes they came very
close even to that dreamland where Bungo Peter adventured
immortally. Oswald would feel a transfiguring presence, a
touch of fantasy and half suspect their glorious companion.

Much of their talk was a kind of story-telling.

''How should we go to the Congo Forest?'' Peter would
ask. ''Would one go by Nairobi?''

''No, that's the other way. We'd have to go——''

And forthwith Nobby and Peter were getting their stuff
together and counting how many porters they would
need. . . .

''One day perhaps we'd come upon a place 'fested with
crocodiles,'' Peter would say.

''We would. You would be pushing rather ahead of the
party with your guns, looking for anything there might be—
pushing through tall reeds far above your head,'' Oswald
would oblige.

''You'd be with me,'' insisted Peter. . . .

It was really story-telling. . . .

It was Peter's habit in those days when he was alone to
meditate on paper. He would cover sheet after sheet with
rapidly drawn scenes of adventure. One day Oswald found

himself figuring in one of these dream pictures. He and
Peter were leading an army in battle. "Capture of Ten
War Elephants" was the legend thereon. But he realized
how clearly the small boy saw him. Nothing was spared of
the darkened, browless side of his face with its asymmetrical
glass eye, the figure of him was very long and lean and bent,
with its arm still in its old sling; and it was drawn manifestly with the utmost confidence and admiration and
love. . . .

Peter's hostility to schools was removed very slowly. The
lessons at High Cross had scarred him badly, and about Miss
Mills clung associations of the utmost dreariness. Still it
was Oswald's instinct to consult the young man on his destiny.

"There's a lot you don't know yet," said Oswald.

"Can't I read it out of books?" asked Peter.

"You can't read everything out of books," said Oswald.
"There's things you ought to see and handle. And things
you can only learn by doing."

Oswald wanted Peter to plan his own school.

Peter considered. "I'd like lessons about the insides of
animals, and about the people in foreign countries—and how
engines work—and all that sort of thing."

"Then we must find a school for you where they teach all
that sort of thing," said Oswald, as though it was merely a
question of ordering goods from the Civil Service Stores. . . .

He had much to learn yet about education.

§ 12

But Oswald was still only face to face with the half of his
responsibility.

One morning he found Peter at the schoolroom table very
busy cutting big letters out of white paper. Beside him was
a long strip of Turkey twill from the dressing-up box that
The Ingle-Nook had plagiarized from the Sheldricks. "I'm
getting ready for Joan," said Peter. "I'm going to put
'Welcome' on this for over the garden gate. And there's to
be a triumphal arch."

Hitherto Peter had scarcely betrayed any interest in Joan

at all, now he seemed able to think of no one else, and Oswald
found himself reduced abruptly from the position of centre
of Peter's universe to a mere helper in the decorations.   But
he was beginning to understand the small boy by this time,
and he took the withdrawal of the limelight philosophically.

When Aunt Phyllis and Joan arrived they found the
flagged path from the "Welcome" gate festooned with chains
of coloured paper (bought with Peter's own pocket-money
and made by him and Oswald, with some slight assistance
and much moral support from Aunt Phœbe in the evening)
to the door.   The triumphal arch had been achieved rather in
the Gothic style by putting the movable Badminton net posts
into a sort of trousering of assorted oriental cloths from the
dressing-up chest, and crossing two heads of giant Heracleum
between them.   Peter stood at the door in the white satin
suit his innocent vanity loved—among other rôles it had
served for Bassanio, Prince Hal, and Antony (over the body
of Cæsar)—with a face of extraordinary solemnity.   Behind
him stood Uncle Nobby.

Joan wasn't quite the Joan that Peter expected.   She was
still wan from her illness and she had grown several inches.
She was as tall as he.   And she was white-faced, so that her
hair seemed blacker than ever, and her eyes were big and
lustrous.   She came walking slowly down the path with her
eyes wide open.   There was a difference, he felt, in her
movement as she came forward, though he could not have
said what it was; there was more grace in Joan now and less
vigour.   But it was the same Joan's voice that cried, "Oh,
Petah! It's lovely!"   She stood before him for a moment
and then threw her arms about him.   She hugged him and
kissed him, and Uncle Nobby knew that it was the smear of
High Cross School that made him wriggle out of her embrace
and not return her kisses.

But immediately he took her by the hand.

"It's better in the playroom, Joan," he said.

"All right, Joan, go on with him," said Oswald, and came
forward to meet Aunt Phyllis.   Aunt Phœbe was on the
staircase a little aloof from these things, as became a woman
of intellect, and behind Aunt Phyllis came Mary, and behind
Mary came the Limpsfield cabman with Aunt Phyllis's trunk

upon his shoulder, and demolished the triumphal arch. But Peter did not learn of that disaster until later, and then he did not mind; it had served its purpose.

The playroom (it was the old nursery rechristened) was indeed better. It was all glorious with paper chains of green and white festooned from corner to corner. On the floor to the right under the window was every toy soldier that Peter possessed drawn up in review array—a gorgeous new Scots Grey band in the front that Oswald had given him. But that was nothing. The big arm-chair had been drawn out into the middle of the room, and on it was *Peter's own lion-skin*. And a piece of red stair-carpet had been put for Joan to go up to the throne upon. And beside the throne was a little table, and on the table was a tinsel robe from Clarkson's and a wonderful gilt crown and a sceptre. Oswald had brought them along that morning.

"The crown is for *you*, Joan!" said Peter. "The sceptre was bought for *you*."

Little white-faced Joan stood stockishly with the crown in one hand and the sceptre in the other. "Put the crown on, Joan," said Peter. "It's yours. It's a rest'ration ceremony."

But she didn't put it on.

"It's lovely—and it's lovely," whispered Joan in a sort of rapture, and stared about her incredulously with her big dark eyes. It was home again—*home*, and Mrs. Pybus had passed like an evil dream in the night. She had never really believed it possible before that Mrs. Pybus could pass away. Even while Aunt Phyllis and Mary had been nursing her, Mrs. Pybus had hovered in the background like something more enduring, waiting for them to pass away as inexplicably as they had come. Joan had heard the whining voice upon the stairs every day and always while she was ill, and once Mrs. Pybus had come and stood by her bedside and remarked like one who maintains an argument, "She'll be 'appy enough 'ere when she's better again."

No more Mrs. Pybus! No more whining scoldings. No more unexpected slaps and having to go to bed supperless. No more measles and uneasy misery in a bed with grey sheets. No more dark dreadful sayings that lurked in the mind like jungle beasts.   She was home, home with Peter, out of that darkness. . . .

And yet—outside was the darkness still. . . .

"Joan," said Peter, trying to rouse her. "There's a cake like a birthday for tea. . . ."

When Oswald came in she was still holding the gilt crown in her hand.

She let Peter take it from her and put it on her head, still staring incredulously about her. She took the sceptre limply. Peter was almost gentle with this strange, staring Joan.

§ 13

For some days Oswald regarded Joan as a grave and thoughtful child. She seemed to be what country people call "old-fashioned." She might have been a changeling. He did not hear her laugh once. And she followed Peter about as if she was his shadow.

Then one day as he cycled over from Chastlands he heard a strange tumult proceeding from a little field on Master's farm, a marvellous mixture of familiar and unfamiliar sounds, an uproar, wonderful as though a tinker's van had met a school treat and the twain had got drunk together. The source of this row was hidden from him by a little coppice, and he dismounted and went through the wood to investigate. Joan and Peter had discovered a disused cowshed with a sloping roof of corrugated iron, and they had also happened upon an abandoned kettle and two or three tin cans. They were now engaged in hurling these latter objects on to the resonant roof, down which they rolled thunderously only to be immediately returned. Joan was no longer a slip of pensive dignity, Peter was no longer a marvel of intellectual curiosities. They were both shrieking their maximum. Oswald had never before suspected Joan of an exceptionally full voice, nor Peter of so vast a wealth of gurgling laughter. "Keep the Pot-A-boilin' " yelled Joan. "Keep the Pot-A-boilin'."

"Hoo!" cried Peter. "Hoo! Go it, Joan. Wow!"

And then, to crown the glory, *the kettle burst*. It came

into two pieces. That was too perfect! The two children
staggered back. Each seized a half of the kettle and kicked
it deliberately. Then they rolled away and fell on their
stomachs amidst the grass, kicking their legs in the air.

But the spirit of rowdyism grows with what it feeds upon.

"Oh, let's do something *reely* awful!" cried Joan. "Let's
do something *reely* awful, Petah!"

Peter's legs became still and stiff with interrogation.

"Oh, Petah!" said Joan. "If I could only smash a window. Frow a brick frough a real window, a Big Glass Window. Just one Glass Window."

"*Where's* a window?" said Peter, evidently in a highly
receptive condition.

From which pitch of depravity Oswald roused him by a
prod in the back. . . .

§ 14

But after that Joan changed rapidly. Colour crept back
into her skin, and a faintly rollicking quality into her bearing. She became shorter again and visibly sturdier, and her
hair frizzed more and stuck out more. Her laugh and her
comments upon the world became an increasingly frequent
embroidery upon the quiet of The Ingle-Nook. She seemed
to have a delusion that Peter was just within earshot, but
only just.

Oswald wondered how far her recent experiences had
vanished from her mind. He thought they might have done
so altogether until one day Joan took him into her confidence
quite startlingly. He was smoking in the little arbour, and
she came and stood beside him so noiselessly that he did not
know she was there until she spoke. She was holding her
hands behind her, and she was regarding the South Downs
with a pensive frown. She was paying him the most beautiful compliment. She had come to consult him.

"Mrs. Pybus said," she remarked, "that every one who
doesn't believe there's a God goes straight to Hell. . . .

"I don't believe there's a God," said Joan, "and Peter
knows there isn't."

For a moment Oswald was a little taken aback by this

simple theology. Then he said, "D'you think Peter's looked everywhere, Joan?"

Then he saw the real point at issue. "One thing you may be sure about, Joan," he said, "and that is that there isn't a Hell. Which is rather a pity in its way, because it would be nice to think of this Mrs. Pybus of yours going there. But there's no Hell at all. There's nothing more dreadful than the dreadful things *in* life. There's no need to worry about Hell."

That he thought was fairly conclusive. But Joan remained pensive, with her eyes still on the distant hills. Then she asked one of those unanswerable children's questions that are all implication, imputation, assumption, misunderstanding, and elision.

"But if there isn't a Hell," said Joan, "what does God do?"

§ 15

It was after Joan had drifted away again from these theological investigations that Oswald, after sitting some time in silence, said aloud and with intense conviction, "I love these children."

He was no longer a stranger in England; he had a living anchorage. He looked out over the autumnal glories of the Weald, dreaming intentions. These children must be educated. They must be educated splendidly. Oswald wanted to see Peter serving the empire. The boy would have pluck —he had already the loveliest brain—and a sense of fun. And Joan? Oswald was, perhaps, not quite so keen in those days upon educating Joan. That was to come later. . . .

After all, the empire, indeed the whole world of mankind, is made up of Joans and Peters. What the empire is, what mankind becomes, is nothing but the sum of what we have made of the Joans and Peters.

CHAPTER THE TENTH

A SEARCHING OF SCHOOLMASTERS

§ 1

SO it was that a systematic intention took hold of the lives of Joan and Peter. They had been snatched apart adventurously and disastrously out of the hands of an aimless and impulsive modernism and dragged off into dusty and decaying corners of the Anglican system. Now they were to be rescued by this Empire worshipper, this disfigured and suffering educational fanatic, and taught——?

What was there in Oswald's mind? His intentions were still sentimental and cloudy, but they were beginning to assume a firm and definite form. Just as the Uganda children were being made into civilized men and women according to the lights and means of the Protectorate government, so these two children had to be made fit rulers and servants of the greatest empire in the world. They had to know all that a ruling race should know, they had to think and act as befitted a leading people. All this seemed to him the simple and obvious necessity of the case. But he was a sick man, fatigued much more readily than most men, given to moods of bitter irritability; he had little knowledge of how he might set about this task, he did not know what help was available and what was impossible. He made enquiries and some were very absurd enquiries; he sought advice and talked to all sorts of people; and meanwhile Joan and Peter spent a very sunny and pleasant November running wild about Limpsfield—until one day Oswald noted as much and packed them off for the rest of the term to Miss Murgatroyd again. The School of St. George and the Venerable Bede was concentrating upon a Christmas production of *Alice in Wonderland*. There could not be very much bad teaching anyhow, and there would be plenty of fun.

How is one to learn where one's children may be educated?

This story has its comic aspects: Oswald went first to the Education Department!

He thought that if one had two rather clever and hopeful children upon whom one was prepared to lavish time and money, an Imperial Education Department would be able to tell an anxious guardian what schools existed for them and the respective claims and merits and inter-relationships of such schools.   But he found that the government which published a six-inch map of the British Isles on which even the meanest outhouse is marked, had no information for the enquiring parent or guardian at all in this matter of schools. An educational map had still to become a part of the equipment of the civilized state.   As it was inconceivable that party capital could be made out of the production of such a map, it was likely to remain a desideratum in Great Britain for many years to come.

In an interview that remained dignified on one side at least until the last, Oswald was referred to the advertisement columns of *The Times* and the religious and educational papers, and to—"a class of educational *agents*," said the official with extreme detachment.   "Usually, of course, people *hear* of schools."

So it was that England still referred back to the happy days of the eighteenth century when our world was small enough for everybody to know and trust and consult everybody, and tell in a safe and confidential manner everything that mattered.

"Oh, my God!" groaned Oswald suddenly, giving way to his internal enemies.   "My God! Here are two children, brilliant children—with plenty of money to be spent on them!   Doesn't the Empire care a twopenny dam what becomes of them?"

"There is an Association of Private Schoolmasters, I believe," said the official, staring at him; "but I don't know if it's any good."

§ 2

Joan was rehearsing a special dance in costume and Peter was word-perfect as the White Knight long before Oswald had found even a hopeful school for either of them. He clung for some time to the delusion that there must exist somewhere a school that would exactly meet Peter's natural and reasonable demand for an establishment where one would learn about "guns and animals, mountains, machines and foreign people," that would give lessons about "the insides of animals" and "how engines work" and "all that sort of thing." The man wanted a school kept by Leonardo da Vinci. When he found a curriculum singularly bare of these vital matters, he began to ask questions.

His questions presently developed into a very tiresome and trying Catechism for Schoolmasters. He did not allow for the fact that most private schoolmasters in England were rather overworked and rather under-exercised men with considerable financial worries. Indeed, he made allowances for no one. He wanted to get on with the education of Joan and Peter—and more particularly of Peter.

His Catechism varied considerably in detail, but always it ran upon the lines of the following questions.

"What sort of boy are you trying to make?"

"How will he differ from an uneducated boy?

"I don't mean in manners, I mean how will he differ in imagination?"

"Yes—I said—imagination."

"Don't you *know* that education is building up an imagination? I thought everybody knew that."

"Then what *is* education doing?"

Here usually the Catechized would become troublesome and the Catechist short and rude. The Catechism would be not so much continued as resumed after incivilities and a silence.

"What sort of curriculum is my ward to go through?"

"Why is he to *do* Latin?"

"Why is he to *do* Greek?"

"Is he going to read or write or speak these languages?"

"Then what is the strange and peculiar benefit of them?"

"What will my ward know about Africa when you have done with him?"

"What will he know about India? Are there any Indian boys here?"

"What will he know about Garibaldi and Italy? About engineering? About Darwin?"

"Will he be able to write good English?"

"Do your boys do much German? Russian? Spanish or Hindustani?"

"Will he know anything about the way the Royal Exchange affects the Empire? But why shouldn't he understand the elementary facts of finance and currency? Why shouldn't every citizen understand what a pound sterling really means? All our everyday life depends on that. What do you teach about Socialism? Nothing! Did you say Nothing? But he may be a member of Parliament some day. Anyhow he'll be a voter."

"But if you can't teach him everything why not leave out these damned classics of yours?" . . .

The record of an irritable man seeking the impossible is not to be dwelt upon too closely. During his search for the boys' school that has yet to exist, Oswald gave way to some unhappy impulses; he made himself distressing and exasperating to quite a number of people. From the first his attitude to scholastic agents was hostile and uncharitable. His appearance made them nervous and defensive from the outset, more particularly the fierce cocking of his hat and the red intensity of his eye. He came in like an accusation rather than an application.

"And tell me, are these all the schools there are?" he would ask, sitting with various printed and copygraphed papers in his hand.

"All we can recommend," the genteel young man in charge would say.

"All you are *paid* to recommend?" Oswald would ask.

"They are the best schools available," the genteel young man would fence.

"Bah!" Oswald would say.

A bad opening. . . .

From the ruffled scholastic agents Oswald would go on in a mood that was bound to ruffle the hopeful school proprietor. Indeed some of these interviews became heated so soon and so extravagantly that there was a complete failure to state even the most elementary facts of the case. Lurid misunderstandings blazed. Uganda got perplexingly into the dispute. From one admirable establishment in Eastbourne Oswald retreated with its principal calling after him from his dignified portico, "I wouldn't take the little nigger at any price."

When his doctor saw him after this last encounter he told him; "You are not getting on as well as you ought to do. You are running about too much. You ought to be resting completely."

So Oswald took a week's rest from school visiting before he tried again.

§ 3

If it had not been for the sense of Joan and Peter growing visibly day by day, Oswald might perhaps have displayed more of the patience of the explorer. But his was rather the urgency of a thirsty traveller who looks for water than the deliberation of a trigonometrical survey. In a little while he mastered the obvious fact that preparatory schools were conditioned by the schools for which they prepared. He found a school at Margate, White Court, which differed rather in quality, and particularly in the quality of its proprietor, than in the nature of its arrangements from the other schools he had been visiting, and to this he committed Peter. Assisted by Aunt Phyllis he found an education for Joan in Highmorton School, ten miles away; he settled himself in a furnished house at Margate to be near them both; and having thus gained a breathing time, he devoted himself to a completer study of the perplexing chaos of upper-class education in England. What was it "up to"? He had his own clear conviction of what it ought to be up to, but the more he saw of existing conditions, the more hopelessly it seemed to be up to either entirely different things or else, in a spirit of intellectual sabotage, up to nothing at all. From the preparatory schools he went on to the great public schools, and from the public schools he went to the universities. He brought to the quest all the unsympathetic detachment of an alien observer and all the angry passion of an anxious patriot. With some suggestions from Matthew Arnold.

"Indolence." "Insincerity." These two words became more and more frequent in his thoughts as he went from one great institution to another. Occasionally the headmasters he talked to had more than a suspicion of his unspoken comments. "Their imaginations are dead within them," said Oswald. "If only they could see the Empire! If only they could forget their little pride and dignity and affectations in the vision of mankind!"

His impressions of headmasters were for the most part taken against a background of white-flannelled boys in playing-fields or grey-flannelled boys in walled court-yards. Eton gave him its river effects and a bright, unforgetable boatman in a coat of wonderful blue; Harrow displayed its view and insisted upon its hill. Physically he liked almost all the schools he saw, except Winchester, which he visited on a rainy day. Almost always there were fine architectural effects; now there was a nucleus of Gothic, now it was time-worn Tudor red brick, now well-proportioned grey Georgian. Most of these establishments had the dignity of age, but Caxton was wealthily new. Caxton was a nest of new buildings of honey-coloured stone; it was growing energetically but tidily; it waved its hand to a busy wilderness of rocks and plants and said, "our botanical garden," to a piece of field and said "our museum group." But it had science laboratories with big apparatus, and the machinery for a small engineering factory. Oswald with an experienced eye approved of its biological equipment. All these great schools were visibly full of life and activity. At times Oswald was so impressed by this life and activity that he felt ashamed of his enquiries; it seemed ungracious not to suppose that all was going well here, that almost any of these schools was good enough and that almost any casual or sentimental considerations, Sydenham family traditions or the like, should suffice to determine which was to have the moulding of Peter. But he had set his heart now on getting to the very essentials of this problem; he was resolved to be blinded by no fair appearances, and though these schools looked as firmly rooted and stoutly prosperous as British oaks and as naturally grown as they, though they had an air of discharging a function as necessary as the beating of a heart and as inevi-

tably, he still kept his grip on the idea that they were artificial things of men's contriving, and still pressed his questions: What are you trying to do? What are you doing?
How are you doing it? How do you fit in to the imperial
scheme of things?

So challenged these various high and head-masters had
most of them the air of men invited to talk of things that
are easier to understand than to say. They were not at all
pompous about their explanations; from first to last Oswald
never discovered the pompous school-master of legend and
history; without exception they seemed anxious to get out of
their gowns and pose as intelligent laymen; but they were not
intelligent laymen, they did not explain, they did not explain,
they waved hands and smiled. They "hoped" they were
"turning out clean English gentlemen." They didn't train
their men specially to any end at all. The aim was to develop a general intelligence, a general goodwill.

"In relation to the empire and its destiny?" said Oswald.

"I should hardly fix it so definitely as that," said Overtone of Hillborough.

"But don't you set before these youngsters some general
aim in life to which they are all to contribute?"

"We rather leave the sort of contribution to them," said
Overtone.

"But you must put something before them of where they
are, where they are to come in, what they belong to?" said
Oswald.

"That lies in the world about them," said Overtone.
"King and country—we don't need to preach such things."

"But what the King signifies—if he signifies anything at
all—and the aim of the country," urged Oswald. "And the
Empire! The Empire—our reality. This greatness of ours
beyond the seas."

"We don't stress it," said Overtone. "English boys are
apt to be suspicious and ironical. Have you read that delightful account of the patriotic lecture in *Stalky and Co?*
Oh, you *should.*"

A common evasiveness characterized all these head-masters
when Oswald demanded the particulars of Peter's curriculum. He wanted to know just the subjects Peter would

study and which were to be made the most important, and
then when these questions were answered he would demand:
"And why do you teach this? What is the particular benefit of that to the boy or the empire? How does this other fit
into your scheme of a clear-minded man?" But it was difficult to get even the first questions answered plainly. From
the very outset he found himself entangled in that long-
standing controversy upon the educational value of Latin
and Greek. His circumstances and his disposition alike disposed him to be sceptical of the value of these shibboleths
of the British academic world. Their share in the time-
table was enormous. Excellent gentlemen who failed to
impress him as either strong-minded or exact, sought to convince him of the pricelessness of Latin in strengthening and
disciplining the mind; Hinks of Carchester, the distinguished
Greek scholar, slipped into his hand at parting a pamphlet
asserting that only Greek studies would make a man write
English beautifully and precisely. Unhappily for his argument Hinks had written his pamphlet neither beautifully
nor precisely. Lippick, irregularly bald and with neglected
teeth, a man needlessly unpleasing to the eye, descanted upon
the Greek spirit, and its blend of wisdom and sensuous
beauty. He quoted Euripides at Oswald and breathed an
antique air in his face—although he knew that Oswald knew
practically no Greek.

"Well," said Oswald, "but compare this," and gave him
back three good minutes of Swahili.

"But what does it mean? It's gibberish to me. A certain melody perhaps."

"In English," Oswald grinned, "you would lose it all.
It is a passage of—oh! quite fantastic beauty." . . .

No arguments, no apologetics, stayed the deepening of
Oswald's conviction that education in the public schools of
Great Britain was not a forward-going process but a habit
and tradition, that these classical school-masters were saying
"nothing like the classics" in exactly the same spirit that
the cobbler said "nothing like leather," because it was the
stuff they had in stock. These subjects were for the most
part being slackly, tediously, and altogether badly taught
to boys who found no element of interest in them, the boys

were as a class acquiring a distaste and contempt for learning thus presented, and a subtle, wide demoralization ensued. They found a justification for cribs and every possible device for shirking work in the utter remoteness and uselessness of these main subjects; the extravagant interest they took in school games was very largely a direct consequence of their intense boredom in school hours.

Such was the impression formed by Oswald. To his eyes these great schools, architecturally so fine, so happy in their out-of-door aspects, so pleasant socially, became more and more visibly whirlpools into which the living curiosity and happy energy of the nation's youth were drawn and caught, and fatigued, thwarted, and wasted. They were beautiful shelters of intellectual laziness—from which Peter must if possible be saved.

But how to save him? There was, Oswald discovered, no saving him completely. Oswald had a profound hostility to solitary education. He knew that except through accidental circumstances of the rarest sort, a private tutor must necessarily be a poor thing. A man who is cheap enough to devote all his time to the education of one boy can have very little that is worth imparting. And education is socialization. Education is the process of making the unsocial individual a citizen. . . .

Oswald's decision upon Caxton in the end, was by no means a certificate of perfection for Caxton. But Caxton had a good if lopsided Modern Side, with big, business-like chemical and physical laboratories, a quite honest and living-looking biological and geological museum, and a pleasant and active layman as headmaster. The mathematical teaching instead of being a drill in examination solutions was carried on in connexion with work in the physical and engineering laboratories. It was true that the "Modern Side" of Caxton taught no history of any sort, ignored logic and philosophy, and, in the severity of its modernity, excluded even that amount of Latin which is needed for a complete mastery of English; nevertheless it did manifestly interest its boys enough to put games into a secondary place. At Caxton one did not see boys playing games as old ladies in hydropaths play patience, desperately and excessively and with a forced enthusiasm, because they had nothing better to do. Even the Caxton school magazine did not give much more than two-thirds of its space to games. So to Caxton Peter went, when Mr. Mackinder of White Court had done his duty by him.

§ 4

Mr. Henderson, the creator of Caxton, was of the large sized variety of schoolmaster, rather round-shouldered and with a slightly persecuted bearing towards parents; his mind seemed busy with many things—buildings, extensions, governors, chapels. Oswald walked with him through a field that was visibly becoming a botanical garden, towards the school playing-fields. Once the schoolmaster stopped, his mind distressed by a sudden intrusive doubt whether the exactly right place had been chosen for what he called a "biological pond." He had to ask various questions of a gardener and give certain directions. But he was listening to Oswald, nevertheless.

Oswald discoursed upon the training of what he called "the fortunate Elite." "We can't properly educate the whole of our community yet, perhaps," he said, "but at least these expensive boys of ours ought to be given everything we can possibly give them. It's to them and their class the Empire will look. Naturally. We ought to turn out boys who know where they are in the world, what the empire is and what it aims to do, who understand something of their responsibilities to Asia and Africa and have a philosophy of life and duty. . . ."

"More of that sort of thing is done," said Mr. Henderson, "than outsiders suppose. Masters talk to boys. Lend them books."

"In an incidental sort of way," said Oswald. "But three-quarters of the boys you miss. . . . Even here, it seems, you must still have your classical side. You must still keep on with Latin and Greek, with courses that will never reach through the dull grind to the stale old culture beyond. Why not drop all that? Why not be modern outright, and leave Eton and Harrow and Winchester and Westminster to go the old ways? Why not teach modern history and modern phi-

losophy in plain English here? Why not question the world
we see, instead of the world of those dead Levantines? Why
not be a modern school altogether?''

The headmaster seemed to consider that idea. But there
were the gravest of practical objections.

''We'd get no scholarships,'' he considered. ''Our boys
would stop at a dead end. They'd get no appointments.
They'd be dreadfully handicapped. . . .

''We're not a complete system,'' said Mr. Henderson.
''No. We're only part of a big circle. We've got to take
what the parents send on to us and we've got to send them
on to college or the professions or what not. It's only part
of a process here—only part of a process.'' . . .

Just as the ultimate excuse of the private schoolmasters
had been that they could do no more than prepare along the
lines dictated for them by the public school, so the public
school waved Oswald on to the university. Thus he came
presently with his questions to the university, to Oxford and
Cambridge, for it was clear these set the pattern of all the
rest in England. He came to Oxford and Cambridge as he
came to the public schools, it must be remembered, with a
fresh mind, for the navy had snatched him straight out of his
preparatory school away from the ordinary routines of an
English education at the tender age of thirteen.

§ 5

Oswald's investigation of Oxford and Cambridge began
even before Peter had entered School House at Caxton. As
early as the spring of 1906, the scarred face under the soft
felt hat was to be seen projecting from one of those brown-
coloured hansom cabs that used to ply in Cambridge. His
bag was on the top and he was going to the University Arms
to instal himself and have ''a good look round the damned
place.'' At times there still hung about Oswald a faint
flavour of the midshipman on leave in a foreign town.

He spent three days watching undergraduates, he prowled
about the streets, and with his face a little on one side,
brought his red-brown eye to bear on the books in bookshop
windows and the display of socks and ties and handkerchiefs

in the outfitters.   In those years the chromatic sock was just
dawning upon the adolescent mind, it had still to achieve the
iridescent glories of its crowning years.   But Oswald found
it symptomatic; *ex pede Herculem.*   He was to be seen surveying the Backs, and standing about among the bookstalls in
the Market Place.   He paddled a Canadian canoe to Byron's
pool, and watched a cheerful group dispose of a huge tea in
the garden of the inn close at hand.   They seemed to joke for
his benefit, neat rather than merry jesting.   So that was
Cambridge, was it?   Then he went on by a tedious cross-
country journey to the slack horrors of one of the Oxford
hotels, and made a similar preliminary survey of the land
here that he proposed to prospect.   There seemed to be more
rubbish and more remainders in the Oxford secondhand
bookshops and less comfort in the hotels; the place was more
self-consciously picturesque, there was less of Diana and
more of Venus about its beauty, a rather blowsy Gothic
Venus with a bad tooth or so.   So it impressed Oswald.   The
glamour of Oxford, sunrise upon Magdalen tower, Oriel,
Pater, and so forth, were lost upon Oswald's toughened mind;
he had spent his susceptible adolescence on a battleship, and
the sunblaze of Africa had given him a taste for colour like
a taste for raw rye whiskey. . . .

He walked about the perfect garden of St. Giles' College
and beat at the head of Blepp, the senior tutor, whose acquaintance he had made in the Athenaeum, with his stock
questions.   The garden of St. Giles' College is as delicate as
fine linen in lavender; its turf is supposed to make American
visitors regret the ancestral trip in the *Mayflower* very bitterly; Blepp had fancied that in a way it answered Oswald.
But Oswald turned his glass eye and his ugly side to the
garden, it might just as well have not been there, and kept
to his questioning; ''What are we making of our boys here?
What are they going to make of the Empire?   What are you
teaching them?   What are you not teaching them?   How
are you working them?   And why?   Why?   What's the
idea of it all?   Suppose presently when this fine October in
history ends, that the weather of the world breaks up; what
will you have ready for the storm?''

Blepp felt the ungraciousness of such behaviour acutely.

It was like suddenly asking the host of some great beautiful dinner-party whether he earned his income honestly. Like shouting it up the table at him. But Oswald was almost as comfortable a guest for a don to entertain as a spur in one's trouser pocket. Blepp did his best to temper the occasion by an elaborate sweet reasonableness.

"Don't you think there's something in our atmosphere?" he began.

"I don't like your atmosphere. The Oxford shops seem grubby little shops. The streets are narrow and badly lit."

"I wasn't thinking of the shops."

"It's where the youngsters buy their stuff, their furniture, and as far as I can see, most of their ideas."

"You'll be in sympathy with the American lady who complained the other day about our want of bathrooms," Blepp sneered.

"Well, *why not?*" said Oswald outrageously.

Blepp shrugged his shoulders and looked for sympathy at the twisted brick chimneys of St. Giles'.

Oswald became jerkily eloquent. "We've got an empire sprawling all over the world. We're a people at grips with all mankind. And in a few years these few thousand men here and at Cambridge and a few thousand in the other universities, have practically to be the mind of the empire. Think of the problems that press upon us as an empire. All the nations sharpen themselves now like knives. Are we making the mentality to solve the Irish riddle here? Are we preparing any outlook for India here? What are you doing here to get ready for such tasks as these?"

"How can I show you the realities that go on beneath the surface?" said Blepp. "You don't see what is brewing to-day, the talk that goes on in the men's rooms, the mutual polishing of minds. Look not at our formal life but our informal life. Consider one college, consider for example Balliol. Think of the Jowett influence, the Milner group— not blind to the empire there, were we? Even that fellow Belloc. A saucy rogue, but good rich stuff. All out of just one college. These are things one cannot put in a syllabus. These are things that defeat statistics."

"But that is no reason why you should put chaff and dry bones into the syllabus," said Oswald. . . .

"This place," said Oswald, and waved his arm at the great serenity of St. Giles', "it has the air of a cathedral close. It might be a beautiful place of retirement for sad and weary old men. It seems a thousand miles from machinery, from great towns and the work of the world."

"Would you have us teach in a foundry?"

"I'd have you teaching something about the storm that seems to me to be gathering in the world of labour. These youngsters here are going to be the statesmen, the writers and teachers, the lawyers, the high officials, the big employers, of tomorrow. But all that world of industry they have to control seems as far off here as if it were on another planet. You're not talking about it, you're not thinking about it. You're teaching about the Gracchi and the Greek fig trade. You're magnifying that pompous bore Cicero and minimizing —old Salisbury for example—who was a far more important figure in history—a greater man in a greater world."

"With all respect to his memory," said Blepp, "but *good Lord!*"

"Much greater. Your classics put out your perspective. Dozens of living statesmen are greater than Cicero. Of course our moderns are greater. If only because of the greatness of our horizons. Oxford and Cambridge ought to be the learning and thinking part of the whole empire, twin hemispheres in the imperial brain. But when I think of the size of the imperial body, its hundreds of nations, its thousands of cities, its tribes, its vast extension round and about the world, the immense problem of it, and then of the size and quality of *this*, I'm reminded of the Atlantosaurus. You've heard of the beast? Its brain was smaller than the ganglia of its rump. No doubt its brain thought itself quite up to its job. It wasn't. Something ate up the Atlantosaurus. These two places, this place, ought to be big enough, and bigly conceived enough, to irradiate our whole world with ideas. All the empire. They ought to dominate the minds of hundreds of millions of men. And they dominate nothing. Leave India and Africa out of it. They do not even dominate England. Think only of your labour at home, of

that huge blind Titan, whom you won't understand, which
doesn't understand you——''

"There again," interrupted Blepp sharply, "you are simply ignorant of what is going on here. Because Oxford has
a certain traditional beauty and a decent respect for the past,
because it doesn't pose and assert itself rawly, you are offended. You do not realize how active we can be, how up-
to-date we are. It wouldn't make us more modern in spirit
if we lived in enamelled bathrooms and lectured in corrugated iron sheds. That isn't modernity. That's your mistake. In respect to this very question of labour, we *have*
got our labour contact. Have you never heard of Ruskin
College? Founded here by an American of the most modern
type, one Vrooman." He repeated the name "Vrooman,"
not as though he loved it but as though he thought it ought
to appeal to Oswald. "I think he came from Chicago."
Surely a Teutonic name from Chicago was modern enough
to satisfy any one! "It is a college of real working-men, of
the Trade Union leader type, the actual horny-handed article,
who come up here—I suppose because they don't agree with
your idea that we deal only in the swathings of mummies.
They at any rate think that we have something to tell the
modern world, something worth their learning. Perhaps
they know their needs better than you do."

Oswald was momentarily abashed. He expressed a desire
to visit this Ruskin College.

Blepp explained he was not himself connected with the
college. "Not quite my line," said Blepp parenthetically;
but he could arrange for a visit under proper guidance, and
presently under the wing of a don of radical tendencies Oswald went.

It seemed to him the most touching and illuminating thing
in Oxford. It reminded him of *Jude the Obscure*.

Ruskin College was sheltered over some stables in a back
street, and it displayed a small group of oldish young men,
for the most part with north-country accents, engaged in
living under austere circumstances—they paid scarcely anything and did all the housework—and doing their best to get
hold of the precious treasure of knowledge and understanding they were persuaded Oxford possessed. They had come

up on their savings by virtue of extraordinary sacrifices.
Graduation in any of the Oxford schools was manifestly impossible to them, if only on account of the Greek bar; the
university had no use for these respectful pilgrims and no
intention of encouraging more of them, and the "principal,"
Mr. Dennis Hird, in the teeth of much opposition, was vamp-
ing a sort of course for them with the aid of a few liberal-
minded junior dons who delivered a lecture when their proper
engagements permitted. There was a vague suggestion of
perplexity in the conversation of the two students with whom
Oswald talked. This tepid drip of disconnected instruction
wasn't what they had expected, but then, what had they expected? Vrooman, the idealist who had set the thing going,
had returned to America leaving much to be explained.
Oswald dined with Blepp at St. Osyth's that night, and
spoke over the port in the common room of these working
men who were "dunning Oxford for wisdom."

Jarlow, the wit of the college, who had been entertaining
the company with the last half-dozen Spoonerisms he had invented, was at once reminded of a little poem he had made,
and he recited it. It was supposed to be by one of these
same Ruskin College men, and his artless rhyming of "Socrates" and "fates" and "sides" and "Euripides," combined
with a sort of modest pretentiousness of thought and intention, was very laughable indeed. Everybody laughed mer-
rily except Oswald.

"That's quite one of your best, Jarlow," said Blepp.

But Oxford had been rubbing Oswald's fur backwards
that day. The common room became aware of him sitting
up stiffly and regarding Jarlow with an evil expression.

"Why the Devil," said Oswald, addressing himself point-
edly and querulously to Jarlow, "shouldn't a working-man
say 'So-*crates?*' We all say 'Paris.' These men do Oxford
too much honour."

§ 6

Perhaps there was a sort of necessity in the educational
stagnation of England during those crucial years before the
Great War. All the influential and important people of the

country were having a thoroughly good time, and if there was a growing quarrel between worker and employer no one saw any reason in that for sticking a goad into the teacher. The disposition of the mass of men is always on the side of custom against innovation. The clear-headed effort of yesterday tends always to become the unintelligent routine of tomorrow. So long as we get along we go along. In the less exacting days of good Queen Victoria the educational processes of Great Britain had served well enough; they still went on because the necessity for a more thorough, coherent, and lucid education had still to be made glaringly manifest. Few people understood the discontent of a Ray Lankester, the fretfulness of a Kipling. Foresight dies when the imagination slumbers. Only catastrophe can convince the mass of people of the possibility of catastrophe. The system had the inertia of a spinning top. The most thoroughly and completely mis-taught of one generation became the mis-teachers of the next. "Learn, obey, create nothing, initiate nothing, have no troublesome doubts," ran the rules of scholarly discretion. "Prize-boy, scholar, fellow, don, pedagogue; prize-boy, scholar, fellow, don"—so spun the circle of the schools. Into that relentless circle the bright, curious little Peters, who wanted to know about the insides of animals and the way of machines and what was happening, were drawn; the little Joans, too, were being drawn. The best escaped complete deadening, they found a use for themselves, but life usually kept them too busy and used them too hard for them ever to return to teach in college or school of the realities they had experienced. And so as Joan and Peter grew up, Oswald became more and more tolerant of a certain rabble rout of inky outsiders who, without authority and dignity, were at least putting living ideas of social function and relationship in the way of adolescent enquiry.

It became manifest to Oswald that the real work of higher education, the discussion of God, of the state and of sex, of all the great issues in life, while it was being elaborately evaded in the formal education of the country, was to a certain extent being done, thinly, unsatisfactorily, pervertedly even by the talk of boys and girls among themselves, by the casual suggestions of tutors, friends, and chance acquaintances, and more particularly by a number of irresponsible journalists and literary men. For example though the higher education of the country afforded no comprehensive view of social inter-relationship at all, the propaganda of the socialists did give a scheme—Oswald thought it was a mistaken and wrong-headed scheme—of economic interdependence. If the school showed nothing to their children of the Empire but a few tiresome maps, Kipling's stories, for all his Jingo violence, did at least breathe something of its living spirit. As Joan and Peter grew up they ferreted out and brought to their guardian's knowledge a school of irresponsible contemporary teachers, Shaw, Wells and the other Fabian Society pamphleteers, the Belloc-Chesterton group, Cunninghame Graham, Edward Carpenter, Orage of *The New Age*, Galsworthy, Cannan; the suffragettes, and the like. If the formal teachers lacked boldness these strange self-appointed instructors seemed to be nothing if not bold. *The Freewoman*, which died to rise again as *The New Freewoman*, existed it seemed chiefly to mention everything that a young lady should never dream of mentioning. Aunt Phœbe's monthly, *Wayleaves*, in its green and purple cover, made a gallant effort to outdo that valiant weekly. Aunt Phœbe was a bright and irresponsible assistant in the education of Oswald's wards. She sowed the house with strange books whenever she came to stay with them. Oswald found Joan reading Oscar Wilde when she was seventeen. He did not interrupt her reading, for he could not imagine how to set about the interruption. Later on he discovered a most extraordinary volume by Havelock Ellis lying in the library, an impossible volume. He read in it a little and then put it down. Afterwards he could not believe that book existed. He thought he must have dreamt about it, or dreamt the contents into it. It seemed incredible that Aunt Phœbe——! . . . He was never quite sure. When he went to look for it again it had vanished, and he did not like to ask for it.

More and more did this outside supplement of education in England press upon Oswald's reluctant attention. Most of these irregulars he disliked by nature and tradition. None of them had the dignity and restraint of the great Victorians, the Corinthian elegance of Ruskin, the Teutonic hammer-blows of Carlyle. Shaw he understood was a lean, red-haired Pantaloon, terribly garrulous and vain; Belloc and Chesterton thrust a shameless obesity upon the public atten-tion; the social origins of most of the crew were appalling, Bennett was a solicitor's clerk from the potteries, Wells a counter-jumper, Orage came from Leeds. Oswald had seen a picture of Wells by Max that confirmed his worst suspi-cions about these people; a heavy bang of hair assisted a cascade moustache to veil a pasty face that was broad rather than long and with a sly, conceited expression; the creature still wore a long and crumpled frock coat, acquired no doubt during his commercial phase, and rubbed together two large, clammy, white, misshapen hands. Except for Cunninghame Graham there was not a gentleman, as Oswald understood the word, among them all. But these writers got hold of the in-telligent young because they did at least write freely where the university teacher feared to tread. They wrote, he thought, without any decent restraint. They seasoned even wholesome suggestions with a flavour of scandalous excite-ment. It remained an open question in his mind whether they did more good by making young people think or more harm by making them think wrong. Progressive dons he found maintained the former opinion. With that support Oswald was able to follow his natural disposition and leave the reading of his two wards unrestrained.

And they read—and thought, to such purpose as will be presently told.

§ 7

But here Justice demands an interlude.

Before we go on to tell of how Joan and Peter grew up to adolescence in these schools that Oswald—assisted by Aunt Phyllis in the case of Joan—found for them, Mr. Mackin-der must have his say, and make the Apology of the School-master. He made it to Oswald when first Oswald visited him and chose his school out of all the other preparatory schools, to be Peter's. He appeared as a little brown man with a hedgehog's nose and much of the hedgehog's indignant note in his voice. He came, shy and hostile, into the drawing-room in which Oswald awaited him. It was, by the by, the most drawing-room-like drawing-room that Oswald had ever been in; it was as if some one had said to a furniture dealer, "People expect me to have a drawing-room. Please let me have exactly the sort of drawing-room that people expect." It displayed a grand piano towards the French window, a large standard lamp with an enormous shade, a pale silk sofa, an Ottoman, a big fern in an ornate pot, and water-colours of Venetian lagoons. In the midst of it all stood Mr. Mackinder, in a highly contracted state, mutely radiating an interrogative "Well?"

"I'm looking for a school for my nephew," said Oswald.

"You want him here?"

"Well— Do you mind if first of all I see something of the school?"

"We're always open to investigation," said Mr. Mackinder, bitterly.

"I want to do the very best I can for this boy. I feel very strongly that it's my duty to him and the country to turn him out—as well as a boy can be turned out."

Mr. Mackinder nodded his head and continued to listen.

This was something new in private schoolmasters. For the most part they had opened themselves out to Oswald, like sunflowers, like the receptive throats of nestlings. They had embraced and silenced him by the wealth of their assurances.

"I have two little wards," he said. "A boy and a girl. I want to make all I can of them. They ought to belong to the Elite. The strength of a country—of an empire—depends ultimately almost entirely on its Elite. This empire isn't overwhelmed with intelligence, and most of the talk we hear about the tradition of statesmanship——"

Mr. Mackinder made a short snorting noise through his nose that seemed to indicate his opinion of contemporary statesmanship.

"You see I take this schooling business very solemnly. These upper-class schools, I say, these schools for the sons of prosperous people and scholarship winners, are really Elite-making machines. They really make—or fail to make —the Empire. That makes me go about asking schoolmasters a string of questions. Some of them don't like my questions. Perhaps they are too elementary. I ask: what is this education of yours up to? What is the design of the whole? What is this preparation of yours for? This is called a Preparatory School. You lay the foundations. What is the design of the building for which these foundations are laid?''

He paused, determined to make Mr. Mackinder say something before he discoursed further.

''It isn't so simple as that,'' was wrung from Mr. Mackinder. ''Suppose we just walk round the school. Suppose we just see the sort of place it is and what we are doing here. Then perhaps you'll be able to see better what we contribute —in the way of making a citizen.''

The inspection was an unusually satisfactory one. White Court was one of the few private schools Oswald had seen that had been built expressly for its purpose. Its class rooms were well lit and well arranged, its little science museum seemed good and well arranged and well provided with diagrams; its gymnasium was businesslike; its wall blackboards unusually abundant and generously used, and everything was tidy. Nevertheless the Catechism for Schoolmasters was not spared. ''Now,'' said Oswald, ''now for the curriculum?''

''We live in the same world with most other English schools,'' Mr. Mackinder sulked. ''This is a preparatory school.''

''What are called English subjects?''

''Yes.''

''How do you teach geography?''

''With books and maps.''

Oswald spoke of lantern slides and museum visits. The cinema had yet to become an educational possibility.

''I do what I can,'' said Mr. Mackinder; ''I'm not a millionaire.''

''Do you *do* classics?''

''We do Latin. Clever boys do a little Greek. In preparation for the public schools.''

''Grammar of course? . . .

''What else? . . .

''French, German, Latin, Greek, bits of mathematics, botany, geography, bits of history, book-keeping, music lessons, some water-colour painting; it's very mixed," said Oswald.

"It's miscellaneous."

Mr. Mackinder roused himself to a word of defence: "The boys don't specialize."

"But this is a diet of scraps," said Oswald, reviving one of the most controversial topics of the catechism. "Nothing can be done thoroughly."

"We are necessarily elementary."

"It's rather like the White Knight in *Alice in Wonderland* packing his luggage for nowhere."

"We have to teach what is required of us," said Mr. Mackinder.

"But what is education up to?" asked Oswald.

As Mr. Mackinder offered no answer to that riddle, Oswald went on. "What *is* Education in England up to, anyhow? In Uganda we knew what we were doing. There was an idea in it. The old native tradition was breaking up. We taught them to count and reckon English fashion, to read and write, we gave them books and the Christian elements, so that they could join on to our civilization and play a part in the great world that was breaking up their little world. We didn't teach them anything that didn't serve mind or soul or body. We saw the end of what we were doing. But half this school teaching of yours is like teaching in a dream. You don't teach the boy what he wants to know and needs to know. You spend half his time on calculations he has no use for, mere formal calculations, and on this dead language stuff——! It's like trying to graft mummy steak on living flesh. It's like boiling fossils for soup."

Mr. Mackinder said nothing.

"And damn it!" said Oswald petulantly; "your school is about as good a school as I've seen or am likely to see. . . .

"I had an idea," he went on, "of just getting the very best out of those two youngsters—the boy especially—of making every hour of his school work a gift of so much power or skill or subtlety, of opening the world to him like a magic book. . . . The boy's tugging at the magic covers. . . ."

He stopped short.

"There are no such schools," said Mr. Mackinder compactly. "This is as good a school as you will find."

And there he left the matter for the time. But in the evening he dined with Oswald at his hotel, and it may be that iced champagne had something to do with a certain relaxation from his afternoon restraint. Oswald had already arranged about Peter, but he wanted the little man to talk more. So he set him an example. He talked of his own life. He represented it as a life of disappointment and futility. "I envy you your life of steadfast usefulness." He spoke of his truncated naval career and his disfigurement. Of the years of uncertainty that had followed. He talked of the ambitions and achievements of other men, of the large hopes and ambitions of youth.

"I too," said Mr. Mackinder, warming for a moment, and then left his sentence unfinished. Oswald continued to generalize. . . .

"All life, I suppose, is disappointment—is anyhow largely disappointment," said Mr. Mackinder presently.

"We get something done."

"Five per cent., ten per cent., of what we meant to do."

The schoolmaster reflected. Oswald refilled his glass for him.

"To begin with I thought, none of these other fellows really know how to run a school. I will, I said, make a nest of Young Paragons. I will take a bunch of boys and get the best out of them, the best possible; watch them, study them, foster them, make a sort of boy so that the White Court brand shall be looked for and recognized. . . ."

He sipped his faintly seething wine and put down the glass.

"Five per cent.," he said; "ten per cent., perhaps." He touched his lips with his dinner-napkin. "I have turned out some creditable boys."

"Did you make any experiments in the subjects you taught?"

"At first. But one of the things we discover in life as we grow past the first flush of beginning, is just how severely we are conditioned. We are conditioned. We seem to be free. And we are in a net. You have criticized my curriculum today pretty severely, Mr. Sydenham. Much that you say is absolutely right. It is wasteful, discursive,

ineffective. Yes. . . . But in my place I doubt if you could
have made it much other than it is. . . .

"One or two things I do. Latin grammar here is taught
on lines strictly parallel with the English and French and
German—that is to say, we teach languages comparatively.
It was troublesome to arrange, but it makes a difference mentally. And I take a class in Formal Logic; English teaching
is imperfect, expression is slovenly, without that. The boys
write English verse. The mathematical teaching too, is as
modern as the examining boards will let it be. Small things,
perhaps. But you do not know the obstacles.

"Mr. Sydenham, your talk today has reminded me of all
the magnificent things I set out to do at White Court, when
I sank my capital in building White Court six and twenty
years ago. When I found that I couldn't control the choice
of subjects, when I found that in that matter I was ruled by
the sort of schools and colleges the boys had to go on to and
by the preposterous examinations they would have to pass,
then I told myself, 'at least I can cultivate their characters
and develop something like a soul in them, instead of crush-
ing out individuality and imagination as most schools do. . . .'

"Well, I think I have a house of clean-minded and cheerful and willing boys, and I think they all tell the truth. . . ."

"I don't know what I'm to do with the religious teaching
of these two youngsters of mine," said Oswald abruptly.
"Practically, they're Godless."

Mr. Mackinder did not speak for a little while. Then he
said, "It is almost unavoidable, under existing conditions,
that the religious teaching in a school should be—formal and
orthodox.

"For my own part—I'm liberal," said Mr. Mackinder,
and added, "very liberal. Let me tell you, Mr. Sydenham,
exactly how I see things."

He paused for a moment as if he collected his views.

"If a little boy has grown up in a home, in the sort of
home which one might describe as God-fearing, if he has
not only heard of God but seen God as a living influence
upon the people about him, then—then, I admit, you have
something real. He will believe in God. He will know God.
God—simply because of the faith about him—will be a know-

able reality.   God is a faith.   In men.   Such a boy's world
will fall into shape about the idea of God.   He will take God
as a matter of course.   Such a boy can be religious from
childhood—yes. . . But there are very few such homes."

"Less, probably, than there used to be?"

Mr. Mackinder disavowed an answer by a gesture of hands
and shoulders.   He went on, frowning slightly as he talked.
He wanted to say exactly what he thought.   "For all other
boys, Mr. Sydenham, God, for all practical purposes, does
not exist.   Their worlds have been made without him; they
do not think in terms of him; and if he is to come into their
lives at all he must come in from the outside—a discovery,
like a mighty rushing wind.   By what is called Conversion.
At adolescence.   Until that happens you must build the soul
on pride, on honour, on the decent instincts.   It is all you
have.   And the less they hear about God the better.   They
will not understand.   It will be a cant to them—a kind of
indelicacy.   The two greatest things in the world have been
the most vulgarized.   God and sex. . . If I had my own
way I would have no religious services for my boys at all."

"Instead of which?"

Mr. Mackinder paused impressively before replying.

"The local curate is preparing two of my elder boys for
Confirmation at the present time."

He gazed gloomily at the tablecloth.   "If one could do as
one liked!" he said.   "If only one could do as one liked!"

But now Oswald was realizing for the first time the eternal tragedy of the teacher, that sower of unseen harvests,
that reaper of thistles and the wind, that serf of custom,
that subjugated rebel, that feeble, persistent antagonist of
the triumphant things that rule him.   And behind that immediate tragedy Oswald was now apprehending for the first
time something more universally tragic, an incessantly recurring story of high hopes and a grey ending; the story of
boys and girls, clean and sweet-minded, growing up into life,
and of the victory of world inertia, of custom drift and the
tarnishing years.

Mr. Mackinder spoke of his own youth.   Quite early in
life had come physical humiliations, the realization that his
slender and delicate physique debarred him from most ac-

tive occupations, and his resolve to be of use in some field where his weak and undersized body would be at no great disadvantage. "I made up my mind that teaching should be my religion," he said.

He told of the difficulties he had encountered in his attempts to get any pedagogic science or training. "This is the most difficult profession in the world," he said, "and the most important. Yet it is not studied; it has no established practice; it is not endowed. Buildings are endowed and institutions, but not teachers." And in Great Britain, in the schools of the classes that will own and rule the country, ninety-nine per cent. of the work was done by unskilled workmen, by low-grade, genteel women and young men. In America, the teachers were nearly all women. "How can we expect to raise a nation nearly as good as we might do under such a handicap?" He had read and learnt what he could about teaching; he had served for small salaries in schools that seemed living and efficient; finally he had built his own school with his own money. He had had the direst difficulties in getting a staff together. "What can one expect?" he said. "We pay them hardly better than shop assistants—less than bank clerks. You see the relative importance of things in the British mind." What hope or pride was there to inspire an assistant schoolmaster to do good work?

"I thought I could make a school different from all other schools, and I found I had to make a school like most other fairly good schools. I had to work for what the parents required of me, and the ideas of the parents had been shaped by their schools. I had never dreamt of the immensity of the resistance these would offer to constructive change. In this world there are incessant changes, but most of them are landslides or epidemics. . . . I tried to get away from stereotyping examinations. I couldn't. I tried to get away from formal soul-destroying religion. I couldn't. I tried to get a staff of real assistants. I couldn't. I had to take what came. I had to be what was required of me. . . .

"One works against time always. Over against the Parents. It is not only the boys one must educate, but the parents—let alone one's self. The parents demand impossible things. I have been asked for Greek and for book-keeping by double-entry by the same parent. I had—I had to leave the matter—as if I thought such things were pos-sible. After all, the Parent is master. One can't run a school without boys.''

"You'd get *some* boys," said Oswald.

"Not enough. I'm up against time. The school has to pay.''

"Can't you hold out for a time? Run the school on a handful of oatmeal?''

"It's running it on an overdraft I don't fancy. You're not a married man, Mr. Sydenham, with sons to consider.''

"No," said Oswald shortly. "But I have these wards. And, after all, there's not only today but tomorrow. If the world is going wrong for want of education——. If you don't give it your sons will suffer.''

"Tomorrow, perhaps. But today comes first. I'm up against time. Oh, I'm up against time.''

He sat with his hands held out supine on the table before him.

"I started my school twenty-seven years ago next Hilary. And it seems like yesterday. When I started it I meant it to be something memorable in schools. . . . I jumped into it. I thought I should swim about. . . . It was like jumping into the rapids of Niagara. I was seized, I was rushed along. . . . Ai! Ai! . . .''

"Time's against us all," said Oswald. "I suppose the next glacial age will overtake us long before we're ready to fight out our destiny.''

"If you want to feel the generations rushing to waste," said Mr. Mackinder, "like rapids—like rapids—you must put your heart and life into a private school.''

CHAPTER THE ELEVENTH

ADOLESCENCE

§ 1

"THE generations rushing to waste like rapids—like rapids. . . ."

Ten years later Oswald found himself repeating the words of the little private schoolmaster.

He was in the gravest perplexity. Joan was now nineteen and a half and Peter almost of age, and they had had a violent quarrel. They would not live in the same house together any longer, they declared. Peter had gone back overnight to Cambridge on his motor bicycle; Joan's was out of order—an embittering addition to her distress—and she had cycled on her push bicycle over the hills that morning to Bishop's Stortford to catch the Cambridge train. And Oswald was left to think over the situation and all that had led to it.

He sat alone in the May sunshine in the little arbour that overlooked his rose garden at Pelham Ford, trying to grasp all that had happened to these stormy young people since he had so boldly taken the care of their lives into his hands. He found himself trying to retrace the phases of their upbringing, and his thoughts went wide and far over the problem of human training. Suddenly he had discovered his charges adult. Joan had stood before him, amazingly grown up—a woman, young, beautiful, indignant.

Who could have foretold ten years ago that Joan would have been declaring with tears in her voice but much stiffness in her manner, that she had "stood enough" from Peter, and calling him "weak."

"He insults all my friends, Nobby," she had said, "and as for his——. He's like that puppy we had who dug up rotten bones we had never suspected, all over the garden.

"Oh! *his women are horrible!*" Joan had cried. . . .

§ 2

Oswald's choice of a permanent home at Pelham Ford had been largely determined by the educational requirements of Joan and Peter. While Peter had been at White Court and Joan at Highmorton School twelve miles away, Oswald had occupied a not very well furnished "furnished house" at Margate. When Peter, after an inquisition by Oswald into English Public Schools, had been awarded at last as a sort of prize, with reservations, to Caxton, Oswald—convinced now by his doctors and his own disagreeable experiences that he must live in England for the rest of his life if he was to hope for any comfort or activity—decided to set up a permanent home with a garden and buildings that would be helpful through days of dullness in some position reasonably accessible from London, Caxton and Margate, and later on from Cambridge, to which they were both predestined. After some search he found the house he needed in the pretty little valley of the Rash, that runs north-eastward from Ware. The Stubland aunts still remained as tenants of The Ingle-Nook, and made it a sort of alternative home for the youngsters.

The country to the north and east of Ware is a country of miniature gorges with frequent water-splashes. The stream widens and crosses the road in a broad, pebbly shallow of ripples just at the end of Pelham Ford, there is a causeway with a white handrail for bicycles and foot passengers beside the ford, and beyond it is an inn and the post office and such thatched, whitewashed homes as constitute the village. Then beyond comes a row of big trees and the high red wall and iron gates of this house Oswald had taken. The church of Pelham Ford is a little humped, spireless building up the hill to the left. The stream brawls along for a time beside the road. Through the gates of the house one looks across a lawn barred by the shadows of big trees, at a blazing flower-garden that goes up a series of terraces to the little red tiled summerhouse that commands the view of the valley. The house is to the right and near the road, a square comfortable eighteenth-century red-brick house with ivy on its shadowed side and fig trees and rose trees towards

the sun.   It has a classical portico, and a grave but friendly
expression.

The Margate house had been a camp, but this was furnished
with some deliberation.   Oswald had left a miscellany of
possessions behind him in Uganda which Muir had packed
and sent on after him when it was settled that there could
be no return to Africa.   The hall befitted the home of a
member of the Plantain Club; African spoils adorned it,
three lions' heads, a white rhinoceros head, elephants' feet,
spears, gourds, tusks; in the midst a large table took the
visitor's hat and stick, and bore a large box for the post.
Out of this hall opened a little close study Oswald rarely
used except when Joan and Peter and their friends were at
home and a passage led to a sunny, golden-brown library possessing three large southward windows on the garden, a room
it had pleased him greatly to furnish, and in which he did
most of his writing.   It had a parquet floor and Oriental rugs
like sunlit flower-beds.   Across the hall, opposite the study,
was a sort of sittingroom-livingroom which was given over
to Joan and Peter.   It had been called the Schoolroom in the
days when their holiday visits had been mitigated by the
presence of some temporary governess or tutor, and now that
those disciplined days were over their two developing personalities still jostled in the one apartment.   A large pleasant drawing-room and a dining-room completed the tale of
rooms on the ground floor.

In this room across the hall there was much that would
have repaid research on the part of Oswald.   The room was
a joint room only when Joan and Peter were without guests
in the house.   Whenever there were guests, whether they
were women or men, Joan turned out and the room became
a refuge or rendezvous for Peter.   It was therefore rather
Peter's than Joan's.   Here as in most things it was Peter's
habit to prevail over Joan.   But she had her rights; she had
had a voice in the room's decoration, a share in its disorder.
The upper bookshelves to the right of the fireplace were hers
and the wall next to that.   Against this stood her bureau,
locked and secure, over and against Peter's bureau.   Oswald
had given them these writing desks three Christmasses ago.
But the mess on the table under the window was Peter's,

and Peter had more than his fair share of the walls.   The stuffed birds and animals and a row of sculls were the result of a "Mooseum" phase of Peter's when he was fourteen. The water-colour pictures were Peter's.   The hearthrug was the lion-skin that Peter still believed had been brought for him from Nairobi by Oswald.

Peter could caricature, and his best efforts were framed here; his style was a deliberate compliment to the incomparable Max.   He had been very successful twice in bringing out the latent fierceness of Joan; one not ungraceful effort was called "The Scalp Dance," the other, less pleasing to its subject, represented Joan in full face with her hands behind her back and her feet apart, "Telling the Whole Troof." Joan, alas! had no corresponding skill for a retort, but she had framed an enlargement of a happy snapshot of Peter on the garden wall.   She had stood below and held her camera up so that Peter's boots and legs were immense and his head dwindled to nothing in perspective.   So seen, he became an embodiment of masculine brutality.   The legend was, "The Camera can Detect what our Eyes Cannot."

One corner of this room was occupied by a pianola piano and a large untidy collection of classical music rolls; right and left of the fireplace the bookshelves bore an assortment of such literature as appealed in those days to animated youth, classics of every period from Plato to Shaw, and such moderns as Compton Mackenzie, Masefield, Gilbert Cannan and Ezra Pound.   Back numbers of *The Freewoman, The New Age, The New Statesman,* and *The Poetry Review* mingled on the lowest shelf.   There was a neat row of philosophical textbooks in the Joan section; Joan for no particular reason was taking the moral science tripos; and a microscope stood on Peter's table, for he was biological. . . .

§ 3

Oswald's domestic arrangements had at first been a grave perplexity.   In Uganda he had kept house very well with a Swahili over-man and a number of "boys"; in Margate this sort of service was difficult to obtain, and the holiday needs of the children seemed to demand a feminine influence of the governess-companion type, a "lady." A succession of refined feminine personalities had intersected these years of Oswald's life. They were all ladies by birth and profession, they all wore collars supported by whalebone about their necks, and they all developed and betrayed a tenderness for Oswald that led to a series of flights to the Climax Club and firm but generous dismissals. Oswald's ideas of matrimony were crude and commonplace; he could imagine himself marrying no one but a buxom young woman of three-and-twenty, and he could not imagine any buxom young woman of three-and-twenty taking a healthy interest in a man over forty with only half a face and fits of fever and fretfulness. When these ladies one after another threw out their gentle intimations he had the ingratitude to ascribe their courage to a sense of his own depreciated matrimonial value. This caused just enough indignation to nerve him to the act of dismissal. But on each occasion he spent the best part of a morning and made serious inroads upon the club notepaper before the letter of dismissal was framed, and he always fell back upon the stock lie that he was going abroad to a Kur-Ort and was going to lock up the house. On each occasion the house was locked up for three or four weeks, and Oswald lived a nomadic existence until a fresh lady could be found. Finally God sent him Mrs. Moxton.

She came in at Margate during an interregnum while Aunt Phyllis was in control. Aunt Phyllis after a reflective interview passed her on to Oswald. She was more like Britannia than one could have imagined possible; her face was perhaps a little longer and calmer and her pink chins rather more numerous.

"I understand," she said, seating herself against Oswald's desk, "that you are in need of some one to take charge of your household."

"Did you—hear?" began Oswald.

"It's the talk of Margate," she said calmly.

"So I understand that you are prepared to be the lady——"

"I am *not* a lady," said Mrs. Moxton with a faint asperity.

"I beg your pardon," said Oswald.

"I am a housekeeper," she said, as who should say: "at

least give me credit for that." "I have had experience with a single gentleman."

There seemed to be an idea in it.

"I was housekeeper to the late Mr. Justice Benlees for some years, until he died, and then unhappily, being in ·receipt of a small pension from him, I took to keeping a boarding-house. Winnipeg House. On the Marine Parade. A most unpleasant and anxious experience." Her note of indignation returned, and the clear pink of her complexion deepened by a shade. "A torrent of Common People."

"Exactly," said Oswald. "I have seen them walking about the town. Beastly new yellow boots. And fast, squeaky little girls in those new floppy white hats. You think you could dispose of the boarding-house?"

Mrs. Moxton compressed her chins slightly in assent.

"It's a saleable concern?"

"There are those," said Mrs. Moxton with a faint sense of the marvels of God's universe in her voice, "who would be glad of it."

He rested his face on his hand and regarded her profile very earnestly with his one red-brown eye—from the beginning to the end of the interview Mrs. Moxton never once looked straight at him. He perceived that she was incapable of tenderness, dissimulation, or any personal relationship, a woman in profile, a woman with a pride in her work, a woman to be trusted.

"You'll *do*," he said.

"Of course, Sir, you will take up my references first. They are a little—old, but I think you will find them satisfactory."

"I have no doubts about your references, Mrs. Moxton, but they shall be taken up nevertheless, duly and in order."

"Thank you, Sir," said Mrs. Moxton, giving him a three-quarter face, and almost looking at him in her pleasure.

And thereafter Mrs. Moxton ruled the household of Oswald according to the laws and habits of the late Mr. Justice Benlees, who had evidently been a very wise, comfortable, and intelligent man. When she came on from the uncongenial furniture at Margate to the comfort and beauty of Pelham Ford she betrayed a certain approval by expanding

an inch or so in every direction and letting out two new
chins, but otherwise she made no remark. She radiated
decorum and a faint smell of lavender. She had, it seemed,
always possessed a black-watered-silk dress and a gold chain.
Even Lady Charlotte approved of her.

For some years Mrs. Moxton enabled Oswald to disregard
the social difficulties that are supposed to surround feminine
adolescence. Joan and Peter got along very well with Pelham Ford as their home, and no other feminine control except an occasional visit from the Stubland aunts. Then Aunt
Charlotte became tiresome because Joan was growing up.
"How can the gal grow up properly," she asked, "even considering what she is, in a house in which there isn't a lady
at the head?"

Oswald reflected upon the problem. He summoned Mrs.
Moxton to his presence.

"Mrs. Moxton," he said, "when Miss Joan is here, I've
been thinking, don't you think she ought to be, so to speak,
mistress of the place?"

"I have been wondering when you would make the change,
Mr. Sydenham," said Mrs. Moxton. "I shall be very pleased
to take my orders from Miss Joan."

And after that Mrs. Moxton used to come to Joan whenever Joan was at Pelham Ford, and tell her what orders she
had to give for the day. And when Joan had visitors, Mrs.
Moxton told Joan just exactly what arrangements Joan was
to order Mrs. Moxton to make. In all things that mattered
Mrs. Moxton ruled Joan with an obedience of iron. Her
curtseys, slow, deliberate and firm, insisted that Joan was a
lady—and had got to be one. She took to calling Joan
"Ma'am." Joan had to live up to it, and did. Visitors increased after the young people were at Cambridge. Junior
dons from Newnham and Girton would come and chaperon
their hostess, and Peter treated Oswald to a variety of samples of the younger male generation. Some of the samples
Oswald liked more than others. And he concealed very carefully from Aunt Charlotte how mixed these young gatherings
were, how light was the Cambridge standard of chaperonage,
and how very junior were some of the junior dons from the
women's colleges.

§ 4

When children are small we elders in charge are apt to suppose them altogether plastic. There are resistances, it is true, but these express themselves at first only in tantrums, in apparently quite meaningless outbreaks; we impose our phrases and values so completely, that such spasmodic opposition seems to signify nothing. We impose our names for things, our classifications with their thousand implications, our interpretations. The child is imitative and obedient by instinct, its personality for the most part latent, warily hidden. That is "hand," we dictate, that is "hat," that is "pussy cat," that is "pretty, pretty," that is "good," that is "nasty," that is "ugly—Ugh!" That again is "fearsome; run away!" There is no discussion. If we know our parental business we are able to establish all sorts of habits, readinesses, dispositions in these entirely plastic days. "Time for Peter to go to bed," uttered with gusto, becomes the signal for an interesting ritual upon which he embarks with dignity. Until some idiot visitor remarks loudly, "Doesn't he *hate* going to bed? I always *hated* going to bed." Whereupon in that matter the seeds of reflection and dissent are sown in the little mind.

And so with most other matters. For a few years of advantage the new mind is clay and we have it to ourselves, and then, still clay, it becomes perceptibly resistent, perceptibly disposed to recover some former shape we have given it or to take an outline of its own. It discovers we are not divine and that even Dadda cannot recall the sunset. It is not only that other minds are coming in to modify and contradict our decisions. We contradict ourselves and it notes the contradiction. And old Nature begins to take an increasing share in the accumulating personality. Apart from what we give and those others give, things bubble up inside it, desires, imaginations, creative dreams. By imperceptible degrees the growing mind slips away from us. A little while ago it seemed like some open vessel into which we could pour whatever we chose; now suddenly it is closed and locked, hiding a fermentation.

Perhaps things have always been more or less so between elders and young, but in the old days of slower change what fathers and mothers had to tell the child, priest and master re-echoed, laws and institutions confirmed, the practice of every one, good or evil, endorsed in black or white. But from the break-up of the Catholic culture in England onward there has been an unceasing conflict between more and more divergent stories about life, and in the last half century that clash has enormously intensified. What began as a war of ideals became at last a chaos. Adolescence was once either an obedience or a rebellion; at the opening of the twentieth century it had become an interrogation and an experiment. One heard very much of the right of the parent to bring up children in his own religion, his own ideas, but no one ever bothered to explain how that right was to be preserved. In Ireland one found near Dublin educational establishments surrounded by ten-foot walls topped with broken glass, protecting a Catholic atmosphere for a few precious and privileged specimens of the Erse nation. Mr. James Joyce in his *Portrait of the Artist as a Young Man*, has bottled a specimen of that Catholic atmosphere for the astonishment of posterity. The rest of the youth of the changing world lay open to every wind of suggestion that blew. The parent or guardian found himself a mere competitor for the attention and convictions of his charges.

§ 5

Through childhood and boyhood and girlhood, Peter's sex and seniority alike had conspired to give him a leadership over Joan. His seemed the richer, livelier mind, he told most of the stories and initiated most of the games; Joan was the follower. That masculine ascendancy lasted until Peter was leaving Caxton; in spite of various emancipating forces at Highmorton. Then in less than a year Joan took possession of herself.

Reserve is a necessary grace in all younger brothers and sisters. Peter spread his reveries as a peacock spreads its tail, but Joan kept her dreams discreetly private. All youth lives much in reverie; thereby the stronger minds anticipate and rehearse themselves for life in a thousand imaginations, the weaker ones escape from it.   Against that early predominance of Peter, Joan maintained her self-respect by extensive secret supplements of the Bungo-Peter saga.   For example she was Bungo-Peter's "Dearest Belovèd."   Peter never suspected how Bungo-Peter and she cuddled up together at the camp fires and were very close and warm every night, until she went off to sleep. . . .

When she was about fourteen Joan's imagination passed out of the phase of myth and saga into the world of romance. The real world drew closer to her. Bungo-Peter vanished; Nobby shrank down to a real Uncle Nobby.   Her childish reveries had disregarded possibility; now the story had to be plausible; it had to join on to Highmorton and The Ingle-Nook and Pelham Ford; its heroine had to be conceivable as the real Joan.   And with the coming of reality, came moods. There were times when she felt dull, and the world looked on her with a grey and stupid face, and other times to compensate her for these dull phases, seasons of unwonted exaltation.   It was as if her being sometimes drew itself together in order presently to leap and extend itself.

In these new phases of expansion she had the most perfect conviction that life, and particularly her life, was wonderful and beautiful and destined to be more and more so.   She began to experience a strange new happiness in mere existence, a happiness that came with an effect of revelation.   It is hard to convey the peculiar delight that invaded her during these phases.   It was almost as if the earth had just been created for her and given to her as a present.   There were moments when the world was a crystal globe of loveliness about her, moments of ecstatic realization of a universal beauty.   The slightest things would suffice to release this sunshine in her soul.   She would discover the intensest delight in little, hitherto disregarded details, in the colour of a leaf held up to the light, or the rhythms of ripples on a pond or the touch of a bird's feather.   There were moments when she wanted to kiss the sunset, and times when she would clamber over the end wall of the garden at Pelham Ford in order to lie hidden and still, with every sense awake, in the big clump of bracken in the corner by the wood beyond.   The smell of

crushed bracken delighted her intensely.   She wanted to be
a nymph then and not a girl in clothes.   And shining summer streams and lakes roused in her a passionate desire to
swim, to abandon herself wholly to the comprehensive sweet
silvery caress of the waters.

In the days of the Saga story, the time of the story had
always been Now—and Never; but in the drama of adolescence the time of all Joan's reveries was Tomorrow; what
she dreamt of now were things that were to be real experiences in quite a little time, when she had grown just a year
or so older, when she was a little taller, when she had left
school, when she was really as beautiful as she hoped to be.

The world about her by example and precept, by plays
and stories and poems and histories, was supplying her with
a rich confusion of material for these anticipatory sketches.
One main history emerged in her fifteenth year.   It went on
for many months.   Joan of Arc was in the making of it, and
Jane Shore, and Nell Gwyn.   At first she was the Lady Joan,
and then she became just Joan Stubland, but always she was
the king's mistress.

From the very beginning Joan had found something splendid and attractive in the word ''mistress.''   It had come to
her first in a history lesson, and then more brightly clad in a
costume novel.   But it was a very glorious and noble kind of
mistress that Joan had in view.   Her ideas of the authority
and duties of a mistress were vague; but she knew that a mistress rules by beauty.   That she ruled Joan never doubted
—or why should she be called mistress?   And she prevailed
over queens, so French history had instructed her.   She made
war and peace.   Joan of Arc was inextricably mixed in with
the vision.   She was a beautiful girl, and she told the king
of France what to do.   At need she led armies.   What else
but a mistress could you call her?   ''Mistress of France,''
magnificent   phrase!   Of   such   ideas   was   Joan   Stubland
woven.   The king perhaps would do injustice, or neglect a
meritorious case.   Then Joan Stubland would appear, watchful and dignified.   ''No,'' she would say.   ''That must not
be.   I am the king's mistress.''

And she wore a kind of light armour.   Without skirts.
Never with skirts.   Joan at fourteen already saw long skirts

ahead of her, and hated them as a man might hate a swamp that he must presently cross knee-deep.

Where the king went Joan went. But he was not the current king, nor his destined successor. She had studied these monarchs in the illustrated papers—and in the news. She did not think much of them. They stood down out of Joan's dream in favour of a younger autocrat. After all, was there not also a young prince, her contemporary, who would some day be king? But in her imagination he was not like his published portraits; instead—and this is curious—he was rather like Peter. He was as much like Peter as any one. This was all of Peter that ever got into her reveries, for there was a curious bar in her mind to Peter being thought of either as her lover or as any one not her lover. Something obscure in her composition barred any such direct imaginations about Peter.

So, contrawise to all established morality and to everything to which her properly constituted teachers were trying to shape her, a chance phrase in a history book filled the imagination of Joan with this dream of a different sort of woman's life altogether. In which one went side by side with a man in a manly way, sharing his power, being dear and beautiful to him. Compared with such a lot who would be one of these wives? Who would stay at home and—as a consequence apparently of the religious ceremony of matrimony—have babies?

The king's mistress story was Joan's dominant reverie, but it was not her only one. It was, so to speak, her serial; it was always "to be continued in our next." But her busy mind, whenever her attention was not fully occupied, was continually spinning romance; beside the serial story there were endless incidental ones. Almost always they were love stories. They were violent and adventurous in substance, full of chases, fights, and confrontations, but Joan did not stint herself of kissing and embraces. There were times when she liked tremendously to think of herself kissing. Most little girls of thirteen or fourteen are thinking with the keenest interest and curiosity about this lover business and its mysteries, and Joan was no exception. She was deeply interested to find she was almost as old as Juliet. Inspired

by Shakespeare, Joan thought quite a lot about balconies and
ladders—and Romeo. Some of her school contemporaries
jested about these things and were very arch and sly. But
she was as shy of talking about love as she was prone to love
reveries. She talked of flowers and poetry and music and
scenery and beautiful things as though they were things in
themselves, but in her heart she was convinced that all the
loveliness that shone upon her in the world was only so much
intimation of the coming loveliness of love.

The outward and visible disposition of Highmorton School
was all against the spirit of such dreams. The disposition
of Highmorton was towards a scorn of males. What Joan
knew surely to be lovely, Highmorton denounced as "soppy."
"Soppy" was a terrible word in boys' schools and girls'
schools alike, a flail for all romance. But in the girls' schools
it was used more particularly against tender thoughts of
men. Highmorton taught the revolt of women from the love
of men—in favour of the love of women. The school re-
sounded always with the achievements of the one important
sex, hitherto held back by man-made laws from demonstrat-
ing an all-round superiority. The staff at Highmorton had
all a common hardness of demeanour; they were without exception suffragettes, and most of them militant suffragettes.
They played hockey with great violence, and let the elder
girls hear them say "damn!" The ones who had any beauty
aspired to sub-virile effects; they impressed small adorers
as if they were sexless angels. There was Miss Oriana Frobisher (science) with the glorious wave in her golden hair
and the flash of lightning in her glasses. She had done great
feats with love, it was said; she had refused a professor of
botany and a fabulously rich widower, and the mathematical
master was "gone" on her. There was Miss Kellaway, dark
and pensive, known to her worshippers as "Queen of the
Night," fragile, and yet a swift and nimble forward. Aunt
Phœbe also had become a leading militant, and Aunt Phyllis,
who wavered on the verge of militancy, continued the Highmorton teaching in the holidays. "Absolute equality between the sexes," was their demand; their moderate demand,
seeing what men were. Joan would have been more than
human not to take the colour of so universal a teaching. And

yet in her reveries there was always one man exempt from that doom of general masculine inferiority. She had no use for a dream lover—unless he was dying of consumption or, Tristram fashion, of love-caused wounds—who could not out-run, out-fence, out-wrestle and out-think her, or for a situation of asserted equality which could not dissolve into caressing devotion.

§ 6

And of these preoccupations with the empire and the duties and destinies of the empire and the collective affairs of mankind, which to Oswald were the very gist and purpose of education, Highmorton taught Joan practically nothing. Miss Jevons, the Head, would speak now and then of "loyalty to the crown" in a rather distant way—Miss Murgatroyd had been wont to do the same thing—and for the rest left politics alone. Except that there was one thing, one supreme thing, the Vote. When first little Joan heard of the Vote at Limpsfield she was inclined to think it was a flattened red round thing rather like the Venerable Bede at the top of the flagstaff. She learned little better at Highmorton. She gathered that women were going to "get the vote" and then they were to vote. They were going to vote somehow against the men and it would make the world better, but there was very little more to it than that. The ideas remained strictly personal, strictly dramatic. Wicked men like Mr. Asquith who opposed the vote were to be cast down; one of the dazzling Pankhurst family, or perhaps Miss Oriana Frobisher, was to take his place. Profound scepticisms about this vote—in her heart of hearts she called it the "old Vote," were hidden by Joan from the general observation of the school. She had only the slightest attacks of that common schoolgirl affliction, schoolmistress love; she never idolized Miss Jevons or Miss Frobisher or Miss Kellaway. Their enthusiasm for the vote, therefore, prevented hers.

Later on it was to be different. She was to find in the vote a symbol of personal freedom—and an excellent excuse for undergraduate misbehaviour.

It is true Highmorton School presented a certain amount

of history and geography to Joan's mind, but in no way as a process in which she was concerned. She grew up to believe that in England we were out of history, out of geography, eternally blessed in a constitution that we could not better, under a crown which was henceforth for ever, so to speak, the centre of an everlasting social tea-party, and that party "politics" in Parliament and the great Vote struggle had taken the place of such real convulsions of human fortune as occurred in other countries and other times. Wars, famine, pestilence; the world had done with them. Nations, kings and people, politics, were for Joan throughout all her schooldays no more than scenery for her unending private personal romance.

But because much has been told here of Joan's reveries it is not to be imagined that she was addicted to brooding. It was only when her mind was unoccupied that the internal story-teller got to work. Usually Joan was pretty actively occupied. The Highmorton ideal of breezy activity took hold of her very early; one kept "on the Go." In school she liked her work, even though her unworshipping disposition got her at times at loggerheads with her teachers; there was so much more in the lessons than there had been at Miss Murgatroyd's. Out of school she became rather a disorderly influence. At first she missed Peter dreadfully. Then she began to imitate Peter for the benefit of one or two small associates with less initiative than her own. Then she became authentically Peter-like. She tried a mild saga of her own in those junior days, and taught her friends to act a part in it as Peter had taught her to be a companion of the great Bungo. She developed the same sort of disposition to go up ladders, climb over walls, try the fronts of cliffs, go through open doors and try closed ones, that used to make Peter such agreeable company. Once or twice she and a friend or so even got lost by the mistress in charge of a school walk, and came home by a different way through the outskirts of Broadstairs. But that led to an awe-inspiring "fuss." Moreover, it took Joan some years to grasp the idea that the physical correction of one's friends is not lady-like. When it came to other girls she perceived that Peter's

way with a girl was really a very good way—better than
either hauteur or pinching. Holding down, for instance, or
the wrist wrench.

All the time that she was at Highmorton Joan found no
friend as good as Peter. Tel Wymark, with the freckles,
became important about Joan's fifteenth birthday as a good
giggling associate, a person to sit with in the back seats of
lectures and debates and tickle to death with dry comments
on the forward proceedings. To turn on Tel quietly and
slowly and do a gargoyle face at her was usually enough to
set her off—or even to pull a straight face and sit as if you
were about to gargoyle. Tel's own humour was by no means
negligible, and she had a store of Limericks, the first Limericks Joan had encountered. Joan herself rarely giggled; on
a few occasions she laughed loudly, but for most comic occasions her laughter was internal, and so this disintegration of
Tel by merriment became a fascinating occupation. It was
no doubt the contrast of her dark restraint that subjected
her to the passionate affection of Adela Murchison.

That affair began a year or so before the friendship with
Tel. Adela was an abundant white-fleshed creature rather
more than a year older than Joan. She came back from the
Easter holidays, stage struck, with her head full of Rosalind.
She had seen Miss Lillah McCarthy as Rosalind in *As You
Like it,* and had fallen violently in love with her. She went
over the play with Joan, and Joan was much fascinated by
the Rosalind masquerade; in such guise Joan Stubland might
well have met her king for the first time. Then Adela and
Joan let their imaginations loose and played at Shakespearian
love-making. They would get together upon walks and steal
apart whenever an opportunity offered. Adela wanted to
kiss a great deal, and once when she kissed Joan she whispered, "It's not Rosalind I love, not Lillah or any one else;
just Joan." Joan kissed her in return. And then something twisted over in Joan's mind that drove her to austerity; suddenly she would have no more of this kissing, she
herself could not have explained why or wherefore. It was
the queerest recoil. "We're being too soppy," she said to
Adela, but that did not in the least express it. Adela be-

came a protesting and urgent lover; she wrote Joan notes, she tried to make scenes, she demanded Was there any one else?

"No," said Joan. "But I don't like all this rot."

"You did!" said Adela with ready tears shining in her pretty eyes.

"And I don't now," said Joan. . . .

Joan herself was puzzled, but she had no material in her mind by which she could test and analyse this revulsion. She hid a dark secret from all the world, she hid it almost from herself, that once before, in the previous summer holidays, one afternoon while she was staying with her aunts at The Ingle-Nook, she had walked over by the Cuspard house on the way to Miss Murgatroyd's. And she had met young Cuspard, grown tall and quaintly good-looking, in white flannels. They had stopped to talk and sat down on a tree together, and suddenly he had kissed her. "You're lovely, Joan," he said. It was an incredible thing to remember, it was a memory so astounding as to be obscure, but she knew as a fact that she had kissed him again and had liked this kissing, and then had had just this same feeling of terror, of enormity, as though something vast clutched at her. It was fantastically disagreeable, not like a real disagreeable thing, but like a dream disagreeable thing. She resolved that in fact it had not happened, she barred it back out of the current of her thoughts, and it shadowed her life for days.

§ 7

The modern world tells the young a score of conflicting stories—more or less distinctly—about every essential thing. While men like Oswald dream of a culture telling the young plainly what they are supposed to be for, what this or that or the other is for, the current method of instruction about God and state and sex alike is a wrangle that never joins issue. For every youth and maiden who is not strictly secluded or very stupid, adolescence is a period of distressful perplexity, of hidden hypotheses, misunderstood hints, checked urgency, and wild stampedes of the imagination. Joan's opening mind was like some ill-defended country across which armies marched. Came the School of St. George and the Venerable Bede, led by Miss Murgatroyd and applauded by Aunt Phœbe, baring its head and feet and knees, casting aside corsets, appealing to nature and simplicity, professing fearlessness, and telling the young a great deal less than it had the air of telling them. Came Highmorton, a bracing wind after that relaxing atmosphere.

But Limpsfield had at least a certain honesty in its limited initiation; Highmorton was comparatively an imposture. With an effect of going right on beyond all established things to something finer and newer, Highmorton was really restoring prudery in a brutalized form. It is no more vigorous to ban a topic by calling it "soppy" and waving a muddy hockey-stick at it in a threatening manner, than it is to ban it by calling it "improper" and primly cutting it dead. There the topic remains.

A third influence had made a contributory grab at Joan; Aunt Charlotte Sydenham's raid on the children's education was on behalf of all that was then most orthodox. Hers was indeed the essential English culture of the earlier Victorian age; a culture that so far as sex went was pure suppression— tempered by the broad hints and tittering chatter of servants and base people. . . .

Stuck away, shut in, in Joan's memory, shut in and disregarded as bees will wax up and disregard the decaying body of some foul intruder, were certain passages with Mrs. Pybus. They carried an impression at once vague and enormous, of a fascinating unclean horror. They were inseparably mixed up with strange incredulous thoughts of hell that were implanted during the same period. Such scenery as they needed was supplied by the dusty, faded furnishings of the little house in Windsor, they had the same faintly disagreeable dusty smell of a home only cleansed by stray wipes with a duster and spiritless sweeping with tea-leaves.

That period had been a dark patch upon the sunlit fabric of Joan's life. Over it all brooded this Mrs. Pybus, frankly dirty while "doing" her house in the morning, then insincerely tidy in the afternoon. She talked continually to, at, and round about Joan. She was always talking. She was an untimely widow prone to brood upon the unpleasant but enormously importunate facts that married life had thrust upon her. She had an irresistible desire to communicate her experiences with an air of wisdom. She had a certain conceit of wisdom. She had no sense of the respect due to the ignorance of childhood. Like many women of her class and type she was too egotistical to allow for childhood.

Never before had Joan heard of diseases. Now she heard of all the diseases of these two profoundly clinical families, the Pybuses and the Unwins. The Pybus family specialized in cancers, "chumors" and morbid growths generally; one, but he was rather remote and legendary, had had an "insec' in 'is 'ed"; the distinction of the Unwins on the other hand was in difficult parturitions. All this stuff was poured out in a whining monologue in Joan's presence as Mrs. Pybus busied herself in the slatternly details of her housework.

"Two cases of cancer I've seen through from the very first pangs," Mrs. Pybus would begin, and then piously, "God grant I never see a third."

"Whatever you do, Joan, one thing I say never do—good though Pybus was and kind. Never marry no one with internal cancer, 'owever 'ard you may be drove. Indigestion, rheumatism, even a wooden leg rather. Better a man that drinks. I say it and I know. It doesn't make it any easier, Joan, to sit and see them suffer.

"You've got your troubles yet to come, young lady. I don't expec' you understand 'arf what I'm telling you. But you will some day. I sometimes think if I 'adn't been kep' in ignorance things might have been better for me—all I bin called upon to go through." That was the style of thing. It was like pouring drainage over a rosebud. First Joan listened with curiosity, then with horror. Then unavailingly, always overpowered by a grotesque fascination, she tried not to listen. Monstrous fragments got through to her cowering attention. Here were things for a little girl to carry off in her memory, material as she sickened for measles for the most terrifying and abominable of dreams.

"There's poor ladies that has to be reg'lar cut open. . . .

"I 'ad a dreadful time when I married Pybus. Often I said to 'im afterwards, you can't complain of *me*, Pybus. The things one lives through! . . .

" 'Is sister's 'usband didn't 'ave no mercy on 'er. . . .

"Don't you go outside this gate, Joan—ever. If one of these 'ere Tramps should get hold of you. . . . I've 'eard of a little girl. . . ."

If a congenial gossip should happen to drop in Joan would be told to sit by the window and look at the "nice picture book"—it was always that one old volume of *The Illustrated London News*—while a talk went on that insisted on being heard, now dropping to harsh whispers, now rising louder after the assurance of Mrs. Pybus:

"Lord! *She* won't understand a word you're saying."

If by chance Mrs. Pybus and her friend drifted for a time from personal or consanguineous experiences then they dealt with crimes. Difficulties in the disposal of the body fascinated these ladies even more than the pleasing details of the act. And they preferred murders of women by men. It seemed more natural to them. . . .

The world changed again. Through the tossing distress of the measles Aunt Phyllis reappeared, and then came a journey and The Ingle-Nook and dear Petah! and Nobby. She was back in a world where Mrs. Pybus could not exist, where the things of which Mrs. Pybus talked could not happen. Yet there was this in Joan's mind, unformulated, there was a passionate stress against its formulation, that all the other things she thought about love and beauty were poetry and dreaming, but this alone of all the voices that had spoken over and about her, told of something real. In the unknown beyond to which one got if one pressed on, was something of that sort, something monstrous, painful and dingy. . . .

Reality!

Wax it over, little dream bees; cover it up; don't think of it! Back to reverie! Be a king's mistress, clad in armour, who sometimes grants a kiss.

§ 8

It was in the nature of Mrs. Pybus to misconceive things. She never grasped the true relationship of Joan and Peter; Mr. Grimes had indeed been deliberately vague upon that point in the interests of the Sydenham family, the use of the Stubland surname for Joan had helped him; and so there dropped into Joan's ears a suggestion that was at the time merely perplexing but which became gradually an established fact in her mind.

"Ow! don't you know?" said Mrs. Pybus to her friend. "Ow, no! She's——" (Her voice sank to a whisper.)

For a time what they said was so confidential as to convey nothing to Joan but a sense of mystery. "Ow 'is mother ever stood 'er in the 'ouse passes my belief," said Mrs. Pybus, coming up to the audible again. "Why! I'd 'ave *killed* 'er. But ladies and gentlemen don't seem to 'ave no natural affections—not wot *I* call affections. There she was brought into the 'ouse and treated just as if she was the little chap's sister."

"She'd be——?" said the friend, trying to grasp it.

" 'Arf sister," said Mrs. Pybus. "Of a sort. Neither 'ere nor there, so to speak. Not in the eyes of the law. And there they are—leastways they was until Lady Charlotte Sydenham interfered."

The friend nodded her head rapidly to indicate intelligent appreciation.

"It isn't like being *reely* brother and sister," said Mrs. Pybus, contemplating possibilities. "It's neither one thing nor another. And all wrop up in mystery as you might say. Why, oo knows? They might go falling in love with each other."

" *'Orrible!*" said Mrs. Pybus's friend.

"It 'ad to be put a stop to," said Mrs. Pybus.

Confirmatory nodding, with a stern eye for the little figure that sat in a corner and pretended to be interested in the faded exploits of vanished royalties, recorded in that old volume of *The Illustrated London News.* . . .

That conversation sank down into the deeps of Joan's memory and remained there, obscured but exercising a dim influence upon her relations with Peter. One phrase sent up a bubble every now and then into her conscious thoughts: "half-sister." It was years after that she began to piece together the hidden riddle of her birth. Mummy and Daddy were away; that had served as well for her as for Peter far beyond the Limpsfield days. It isn't until children are in their teens that these things interest them keenly. It wasn't a thing to talk about, she knew, but it was a thing to puzzle over. Who was really her father? Who was her mother? If she was Peter's half-sister, then either his father was not hers or his mother. . . .

When people are all manifestly in a plot to keep one in the dark one does not ask questions.

§ 9

After the first violent rupture that Mr. Grimes had organized, Joan and Peter parted and met again in a series of separations and resumptions. They went off to totally dissimilar atmospheres, Joan to the bracing and roughening air of Highmorton and Peter first to the brightness of White Court and then to the vigorous work and play of Caxton; and each time they returned for the holidays to Margate or Limpsfield or Pelham Ford changed, novel, and yet profoundly familiar. Always at first when holidays brought them together again they were shy with each other and intensely egotistical, anxious to show off their new tricks and make the most of whatever small triumphs school life had given them. Then in a day or so they would be at their ease together like a joint that has been dislocated and has slipped into place again. Cambridge at last brought them nearer together, and ended this series of dislocations. After much grave weighing of the situation by Miss Fairchild, the principal of Newton Hall, Peter, when Joan came up, was given the status of a full brother.

They grew irregularly, and that made some quaint variations of relationship. Peter, soon after he went to Caxton, fell to expanding enormously. He developed a chest, his limbs became great things. There was a summer bitten into Joan's memory when he regarded her as nothing more than a "leetle teeny female tick," and descanted on the minuteness of her soul and body. But he had lost some of his lightness, if none of his dexterity and balance, as a climber, and Joan got her consolations among the lighter branches of various trees they explored. Next Christmas Joan herself had

done some serious growing, and the gap was not so wide.
But it was only after her first term at Newnham that Joan
passed from the subservience of a junior to the confidence of
a senior. She did it at a bound. She met him one day in
the narrow way between Sidney Street and Petty Cury.
Her hair was up and her eyes were steady; most of her legs
had vanished, and she had clothes like a real woman. We
do not foregather even with foster brothers in the streets of
Cambridge, but a passing hail is beyond the reach of discipline. "Hullo, Petah!" she said, "what a gawky great
thing you're getting!"

Peter, a man in his second year, was so taken aback he had
no adequate reply.

"You've grown too," he said, "if it comes to that";—a
flavourless reply. And there was admiration in his eyes.

An encounter for subsequent regrets. He thought over it
afterwards. The cheek of her! It made his blood boil.

"So long, Petah," said Joan, carrying it off to the end....

They were sterner than brother and sister with each other.
There was never going to be anything "soppy" between
them. At fourteen, when Peter passed into the Red Indian
phase of a boy's development, when there can be no more
"blubbing," no more shirking, he carried Joan with him.
She responded magnificently to the idea of pluck. Spartan
ideals ruled them both. And a dark taciturnity. Joan
would have died with shame if Peter had penetrated the
secret romance of Joan Stubland, and the days of Peter's
sagas were over for ever. When Peter was fifteen he was
consumed by a craving for a gun, and Oswald gave him one.
"But kill," said Oswald. "If you let anything get away
wounded——"

Peter took Joan out into the wood at the back. He missed
a pigeon, and then he got one.

"Pick it up, Joan," he said, very calmly and grandly.

Joan was white to the lips, but she picked up the blood-
stained bird in silence. These things had to happen.

Then out of a heap of leaves in front darted a rabbit. Lop,
lop, lop, went its little white scut. *Bang!* and over it rolled,
but it wasn't instantly killed. Horror came upon Joan.
She was nearest; she ran to the wretched animal, which was

lying on its side and kicking automatically, and stood over it. Its eyes were bright and wide with terror. "Oh, how am I to *kill* it?" she cried, with agony in her voice; "what am I to do-o?" She wrung her hands. She felt she was going to pieces, giving herself away, failing utterly. Peter would despise her and jeer at her. But the poor little beast! The poor beast! There is a limit to pride. She caught it up. "Petah!" she cried quite pitifully, on the verge of a whimper.

Peter had come up to her. He didn't look contemptuous. He was white-lipped too. She had never seen him look scared before. He snatched the rabbit from her and killed it by one, two, three—she counted—quick blows—she didn't see. But she had met his eyes, and they were as distressed as hers. Just for a moment.

Then he was a fifth form boy again. He examined his victim with an affectation of calm. "Too far back," he said. "Bad shot. Mustn't do that again." . . .

The rabbit was quite still and limp now, dangling from Peter's hand, its eye had glazed, blood dripped and clotted at its muzzle, but its rhythmic desperate kicking was still beating in Joan's brain.

Was this to go on? Could she go on?

Peter's gun and the pigeon were lying some yards away. He regarded them and then looked down at the rabbit he held.

"Now I know I can shoot," he said, and left the sentence unfinished.

"Bring the pigeon, Joan," he said, ending an indecision, and picked up his gun and led the way back towards the house. . . .

"We got a pigeon and a rabbit," Joan babbled at tea to Oswald. "Next time, Petah's going to let me have the gun."

Our tone was altogether sporting.

But there was no next time. There were many unspoken things between Joan and Peter, and this was to be one of them. For all the rest of their lives neither Joan nor Peter went shooting again. Men Peter was destined to slay—but no more beasts. Necessity never compelled them, and it would have demanded an urgent necessity before they would have faced the risk of seeing another little furry creature twist and wriggle and of marking how a bright eye glazes over. But they were both very bitterly ashamed of this distressing weakness. They left further shooting for "tomorrow," and it remained always tomorrow. They said nothing about their real feelings in the matter, and Peter cleaned and oiled his new gun very carefully and hung it up conspicuously over the mantelshelf of their common room, ready to be taken down at any time—when animals ceased to betray feeling.

<h2 style="text-align:center">§ 10</h2>

Joan and Peter detested each other's friends from the beginning. The quarrel that culminated in that amazing speech of Joan's, had been smouldering between them for a good seven years. It went right back to the days when they were still boy and girl.

To begin with, after their first separation they had had no particular friends; they had had acquaintances and habits of association, but the mind still lacks the continuity necessary for friendship and Euclid until the early teens. The first rift came with Adela Murchison. Joan brought her for the summer holidays when Peter had been just a year at Caxton.

That was the first summer at Pelham Ford. Aunt Phyllis was with them, but Aunt Phœbe was in great labour with her first and only novel, a fantasia on the theme of feminine genius, "These are my Children, or Mary on the Cross." (It was afterwards greatly censored. Boots, the druggist librarian, would have none of it.) She stayed alone, therefore, at The Ingle-Nook, writing, revising, despairing, tearing up and beginning again, reciting her more powerful passages to the scarlet but listening ears of Groombridge and the little maid, and going more and more unkempt, unhooked, and unbuttoned. Oswald, instead of resorting to the Climax Club as he was apt to do when Aunt Phœbe was imminent, abode happily in his new home.

Adela was a month or so older than Peter and, what annoyed him to begin with, rather more fully grown. She was, as she only too manifestly perceived, a woman of the world in comparison with both of her hosts. She was still deeply in love with Joan, but by no means indifferent to this dark boy who looked at her with so much of Joan's cool detachment.

Joan's romantic dreams were Joan's inmost secret, Adela's romantic intentions were an efflorescence. She was already hoisting the signals for masculine surrender. She never failed to have a blue ribbon astray somewhere to mark and help the blueness of her large blue eyes. She insisted upon the flaxen waves over her ears, and secretly assisted them to kink. She had a high colour. She had no rouge yet in her possession but there was rouge in her soul, and she would rub her cheeks with her hands before she came into a room. She discovered to Joan the incredible fact that Oswald was also a man.

With her arm round Joan's waist or over her shoulder she would look back at him across the lawn.

"I say," she said, "he'd be *frightfully* good-looking—if it wasn't for *that*."

And one day, "I wonder if Mr. Sydenham's ever been in love."

She lay in wait for Oswald's eye. She went after him to ask him unimportant things.

Once or twice little things happened, the slightest things, but it might have seemed to Joan that Oswald was disposed to flirt with Adela. But that was surely impossible. . . .

The first effect of the young woman upon Peter was a considerable but indeterminate excitement. It was neither pleasurable nor unpleasurable, but it hung over the giddy verge of being unpleasant. It made him want to be very large, handsome and impressive. It also made him acutely ashamed of wanting to be very large, handsome and impressive. It turned him from a simple boy into a conflict of motives. He wanted to extort admiration from Adela. Also he wanted to despise her utterly. These impulses worked out to no coherent system of remarks and gestures, and he became awkward and tongue-tied.

Adela wanted to be shown all over the house and garden. She put her arm about Joan in a manner Peter thought offensive. Then she threw back her hair at him over her shoulder and said, shooting a glance at him, "You come too."

Cheek!

Still, she was a guest, and so a fellow had to follow with his hands in his pockets and watch his own private and particular Joan being ordered about and—what was somehow so much more exasperating—*pawed* about.

At what seemed to be the earliest opportunity Peter excused himself, and went off to the outhouse in which he had his tools and chemicals and things. He decided he would rig up everything ready to make Sulphuretted Hydrogen—although he knew quite well that this was neither a large, handsome, nor impressive thing to do. And then he would wait for them to come along, and set the odour going.

But neither of the girls came near his Glory Hole, and he was not going to invite them. He just hovered there unvisited, waiting with his preparations and whistling soft melancholy tunes. Finally he made a lot of the gas, simply because he had got the stuff ready, and stank himself out of his Glory Hole into society again.

At supper, which had become a sort of dinner that night, Adela insisted on talking like a rather languid, smart woman of the world to Nobby. Nobby took her quite seriously. It was perfectly sickening.

"D'you hunt much?" said Adela.

"Not in England," said Nobby. "There's too many hedges for me. I've a sailor's seat."

"All my people hunt," said Adela. "It's rather a bore, don't you think, Mr. Sydenham?"

Talk like that!

Two days passed, during which Peter was either being bored to death in the company of Adela and Joan or also bored to death keeping aloof from them. He cycled to Ware with them, and Adela's cycle had a change speed arrangement with a high gear of eighty-five that made it difficult to keep ahead of her. Beast!

And on the second evening she introduced a new card game, Demon Patience, a scrambling sort of game in which you piled on aces in the middle and cried "Stop!" as soon as your stack was out. It was one of those games, one of those inferior games, at which boys in their teens are not nearly as quick as girls, Peter discovered. But presently Joan began to pull ahead and beat Adela and Peter. The two girls began to play against each other as if his poor little spurts didn't amount to anything. They certainly didn't amount to very much.

Adela began to play with a sprawling eagerness. Her colour deepened; her manners deteriorated. She was tormented between ambition and admiration. When Joan had run her out for the third time, she cried, "Oh, Joan, you Wonderful Darling!"

And clutched and kissed her! . . .

All the other things might have been bearable if it had not been for this perpetual confabulating with Joan, this going off to whisper with Joan, this putting of arms round Joan's neck, this whispering that was almost kissing Joan's ear. One couldn't have a moment with Joan. One couldn't use Joan for the slightest thing. It would have been better if one hadn't had a Joan.

On the mill-pond there was a boat that Joan and Peter were allowed to use. On the morning of the fifth day Joan found Peter hanging about in the hall.

"Joan."

"Yes?"

"Come and muck about in Baker's boat."

"If Adela——"

"Oh, *leave* Adela! We don't want her. She'd stash it all up."

"But she's a visitor!"

"Pretty rotten visitor! What did you bring her here for? She's rotten."

"She's not. She's all right. You're being horrid rude to her. Every chance you get. I like her."

"Silly tick, she is!"

"She's taller than you are, anyhow."

"Nyar Nyar Nyar Nyar," said Peter in a singularly ineffective mockery of Adela's manner. Adela appeared, descending the staircase. Peter turned away.

"Peter wants to go in the boat on the mill-pond," said Joan, as if with calculated wickedness.

"Oh! I *love* boats!" said Adela.

What was a chap to do but go?"

But under a thin mask of playfulness Peter splashed them both a lot—especially Adela. And in the evening he refused to play at Demon Patience and went and sat by himself to draw. He tried various designs. He was rather good at drawing Mr. Henderson, and he did several studies of him. Then the girls, who found Demon Patience slow with only two players, came and sat beside him. He was inspired to begin an ugly caricature of Adela.

He began at the eyes.

Joan knew him better than Adela. She saw what was coming. Down came her little brown paw on the paper. "No, you don't, Petah," she said.

Peter looked into her face, hot against his, and there was a red light in his eyes.

"Leago, Joan," he said.

A struggle began in which Adela took no share.

The Sydenham blood is hot blood, and though it doesn't like hurting rabbits it can be pretty rough with its first cousins. But Joan was still gripping the crumpled half of the offending sheet when Aunt Phyllis, summoned by a scared Adela, came in. The two were on the hearthrug, panting, and Joan's teeth were deep in Peter's wrist; they parted and rose somewhat abashed. "My *dears!*" cried Aunt Phyllis.

"We were playing," said Joan, flushed and breathless, but honourably tearless.

"Yes," said Peter, holding his wrist tight. "We were playing."

"Romping," said Aunt Phyllis. "Weren't you a little rough? Adela, you know, isn't used to your style. . . ."

After that, Peter shunned further social intercourse. He affected a great concentration upon experimental chemistry and photography, and bicycled in lonely pride to Waltham Cross, Baldock, and Dunmow. He gave himself up to the roads of Hertfordshire. When at last Adela departed it made no difference in his aloofness. Joan was henceforth as nothing to him; she was just a tick, a silly little female tick, an associate of things that went "Nyar Nyar Nyar." He hated her. At least, he would have hated her if there was anything that a self-respecting Caxtonian could hate in a being so utterly contemptible. (Yet at the bottom of his heart he loved and respected her for biting his wrist so hard.)

Deprived of Adela, Joan became very lonely and forlorn. After some days there were signs of relenting on the part of Peter, and then came his visitor, Wilmington, a boy who had gone with him from White Court to Caxton, and after that there was no need of Joan. With a grim resolution Peter shut Joan out from all their pursuits. She was annihilated.

The boys did experimental chemistry together, made the most disgusting stinks, blew up a small earthwork by means of a mine, and stained their hands bright yellow; they had long bicycle rides together, they did "splorjums" in the wood, they "mucked about" with Baker's boat. Joan by no effort could come into existence again. Once or twice as Peter was going off with Wilmington, Peter would glance back and feel a gleam of compunction at the little figure that watched him going. But she had her Adelas. She and Adela wrote letters to each other. She could go and write to her beastly Adela now. . . .

"Can't Joan come?" said Wilmington.

"She's only a tick," said Peter.

"She's not a bad sort of tick," said Wilmington.

(What business was it of his?)

Joan fell back on Nobby, and went for walks with him in the afternoon.

Then came a complication. Towards the end Wilmington got quite soppy on Joan. It showed.

Aunt Phyllis suggested charades for the evening hour after dinner. Wilmington and Peter played against each other, and either of them took out any people he wanted to act with him. Aunt Phyllis was a grave and dignified actress and Nobby could do better than you might have expected. Peter did Salome. (Sal—owe—me; doing sal volatile for Sal.) He sat as Herod, crowned and scornful with the false black beard, and Joan danced and afterwards brought the football in on a plate. Aunt Phyllis did pseudo-oriental music. But when Wilmington saw Joan dance he knew what it was to be in love. He sat glowering passion. For a time he remained frozen rigid, and then broke into wild hand-clapping. His ears were bright red, and Aunt Phyllis looked at him curiously. It was with difficulty that his clouded mind could devise a charade that would give him a call upon Joan. But he thought at last of Milton. (Mill—tun.)

"I want you," he said.

"Won't Aunty do?"

"No, *you*. It's got to be a girl."

He held the door open for her, and stumbled going out of the room. He was more breathless and jerky than ever outside. Joan heard his exposition with an unfriendly expression.

"And what am I to do then?" she asked. . . .

"And then? . . ."

They did "Mill" and "Tun" pretty badly. Came Wilmington's last precious moments with her. He broke off in his description of Milton blind and Joan as the amanuensis daughter. "Joan," he whispered, going hoarse with emotion. "Joan, you're lovely. I'd die for you."

A light of evil triumph came into Joan's eyes.

"Ugly thing!" said Joan, "what did you come here for? You've spoilt my holidays. Let *go* of my hand! . . . Let's go in and do our tableau."

And afterwards when Wilmington met Joan in the passage she treated him to a grimace that was only too manifestly intended to represent his own expression of melancholy but undying devotion. In the presence of others she was coolly polite to him.

Peter read his friend like a book, but refrained from injurious comment, and Wilmington departed in a state of grave nervous disarray.

A day passed. There was not much left now of the precious holidays. Came a glowing September morning.

"Joe-un," whooped Peter in the garden—in just the old note.

"Pee-tah!" answered Joan, full-voiced as ever, distant but drawing nearer.

"Come and muck about in Baker's boat."

"Right-o, Petah!" said Joan, and approached with a slightly prancing gait.

§ 11

Growing out of his Red Indian phase Peter moved up into the Lower Sixth and became a regular cynical man of the world with an air of knowing more than a thing or two. He was, in fact, learning a vast number of things that are outside the books; and rearranging many of his early shocks and impressions by the help of a confusing and increasing mixture of half-lights. The chaotic disrespect of the young went out of his manner in his allusion to school affairs, he no longer spoke of various masters as "Buzzy," "Snooks," and "the Croker," and a curious respectability had invaded his demeanour. The Head had had him in to tea and tennis. The handle of the prefect's birch was perhaps not more than a year now from his grip, if he bore himself gravely. He reproached Joan on various small occasions for "thundering bad form," and when Wilmington came, a much more wary and better-looking Wilmington with his heart no longer on his sleeve, the conversation became, so to speak, political. They talked at the dinner-table of the behaviour of so-and-so and this-and-that at "High" and at "Bottoms" and on "the Corso"; they discussed various cases of "side" and "cheek," and the permanent effect of these upon the standing and reputations of the youths concerned; they were earnest to search out and know utterly why Best did not get his colours and whether it was just to "super" old Rawdon. They discussed the question of superannuation with Oswald very gravely. "Don't you think," said Oswald, "if a school takes a boy on, it ought to see him through?"

"But if he doesn't work, sir?" said Wilmington.

"A school oughtn't to produce that lassitude," said Oswald.

"A chap ought to *use* a school," said Peter.

That was a new point of view to Oswald and Joan.

Afterwards came Troop, a larger boy than either Peter or Wilmington, a prefect, a youth almost incredibly manly in his manner, and joined on to these discussions. Said Oswald, "There ought not to be such a thing as superannuation. A man ought not to be let drift to the point of unteachable incapacity. And then thrown away. Some master ought to have shepherded him in for special treatment.''

"They don't look after us to that extent, sir,'' said Troop.

"Don't they teach you? Or fail to teach you?''

"It's the school teaches us,'' said Peter, as though it had just occurred to him.

"Still, the masters are there,'' said Oswald, smiling.

"The masters are there,'' Troop acquiesced. "But the life of the school is the tradition. And a big chap like Rawdon hanging about, too big to lick and too stupid for responsibility—— It breaks things up, sir.''

Oswald was very much interested in this prefect's view of the school life. Behind his blank mask he engendered questions; his one eye watched Troop and went from Troop to Peter. This manliness in the taught surprised him tremendously. Peter was acquiring it rapidly, but Troop seemed to embody it. Oswald himself had been a man early enough and had led a hard life of mutual criticism and exasperation with his fellows, but that had been in a working reality, the navy; this, he reflected, was a case of cocks crowing inside the egg. These boys were living in a premature autonomous state, an aristocratic republic with the Head as a sort of constitutional monarch. There was one questionable consequence at least. They were acquiring political habits before they had acquired wide horizons. Were the political habits of a school where all the boys were of one race and creed and class, suitable for the problems of a world's affairs?

Troop, under Oswald's insidious leading, displayed his ideas modestly but frankly, and they were the ideas of a large child. Troop was a good-looking, thoroughly healthy youth, full of his grave responsibilities towards the school and inclined to claim a liberal attitude. He was very great upon his duty to "make the fellows live decently and behave decently.'' He was lured into a story of how one youth with a tendency to long hair had been partly won and partly driven to a more seemly coiffure; how he had dealt with a games shirker, and how a fellow had been detected lending socialist pamphlets—"not to his friends, sir, I shouldn't mind that so much, but pushing them upon any one''—and restrained. "Seditious sort of stuff, sir, I believe. No, I did not *read* it, sir." Troop was for cold baths under all circumstances, for no smoking under sixteen and five foot six, and for a simple and unquestioning loyalty to any one who came along and professed to be in authority over him. When he mentioned the king his voice dropped worshipfully. Upon the just use of the birch Troop was conscientiously prolix. There were prefects, he said, who "savaged" the fellows. Others swished without judgment. Troop put conscience into each whack.

Troop's liberalism interested Oswald more than anything else about him. He was proud to profess himself no mere traditionalist; he wanted Caxton to "broaden down from precedent to precedent." Indeed he had ambitions to be remembered as a reformer. He hoped, he said, to leave the school "better than he found it"—the modern note surely. His idea of a great and memorable improvement was to let the Upper Fifth fellows into the Corso after morning service on Sunday. He did not think it would make them impertinent; rather it would increase their self-respect. He was also inclined to a reorganization of the afternoon fagging "to stop so much bawling down the corridor." There ought to be a bell—an electric bell—in each prefect's study. No doubt that was a bit revolutionary—Troop almost smirked. "It's all very well for schools like Eton or Winchester to stick to the old customs, sir, but we are supposed to be an Up-to-Date school. Don't you think, sir?" The egg was everything to this young cockerel; the world outside was naught. Oswald led him on from one solemn puerility to another, and as the big boy talked in his stout man-of-the-world voice, the red eye roved from him to Peter and from Peter back to Troop. Until presently it realized that Peter was watching it as narrowly. "What does Peter really think of this stuff?" thought Oswald. "What does Nobby really think of this stuff?" queried Peter.

"I suppose, some day, you'll leave Caxton," said Oswald.

"I shall be very sorry to, sir," said Troop sincerely.

"Have you thought at all——"

"Not yet, sir. At least——"

"Troop's people," Peter intervened, "are Army people."

"I see," said Oswald.

Joan listened enviously to all this prefectorial conversation. At Highmorton that sort of bossing and influencing
was done by the junior staff. . . .

Oswald did his best to lure Troop from his administrative
preoccupations into general topics. But apparently some
one whom Troop respected had warned him against general
topics. Oswald lugged and pushed the talk towards religion, Aunt Phyllis helping, but they came up against a
stone wall. "My people are Church of England," said
Troop, intimating thereby that his opinions were banked with
the proper authorities. It was not for him to state them.
And in regard to politics, "All my people are Conservative."
One evening Oswald showed him a portfolio of drawings
from various Indian temples, and suggested something of the
complex symbolism of the figures. Troop thought it was
"rather unhealthy." But—turning from these monstrosi-
ties—he had hopes for India. "My cousin tells me, sir, that
cricket and polo are spreading very rapidly there." "Polo,"
said Oswald, "is an Indian game. They have played it for
centuries. It came from Persia originally." But Troop
was unable to imagine Indians riding horses; he had the
common British delusion that the horse and the ship were
both invented in our islands and that all foreign peoples are
necessarily amateurs at such things. "I thought they rode
elephants," said Troop with quiet conviction. . . .

Troop was not only a great experience for Oswald, he also
exercised the always active mind of Joan very considerably.

Peter, it seemed, hadn't even mentioned her beforehand.

"Hullo!" said Troop at the sight of her. "Got a sister?"

"Foster-sister," said Peter, minimizing the thing. "Joan,
this is Troop."

Joan regarded him critically. "Can he play D.P.?"

"Not one of my games," said Troop, who was chary of all
games not usually played.

"It's a game like Snap," said Peter with an air of casual
contempt, and earned a bright scowl.

For a day or so Troop and Joan kept aloof, watching one
another. Then she caught him out rather neatly twice at
single wicket cricket; he had a weakness for giving catches
to point and she had observed it. "Caught!" he cried ap-

provingly. Also she snicked and slipped and at last slogged boldly at his patronizing under-arm bowling. "Here's a Twister," he said, like an uncle speaking to a child.

Joan smacked it into the cedar. *"Twister!"* quoth Joan, running.

After that he took formal notice of her, betraying a disposition to address her as "Kid." (Ralph Connor was at that time adding his quota to the great British tradition. It is true he wrote in American about cowboys—but a refined cowboy was the fullest realization of an English gentleman's pre-war ideals—and Ralph Connor's cowboys are essentially refined. Thence came the "Kid," anyhow.) But Joan took umbrage at the "Kid." And she disliked Troop's manner and influence with Peter. And the way Peter stood it. She did not understand what a very, very great being a prefect is in an English public school, she did not know of Troop's superbness at rugger, it seemed to her that it was bad manners to behave as though a visit to Pelham Ford were an act of princely condescension. She was even disposed to diagnose Troop's largeness, very unjustly, as fat. So she pulled up Troop venomously with "My name's not Kit, it's Joan. J.O.A.N."

"Sorry!" said Troop. And being of that insensitive class whose passions are only to be roused by a smacking, he began to take still more notice of her. She was, he perceived, a lively Kid. He felt a strong desire to reprove and influence her. He had no suspicion that what he really wanted to do was to interest Joan in himself.

Joan's tennis was incurably tricky. Troop's idea of tennis was to play very hard and very swiftly close over the net, but without cunning. Peter and Wilmington followed his lead. But Joan forced victory upon an unwilling partner by doing unexpected things.

Troop declared he did not mind being defeated, but that he was shocked by the spirit of Joan's play. It wasn't "sporting."

"Those short returns aren't done, Kid," he said.

"I do them," said Joan. "Ancient."

Peter and Wilmington were visibly shocked, but Troop showed no resentment at the gross familiarity.

"But if every one did them!" he reasoned.

"I could take them," said Joan. "Any one could take them who knew how."

The dispute seemed likely to die down into unverifiable assertions.

"Peter can take them," said Joan. "He drops them back. But he isn't doing it today."

Peter reflected. Troop would never understand, but there was something reasonable in Joan's line. "I'll see to Joan," he said abruptly, and came towards the middle of the net.

The game continued on unorthodox but brilliant lines. "I don't call this tennis," said Troop.

"If you served to her left," said Peter.

"But she's a girl!" protested Troop. "*Serve!*"

He made the concessions that are proper to a lady, and Joan scored the point after a brief rally with Peter. "Game," said Joan.

Troop declared he did not care to play again. It would put him off tennis. "Take me as a partner," said Joan. "No—I don't think so, thanks," said Troop coldly.

Every one became thoughtful and drifted towards the net. Oswald approached from the pergola, considering the problem.

"I've been thinking about that sort of thing for years," he remarked, strolling towards them.

"Well, sir, aren't you with me?" asked Troop.

"No. I'm for Joan—and Peter."

"But that sort of trick play——"

"No. The way to play a game is to get all over the game and to be equal to anything in it. If there is a stroke or anything that spoils the game it ought to be barred by the rules. Apart from that, a game ought to be worked out to its last possibility. Things oughtn't to be barred in the interests of a few conventional swipes. This cutting down of a game to just a few types of stroke——"

Peter looked apprehensive.

"It's laziness," said Oswald.

Troop was too puzzled to be offended. "But you have to work tremendously hard, sir, at the proper game."

"Not mentally," said Oswald. "There's too much good

form in all our games. It's just a way of cutting down a game to a formality.''

"But, for instance, sir, would you bowl grounders at cricket?''

"If I thought the batsman had been too lazy to learn what to do with them. Why not?''

"If you look at it like *that,* sir!'' said Troop and had no more to say. But he went away marvelling. Oswald was a V.C. Yet he looked at games like—like an American, he played to win; it was enough to perplex any one. . . .

"Must confess I don't see it,'' said Troop when Oswald had gone. . . .

When at last Troop and Wilmington departed Oswald went with them to the station—the luggage was sent on in the cart—and walked back over the ploughed ridge and up the lane with Peter. For a time they kept silence, but Troop was in both their minds.

"He's a good sort,'' said Peter.

"Admirable—in some ways.''

"I thought,'' said Peter, "you didn't like him. You kept on pulling his leg.''

So Peter had seen.

"Well, he doesn't exercise his brain very much,'' said Oswald.

"Stops short at his neck,'' said Peter. "Exercise, I mean.''

"You and Troop are singularly unlike each other,'' said Oswald.

"Oh, that's exactly it. I can't make out why I like him. If nothing else attracted me, that would.''

"Does he know why he likes you?''

"Hasn't the ghost of an idea. It worries him at times. Makes him want to try and get all over me.''

"Does he—at all?''

"Lots,'' said Peter. "I fag at the blessed Cadet Corps simply because I like him. At rugger he's rather a god, you know. And he's a clean chap.''

"He's clean.''

"Oh, he's clean. It's catching,'' said Peter, and seemed to reflect. "And in a sort of way lately old Troop's taken to swatting. It's pathetic." Then with a shade of anxiety, "I don't think for a moment he twigged you were pulling his leg."

Oswald came to the thing that was really troubling him. "Allowing for his class," said Oswald, "that young man is growing up to an outlook upon the world about as broad and high as the outlook of a bricklayer's labourer."

Peter reflected impartially, and Oswald noted incidentally what a good profile the boy was developing.

"A Clean, Serious bricklayer's labourer," said Peter, weighing his adjectives carefully.

"But he may go into Parliament, or have to handle a big business," said Oswald.

"Army for Troop," said Peter, "via a university commission."

"Even armies have to be handled intelligently nowadays," said Oswald.

"He'll go into the cavalry," said Peter, making one of those tremendous jumps in thought that were characteristic of himself and Joan.

§ 12

A day or so after Troop's departure Peter waylaid Oswald in the garden. Peter, now that Troop had gone, was amusing himself with dissection again—an interest that Troop had disposed of as a "bit morbid." Oswald thought the work Peter did neat and good; he had to brush up his own rather faded memories of Huxley's laboratory in order to keep pace with the boy.

"I wish you'd come to the Glory Hole and look at an old rat I dissected yesterday. I want to get its solar plexus and I'm not sure about it. I've been using acetic acid to bring out the nerves, but there's such a lot of white stuff about. . . ."

The dissection was a good piece of work, the stomach cleaned out and the viscera neatly displayed. Very much in evidence were eight small embryo rats which the specimen under examination, had not science overtaken her, would presently have added to the rat population of the world.

"The old girl's been going it," said Peter in a casual tone, and turned these things over with the handle of his scalpel. "Now is all *this* stuff solar plexus, Nobby?" . . .

The next morning Oswald stopped short in the middle of his shaving, which in his case involved the most tortuous deflections and grimacings. "It's all right with the boy," he said to himself.

"I *think* it's all right.

"No nonsense about it anyhow.

"But what a tortuous, untraceable business the coming of knowledge is! Curiosity. A fad for dissecting. An instinct for cleanliness. Pride. A bigger boy like Troop. . . . Suppose Troop had been a different sort of boy? . . .

"But then I suppose Peter and he wouldn't have hit it off together."

Oswald scraped, and presently his mind tried over a phrase.

"Inherent powers of selection," said Oswald. "Inherent. . . . I suppose I picked my way through a pretty queer lot of stuff. . . ."

He stood wiping his safety-razor blade.

"There was more mystery in my time and more emotion. This is better. . . .

"Facts are clean," said Oswald, uttering the essential faith with which science has faced vice and priestcraft, magic and muddle and fear and mystery, the whole world over.

"Facts are clean."

§ 13

Joan followed a year after Peter to Cambridge. She entered at Newton Hall. Both Oswald and Aunt Phyllis preferred Newnham to Girton because of the greater freedom of the former college. They agreed that, as Oswald put it, if women were to be let out of purdah they might as well be let right out.

Coming from Highmorton to Newnham was like emerging from some narrow, draughty passage in which one marches muddily with a whispering, giggling hockey team all very much of a sort, into a busy and confused market-place, a rather squabbling and very exciting market-place, in which there is the greatest variety of sorts. And Joan's mind, too, was opening out in an even greater measure. A year or so ago she was a spirited, intelligent animal, a being of dreams and unaccountable impulses; in a year or so's time she was to become a shaped and ordered mind, making plans, controlling every urgency, holding herself in relation to a definite conception of herself and the world. We have still to gauge the almost immeasurable receptivity of those three or four crucial years. We have still to grasp what the due use of those years may mean for mankind.

Oswald had been at great pains to find out what was the best education the Empire provided for these two wards of his. But his researches had brought him to realize chiefly how poor and spiritless a thing was the very best formal education that the Empire could offer. It seemed to him, in the bitter urgency of his imperial passion, perhaps even poorer than it was. There was a smattering of Latin, a thinner smattering of Greek, a little patch of Mediterranean history and literature detached from past and future—all university history seemed to Oswald to be in disconnected fragments—but then he would have considered any history fragmentary that did not begin with the geological record and end with a clear tracing of every traceable consequence of the "period" in current affairs; there were mathematical specializations that did not so much broaden the mind as take it into a gully, modern and mediaeval language specializations, philosophical studies that were really not philosophical studies at all but partial examinations of remote and irrelevant systems, the study of a scrap of Plato or Aristotle here, or an excursion (by means of translations) into the Hegelian phraseology there. This sort of thing given out to a few thousand young men, for the most part greatly preoccupied with games, and to a few hundred young women, was all that Oswald could discover by way of mental binding for the entire empire. It seemed to him like innervating a body as big as the world with a brain as big as a pin's head. As Joan and Peter grew out of school and went up to Cambridge they became more and more aware of a note of lamentation and woe in the voice of their guardian. He talked at them, over their heads at lunch and dinner, to this or that visitor. He also talked to them. But he had a great dread of preachments. They were aware of his general discontent with the education he was giving them, but as yet they had no standards by which to judge his charges. Over their heads his voice argued that the universities would give them no access worth considering to the thoughts and facts of India, Russia, or China, that they were ignoring something stupendous called America, that their political and economic science still neglected the fact that every problem in politics, every problem in the organization of production and social co-operation is a psychological problem; and that all these interests were supremely urgent interests, and how the devil was one going to get these things in? But one thing Joan and Peter did grasp from these spluttering dissertations that flew round and about them. They had to find out all the most important things in life for themselves.

Perhaps the problem of making the teacher of youth an inspiring figure is an insoluble one. At any rate, there was no great stir evoked in Joan and Peter by the personalities of any of their university tutors, lecturers, and professors. These seemed to be for the most part little-spirited, gossiping men. They had also an effect of being underpaid; they had been caught early by the machinery of prize and scholarship, bred, "in the menagerie"; they were men who knew nothing of the world outside, nothing of effort and adventure, nothing of sin and repentance. Not that there were not whispers and scandals about, but such sins as the dons knew of were rather in the nature of dirty affectations, got out of Petronius and Suetonius and practised with a tremendous sense of devilment behind locked doors, than those graver and larger sins that really distress and mar mankind. As Joan and Peter encountered these master minds, they appeared as gowned and capped individuals, hurrying to lecture-rooms, delivering lectures that were often hasty and indistinct, making obscure but caustic allusions to rival teachers, parrying the troublesome inquiring student with an accustomed and often quite pretty wit. With a lesser subtlety and a greater earnestness the women dons had fallen in with this tradition. There were occasional shy personal contacts.

But at his tea or breakfast the don was usually too anxious to impress Peter with the idea that he himself was really only a sort of overgrown undergraduate, to produce any other effect at all.

Into the Cambridge lecture rooms and laboratories went Joan and Peter, notebook in hand, and back to digestion in their studies, and presently they went into examination rooms where they vindicated their claim to have attended to textbook and lecture. In addition Peter did some remarkably good sketches of tutors and professors and fellow students. This was their "grind," Joan and Peter considered, a drill they had to go through; it became them to pass these tests creditably—if only to play the game towards old Nobby. Only with Peter's specialization in biology did he begin to find any actuality in these processes. He found a charm in phylogenetic speculations; and above the narrow cañons of formal "research" there were fascinating uplands of wisdom. Upon those uplands there lay a light in which even political and moral riddles took on a less insoluble aspect. But going out upon those uplands was straying from the proper work. . . . Joan got even less from her moral philosophy. Her principal teacher was a man shaped like a bubble, whose life and thought was all the blowing of a bubble. He claimed to have *proved* human immortality. It was, he said, a very long and severe logical process. About desire, about art, about social association, about love, about God—for he knew also that there was no God—it mattered not what deep question assailed him, this gifted being would dip into his Hegelian suds and blow without apparent effort, and there you were—as wise as when you started! And off the good man would float, infinitely self-satisfied and manifestly absurd.

But even Peter's biology was only incidentally helpful in answering the fierce questions that life was now thrusting upon him and Joan. Nor had this education linked them up to any great human solidarity. It was like being guided into a forest—and lost there—by queer, absent-minded men. They had no sense of others being there too, upon a common adventure. . . .

"And it is all that I can get for them!" said Oswald. "Bad as it is, it is the best thing there is."

He tried to find comfort in comparisons.

"Has any country in the world got anything much better?"

§ 14

One day Oswald found himself outside Cambridge on the Huntingdon road. It was when he had settled that Peter was to enter Trinity, and while he was hesitating between Newnham and Girton as Joan's destiny. There was a little difficulty in discovering Girton. Unlike Newnham, which sits down brazenly in Cambridge, Girton is but half-heartedly at Cambridge, coyly a good mile from the fountains of knowledge, hiding its blushes between tall trees. He was reminded absurdly of a shy, nice girl sitting afar off until father should come out of the public-house. . . .

He fell thinking about the education of women in Great Britain.

At first he had been disposed to think chiefly of Peter's education and to treat Joan's as a secondary matter; but little by little, as he watched British affairs close at hand, he had come to measure the mischief feminine illiteracy can do in the world. In no country do the lunch and dinner-party, the country house and personal acquaintance, play so large a part in politics as they do in Great Britain. And the atmosphere of all that inner world of influence is a woman-made atmosphere, and an atmosphere made by women who are for the most part untrained and unread. Here at Girton and Newnham, and at Oxford at Somerville, he perceived there could not be room for a tithe of the girls of the influential and governing classes. Where were the rest? English womanhood was as yet only nibbling at university life. Where were the girls of the peerage, the county-family girls and the like? Their brothers came up, but they stayed at home and were still educated scarcely better than his Aunt Charlotte had been educated forty years ago—by a genteel person, by a sort of mental maid who did their minds as their maids did their hair for the dinner-table.

"No wonder," he said, "they poison politics and turn it all into personal intrigues. No wonder they want religion to be just a business of personal consolations. No wonder every sort of charlatan and spook dealer, fortune-teller and magic healer flourishes in London. Well, Joan anyhow shall have whatever they can give her here. . . .

"It's better than nothing. And she'll talk and read. . . ."

§ 15

But school and university are only the formal part of education. The larger part of the education of every human being is and always has been and must be provided by the Thing that Is. Every adult transaction has as its most important and usually most neglected aspect its effect upon the minds of the young. Behind school and university the Empire itself was undesignedly addressing Joan and Peter. It was, so to speak, gesticulating at them over their teachers' heads and under their teachers' arms. It was performing ceremonies and exhibiting spectacles of a highly suggestive nature.

In a large and imposing form certain ideas were steadfastly thrust at Joan and Peter. More particularly was the idolization of the monarchy thrust upon them. In terms of zeal and reverence the press, the pulpit, and the world at large directed the innocent minds of Joan and Peter to the monarch as if that individual were the Reason, the Highest Good and Crown of the collective life. Nothing else in the world of Joan and Peter got anything like the same tremendous show. Their early years were coloured by the reflected glories of the Diamond Jubilee; followed the funeral pomps of Queen Victoria, with much mobbing of negligent or impecunious people not in black by the loyal London crowd; then came the postponed and then the actual coronation of King Edward, public prayings for his health, his stupendous funeral glories; succeeded by the coronation of King George, and finally, about the time that Joan followed Peter up to Cambridge, the Coronation Durbar. The multitude which could not go to India went at least to the Scala cinema, and saw the adoration in all its natural colours. Reverent crowds choked that narrow by-street. Across all the life and activities of England, across all her intellectual and moral effort, holding up legislation, interfering with industry, stopping the traffic, masking every reality of the collective life, these vast formalities trailed with a magnificent priority. Nothing was respected as they were respected! Sober statesmen were seen invested in strange garments that no sensible person would surely wear except for the gravest reasons; the archbishops and bishops were discovered bent with reverence, invoking the name of God freely, blessing the Crown with the utmost gravity, investing the Sovereign with Robe and Orb, Ring and Sceptre, anointing him with the Golden Coronation Spoon. Either the Crown was itself a matter of altogether supreme importance to the land or else it was the most stupendous foolery that ever mocked and confused the grave realities of a great people's affairs.

The effect of it upon the minds of our two young people was—complicating. How complicating it is few people realize who have not closely studied the educational process of the British mind as a whole. Then it becomes manifest that the monarch, the state church, and the system of titles and social precedence centering upon the throne, constitute a system of mental entanglements against which British education struggles at an enormous disadvantage. The monarchy in Great Britain is a compromise that was accepted by a generation regardless of education and devoid of any sense of the future. It is now a mask upon the British face; it is a gaudy and antiquated and embarrassing wrapping about the energies of the nation. Because of it Britain speaks to her youth, as to the world, with two voices. She speaks as a democratic republic, just ever so little crowned, and also she speaks as a succulently loyal Teutonic monarchy. Either she is an adolescent democracy whose voice is breaking or an old monarchy at the squeaking stage. Now her voice is the full strong voice of a great people, now it pipes ridiculously. She perplexes the world and stultifies herself.

That was why her education led up to no such magnificent exposition and consolidation of purpose as Oswald dreamt of for his wards. Instead, the track presently lost itself in a maze of prevarications and evasions. The country was double-minded, double-mindedness had become its habit, and it had lost the power of decision. Every effort to broaden and modernize university education in Britain encountered insurmountable difficulties because of this fundamental dispersal of aim. The court got in the way, the country clergy got in the way, the ruling-class families got in the way. It is impossible to turn a wandering, chance-made track into a good road until you know where it is to go. And that question of destination was one that no Englishman before the war could be induced to put into plain language. Double-mindedness had become his second nature. From the very outset it had taken possession of him. When a young American goes to his teacher to ask why he should serve his state, he is shown a flag of thirteen stripes and eight and forty stars and told a very plain and inspiring history. His relations to his country are thenceforward as simple and unquestionable as a child's to its mother. He may be patriotic or unpatriotic as a son may be dutiful or undutiful, but he will not be muddle-headed. But when Joan and Peter first began to realize that they belonged to the British Empire they were shown a little old German woman and told that reverence for her linked us in a common abjection with the millions of India. They were told also that really this little old lady did nothing of the slightest importance and that the country was the freest democracy on earth, ruled by its elected representatives. And each of these preposterously contradictory stories pursued them in an endless series of variations up to adolescence. . . .

To two naturally clear-headed young people it became presently as palpably absurd to have a great union of civilized states thus impersonated as it is to have Wall impersonated by Snout the Tinker in *A Midsummer Night's Dream*. They were already jeering at royalty and the church with Aunt Phyllis long before they went up to Cambridge. There they found plenty of associates to jeer with them. And there too they found a quite congenial parallel stream of jeering against Parliament, which pretended to represent the national mind and quality, but which was elected by a method that manifestly gave no chance to any candidate who was not nominated by a party organization. In times of long established peace, when the tradition of generations has established the illusion of the profoundest human security, men's minds are not greatly distressed by grotesqueness and absurdity in their political forms. It is all part of the humour and the good-humour of life. When one believes that all the tigers in the jungle are dead, it is quite amusing to walk along the jungle paths in a dressing-gown with a fan instead of a gun. Joan and Peter grew up to the persuasion that the crown above them was rather a good joke, and that Parliament and its jobs and party flummery were also a joke, and that the large, deep rottenness in this British world about them was perhaps in the nature of things and anyhow beyond their altering. They too were becoming double-minded according to the tradition of the land.

Yet beneath this acquiescence in the deep-rooted political paradox of Britain they were capable of the keenest interest in a number of questions that they really believed were alive. It became manifest to them that this great golden preposterous world was marred by certain injustices and unkindnesses. Something called Labour they heard was unhappy and complained of unfair treatment, certain grumblings came from India and Ireland, and there was a curiously exciting subject which demanded investigation and reforming activities called the sex question. And generally there seemed to be, for no particular reason, a lot of restrictions upon people's conduct.

In addition Peter had acquired from Oswald, rather by way of example than precept, a very definite persuasion, and Joan had acquired a persuasion that was perhaps not quite so clearly and deeply cut, that to make it respectable there ought to be something in one's life in the nature of special work. In Oswald's case it was his African interest. Peter thought that his own work might perhaps be biological. But that one's work ought to join on to the work of the people or that all the good work in the world should make one whole was a notion that had not apparently entered Peter's mind. Oswald with his dread of preachments was doubtful about any deliberate dissertations in the matter. He got

Peter to begin the *Martyrdom of Man,* which had so profoundly affected his own life, but Peter expressed doubts about the correctness of Reade's Egyptian history, and put the book aside and did not go on reading it.

At times Oswald tried to say something to Joan and Peter of his conception of the Empire as a great human enterprise, playing a dominating part in the establishment of a world peace and a world civilization, and giving a form and direction and pride to every life within it.   But these perpetual noises of royalty in its vulgarest, most personal form, the loyalist chatter of illiterate women and the clamour of the New Imperialism to "tax the foreigner" and exploit the empire for gain, drowned his intention while it was still unspoken in his mind.   There were moments when he could already ask himself whether this empire he had shaped his life to serve, this knightly empire of his, enlightened, righteous, and predominant, was anything better than a dream— or a lie.

§ 16

When Joan left Highmorton she came into the market-place of ideas. She began to read the newspaper. She ceased to be a leggy person with a skirt like a kilt and a dark shock of hair not under proper control; instead, she became visibly a young lady, albeit a very young young lady, and suddenly all adult conversation was open to her.

Under the brotherly auspices of Peter she joined the Cambridge University Fabian Society. Peter belonged to it, but he explained that he didn't approve of it.   He was in it for its own good.   She also took a place in two suffrage organizations, and subscribed to three suffrage papers.   Tel Wymark, who was also in Newton Hall, introduced her to the Club of Strange Faiths, devoted to "the impartial examination of all religious systems."   And she went under proper escort to the First Wednesday in Every Month Teas in Bunny Cuspard's rooms. Bunny was an ex-collegiate student, he had big, comfortable rooms in Siddermorton Street, and these gatherings of his were designed to be discussions, very memorable discussions of the most advanced

type, about this and that.   As a matter of fact they consisted
in about equal proportions of awkward silences, scornful
treatment of current reputations, and Bunny, in a loose, in-
accurate way, spilling your tea or handing you edibles.
Bunny's cakes and sandwiches were wonderful; in that respect he was a born hostess.   Junior dons and chance visitors
to Cambridge would sometimes drift in to Bunny's intellectual feasts, and here it was that Joan met young Winterbaum
again.

Young Winterbaum was rather a surprise. He had got
his features together astonishingly since the days of Miss
Murgatroyd's school; he had grown a moustache, much more
of a moustache than Peter was to have for years yet, and
was altogether remarkably grown up and a man of the
world. "Funny lot," he remarked to Joan when he had
sat down beside her. "Why do *you* come to Cambridge?"

"My people make me come up here," he explained; "family considerations, duty to the old country, loyalty to the old
college, and all that. But I'd rather be painting. It's the
only live thing just now. You up to anything?"

"Ears and eyes and mouth wide open," said Joan.

"This show isn't worth it. Do you ever drift towards
Chelsea?"

Joan said she went to Hampstead now and then; she stayed
sometimes with the Sheldricks, who were in a congested house
on Downshire Hill now, and sometimes with Miss Jepson.
Henceforth, now that she was no longer under the Highmorton yoke, she hoped to be in London oftener.

"Did you see the Picasso show?" asked Winterbaum.

She had not.

"You missed something," said young Winterbaum, just
like old times. "Picasso, Mancini; these are the gods of my
idolatry. . . ."

Bunny Cuspard interrupted clumsily with some specially
iced cakes. Joan, accepting a cake, discovered Wilmington
talking absentmindedly to her chaperon and looking Pogroms
at Winterbaum. So Joan, pleased rather than excited by
this chance evidence of a continuing interest, lifted up a face
of bright recognition and smiled and nodded to Wilmington. . . .

§ 17

It was the ambition of Mrs. Sheldrick and her remaining daughters—some of them had married—to make their home on Downshire Hill "a little bit of the London *Quartier Latin.*"

Mr. Sheldrick had worn out the large, loose, tweed suit that had held him together for so long, he had gone to pieces altogether and was dead and buried, and the Sheldricks were keeping a home together by the practice of decorative arts and promiscuous hospitalities. Mrs. Sheldrick was writing a little in the papers of the weaker among the various editors who lived within her social range; little vague reviews and poems she wrote, with a quiet smile, that were not so much allusive as with an air of having recently had a flying visit from an allusion that was unable to stay. Sydney Sheldrick was practising sculpture, and Babs was attending the London School of Dramatic Art, to which Adela Murchison had also found her way. Antonia, the eldest, was in business, making djibbah-like robes.

There was downstairs and the passage and staircase and upstairs, a sitting-room in front, and a sort of oriental lounge (that later in the evening became the bedroom of Antonia and Babs) behind. It had all been decorated in the most modern style by Antonia in a very blue blue that seemed a little threadbare in places and very large, suggestive shapes of orange, with a sort of fringe of black and white chequers and a green ceiling with harsh pink stars. And the chairs, except for the various ottomans and cosy corners which were in faded blue canvas, had been painted bright pink or grey.

Into this house they gathered, after nine and more particularly on Saturdays, all sorts of people who chanced to be connected by birth, marriage, misfortune, or proclivity with journalism or the arts. Hither came Aunt Phœbe Stubland, and read a paper called insistently: *Watchman, What of the Night? What of it?* and quite up to its title; and hither too came Aunt Phyllis Stubland, quietly observant. But quite a lot of writers came. And in addition there were endless conspirators. There was Mrs. O'Grady, the beauti-

ful Irish patriot, who was always dressed like a procession
of Hibernians in New York, and there was Patrick Lynch,
a long, lax black object, ending below in large dull boots,
and above in a sad white face under wiry black hair, grieving for ever that grief for Ireland—*Cathleen ni Houlihan*
and all the rest of it—that only these long, black, pale Irishmen can understand. And there was Eric Schmidt, who
was rare among Irish patriots because of his genuine knowledge of Erse. All these were great conspirators. Then
there was Mrs. Punk, who had hunger-struck three times,
and Miss Corcoran-Deeping the incendiary. And American
socialists. And young Indians. And one saw the venerable
figure of Mr. Woodjer, very old now and white and deaf
and nervous and indistinct, who had advocated in several
beautiful and poetical little volumes a new morality that
would have put the wind up of the Cities of the Plain.
And Winterbaum drifted in, but cautiously, as doubting
whether it wasn't just "a bit too marginal," to bring away
his two frizzy-haired sisters, very bright-eyed and eager,
rapid-speaking and *au fait,* and wonderfully bejewelled for
creatures so young. They were going in for dancing; they
did Spanish dances, stupendously clicking down their red
heels with absolute precision together; they took the Sheldricks on the way to the Contangos or the Mondaines or the
Levisons, or even to the Hoggenheimers; they glittered at
Downshire Hill like birds of Paradise, and had the loveliest
necks and shoulders and arms. Outside waited young Winterbaum's coupé—a very smart little affair in black and
cream, with an electric starter wonderfully fitted.

Here too came young Huntley, who had written three
novels before he was twenty-two, and who was now thirty
and quite well known, not only as a novelist of reputation,
but as a critic eminently unpopular with actor managers;
a blond young man with a strong profile, a hungry, scornful
expression and a greedy, large blue eye that wandered about
the crush as if it sought something, until it came to rest
upon Joan. Thereafter Mr. Huntley's other movements and
conversation were controlled by a resolution to edge towards
and overshadow and dominate Joan with the profile as much
as possible.

Joan, by various delicacies of perception, was quite aware of these approaches without seeming at any time to regard Huntley directly; and by a subtlety quite imperceptible to him she drifted away from each advance. She did not know who he was, and though the profile interested her, his steadfast advance towards her seemed to be premature. Until suddenly an apparently quite irrelevant incident spun her mind round to the idea of encouraging him.

The incident was the arrival of Peter.

Early in the afternoon he had vanished from Mrs. Jepson's, where he and Joan were staying; he had not come in to dinner, and now suddenly he appeared conspicuously in this gathering of the Sheldricks', conspicuously in the company of Hetty Reinhart, who was to Joan, for quite occult reasons, the most detestable of all his large circle of detestable friends. That alone was enough to tax the self-restraint of an exceedingly hot-tempered foster sister. (So this was what Peter had been doing with his time! This had been his reason for neglecting his own household! At the *Petit Riche*, or some such place—with *her!* A girl with a cockney accent! A girl who would stroke your arm as soon as speak to you! . . .) But though the larger things in life strain us, it is the smaller things that break us. What finally turned Joan over was a glance, a second's encounter with Peter's eye. Hetty had sailed forward with that extraordinary effect of hers of being a grown-up, experienced woman, to greet Mrs. Sheldrick, and Peter stood behind, disregarded. (His expression of tranquil self-satisfaction was maddening.) His eye went round the room looking, Joan knew, for two people. It rested on Joan.

The question that Peter was asking Joan mutely across the room was in effect this: "Are you behaving yourself, Joan?"

Then, not quite reassured by an uncontrollable scowl, Peter looked away to see if some one else was present. Some one else apparently wasn't present, and Joan was unfeignedly sorry.

He was looking for Mir Jelalludin, the interesting young Indian with the beautifully modelled face, whom Joan had met and talked to at the Club of Strange Faiths. At the

Club of Strange Faiths one day she had been suddenly
moved to make a short speech about the Buddhist idea of
Nirvana, which one of the speakers had described as extinction. Making a speech to a little meeting was not a very
difficult thing for Joan; she had learnt how little terrible a
thing is to do in the Highmorton debating society, where
she had been sustained by a grim determination to score off
Miss Frobisher. She said that she thought the real intention was not extinction at all, but the escape of the individual
consciousness after its living pilgrimage from one incarnate
self to another into the universal consciousness. That was
the very antithesis of extinction; one lost oneself indeed,
but one lost oneself not in darkness and non-existence, but
in light and the fullness of existence. There was all the
difference between a fainting fit and ecstasy between these
two conceptions. And it was true of experience that one
was least oneself, least self-conscious and egotistical at one's
time of greatest excitement.

Mir Jelalludin received these remarks with earnest applause. He made as if to speak after her, rose in his place,
and then hastily sat down. Afterwards he came and spoke
to her, quite modestly and simply, without the least imper-
tinence.

He explained, with a pleasant staccato accent and little
slips in his pronunciation that suggested restricted English
conversation and much reading of books, how greatly he had
been wanting to say just what she had said, "so bew-ti-
fully," but he had been restrained by "impafction of the
pronunsation. So deefi'clt, you know." One heard English people so often not doing justice to Indian ideas so that
it was very pleasant to hear them being quite sympathetically
put.

There was something very pleasing in the real intellectual
excitement that had made him speak to her, and there was
something very pleasing to the eye in the neat precision with
which his brown features were chiselled and the decisive accuracy of every single hair on his brow. He was, he explained, a Moslem, but he was interested in every school of Indian thought. He was afraid he was not very orthodox, and
he showed a smile of the most perfect teeth. There had always

been a tendency to universalism in Indian thought, that affected even the Moslem. Did she know anything of the
Brahmo Somaj? Had she read any novel of Chatterji's
There was at least one great novel of his the English ought
to read, the *Ananda Math*. No one could understand Indian thought properly who had not read it. He had a translation of it into English—which he would lend her.

Would she be interested to read it?

Might he send it to her?

Joan's chaperon was a third year girl who put no bar
upon these amenities. Joan accepted the book and threw
out casually that she sometimes went to Bunny Cuspard's
teas. If Mr. Jelalludin sent her Chatterji's book she could
return it to Bunny Cuspard's rooms.

It was in Bunny Cuspard's room that Peter had first
become aware of this exotic friendship. He discovered his
Joan snugly in a corner listening to an explanation of the
attitude of Islam towards women. It had been enormously
misrepresented in Christendom. Mr. Jelalludin was very
earnest in his exposition, and Joan listened with a pleasant
smile and regarded him pleasantly and wished that she
could run her fingers just once along his eyebrow without
having her motives misunderstood.

But at the sight of his Joan engaged in this confabulation
Peter suddenly discovered all the fiercest traits of race pride.
He fretted about the room and was rude to other people and
watched a book change hands, and waited scarcely twenty
seconds after the end of Joan's conversation before he came
up to her.

"I say, Joan," he said, "you can't go chumming with
Indians anyhow."

"Peter," she said, "we've chummed with India."

"Oh, nonsense! Not socially. Their standards are different."

"I hope they are," said Joan. "The way you make these
Indian boys here feel like outcasts is disgraceful."

"They're different. The men aren't uncivil to them.
But it isn't for you——"

"It's for all English people to treat them well. He's a
charming young man."

"It isn't *done*, Joan."

"It's going to be, Petah."

"You're meeting him again?"

"If I think proper."

"Oh!" said Peter, baffled for the time. "All *right*, Joan."

A fierce exchange of notes followed. "Don't you understand the fellow's a polygamist?" Peter wrote. "He keeps his women in purdah. No decent woman could be talked to in India as he talked to you. Not even an introduction. Personally, I've no objection to any friends you make provided they are decent friends. . . ."

"He isn't a polygamist," Joan replied. "I've asked him. And every one says he's a first-rate cricketer. As for decent friends, Peter——"

The issue had been still undecided when they came down for the Christmas vacation.

So far Joan had maintained her positions without passion. But now suddenly her indignation at Peter's interference flared to heaven. That he should come here, hot from Soho, to tyrannize over *her!* Indians indeed! As if Hetty Reinhart wasn't worse than a Gold Coast nigger! . . .

The only outward manifestation of this wild storm of resentment had been her one instant's scowl at Peter. Thereafter Joan became again the quiet, intelligently watchful young woman she had been all that evening. But now she turned herself through an angle of about thirty degrees towards Huntley, who was talking to old Mrs. Jex, the wonder of Hampstead, who used to know George Eliot and Huxley, the while he was regarding Joan with sidelong covetousness. Joan lifted her eyes towards him with an expression of innocent interest. The slightly projecting blue eyes seemed to leap in response.

Mrs. Jex was always rather inattentive to her listener when she was reciting her reminiscences, and Huntley was able to turn away from her quietly without interrupting the flow.

The Sheldrick circle scorned the formalities of introductions. "Are you from the Slade school?" said Huntley.

"Cambridge," said Joan.

"My name's Gavan Huntley."

But this was going to be more amusing than Joan had expected. This was a real live novelist—Joan's first. Not a fortnight ago she had read *The Pernambuco Bunshop*, and thought it rather clever and silly.

"Not *the* Gavan Huntley?" she said.

His face became faintly luminous with satisfaction. "Just Gavan Huntley," he said with a large smile.

"The Pernambuco Bunshop?" she said.

"Guilty," he pleaded, smiling still more naïvely.

One had expected something much less natural in a novelist.

"I *loved* it," said Joan, and Huntley was hers to do what she liked with. Joan's idea of a proper conversation required it to be in a corner. "Do Sheldricks never sit down?" she asked. "I've been standing all the evening."

"They can't," he said confidentially. "They're the other sort of Dutch doll, the cheap sort, that hasn't got joints at the knees."

"Antonia sometimes leans against the wall."

"Her utmost. The next thing would be to sit on the floor with her legs straight out. I've seen her do that. But there is a sort of bench on the staircase landing."

Thither they made their way, and there presently Peter found them.

He found them because he was making for that very corner in the company of Sydney Sheldrick. "Hullo!" said Sydney. "That you, Joan?"

"We've taken this corner for the evening," said Huntley, laying a controlling hand on Joan's pretty wrist.

Joan and Peter regarded each other darkly.

"There ought to be more seats about somewhere," said Sydney. "Come up to the divan, old Peter. . . ."

Of course Peter must object to Huntley. They were scarcely out of the Sheldricks' house when he began. "That man Huntley's a bad egg, Joan. Everybody knows it."

For a time they disputed about Huntley.

"Peter," said Joan, with affected calm, "is there any man, do you think, to whom so—so untrustworthy a girl as I am might safely talk?"

Peter seemed to consider. "There's chaps like Troop," he said.

"Troop!" said Joan, relying on her intonation.

"It isn't that you're untrustworthy," said Peter.

"Fragile?"

"It's the look and tone of things."

"I wonder how you get these ideas."

"What ideas?"

"Of how I behave in a corner with Jelalludin or Gavan Huntley."

"I haven't suggested anything."

"You've suggested everything. Do you think I collect stray kisses like Sydney Sheldrick? Do you think I'm a dirty little—little—cocotte like Hetty Reinhart?"

"*Joan!*"

"*Well,*" said Joan savagely, and said no more.

Peter came to the defence of Hetty belatedly. "How can you say such things of Hetty?" he asked. "What can you know about her?"

"Pah! I can smell what she is across a room. Do you think I'm an absolute young fool, Peter?"

"You've got no right, Joan——"

"Why argue, Peter, why argue? When things are plain. Can't you go your own way, Peter"—Joan was annoyed to find suddenly that she was weeping. Tears were running down her face. But the road was dark, and perhaps if she gave no sign Peter would not see. "You go your own way, Peter, go your own way, and let me go mine."

Peter was silent for a little while. Then compunction betrayed itself in his voice.

"It's you I'm thinking of, Joan. I can't bear to see you make yourself cheap."

"Cheap! And *you?*"

"I'm different. I'm altogether different. A man is."

Silence for a time. Joan seemed to push back her hair, and so smeared the tears from her face.

"We interfere with each other," she said at last. "We interfere with each other. What is the good of it? You've got to go your way and I've got to go mine. We used to have fun—lots of fun. *Now. . . .*"

She couldn't say any more for a while.

"I'm going my own way, Peter. It's a different way——
Leave me alone. Keep off!"

They said no more. When they got in they found Miss
Jepson sitting by the fire, and she had got them some
cocoa and biscuits. The headache that had kept her from
the Sheldrick festival had lifted, and Joan plunged at once
into a gay account of the various people she had seen that
evening—saving and excepting Gavan Huntley. But Peter
stood by the fireplace, silent, looking down into the fire, sulking or grieving. All the while that Joan rattled on to Miss
Jepson she was watching him with almost imperceptible
glances and wondering whether he sulked or grieved. Did
he feel as she felt? If he sulked—well, confound him!
But what if this perplexing dissension hurt him as much as
it was hurting her!

§ 18

Joan had long since lost that happiness, that perfect
assurance, that intense appreciation of the beauty in things
which had come to her with early adolescence. She was
troubled and perplexed in all her ways. She was full now
of stormy, indistinct desires and fears, and a gnawing, indefinite impatience. No religion had convinced her of a purpose in her life, neither Highmorton nor Cambridge had
suggested any mundane devotion to her, nor pointed her
ambitions to a career. The only career these feminine schools
and colleges recognized was a career of academic successes
and High School teaching, intercalated with hunger strikes
for the Vote, and Joan had early decided she would rather
die than teach in a High School. Nor had she the quiet
assurance her own beauty would have given her in an earlier
generation of a discreet choice of lovers and marriage and
living "happily ever afterwards." She had a horror of
marriage lurking in her composition; Mrs. Pybus and Highmorton had each contributed to that; every one around her
spoke of it as an entire abandonment of freedom. Moreover there was this queerness about her birth—she was beginning to understand better now in what that queerness

consisted—that seemed to put her outside the customary ceremonies of veil and orange blossoms. Why did they not tell her all about it—what her mother was and where her mother was? It must be a pretty awful business, if neither Aunt Phyllis nor Aunt Phœbe would ever allude to it. It would have to come out—perhaps some monstrous story—before she could marry. And who could one marry? She could not conceive herself marrying any of these boys she met, living somewhere cooped up in a little house with solemn old Troop, or under the pursuing eyes, the convulsive worship, of Wilmington. She had no object in life, no star by which to steer, and she was full of the fever of life. She was getting awfully old. She was eighteen. She was nineteen. Soon she would be twenty.

All her being, in her destitution of any other aim that had the slightest hold upon her imagination, was crying out for a lover.

It was a lover she wanted, not a husband; her mind made the clearest distinction between the two. He would come and unrest would cease, confusion would cease and beauty would return. Her lover haunted all her life, an invisible yet almost present person. She could not imagine his face nor his form, he was the blankest of beings, and yet she was so sure she knew him that if she were to see him away down a street or across a crowded room, instantly, she believed, she would recognize him. And until he came life was a torment of suspense. Life was all wrong and discordant, so wrong and discordant that at times she could have hated her lover for keeping her waiting so wretchedly.

And she had to go on as though this suspense was nothing. She had to disregard this vast impatience of her being. And the best way to do that, it seemed to her, was to hurry from one employment to another, never to be alone, never without some occupation, some excitement. Her break with. Peter had an extraordinary effect of release in her mind. Hitherto, whatever her resentment had been she had admitted in practice his claim to exact a certain discretion from her; his opinion had been, in spite of her resentment, a standard for her. Now she had no standard at all—unless it was a rebellious purpose to spite him. On Joan's personal conduct the thought of Oswald, oddly enough, had scarcely any influence at all. She adored him as one might a political or historical hero; she wanted to stand well in his sight, but the idea of him did not pursue her into the details of her behaviour at all. He seemed preoccupied with ideas and unobservant. She had never had any struggle with him; he had never made her do anything. And as for Aunts Phyllis and Phœbe—while the latter seemed to make vague gestures towards quite unutterable liberties, the former maintained an attitude of nervous disavowal. She was a woman far too uncertain-minded for plain speaking. She was a dear. Clearly she hated cruelty and baseness; except in regard to such things she set no bounds.

Hitherto Joan had had a very few flirtations; the extremest thing upon her conscience was Bunny Cuspard's kiss. She had the naturally shilly-shally of a girl; she was strongly moved to all sorts of flirtings and experimentings with love, and very adventurous and curious in these matters; and also she had a system of inhibitions, pride, hesitation, fastidiousness, and something beyond these things, a sense of some ultimate value that might easily be lost, that held her back. Rebelling against Peter had somehow also set her rebelling against these restraints. Why shouldn't she know this and that? Why shouldn't she try this and that? Why, for instance, was she always "shutting up" Adela whenever she began to discourse in her peculiar way upon the great theme? Just a timid prude she had been, but now——.

And all this about undesirable people and unseemly places, all this picking and choosing as though the world was mud; what nonsense it was! She could take care of herself surely!

She began deliberately to feel her way through all her friendships to see whether this thing, passion, lurked in any · of them. It was an interesting exercise of her wits to try over a youth like old Troop, for example; to lure him on by a touch of flattery, a betrayal of warmth in her interest, to reciprocal advances. At first Troop wasn't in the least in love with her, but she succeeded in suggesting to him that he was. But the passion in him released an unsuspected fund of egotistical discourse; he developed a disposition to explain himself and his mental operations in a large, flattering way both by word of mouth and by letter. Even when he was roused to a sense of her as lovable, he did not become really interested in her but only in his love for her. He arrived at one stride at the same unanalytical acceptance of her as of his God and the Church and the King and his parents and all the rest of the Anglican system of things. She was his girl—"the kid." He really wasn't interested in those other things any more than he was in her; once he had given her her rôle in relation to him his attention returned to himself. The honour, integrity, and perfection of Troop were the consuming occupations of his mind. This was an edifying thing to discover, but not an entertaining thing to pursue; and after a time Joan set herself to avoid, miss, and escape from Troop on every possible occasion. But Troop prided himself upon his persistence. He took to writing her immense, ill-spelt, manly letters, with sentences beginning: "You understand me very little if——." It was clear he was hers only until some simpler, purer, more receptive and acquisitive girl swam into his ken.

Wilmington, on the other hand, was a silent covetous lover. Joan could make him go white, but she could not make him talk. She was a little afraid of him and quite sure of him. But he was not the sort of young man one can play with, and she marvelled greatly that any one could desire her so much and amuse her so little. Bunny Cuspard was a more animated subject for experiment, and you could play with him a lot. He danced impudently. He could pat Joan's shoulder, press her hand, slip his arm round her waist and bring his warm face almost to a kissing contact as though it was all nothing. Did these approaches warm her blood? Did she warm his? Anyhow it didn't matter, and it wasn't anything.

Then there was Graham Prothero, a very good-looking friend of Peter's, whom she had met while skating. He had a lively eye, and jumped after a meeting or so straight into Joan's dreams, where he was still more lively and good-looking. She wished she knew more certainly whether she had got into his dreams.

Meanwhile Joan's curiosity had not spared Jelalludin.

She had had him discoursing on the beauties of Indian love, and spinning for her imagination a warm moonlight vision of still temples reflected in water tanks, of silvery water shining between great lily leaves, of music like the throbbing of a nerve, of brown bodies garlanded with flowers. There had been a loan of Rabindranath Tagore's love poems. And once he had sent her some flowers.

Any of these youths she could make her definite lover she knew, by an act of self-adaptation and just a little reciprocal giving. Only she had no will to do that. She felt she must not will anything of the sort. The thing must come to her; it must take possession of her. Sometimes, indeed, she had the oddest fancy that perhaps suddenly one of these young men would become transfigured; would cease to be his clumsy, ineffective self, and change right into that wonderful, that compelling being who was to set all things right. There were moments when it seemed about to happen. And then the illusion passed, and she saw clearly that it was just old Bunny or just staccato Mir Jelalludin.

In Huntley, Joan found something more intriguing than this pursuit of the easy and the innocent. Huntley talked with a skilful impudence that made a bold choice of topics seem the most natural in the world. He presented himself as a leader in a great emancipation of women. They were to be freed from "the bondage of sex." The phrase awakened a warm response in Joan, who was finding sex a yoke about her imagination. Sex, Huntley declared, should be as incidental in a woman's life as it was in a man's. But before that could happen the world must free its mind from the "superstition of chastity," from the idea that by one single step a woman passed from the recognizable into an impossible category. We made no such distinction in the case of men; an artist or a business man was not suddenly thrust out of the social system by a sexual incident. A woman was either Mrs. or Miss; a gross publication of elemental facts that were surely her private affair. No one asked whether a man had found his lover. Why should one proclaim it in the case of a woman by a conspicuous change of her name? Here, and not in any matter of votes or economics was the real feminine grievance. His indigna-

tion was contagious. It marched with all Joan's accumulated prejudice against marriage, and all her growing resentment at the way in which emotional unrest was distracting and perplexing her will and spoiling her work at Cambridge. But when Huntley went on to suggest that the
path to freedom lay in the heroic abandonment of the "fetish
of chastity," Joan was sensible of a certain lagging of spirit.
A complex of instincts that conspired to adumbrate that
unseen, unknown, and yet tyrannous lover, who would not
leave her in peace and yet would not reveal himself, stood
between her and the extremities of Huntley's logic.

There were moments when he seemed to be pretending
to fill that oppressive void; moments when he seemed only to
be hinting at himself as a possible instrument of freedom.
Joan listened to him gravely enough so long as he theorized;
when he came to personal things she treated him with the
same experimental and indecisive encouragement that she
dealt out to her undergraduate friends. Huntley's earlier
pose of an intellectual friend was attractive and flattering;
then he began to betray passion, as it were, unwittingly. At
a fancy dress dance at Chelsea—and he danced almost as well
as Joan—he became moody. He was handsome that night
in black velvet and silver that betrayed much natural grace;
Joan was a nondescript in black and red, with short skirts
and red beads about her pretty neck. "Joan," he said suddenly, "you're getting hold of me. You're disturbing me."
He seemed to soliloquize. "I've not felt like this before."
Then very flatteringly and reproachfully, "You're so
damned intelligent, Joan. And you dance—as though God
made you to make me happy." He got her out into an open
passage that led from the big studio in which they had been
dancing, to a yard dimly lit by Chinese lanterns, and at the
dark turn of the passage kissed her more suddenly and violently than she had ever been kissed before. He kissed her
lips and held her until she struggled out of his arms. Up
to that moment Joan had been playing with him, half attracted and half shamming; then once more came the black
panic that had seized her with Bunny and Adela.

She did not know whether she liked him now or hated him.
She felt strange and excited. She made him go back with

her into the studio. "I've got to dance with Ralph Winter-baum," she said.

"Say you're not offended," he pleaded.

She gave him no answer. She did not know the answer. She wanted to get away and think. He perceived her confused excitement and did not want to give her time to think. She found Winterbaum and danced with him, and all the time, with her nerves on fire, she was watching Huntley, and he was watching her. Then she became aware of Peter regarding her coldly, over the plump shoulder of a fashion-plate artist. She went to him as soon as the dance was over.

"Peter," she said, "I want to go home."

He surveyed her. She was flushed and ruffled, and his eyes and mouth hardened.

"It's early."

"I want to go home."

"Right. You're a bit of a responsibility, Joan."

"Don't, then," she said shortly, and turned round to greet Huntley as though nothing had happened between them.

But she kept in the light and the crowd, and there was a constraint between them. "I want to talk to you more," he said, "and when we can talk without some one standing on one's toes all the time and listening hard. I wish you'd come to my flat and have tea with me one day. It's still and cosy, and I could tell you all sorts of things—things I can't tell you here."

Joan's dread of any appearance of timid virtue was overwhelming. And she was now blind with rage at Peter—why, she would have been at a loss to say. She wanted to behave outrageously with Huntley. But in Peter's sight. This struck her as an altogether too extensive invitation.

"I've never noticed much restraint in your conversation," she said.

"It's the interruptions I don't like," he said.

"You get me no ice, you get me no lemonade," she complained abruptly.

"That's what my dear Aunt Adelaide used to call changing the subject."

"It's the cry of outraged nature."

"But I saw you having an ice—not half an hour ago."

"Not the ice I wanted," said Joan.

"Distracting Joan! I suppose I must get you that ice. But about the tea?"

"I *hate* tea," said Joan, with a force of decision that for a time disposed of his project.

Just for a moment he hovered with his eye on her, weighing just what that decision amounted to, and in that moment she decided that he wasn't handsome, that there was something *unsound* about his profile, that he was pressing her foolishly. And anyhow, none of it really mattered. He was nothing really. She had been a fool to go into that dark passage, she ought to have known her man better; Huntley had been amusing hitherto and now the thing had got into a new phase that wouldn't, she felt, be amusing at all; after this he would pester. She hated being kissed. And Peter was a beast. Peter was a hateful beast. . . .

Joan and Peter went home in the same taxi—in a grim silence. Yet neither of them could have told what it was that kept them hostile and silent.

§ 19

But Joan and Peter were not always grimly silent with one another. The black and inexplicable moods came and passed again. Between these perplexing mute conflicts of will, they were still good friends. When they were alone together they were always disposed to be good friends; it was the presence and excitement and competition of others that disturbed their relationship; it was when the species invaded their individualities and threatened their association with its occult and passionate demands. They would motor-cycle together through the lanes and roads of Hertfordshire, lunch cheerfully at wayside inns, brotherly and sisterly, relapse again into mere boy and girl playfellows, race and climb trees, or, like fellow-students, share their common room amicably, dispute over a multitude of questions, and talk to Oswald. They both had a fair share of scholarly ambition and read pretty hard. They had both now reached the newspaper-reading stage. Peter was beginning to take an interest in politics, he wanted to discuss socialism and economic organization thoroughly; biological work alone among all scientific studies carries a philosophy of its own that illuminates these questions, and Oswald was happy to try over his current interests in the light of these fresh, keen young minds. Peter was a discriminating advocate of the ideas of Guild socialism; Oswald was still a cautious individualist drifting towards Fabianism. The great labour troubles that had followed the Coronation of King George had been necessary to convince him that all was not well with the economic organization of the empire. Hitherto he had taken economic organization for granted; it wasn't a matter for Sydenhams.

Pelham Ford at such times became a backwater from the main current of human affairs, the current that was now growing steadily more rapid and troubled. Thinking could go on at Pelham Ford. There were still forces in that old-world valley to resist the infection of intense impatience that was spreading throughout the world. The old red house behind its wall and iron gates seemed as stable as the little hills about it; the road and the row of great trees between the stream and the road, the high pathway and the ford and the village promised visibly to endure for a thousand years. It was when Aunt Phyllis or Aunt Phœbe descended upon the place to make a party, ''get a lot of young people down and brighten things up,'' or when the two youngsters went to London together into the Sheldrick translation of the *Quartier Latin,* or when they met in Cambridge in some crowded chattering room that imagination grew feverish, fierce jealousies awoke, temperaments jarred, and the urge of adolescence had them in its clutch again.

It was during one of these parties at Pelham Ford that Joan was to happen upon two great realizations, realizations of so profound an effect that they may serve to mark the end for her of this great process of emotional upheaval and discovery that is called adolescence. They left her shaped. They came to her in no dramatic circumstances, they were mere conversational incidents, but their effect was profound and conclusive.

In the New Year of 1914 Oswald was to take Peter to

Russia for three weeks. Before his departure, Aunt Phœbe had insisted that there should be a Christmas gathering of the young at Pelham Ford. They would skate or walk or toboggan or play hockey by day, and dress up and dance or improvize charades and burlesques in the evening. One or two Sheldricks would come, Peter and Joan could bring down any stray friends who had no home Christmas to call them, and Aunts Phyllis and Phœbe would collect a few young people in London.

The gathering was from the first miscellaneous. Christmas is a homing time for the undergraduates of both sexes, such modern spirits as the home failed to attract used to go in those days in great droves to the Swiss winter sports, and Joan found nobody but an ambitious Scotch girl whom she knew but slightly and Miss Scroby the historian, who was rather a friend for Aunt Phyllis than herself. Peter discovered that Wilmington intensely preferred Pelham Ford to his parental roof, and brought also two other stray men, orphans. This selection was supplemented by Aunt Phœbe, who had latterly made Hetty Reinhart her especial protégée. She descanted upon the obvious beauty of Hetty and upon the courage that had induced Hetty to leave her home in Preston and manage for herself in a great lonely studio upon Haverstock Hill. "The bachelor woman," said Aunt Phœbe; "armed with a latchkey and her purity. A vote shall follow. Hetty is not one of the devoted yet. But I have my hopes. We need our Beauty Chorus. Hetty shall be our Helen, and Holloway our Troy."

So with Peter's approval Hetty was added to the list before Joan could express an opinion, and appeared with a moderate sized valise that contained some extremely exiguous evening costumes, and a steadfast eye that rested most frequently on Peter. In addition Aunt Phœbe brought two Irish sisters, one frivolous, the other just recuperating from the hunger-strike that had ended her imprisonment for window-breaking in pursuit of the Vote, and a very shy youth of seventeen, Pryce, the caddie-poet. Huntley was to constitute a sort of outside element in the party, sharing apartments with young Sopwith Greene the musician, in the village about half a mile away. These two men were to work

and keep away when they chose, and come in for meals and
sports as they thought fit. At the eleventh hour had come a
pathetic and irresistible telegram from Adela Murchison:

Alone Xmas may I come wire if inconvenient.

and she, too, was comprehended.

The vicarage girls were available for games and meals
except on Sunday and Christmas Day; there was a friendly
family of five sons and two daughters at Braughing, a chal-
lenging hockey club at Bishop's Stortford, and a scratch collection at Newport available by motor-car for a pick-up
match if the weather proved, as it did prove, too open for
skating.

Oswald commonly stood these Aunt parties for a day or
so and then retreated to the Climax Club. Always beforehand he promised himself great interest and pleasure in the
company of a number of exceptionally bright and representative youths and maidens of the modern school, but always
the actual gathering fatigued him and distressed him. The
youths and maidens wouldn't be representative, they talked
too loud, too fast and too inconsecutively for him, their wit
was too rapid and hard—and they were all over the house.
It was hard to get mental contacts with them. They paired
off when there were no games afoot, and if ever talk at table
ceased to be fragmentary Aunt Phœbe took control of it. In
a day or so he would begin to feel at Pelham Ford like a
cat during a removal; driven out of his dear library, which
was the only available room for dancing, he would try to
work in his unaccustomed study, with vivid, interesting young
figures passing his window in groups of two or three, or only
too audibly discussing the world, each other, and their general arrangements, in the hall.

His home would have felt altogether chaotic to him but
for the presence, the unswerving, if usually invisible, presence of Mrs. Moxton, observing times and seasons, providing
copious suitable meals, dominating by means of the gong, replacing furniture at every opportunity, referring with a
calm dignity to Joan as the hostess for all the rules and sanc-
tions she deemed advisable. From unseen points of view one
felt her eye. One's consolation for the tumult lay in one's

confidence in this discretion that lay behind it.   Even Aunt
Phœbe's way of speaking of "our good Moxton" did not
mask the facts of the case.   Pelham Ford was ruled.   At
Pelham Ford even Aunt Phœbe came down to meals in time.
At Pelham Ford no fire, once lit, ever went out before it was
right for it to do so.   You might in pursuit of facetious
ends choose to put your pyjamas outside your other clothes,
wrap your window curtains about you, sport and dance, and
finally, drawn off to some other end, abandon these wrap-
pings in the dining-room or on the settee on the landing.
When you went to bed your curtains hung primly before
your window again, and your pyjamas lay folded and re-
proved upon your bed.

The disposition of the new generation to change its clothes,
adopt fantastic clothes, and at any reasonable excuse get
right out of its clothes altogether, greatly impressed Oswald.
Hetty in particular betrayed a delight in the beauties of her
own body with a freedom that in Oswald's youth was permitted only to sculpture.   But Adela made no secrets of
her plump shoulders and arms, and Joan struck him as insensitive.   Skimpiness was the fashion in dress at that time.
No doubt it was all for the best, like the frankness of Spartan maidens.   And another thing that brought a flavour of
harsh modernity into the house was the perpetual music and
dancing that raged about it.   There was a pianola in the
common room of Joan and Peter, but when they were alone
at home it served only for an occasional outbreak of Bach,
or Beethoven, or Chopin.   Now it was in a state of almost
continuous eruption.   Aunt Phyllis had ordered a number
of rolls of dance music from the Orchestrelle library, and
in addition she had brought down a gramophone.   Never before had music been so easy in the world as it was in those
days.   In Oswald's youth music, good music, was the rare
privilege of a gifted few, one heard it rarely and listened
with reverence.   Nowadays Joan could run through a big
fragment of the Ninth Symphony, giving a rendering far
better than any but a highly skilled pianist could play, while
she was waiting for Peter to come to breakfast.   And this
Christmas party was pervaded with One Steps and Two
Steps, pianola called to gramophone and gramophone to

pianola, and tripping feet somewhere never failed to respond. Most of these young people danced with the wildest informality. But Hetty and the youngest Irish girl were serious propagandists of certain strange American dances, the Bunny Hug, and the Fox Trot; Sopwith Greene and Adela tangoed and were getting quite good at it, and Huntley wanted to teach Joan an Apache dance. Joan danced by rule and pattern or by the light of nature as occasion required.

The Christmas dinner was at one o'clock, a large disorderly festival. Gavan Huntley and Sopwith Greene came in for it. Oswald carved a turkey, Aunt Phyllis dispensed beef; the room was darkened and the pudding was brought in flaming blue and distributed in flickering flames. Mincepies, almonds and raisins, Brazil nuts, oranges, tangerines, Carlsbad plums, crystallized fruits and candied peel; nothing was missing from the customary feast. Then came a mighty banging of crackers, pre-war crackers, containing elaborate paper costumes and preposterous gifts. Wilmington ate little and Huntley a great deal, and whenever Joan glanced at them they seemed to be looking at her. Hetty, flushed and excited, became really pretty in a paper cap of liberty, she waved a small tricolour flag and knelt up in her chair to pull crackers across the table; Peter won a paper cockscomb and was moved to come and group himself under her arm and crow as "Vive la France!" The two Irish girls started an abusive but genial argument with Sopwith Greene upon the Irish question. Aunt Phœbe sat near Aunt Phyllis and discoursed on whether she ought to go to prison for the Vote. "I try to assault policemen," she said. "But they elude me." One of Peter's Cambridge friends, it came to light, had been present at a great scene in which Aunt Phœbe had figured. He emerged from his social obscurity and described the affair rather amusingly.

It had been at an Anti-Suffrage meeting in West Kensington, and Aunt Phœbe had obtained access to the back row of the platform by some specious device. Among the notabilities in front Lady Charlotte Sydenham and her solicitor had figured. Lady Charlotte had entered upon that last great phase in a woman's life, that phase known to the vulgar observer as "old lady's second wind." It is a phase often of great Go and determination, a joy to the irreverent young and a marvel and terror to the middle-aged. She had taken to politics, plunged into public speaking, faced audiences. It was the Insurance Act of 1912 that had first moved her to such publicity. Stung by the outrageous possibility of independent-spirited servants she had given up her usual trip to Italy in the winter and stayed to combat Lloyd George. From mere subscriptions and drawing-room conversations and committees to drawing-room meetings and at last to public meetings had been an easy series of steps for her. At first a mere bridling indignation on the platform, she presently spoke. As a speaker she combined reminiscences of Queen Elizabeth at Tilbury and Marie Antoinette on the scaffold with vast hiatuses peculiar to herself. "My good people," she would say, disregarding the more conventional methods of opening, "have we neglected our servants or have we not? Is any shop Gal or factory Gal half so well off as a servant in a good house? Is she? I ask. The food alone! The morals! And now we are to be taxed and made to lick stamps like a lot of galley-slaves to please a bumptious little Welsh solicitor! For my part I shall discontinue all my charitable subscriptions until this abominable Act is struck off the Statute Book. Every one. And as for buying these Preposterous stamps—— Rather than lick a stamp I will eat skilly in prison. Stamps indeed. I'd as soon lick the man's boots. That's all I have to say, Mr. Chairman (or 'My Lord,' or 'Mrs. Chairman,' as the case might be). I hope it will be enough. Thank you." And she would sit down breathing heavily and looking for eyes to meet.

For the great agitation against the Insurance Act that sort of thing sufficed, but when it came to testifying against an unwomanly clamour for votes, the argument became more complicated and interruptions difficult to handle, and after an unpleasant experience when she was only able to repeat in steadily rising tones, "I am not one of the Shrieking Sisterhood" ten times over to a derisive roomful, she decided to adopt the more feminine expedient of a spokesman. She had fallen back upon Mr. Grimes, who like all solicitors had his parliamentary ambitions, and she took him about with her

in the comfortable brown car that had long since replaced the
white horse, and sat beside him while he spoke and approved
of him with both hands.   Mr. Grimes had been addressing the
meeting when Aunt Phœbe made her interruption.   He had
been arguing that the unfitness of women for military service
debarred them from the Vote.   ''Let us face the facts,'' he
said, drawing the air in between his teeth.   ''Ultimately—
ultimately all social organization rests upon Force.''

It was just at this moment that cries of ''Order, Order,''
made him aware of a feminine figure close beside him.   He
turned to meet the heaving wrath of Aunt Phœbe's face.
There was just an instant's scrutiny.   Then he remembered,
he remembered everything, and with a wild shriek leapt clean
off the platform upon the toes of the front row of the audience.

''If you *touch* me!'' he screamed. . . .

The young man told the incident briefly and brightly.

''Thereby hangs a tale,'' said Aunt Phœbe darkly, and
became an allusive Sphinx for the rest of the dinner.

''I shook that man,'' she said at last to Pryce.

''What—*him?*'' said Pryce, staring round-eyed at the
young man from Cambridge.

''No, the man at the meeting.''

''What—afterwards?'' said Pryce, lost and baffled.

''No,'' said Aunt Phœbe; *''before.''*

Pryce tried to look intelligent, and nodded his head very
fast to conceal the fear and confusion in his mind.

Amidst all these voices and festivities sat Oswald, with a
vast paper cap shaped rather like the dome of a Russian
church cocked over his blind side, listening distractedly,
noting this and that, saying little, thinking many things.

The banquet ended at last, and every one drifted to the
library.

Affairs hovered vaguely for a time.   Peter handed cigarettes about.   Some one started the gramophone with a Two
Step that set every one tripping.   Hetty with a flush on her
cheek and a light in her eyes was keeping near Peter; she
seized upon him now for a dance that was also an embrace.
Peter laughed, nothing loath.   ''Oh! but this is glorious!''
panted Hetty.

"Come and dance, too, Joan," said Wilmington.

"It's stuffy!" said Joan.

Oswald, contemplating a retreat to his study armchair, found her presently in the hall dressed to go out with Huntley.

"We're going over the hill to see the sunset," Joan explained. "It's too stuffy in there."

Oswald met Huntley's large grey eye for a moment. He had an instinctive distrust of Huntley. But on the other hand, surely Joan had brains enough and fastidiousness enough not to lose her head with this—this phosphorescent fish of a novelist.

"Right-o," said Oswald, and hovered doubtfully.

Aunt Phœbe appeared on the landing above carrying off a rather reluctant Miss Scroby to her room for a real good talk; a crash and an unmistakable giggle proclaimed a minor rag in progress in the common room across the hall in which Sydney Sheldrick was busy. The study door closed on Oswald. . . .

Joan and Huntley passed by outside his window. He sat down in front of his fire, poked it into a magnificent blaze, lit a cigar and sat thinking. The beat of dancing, the melody of the gramophone and a multitude of less distinct sounds soaked in through the door to him.

He was, he reflected, rather like a strange animal among all this youth. They treated him as something remotely old; he was one-and-fifty, and yet this gregarious stir and excitement that brightened their eyes and quickened their blood stirred him too. He couldn't help a feeling of envy; he had missed so much in his life. And in his younger days the pace had been slower. These young people were actually noisier, they were more reckless, they did more and went further than his generation had gone. In his time, with his sort of people, there had been the virtuous life which was, one had to admit it, slow, and the fast life which was noisily, criminally, consciously and vulgarly vicious. This generation didn't seem to be vicious, and was anything but slow. How far did they go? He had been noting little things between Peter and this Reinhart girl. What were they up to between them? He didn't understand. Was she manœuvring to marry the boy? She must be well on the way to thirty, twenty-six or twenty-seven perhaps, she hadn't a young girl's look in her eyes. Was she just amusing herself by angling for calf-love? Was she making a fool of Peter? Their code of manners was so easy; she would touch his hands, and once Peter had stroked her bare forearm as it lay upon the table. She had looked up and smiled. Leaving her arm on the table. One could not conceive of Dolly permitting such things. Was this an age of daring innocence, or what was coming to the young people?

Joan seemed more dignified than the others, but she, too, had her quality of prematurity. At her age Dolly had dressed in white with a pink sash. At least, Dolly must have been *about* Joan's age when first he had seen her. Eighteen—seventeen? Of course a year or so makes no end of difference just at this age. . . .

From such meditations Oswald was roused by the tumult of a car outside. He took a wary glimpse from his window at this conveyance, and discovered that it was coloured an unusual bright chocolate colour, and had its chauffeur—a depressed-looking individual—in a livery to match. He went out into the hall to discover the large presence, the square face, the "whisker," and the china-blue eyes of Lady Charlotte Sydenham. He knew she was in England, but he had had no idea she was near enough to descend upon them. She stood in the doorway surveying the Christmas disorder of the hall. Some one had adorned Oswald's stuffed heads with paper caps, the white rhinoceros was particularly motherly with pink bonnet-strings under its throat, a box of cigarettes had been upset on the table amidst various hats, and half its contents were on the floor, which was also littered with scraps of torn paper from the crackers; from the open door of the library came the raucous orchestration of the gramophone, and the patter and swish of dancers.

"I thought you'd be away," said Aunt Charlotte, a little checked by the sight of Oswald. "I'm staying at Minchings on my way to sit on the platform at Cambridge. We're raising money to get those brave Ulstermen guns. Something has to be done if these Liberals are not to do as they like with us. They and their friends the priests. But I *knew* there'd

be a party here. And those aunts. So I came. . . . Who
are all these young people you have about?"

"Miscellaneous friends," said Oswald.

"You've got a touch of grey in your hair," she noted.

"I must get a big blond wig," he said.

"You might do worse."

"You're looking as fresh as paint," he remarked, scrutinizing her steadfastly bright complexion. "Is that the faithful Unwin sitting and sniffing in the car? It's a rennet
face."

"She can sit," said Lady Charlotte. "I shan't stay ten
minutes, and she's got a hot-water bottle and three rugs.
But being so near I had to come and see what was being done
with those wards of mine."

"Former wards," Oswald interjected.

"The Gal I passed. Where is Master Stubland? I'll just
look at him. Is he one of these people making a noise in
here?"

She went to the door of the library and surveyed the scene
with an aggressive lorgnette. The furniture had been thrust
aside with haste and indignity, the rugs rolled up from the
parquet floor, and Babs Sheldrick was presiding over the
gramophone and helping and interrupting Sydney in the
instruction of Wilmington, of Peter and Hetty and of Adela
and Sopwith Greene in some special development of the tango.
All the young people still wore their paper caps and were
heated and dishevelled. In the window-seat the convalescent
suffragette was showing wrist tricks to one of the young men
from Cambridge. "Party!" said Lady Charlotte. "Hig-
gledy-piggledy I call it. Which is Peter?"

Peter was indicated.

"Well, he's grown! Who's that fast-looking girl he's
hugging?"

Peter detached himself from Hetty and came forward.

His ancient terror of the whisker-woman still hung about
him, but he made a brave show of courage. "Glad you've
not forgotten us, Lady Charlotte," he said.

"Not much Stubland about *him*," she remarked to Oswald.
"There's a photograph of you before you blew your face
off—"

"It's his mother he's like," said Oswald, laying a hand on Peter's shoulder.

"I never saw a family harp on themselves more than the Sydenhams," the lady declared. "It's like the Habsburg chin. . . . This one of the new improper dances, Peter?"

"*Honi soit*," said Peter.

"People have been whipped at the cart's tail for less. In my mother's time no decent woman waltzed. Even—in crinolines. Now a waltz isn't close enough for them."

The gramophone came to an end and choked. "Thank goodness!" said Lady Charlotte.

"Won't you dance yourself, Lady Charlotte?" said Peter, standing up to her politely.

The hard blue eye regarded him with a slightly impaired disfavour, but the old lady made no reply.

They heard the startled voice of the youth from Cambridge. "It's *her!*" . . .

But the sting of the call was at its end.

"So that's Peter," said Lady Charlotte, as the chauffeur and Oswald assisted her back into her liver-coloured car. "I told you I saw the Gal?"

"Joan?"

"I passed her on the road half a mile from here. Came upon her and her 'gentleman friend'—I suppose she'd call him—as we turned a corner. A snap-shot so to speak. It's the walking-out instinct. Blood will tell. I saw her, but she didn't see me. Lost, she was, to things mundane. But it was plain enough how things were. A tiff. Some lovers' quarrel. Wake *up*, Unwin."

"What do you mean?"

"What I say," said Lady Charlotte.

"That fellow Huntley!"

"*Ha!* So now you'll lock the stable door! What else was to be expected?"

"But this is nonsense!"

"I may be mistaken. I hope I am mistaken. I just give you my impression. I'm not a fool, Oswald, though it's always been your pleasure to treat me as one. Time shows."

There was a pause while rugs with loud monograms were adjusted about her.

"Well, I'm glad I came over. I wanted to see the Great
Experiment. I said at the time it can't end well. Bad in
the beginnings. No woman to help him—except for those
two Weird Sisters. No religion. You see? The boy's a
young Impudence. The girl's in some mess already. What
did I tell you?"

Oswald was late with his recovery.

"Look here, auntie! you keep your libellous mind off my
wards."

"Home, Parbury!" said Lady Charlotte to the chocolate-
uniformed chauffeur.

She fired a parting shot.

"I warned you long ago, you'd get the Gal into a thoroughly false position. . . ."

She was getting away after her raid with complete impunity. Never before had she scored like this. Was Oswald
growing old? She made her farewell of him with a stately
gesture of head and hand. She departed disconcertingly
serene. A flood of belated repartee rushed into Oswald's
mind. But except for a violent smell of petrol and a cloud
of smoke and a kind of big scar of chocolate on the retina
nothing remained now of Lady Charlotte.

In the hall he paused before a mirror and examined that
touch of grey.

§ 20

But it had not been a lovers' quarrel that had blinded
Joan to the passing automobile. It had been the astounding
discovery of her real relationship to Peter. So astounding
had that been that at the moment she was not only regardless
of the passing traffic but oblivious of Huntley and every
other circumstance of her world.

Huntley was not one of those people who love; he was a
pursuing egotist with an unwarrantable scorn for the intelligence of his fellow-creatures. He liked to argue and show
people that they were wrong in a calm, scornful manner;
The Pernambuco Bun-shop was a very sarcastic work.
He was violently attracted by the feminine of all ages; it
fixed his attention with the vast possibilities of admiration

and triumph it offered him. And he had greedy desires. Joan attracted him at first because she was admired. He saw how Wilmington coveted her. She had a prestige in her circle. She had, too, a magnetism of her own. Before he realized the slope down which he slid, he wanted her so badly that he thought he was passionately in love. It kept him awake of nights, and distracted him from his work. He did not want to marry her. That was against his principles. That was the despicable way of ordinary human beings. He lived on a higher plane. But he wanted her as a monkey wants a gold watch—he wanted this new, fresh, lovely and beautiful thing just to handle and feel as his own.

There was little charm about Huntley and less companionship. He was too arrogant for companionship. But he abounded in ideas, he knew much, and so he interested her. He talked. He pursued her with the steadfast scrutiny of his large grey eyes—and with arguments. He tried to argue and manœuvre Joan into a passionate love for him.

Well, Joan had a broad brow; she thought things over; she was amenable to ideas.

He harped on "freedom." He carried freedom far beyond the tempered liberties of ordinary human association. Any ordinary belief was by his standards a limitation of freedom. There was a story that he had once been caught burgling a house in St. John's Wood and had been let off by the magistrate only because the crime seemed absolutely motiveless. No doubt he had been trying to convince himself of his freedom from prejudice about the rights of property. He had an obscure idea that he could induce Joan to plunge into wild depravities merely to prove himself free from her own decent instincts. But he was ceasing to care for his argument if only he could induce her.

There was a moment when he said, "Joan, you are the one woman"—he always called her a woman—"who could make me marry her."

"I'll spare you," said Joan succinctly.

"Promise me that."

"Promise."

"Anyhow."

"Anyhow."

On this Christmas afternoon he discoursed again upon freedom. "You, Joan, might be the freest of the free, if only you chose. You are absolutely your own mistress. Absolutely."

"I have a guardian," she said.

"You're of age."

"No; I'm nineteen."

"You—it happens, were of age at eighteen, Joan." He watched her face. He had been burning to get to this point for weeks. "Even about your birth there was freedom."

"So *you* know that."

"Icy voice! To me it seems the grandest thing. When I reflect that I, alas! was born in loveless holy wedlock I grit my teeth."

"Oh! I don't care. But how do you know?"

"It's fairly well known, Joan. It's no very elaborate secret. I've got a little volume of your father's poetry."

She hesitated. "I didn't know my father wrote poetry," she said.

"It was all Will Sydenham ever did that was worth doing —except launch you into the world. He was a dramatic critic and something of a journalist, I believe. Stoner of the *Post* knew him quite well. But all this is ancient history to you."

"It isn't. Nobody has told me. . . . I didn't know."

"But what did you think?"

"Never mind what I thought. Every one doesn't talk with your freedom. I've never been told. Who was my mother?"

"Stoner says she died in hospital. Soon after you were born. He never knew her name."

"Wasn't it Stubland?"

"Lord, No! Why should it be?"

"But then——"

"That's one of the things that makes you so splendidly new, Joan. You start clean in the world—like a new Eve. Without even an Adam to your name. Fatherless, motherless, sisterless, brotherless. You fall into the world like a meteor!"

She stood astonished at the way in which she had blundered. Brotherless! If Huntley had not drawn her back by the arm Lady Charlotte's car would have touched her. . . .

§ 21

That night some one tapped at the bedroom door of Aunt Phyllis. "Come in," she cried, slipping into her dressing-gown, and Joan entered. She was still wearing the dress of spangled black in which she had danced with Huntley and Wilmington and Peter. She went to her aunt's fire in silence and stood over it, thinking.

"You're having a merry Christmas, little Joan?" said Aunt Phyllis, coming and standing beside her.

"Ever so merry, Auntie. We go it—don't we?"

Aunt Phyllis looked quickly at the flushed young face beside her, opened her mouth to speak and said nothing. There was a silence, it seemed a long silence, between them. Then Joan asked in a voice that she tried to make off-hand, "Auntie. Who was my father?"

Aunt Phyllis was deliberately matter-of-fact. "He was the brother of Dolly—Peter's mother."

"Where is he?"

"He was killed by an omnibus near the Elephant and Castle when you were two years old."

"And my mother?"

"Died three weeks after you were born."

Joan was wise in sociological literature. "The usual fever, I suppose," she said.

"Yes," said Aunt Phyllis.

"Do you know much about her?"

"Very little. Her name was Debenham. Fanny Debenham."

"Was she pretty?"

"I never saw her. It was Dolly—Peter's mother—who went to her. . . ."

"So that's what I am," said Joan, after a long pause.

"Only we love you. What does it matter? Dear Joan of my heart," and Aunt Phyllis slipped her arm about the girl's shoulder.

But Joan stood stiff and intent, not answering her caress.
"I knew—in a way," she said.

The thought that consumed her insisted upon utterance.
"So I'm not Peter's half-sister," she said.

"But have you thought——?"

Joan remained purely intellectual. "I've thought dozens
of things. And I thought at last it was that. . . . Why was
I called Stubland? I'm not a Stubland."

"It was more convenient. It grew up."

"It put me out. It has sent me astray. . . ."

She remained for a time taking in this new aspect of things
so intently as to be regardless of the watcher beside her.
Then she roused herself to mask her extravagant preoccupation. "You're no relation then of mine?" she said.

"No."

"You've been so kind to me. A mother. . . ."

Aunt Phyllis was weeping facile tears. "Have I been
kind, dear? Have I seemed kind? I've always wanted to
be kind. And I've loved you, Joan, my dear. And love
you."

"And Nobby?"

"Nobby too."

"You've been bricks to me, both of you. No end. Aunt
Phœbe too. And Peter——? Does Peter know? Does he
know what I am?"

"I don't know. I don't know what he knows, Joan."

"If it hadn't been for the same surname. Joan Debenham. . . . I've had fancies. I've thought Nobby, perhaps,
was my father. . . . Queer! . . . Why did you people bother
yourselves about me?"

"My dear, it was the most natural thing in the world."

"I suppose it was—for you. You've been so decent——"

"Every woman wants a daughter," said Aunt Phyllis in
a whisper, and then almost inaudibly; "you are mine."

"And the tempers I've shown. The trouble I've been.
All these years. I wonder what Peter knows? He must
suspect. He must have ideas. . . . Joan Debenham—from
outside."

She stood quite still with the red firelight leaping up to

light her face, and caressing the graceful lines of her slender
form. She stood for a time as still as stone. Had she, after
all, a stony heart? Aunt Phyllis stood watching her with a
pale, tear-wet, apprehensive face. Then abruptly the girl
turned and held out her arms.

"Can I ever thank you?" she cried, with eyes that now
glittered with big tears. . . .

Presently Aunt Phyllis was sitting in her chair stroking
Joan's dark hair, and Joan was kneeling, staring intently at
some strange vision in the fire. "Do you mind my staying
for a time?" she asked. "I want to get used to it. It's just
as though there wasn't anything—but just here. I've lost
my aunt—and found a mother."

"My Joan," whispered Aunt Phyllis. "My own dear
Joan."

"Always I have thought Peter was my brother—always.
My half brother. Until today."

§ 22

It was Adela who inflicted Joan's second shock upon her,
and drove away the last swirling whispers of adolescent
imaginations and moon mist from the hard forms of reality.
This visit she had seemed greatly improved to Joan; she was
graver. Visibly she thought, and no longer was her rolling
eye an invitation to masculine enterprise. She came to
Joan's room on Boxing Day morning to make up dresses
with her for the night's dance, and she let her mind run as
she stitched. Every one was to come in fancy dress; the
vicarage girls would come and the Braughing people. Every
one was to represent a political idea. Adela was going to be
Tariff Reform. All her clothes were to be tattered and unfinished, she said, even her shoes were to have holes. She
would wear a broken earring in one ear. "I don't quite see
your point," said Joan.

"Tariff Reform means work for all, dear," Adela explained gently.

Days before Joan had planned to represent Indian Nationalism. It was a subject much in dispute between her and
Peter, whose attitude to India and Indians seemed to her

unreasonably reactionary—in view of all his other opinions. She could never let her controversies with Peter rest; the costume had been aimed at him. She was going to make up her complexion with a little brown, wear a sari, sandals on bare feet, and a band of tinsel across her forehead. She had found some red Indian curtain stuff that seemed to be adaptable for the sari. She worked now in a preoccupied manner, with her mind full of strange thoughts. Sometimes she listened to what Adela was saying, and sometimes she was altogether within herself. But every now and then Adela would pull her back to attention by a question.

"Don't you think so, Joan?"

"Think what?" asked Joan.

"Love's much more *our* business than it is theirs."

That struck Joan. "Is it?" she asked. She had thought the shares in the business were equal and opposite.

"All this waiting for a man to discover himself in love with you; it's rot. You may wait till Doomsday."

"Still, they do seem to fall in love." ·

"With any one. A man's in love with women in general, but women fall in love with men in particular. We're the choosers. Naturally. We want a man, that man and no other, and all our own. They don't feel like that. And we have to hang about pretending they choose and trying to make them choose without seeming to try to make them. Well, we're altering all that. When I want a man——"

Adela's pause suggested a particular reference.

"I'll get him somehow," she said intently.

"If you mean to get him—if you don't mind much the little things that happen meanwhile—you'll get him," said Adela, as though she repeated a creed. "But, of course, you can't make terms. When a man knows that a woman is his, when he's sure of it—absolutely, then she's got him for good. Sooner or later he must come to her. I haven't had my eyes open just for show, Joan, this last year or so."

"Good luck, Adela," said Joan.

Adela attempted no pretences. "It stands to reason if you love a man——" Her eyes filled with tears. "Love his very self. You can make him happy and safe. Be his line of least resistance. But the meanwhile is hard——"

Adela stitched furiously.

"That's why you came down here?" Joan asked.

"You haven't seen?" Adela's preoccupation with Sop-with Greene had been the most conspicuous fact in the party. "Once or twice a gleam," said Joan.

"Ask him to play tonight, dear," said Adela. "Some of his own things."

But now the last checks upon Adela's talk were removed. She wanted to talk endlessly and unrestrainedly about love. She wanted to hear herself saying all the generosities and devotions she contemplated. "There's no bargain in love," said Adela. "You just watch and give." Running through all her talk was a thread of speculation; she was obsessed by the idea of the relative blindness and casualness of love in men. "We used to dream of lovers who just concentrated upon us," she said. "But there's something nimmy-pimmy in a man concentrating on a woman. He ought to have a Job, something Big, his Art, his Aim—Something. One wouldn't really respect a man who didn't do something Big. Love's a nuisance to a real man, a disturbance, until some woman takes care of him."

"Couldn't two people—take care of each other?" asked Joan.

"Oh, that's Ideal, Joan," said Adela as one who puts a notion aside. "A man takes his love where he finds it. On his way to other things. The easier it is to get the better he likes it. That's why, so often, they take up with any—sort of creature. And why one needn't be so tremendously jealous. . . ."

Adela reflected. "*I* don't care a bit about him and Hetty."

"Hetty Reinhart?"

"Everybody talked about them. Didn't you hear? But of course you were still at school. Of course there's that studio of hers. You know about her? Yes. She has a studio. Most convenient. She does as she pleases. It amused him, I suppose. Men don't care as we do. They're just amused. Men can fall in love for an afternoon—and out of it again. He makes love to her and he's not even jealous of her. Not a bit. He doesn't seem to mind a rap about Peter.''

She babbled on, but Joan's mind stopped short.

"Adela," she said, "what is this about Hetty and Peter?"

"The usual thing, I suppose, dear. You don't seem to hear of *anything* at Cambridge.''

"But you don't mean——?"

"Well, I know *something* of Hetty. And I've got eyes.''

"You mean to say she's—she's *got* Peter?"

"It shows plainly enough.''

"*My* Peter!" cried Joan sharply.

"You're not an Egyptian princess," said Adela.

"You mean—he's gone—Peter's gone—to her studio? That—things like that have happened?"

Adela stared at her friend. "These things *have* to happen, Joan.''

"But he's only a boy yet.''

"She doesn't think he's a boy. Why! he's almost of age! Lot of boy about Peter!''

"But do you mean——?"

"I don't mean anything, Joan, if you're going to look like that. You've got no right to interfere in Peter's love affairs. Why should you? Don't we all live for experience?''

"But," said Joan, "Peter is different.''

"No. No one is different," said Adela.

"But I tell you he's *my* Peter.''

"He's your brother, of course.''

"*No!*"

"Your half brother then. Everybody knows that, Joan—thanks to the Sheldricks. A sister can't always keep her brothers away from other girls.''

Joan was on the verge of telling Adela that she was not even Peter's half sister, but she restrained herself. She stuck to the thing that most concerned her now.

"It's spoiling him," she said. "It will make a mess of him. Why! he may think that is love, that!—slinking off to a studio. The nastiness! And she's had a dozen lovers. She's a common thing. She just strips herself here and shows her arms and shoulders because she's—just that.''

"She's really in love with him anyhow," said Adela. "She's gone on him. It's amusing."

"Love! *That*—love! It makes me sick to think of it," said Joan.

"A man isn't made like that," said Adela. "Peter has to go his own way."

"Peter," said Joan, "who used to be the cleanest thing alive."

"Good sisters always feel like that," said Adela. "I know how shocked I was when first I heard of Teddy. . . . It isn't the same thing to men, Joan. It isn't indeed. . . ."

"*Dirty* Peter," said Joan with intense conviction. "Of course I've known. Of course I've known. Any one could see. Only I wouldn't know."

She thrust the striped red stuff for her Indian dress from her.

"I shan't be Indian Nationalism, Adela, after all. Somehow I don't care to be. Why should I cover myself up in this way?"

"You'd look jolly."

"No. I want something with black in it. And red. And my arms and shoulders showing. Why shouldn't we all dress down to Hetty? She has the approval of the authorities. Aunt Phœbe applauds every stitch she takes off. Freedom—with a cap of Liberty."

"Hetty said something about being Freedom," hesitated Adela.

"Then I shall come as Anarchy," said Joan, staring at the red stuff upon the table before her.

Came a pause.

"I don't see why Peter should have all the fun in life," said Joan.

§ 23

Joan as Anarchy made a success that evening at Pelham Ford. In the private plans of Hetty Reinhart that success had not been meant for Joan. Hetty as Freedom gave the party her lithe arms, her slender neck, and so much of her back that the two vicarage girls, who had come very correctly in powder and patches as Whig and Tory, were sure that it was partly accidental. On Hetty's dark hair perched a Phrygian cap, and she had a tricolour skirt beneath a white bodice that was chiefly decolletage and lace. About her neck was a little band of black which had nothing to do with Freedom; it was there for the sake of her slender neck. She was much more like *La Vie Parisienne.* She was already dancing with Peter when Joan, who had delayed coming down until the music began, appeared in the doorway. Nobby, wrapped in a long toga-like garment of sun-gold and black that he alleged qualified him to represent Darkest Africa, was standing by the door, and saw the effect of Joan upon one of the Braughing boys before he discovered her beside him.

Her profile was the profile of a savage. She lifted her clear-cut chin as young savage women do, and her steady eyes regarded Hetty and Peter. Her black hair was quite unbound and thrown back from her quiet face, and there was no necklace, no bracelet, not a scrap of adornment nor enhancement upon her arms or throat. It had not hitherto occurred to Oswald that his ward had the most beautiful neck and shoulders in the world, or that Joan was as like what Dolly once had been as a wild beast is like a cherished tame one. But he did presently find these strange ideas in his mind.

Her dress was an exiguous scheme of slashes and tatters in black and bright red. She was bare ankled—these modern young people thought nothing of that—but she had white dancing shoes upon her feet.

"Joan!" said Huntley, advancing with an air of proprietorship.

"No," said Joan with a gesture of rejection. "I don't want to dance with any one in particular. I'm going to dance alone."

"Well—dance!" said Huntley with a large courtly movement of a white velvet cloak all powdered with gold crosses and fleur-de-lys, that he pretended was a symbol of Reaction.

"When I choose," said Joan. "And as I choose."

Across the room Peter was staring at her, and she was looking at Peter. He tripped against Hetty, and for a little interval the couple was out of step. "Come on, Peter," said Hetty, rallying him.

Joan appeared to forget Peter and every one.

There was dancing in her blood, and this evening she meant to dance. Her body felt wonderfully light and as supple as a whip under her meagre costume. There was something to be said for this semi-nudity after all. The others were dancing a two-step with such variations as they thought fit, and there was no objection whatever at Pelham Ford to solo enterprises. Joan could invent dances. She sailed out into the room to dance as she pleased.

Oswald watched her nimble steps and the whirling rhythms of her slender body. She made all the others seem over-dressed and clumsy and heavy. Her face had a grave pre-occupied expression.

Huntley stood for a moment or so beside Oswald, and then stepped out after her to convert her dance into a duet. He too was a skilful and inventive dancer, and the two coquetted for a time amidst the other couples.

Then Joan discovered Wilmington watching her and Hunt-ley from the window bay. She danced evasively through Huntley's circling entanglements, and seized Wilmington's hand and drew him into the room.

"I can't dance, Joan," he said, obeying her. "You *know* I can't dance."

"You have to dance," she said, aglow and breathing swiftly. "Trust me."

She took and left his hands and took them again and turned him about so skilfully that a wonderful illusion was produced in Wilmington's mind and in those about him that indeed he could dance. Huntley made a crouching figure of jealousy about them; he spread himself and his cloak into fantastic rhombs—and then the music ceased. . . .

"The Argentine Tango!" cried Huntley. "Joan, you *must* tango."

"Never."

"Dance Columbine to my Harlequin then."

"And stand on your knee? I should break it."

"Try me," said Huntley.

"Kneel," said Joan. "Now take my hands. Prepare for

the shock." And she leapt lightly to his knee and posed for a second, poised with one toe on Huntley's thigh, and was down again.

"Do it again, Joan," he cried with enthusiasm. "Do it again."

"Let us invent dances," cried Aunt Phyllis. "Let us invent dances. Couldn't we dance charades?"

"Let them dance as nature meant them to," said Aunt Phœbe's deepest tones. *"Madly!"*

"Shall we try that Tango we did the other night?" said Hetty, coming behind Peter.

Peter had come forward to the group in the centre of the room. Old habits were strong in him, and he had a vague feeling that this was one of the occasions when Joan ought to be suppressed. "We're getting chaotic," he said.

"You see, Peter, I'm Anarchy," said Joan.

"An ordered Freedom is the best," said Peter without reflecting on his words.

"Nobby, I want to dance with you," said Joan.

"I've never danced anything but a Country Dance—you know the sort of thing in which people stand in rows—in my life," said Oswald.

"A country dance," cried Joan. "Sir Roger de Coverley."

"We want to try a fox-trot we know," complained one of the Braughing guests.

Two parties became more and more distinctly evident in the party. There was a party which centred around Hetty and the Sheldrick girls, which was all for the rather elaborately planned freak dances they had more or less learnt in London, the Bunny-Hugs, the Fox-Trot, and various Tangoes. Most of the Londoners were of this opinion, Sopwith Greene trailed Adela with him, and Huntley was full of a passionate desire to guide Joan's feet along the Tango path. But Joan's mind by a kind of necessity moved contrariwise to Hetty's. Either, she argued, they must dance in the old staid ways— Oswald and the Vicarage girls applauding—or dance as the spirit moved them.

"Oh, dance your old Fox-Trots," she cried, with a gesture that seemed to motion Huntley and Hetty together. "Have

your music all rattle and rag-time like sick people groaning
in trains.   That's neither here nor there.   I want to dance
to better stuff than that.   Come along, Willy.''

She seized on Wilmington's arm.

''But where are you going?'' cried Huntley.

''I'm going to dance Chopin in the hall—to the pianola.''

''You're going to play,'' she told Wilmington.

''But you can't,'' said Peter.

Joan disappeared with her slave.   A light seemed to go out
from the big library as she went.   ''Now we can get on,''
said Hetty, laying hands on her Peter.

For a time the Fox-Trot ruled.   The Vicarage girls didn't
do these things, and drifted after Joan.   So did Oswald.
Towards the end the dancers had a sense of a cross-current of
sound in the air, of some adverse influence thrown across their
gymnastics.   When their own music stopped, they became
aware of that crying voice above the thunder, the Revolutionary Etude.

There was a brief listening pause.   ''Now, how the
deuce,'' said Huntley, ''can she be dancing *that?*''

He led the way to the hall. . . .

''I'm tired of dancing,'' whispered Hetty.   ''Stay back.
They're all going.   I want you to kiss the little corner of
my mouf.''

Peter looked round quickly, and seized his privilege with
unseemly haste.   ''Let's see how Joan is dancing that old
row,'' he said. . . .

Animation, boldness, and strict relegation of costume to
its function of ornament had hitherto made Hetty the high
light of this little gathering.   She was now to realize how
insecure is this feminine predominance in the face of fresher
youth and greater boldness.   And Joan was full of a pretty
girl's discovery that she may do all that she dares to do.
For a time—and until it is time to pay.

Life had intoxicated Joan that night.   A derision of seem-
liness possessed her.   She was full of impulse and power.
She felt able to dominate every one.   At one time or other she
swept nearly every man there except Oswald and Peter and
Pryce into her dancing.   Two of the Braughing youths fell
visibly in love with her, and Huntley lost his head, badgered

her too much to dance, and then was offended and sulked in a manner manifest to the meanest capacity. And she kissed Wilmington.

That was her wildest impulse. She came into the study where he was playing the pianola for her dancing. She wanted him to change the roll for the first part of the Kreutzer Sonata, and found herself alone with him. She loved him because he was so completely and modestly hers. She bent over him to take off the roll from the instrument, and found her face near his forehead. "Dear old Willy," she whispered, and put her hand on his shoulder and brushed his eyebrows with her lips.

Then she was remorseful.

"It doesn't mean anything, Willy," she said.

"I know it doesn't," he said in a voice of the deepest melancholy.

"Only you are a dear all the same," she said. "You are clean. You're *right*."

"If it wasn't for my damned Virtues——" said Wilmington. "But anyhow. Thank you, Joan—very much. Shall I play you this right through?"

"A little slowly," she said. "It's marked too fast," and went towards the open door.

Then she flitted back to him. . . . Her intent face came close to his. "I don't love any one, Willy," she said. "I'm not the sort. I just dance."

They looked at each other.

"I love *you*," said Wilmington, and watched her go.

But she had made him ridiculously happy. . . .

She danced through the whole Kreutzer Sonata. The Kreutzer Sonata has always been a little dirty since Tolstoy touched it. Tolstoy pronounced it erotic. There are men who can find a lascivious import in a Corinthian capital. The Kreutzer Sonata therefore had a strong appeal to Huntley's mind. These associations made it seem to him different from other music, just as calling this or that substance a "drug" always dignified it in his eyes with the rich suggestions of vice. He read strange significances into Joan's choice of that little music as he watched her over the heads of the Braughing girls. But Joan just danced.

At supper she found herself drifting to a seat near Peter. She left him to his Hetty, and went up the table to a place under Oswald's black wing. The supper at Pelham Ford was none of your stand-up affairs. Mrs. Moxton's ideas of a dance supper were worthy of Britannia. Oswald carved a big turkey and Peter had cold game pie, and Aunt Phyllis showed a delicate generosity with a sharp carver and a big ham. There were hot potatoes and various salads, and jugs of lemonade and claret cup for every one, and whisky for the mature. Joan became a sober enquirer about African dancing.

"It's the West Coast that dances," said Oswald. "There's richer music on the West Coast than all round the Mediterranean."

"All this American music comes from the negro," he declared. "There's hardly a bit of American music that hasn't colour in its blood."

After supper Joan was the queen of the party. Adela was in love with her again, as slavish as in their schooldays, and the Sheldricks and the Braughing boys and girls did her bidding. "Let's do something processional," said Joan. "Let us dress up and do the Funeral March of a Marionette."

Hetty didn't catch on to that idea, and Peter was somehow overlooked. Most of the others scampered off to get something black and cast aside anything too coloured. Aunt Phyllis knew of some black gauze and produced it. There were black curtains in the common room, and these were seized upon by Huntley and Wilmington. They made a coffin of the big black lacquered post-box in the hall, and a bier of four alpenstocks and a drying-board from the scullery.

Joan was chief mourner, and after the Funeral March was over danced the sorrows of life before the bier to the first part of the Fifth Symphony.

Hetty and Peter sat close together and yet unusually apart upon the broad window-seat. Hetty looked tired and Peter seemed inattentive. Perhaps they had a little overdone each other's charm that Christmas.

And only once more that evening did it happen that Peter and Joan met face to face. Nearly everybody poured out

into the garden to see the guests go off. The Braughing people crowded hilariously into a car; the others walked. The
weather had suddenly hardened, a clear dry cold made the
paths and road very like metal, and not the littlest star was
missing from the quivering assembly in the sky.

"We'll have skating yet," cried the Braughing party.

Adela and Joan and Wilmington and Pryce came with
Huntley and Greene and the vicarage girls along the road and
over the ice-bound water-splash as far as the vicarage gate.
"Too cooold to say good-bye," cried Joan. "Oh, my *poor*
bare legs!" and led a race back.

Adela was left far behind, but neither Wilmington nor
Pryce would let Joan win without a struggle. The three
shot in through the wide front door almost abreast, and
Joan ran straight at Peter and stopped short within two
feet of him.

"I've won!" said Joan.

Just for an instant the two looked at one another, and it
seemed to Joan afterwards that she had seen something
then in Peter's eyes, something involuntary that she had
caught just once before in them—when she had come upon
him by chance in Petty Cury when first she had gone up
to Cambridge.

A silly thing to think about! What did it matter? What
did anything matter? Life was a dance, and Joan, thank
heaven! could dance. Peter was just nothing at all. Nothing at all. Nothing at all.

"I wonder, Joan, how many miles you have pranced tonight!" said Aunt Phyllis, kissing her good night.

"Joan," said Adela, "you *are* The Loveliest." . . .

For a minute or so Joan stood in front of her looking-
glass, studying a flushed, candle-lit figure. . . .

"Pah!" she said at last. "*Hetty!*" and flung her scanty
clothes aside.

She caught the reflection of herself in the mirror again.
She spread out her hands in a gesture to the pretty shape
she saw there, and stood.

"What's the Good of it?" she said at last.

As soon as Joan's head touched the pillow that night she

fell asleep, and she slept as soundly as a child that had been thoroughly naughty and all at sixes and sevens, and that has been well slapped and had a good cry to wind up with, and put to bed. In all the world there is no sounder sleep than that.

CHAPTER THE TWELFTH

THE WORLD ON THE EVE OF WAR

§ 1

OSWALD sat in the March sunshine that filled and warmed his little summerhouse, and thought about Joan and Peter. . . .

His sudden realization of Joan's mental maturity, the clear warning it brought to him that the task and opportunity of education was passing out of his hands, that already the reckoning of consequences was beginning for both his wards, set his mind searching up and down amidst the memories of his effort, to find where he could have slipped, where blundered and failed. He perceived now how vague had been the gesture with which he had started, when he proclaimed his intention to give them "the best education in the world."

The best education in the world is still to seek, and while he had been getting such scraps of second best for them as he could, the world itself, nature, tradition, custom, suggestion, example and accident, had moulded them and made them. When he measured what had been done upon these youngsters by these outward things and compared it with their deliberate education, the schoolmaster seemed to him to be still no more than a half-hearted dwarf who would snare the white horses of a cataract with a noose of packthread.

"The generations running to waste—like rapids."

But there are stronger harnessings than packthreads, and there are already engineers in the world who, by taking thought and patient work, can tame the maddest torrent that ever overawed the mind of man. In the end perhaps all torrents will be tamed, and knowledge and purpose put an end to aimless adventure. The schoolmaster will not always be a dwarf. . . .

As our children grow beyond our control we begin to learn something of the reality of education. The world had Joan and Peter now; at the most Oswald could run and shout advice from the bank as they went down the rush. But he knew that he could have done more for them, and that with a different world he could have done infinitely more for them in their receptive years. They were the children of an age; their restless fever of impulse was but their individual share in a great fever. The whole world now was restless, out of touch with any standards, and manifestly drifting towards great changes.

Neither Joan nor Peter seemed to have any definite purpose in life. Their impulses were not focused. They were drawn hither and thither. That was the essential failure of their adolescence. Their education had done many good things for them, but it had left their wills as spontaneous, indefinite and unsocial as the will of a criminal. Physically Oswald and the world had done well by them; they were clean-blooded, well grown, well exercised animals; they belonged to a generation of youth measurably taller, finer, and more beautiful than any generation before them. They were swift-footed and nimble. Mentally, too, they were swift and clear. It was not that their ideas were confused but their wills. Each of them could speak and read and write three languages quite well, they could draw well and Peter could draw brilliantly, they were alive to art and music, they read widely, they had the dispassionate, wide, scientific vision of the world. But being so fine and clean it was all the more distressing to realize that these two young people now faced the world with no clear will in them about it or themselves, that Joan seemed consumed with discontents and this dark personal quarrel with Peter, and that Peter could be caught and held by a mere sensual adventure. Hetty Reinhart kept him busy with notes and situations; having created a necessity she went on to create a jealous rivalry. He would be sometimes excited and elated, sometimes manifestly angry and sulky; and his work at Cambridge, which for two years had been conspicuously brilliant, was falling away.

Until Joan's angry outspokenness had forced these facts

upon his attention, Oswald had shirked their realization. He had seen with his one watchful eye, but he had not willed to see. A score of facts had lain, like disagreeable letters that one hesitates to answer, uncorrelated in his mind. The disorders of the Christmas party had indeed left him profoundly uneasy. With the new year he went with Peter on a trip to Russia. He wanted the youngster to develop a vision of the European problem, for Peter seemed blind to the importance of international things. They had crossed to Flushing, travelled straight through to Berlin, gone about Berlin for a few days, run on to St. Petersburg—it was not yet Petrograd—visited a friendly house near the Valdai Hills, spent a busy week in and about Moscow, and returned by way of Warsaw. They saw Germany already trained like an athlete for the adventure of the coming war, and Russia great and disorderly, destined to be taken unawares. Then they returned to England to look again at their own country with eyes refreshed by these contrasts. And all the time Oswald watched Peter and speculated about the thoughts and ideas hidden in Peter's head.

§ 2

This Russian trip had been precipitated by a sudden opportunity. Originally Oswald had planned a Russian tour for his wards on a more considerable scale. Among the unsolved difficulties of this scheme had been his ignorance of Russian. He had thought of employing a courier—but a courier can be a tiresome encumbrance. His friend Bailey, who was an enthusiast for Russia and spoke Russian remarkably well for an Englishman, wrote from Petrograd offering to guide Oswald and Peter about that city, suggesting a visit to a cousin who had married a Russian landowner in Novgorod, and a week or so in Moscow, where some friends of Bailey's would keep a helpful eye on the travellers. It was too good a chance to lose. There was some hasty buying of fur-lined gloves, insertion of wadding under the fur of Oswald's fur coat, and the purchase of a suitable outfit for Peter.

Bailey had his misogynic side, Oswald knew; he thought

women troublesome millinery to handle; and he did not include Joan in the invitation.   On the whole Oswald did
not regret that omission, because it gave him so excellent a
chance of being alone with Peter for long spells, and getting
near his private thoughts.

It was an expedition that left a multitude of vivid impressions upon the young man's memory; the still, cold,
starry night of the departure from Harwich, the lit decks,
the black waters, the foaming wake caught by the ship's
lights, the neat Dutch landscape with its black and white
cows growing visible as day broke, shivering workers under
a chill, red-nosed dawn pouring down by a path near the
railway into the factories of some industrial town; the long
flat journey across Germany; the Sieges-Allée and the war
trophies and public buildings of Berlin; the Sunday morning crowd upon Unter den Linden; the large prosperity of
the new suburbs of Berlin; north Germany under an iron
frost, a crowd of children sliding and skating near Königs-
berg; the dingier, vaster effects of Russia, streets in Petrograd with the shops all black and gold and painted with shining pictures of the goods on sale to a population of illiter-
ates, the night crowd in the People's Palace; a sledge drive
of ten miles along the ice of a frozen river, a wooden country house behind a great stone portico, and a merry house
party that went scampering out after supper to lie on the
crisp snow and see the stars between the tree boughs; the
chanting service in a little green-cupolaed church and a
pretty village schoolmistress in peasant costume; the great
red walls of the Kremlin rising above the Moskva and the
first glimpse of that barbaric caricature, the cathedral of
St. Basil; the painted magnificence of the Troitzkaya mon-
astery; a dirty, evil-smelling little tramp with his bundle and
kettle, worshipping unabashed in the Uspenski cathedral;
endless bearded priests, Tartar waiters with purple sashes,
a whole population in furs and so looking absurdly wealthy
to an English eye; a thousand such pictures, keen, bright
and vivid against a background of white snow. . . .

The romanticism of the late Victorians still prevailed in
Oswald's mind.   The picturesqueness of Russia had a great
effect upon him.   From the passport office at Wirballen with

its imposing green-uniformed guards and elaborate ceremonies onward into Moscow, he marked the contrast with
the trim modernity of Germany. The wild wintry landscape of the land with its swamps and unkempt thickets of
silver birch, the crouching timber villages with their cupo-
laed churches, the unmade roads, the unfamiliar lettering
of the stations, contributed to his impression of barbaric
greatness. After the plainly ugly, middle-class cathedral
of Berlin he rejoiced at the dark splendours, the green serpentine and incense, of St. Isaac's; he compared the frozen
Neva to a greater Thames and stood upon the Troitzki Bridge
rejoicing over the masses of the fortress of St. Peter and
St. Paul. In Petrograd he said, "away from here to the
North Pole is Russia and the Outside, the famine-stricken
north, the frozen fen and wilderness, the limits of mankind."
Moscow made him talk of the mingling of east and west,
western and eastern costumes jostled in the streets. He was
surprised at the frequency of Chinamen. "Away from here
to Vladivostok," he said, "is Russia and all Asia. North,
west, east and south there is limitless land. We are an
island people. But here one feels the land masses of the
earth."

Peter was preoccupied with a gallant attempt to master
colloquial Russian in a fortnight by means of a *Russian
Self-Taught* he had bought in London; he did not thrust his
conversation between Bailey and Oswald, but sometimes when
he was alone with his guardian and the mood took him he
would talk freely and rather well. He had been reading
abundantly and variously; it was evident that at Cambridge he belonged to a talking set. If he had no directive
form in his mind he had at any rate something like a systematic philosophy.

It was a profoundly sceptical philosophy. There were
moments when Oswald was reminded of Beresford's "Hamp-
denshire Wonder," who read through all human learning
and literature before the age of five, and turned upon its
instructor with "Is this *all?*" Peter looked at the world
into which he had come, at the Kings and Kaisers demanding
devotion to "our person," at the gentlemen waving flags
and talking of patriotism and service to empires and races

and "nationality," at the churches and priests pursuing their "policies," and in effect he turned to Oswald with the same question. In the background of his imagination it was only too manifest that the nymphs—with a general family resemblance to Hetty Reinhart—danced, and he heard that music of the senses which the decadent young men of the *fin de siècle* period were wont to refer to as "the pipes of Pan."

He and Oswald looked together at Moscow in the warm light of sunset. They were in the veranda of a hill-side restaurant which commanded the huge bend of the river between the Borodinski and the Kruimski bridges. The city lay, wide and massive, along the line of the sky, with little fields and a small church or so in the foreground. The six glittering domes of the great Church of the Redeemer rose in the centre against the high red wall and the clustering palaces and church cupolas of the Kremlin. Left and right of the Kremlin the city spread, a purple sea of houses and walls, flecked with snowy spaces and gemmed with red reflecting windows, through which the river twisted like a silver eel. Moscow is a city of crosses, every church has its bulbous painted cupola and some have five or six, and every cupola carries its brightly gilded two-armed cross. The rays of the setting sun was now turning all these crosses to pale fire.

Oswald, in spite of his own sceptical opinions, was a little under the spell of the "Holy Russia" legend. He stood with his foot on a chair and rested his jaw on his hand, with the living side of his face turned as usual towards his ward, and tried to express the confused ideas that were stirring in his mind. "This isn't a city like the cities of western Europe, Peter," he said. "This is something different. Those western cities, they grow out of the soil on which they stand; they are there for ever like the woods and hills; there is no other place for London or Rouen or Rome except just where it stands; but this, Peter, is a Tartar camp, frozen. It might have been at Nijni-Novgorod or Yaroslav or Kazan. It might be anywhere upon the Russia plain; only it happens to be here. It's a camp changed to wood and brick and plaster. That's the headquarters camp there, the Tsar's pavilions. And all these crosses everywhere are like the standards outside the tents of the captains.''

''And where is it going?'' said Peter, looking at Moscow over his fur collar, with his hands deep in his overcoat pockets.

''Asia advancing on Europe—with a new idea. . . . One understands Dostoevsky better when one sees this. One begins to realize this Holy Russia, as a sort of epileptic genius among nations—like his Idiot, insisting on moral truth, holding up the cross to mankind.''

''*What* truth?'' asked Peter.

''They seem to have the Christian idea. In a way we Westerns don't. Dostoevsky, Tolstoy, and their endless schools of dissent have a character in common. Christianity to a Russian means Brotherhood.''

''If it means anything,'' said Peter.

The youngster reflected.

''I wonder, is there really this Russian idea? I don't believe very much in these national ideas.''

''Say national character then. This city with its endless crosses is so in harmony with Russian music, Russian art, Russian literature.''

''Any city that had to be built here would have to look more or less like this,'' said Peter.

''If it were built by Americans?''

''If they'd lived here always,'' said Peter. ''But we're arguing in a circle. If they'd lived here always the things that have made the Russians Russians, would have made them Russians. I've gone too far. Of course there *is* a Russian character. They're wanderers, body and brain. Men of an endless land. But——''

''Well?''

''Not much of a Russian idea to it. . . . I don't believe a bit in all these crosses.''

''You mean as symbols of an idea?''

''Yes. Of course the cross has meant *something* to people. It must have meant tremendous things to some people. But men imitate. One sticks up a cross because it means all sorts of deep things to him. Then the man down the road thinks he will have a cross too. And the man up the road doesn't quite see what it's all about but doesn't like to be out of it. So they go on, until sticking up crosses becomes a habit. It becomes a necessity. They'd be shocked to see a new church without four or five crosses on it. They organize a business in golden crosses. Everybody says, 'You *must* have a cross.' Long ago every one has forgotten that deep meaning. . . ."

"H'm," said Oswald, "you think that?"

"It's just a crowd," said Peter, thinking aloud. "Underneath the crosses it's just a swarming and breeding of men. . . . Like any other men."

"But don't you think that all that million odd down there is held together by a distinctive idea? Don't you feel sometimes the Russian idea about you—like the smell of burnt wood on the breeze?"

"Well, call it a breeze," said Peter. "It's like a breeze blowing over mud. It blows now and then. It's forgotten before it is past. What does it signify?"

He was thinking as he talked. Oswald did not want to interrupt him, and just smiled slightly and looked at Peter for more.

"I don't think there's any great essential differences between cities," said Peter. "It's easy to exaggerate that. Mostly the differences are differences of scenery. Beneath the differences it's the same story everywhere; men shoving about and eating and squabbling and multiplying. We might just as well be looking at London from Hampstead bridge so far as the human facts go. Here things are done in red and black and gold against a background of white snow; there they are done in drab and grey and green. This is a land of dull tragedy instead of dull comedy, gold crosses on green onions instead of church spires, extremes instead of means, but it's all the same old human thing. Even the King and Tsar look alike, there's a state church here, dissenters, landowners. . . ."

"I suppose there is a sort of parallelism," Oswald conceded. . . .

"We're not big enough yet for big ideas, the Russian idea, or the Christian idea or any such idea," said Peter. "Why pretend we have them?"

"Now that's just it," said Oswald, coming round upon him with an extended finger. "Because we want them so badly."

"Does every one?"

"Yes. Consciously or not. That's where you and I are at issue, Peter."

"Oh, I don't *see* the ideas at work!" cried Peter. "Except as a sort of flourish of the mind. But look at the everyday life. Wherever we have been—in London, Paris, Italy, Berlin, here, we see every man who can afford it making for the restaurants and going where there are women to be got. Hunger, indulgence, and sex, sex, sex, sex." His voice was suddenly bitter. He turned his face to Oswald for a moment. "We're too little. These blind impulses—— I suppose there's a sort of impulse to Beauty in it. Some day perhaps these forces will do something—drive man up the scale of being. But as far as *we've* got——!"

He stared at Moscow again.

He seemed to have done.

"You think we're oversexed?" said Oswald after a pause.

The youngster glanced at his guardian.

"I'm not blind," he fenced.

Then he laughed with a refreshing cheerfulness. "It's youthful pessimism, Nobby. My mind runs like this because it's the fashion. We get so dosed with Schopenhauer and Nietzsche—usually at second hand. We all *try* to talk like this. Don't mind me."

Oswald smiled back.

"Peter, you drive my spirit back to the Victorians," he said. "I want to begin quoting Longfellow to you. 'Life is real, life is earnest——' "

"No!" Peter countered. "But it ought to be."

"Well, it becomes so. We have Science, and out of Science comes a light. We shall see the Will plainer and plainer."

"The Will?" said Peter, turning it over in his mind.

"Our own will then," said Oswald. "Yours, mine, and every right sort of man's."

Peter seemed to consider it.

"It won't be a national will, anyhow," he said, coming

back to Moscow. "It won't be one of these national ideas.
No Holy Russia—or Old England for the matter of that.
They're just—human accumulations. No. I don't know
of this Will at all—*any* will, Nobby. I can't see or feel this
Will. I wish I could. . . ."

He had said his say. Oswald turned again to the great
spectacle of the city. Did all those heavenward crosses now
sinking into the dusk amount to no more than a glittering
emanation out of the fen of life, an unmeaning *ignis fatuus,*
born of a morass of festering desires that had already forgotten it? Or were these crosses indeed an appeal and a
promise? Out of these millions of men would Man at last
arise? . . .

Slowly, smoothly, unfalteringly, the brush of the twilight
had been sweeping its neutral tint across the spectacle, painting out the glittering symbols one by one. A chill from outer
space fell down through the thin Russian air, a dark transparent curtain. Oswald shivered in his wadded coat.
Abruptly down below, hard by a ghostly white church, one
lamp and then another pricked the deepening blue. A little
dark tram-car that crept towards them out of the city ways to
fetch them back into the city, suddenly became a glow-
worm. . . .

§ 3

Twenty years before Oswald would not have talked in
this fashion of the Will. Twenty years before, the social and
political order of the world had seemed so stable to an English mind that the thought of a sustaining will was superfluous. Queen Victoria and the whole system had an air of
immortal inertia. The scientific and economic teachings
under which Oswald's ideas had been shaped recognized no
need for wilfully co-ordinated efforts. The end of education, they indicated, was the Diffusion of Knowledge. Victorian thought in England took good motives for granted,
seemed indeed disposed to regard almost any motive as
equally good for the common weal. Herbert Spencer, that
philosopher who could not read Kant, most typical of all
English intelligences in those days, taught that if only
there were no regulation, no common direction, if every one

were to pursue his own individual ends unrestrained, then by a sort of magic, chaos, freed from the interference of any collective direction, would produce order. His supreme gift to a generation of hasty profiteers was the discovery that the blind scuffle of fate could be called "Evolution," and so given an air of intention altogether superior to our poor struggles to make a decent order out of a greedy scramble. For some decades, whatever sections of British life had ceased to leave things to Providence and not bother—not bother—were leaving them to Evolution—and still not bothering. . . .

It was because of Oswald's discovery of the confused and distressed motives of Joan and Peter and under the suggestions of the more kinetic German philosophy that was slowly percolating into English thought, that his ideas were now changing their direction. Formerly he had thought of nations and empires as if they were things in themselves, loose shapes which had little or nothing to do with the individual lives they contained; now he began to think that all human organizations, large and small alike, exist for an end; they are will forms; they present a purpose that claims the subordination of individual aims. He began to see states and nations as things of education, beings in the minds of men.

The parallelism of Russia and Britain which Peter had made, struck Oswald as singularly acute. They had a closer parallelism with each other than with France or Italy or the United States or Germany or any of the great political systems of the world. Russia was Britain on land. Britain was Russia in an island and upon all the seas of the globe. One had the dreamy lassitude of an endless land horizon, the other the hardbitten practicality of the salt seas. One was deep-feeling, gross, and massively illiterate, the other was pervaded by a cockney brightness. But each was trying to express and hold on to some general purpose by means of forms and symbols that were daily becoming more conspicuously inadequate. And each appeared to be moving inevitably towards failure and confusion.

One afternoon during their stay in Petrograd, Bailey took Oswald and Peter to see a session of the Duma. They drove

in a sledge down the Nevski Prospekt and by streets of
ploughed-up and tumbled snow, through which struggled
an interminable multitude of sledges bringing firewood into
the city, to the old palace of the favourite Potemkin, into
which the Duma had in those days been thrust.   The Duma
was sitting in a big adapted conservatory, and the three
visitors watched the proceedings from a little low gallery
wherein the speakers were almost inaudible.   Bailey pointed
out the large proportion of priests in the centre and explained the various party groups; he himself was very
sympathetic with the Cadets.   They were Anglo-maniac;
they idealized the British constitution and thought of a limited monarchy—in the land of extremes. . . .

Oswald listened to Bailey's exposition, but the thing that
most gripped his attention was the huge portrait of the Tsar
that hung over the gathering.   He could not keep his eyes
off it.   There the figure of the autocrat stood, with its sidelong, unintelligent visage, four times as large as life, dressed
up in military guise and with its big cavalry boots right
over the head of the president of the Duma.   That portrait
was as obvious an insult, as outrageous a challenge to the
self-respect of Russian men, as a gross noise or a foul gesture
would have been.

"You and all the empire exist for *ME*," said that foolish-
faced portrait, with its busby a little on one side and its weak
hand on its sword hilt. . . .

It was to that figure they asked young Russia to be loyal.

That dull-faced Tsar and the golden crosses of Moscow
presented themselves as Russia to the young.   A heavy-
handed and very corrupt system of repression sustained their
absurd pretensions.   They had no sanction at all but that
they existed—through the acquiescences of less intelligent
generations.   The aged, the prosperous, the indolent, the
dishonest, the mean and the dull supported them in a vast
tacit conspiracy.   Beneath such symbols could a land under
the sting of modern suggestions ever be anything but a will
welter, a confusion of sentiments and instincts and wilful-
ness?   Was it so wonderful that the world was given the
stories of Artzibachev as pictures of the will forms of the
Russian young?

§ 4

Through all that journey Oswald was constantly comparing
Peter with the young people he saw.   On two occasions he
and Peter went to the Moscow Art Theatre.   Once they saw
Hamlet in Russian, and once Tchekhov's *Three Sisters;*
and each was produced with a completeness of ensemble, an
excellence of mechanism and a dramatic vigour far beyond
the range of any London theatre.   Here in untidy, sprawling, slushy Moscow shone this diamond of co-operative effort
and efficient organization.   It set Oswald revising certain
hasty generalizations about the Russian character. . . .

But far more interesting than the play to him was the
audience.   They were mostly young people, and some of
them were very young people; students in uniform, bright-
faced girls, clerks, young officers and soldiers, a sprinkling
of intelligent-looking older people of the commercial and
professional classes; each evening showed a similar gathering, a very full house, intensely critical and appreciative.
It was rather like the sort of gathering one might see in the
London Fabian Society, but there were scarcely any earnest
spinsters and many more young men.   The Art Theatre, like
a magnet, had drawn its own together out of the vast barbaric medley of western and Asiatic, of peasant, merchant,
priest, official and professional, that thronged the Moscow
streets.   And they seemed very delightful young people.

His one eye wandered from the brightly-lit stage to the
rows and rows of faces in the great dim auditorium about
him, rested on Peter, and then went back to those others.
This, then, must be a sample of the Intelligentzia.   These
were the youth who figured in so large a proportion of recent
Russian literature.   How many bright keen faces were there!
What lay before them? . . .

A dark premonition crept into his mind of the tragedy of
all this eager life, growing up in the clutch of a gigantic
political system that now staggered to its end. . . .

This youth he saw here was wonderfully like the new generation that was now dancing its way into his house at Pelham Ford. . . .

It was curious to note how much more this big dim house-ful of young Muscovites was like a British or an American audience than it was to a German gathering. Perhaps there were rather more dark types, perhaps more high cheekbones; it was hard to say. . . .

But all the other north temperate races, it seemed to Oswald, as distinguished from the Germans, had the same suggestion about them of unco-ordinated initiatives. Their minds moved freely in a great old system that had lost its hold upon them. But the German youths were co-ordinated. They were tremendously co-ordinated. Two Sundays ago he and Peter had been watching the Sunday morning parade along Unter den Linden. They had gone to see the white-trousered guards kicking their legs out ridiculously in the goose step outside the Guard House that stands opposite the Kaiser's Palace, they had walked along Unter den Linden to the Brandenburger Tor, and then, after inspecting that vainglorious trophy of piled cannon outside the Reichstag, turned down the Sieges Allée, and so came back to the Adlon by way of the Leipziger Platz. Peter had been alive to many things, but Oswald's attention had been concentrated almost exclusively on the youngsters they were passing, for the most part plump, pink-faced students in corps caps, very erect in their bearing and very tight in their clothes. They were an absolutely distinct variety of the young human male. A puerile militarism possessed them all. They exchanged salutations with the utmost punctilio. While England had been taking her children from the hands of God, and not so much making them as letting them develop into notes of interrogation, Germany without halt or hesitation had moulded her gift of youth into stiff, obedient, fresh soldiers.

There had been a moment like a thunderclap while Oswald and Peter had been near the Brandenburger Tor. A swift wave of expectation had swept through the crowd; there had been a galloping of mounted policemen, a hustling of traffic to the side of the road, a hasty lining up of spectators. Then with melodious tootlings and amidst guttural plaudits, a big white automobile carrying a glitter of uniforms had gone by, driven at a headlong pace. *"Der Kaiser!"* Just for a moment the magnificence hung in the eye—and passed.

What had they seen?   Cloaks, helmets, hard visages, one distinctive pallid face; something melodramatic, something eager and in a great hurry, something that went by like the sound of a trumpet, a figure of vast enterprise in shining armour, with mailed fist.   This was the symbol upon which these young Germans were being concentrated.   This was the ideal that had gripped them.   Something very modern and yet romantic, something stupendously resolute.   Going whither?   At any rate, going magnificently somewhere. That was the power of it.   It *was* going somewhere.   For good or bad it was an infinitely more attractive lead than the cowardly and oppressive Tsardom that was failing to hold the refractory minds of these young Russians, or the current edition of the British imperial ideal, twangling its idiotic banjo and exhorting Peter and his generation to "tax the foreigner" as a worthy end and aim in life.

Oswald, with his eye on the dim, preoccupied audience about him, recalled a talk that he and Peter had had with a young fellow-traveller in the train between Hanover and Berlin.   It had been a very typical young German, glasses and all; and his clothes looked twice as hard as Peter's, and he sat up stiffly while Peter slouched on the seat.   He evidently wanted to air his English, while Peter had not the remotest desire to air his German, and only betrayed a knowledge of German when it was necessary to explain some English phrase the German didn't quite grasp.   The German wanted to know whether Oswald and Peter had been in Germany before, where they were going, what they thought of it, what they were going to think of Berlin.

Responding to counter questions he said he had been twice to England.   He thought England was a great country.   "Yes—but not systematic.   No!"

"You mean undisciplined?"

Yes, it was perhaps undisciplined he meant.

Oswald said that as a foreigner he was most struck by the tremendous air of order in north Germany.   The Germans were orderly by nature.   The admission proved an attractive gambit.

The young German questioned Oswald's view that the Germans were naturally orderly.   Hard necessity had made them so. They had had to discipline themselves, they had been obliged to develop a Kultur—encircled by enemies. Now their Kultur was becoming a second nature. Every nation, he supposed, brought its present to mankind. Germany's was Order, System, the lesson of Obedience that would constantly make her more powerful. The Germans were perforce a thorough people. Thorough in all they did. Although they had come late into modern industrialism they had already developed social and economic organization far beyond that of any other people. Nicht wahr? Their work was becoming necessary to the rest of mankind. In Russia, for example, in Turkey, in Italy, in South America, it was more and more the German who organized, developed, led. "Though we are fenced round," he said, "still—we break out."

There was something familiar and yet novel in all this to Oswald. It was like his first sensation upon reading Shakespeare in German. It was something very familiar— in an unfamiliar idiom. Then he recognized it. This was exactly his own Imperialism—Teutonized. The same assertion of an educational mission. . . .

"Everywhere we go," said the young German, "our superior science, our higher education, our better method prevails. Even in your India——"

He smiled and left that sentence unfinished.

"But your militarism, your sabre rule here at home; this Zabern business; isn't that a little incompatible with this idea of Germany as a great civilizing influence permeating the world?"

"Not at all," said the young German, with the readiness of a word-perfect actor. "Behind our missionaries of order we must have ready the good German sword."

"But isn't the argument of force apt to be a little—decivilizing?"

The young German did not think so. "When I was in England I said, there are three things that these English do not properly understand to use, they are the map or index, the school, and—the sword. Those three things are the triangle of German life. . . ."

That hung most in Oswald's mind. He had gone on

talking to the young German for a long time about the differences of the British and the German way. He had made Peter and the youngster compare their school and college work, and what was far more striking, the difference in pressure between the two systems. "You press too hard," he said. "In Alsace you have pressed too hard—in Posen."

"Perhaps we sometimes press—I do not know," said the young German. "It is the strength of our determination. We are impatient. We are a young people." For a time Oswald had talked of the methods of Germany in the Cameroons and of Britain on the Gold Coast, where the German had been growing cacao by the plantation system, turning the natives into slaves, while the British, with an older experience and a longer view, had left the land in native hands and built up a happy and loyal free cultivation ten times as productive mile for mile as the German. It seemed to him to be one good instance of his general conception of Germany as the land of undue urgency. "Your Wissmann in East Africa was a great man—but everywhere else you drive too violently. You antagonize." North Germany everywhere, he said, had the same effect upon him of a country "going hard."

"Germany may be in too much of a hurry," he repeated.

"We came into world-politics late," said the young German, endorsing Oswald's idea from his own point of view. "We have much to overtake yet." . . .

The Germans had come into world-politics late. That was very true. They were naïve yet. They could still feed their natural egotism on the story of a world mission. The same enthusiasms that had taken Russia to the Pacific—and to Grand Ducal land speculation in Manchuria—and the English to the coolie slavery of the Rand, was taking these Germans now—whither? Oswald did not ask what route to disillusionment Germany might choose. But he believed that she would come to disillusionment. She was only a little later in phase than her neighbours; that was all. In the end they would see that that white-cloaked heroic figure in the automobile led them to futility as surely as the skulking Tsar. Not that way must the nations go. . . .

Oswald saw no premonition of a world catastrophe in this

German youngster's devotion to an ideal of militant aggression, nor in the whole broad spectacle of straining preparation across which he and Peter travelled that winter from
Aix to Wirballen. He was as it were magically blind. He
could stand on the Hanover platform and mark the largeness
of the station, the broad spreading tracks, the endless sid-
ings, the tremendous transport preparations, that could have
no significance in the world but military intention, and still
have no more to say than, ''These Germans give themselves
elbow-room on their railways, Peter. I suppose land is
cheaper.'' He could see nothing of the finger of fate pointing straight out of all this large tidy preparedness at Peter
and their fellow-passengers and all the youth of the world.
He thought imperialistic monarchy was an old dead thing
in Russia and in Britain and in Germany alike.

In Berlin indeed in every photographer's was the touched-
up visage of the Kaiser, looking heroic, and endless post-
cards of him and of his sons and of the Kaiserin and
little imperial grandchildren and the like; they were as
dull and dreary-looking as any royalties can be, and it
was inconceivable to Oswald that such figures could really
rule the imagination of a great people. He did not realize
that all the tragedy in the world might lie behind the
words of that young German, ''we came into world-politics
late,'' behind the fact that the German imperialist system
was just a little less decayed, a little less humorous, a little
less indolent and disillusioned than either of its great paral-
lels to the east and west. He did not reflect that no system
is harmless until its hands are taken off the levers of power.
He could still believe that he lived in an immensely stable
world, and that these vast forms of kingdom and empire, with
their sham reverences and unmeaning ceremonies and obligations, their flags and militancy and their imaginative
senility, threatened nothing beyond the negative evil of un-
inspired lives running to individual waste. That was the
thing that concerned him. He saw no collective fate hanging over all these intent young faces in the Moscow Art
Theatre, as over the strutting innocents of patriotic Berlin;
he had as yet no intimation of the gigantic disaster that was
now so close at hand, that was to torment and shatter the

whole youth of the world, that was to harvest the hope and energy of these bright swathes of life. . . .

He glanced at Peter, intent upon the stage.

Peter lay open to every impulse. That was Oswald's supreme grievance then against Tsars, Kings, and Churches. They had not been good enough for Peter. That seemed grievance enough.

He did not imagine yet that they could murder the likes of Peter by the hundred thousand, without a tremor.

He loved the fine lines of the boy's profile, he marked his delicate healthy complexion. Peter was like some wonderful new instrument in perfect condition. And all these other youngsters, too, had something of the same clean fire in them. . . .

Was it all to be spent upon love-making and pleasure-seeking and play? Was this exquisite hope and desire presently to be thrown aside, rusted by base uses, corroded by self-indulgence, bent or broken? "The generations running to waste—like rapids. . . ."

He still thought in that phrase. The Niagara of Death so near to them all now to which these rapids were heading, he still did not hear, did not suspect its nearness. . . .

And Joan——. From Peter his thoughts drifted to Joan. Joan apparently could find nothing better to do in life than dance. . . .

Suddenly Peter took a deep breath, sat back, and began to clap. The whole house broke out into a pelting storm of approval.

"Ripping!" said Peter. "Oh! ripping."

He turned his bright face to Oswald. "They do it so well," he said, smiling. "I had forgotten it was in Russian. I seemed to understand every word."

Oswald turned his eye again to *Hamlet* in Gordon Craig's fantastic setting—which Moscow in her artistic profusion could produce when London was too poor to do so.

§ 5

Very similar were the thoughts in Oswald's mind three months later, three months nearer the world catastrophe, as he sat in his summerhouse after Joan had told him of her quarrel with Peter.

Her denunciation of Peter had had the curious effect upon him of making him very anxious about her. So far as Peter went, what she had told him had but confirmed and made definite what he had known by instinct since the Christmas party. His mind was used now to the idea of Peter being vicious. But he was very much shocked indeed at the discovery that Joan was aware of Peter's vices. That was a new jolt to his mind. In many things Joan and Peter had changed his ideas enormously, but so far he had retained not only his wardroom standards with regard to the morals of a youth, but also his romantic ideals of feminine purity with regard to a girl. He still thought of his own womenkind as of something innocent, immaculate and untouchable, beings in a different world from the girls who "didn't mind a bit of fun" and the women one made love to boldly.

But now he had to face the fact—Joan had forced it upon him—this new feminine generation wasn't divided in that obvious way. The clean had knowledge, the bold were not outcast and apart. The new world of women was as mixed as the world of men. He sat in his summerhouse thinking of his Joan's flushed face, her indignant eyes, her outspoken words.

"It was a *woman's* face," he whispered. . . .

And he was realizing too how much more urgent the ending of adolescence was becoming with a girl than it could ever be with a boy. Peter might tumble into a scrape or so and scramble out again, not very much the worse for it, as he himself had done. But Joan, with all the temerity of a youth, might be making experiments that were fatal. He had not been watching her as he had watched Peter. Suddenly he woke up to this realization of some decisive issue at hand. Why was she so whitely angry with Peter? Why did she complain of having to "stand too much" from Peter? Her abuse of his friends had the effect of a counter attack. Was there some mischief afoot from which Peter restrained her? What men were there about in Joan's world?

There was something slimy and watchful about this fellow Huntley. Could there be more in that affair than one liked

to think? . . . Or was there some one unknown in London
or in Cambridge?

She and Peter were quarrelling about the Easter party.
It would apparently be impossible to have any Easter party
this year, since both wanted to bar out the other one's friends.
And anyhow there mustn't be any more of this Hetty
Reinhart business at Pelham Ford. That must stop. It
ought never to have happened. . . . He would take Peter
over to Dublin. They could accept an invitation he had had
from Graham Powys out beyond Foxrock, and they could
motor into Dublin and about the country, and perhaps the
Irish situation might touch the boy's imagination. . . .

Joan could go to her aunts at The Ingle-Nook. . . .

Should he have a talk to Aunt Phyllis about the girl?

It was a pity that Aunt Phyllis always lost her breath
and was shaken like an aspen leaf with fine feeling whenever
one came to any serious discussion with her. If it wasn't
for that confounded shimmer in her nerves and feelings, she
would be a very wise and helpful woman. . . .

§ 6

Oswald's thoughts ranged far and wide that morning.

Now he would be thinking in the most general terms of
life as he conceived it, now he would be thinking with vivid
intensity about some word or phrase or gesture of Joan
and Peter.

He was blind still to the thing that was now so close to
all his world; nevertheless a vague uneasiness about the
trend of events was creeping into his mind and mixing with
his personal solicitudes. Many men felt that same uneasiness in those feverish days—as if Death cast his shadow upon
them before he came visibly into their lives.

Oswald belonged to that minority of Englishmen who think
systematically, whose ideas join on. Most Englishmen, even
those who belong to what we call the educated classes, still
do not think systematically at all; you cannot understand
England until you master that fact; their ideas are in
slovenly detached little heaps, they think in ready-made

phrases, they are honestly capable therefore of the most grotesque inconsistencies. But Oswald had built up a sort of
philosophy for himself, by which he did try his problems
and with which he fitted in such new ideas as came to him.
It was a very distinctive view of life he had; a number of influences that are quite outside the general knowledge of English people had been very powerful in shaping it.   Biological
science, for example, played a quite disproportionate part in
it.   Like the countrymen of Metchnikoff, most of the countrymen of Darwin and Huxley believe firmly that biological
science was invented by the devil and the Germans to
undermine the Established Church. But Oswald had been
exceptional in the chances that had turned his attention to
these studies. And a writer whose suggestions had played
a large part in shaping his ideas about education and social
and political matters was J. J. Atkinson. He thought Atkinson the most neglected of all those fine-minded Englishmen England ignores. He thought Lang and Atkinson's
Social Origins one of the most illuminating books he had
ever read since Winwood Reade's *Martyrdom of Man.*
No doubt it will be amusing to many English readers that
Oswald should have mixed up theories of the origins and
destinies of mankind with his political views and his anxieties about Joan's behaviour and Peter's dissipations but
he did. It was the way of his mind. He perceived a connexion between these things.

The view he had developed of human nature and human
conditions was saturated with the idea of the ancestral ape.
In his instincts, he thought, man was still largely the creature of the early Stone Age, when, following Atkinson, he
supposed that the human herd, sex linked, squatted close
under the dominion of its Old Man, and hated every stranger.
He did not at all accept the Aristotelian maxim that man
is "a political animal." He was much more inclined to
Schopenhauer's comparison of human society to a collection
of hedgehogs driven together for the sake of warmth. He
thought of man as a being compelled by circumstances of his
own inadvertent creation to be a political animal in spite of
the intense passions and egotisms of his nature. Man he
judged to be a reluctant political animal. Man's prehensile

hand has given him great possibilities of experiment, he is a restless and curious being, knowledge increases in him and brings power with it. So he jostles against his fellows. He becomes too powerful for his instincts. The killing of man becomes constantly more easy for man. The species must needs therefore become political and religious, tempering its intense lusts and greeds and hostilities, if it is to save itself from self-destruction. The individual man resists the process by force and subterfuge and passivity at every step. Nevertheless necessity still finds something in the nature of this fiercest of its creatures to work upon. In the face of adult resistance necessity harks back to plastic immaturity. Against the narrow and intense desires of the adult man, against the secretive cunning and dispersiveness of our ape heredity, struggle the youthful instincts of association. Individualism is after all a by-path in the history of life. Every mammal begins by being dependent and social; even the tiger comes out of a litter. The litter is brotherhood. Every mother is a collectivist for her brood. A herd, a tribe, a nation, is only a family that has delayed dispersal, stage by stage, in the face of dangers. All our education is a prolongation and elaboration of family association, forced upon us by the continually growing danger of the continually growing destructiveness of our kind.

And necessity has laid hold of every device and formula that will impose self-restraint and devotion upon the lonely savagery of man, that will help man to escape race-suicide. In spite of ever more deadly and far-reaching weapons, man still escapes destruction by man. Religion, loyalty, patriotism, those strange and wonderfully interwoven nets of superstition, fear, flattery, high reason and love, have subjugated this struggling egotistical ape into larger and larger masses of co-operation, achieved enormous temporary securities. But the ape is still there, struggling subtly. Deep in every human individual is a fierce scepticism of and resentment against the laws that bind him, and the weaker newer instincts that would make him the servant of his fellow man.

Such was Oswald's conception of humanity. It marched with all his experiences of Africa, where he had struggled to weave the net of law and teaching against warrior, slave-

trader, disease and greed. It marched now with all the appearances of the time. So it was he saw men.

It seemed to him that the world that lay behind the mask of
his soft, sweet Hertfordshire valley, this modern world into
which Joan and Peter had just rushed off so passionately,
was a world in which the old nets of rule and convention
which had maintained a sufficiency of peace and order in
Europe for many generations of civilization, were giving
way under the heavy stresses of a new time. Peoples were
being brought too closely together, too great a volume of suggestions poured into their minds, criticism was vivid and destructive; the forms and rules that had sufficed in a less
crowded time were now insufficient to hold imaginations and
shape lives. Oswald could see no hope as yet of a new net
that would sweep together all that was bursting out of the
old. His own generation of the 'eighties and 'nineties, under a far less feverish urgency, had made its attempt to
patch new and more satisfactory network into the rotting
reticulum, but for the most part their patches had done no
more than afford a leverage for tearing. He had built his
cosmogony upon Darwin and Winwood Reade, his religion
upon Cotter Morrison's *Service of Man;* he had interwoven with that a conception of the Empire as a great
civilizing service. That much had served him through the
trying years at the end of adolescence, had in spite of strong
coarse passions made his life on the whole a useful life.
King, church, and all the forms of the old order he had been
willing to accept as a picturesque and harmless paraphernalia upon these structural ideas to which he clung. He
had been quite uncritical of the schoolmaster. Now with
these studies of education that Joan and Peter had forced
upon him, he was beginning to realize how encumbering and
obstructive the old paraphernalia could be, how it let in indolence, stupidity, dishonesty, and treachery to the making
of any modern system. A world whose schools are unreformed is an unreformed world. Only in the last year or so
had he begun to accept the fact that for some reason these
dominant ideas of his, this humanitarian religion which had
served his purpose and held his life and the lives of a generation of liberal-minded Englishmen together, had no grip-

ping power upon his wards. This failure perplexed him profoundly. Had his Victorian teachers woven prematurely, or had they used too much of the old material? Had they rather too manifestly tried to make the best of two worlds—leaving the schools alone? Must this breaking down of strands that was everywhere apparent, go still further? And if so, how far would the breaking down have to go before fresh nets could be woven?

If Oswald in his summerhouse in the spring of 1914 could see no immediate catastrophe ahead, he could at least see that a vast disintegrative process had begun in the body of European civilization. This disintegration, he told himself, was a thing to go on by stages, to be replaced by stages; it would give place to a new order, a better order, "someday"; everything just and good was going to happen someday, the liberation of India, the contentment of Ireland, economic justice, political and military efficiency. It was all coming—always coming and never arriving, that new and better state of affairs. What did go on meanwhile was disintegration. The British mind hates crisis; it abhors the word "Now." It believes that you can cool water for ever and that it will never freeze, that you can saw at a tree for ever and that it will never fall, that there is always some sand left above in the hour-glass. When the English Belshazzar sees the writing on the wall, he welcomes the appearance of a new if rather sensational form of publication, and he sits back to enjoy it at his leisure. . . .

The nets were breaking, but they would never snap. That in effect was Oswald's idea in 1913. The bother, from his point of view, was that they had let out Joan and Peter to futility.

There is a risk that the catastrophic events of 1914 may blind the historian to the significance of the spinning straws of 1913. But throughout Europe the sands were trickling before the avalanche fell. The arson of the suffragettes, the bellicose antics of the Unionist leaders in Ulster, General Gough's Curragh mutiny, were all parts of the same relaxation of bonds that launched the grey-clad hosts of Germany into Belgium. Only the habits of an immense security could have blinded Oswald to the scale and imminence of the disaster. The world had outgrown its ideas and its will.

Already people are beginning to forget the queer fevers that ran through the British community in 1913. For example there was the violent unrest of the women. That may exercise the historian in the future profoundly. Probably he will question the facts. Right up to the very outbreak of the war there was not a week passed without some new ridiculous outrage on the part of the militant suffragettes. Now it was a fine old church would be burnt, now a well-known country house; now the mania would take the form of destroying the letters in pillar-boxes, now the attack was upon the greens of the golf links. Public meetings ceased to be public meetings because of the endless interruptions by shrill voices crying "Votes for women!" One great triumph of the insurgents was a raid with little hammers upon the west-end shop-windows. They burnt the tea pavilion in Kew Gardens, set fire to unoccupied new buildings, inaugurated a campaign of picture-slashing at the public exhibitions. For a time they did much mischief to the cushions and fittings of railway carriages. Churches had to be locked up and museums closed on account of them. Poor little Pelham Ford church had had to buy a new lock against the dangers of some wandering feminist. And so on and so on. But this revolt of the women was more than a political revolt. That concentration upon the Vote was the concentration of a vast confused insurgence of energy that could as yet find no other acceptable means of expression. New conditions had robbed whole strata of women of any economic importance, new knowledge had enormously diminished the need for their domestic services, the birth-rate had fallen, the marriage age had risen, but the heedless world had made no provision for the vitality thus let loose. The old ideals of a womanly life showed absurd in the light of the new conditions. Why be pretty and submissive when nobody wants you? Why be faithful with no one to be faithful to? Why be devoted in a world which has neither enough babies nor lovers nor even its old proportion of helpless invalids to go round? Why, indeed, to come to the very heart of the old ideal, keep chaste when there is no one to keep chaste for? Half the intelligent women in that world had stood as Joan had done, facing their own life and beauty and asking desperately "What is the Good of it?"

But while the old nets rotted visibly, there were no new nets being woven. There was everywhere the vague expectation of new nets, of a new comprehensiveness, a new way of life, but there was no broad movement towards any new way of life. Everywhere the old traditions and standards and institutions remained, discredited indeed and scoffed at, but in possession of life. Energetic women were reaching out in a mood of the wildest experiment towards they knew not what. It was a time of chaotic trials. The disposition of the first generation of released women had been towards an austere sexlessness, a denial of every feminine weakness, mental and physical, and so by way of Highmorton and hockey to a spinsterish, bitter competition with men. A few still bolder spirits, and Aunt Phœbe Stubland was among these pioneers, carried the destructive "Why not?" still further. Grant Allen's *Woman Who Did* and Arthur's infidelities were but early aspects of a wide wave of philoprogenitive and eugenic sentimentality. The new generation carried "why not?" into the sphere of conduct with amazing effect.

Women are the custodians of manners, and mothers and hostesses who did not dream of the parallelism of their impulse with militancy, were releasing the young to an unheard-of extravagance of dress and festival. Joan could wear clothes at a Chelsea dance that would have shocked a chorus girl half a century before; she went about London in the small hours with any casual male acquaintance; so far as appearances went she might have been the most disreputable of women. She yielded presently to Huntley's persistence and began dancing the tango with him. It was the thing to slip away from a dance in slippers and a wrap, and spend an hour or so careering about London in a taxi or wandering on Hampstead Heath. Joan's escapades fretted the sleeping tramps upon the Thames Embankment. London, which had hitherto dispersed its gatherings about eleven and got to bed as a rule by midnight, was aspiring in those days to become nocturnal. The restaurants were obliged to shut early, but a club was beyond such regulations. Neces-

sity created the night club, which awoke about eleven and
closed again after a yawning breakfast of devilled bones.

A number of night clubs were coming into existence, to
the particular delight of young Winterbaum. His boyish
ambition for Joan was returning. He had seen her dance
and heard her dancing praised. Vulgar people made wild
vulgar guesses in his hearing at what lay behind her grave
and sometimes sombre prettiness. He pretended to be very
discreet about that. It became the pride of his life to appear at some crowded night club in possession of Joan; he
did not know what people thought of her or of him but he
hoped for the worst. He wore the most beautiful buttons on
his white waistcoat and the most delicate gold chain you can
imagine. In the cloakroom he left a wonderful overcoat and
a wonderful cane. Sometimes he encouraged the ringlets
in his hair and felt like Disraeli, and sometimes he restrained
them and felt like a cold, cynical Englishman of the darker
sort. He would sit swelling with pride beside Joan, and
nod to painted women and heavy men; he knew no end of
people. He did not care what sort of people they were so
long as he knew them. It was always his ambition to be seen
drinking champagne with Joan. Joan had no objection in
the world, but she could not bring herself to swallow a drink
that tasted, she thought, like weak vinegar mixed with a
packet of pins and that went up your nose and made your
brain swing slowly to and fro on its axis for the rest of the
evening. So she just drank nothing at all.

She would sit at her table with her pretty bare arms folded
under her like the paws of a little cat, with her face, that
still had the delicacy and freshness of a child's, as intent as
any intelligent child's can be on the jumble of people before
her, and her sombre eyes, calm and beautiful, looking at
smart London trying at last to take its pleasures gaily.
Perhaps some fortunate middle-aged gentleman of Winterbaum's circle would be attempting to charm her by brilliant
conversation, as, for instance Sir Joseph Lystrom, with a full-
mouthed German flavour in his voice, in this style: "Pretty
cheap here this evening somehow, eh? *What?*" Somewhere in the back of Sir Joseph's mind was the illusion that
by barking in this way and standing treat profusely, lay

the road to a girl's young love. Somewhen perhaps—who
knows?—he may have found justification for that belief.
Joan had long since learnt how to turn a profile to these
formal attentions, and appear to be interested without hearing or answering a word.

Or sometimes it would be Huntley. Huntley had lately
taken to dodging among the night clubs to which he had
access, when Joan was in London. Usually such nights
ended in futility, but occasionally he was lucky and found
Joan. Then he would come and talk and suggest ideas to
her. He still remained the most interesting personality in
her circle. She pretended to Winterbaum and herself to be
bored by his pursuit, but indeed she looked for it. Except
for Winterbaum and Huntley and Winterbaum's transitory
introductions, she remained a detached figure in these places.
Sometimes quite good-looking strangers sat a little way off
and sought to convey to her by suitable facial expression the
growth of a passionate interest in her. She conveyed to them
in return that they were totally invisible to her, resisting at
times a macabre disposition to take sights at them suddenly
and amazingly or put out her tongue. Sometimes women
of the great Winterbaum circle would make a fuss of her.
They called her a "dear child." They would have been
amazed at the complete theoretical knowledge a dear child
of unrestricted reading could possess of them and their
little ways.

"So this is the life of pleasure," thought the dear child.
"Well!"

And then that same question that Peter seemed always to
be asking of Oswald: "Is this *all*?"

When she danced in these places she danced with a sort
of contempt. And the sage, experienced men who looked at
her so knowingly never realized how much they imagined
about her and how little they knew.

She would sit and think how indecent it was to be at the
same time old and dissipated. Some of these women here,
she perceived, were older than her aunts Phœbe and Phyllis,
years older. Their faces were painted and done most amazingly—Joan knew all about facial massage and the rest of it
—and still they were old faces. But their poor bodies were

not nearly so old as their faces, that was the tragedy of them.
Joan regarded the tremendous V decolletage of a lively
grandmother before her, and the skin of the back shone as
young as her own.   The good lady was slapping the young
gentleman next to her with a quite smooth and shapely arm.
Joan speculated whether the old fashion of the masked ball
and the Venetian custom of masks which she had been reading about that day in Voltaire's *Princesse de Babylone,*
might not have something to do with that.   But—she reverted—only young people ought to make love at all.   Her
aunts didn't; Oswald didn't.   And Oswald was years
younger than some of the men here, and in Joan's eyes at
least far more presentable.   He had a scarred face indeed
but a clean skin; some of the old men here had skins one
would shiver to touch, and the expressions of evil gargoyles.
She let her thoughts dwell—not for the first time—on Oswald
and a queer charm he had for her.   Never in all her life
had she known him do or say a mean, dishonest, unjust, or
unkind thing.   In some ways he was oddly like Peter, but
wise and gentle—and not exasperating. . . .

But all this playing with love in London was detestable,
all of it.   This was really a shameful place.   It was shameful to be here.   Love—mixed up with evening dress and
costly clothes and jewellery and nasty laughter and cigars,
strong cigars and drink that slopped about.   It was disgusting.   These people made love after their luncheons and dinners and suppers.   Pigs!   They were all pigs.   They looked
like pigs.   If ever she made love it should be in the open
air, in some lovely place with blue mountains in the distance,
where there were endless wild flowers, where one could swim.
No man she had ever talked with of love had really understood anything of the beauty of love and the cleanness of
love—except Mir Jelaluddin.   And he had a high-pitched
voice and a staccato accent—and somehow. . . . One ought
not to be prejudiced against a dark race, but somehow it was
unthinkable. . . .

Joan sat in the night club dreaming of a lover, and the
men about her glanced furtively at her face, asking themselves, "Can it be I?" men with red ears, men with greasy
hair, men with unpleasing necks and clumsy gestures; bald

men, fat men, watery-eyed men, cheats, profiteers, usurers, snobs, toadies, successful old men of every sort and young men who had done nothing and for the most part never would. "Can it be I?" they surmised dimly, seeing her pensive eyes. And she was dreaming of a lithe, white, slender figure, strong and clean. He would hunt among the mountains, he would swim swift rivers; he would never drink strong drink nor reek of smoke. . . .

At this moment young Winterbaum became urgent with his beautiful gold cigarette case. Joan took a cigarette and lighted it, and sat smoking with her elbows side by side on the table.

"You're not bored?" said young Winterbaum.

"Oh, no. I'm watching people. I don't want to talk."

"Oh! not at all?" said young Winterbaum.

"So long as one has to talk," he said after reflection and with an air of cleverness, "one isn't really friends."

"Exactly," said Joan, and blew smoke through her nose.

What was it she had been thinking about? She could not remember, the thread was broken. She was sorry. She had a vague memory of something pleasant. . . . She fell into a fresh meditation upon Jews. All Jews, she thought, ought to grow beards. At least after they were thirty. They are too dark to shave, and besides there is a sort of indignity about their beaked shaven faces. A bearded old Jew can look noble, a moustached old Jew always looked like an imitation of a Norman gentleman done in cheaper material. But that of course was exactly what he was. . . .

Why did men of forty or fifty always want to dance with and make love to flappers? Some of these girls here must be two or three years younger than herself. What was the interest? They couldn't talk; they weren't beautiful; one could see they weren't beautiful. And they laughed, good God! how they laughed! Girls ought to be taught to laugh, or at any rate taught not to laugh offensively. Laughter ought to be a joyful, contagious thing, jolly and kind, but these shrieks! How few of these people looked capable of real laughter! They just made this loud chittering sound. Only human beings laugh. . . .

In this manner the mind of Joan was running on the

evening when she saw Peter and Hetty come into the club which tried to live up to the name of "The Nest of the Burning Phœnix." Some tango experts had just relinquished the floor and there was a space amidst the throng when Hetty made her entry. Hetty had made a great effort, she was in full London plumage, and her effect was tremendous. About her little bold face was a radiant scheme of peacock's feathers, her slender neck carried a disc a yard and a quarter wide; her slender, tall body was sheathed in black and peacock satin; she wore enormous earrings and a great barbaric chain. Her arms were bare except for a score of bangles, and she had bare sandalled feet. She carried her arrow point of a chin triumphantly. Peter was not her only attendant. There was also another man in her train whom every one seemed to recognize, a big, square-faced, handsome man of thirty-five or so who made Peter look very young and flimsy. "She's got Fred Beevor!" said Winterbaum with respect, and dropped the word "Million." Peter's expression was stony, but Joan judged he was not enjoying himself.

There were very few unoccupied chairs and tables, but opposite Joan were two gilt seats and another disengaged at a table near at hand. Hetty was too busy with her triumph to note Joan until Beevor had already chosen this place. With a slight awkwardness the two parties mingled. Young Winterbaum at least was elated. Beevor after a few civilities to Joan let it appear that Hetty preoccupied him. Peter was evidently not enjoying himself at all. Joan found him seated beside her and silent.

Joan knew that it is the feminine rôle to lead conversation, but it seemed to her rather fun to have to encourage a tongue-tied Peter. A malicious idea came into her head.

"Well, Petah," she said; "why don't you say I oughtn't to be here?"

Peter regarded her ambiguously. He had an impulse.

"No decent people ought to be here," he said quietly. "Let's go home, Joan."

Her heart jumped at the suggestion. All her being said yes. And then she remembered that she had as much right to have a good time as Peter. If she went back with him it

would be like giving in to him; it would be like admitting his
right to order her about.   And besides there was Hetty.   He
wasn't really disgusted.   All he wanted to do really was to
show off because he was jealous of Hetty.   He didn't want
to go home with Joan.   She wasn't going to be a foil for
Hetty anyhow.   And finally, once somewhere he had refused
her almost exactly the same request.   She checked herself
and considered gravely.   A little touch of spite crept into
her expression.

"No," she said slowly.   "No. . . . I've only just come,
Petah."

"Very well," said Peter.   "*I* don't mind.   If you like
this sort of thing——"

He said no more, sulking visibly.

Joan resolved to dance at the first opportunity, and to
dance in a bold and reckless way—so as thoroughly to exasperate Peter.   She looked about the room through the smoke-
laden atmosphere in the hope of seeing Huntley. . . .

She and Peter sat side by side, feeling very old and experienced and worldly and up-to-date.   But indeed they
were still only two children who ought to have been packed
off to bed hours before.

§ 7

The disorder in the world of women, the dissolution of
manners and restraints, was but the more intimate aspect of
a universal drift towards lawlessness.   The world of labour
was seething also with the same spirit of almost aimless
insurrection.   In a world of quickened apprehensions and
increasing stimulus women were losing faith in the rules of
conduct that had sufficed in a less exacting age.   Far profounder and more dangerous to the established order were the
scepticisms of the workers.   The pretensions of the old social
system that trade unionism had scarcely challenged were
now being subjected throughout all western Europe to a
pitiless scrutiny by a new and more educated type of em-
ployé.

The old British trade unionism had never sought much
more than increased wages and a slightly higher standard

of life; its acceptance of established institutions had been artlessly complete; it had never challenged the authority nor the profits of the proprietor. It had never proposed more than a more reasonable treaty with the masters, a fairer sharing of the good gifts of industry. But infatuated by the evil teachings of an extreme individualism, a system of thought which was indeed never more than a system of base excuses dressed up as a philosophy, the directing and possessing classes had failed altogether to agree with their possible labour adversary quickly while they were yet in the way with him. They had lacked the intelligence to create a sympathetic industrial mentality, and the conscience to establish a standard of justice. They left things alone until the grit of a formless discontent had got into every cog of the industrial machinery. Too late, the employers were now conceding the modest demands that labour had made in the 'eighties and 'nineties, they were trying to accept the offers of dead men; they found themselves face to face with an entirely less accommodating generation. This new labour movement was talking no longer of shorter hours and higher pay but of the social revolution. It did not demand better treatment from the capitalist; it called him a profiteer and asked him to vanish from the body politic. It organized strikes now not to alter the details of its working conditions as its predecessor had done, but in order to end the system by making it impossible. In Great Britain as on the Continent, the younger generation of labour was no longer asking to have the harness that bound it to the old order made easier and lighter; it was asking for a new world.

The new movement seemed to men of Oswald's generation to come as thunderstorms will sometimes come, as the militant suffragette had seemed to come, suddenly out of a clear sky. But it was far more ominous than the suffragette movement, for while that made one simple explicit demand, this demanded nothing short of a new economic order. It asked for everything and would be content with nothing. It was demanding from an old habitual system the supreme feat of reconstruction. Short of that vague general reconstruction it promised no peace. Higher wages would not pacify it; shorter hours would not pacify it. It threatened sabotage of every sort, and a steady, incessant broadening antagonism of master and man. Peter, half sympathetic and half critical, talked about it to Oswald one day.

"They all say, 'I'm a Rebel!'" said Peter. "'Rebel' is their cant word."

"Yes, but rebel against what?"

"Oh! the whole system."

"They have votes."

"They get humbugged, they say. They do, you know. The party system is a swindle, and everybody understands that. Why don't we clean it up? P.R.'s the only honest method. They don't understand how it is rigged, but they know it is rigged. When you talk about Parliament they laugh."

"But they have their Unions."

"They don't trust their leaders. They say they are got at. They say they are old-fashioned and bluffed by the politicians. . . . They are. . . ."

"Then what do they want?"

"Just to be out of all this. They are bored to tears by their work, by the world they have to live in, by the pinched mean lives they have to lead—in the midst of plenty and luxury—bored by the everlasting dulness and humbug of it all."

"But how are they going to alter it?"

"That's all vague. Altogether vague. Cole and Mellor and those Cambridge chaps preach Guild Socialism to them, but I don't know how far they take it in—except that they agree that profit is unnecessary. But the fundamental fact is just blind boredom and the desire to smash up things. Just on the off chance of their coming better. The employer has been free to make the world for them, and this is the world he has made. Damn him! That's how they look at it. They are bored by his face, bored by his automobile, bored by his knighthood, bored by his country house and his snob of a wife——"

"But what can they do?"

"Make things impossible."

"They can't run things themselves."

"They aren't convinced of that. Anyhow if they smash

up things the employer goes first, and he's the chap they seem to be principally after——''

Peter reflected. Then he gave a modern young English-man's view of the labour conflict. ''The employers have been pretty tidy asses not to see that their workpeople get a better, more amusing life than they do. It was their busi-ness and their interest to do so. It could have been managed easily. But they're so beastly disloyal. And so mean. They not only sweat labour themselves but they won't stir a finger to save it from jerry-built housing, bad provisioning, tally-men, general ugliness, bad investments, rotten insurance companies—every kind of rotten old thing. Any one may help kill *their* sheep. They've got no gratitude to their workers. They won't even amuse them. Why couldn't they set up decent theatres for them, and things like that? It's so stupid of them. These employers are the most dangerous class in the community. There's enough for every one now-adays and over. It's the first business of employers to see workpeople get their whack. What good are they if they don't do that? But they never have. Labour is convinced now that they never will. They run about pretending to be landed gentry. They've got their people angry and bitter now, they've destroyed public confidence in their ways, and it serves them jolly well right if the workmen make things impossible for them. I think they will. I hope they will.''

''But this means breaking up the national industries,'' said Oswald. ''Where is this sort of thing going to end?''

''Oh! things want shaking up,'' said Peter.

''Perhaps,'' he added, ''one *must* break up old things before one can hope for new. I suppose the masters won't let go while they think there's a chance of holding on. . . .''

He had not a trace left of the Victorian delusion that this might after all be the best of all possible worlds. He thought that our politicians and our captains of industry were very poor muddlers indeed. They drifted. Each one sat in his own works, he said, and ran them for profit without caring a rap whither the whole system was going. Compared with Labour even their poverty of general ideas was amazing. Peter, warming with his subject, walked to and fro across the Pelham Ford lawn beside Oswald, proposing to rearrange industrialism as one might propose to reshuffle a pack of cards.

"But suppose things smash up," said Oswald.

"Smash up," did not seem to alarm Peter.

"Nowadays," said Peter, "so many people read and write, so much has been thought out, there is so big a literature of ideas in existence, that I think we could recover from a very considerable amount of smashing. I'm pro-smash. We have to smash. What holds us back are fixed ideas. Take Profit. We're used to Profit. Most business is done for profit still. But why should the world tolerate profit at all? It doesn't stimulate enterprise; it only stimulates knavery. And Capital, Financial Capital is just blackmail by gold—gold rent. We think the state itself even can't start a business going or employ people without first borrowing money. Why should it borrow money? Why not, for state purposes, create it? Yes. No money would be any good if it hadn't the state guarantee. Gold standard, fixed money fund, legitimate profits and so on; that's the sort of fixed idea that gets in the way nowadays. It won't get out of the way just for reason's sake. The employers keep on with these old fixed ideas, naturally, because so it is they have been made, but the work-people believe in them less and less. There must be a smash of some sort—just to shake ideas loose. . . ."

Oswald surveyed his ward. So this was the young man's theory. Not a bad theory. Fixed Ideas!

"There's something to be said for this notion of Fixed Ideas," he said. "Yes. But isn't this 'I'm a Rebel' business, isn't that itself a Fixed Idea?"

"Oh certainly!" said Peter cheerfully. "We poor human beings are always letting our ideas coagulate. That's where the whole business seems to me so hopeless. . . ."

§ 8

In the 'eighties and 'nineties every question had been positive and objective. "People," you said, "think so and so. *Is it right?*" That seemed to cover the grounds for discussion in those days. One believed in a superior universal reason to which all decisions must ultimately bow. The new generation was beginning where its predecessors left off, with what had been open questions decided and carried beyond discussion. It was at home now on what had once been battlefields of opinion. The new generation was reading William James and Bergson and Freud and becoming more and more psychological. "People," it said, "think so and so. Why do they do so?"

So when at last Oswald carried off Peter to Dublin—which he did not do at Easter as he had planned but at Whitsuntide for a mere long week-end—to see at close hand this perplexing Irish Question that seemed drifting steadily and uncontrollably towards bloodshed, he found that while he was asking "who is in the right and who is in the wrong here? Who is most to blame and who should have the upper hand?" Peter was asking with a terrible impartiality, "Why are *all* these people talking nonsense?" and "Why have they got their minds and affairs into this dangerous mess?" Sir Horace Plunkett, Peter had a certain toleration for; but it was evident he suspected A.E. Peter did not talk very much, but he listened with a bright scepticism to brilliant displays of good talk—he had never heard such good anecdotal talk before—and betrayed rather than expressed his conviction that Nationalism, Larkinism, Sinn Feinism, Ulsterism and Unionism were all insults to the human intelligence, material for the alienist rather than serious propositions.

It wasn't that he felt himself to be in possession of any conclusive solution, or that he obtruded his disbelief with any sense of superiority. In spite of his extreme youth he did not for a moment assume the attitude of a superior person. Life was evidently troubling him profoundly, and he was realizing that there was no apparent answer to many of his perplexities. But he was at least trying hard to get an answer. What shocked him in the world of Dublin was its manifest disinclination to get any answer to anything. They jeered at people who sought solutions. They liked the fun of disorder; it gave more scope for their irrepressible passion for character study. He began to recognize one particular phrase as the keynote of Dublin's animation: "Hev ye hurrd the letest?"

On the Sunday afternoon of their stay in Dublin, Powys
motored them through the city by way of Donnybrook and
so on round the bay to Howth to see the view from Howth
Head. Powys drove with a stray guest beside him. Behind,
Peter imparted impressions to Oswald.

"I don't like these high walls," he said. "I've never seen
such a lot of high walls. . . . It's just as if they all shut
themselves in from one another."

"Fixed Ideas, Peter?"

"They *are* rather like Fixed Ideas. I suppose high walls
are fun to climb over and throw things over. But—it's un-
civilized."

"Everybody," grumbled Peter, "is given to fixed ideas,
but the Irish have 'em for choice. All this rot about Ireland
a Nation and about the Harp, which isn't properly their symbol, and the dear old Green Flag which isn't properly their
colour! . . . They can't believe in that stuff nowadays. . . .
But *can* they? In our big world? And about being a Black
Protestant and pretending Catholics are poison, or the other
way round. What are Protestants and Catholics now? . . .
Old dead squabbles. . . . Dead as Druids. . . . Keeping up
all that bickering stuff, when a child of eight ought to
know nowadays that the Christian God started out to be a
universal, charitable God. . . . If Christ came to Dublin the
Catholics and Protestants would have a free fight to settle
which was to crucify Him. . . ."

"It's the way with them," said Oswald. "We've got to
respect Irish opinion."

"It doesn't respect itself. Everywhere else in the world,
wherever we have been, there's been at least something like
the germ of an idea of a new life. But here! When you
get over here you realize for the first time that England is
after all a living country trying to get on to something—
compared with this merry-go-round. . . . It's exactly like a
merry-go-round churning away. It's the atmosphere of a
country fair. An Irishman hasn't any idea of a future at
all, so far as I can see—except that perhaps his grandchildren
will tell stories of what a fine fellow he was. . . ."

The automobile halted for a moment at cross roads, and the
finger-post was in Erse characters.

"Look at *that!*" said Peter with genuine exasperation. "And hardly a Dubliner knows fifty words of the language! It's foolery. If we were Irish I suppose we should smother London with black-letter. We should go on pretending that we, too, were still Catholics and Protestants. The pseudo-Protestants would hang Smithfield with black on account of the martyrs, and the pseudo-Catholics would come and throw the meat about on Fridays. Chesterton and Belloc would love it anyhow." . . .

Oswald was not sure of the extent of Peter's audience. "The susceptibilities of a proud people, Peter," he whispered, with his eye on the back of their host.

"Bother their susceptibilities. Much they care for *our* susceptibilities. The worst insult you can offer a grown-up man is to humour him," said Peter. "What's the good of pretending to be sympathetic with all this Wearing of the Green. It's like our White Rose League. Let 'em do it by all means if they want to, but don't let's pretend we think it romantic and beautiful and all the rest of it. It's just posing and dressing up, and it's a nuisance, Nobby. All Dublin is posing and dressing up and playing at rebellion, and so is all Ulster. The Volunteers of the eighteenth century all over again. It's like historical charades. And they've pointed loaded guns at each other. Only idiots point loaded guns. Why can't we English get out of it all, and leave them to pose and dress up and then tell anecdotes and anecdotes and anecdotes about it until they are sick of it? If ever they are sick of it. Let them have their Civil War if they want it; let them keep on with Civil Wars for ever; what has it got to do with us?"

"You're a Home Ruler then," said Oswald.

"I don't see that we English do any good here at all. What are we here for anyhow? The Castle's just another Fixed Idea, something we haven't the mental vigour to clear away. Nobody does any good here. We're not giving them new ideas, we're not unifying them, we're not letting Ireland out into the world—which is what she wants—we're not doing anything but just holding on."

"What's that?" said Powys suddenly over his shoulder.

"Peter's declaring for Home Rule," said Oswald.

"After his glimpse of the slums of Dublin?"

"It's out of malice. He wants to leave Irishmen to Irishmen."

"Ulster says *No!*" said Powys. "Tell him to talk to Ulster," and resumed a conversation he had interrupted with the man beside him.

At the corner where Nassau Street runs into Grafton Street they were held up for some lengthy minutes by a long procession that was trailing past Trinity College and down Grafton Street. It had several bands, and in the forefront of it went National Volunteers in green uniforms, obviously for the most part old soldiers; they were followed by men with green badges, and then a straggle of Larkinites and various Friendly Societies with their bands and banners, and then by a long dribble of children and then some workgirls, and then a miscellany of people who had apparently fallen in as the procession passed because they had nothing else to do. As a procession it was tedious rather than impressive. The warm afternoon—it was the last day in May—had taken the good feeling out of the walkers. Few talked, still fewer smiled. The common expression was a long-visaged discontent, a gloomy hostile stare at the cars and police cordon, an aimless disagreeableness. They were all being very stern and resolute about they did not quite know what. They meant to show that Dublin could be as stern and resolute as Belfast. Between the parts of the procession were lengthy gaps. It was a sunshiny, dusty afternoon, and the legs of the processionists were dusty to the knees, their brows moist, and their lips dry. There was an unhurried air about them of going nowhere in particular. It was evident that many of their banners were heavy. "What's it all about?" asked Oswald.

"Lord knows," said Powys impatiently. "It's just a demonstration."

"Is that all? Why don't we cut across now and get on?"

"There's more coming. Don't you hear another band?"

"But the police could hold it up for a minute and let all these tramcars and automobiles across."

"There'd be a fight," said Powys. "They daren't." . . .

"And I suppose this sort of thing is going on in the north too?" asked Oswald after a pause.

"Oh! everywhere," said Powys. "Orange or Green. But they've got more guns up north."

"These people don't really want Ireland a Nation and all the rest of it," said Peter.

"*Oh?*" said Powys, staring at him.

"Well, look at them," said Peter. "You can see by their faces. They're just bored to death. I suppose most people *are* bored to death in Ireland. There's nothing doing. England just holds them up, I suppose. And it's an island— rather off the main line. There's nothing to get people's minds off these endless, dreary old quarrels. It's all they have. But they're bored by it. . . ."

"And that's why we talk nothing but anecdotes, Peter, eh?" Powys grinned.

"Well, you *do* talk a lot of anecdote," said Peter, who hadn't realized the sharpness of his host's hearing.

"Oh! we do. I don't complain of your seeing it. It isn't your discovery. Have you read or heard the truest words that were ever said of Ireland—by that man Shaw? In *John Bull's Other Island*. . . . That laughing scene about the pig. 'Nowhere else could such a scene cause a burst of happiness among the people.' That's the very guts of things here; eh?"

"It's his best play," said Oswald, avoiding too complete an assent.

"It gets there," Powys admitted, "anyhow. The way all them fools come into the shanty and snigger." . . .

The last dregs of the procession passed reluctantly out of the way. It faded down Grafton Street into a dust cloud and a confusion of band noises. The policemen prepared to release the congested traffic. Peter leaned out to count the number of trams and automobiles that had been held up. He was still counting when the automobile turned the corner.

They shook Dublin off and spun cheerfully through the sunshine along the coast road to Howth. It was a sparkling bright afternoon, and the road was cheerful with the prim

happiness of many couples of Irish lovers.   But that afternoon peace was the mask worn by one particular day.   If the
near future could have cast a phantom they would have seen
along this road a few weeks ahead of them the gun-runners
of Howth marching to the first foolish bloodshed in Dublin
streets. . . .

They saw Howth Castle, made up now by Lutyens to look
as it ought to have looked and never had looked in the past.
The friend Powys had brought wanted to talk to some of
the castle people, and while these two stayed behind Oswald
and Peter went on, between high hedges of clipped beech and
up a steep, winding path amidst great bushes of rhododendron in full flower to the grey rock and heather of the crest.
They stood in the midst of one of the most beautiful views
in the world.   Northward they looked over Ireland's Eye at
Lambay and the blue Mourne mountains far away; eastward
was the lush green of Meath, southward was the long beach of
the bay sweeping round by Dublin to Dalkey, backed by
more blue mountains that ran out eastward to the Sugar
Loaf.   Below their feet the pale castle clustered amidst its
rich greenery, and to the east, the level blue sea sustained
one single sunlit sail.   It was rare that the sense of beauty
flooded Peter, as so often it flooded Joan, but this time he was
transported.

"But this is altogether beautiful," he said, like one who
is taken by surprise.

And then as if to himself: "How beautiful life might be!
How splendid life might be!"

Oswald was standing on a ledge below Peter, and with his
back to him.   He waited through a little interval to see if
Peter would say any more.   Then he pricked him with "only
it isn't."

"No," said Peter, with the sunlight gone out of his voice.
"It isn't."

He went on talking after a moment's reflection.

"It's as if we were hypnotized and couldn't get away
from mean things, beastly suspicions, and stale quarrels.   I
suppose we are still half apes.   I suppose our brains *set* too
easily and rapidly.   I suppose it's easy to quarrel yet and

still hard to understand.   We take to jealousy and bitterness
as ducklings take to water.   Think of that stale, dusty procession away there!''

Oswald's old dream vision of the dark forest came back
to his mind.   "Is there no way out, Peter?" he said.

"If some great idea would take hold of the world!" said
Peter. . . .

"There have been some great ideas," said Oswald. . . .

"If it would take hold of one's life," Peter finished his
thought. . . .

"There has been Christianity," said Oswald.

"Christianity!" Peter pointed at the distant mist that was
Dublin.   "Sour Protestants," he said, "and dirty priests
setting simple people by the ears."

"But that isn't true Christianity."

"There isn't true Christianity," said Peter compactly. . . .

"Well, there's love of country then," said Oswald.

"That Dublin corporation is the most patriotic and nation-
alist in the world.   Fierce about it.   And it's got complete
control there.   It's green in grain.   No English need apply.
. . . From the point of view of administration that town is
a muck heap—for patriotic crowings.   Look at their dirty,
ill-paved streets.   Look at their filthy slums!   See how they
let their blessed nation's children fester and die!"

"There are bigger ideas than patriotism.   There are ideas
of empire, the Pax Britannica."

"Carson smuggling guns."

"Well, is there nothing?   Do *you* know of nothing?"

Oswald turned on his ward for the reply.

"There's a sort of idea, I suppose."

"But what idea?"

"There's an idea in our minds."

"But what is it, Peter?"

"Call it Civilization," Peter tried.

"I believe," he went on, weighing his words carefully, "as
you believe really, in the Republic of Mankind, in universal
work for a common end—for freedom, welfare, and beauty.
Haven't you taught me that?"

"*Have* I taught you that?"

"It seems to me to be the commonsense aim for all human-

ity. You're awake to it. You've awakened me to it and I
believe in it. But most of this world is still deep in its old
Fixed Ideas, walking in its sleep. And it won't wake up.
It won't wake up. . . . What can we *do?* We've got to a
sort of idea, it's true. But here are these Irish, for example,
naturally wittier and quicker than you or I, hypnotized by
Orange and Green, by Protestant and Catholic, by all these
stale things—drifting towards murder. It's murder is coming here. You can smell the bloodshed coming on the air—
and we can't do a thing to prevent it. Not a thing. The
silliest bloodshed it will be. The silliest bloodshed the world
has ever seen. We can't do a thing to wake them up. . . .

"We're *in* it," said Peter in conclusion. "We can't even
save ourselves."

"I've been wanting to get at your political ideas for a
long time," said Oswald. "You really think, Peter, there
might be a big world civilization, a world republic, did you
call it?—without a single slum hidden in it anywhere, with
the whole of mankind busy and happy, the races living in
peace, each according to its aptitudes, a world going on—
going on steady and swift to still better things."

"How can one believe anything else? Don't you?"

"But how do we get there, Peter?"

"Oh, how do we get there?" echoed Peter. "How do we
get there?"

He danced a couple of steps with vexation.

"I don't *know,* Nobby," he cried. "I don't know. I
can't find the way. I'm making a mess of my life. I'm not
getting on with my work. You *know* I'm not. . . . Either
we're mad or this world is. Here's all these people in Ireland letting a solemn humbug of a second-rate lawyer with
a heavy chin and a lumpish mind muddle them into a civil
war—and *that's* reality! That's life! The solemn League
and Covenant—copied out of old history books! That's
being serious! And over there in England, across the sea,
muddle and muck and nonsense indescribable. Oh! and
we're *in* it!"

"But aren't there big movements afoot, Peter, social reform, the labour movement, the emancipation of women, big
changes like that?"

"Only big discontents."

"But doesn't discontent make the change?"

"It's just boredom that's got them. It isn't any disposition to *make*. Labour is bored, women are bored, all Ireland is bored. I suppose Russia is bored and Germany is getting bored. She is boring all the world with her soldiering. How bored they must be in India too—by us! The day bores its way round the earth now—like a mole. Out of sight of the stars. But boring people doesn't mean making a new world. It just means boring on to decay. It just means one sort of foolish old fixed idea rubbing and sawing against another, until something breaks down. . . . Oh! I want to get out of all this. I don't *like* this world of ours. I want to get into a world awake. I'm young and I'm greedy. I've only got one life to live, Nobby. . . . I want to spend it where something is being made. Made for good and all. Where clever men can do something more than sit overlong at meals and tell spiteful funny stories. Where there's something better to do than play about with one's brain and viscera! . . ."

§ 9

In the days when Peter was born the Anglican system held the Empire with apparently invincible feelings of security and self-approval; it possessed the land, the church, the army, the foreign office, the court. Such people as Arthur and Dolly were of no more account than a stray foreign gipsy by the wayside. When Peter came of age the Anglican system still held on to army, foreign office, court, land, and church, but now it was haunted by a sense of an impalpable yet gigantic antagonism that might at any time materialize against it. It had an instinctive perception of the near possibility of a new world in which its base prides could have no adequate satisfaction, in which its authority would be flouted, its poor learning despised, and its precedents disregarded. The curious student of the history of England in the decade before the Great War will find the clue to what must otherwise seem a hopeless tangle in the steady, disingenuous, mischievous antagonism of the old Anglican system to every kind of change that might bring nearer the dreaded processes of modernization. Education, and particularly university, reform was blocked, the most necessary social legislation fought against with incoherent passion, the lightest, most reasonable taxation of land or inheritance resisted.

Wherever the old system could find allies it snatched at them and sought to incorporate them with itself. It had long since taken over the New Imperialism with its tariff schemes and its spirit of financial adventure. It had sneered aloof when the new democracy of the elementary schools sought to read and think; it had let any casual adventurer to supply that reading; but now the creator of *Answers* and *Comic Cuts* ruled the *Times* and sat in the House of Lords. It was a little doubtful still whether he was of the new order or the old, whether he was not himself an instalment of revolution, whether the Tories had bought him or whether he had bought them, but at any rate he did for a time seem to be serving the ends of reaction.

To two sources of strength the Anglicans clung with desperate resolution, India and Ulster. From India the mass of English people were shut and barred off as completely as any foreigners could have been. India was the preserve of the "ruling class." To India the good Anglican, smitten by doubts, chilled by some disrespectful comment or distressed by some item of progress achieved, could turn, leaving all thoughts of new and unpleasant things behind him; there in what he loved to believe was the "unchanging East" he could recover that sense of walking freely and authoritatively upon an abundance of inferior people which was so necessary to his nature, and which was being so seriously impaired at home. The institution of caste realized his secret ideals. From India he and his womankind could return refreshed, to the struggle with Liberalism and all the powers of democratic irreverence in England. And Ulster was a still more precious stronghold for this narrow culture. From the fastness of Ulster they could provoke the restless temperament of the Irish to a thousand petty exasperations of the English, and for Ulster, "loyal Ulster," they could appeal to the generous partisanship of the English against their native liberalism. More and more did it become evident that Ulster was the key-

stone of the whole Anglican ascendancy; to that they owed
their grip upon British politics, upon army, navy, and education; they traded—nay! they existed—upon the open Irish
sore. With Ireland healed and contented England would
be lost to them. England would democratize, would Ameri-
canize. The Anglicans would vanish out of British life as
completely as the kindred Tories vanished out of America
at the close of the eighteenth century. And when at last,
after years of confused bickering, a Home Rule Bill became
law, and peace between the two nations in Ireland seemed
possible, the Anglicans stepped at once from legal obstruction to open treason and revolt. The arming of Ulster to
resist the decision of Parliament was incited from Great
Britain, it was supported enthusiastically by the whole of the
Unionist party in Great Britain, its headquarters were in the
west end of London, and the refusal of General Gough to
carry out the precautionary occupation of Ulster was hailed
with wild joy in every Tory home. It was not a genuine
popular movement, it was an artificial movement for which
the landowning church people of Ireland and England were
chiefly responsible. It was assisted by tremendous exertions
on the part of the London yellow press. When Sir Edward
Carson went about Ulster in that warm June of 1914, review-
ing armed men, promising "more Mausers," and pouring out
inflammatory speeches, he was manifestly preparing bloodshed. The old Tory system had reached a point where it
had to kill men or go.

And it did not mean to go; it meant to kill. It meant to
murder men.

If youth and the new ideas were to go on with the world,
the price was blood.

Ulster was a little country; altogether the dispute did not
affect many thousands of men, but except for the difference
in scale there was indeed hardly any difference at all between
this scramble towards civil conflict in Ireland and the rush,
swift and noiseless, that was now carrying central Europe
towards immeasurable bloodshed. To kill and mutilate and
waste five human beings in a petty riot is in its essence no
less vile a crime than to kill and mutilate and waste twenty

millions.   While the British Tories counted their thousands, the Kaiser and his general staff reckoned in millions; while the British "loyalists" were smuggling a few disused machine-guns from Germany, Krupp's factories were turning out great guns by the hundred.   But the evil thing was the same evil thing; a system narrow and outworn, full of a vague fear of human reason and the common sense of mankind, full of pride and greed and the insolent desire to trample upon men, a great system of false assumptions and fixed ideas, oppressed by a thirsty necessity for reassurance, was seeking the refreshment of loud self-assertion and preparing to drink blood.   The militarist system that centred upon Potsdam had clambered to a point where it had to kill men or go.   The Balkans were the Ulster of Europe.   If once this Balkan trouble settled down, an age of peace might dawn for Europe, and how would Junkerdom fare then, and where would Frau Bertha sell her goods?   How would the War Lord justify his glories to the social democrat? . . .

But Oswald, like most Englishmen, was not attending very closely to affairs upon the Continent.   He was preoccupied with the unreason of Ulster.

Recently he had had a curious interview with Lady Charlotte Sydenham, and her white excited face and blazing blue eyes insisted now upon playing the part of mask to the Ulster spirit in his thoughts.   She had had to call him in because she had run short of ready money through over-subscription to various schemes for arming the northern patriots.   She had sat at her writing-desk with her cap a little over one eye, as though it was a military cap, and the tuft of reddish hair upon her cheek more like bristles than ever, and he had walked about the room contriving disagreeable things to say to her after his wont.   He was disinclined to let her have more money, he confessed; she ought to have had more sense, he said, than to write off big cheques, cheques beyond her means, in support of this seditious mischief.   If she asked these people who had taken her money, probably they would let her have some back to go on with.

This enraged her nicely, as he had meant it to do.   She scolded at him.   A nice Sydenham he was, to see his King

insulted and his country torn apart.   He who had once worn
the Queen's uniform.   Thank God! she herself was a Parminter and belonged to a sounder strain!

"It's you who are insulting the King," Oswald interpolated, "trying to defy his Acts in Parliament."

"*Oh!*" cried Lady Charlotte, banging the desk with her
freckled fist.   "Oh! Parliament!   I'd shoot 'em down!
First that vile Budget, then the attack on the Lords."

"They passed the Parliament Act," said Oswald.

"To save themselves from being swamped in a horde of
working-men peers—sitting there in their caps with their
dirty boots on the cushions.   Lord Keir Hardie!   You'll
want Lord Chimneysweep and Viscount Cats-meatman next.
. . . Then came that abominable Insurance Act—one thing
worse than another!   Setting class against class and giving
them ideas!   Then we gave up South Africa to the Boers
again!   What did we fight for?   Didn't we buy the country
with our blood?   Why, my poor cousin Rupert Parminter
was a prisoner in Pretoria for a whole year—thirteen weary
months!   For nothing!   And now Ireland is to be handed
over to priests and rebels.   To *Irishmen!*   And I—I am not
to lift a finger, not a finger, to save my King and my Country
and my God—when they are all going straight to the Devil!"

"H'm," said Oswald, rustling the counterfoils in his hand.
"But you *have* been lifting your finger, you know!"

"If I could give more——"

"You *have* given more."

"I'd give it."

"Won't Grimes make a friendly advance?   But I suppose
you're up to the neck with Grimes. . . . I wonder what interest that little swindler charges you."

The old lady could not meet the mild scrutiny of his eye.
"You come here and grin and mock while your country is
being handed over to a gang of God-knows-whos!" she said,
staring at her inkpot.

"To whom probably it belongs as much as it does to me,"
said Oswald.

"Thank God the army is sound," said Aunt Charlotte.
"Thank God this doesn't end with your Parliaments!   Mark
my words, Oswald!   On the day they raise their Home Rule

flag in Ireland there will be men shot down—men shot down.
A grim lesson.''

"Some perhaps killed by your own particular cheques,''
said Oswald. "Who knows?''

"I hope so,'' said Lady Charlotte, with a quiver of deep
passion in her voice. "I hope so sincerely. If I could think
I had caused the death of one of those traitors. . . . If it
could be Lloyd George!'' . . .

But that was too much apparently even for Lady Charlotte to hope for.

Oswald, when he had come to her, had fully intended to let
her have money to go on with, but now he was changing his
mind. He had thought of her hitherto just as a grotesque
figure in his life, part of the joke of existence, but now with
this worry of the Irish business in his mind he found himself
regarding her as something more than an individual. She
seemed now to be the accentuated voice of a whole class, the
embodiment of a class tradition. He strolled back from the
window and stood with his hands deep in his trouser pockets
—which always annoyed her—and his head on one side, focus-
ing the lady.

"My dear Aunt,'' he said, "what right have you to any
voice in politics at all? You know, you're pretty—ungracious. The world lets you have this money—and you spend
it in organizing murder.''

"*The world lets me have this money!*'' cried Lady Charlotte, amazed and indignant. "Why!'' she roared, "it's MY
money!''

In that instant the tenets of socialism, after a siege lasting
a quarter of a century, took complete possession of Oswald's
mind. In that same instant she perceived it. "Any one can
see you're a Liberal and a Socialist yourself,'' she cried.
"You'd shake hands with Lloyd George tomorrow. Yes, you
would. Why poor foolish Vincent made *you* trustee——!
He might have known! *You* a sailor! A faddy invalid!
Mad on blacks. I suppose you'd give your precious Baganda
Home Rule next! And him always so sound on the treatment of the natives! Why! he kicked a real judge—a native
judge—Inner Temple and all the rest of it—out of his railway compartment. Kicked him. Bustled him out neck and

crop. Awayed with him! Oh, if he could see you now! Insulting me! Standing up for all these people, blacks, Irishmen, strikers, anything. Sneering at the dear old Union Jack they want to tear to pieces.''

"Well," said Oswald as she paused to take breath. "You've got yourself into this mess and you must get along now till next quarter day as well as you can. I can't help you and you don't deserve to be helped.''

"You'll not let me spend my own money?''

"You've fired off all the money you're entitled to. You'll probably kill a constable—or some decent little soldier boy from Devon or Kent. . . . Good God! Have you *no* imagination? . . .''

It was the most rankling encounter he had ever had with her. Either he was losing tolerance for her or she was indeed becoming more noisy and ferocious. She haunted his thoughts for a long time, and his thoughts of her, so intricate is our human composition, were all mixed up with sympathy and remorse for the petty cash troubles in which he had left her. . . .

But what a pampered, evil soul she had always been! Never in all her life had she made or grown or got one single good thing for mankind. She had lived in great expensive houses, used up the labour of innumerable people, bullied servants, insulted poor people, made mischief. She was like some gross pet idol that mankind out of whim kept for the sake of its sheer useless ugliness. He found himself estimating the weight of food and the tanks of drink she must have consumed, the carcases of oxen and sheep, the cartloads of potatoes, the pyramids of wine bottles and stout bottles she had emptied. And she had no inkling of gratitude to the careless acquiescent fellow-creatures who had suffered her so long and so abundantly. At the merest breath upon her clumsy intolerable dignity she clamoured for violence and cruelty and killing, and would not be appeased. An old idol! And she was only one of a whole class of truculent, illiterate harridans who were stirring up bad blood in half the great houses of London, and hurrying Britain on to an Irish civil war. No! She wasn't as funny as she seemed.

Not nearly so funny.   She was too like too many people for
that.   Too like most people?

Did that go too far?

After all there was a will for good in men; even this weary
Irish business had not been merely a conflict of fixed ideas,
there had been, too, real efforts on the part of countless people
to get the tangle straightened out.   There were creative
forces at work in men—even in Ireland.   And also there
was youth.

His thoughts came back to the figure of Peter, standing
on the head of Howth and calling for a new world.

"I'll pit my Peter," he said, "against all the Aunt Charlottes in creation. . . . In the long run, that is."

He was blind—was not all Europe blind?—to the vast
disaster that hung over him and his and the whole world, to
the accumulated instability of the outworn social and political
façade that now tottered to a crash.   Massacre, famine, social
confusion, world-wide destruction, long years of death and
torment were close at hand; the thinnest curtain of time, a
mere month of blue days now, hung between him and the
thunderous overture of the world disaster.

"I pit my Peter," he repeated, "against all the Aunt
Charlottes in creation."

§ 10

All novels that run through the years of the great war must
needs be political novels and fragments of history.   In
August, 1914, that detachment of human lives from history,
that pretty picaresque disorder of experiences, that existence
like a fair with ten thousand different booths, which had
gone on for thousands of years, came to an end.   We were
all brought into a common drama.   Something had happened
so loud and insistent that all lives were focused upon it; it
became a leading factor in every life, the plot of every story,
the form of all our thoughts.   It so thrust itself upon mankind that the very children in the schools about the world
asked "why has this thing happened?" and could not live

on without some answer. The Great War summoned all
human beings to become political animals, time would brook
no further evasion. August, 1914, was the end of adventure
and mental fragmentation for the species; it was the polar-
ization of mankind.

Other books have told, innumerable books that have yet
to come will tell, of the rushing together of events that culminated in the breach of the Belgian frontier by the German
hosts. Our story has to tell only of how that crisis took to
itself and finished and crowned the education of these three
people with whom we are concerned. Of the three, Oswald
and Joan spent nearly the whole of July at Pelham Ford.
Peter came down from Cambridge for a day or so and then,
after two or three days in London for which he did not
clearly account, he went off to the Bernese Oberland to climb
with a party of three other Trinity men. There was a vague
but attractive project at the back of his mind, which he did
not confide to Oswald or Joan, of going on afterwards into
north Italy to a little party of four or five choice spirits
which Hetty was to organize. They could meet on the other
side of the Simplon. Perhaps they would push on into
Venezia. They would go for long tramps amidst sweet
chestnut trees and ripening grapes, they would stay in the
vast, roomy, forgotten inns of sleepy towns whose very stables
are triumphs of architecture, they would bathe amidst the
sunlit rocks of quiet lakes. Wherever they went in that land
the snow and blue of the distant Alps would sustain the sweet
landscape as music sustains a song.

Hetty had made it all fantastically desirable. She had
invented it and woven details about it one afternoon in her
studio. She knew north Italy very well; it was not the first
amusing journey in that soft, delicious land that she had
contrived. Peter was tremendously excited to think of the
bright possibilities of such an adventure, and yet withal
there was a queer countervailing feeling gnawing amidst his
lusty anticipations. Great fun it would be, tremendous fun,
with a little spice of sin in it, and why not? Only somehow
he had a queer unreasonable feeling that Joan ought to share
his holidays. Old Joan who looked at him with eyes that
held a shadow of sorrow; who made him feel that she knew

more than she could possibly know. He wished Joan, too, had some spree in contemplation—not of course quite the same sort of spree. A decent girl's sort of spree. Just the tramp part. He wished he could tell Joan of what was in hand, that there wasn't this queer embarrassment between them. Joan had her car of course. . . .

Oswald had recently bought Joan a pretty little ten-horse-power Singer car, a two-seater, in which she was to run about the country at her own free will. It was one of several attempts he had recently made to brighten life for Joan. He was beginning to watch her very closely; he did not clearly understand the thoughts and imaginations that made her so grave and feverish at times, but he knew that she was troubled. The girl's family resemblance to his Dolly had caught his mind. He thought she was more like Dolly than she was because her image constantly before him was steadily replacing Dolly's in his mind. And he liked very much to sit beside her and watch her drive. At five-and-forty miles an hour her serene profile was divine. She had a good mechanical intelligence and her nerve was perfect; the little car lived in her hands and had the precision of movement of an animal.

They ran across country to Warwick and Stratford-on-Avon, and slept the night in Warwick; they went to New market and round to Chelmsford and Dovercourt, which was also an over-night excursion. These were their longer expeditions. They made afternoon runs to St. Albans, Hitchin, Baldock, Bedford, Stevenage and Royston. Almost every fine day they made some trip. While she drove or while they walked about some unfamiliar town the cloud seemed to lift from Joan's mind, she became as fresh and bright as a child. And she talked more and more freely to Oswald. She talked more abundantly than Peter and much less about ideas. She talked rather of scenery and customs and atmospheres. She seemed to have a far more concrete imagination than Peter, to accept the thing that was with none of his reluctance. She would get books about Spain, about the South Sea Islands, about China, big books of travel and description, from the London Library, and so assimilate them that she seemed to be living imaginatively for days together in these alien atmospheres. She wanted to know about Uganda. She was curious about the native King. There were times when Oswald was reminded of some hungry and impatient guest in a restaurant reading over an over-crowded and perplexing menu.

She did not read many plays or novels nor any poetry. She mentioned casually one day to Oswald that such reading either bored her or disturbed her. She read a certain amount of philosophy, but manifestly now as a task. And she was incessantly restless. She had no mother nor sisters, no feminine social world about her; she suffered from a com-plete lack of all those distracting and pacifying routines and all those restraints of habit and association that control the lives of more normally placed girls. Her thoughts, stimu-lated by her uncontrolled reading, ran wild. One morning she was up an hour before dawn, and let herself out of the house and walked over the hills nearly to Newport before breakfast, coming back with skirts and shoes wet with dew and speckled with grass seeds and little burrs. She spent that afternoon asleep in the hammock. And she would play fitfully at the piano or the pianola after dinner and then wander out, a restless white sprite, into the garden. One night early in the month she persuaded Oswald to go for a long moonlight walk with her along the road to Ware.

There was a touch of dream quality in that walk for both of them. They had never been together in moonlight before. She ceased to be Joan and became at once something very strange and wonderful and very intimate, a magic phantom of womanhood, a creature no longer of flesh and blood but of pallor and shadow, whose hair was part of the universal dusk and her eyes two stars. And he, too, walking along and some-times talking as if he talked to the lonely sky, and sometimes looking down out of the dimness closely at her, he had lost his age and his scars and become the utmost dignity of a man. They walked sometimes on a road of misty brightness and sometimes through deep pools of shadow and sometimes amidst the black bars and lace cast by tree stems and tree branches, and she made him talk of the vast spaces of Africa and the long trails through reed and forest, and of great animals standing still and invisible close at hand, hidden by the trickery of their colourings, and how he had gone all alone into the villages of savage people who had never before set eyes on a European. And she talked with a whisper and sigh in her voice of how she, too, would like to go into wild and remote lands—"if I could go off with a man like you." And it seemed to him for a time that this sweet voice beside him was not truly Joan's but another's, and that he walked once more with the dearest wish he had ever wished in his life.

He talked to her of moonlight and starlight in the tropics, of a wonderful pale incandescence that shines out above the grave of the sunset when the day has gone, of fireflies and of phosphorescent seas, and of the distant sounds of drumming and chanting and the remote blaze of native bonfires seen through black tree stems in the night. He talked, too, of the howling of beasts at night, and of the sudden roaring of lions, and at that she drew closer to him.

When at last it was time for her to turn she did not want to turn. "I have been happy," she said. "I have been happy. Let us go on. Why should we go back?"

As if she was not always happy. She pulled at his arm like a child. . . .

And as they came home she came close to him, and for long spaces they said not a word to one another.

But at the water splash in the village she had a queer impulse. The water splash appeared ahead of them, an incessant tumult of silver in which were set jewels of utter blackness and shining diamonds. She looked and tugged him by the arm.

"Let us walk through the water, dear Nobby!" she said. "I want to feel it about my feet. Do! Do! Do! It will hardly cover our shoes. . . ."

A queer impulse that was of hers but, what was queerer, it found the completest response in him. "All right," he said, as though this was the most commonplace suggestion possible; and very gravely, and as if it was some sort of rite, he let her lead him through the water. They were indeed both very grave. . . .

They walked up to the house in silence. . . .

"Good night, Nobby dear," said Joan, leaning suddenly

over by the newel of the stairs, and kissed him, as the moonlight kisses, a kiss as soft and cool as ever awakened Endy-
mion. . . .

Life was at high tide in Joan that July, and everything in
her was straining at its anchors. All her being was flooded
with the emotional intimations that she was a woman, that
she had to be beautiful and hasten to meet exquisite and profoundly significant experiences; none of her instincts told
her that the affairs of the world drew to an issue that would
maim and kill half the youths she knew and torment and
alter her own and every life about her. She was haunted
and distressed day and night—for the trouble got into her
dreams—by Peter's evident love-making with Hetty and
Huntley's watchful eyes, and she saw nothing of the red eyes
of war and the blood-lust that craved for all her generation.
Peter was making love—making love to Hetty. Peter was
making love to Hetty. And Joan was left at home in a fever
of desertion. Her brotherhood with Peter which had been
perhaps the greatest fact of her girlhood was breaking down
under the exasperation of their separation and her jealousy,
and Huntley was steadily and persistently invading her
imagination. . . .

Women and men alike are love-hungry creatures; women
even more so than men. It is not beauty nor strength nor
goodness that hearts go to so much as attention. To know
that another human being thinks of us, esteems us above
all our secret estimates, has a steadfast and consuming need
of us, is the supreme reassurance of life. And when women's
hearts are distressed by vague passions and a friendless insecurity they will go out very readily even to a cripple who
watches and waits.

Huntley was one of those men for whom women are the
sole interest in life. If he had been obliged to master a
mathematical problem he would have thought he struggled
with a Muse and so achieved it. He watched them and waylaid them for small and great occasions. He understood completely these states of wild impatience that possess the feminine mind. He had no brotherliness nor fatherliness in his
composition: his sole conception of this trouble of the un-
mated was of an opportunity for himself. A little patience,

a little thought—and it was very delightful thought, a little pleasant skill, and all this vague urgency would become a gift for him.

But never before had Huntley met any one so fresh and youthfully beautiful as Joan. There were times when he could doubt whether he was the magnetizer or the magnetized. He had kissed her but he was not sure that she had kissed him. Some day she should kiss him of her own free will. He thought now almost continuously of Joan. The only work he could get on with was a novel into which he put things he had imagined about Joan. He wrote her long letters and planned for days to get an hour's conversation with her. And he would go for long walks and spend all the time composing letters or scheming dramatic conversations that never would happen in reality because Joan missed all her cues.

It was rather by instinct than by any set scheme that he did his utmost to convert her vague unrest into a discontent with all her circumstances, to shape her thoughts to the idea that her present life was a prison-house of which he held the key of escape. He suggested in a score of different ways to her mind that outside her present prison was a wonderland of beauty and excitement. He was clever enough to catch from her talk her love of the open, of fresh air and sunlight. He had more than a suspicion of Hetty Reinhart's plans; he conveyed them by shadowy hints. Why should not Joan too defy convention? She could tell Oswald a story of a projected walk with some other girl at Cambridge, and slip away to Huntley. They had always been the best of companions. Why shouldn't they take a holiday together?

And why not?

What was there to fear? Couldn't she trust Huntley? Couldn't she trust herself?

To which something deep in Joan's composition replied that this was but playing with passion and romance, and she wanted passion and romance. She wanted a reality—unendurably. And it was clear as day to her that she did not want passion and romance with Huntley. He was a strange being to her really, not differing as man does from woman but as dog does from cat; hidden deep down perhaps was some mysterious difference of race; he could amuse her and interest her because he was queer and unexpected, but he was not of her kind.   Like to like was the way of the Sydenham blood.   He offered and pointed to all that seemed to her necessary to make life right and to end this aching suspense —except that he was a stranger. . . .

The long sunny days of June dragged by.   Suppose after all she were to slip away to Huntley.   It would be a spree, it would be an excitement.   Did he matter so much after all? . . .

Peter sent a postcard and said he thought he would go on "with some people into Italy."

She had known—all along—that that was coming.

She went out the night after that postcard came into the garden alone.   It was a still and sultry evening, and she stifled even in the open air.   She wanted to go up into the arbour and to sit there and think.   She could not understand the quiver of anger that ran through her being like the shiver of the current on the surface of a stream.   All the trees and bushes about her were dark and shapeless lumps of blackness and as she went up the path she trod on two snails.

"Damn them!" she said at the second scrunch.   "Phew! What a night.   Full of things that crawl about in the darkness.   Full of *beastly* things. . . ."

A little owl mewed and mocked wickedly among the trees.

There was no view out of the black arbour, only the sense of a darkened world.   A thin ineffectual moon crescent was sinking westward, and here and there were spiritless stars.   A strange, huge shape of clouds, a hooded figure of the profoundest blue, brooded in a sky of luminous pale yellow over the land to the south and east, and along the under fringe of its skirts ever and again there ran a flicker of summer lightning.   "And I am to live here!   I am to live here while life runs by me," she said.

She would go to Huntley.   No brother and sister business though!   She would go to Huntley and end all this torment.

But she couldn't! . . .

"Why have I no will?" she cried harshly.

She did not love Huntley. That did not matter. She would *make* herself love Huntley. . . .

She went out upon the terrace and stood very still, looking down upon the house and thinking hard.

Could she love no one? If so, then it might as well be Huntley she went to as any one? All these boys, Troop, Winterbaum, Wilmington—they were nothing to her. But she wanted to live. Was it perhaps that she did love some one—who stood, invisible and unregarded, possessing her heart?

Her mind halted on that for a time and then seemed to force itself along a certain line that lay before it. Did she love Oswald? She did. More than any of them—far more. The other night most certainly she had been in love with him. When he walked through the water with her—absurdly grave——! She could have flung her arms about him then. She could have clung to him and kissed him. Of course she must be in love with him. . . . But he was not in love with her! . . . And yet that moonlit evening it seemed——?

Suppose it were Oswald and not Huntley who beckoned.

Love for Huntley—love him where you would—though you loved him in the most beautiful scenery in the world—would still be something vulgar, still be this dirty love of the studios, still a trite disobedience, a stolen satisfaction, after the fashion of the Reinhart affair. But Oswald was a great man, a kind and noble giant, who told no lies, who played no tricks. . . .

If he were to love one——! . . .

She stood upon the terrace looking down upon the lit house, trembling with this thought that she loved Oswald and holding fast to it—for fear of another thought that she dared not think, that lay dark and waiting outside her consciousness, a poor exile thought, utterly forbidden.

§ 11

Joan stood in the darkness on the turf outside Oswald's open window, and watched him.

He was so deep in thought that he had not noted the soft sounds of her approach. The only light in the room was his study lamp, and his face was in shadow while his hands rested on the open Atlas in front of him and were brightly lit. They were rather sturdy white hands with broad thumbs, exactly like Peter's. Presently he stirred and pulled the Atlas towards him, and turned the page over to another map. The fingers of his left hand drummed on the desk.

He looked up abruptly, and she came to the window and leant forward into the room, with her arms folded on the sill.

"You're as still as the night, Joan," he said.

"There's thunder brewing."

"There's war brewing, Joan."

"Why do you sit poring over that map?"

"Because there are various people called Croats and Slovenes and Serbs and they are beginning to think they are one people and ought to behave as one people, and some of them are independent and some are under the Austrians and some are under the Italians."

"What has that got to do with us?" said Joan.

She followed her question up with another. "Is it a fresh Balkan war?"

"Something bigger than that," said Oswald. "Something very much bigger—unless we are careful."

His tone was so grave that Joan caught something of his gravity. She stepped in through the window. "Where are all these people?" she said. She thought it was characteristic of him to trouble about these distant races and their entanglements. But she wished he could have a keener sense of the perplexities that came nearer him. She came and leant over him while he explained the political riddle of Austria and Eastern Europe to her. . . .

"We are too busy with the Irish trouble," he said. "I am afraid of Germany. If that fool Carson and these Pankhurst people had been paid to distract our minds from what is happening, they could not do the work better. Big things are happening—oh! big things."

She tried to feel their bigness. But to her all such political talk was still as unreal as things one reads about in histories, something to do with maps and dates, something you can "get up" and pass examinations in, but nothing that touches the warm realities of personal life and beauty. Yet it pleased her to think that this Oswald she loved could reach up to these things, so that he partook of the nature of the great beings who cared for them like Gladstone or Lincoln, and was not simply a limited real person like Troop or Wilmington or Peter. (He was really like a great Peter, like what Peter ought to be.) He seemed preoccupied as if he did not feel how close she was about him, how close her beauty came to him. She sat now on the arm of his chair behind him, with her face over his shoulder. Her body touched his shoulders, by imperceptible degrees she brought her cheek against his crisp hair, where it pressed no heavier than a shadow.

She had no suspicion how vividly he was aware of her nearness.

As he discoursed to her upon the text of the maps before them, a deep undercurrent of memories and feelings of quite a different quality ran contrariwise through his mind. "We are getting nearer than we have ever been to a big European war, a big break-up! People do not understand, do not begin to dream of the smash-up that that would be. There is scarcely a country that may not be drawn in."

So he spoke. And below that level of thought he was irritated to feel that such thought could not wholly possess him. Far more real to him were the vague suggestions of love and the summer night and the dusky nearness of this Joan, this phantom of Dolly, for more and more were Joan and Dolly blending together in his emotional life, this dearness and sweetness that defied all reasoning and explanation. And cutting across both these streams of thought and feeling came a third stream of thought. Joan's intonations in every word she spoke betrayed her indifference to the great net of political forces in which the world struggled. She was no more deeply interested than if he had been discussing some problem at chess or some mathematical point. She was not deeply interested and he was not completely interested, and yet this question that was slipping its hold on their attention might involve the lives and welfare of millions. . . .

He struggled with his conception of a world being hauled
to its destruction in a net of vaguely apprehended ideas, of
ordinary life being shattered not by the strength but by the
unattractive feebleness of its political imaginings. "People
do not understand," he repeated, trying to make this thing
real to himself. "All Europe is in danger."

He turned upon her with a betrayal of irritation in his
voice. "You think all this matters nothing to us," he said.
"But it does. If Austria makes war in Serbia, Russia will
come in. If Russia comes in, France comes in. That brings
in Germany. We can't see France beaten again. We can't
have that."

But Joan had still the child's belief that somewhere, somehow, behind all the ostensible things of the world, wise
adults in its interests have the affairs of mankind under control. "They won't let things go as far as that," she said.

Oswald reflected upon that. How sure this creature was
of her world!

"Until Death and Judgment come, Joan," he said, "there
is neither Death nor Judgment."

That saying and his manner of saying it struck hard on
her mind. Before she went to sleep that night she found
herself trying to imagine what war was really like. . . .

And next day she was thinking of war. Would Peter perhaps have to be a soldier if there was a real great war?
Would all her young men go soldiering? Would Oswald go?
And what was there for a girl to do in war-time? She
hated the idea of nursing, but she supposed she would have to
nurse. Far rather would she go under fire and rescue
wounded men. Had modern war no use for a Joan of Arc?
. . . She sank to puerile visions of a girl in a sort of Vivandi-
ère uniform upholding a tattered flag under a heavy fire.
. . . It couldn't last very long. . . . It would be exciting.
. . . But all this was nonsense; there would be no war.
There would be a conference or an arbitration or something
dull of that sort, and all this stir and unrest would subside
and leave things again—as they had been. . . .

Swiftly and steadfastly now the world was setting itself
to tear up all the scenery of Joan's world and to smash and
burn its every property. If it had not been for the sug-

gestion of Oswald's deepening preoccupation one may doubt whether Joan would have heeded the huge rush of events in Europe until the moment of the crash. But because of him she was drawn into the excitement. From the twenty-fifth of July, which was the day when the news of the Austrian ultimatum to Serbia appeared in the English newspapers, through the swift rush of events that followed, the failure of the Irish Conference at Buckingham Palace to arrive at any settlement upon the Irish question, the attempts of Sir Edward Grey to arrest the march of events in Eastern Europe, the unchallenged march of five thousand men with machine-guns through Belfast, the shooting upon the crowd in Dublin after the Howth gun-running, the consequent encouragement of Germany and Austria to persist in a stiff course with Russia because of the apparent inevitability of civil war in Ireland, right up to the march of the Germans into Luxembourg on the first of August, Joan followed with an interest that had presently swamped her egotistical eroticism altogether.

The second of August was a Sunday and brought no papers to Pelham Ford, but Joan motored to Bishop's Stortford to get an *Observer*. Monday was Bank Holiday; the belated morning paper brought the news of the massacre of Belgian peasants by the Germans at Visé. The Germans were pouring into Belgium, an incredible host of splendidly armed men. Tuesday was an immense suspense for Oswald and Joan. They were full of an uncontrollable indignation against Germany. They thought the assault on Belgium the most evil thing that had ever happened in history. But it seemed as though the Government and the country hesitated. *The Daily News* came to hand with a whole page advertisement in great letters exhorting England not to go to war for Belgium.

"But this is Shame!" cried Oswald. "If once the Germans get Paris——! It is Shame and Disaster!"

The postman was a reservist and had been called up. All over the country the posts were much disorganized. It was past eleven on the sunniest of Wednesdays when Joan, standing restless at the gates, called to Oswald, who was fretfully pacing the lawn, that the papers were coming.

She ran down the road to intercept the postman, and came back with a handful of letters and parcels. Newspapers were far more important than any personal letters that morning. She gave Oswald the newspaper package to tear open, and snatched up *The Daily News* as it fell out of the enveloping *Times*.

There was a crisp rustling of the two papers.

Oswald's fear of his country's mental apathy, muddle-headedness, levity, and absolute incapacity to grasp any great situation at all, had become monstrous under the stresses of these anxious days. Up to the end he feared some politicians' procrastination, some idiot dishonesty and betrayal, weak palterings with a challenge as high as heaven, with dangers as plain as daylight. . . .

"Thank God!" he cried. "It is War!"

CHAPTER THE THIRTEENTH

JOAN AND PETER GRADUATE

§ 1

SO it was, with a shock like the shock of an unsuspected big gun fired suddenly within a hundred yards of her, that the education of Joan and her generation turned about and entered upon a new and tragic phase. Necessity had grown impatient with the inertia of the Universities and the evasions of politicians. Mankind must learn the duties of human brotherhood and respect for the human adventure, or waste and perish; so our stern teacher has decreed. If in peace time we cannot learn and choose between those alternatives, then through war we must. And if we will in no manner learn our lesson, then——. The rocks are rich with the traces of ineffective creatures that the Great Experimenter has tried and thrown aside. . . .

All these young people who had grown up without any clear aims or any definite sense of obligations, found themselves confronted, without notice, without any preparation, by a world crisis that was also a crisis of life or death, of honour or dishonour for each one of them. They had most of them acquired the habit of regarding the teachers and statesmen and authorities set up over their lives as people rather on the dull side of things, as people addicted to muddling and disingenuousness in matters of detail; but they had never yet suspected the terrific insecurity of the whole system—until this first thunderous crash of the downfall. Even then they did not fully realize themselves as a generation betrayed to violence and struggle and death. All human beings, all young things, are born with a conviction that all is right with the world. There is mother to go to and father to go to, and behind them the Law; for most of the generation that came before Joan and Peter the delu-

443

sion of a great safety lasted on far into adult life; only
slowly, with maturity, came the knowledge of the flimsiness
of all these protections and the essential dangerousness of
the world. But for this particular generation the disillusionment came like an unexpected blow in the face. They were
preparing themselves in a leisurely and critical fashion for
the large, loose prospect of unlimited life, and then abruptly
the world dropped its mask. That pampered and undisciplined generation was abruptly challenged to be heroic beyond all the precedents of mankind. Their safety, their freedom ended, their leisure ended. The first few days of August, 1914, in Europe, was a spectacle of old men planning
and evading, lying and cheating, most of them so scared by
what they were doing as completely to have lost their heads,
and of youth and young men everywhere being swept from
a million various employments, from a million divergent interests and purposes, which they had been led to suppose were
the proper interests and purposes of life, towards the great
military machines that were destined to convert, swiftly and
ruthlessly, all their fresh young life into rags and blood and
rotting flesh. . . .

But at first the young had no clear sense of the witless
futility of the machine that was to crush their lives. They
did not understand that there was as yet no conception of a
world order anywhere in the world. They had taken it for
granted that there was an informal, tacitly understood world
order, at which these Germans—confound them!—had suddenly struck.

Peter and his friends were so accustomed to jeer at the
dignitaries of church and state and at kings and politicians
that they could not realize that such dwarfish and comic characters could launch disaster upon a whole world. They
sat about a little table in a twilit arbour on the way down
from Bel-Alp—Peter was to leave the climbers and join the
Italian party at Brigue—and devoured omelette and veal
and drank Yvorne, and mocked over the Swiss newspapers.

"Another ultimatum!" said one cheerful youth. "Holland will get it next."

"He's squirting ultimatums. Like a hedgehog throwing
quills."

"I saw him in Berlin," said Peter. "He rushed by in an automobile. He isn't a human being. He's more like Mr. Toad in *The Wind in the Willows*. . . ."

"All the French have gone home; all the Germans," said Troop. "I suppose we ought to go."

"I've promised to go to Italy," said Peter.

"War is war," said Troop, and stiffened Peter's resolution.

"I'm not going to have my holidays upset by a theatrical ass in a gilt helmet," said Peter.

He got down to Brigue next day, and the little town was bright with uniforms, for the Swiss were mobilizing. He saw off his mountaineering friends in the evening train for Paris. "You'd better come," said Troop gravely, hanging out of the train.

Peter shook his head. His was none of your conscript nations. No. . . .

He dined alone; Hetty and her two friends were coming up from Lausanne next day. In the reading-room he found the *Times* with the first news of the invasion of Belgium. Several of the villagers of Visé had turned out with shot guns, and the Germans had performed an exemplary massacre for the discouragement of franc-tireurs. Indignation had been gathering in Peter during the day. He swore aloud and flung down the paper. "Is there no one sane enough to assassinate a scoundrel who sets things loose like this?" he said. He prowled about the little old town in the moonlight, full of black rage against the Kaiser. He felt he must go back. But it seemed to him a terrible indignity that he should have to interrupt his holiday because of the ambition of a monarch. "Why the devil can't the Germans keep him on his chain?" he said, and then, "Shooting the poor devils—like rabbits!"

Hetty and her friends arrived in the early train next morning, all agog about the war. They thought it a tremendous lark. They were not to get out at Brigue, it was arranged; Peter was to be on the platform with his rucksack and join them. He kept the appointment, but he was a very scowling Peter in spite of the fact that Hetty was gentle and tremulous at the sight of him in her best style. "This train is an hour late," said Peter, sitting down beside her. "That accursed fool at Potsdam is putting all our Europe out of gear.'' . . .

For three days he was dark, preoccupied company. ''Somebody ought to assassinate him,'' he said, harping on that idea. ''Have men no self-respect at all?''

He felt he ought to go back to England, and the feeling produced a bleak clearness in his mind. It was soft sunshine on the lake of Orta, but east wind in Peter's soul. He disliked Hetty's friends extremely; he had never met them before; they were a vulgar brace of sinners he thought, and they reflected their quality upon her. The war they considered was no concern of theirs; they had studio minds. The man was some sort of painter, middle-aged, contemptuous, and with far too much hair. He ought to have been past this sort of spree. The girl was a model and had never been in Italy before. She kept saying, ''O, the *sky!*'' until it jarred intolerably. The days are notoriously longer on the lake of Orta than anywhere else in the world; from ten o'clock in the morning to lunch time is about as long as a week's imprisonment; from two to five is twice that length; from five onward the course of time at Orta is more normal. Hetty was Hetty, in the tradition of Cleopatra, but could Cleopatra hold a young man whose mind was possessed by one unquenchable thought that he had been grossly insulted and deranged by an exasperating potentate at Potsdam who was making hay of his entire world, and that he had to go at once and set things right, and that it was disgraceful not to go?

He broached these ideas to Hetty about eleven o'clock on their first morning upon the lake. They were adrift in a big tilted boat in the midst of a still, glassy symmetry of mountain-backed scenery and mountain-backed reflections, and the other couple was far away, a little white dot at the head of a V of wake, rowing ambitiously to the end of the lake.

''You can't go,'' said Hetty promptly. . . .

''But I have come all the way to Italy for you!'' cried Hetty. . . .

This was a perplexing problem for the honour of a young man of one-and-twenty. He argued the case—weakly. He had an audience of one, a very compelling one. He decided to remain. In the night he woke up and thought of Troop. Old Troop must be in England by now. Perhaps he had already enlisted. Ever since their school days he and Troop had had a standing dispute upon questions of morals and duty. There was something dull and stiff about old Troop that drove a bright antagonist to laxity, but after all——? Troop had cut off clean and straight to his duty. . . . Because Troop wasn't entangled. He had kept clear of all this love-making business. . . . There was something to be said for Troop's point of view after all. . . .

The second day Peter reopened the question of going as they sat on a stone seat under the big, dark trees on the Sacro Monte, and looked out under the drooping boughs upon the lake, and Hetty had far more trouble with him. He decided he could not leave her. But he spent the hours between tea and dinner in reading all the war news he could find—translating the Italian with the aid of a small conversation dictionary. Something had happened in the North Sea, he could not make out exactly what it was, but the Germans had lost a ship called the *Königin Luise,* and the British a battleship—was it a battleship?—the *Amphion.* Beastly serious that!—a battleship. There was something vague, too, about a fleet encounter, but no particulars. It was a bore getting no particulars. Here close at hand in the Mediterranean there had been, it was said, a naval battle in the Straits of Messina also; the *Panther* was sunk; and the Germans had had a great defeat at Liége. The British army was already landing in France. . . .

Upon his second decision to remain Peter reflected profoundly that night.

The standing dispute between him and Troop upon the lightness or seriousness of things sexual returned to his mind. Troop, Peter held, regarded all these things with a portentous solemnity, a monstrous sentimentality. Peter, Troop maintained, regarded them with a dangerous levity. Troop declared that love, "true love," was, next to "honour," the most tremendous thing in life; he was emphatic upon "purity." Peter held that love was as light and pleasant and incidental a thing as sunshine. You said, "Here's a

jolly person!'' just as you said, ''Here's a pretty flower!''
There had been, he argued, a lot of barbaric ''Taboos'' in
these matters, but the new age was dropping all that. He
called Troop's idea of purity ''ceremonial obsession.'' Both
talked very freely of ''cleanness'' and meant very different
things: Troop chiefly abstinence and Peter baths. Peter
had had the courage of his opinions; but once or twice
he had doubted secretly whether, after all, there weren't de-
filements beyond the reach of mere physical cleansing. One
dismissed that sort of thing as ''reaction.'' All these disputes were revived now in his memory in the light of this
one plain, disconcerting fact: Troop had gone straight home
to enlist and he himself was still in Italy. Weakening of
moral fibre? Loss of moral fibre?

The next day, in the boat, Peter reopened the question of
his departure.

''You see, Hetty,'' he said, ''if there was conscription in
England—I shouldn't feel so bound to go.''

''But then you would be bound to go.''

''Well, then I could be a decent deserter—for love's sake.
But when your country leaves it to you to come back or not
as you think fit—then, you know, you're bound—in honour.''

Hetty dabbled her hand over the side of the boat. ''Oh—
go!'' she said.

''Yes,'' said Peter over the oars, and as if ashamed, ''I
must go—I must. There is a train this afternoon which
catches the express at Domo d'Ossola.''

He rowed for a while. Presently he stole a glance at
Hetty. She was lying quite still on her cushion under the
tilt, staring at the distant mountains, with tears running
down her set face. They were real tears. ''Three days,''
she said choking, and at that rolled over to weep noisily upon
her arms.

Peter sat over his oars and stared helplessly at her emotion.

A familiar couplet came into his head, and remained unspoken because of its striking inappropriateness:

> "I could not love thee, dear, so much,
> Loved I not honour more."

Presently Hetty lay still. Then she sat up and wiped at
a tear-stained face.

"If you must go," said Hetty, "you must go. But why
you didn't go from Brigue——!"

That problem was to exercise Peter's mind considerably
in the extensive reflections of the next few days and nights.
"And I have to stick in Italy with those two Bores!" . . .

But the easy flexibility of Hetty's temperament was a large
part of her charm.

"I suppose you ought to go, Peter," she said, "really.
I had no business to try and keep you. But I've had so
little of you. And I love you."

She melted. Peter melted in sympathy. But he was much
relieved. . . .

She slipped into his bedroom to help him pack his rucksack, and she went with him to the station. "I wish I was a
man, too," she said. "Then I would come with you. But
wars don't last for ever, Peter. We'll come back here."

She watched the train disappear along the curve above
the station with something like a sense of desolation. Then
being a really very stout-hearted young woman, she turned
about and went down to the telegraph office to see what
could be done to salvage her rent and shattered holiday.

And Peter, because of these things, and because of certain
delays at Paris and Havre, for the train and Channel services were getting badly disorganized, got to England six
whole days later than Troop.

§ 2

This passion of indignation against Germany in which
Peter enlisted was the prevailing mood of England during
the opening months of the war. The popular mind had
seized upon the idea that Europe had been at peace and
might have remained at peace indefinitely if it had not been
for the high-handed behaviour, first of Austria with Serbia,
and then of Germany with Russia. The belief that on the
whole Germany had prepared for and sought this war was no
doubt correct, and the spirit of the whole nation rose high
and fine to the challenge. But that did not so completely

exhaust the moral factors in the case as most English people, including Peter, supposed at that time.

Neither Peter nor Joan, although they were members of the best educated class in the community and had been given the best education available for that class, had any but the vaguest knowledge of what was going on in the political world. They knew practically nothing of what a modern imperial system consisted, had but the vaguest ideas of the rôle of Foreign Office, Press and Parliament in international affairs, were absolutely ignorant of the direction of the army and navy, knew nothing of the history of Germany or Russia during the previous half-century, or the United States since the Declaration of Independence, had no inklings of the elements of European ethnology, and had scarcely ever heard such words, for example, as Slovene, or Slovak, or Ukrainian. The items of foreign intelligence in the newspapers joined on to no living historical conceptions in their minds. Between the latest history they had read and the things that happened about them and in which they were now helplessly involved, was a gap of a hundred years or more; the profound changes in human life and political conditions brought about during that hundred years by railways, telegraphs, steam shipping, steel castings and the like, were all beyond the scope of their ideas. For Joan history meant stories about Joan of Arc, Jane Shore, the wives of Henry the Eighth, James I. and his Steenie, Charles the Second, and suchlike people, winding up with the memoirs of Madame d'Arblay; Peter had ended his historical studies when he went on to the modern side at Caxton—it would have made little difference so far as modern affairs were concerned if he had taken a degree in history—and was chiefly conversant with such things as the pedigree of the Electress Sophia of Hanover, the Constitutions of Clarendon, the statute of Mortmain, and the claims of Edward the Third and Henry the Fifth to the crown of France. Neither of them knew anything at all of India except by way of Kipling's stories and the Coronation Durbar pictures. If the two of them had rather clearer ideas than most of their associates about the recent opening up and partition of Africa

it was because Oswald had talked about those things.   But
the jostling for empire that had been going on for the past
fifty years all over the world, and the succession of Imperialist theories from Disraeli to Joseph Chamberlain and from
Bismarck to Treitschke, had no place in their thoughts.   The
entente cordiale was a phrase of no particular significance to
them.   The State in which they lived had never explained
to them in any way its relations to them nor its fears and
aims in regard to the world about it.   It is doubtful, indeed,
if the State in which they lived possessed the mentality to
explain as much even to itself.

How far the best education in America or Germany or any
other country was better, it is not for us to discuss here,
nor how much better education might be.   This is the story
of the minds of Joan and Peter and of how that vast system
of things hidden, things unanalysed and things misrepresented and obscured, the political system of the European
"empires" burst out into war about them.   The sprawling,
clumsy, heedless British State, which had troubled so little
about taking Peter into its confidence, displayed now no hesitation whatever in beckoning him home to come and learn as
speedily as possible how to die for it.

The tragedy of youth in the great war was a universal
tragedy, and if the German youths who were now, less freely
and more systematically, beating Peter by weeks and months
in a universal race into uniform, were more instructed than
he, they were also far more thoroughly misinformed.   If
Peter took hold of the war by the one elemental fact that
Belgium had been invaded most abominably and peaceful
villagers murdered in their own fields, the young Germans
on the other hand had been trained to a whole system of false
interpretations.   They were assured that they fought to
break up a ring of threatening enemies.   And that the whole
thing was going to be the most magnificent adventure in history.   Their minds had been prepared elaborately and persistently for this heroic struggle—in which they were to
win easily.   They had been made to believe themselves a race
of blond aristocrats above all the rest of mankind, entitled
by their moral and mental worth to world dominion.   They

believed that now they did but come to their own. They
had been taught all these things from childhood; how could
they help but believe them?

Peter arrived, tired and dirty, at Pelham Ford in the
early afternoon. Oswald and Joan were out, but he bathed
and changed while Mrs. Moxton got him a belated lunch.
As he finished this Joan came into the dining-room from a
walk.

"Hullo, Petah," she said, with no display of affection.

"Hullo, Joan."

"We thought you were never coming."

"I was in Italy," said Peter.

"H'm," said Joan, and seemed to reckon in her mind.

"Nobby is in London," she said. "He thinks he might
help about East Africa. It's his country practically. . . .
Are you going to enlist?"

"What else?" said Peter, tapping a cigarette on the table.
"It's a beastly bore."

"Bunny's gone," said Joan. "And Wilmington."

"They've written?"

"Willy came to see me."

"Heard from any of the others?"

"Oh! . . . Troop."

"Enlisted?"

"Cadet."

"Any one else?"

"No," said Joan, and hovered whistling faintly for a
moment and then walked out of the room. . . .

She had been counting the hours for four days, perplexed
by his delay; his coming had seemed the greatest event in
the world, for she had never doubted he would come back
to serve, and now that he had come she met him like this!

§ 3

They dressed for dinner that night because Oswald came
back tired and vexed from London and wanted a bath
before dining. "They seemed to be sending everybody to
East Africa on the principle that any one who's been there

before ought not to go again," he grumbled. "I can't see any other principle in it." He talked at first of the coming East African campaign because he hesitated to ask Peter what he intended to do. Then he went on to the war news. The Germans had got Liége. That was certain now. They had smashed the forts to pieces with enormous cannon. There had been a massacre of civilians at Dinant. Joan did not talk very much, but sat and watched Peter closely with an air of complete indifference.

There was a change in him, and she could not say exactly what this change was. The sunshine and snow glare and wind of the high mountains had tanned his face to a hard bronze and he was perceptibly leaner; that made him look older perhaps; but the difference was more than that. She knew her Peter so well that she could divine a new thought in him.

"And what are you going to do, Peter?" said Oswald, coming to it abruptly.

"I'm going to enlist."

"In the ranks, you mean?" Oswald had expected that.

"Yes."

"You ought not to do that."

"Why not?"

"You have your cadet corps work behind you. You ought to take a commission. We shan't have too many officers."

Peter considered that.

"I want to begin in the ranks. . . . I want discipline."

(Had some moral miracle happened to Peter? This was quite a new note from our supercilious foster brother.)

"You'll get discipline enough in the cadet corps."

"I want to begin right down at the bottom of the ladder."

"Well, if you get a rotten drill sergeant, I'm told, it's disagreeable."

"All the better."

"They'll find you out and push you into a commission," said Oswald. "If not, it's sheer waste."

"Well, I want to feel what discipline is like—before I give orders," said Peter. "I want to be told to do things and asked why the devil I haven't done 'em smartly. I've been going too easy. The ranks will brace me up."

(Yes, this was a new note. Had that delay of four or five

days anything to do with this? . . . Joan, with a start, discovered that she was holding up the dinner, and touched the electric bell at her side for the course to be changed.)

"I suppose we shall all have to brace up," said Oswald. "It still seems a little unreal. The French have lost Mulhausen again, they say, but they are going strong for Metz. There's not a word about our army. It's just crossed over and vanished. . . ."

(Queer to sit here, dining in the soft candlelight, and to think of the crowded roads and deploying troops, the thudding guns and bursting shells away there behind that veil of secrecy—millions of men in France and Belgium fighting for the world. And Peter would go off tomorrow. Presently he would be in uniform; presently he would be part of a marching column. He would go over—into the turmoil. Beyond that her imagination would not pass.)

"I wish I could enlist," said Joan.

"They're getting thousands of men more than they can handle as it is," said Oswald. "They don't want you."

"You'd have thought they'd have had things planned and ready for this," said Peter.

"Nothing is ready," said Oswald. "Nothing is planned. This war has caught our war office fast asleep. It isn't half awake even now."

"There ought to be something for women to do," said Joan.

"There ought to be something for every one to do," said Oswald bitterly, "but there isn't. This country isn't a State; it's a crowd adrift. Did you notice, Peter, as you came through London, the endless multitudes of people just standing about? I've never seen London like that before. People not walking about their business, but just standing." . . .

Peter told of things he had seen on his way home. "The French are in a scowling state. All France scowls at you, and Havre is packed with bargains in touring cars—just left about—by rich people coming home. . . ."

So the talk drifted. And all the time Joan watched Peter as acutely and as unsuspectedly as a mother might watch a grown-up son. Tomorrow morning he would go off and join up. But it wasn't that which made him grave. New experiences always elated Peter. And he wouldn't be afraid; not he. . . . She had been let into the views of three other young men who had gone to war already; Troop had written, correctly and consciously heroic, "*Some of the chaps seem to be getting a lot of emotion into it,*" said Troop. "*It's nothing out of the way that I can see. One just falls into the line of one's uncles and cousins.*"

Wilmington had said: "I just wanted to see you, Joan. I'm told I'll be most useful as a gunner because of my mathematics. When it comes to going over, you won't forget to think of me, Joan?"

Joan answered truthfully. "I'll think of you a lot, Billy."

"There's nothing in life like you, Joan," said Wilmington in his white expressionless way. "Well, I suppose I'd better be going."

But Bunny had discoursed upon fear. "*I've enlisted,*" he wrote, "*chiefly because I'm afraid of going Pacifist right out—out of funk. But it's hell, Joan. I'm afraid in my bones. I hate bangs, and they say the row of modern artillery is terrific. I've never seen a dead body, a human dead body, I mean, ever. Have you? I would go round a quarter of a mile out of my way any time to dodge a butcher's shop. I was sick when I found Peter dissecting a rabbit. You know, sick, à la Manche. No metaphors. I shall run away, I know I shall run away. But we've got to stop these beastly Germans anyhow. It isn't killing the Germans I shall mind—I'm fierce on Germans, Joan; but seeing the chaps on stretchers or lying about with all sorts of horrible injuries.*"

Sheets of that sort of thing, written in an unusually bad handwriting—apparently rather to comfort himself than to sustain Joan.

Well, it wasn't Peter's way to think beforehand of being "on stretchers or lying about," but Bunny's scribblings had got the stretchers into Joan's thoughts. And it made her wish somehow that Peter, instead of being unusually grave and choosing to be a ranker, was taking this job with his usual easy confidence and going straight and gaily for a commission.

After dinner they all sat out in garden chairs, outside the library window, and had their coffee and smoked. Joan got her chair and drew it close to Peter's. Two hundred miles away and less was battle and slaughter, perhaps creeping nearer to them, the roaring of great guns, the rattle of rifle fire, the hoarse shouts of men attacking, and a gathering harvest of limp figures "on stretchers and lying about"; but that evening at Pelham Ford was a globe of golden serenity. Not a leaf stirred, and only the little squeaks and rustlings of small creatures that ran and flitted in the dusk ruffled the quiet air.

Oswald made Peter talk of his climbing. "My only mountain is Kilimanjaro," he said. "No great thing so far as actual climbing goes." Peter had begun with the Dolomites, had gone over to Adelboden, and then worked round by the Concordia Hut to Bel Alp. "Was it very beautiful?" asked Joan softly under his elbow.

"You could have done it all. I wish you had come," said Peter.

There was a pause.

"And Italy?" said Joan, still more softly.

"Where did you go in Italy, Peter?" said Oswald, picking up her question.

Peter gave a travel-book description of Orta and the Isle of San Giulio.

Joan sat as still and watchful as a little cat watching for a mouse. (Something had put Peter out in Italy.)

"It's off the main line," said Peter. "The London and Paris papers don't arrive, and one has to fall back on the *Corriere della Sera*."

"Very good paper too," said Oswald.

"News doesn't seem so real in a language you don't understand."

He was excusing himself. So he was ashamed to that extent. That was what was bothering him. One might have known he wouldn't care for—those other things. . . .

Late that night Joan sat in her room thinking. Presently she unlocked her writing-desk and took out and re-read a let-

ter. It was from Huntley in Cornwall, and it was very
tender and passionate. *"The world has gone mad, dearest,"*
it ran; *"but we need not go mad. The full moon is slipping
by. I lay out on the sands last night praying for you to
come, trying to will you to come. Oh—when are you coming?"* . . .

And much more to the same effect. . . .

Joan's face hardened. "Po'try," she said. She took
a sharpened pencil from the glass tray upon her writing-
table and regarded it. The pencil was finely pointed—too
finely pointed. She broke off the top with the utmost care
and tested the blunt point on her blotting-paper to see if it
was broad enough for her purpose. Then she scrawled her
reply across his letter—in five words: *"You ought to enlist.
Joan,"* and addressed an envelope obliquely in the same uncivil script.

After which she selected sundry other letters and a snap-
shot giving a not unfavourable view of Huntley from her
desk, and having scrutinized the latter for an interval, tore
them all carefully into little bits and dropped them into her
wastepaper basket. She stood regarding these fragments
for some time. "I might have gone to him," she whispered
at last, and turned away.

She blew out her candle, hesitated by her bedside, and
walked to the open window to watch the moon rise.

She sat upon her window-sill like a Joan of marble for a
long time. Then she produced one of those dark sayings
with which she was wont to wrap rather than express her profounder thoughts.

"Queer how suddenly one discovers at last what one has
known all along. . . . Queer. . . .

"Well, *I* know anyhow." . . .

She stood up at last and yawned. "But I don't like war,"
said Joan. "Stretchers! Or lying about! Groaning. In
the darkness. Boys one has danced with. Oh! beastly.
Beastly!"

She forgot her intention of undressing, put her foot on
the sill, and rested chin on fist and elbow on knee, scowling
out at the garden as though she saw things that she did not
like there.

§ 4

So it was that Joan saw the beginning of the great winnowing of mankind, and Peter came home in search of his duty.

Within the first month of the war nearly every one of the men in Joan's world had been spun into the vortex; hers was so largely a world of young or unattached people, with no deep roots in business or employment to hold them back. Even Oswald at last, in spite of many rebuffs, found a use for himself in connection with a corps of African labourers behind the front, and contrived after a steady pressure of many months towards the danger zone, to get himself wounded while he was talking to some of his dear Masai at an ammunition dump. A Hun raider dropped a bomb, and some flying splinters of wood cut him deeply and extensively. The splinters were vicious splinters; there were complications; and he found himself back at Pelham Ford before the end of 1916, aged by ten years. The Woman's Legion captured Joan from the date of its formation, and presently had her driving a car for the new Ministry of Munitions, which came into existence in the middle of 1915.

Her career as a chauffeuse was a brilliant one. She lived, after the free manner of the Legion, with Miss Jepson at Hampstead; she went down every morning to her work, she drove her best and her best continually improved, so that she became distinguished among her fellows. The Ministry grew aware of her and proud of her. A time arrived when important officials quarrelled to secure her for their journeys. Eminent foreign visitors invariably found themselves behind her.

"But she drives like a man," they would say, a little breathlessly, after some marvellously skidded corner.

"All our girls drive like this," the Ministry of Munitions would remark, carelessly, loyally, but untruthfully.

Joan's habitual wear became khaki; she had puttees and stout boots and little brass letterings upon her shoulders and sleeves, and the only distinctive touches she permitted herself were the fur of her overcoat collar and a certain foppery about her gauntlets. . . .

Extraordinary and profound changes of mood and relationship occurred in the British mind during those first two
years of the war, and reflected themselves upon the minds
of Joan and Peter. To begin with, and for nearly a year,
there was a quality of spectacularity about the war for the
British. They felt it to be an immense process and a
vitally significant process; they read, they talked, they
thought of little else; but it was not yet felt to be an intimate
process. The habit of detachment was too deeply ingrained.
Great Britain was an island of onlookers. To begin with
the war seemed like something tremendous and arresting going on in an arena. "Business as usual," said the business
man, putting up the price of anything the country seemed to
need. There was a profound conviction that British life
and the British community were eternal things; they might
play a part—a considerable part—in these foreign affairs;
they might even have to struggle, but it was inconceivable
that they should change or end. September and October in
1914 saw an immense wave of volunteer enthusiasm—enthusiasm for the most part thwarted and wasted by the unpre-
paredness of the authorities for anything of the sort, but it
was the enthusiasm of an audience eager to go on the stage;
it was not the enthusiasm of performers in the arena and
unable to quit the arena, fighting for life or death. To
secure any sort of official work was to step out of the undistinguished throng. In uniform one felt dressed up and
part of the pageant. Young soldiers were self-conscious in
those early days, and inclined to pose at the ordinary citizen.
The ordinary citizen wanted to pat young soldiers on the
back and stand them drinks out of his free largesse. They
were "in it," he felt, and he at most was a patron of the
affair.

That spectacularity gave way to a sense of necessary participation only very slowly indeed. The change began as
the fresh, bright confidence that the Battle of the Marne had
begotten gave place to a deepening realization of the difficulties on the road to any effective victory. The persuasion
spread from mind to mind that if Great Britain was to fight
this war as she had lived through sixty years of peace, the
gentleman amateur among the nations, she would lose this

war. The change of spirit that produced its first marked result in the creation of the Ministry of Munitions with a new note of quite unofficial hustle, and led on through a series of inevitable steps to the adoption of conscription, marks a real turning about of the British mind, the close of a period of chaotic freedom almost unprecedented in the history of communities. It was the rediscovery of the State as the necessary form into which the individual life must fit.

To the philosophical historian of the future the efforts of governing and leading people in Great Britain to get wills together, to explain necessities, to supplement the frightful gaps in the education of every class by hastily improvised organizations, by speeches, press-campaigns, posters, circulars, cinema shows, parades and proclamations; hasty, fitful, ill-conducted and sometimes dishonestly conducted appeals though they were, will be far more interesting than any story of battles and campaigns. They remind one of a hand scrambling in the dark for something long neglected and now found to be vitally important; they are like voices calling in a dark confusion. They were England seeking to comprehend herself and her situation after the slumber of two centuries. But to people like Joan and Peter, who were not philosophical historians, the process went on, not as a process, but as an apparently quite disconnected succession of events. Imperceptibly their thoughts changed and were socialized. Joan herself had no suspicion of the difference in orientation between the Joan who stood at her bedroom window in August, 1914, the most perfect spectator of life, staring out at the darkness of the garden, dumbly resenting the call that England was making upon the free lives of all her friends, and the Joan of 1917, in khaki and a fur-collared coat, who slung a great car with a swift, unerring confidence through the London traffic and out to Woolwich or Hendon or Waltham or Aldershot or Chelmsford or what not, keen and observant of the work her passengers discussed, a conscious part now of a great and growing understanding and criticism and will, of a rediscovered unity, which was England— awakening.

Youth grew wise very fast in those tremendous years. From the simple and spectacular acceptance of every obvious

appearance, the younger minds passed very rapidly to a
critical and intricate examination. In the first blaze of
indignation against Germany, in the first enthusiasm, there
was a disposition to trust and confide in every one in a position of authority and responsibility. The War Office was
supposed—against every possibility—to be planning wisely
and acting rapidly; the wisdom of the Admiralty was taken
for granted, the politicians now could have no end in view
but victory. It was assumed that Sir Edward Carson could
become patriotic, Lord Curzon self-forgetful, Mr. Asquith
energetic, and Mr. Lloyd George straightforward. It was
indeed a phase of extravagant idealism. Throughout the
opening weeks of the war there was an appearance, there
was more than an appearance, of a common purpose and a
mutual confidence. The swift response of the Irish to the
call of the time, the generous loyalty of India, were like intimations of a new age. The whole Empire was uplifted; a
flush of unwonted splendour suffused British affairs.

Then the light faded again. There was no depth of understanding to sustain it; habit is in the long run a more
powerful thing than even the supremest need. In a little
time all the inglorious characteristics of Britain at peace,
the double-mindedness, the slackness, were reappearing
through the glow of warlike emotion. Fifty years of under-
education are not to be atoned for in a week of crisis. The
men in power were just the same men. The inefficient were
still inefficient; the individualists still self-seeking. The party
politicians forgot their good resolutions, and reverted to
their familiar intrigues and manœuvres. Redmond and
Ireland learnt a bitter lesson of the value of generosity in
the face of such ignorant and implacable antagonists as the
Carsonites. Britain, it became manifest, had neither the
greatness of education nor yet the simplicity of will to make
war brilliantly or to sustain herself splendidly. At every
point devoted and able people found themselves baffled by
the dull inertias of the old system. And the clear flame
of enthusiasm that blazed out from the youth of the country
at the first call of the war was coloured more and more by
disillusionment as that general bickering which was British
public life revived again, and a gathering tale of waste, fail-

ure, and needless suffering mocked the reasonable expectation
of a swift and glorious victory.

The change in the thought and attitude of the youth of
Britain is to be found expressed very vividly in the war
poetry of the successive years. Such glowing young heroes
as Julian Grenfell and Rupert Brooke shine with a faith
undimmed; they fight consciously, confident of the nearness
of victory; they sing and die in what they believe to be a
splendid cause and for a splendid end. An early death in
the great war was not an unmitigated misfortune. Three
years later the young soldier's mind found a voice in such
poetry as that of young Siegfried Sassoon, who came home
from the war with medals and honours only to denounce the
war in verse of the extremest bitterness. His song is no
longer of picturesque nobilities and death in a glorious cause;
it is a cry of anger at the old men who have led the world to
destruction; of anger against the dull, ignorant men who can
neither make war nor end war; the men who have lost the
freshness and simplicity but none of the greed and egotism
of youth. Germany is no longer the villain of the piece.
Youth turns upon age, upon laws and institutions, upon the
whole elaborate rottenness of the European system, saying:
*"What is this to which you have brought us? What have
you done with our lives?"*

No story of these years can ever be true that does not
pass under a shadow. Of the little group of youths and
men who have figured in this story thus far, there was
scarcely one who was not either killed outright or crippled
or in some way injured in the Great War—excepting only
Huntley. Huntley developed a deepening conscience against
warfare as the war went on, and suffered nothing worse than
some unpleasant half-hours with Tribunals and the fatigues
of agricultural labour. Death, which had first come to Joan
as a tragic end to certain "kittays," was now the familiar
associate of her every friend. Her confidence in the safety
of the world, in the wisdom of human laws and institutions,
in the worth and dignity of empires and monarchs, and the
collective sanity of mankind was withdrawn as a veil is
withdrawn, from the harsh realities of life.

Wilmington, with his humourless intensity, was one of

the first to bring home to her this disillusionment and tragedy of the youth of the world. He liked pure mathematics; it was a subject in which he felt comfortable. He had worked well in the first part of the mathematical tripos, and he was working hard in the second part when the war broke out. He fluctuated for some days between an utter repudiation of all war and an immediate enlistment, and it was probably the light and colour of Joan in his mind that made Wilmington a warrior. War was a business of killing, he decided, and what he had to do was to apply himself and his mathematics to gunnery as efficiently as possible, learning as rapidly as might be all that was useful about shells, guns and explosives, and so get to the killing of Germans thoroughly, expeditiously, and abundantly. He was a particularly joyless young officer, white-faced and intent, with an appearance of scorn that presently developed from appearance into reality, for most of his colleagues. He was working as hard and as well as he could. At first with incredulity and then with disgust he realized that the ordinary British officer was not doing so. They sang songs, they ragged, they left things to chance, they thought blunders funny, they condoned silliness and injustice in the powers above. He would not sing nor rag nor drink. He worked to the verge of exhaustion. But this exemplary conduct, oddly enough, did not make him unpopular either with the junior officers or with his seniors. The former tolerated him and rather admired him; the latter put work upon him and sought to promote him.

In quite a little while as it seemed—for in those days, while each day seemed long and laborious and heavy, yet the weeks and months passed swiftly—he was a captain in France, and before the end of 1915 he wrote to say that his major had left him practically in command of his battery for three weeks. He had been twice slightly wounded by that time, but he got little leisure because he was willing and indispensable.

He wrote to Joan very regularly. He was a motherless youth, and Joan was not only his great passion but his friend and confidante. His interest in his work overflowed into his letters; they were more and more about gunnery and the art of war, which became at last, it would seem, a serious rival to Joan in his affections. He described ill, but he would send her reasoned statements of unanswerable views. He could not understand why considerations that were so plain as to be almost obvious, were being universally disregarded by the Heads and the War Office. He appealed to Joan to read what he had to say, and tell him whether he or the world was mad. When he came back on leave in the spring of 1916, she was astonished to find that he was still visibly as deeply in love with her as ever. The fact of it was he had words for his gunnery and military science, but he had no words, and that was the essence of his misfortune, for his love for Joan.

But the burthen of his story was bitter disillusionment at the levity with which his country could carry on a war that must needs determine the whole future of mankind. He would write out propositions of this sort: "It is manifest that success in warfare depends upon certain primary factors, of which generalship is one. No country resolute to win a war will spare any effort to find the *best men,* and make them its generals and leaders irrespective of every other consideration. No honourable patriots will permit generals to be appointed by any means except the *best selective methods,* and no one who cares for his country will obstruct (1) the *promotion,* (2) *trying over,* and (3) *prompt removal,* if they fail to satisfy the most exacting tests, of all possible men. And next consider what sort of men will be the best commanders. They must be *fresh-minded young men.* All the great generals of the world, the supreme cases, the Alexanders, Napoleons, and so on, have shown their quality before thirty even in the days when strategy and tactics did not change very greatly from year to year, and now when the material and expedients of war make warfare practically a *new thing* every few years, the need for fresh young commanders is far more urgent than ever it has been. But the British army is at present commanded by oldish men who are manifestly of not more than mediocre intelligence, and who have no knowledge of this new sort of war that has arisen. It is a war of guns and infantry—with aeroplanes

coming in more and more—and most of the higher positions
are held by cavalry officers; the artillery is invariably commanded by men unused to the handling of such heavy guns
as we are using, who stick far behind our forward positions
and decline any practical experience of our difficulties.
They put us in the wrong positions, they move us about absurdly; young officers have had to work out most of the
problems of gun-pits and so forth for themselves—against
resistance and mere stupid interference from above.   The
Heads have no idea of the kind of work we do or of the
kind of work we could do.   They are worse than amateurs;
they are unteachable fossils.   But why is this so?   If the
country is serious about the war, why does it permit it?   If
the Government is serious about the war, why does it permit
it?   If the War Office is serious about the war, why does it
permit it?   If G.H.Q. is serious about the war, why does it
permit it?   What is wrong?   There is a hitch here I don't
understand.   Am I over-serious, and is all this war really
some sort of gross, grim joke, Joan?   Do I take life too seriously?

"Joan, in this last push this battery did its little job
right; we cut all the wire opposite us and blew out every
blessed stake.   We made a nice tidy clean up.   It was quite
easy to do, given hard work.   If I hadn't done it I ought
either to have been shot for neglect or dismissed for incapacity.   But on our left it wasn't done.   Well, there were
at least a hundred poor devils of our infantrymen on that
wire, a hundred mothers' sons, hanging like rags on it or
crumpled up below.   I saw them.   It made me sick.   And
I saw the chap who was chiefly responsible for that, Major
Clutterwell, a little bit screwed, being the life and soul of a
little party in Hazebrouck three days after!   He ought to
have been the life and soul of a hari kari party, but either
he is too big a cad or too big a fool—or both.   The way
they shy away our infantrymen over here is damnable.
They are the finest men in the world, I'm convinced; they
will go at anything, and the red tabs send them into impossible jobs, fail to back them up—always they fail to back
them up; they neglect them, Joan; they neglect them even

when they are fighting and dying! There are men here, colonels, staff officers, I would like to beat about the head with an iron bar. . . .''

This was an unusually eloquent passage. Frequently his letters were mainly diagram to show for example how we crowded batteries to brass away at right angles to the trenches when we ought to enfilade them, or some such point. Sometimes he was trying to establish profound truths about the proper functions of field guns and howitzers. For a time he was gnawing a bitter grievance. ''I was told to shell a line I couldn't reach. The contours wouldn't allow of it. You can do a lot with a shell, but you cannot make it hop slightly and go round a corner. There is a definite limit to the height to which a gun will lob a shell. I tried to explain these elementary limitations of gunfire through the telephone, and I was told I should be put under arrest if I did not obey orders. I wasn't up against a commander, I wasn't up against an intelligence; I was up against a silly old man in a temper. So I put over a barrage about fifty yards beyond the path—the nearest possible. Every one was perfectly satisfied—the Boche included. Thus it is that the young officer is subdued to the medium he works in.''

At times Wilmington would embark on a series of propositions to demonstrate with mathematical certitude that if the men and material wasted at Loos had been used in the Dardanelles, the war would have been decided by the end of 1915. But the topic to which his mind recurred time after time was the topic of efficient leadership. ''Modern war demands continuity of idea, continuity of will, and continuous progressive adaptation of means and methods,'' he wrote —in two separate letters. In the second of these he had got on to a fresh notion. ''Education in England is a loafer education; it does not point to an end; it does not drive through; it does not produce *minds that can hold out* through a long effort. The young officers come out here with the best intentions in the world, but one's everyday life is shaped not by our intentions but our habits. Their habits of mind are loafing habits. They learnt to loaf at school. Caxton, I am now convinced, is one of the best schools in England; but even at Caxton we did not fully acquire the *habit of steadfast haste* which modern life demands. Everything that gets done out here is done by a spurt. With the idea behind it of presently doing nothing. The ordinary state of everybody above the non-commissioned ranks is loafing. At the present moment my major is shooting pheasants; the batteries to the left of us are cursing because they have to shift—it holds up their scheme for a hunt. Just as though artillery work wasn't the most intense sport in the world—especially now that we are going to have kite balloons and do really scientific observing. Even the conscientious men of the Kitchener-Byng school don't really seem to me to *get on;* they work like Trojans at established and routine stuff but they don't keep up inquiry. They are human, all too human. Man is a sedentary animal, and the schoolmaster exists to prevent his sitting down comfortably.'' This from Wilmington without a suspicion of jesting. ''This human weakness for just living can only be corrected in schools. The more I scheme about increasing efficiency out here, the more I realize that it can't be done here, that one has to go right back to the schools and begin with *a more continuous urge.* When this war is over I shall try to be a schoolmaster. I shall hate it most of the time, but then I hate most things. . . .''

But Wilmington never became a schoolmaster. He got a battery of six-inch guns just before the Somme push in 1916, and he went forward with them into positions he chose and built up very carefully, only to be shifted against his wishes almost at once to a new and, he believed, an altogether inferior position. He was blown to nothingness by a German shell while he was constructing a gun pit.

§ 6

Wilmington was not the first of Joan's little company to be killed. Joan had the gift of friendship. She was rare among girls in that respect. She was less of an artist in egotism than most of her contemporaries; there were even times when she could be self-forgetful to the pitch of untidiness. Two other among that handful of young soldiers who were killed outright and who had been her friends, wrote to her with some regularity right up to the times of their deaths, and found a comfort in doing so. They wrote to her at first upon neat notepaper adorned with regimental crests, but their later letters as they worked their slow passages towards the place of death were pencilled on thin paper. She kept them all. She felt she could have been a good sister to many brothers.

One of these two who died early was Winterbaum. She did not hear from this young man of the world for some weeks after the declaration of war. Then came a large photograph of himself in cavalry uniform, and a manly, worldly letter strongly reminiscent of Kipling and anticipatory of Gilbert Frankau. "There is something splendid about this life after all," he wrote. "It's good to be without one's little luxuries for a space, democratically undistinguished among one's fellows. It's good to harden up until nothing seems able to bruise one any more. I bathed yesterday, without water, Joan—just a dry towel, and that not over clean—was all that was available. After this is all over I shall have such an appetite for luxury—I shall be fierce, Joan."

Those early days were still days of unrestricted plenty, and the disposition of the British world was to pet and indulge everything in khaki. Young Winterbaum wore his spurs and the most beautiful riding-breeches to night clubs and great feasts in the more distinguished restaurants. He took his car about with him, his neat little black-and-white car, fitted with ivory fopperies. He tried hard to take it with him to France. From France his scribbled letters became more and more heroic in tone. "Poor David has been done in," he said. "I am now only three from the Contango peerage. Heaven send I get no nearer! No Feudal dignities for me. I would give three gilded chambers at any time for one reasonably large and well-lit studio. And—I have a kind of affection for my cousins."

His prayer was answered. He got no nearer to the Contango peerage. The powers above him decided that a little place called Loos was of such strategic value to the British army as to be worth the lives of a great number of young men, and paid in our generous British fashion even more than the estimate. Winterbaum was part of the price. No particulars of his death ever came to Joan and Peter. The attack began brightly, and then died away. There was a failure to bring up reserves and grasp opportunity. Winterbaum vanished out of life in the muddle—one of thousands. He was the first of the little company of Joan's friends to be killed.

Bunny Cuspard spread a less self-conscious, more western, and altogether more complicated psychology before Joan's eyes. Like Wilmington he had faltered at the outset of the war between enlistment and extreme pacifism, but unlike Wilmington he had never reconciled himself to his decision. Bunny was out of sympathy with the fierceness of mankind; he wanted a kindly, prosperous, rather funny world where there is nothing more cruel than gossip; that was the world he was fitted for. He repeated in his own person and quality the tragedy of Anatole France. He wanted to assure the world and himself that at heart everything was quite right and magnificent fun, to laugh gaily at everything, seeing through its bristling hostilities into the depth of genial absurdity beneath.

And so often he could find no genial absurdity.

He had always pretended that discovering novel sorts of cakes for his teas or new steps for dances was the really serious business of life. One of his holiday amusements had been "Little Wars," which he played with toy soldiers and little model houses and miniature woods of twigs and hills of boarding in a big room at his Limpsfield home. He would have vacation parties for days to carry out these wars, and he and his guests conducted them with a tremendous seriousness. He had elaborated his miniature battle scenery more and more, making graveyards, churches, inns, walls, fences— even sticking absurd notices and advertisements upon the walls, and writing epitaphs upon his friends in the graveyard. He had loved the burlesque of it. He had felt that it brought history into a proper proportion to humour. But one of the drawbacks had always been that as the players lay upon the floor to move their soldiers and guns about they crushed down his dear little toy houses and woods. . . .

His mind still fought desperately to see the war as a miniature.

He got to a laugh ever and again by a great effort, but some of the things that haunted his imagination would not under any circumstances dissolve in laughter. Things that other people seemed to hear only to dismiss remained to suppurate in his mind. One or two of the things that were most oppressive to him he never told Joan. But she had a glimpse now and then of what was there, through the cracks in his laughter.

He had heard a man telling a horrible story of the opening bombardment of Ypres by the Germans. The core of the story was a bricked tunnel near the old fortifications of the town, whither a crowd of refugees had fled from the bombardment, and into which a number of injured people had been carried. A shell exploded near the exit and imprisoned all those people in a half-light without any provisions or help. There was not even drinking-water for the wounded. A ruptured drain poured a foul trickle across the slimy floor on which the wounded and exhausted lay. Now quite near and now at a distance the shells were still bursting, and through that thudding and uproar, above all the crouching and murmuring distresses of that pit of misery sounded the low, clear, querulous voice of a little girl who was talking as she died, talking·endlessly of how she suffered, of how her sister could not come to help her, of her desire to be taken away; a little, scolding indignant spirit she was, with a very clear explicit sense of the vast impropriety of everything about her.

"Why does not some one come?"

"Be tranquil," an old woman's voice remonstrated time after time. "Help will come."

But for most of the people in the tunnel help never came. Through a slow, unhurrying night of indescribable pain and discomfort, in hunger, darkness, and an evil stench, their lives ebbed away one by one. . . .

That dark, dreadful, stinking place, quivering to the incessant thunder of guns, sinking through twilight into night, lit by flashes and distant flames, and passing through an eternity of misery to a cold, starving dawn, threaded by the

child's shrill voice, took a pitiless grip upon Bunny's imagination. He could neither mitigate it nor forget it.

How could one laugh at the Kaiser with this rankling in
his mind? He could not fit it into any merry scheme of
things, and he could not bear any scheme that was not merry;
and not to be able to fit dreadful things into a scheme that
does at last prevail over them was, for such a mind as
Bunny's, to begin to drift from sanity.

The second story that mutely reinforced the shrill indict-
ment of that little Belgian girl was a description he had
heard of some poor devil being shot for cowardice at dawn.
A perplexed, stupid youth of two- or three-and-twenty, with
little golden hairs that gleamed on a pallid cheek, was led
out to a heap of empty ammunition boxes in a desolate and
mutilated landscape of mud and splintered trees under a
leaden sky, and set down on a box to die. It was as if Bunny
had seen that living body with his own eyes, the body that
jumped presently to the impact of the bullets and lurched
forward, and how the officer in command—who had been himself but a little child in a garden a dozen years or more ago—
came up to the pitiful prostrate form and put his revolver to
the head behind the ear that would never hear again and
behind the eye that stared and glazed, and pulled the trigger
"to make sure."

Bunny could feel that revolver behind his own ear. It
felt as a dental instrument feels in the mouth.

"Oh, my God!" cried Bunny; "oh, my God!" starting up
from his sack of straw on the floor in his billet in the middle
of the night.

"Oh! *shut* it!" said the man who was trying to sleep beside him.

"Sorry!" said Bunny.

"You keep it for the Germans, mate."

"Oh! Oh! If I could kill this damned Kaiser with ten
thousand torments!" whispered Bunny, quieting down. . . .

These were not the only stories that tormented Bunny's
mind, but they were the chief ones. Others came in and
went again—stories of the sufferings of wounded men, of almost incredible brutalities done to women and children and
helpless people, and of a hundred chance reasonless horrors;

they came in with an effect of support and confirmation to these two principal figures—the shrill little girl making her bitter complaint against God and the world which had promised to take care of her, and had scared her horribly and torn her limbs and thrust her, thirsty and agonized, into a stinking drain to die; and the poor puzzled lout, caught and condemned, who had to die so dingily and submissively because his heart had failed him. Against the grim instances of their sombre and squalid fates the soul of Bunny battled whenever, by night or day, thought overtook him in his essential and characteristic resolve to see life as "fun"—as "great fun."

These two fellow-sufferers in life took possession of his imagination because of their intense kindred with himself. So far as he got his riddle clear it was something after this fashion: "Why, if the world is like this, why are we in it? What am I doing in this nightmare? Why are there little girls and simple louts—and me?"

The days drew near when he would have to go to the front. He wrote shamelessly to Joan of his dread of that experience.

"*It's the mud and dirtiness and ugliness,*" he said. "*I am a domestic cat, Joan—an indoor cat. . . .*

"*I've got a Pacifist temperament. . . .*

"*All the same, Joan, the Germans started this war. If we don't beat them, they will start others. They are intolerable brutes—the Junkers, anyhow. Until we get them down they will go on kicking mankind in the stomach. It is their idea of dignified behaviour. But we are casting our youth before swine. . . . Why aren't there more assassins in the world? Why can't we kill them by machinery—painlessly and cleanly? We ought to be cleverer than they are.*"

There was extraordinarily little personal fear in Bunny. He was not nearly so afraid of the things that would happen to him as of the things that would happen about him. He hated the smashing even of inanimate things; a broken-down chair or a roofless shed was painful to him. Whenever he thought of the trenches he thought of treading and slipping in the dark on a torn and still living body. . . .

He stuck stoutly to his reasoning that England had to fight

and that he had to fight; but hidden from Joan, hidden from every living soul, he kept a secret resolve. It was, he knew, an entirely illogical and treasonable resolve, and yet he found it profoundly comforting. He would never fire his rifle so that it would hurt any one even by chance, and he would never use his bayonet. He would go over the top with the best of them, and carry his weapons and shout.

If it came to close fighting he would go for a man with his hands and try to disarm him.

But this resolve was never put to the test. The Easter newspapers of 1916 arrived with flaming headlines about an insurrection in Dublin and the seizure of the Post Office by the rebels. Oddly enough, this did not shock Bunny at all. It produced none of the effect of horror and brutality that the German invasion of Belgium had made upon his mind. It impressed him as a "rag"; as the sort of rag that they got up to at Cambridge during seasons of excitement. He was delighted by the seizure of the Post Office, by the appearance of a revolutionary flag and the issue of Republican stamps. It was as good as "Little Wars"; it was "Little Revolutions." He didn't like the way they had shot a policeman outside Trinity College, but perhaps that report wasn't true. The whole affair had restored that flavour of adventure and burlesque that he had so sadly missed from the world since the war began.

He had always idealized the Irish character as the pleasantest combination of facetiousness and generosity. When he found himself part of a draft crossing to Dublin with his back to the grim war front, his spirits rose. He could forget that nightmare for a time. He was going to a land of wit and laughter which had rebelled for a lark. He felt sure that the joke would end happily and that he would be shaking hands with congenial spirits still wearing Sinn Fein badges before a fortnight was out. Perhaps he would come upon Mrs. O'Grady or Patrick Lynch, whom he had been accustomed to meet at the Sheldricks'. He had heard they were in it. And when the whole business had ended brightly and cheerfully then all those clever and witty people would grow grave and helpful, and come back with him to join in that temporarily neglected task of fighting on the western front against an iron brutality that threatened to overwhelm the world.

He was still in this cheerful vein two days later as he was crossing St. Stephen's Green. His quaint, amiable face was smiling pleasantly and he was marching with a native ungainliness that no drill-sergeant could ever overcome, when something hit him very hard in the middle of the body.

He knew immediately that he had been shot.

He was not dismayed or shocked by this, but tremendously interested.

All other feelings were swamped in his surprise at a curious contradiction. He had felt hit behind, he was convinced he had been hit behind, but what was queer about it was that he was spinning round as though he had been hit in front. It gave him a preposterous drunken feeling. His head was quite clear, but he was altogether incapable of controlling these spinning legs of his, which were going round backward. His facile sense of humour was aroused. It was really quite funny to be spinning backwards in this way. It was like a new step in dancing. His hilarity increased. It was like the maddest dancing they had ever had at Hampstead or Chelsea. The "backwards step." He laughed. He had to laugh; something was tickling his ribs and throat. His whole being laughed. He laughed a laugh that became a rush of hot blood from his mouth. . . .

The soul of Bunny, for all I know, laughs for ever among the stars; but it was a dead young man who finished those fantastic gyrations.

He paused and swayed and dropped like an empty sack, and lay still in St. Stephen's Green, the modest contribution of one happy Sinn Fein sniper to the Peace of Mankind.

Perhaps Bunny was well out of a life where there can be little room for Bunnyism for many years to come, and lucky to leave it laughing. And as an offset to his loss we have to count the pleasant excitement of Ireland in getting well back into the limelight of the world's affairs, and the bright and glowing gathering of the armed young heroes who got away, recounting their deeds to one another simultaneously in some

secure place, with all the rich, tumultuous volubility of the
Keltic habit.

"Did ye see that red-haired fella I got in the square, boys?
. . . Ah, ye should have seen that fella I got in the square."

§ 7

But not all the world of Joan was at war. The Sheldrick
circle, for example, after some wide fluctuations during which
Sydney almost became a nurse and Babs nearly enlisted into
the Women's Legion, took a marked list under the influence
of one of the sons-in-law towards pacifism. Antonia, who
had taken two German prizes at school, was speedily provoked
by the general denunciation of "Kultur" into a distinctly
pro-German attitude. The Sheldrick circle settled down on
the whole as a pro-German circle, with a poor opinion of
President Wilson, a marked hostility to Belgians, and a disposition to think the hardships of drowning by U-boats much
exaggerated.

The Sheldricks were like seedlings that begin flourishing
and then damp off. From amusing schoolfellows they had
changed into irritating and disappointing friends. Energy
leaked out of them at adolescence. They seemed to possess
the vitality for positive convictions no longer, they displayed
an instinctive hostility to any wave of popular feeling that
threatened to swamp their weak but still obstinate individualities. Their general attitude towards life was one of protesting refractoriness. Whatever it was that people believed
or did, you were given to understand by undertones and ab-
stinencies that the Sheldricks knew better, and for the most
exquisite reasons didn't. All their friends were protesters
and rebels and seceders, or incomprehensible poets or inexplicable artists. And from the first the war was altogether too big and strong for them. Confronted by such
questions as whether fifty years of belligerent preparation,
culminating in the most cruel and wanton invasion of a
peaceful country it is possible to imagine, was to be resisted
by mankind or condoned, the Sheldricks fell back upon the

counter statement that Sir Edward Grey, being a landowner, was necessarily just as bad as a German Junker, or that the Government of Russia was an unsatisfactory one.

In a few months it was perfectly clear to the Sheldricks that they would have nothing to do with the war at all. They were going to ignore it. Sydney just went on quietly doing her little statuettes that nobody would buy, little portrait busts of her sisters and such-like things; now and then her mother contrived to get her a commission. Babs kept on trying to get a part in somebody's play; Antonia continued to produce djibbahs in chocolate and grocer's blue and similar tints. One saw the sisters drifting about London in costumes still trailingly pre-Raphaelite when all the rest of womankind was cutting its skirts shorter and shorter, their faces rather pained in expression and deliberately serene, ignoring the hopes and fears about them, the stir, the huge effort, the universal participation. It was not their affair, thank you. They were not going to wade through this horrid war; they were going round.

Every time Joan went to see them, either they had become more phantomlike and incredible, or she had become coarser and more real. Would they ever get round? she asked herself; and what would they be like when at last they attempted, if ever they attempted, to rejoin the main stream of human interests again?

They kept up their Saturday evenings, but their gatherings became thinner and less and less credible as the war went on. The first wave of military excitement carried off most of the sightly young men, and presently the more capable and enterprising of the women vanished one after another to nurse, to join the Women's Legion, to become substitute clerks and release men to volunteer, to work in canteens and so forth. There was, however, a certain coming and going of ambiguous adventurers, who in those early days went almost unchallenged between London and Belgium on ambulance work, on mysterious missions and with no missions at all. Belgian refugees drifted in and, when they found a lack of sympathy for their simple thirst for the destruction of Germans under all possible circumstances, out again. Then Ireland called her own, and Patrick Lynch went off to die a martyr's death with arms in his hands after three days of the most exhilarating mixed shooting in the streets of Dublin. Antonia discovered passionate memories as soon as he was dead, and nobody was allowed to mention the name of Bunny in the Sheldrick circle for fear of spoiling the emotional atmosphere. Hetty Reinhart, after some fluctuations, went khaki, flitted from one ministry to another in various sorts of clerical capacities, took such opportunities as offered of entertaining young officers lonely in our great capital, and was no more seen in Hampstead. What was left of this little group in the Hampstead *Quartier Latin* drew together into a band of resistance to the creeping approach of compulsory service.

Huntley's lofty scorn of the war had intensified steadily; the harsh disappointment of Joan's patriotism had stung him to great efforts of self-justification, and he became one of the most strenuous writers in the extreme Pacifist press. Not an act or effort of the Allies, he insisted, that was not utterly vile in purpose and doomed to accelerate our defeat. Not an act of the enemy's that was not completely thought out, wisely calculated, and planned to give the world peace and freedom on the most reasonable terms. He was particularly active in preparing handbills and pamphlets of instruction for life-long Conscientious Objectors to war service who had not hitherto thought about the subject. Community of view brought him very close in feeling to both Babs and Sydney Sheldrick. There was much talk of a play he was to write which was to demonstrate the absurdity of Englishmen fighting Germans just because Germans insisted upon fighting Englishmen, and which was also to bring out the peculiarly charming Babsiness of Babs. He studied her thoroughly and psychologically and physiologically and intensively and extensively.

By a great effort of self-control he abstained from sending his writings to Joan. Once however they were near meeting. On one of Joan's rare calls Babs told her that he was coming to discuss the question whether he should go to prison and hunger-strike, or consent to take up work of national importance. Babs was very full of the case for each alternative. She was doubtful which course involved the greatest moral courage. Moral courage, it was evident, was being carried to giddy heights by Huntley. It would be pure hypocrisy, he felt, to ignore the vital value of his writings, and while he could go on with these quite comfortably while working as a farm hand, with a little judicious payment to the farmer, their production would become impossible in prison. He must crucify himself upon the cross of harsh judgments, he felt, and take the former course. He wanted to make his views exactly clear to every one to avoid misunderstanding.

Joan hesitated whether she should stay and insult him or go, and chose the seemlier course.

§ 8

Joan was already driving a car for the Ministry of Munitions before Peter got himself transferred from the ranks of the infantry to the Royal Flying Corps. Peter's career as an infantryman never took him nearer to the western front than Liss Forest. Then he perceived the error of his ways and decided to get a commission in the Royal Flying Corps. In those days the Flying Corps was still a limited and inaccessible force with a huge waiting list, and it needed a considerable exertion of influence to secure a footing in that select band. . . . But at last a day came when Peter, rather self-conscious in his new leather coat and cap, walked out from the mess past a group of chatting young pilots towards the aeroplane in which he was to have his first experience of flight.

He had a sense of being scrutinized, but indeed hardly any one upon the aerodrome noted him. This sense of an audience made him deliberately casual in his bearing. He saluted his pilot in a manner decidedly offhand. He clambered up through struts and wire to the front seat as if he was a clerk ascending the morning omnibus, and strapped himself in as if it hardly mattered whether he was strapped in or not.

"Contact, sir," said the mechanic. "Contact," came the pilot's voice from behind. The engine roared, a gale swept backwards, and Peter vibrated like an aspen leaf.

The wheels were cleared, the mechanics jumped aside, and Peter was careering across the grass in a series of light leaps, and then his progress became smoother. He did not perceive at first the reason for this sudden steadying of the machine. He found himself tilting upward. He was off the ground. He had been off the ground for some seconds. He looked over the side and saw the grass fifty feet below, and the black shadow of the aeroplane, as if it fled before them, rushing at a hedge, doubling up at the hedge, and starting again in the next field. And up he went.

Peter stared at fields, hedges, trees, sheds and roadways growing small below him. He noted cows in plan and an automobile in plan, in a lane, going it seemed very slowly indeed. It was a stagnant world below in comparison with his own forward sweep. His initial nervousness and self-consciousness had passed away. He was enormously interested and delighted. He was trying to remember when it was that Nobby had said: "I doubt if we'll see that in my lifetime—or yours." It was somewhen long ago at Limpsfield. Quite early. . . .

And then abruptly Peter was clutching the side with his thick-gloved hand; the aeroplane was coming round in a close curve and banking steeply, very steeply. For a moment it seemed as though there was nothing at all between him and England below. If he fell out——!

He looked over his shoulder and met the hard regard of a pair of steel-blue eyes.

He remembered that after all he was under observation. This was no mere civilian's joy ride. He affected a concentration upon the scenery. The aeroplane swung slowly back again to the level, and his hand left the side. . . .

They were going up very rapidly now. The world seemed to be rolling in at the edges of a great circle that grew constantly larger. Away to the left were broad spaces of brown sand, and grey rippled and smooth shining water channels, and beyond, the sapphire sea; beneath and to the right were fields, houses, villages, woods, and a distant range of hills that seemed to be coming nearer. The scale was changing and everything was becoming maplike. Cows were little dots now and men scarcely visible. . . . And then suddenly all the scenery seemed to be rushing upward before Peter's eyes and he had a feeling like the feeling one has in a lift when it starts—a down-borne feeling. He affected indifference, and gave the pilot his whistling profile. Down they swept, faster than a luge on the swiftest ice run, until one could see the ditches in the shadows beneath the hedges and cows were plainly cows again, and then once more they were heeling over and curving round. But Peter had been ready for that this time; he had been telling himself over and over again that he was strapped in. He betrayed no surprise. He was getting more and more exhilarated.

And then they were climbing again and soaring straight out towards the sea. Up went this roaring dragonfly in which Peter was sitting, at a hundred and twenty miles or so per hour, leaving the dwindling land behind.

Up they went and up, until the world seemed nearly all sea and the coast was far away; they mounted at last above a little white cloud puff and then above a haze of clouds, and when Peter looked down he saw at a vast distance below, through a clear gap in that filmy cloud fabric, three ships smaller than any toys. Of the men he could distinguish nothing. How sweet the cold clear air had become!

And high above the world, in the lonely sky above the cloud fleece, the pilot saw fit to spring a surprise upon Peter.

He was not of the genial and considerate order of teachers; he believed in weeding out duds as swiftly as possible. He had an open mind as to whether this rather over-intelligent-looking beginner might not, under certain circumstances, squeal. So he just tried him and, without a note of preparation, looped the loop with him.

The propeller that span before the eyes of Peter dipped. Peter bowed in accord with it. It dipped more and more steeply, until the machine was almost nose down, until Peter was looking at the sea and the land as one sits and looks at a wall. He was tilted down and down until he was face downward. And then as abruptly he was tilted up; it was like being in a swing; the note of the engine altered as if a hand swept up a scale of notes; the sea and the land seemed to fall away below him as though he left them for ever, and the blue sky swept down across his field of vision like a curtain; he was, so to speak, on his back now with his legs in the air, looking straight at the sky, at nothing but sky, and expecting to recover. For a vast second he waited for the swing to end. This was surely the end of the swing. . . .

Only—most amazingly—he didn't recover! He wanted to say, "Ouch!" He was immensely surprised—too surprised to be frightened. He went over backwards—in an instant—and the sea and the land reappeared above the sky and also came down like curtains, too, and then behold! the aeroplane was driving down and the world was in its place again far below.

"The Loop!" whispered Peter, a little dazed, and glanced back at his pilot and smiled. This was no perambulator excursion. "The Loop—first trip!"

The blue eyes seemed a little less hard, the weather-red face was smiling faintly.

Then gripped by an irresistible power, Peter found himself going down, down, down almost vertically. The pilot had apparently stopped the engine. . . .

Peter watched the majestic expansion of the landscape as they fell. They had come back over the land. Far away he could see the aerodrome like a scattered collection of little toy huts, and growing bigger and bigger every instant. He sat quite still, for it was all right—it must be all right. But now they were getting very near the ground, and it was still rushing up to meet them, and pouring outwardly as it rose. A cat now would be visible. . . .

It *was* all right. The engine picked up with a roar like a score of lions, and the pilot levelled out a hundred feet above the trees. . . .

Then presently they were dropping to the aerodrome again; down until the hedges were plain and the grazing cattle close and distinct; and then, with a sense of infinite regret, Peter perceived that they were back on the turf again and that the flight was over. They danced lightly over the turf. Their rush slowed down. They taxied gently up to the hangar and the engine shuddered and, with a pathetic drop to silence, stopped. . . .

A little stiffly, Peter unbuckled himself and stretched and set himself to clamber to the ground.

His weather-bitten senior nodded to him and smiled faintly. . . .

Peter walked towards the mess. It was wonderful—and intensely disappointing in that it was so soon over. There were still great pieces of the afternoon left. . . .

§ 9

The aerodrome was short of machines and instructors, and he had to wait a couple of weeks before he could get into the air a second time.

He worked sedulously to gather knowledge during that waiting interval, and his first real lesson found him a very alert and ready pupil. This time the dual control was at his disposal, and for a straight or so the pilot left things to him altogether. Came half a dozen other lessons, and then Peter found himself sitting alone in a machine outside the great sheds, watched closely by a knot of friendly rivals, and, for the first time on his own account, conducting that duologue he had heard now so often on other lips. "Switch off." . . . "Suck in." "Contact!"

He started across the ground. His first sensations bordered on panic. Hitherto the machines he had flown in had been just machines; now this one, this one was an animal; it started out across the aerodrome like a demented ostrich, swerving wildly and trying to turn round. Always before this, the other man had done the taxi business on the ground. It had never occurred to Peter that it involved any difficulty. Peter's heart nearly failed him in that opening twenty seconds; he was convinced he was going to be killed; and then he determined to get up at any cost. At any rate he wouldn't smash on the ground. He let out the accelerator, touched his controls, and behold he was up—he was up! Instantly the machine ceased to resemble a floundering ostrich, and became a steady and dignified carinate, swaying only slightly from wing to wing. Up he went over the hedges, over the trees, beyond, above the familiar field of cows. The moment of panic passed, and Peter was himself again.

He had got right outside the aerodrome and he had to

bank and bring her round. Already he had done that successfully a number of times with an instructor to take care
of him. He did it successfully now. His confidence grew.
Back he buzzed and droned, a hundred feet over the aerodrome. He made three complete circuits, rose outside the
aerodrome and came down, making a good landing. He was
instantly smitten with the intensest regret that he had not
made eight or nine circuits. It was a mere hop. Any man
of spirit would have gone on. There were four hours of daylight yet. He might have gone up; he might have tried a
spiral. . . . *Damn!*

But the blue eyes of the master approved him.

"Couldn't have made a better landing, Stubland," said the
master. "Try again tomorrow. Follow it up close. Short
and frequent doses. That's the way."

Peter had made another stage on his way to France.

Came other solo flights, and flights on different types of
machines, and then a day of glory and disobedience when,
three thousand feet above the chimneys of a decent farm-
house, Peter looped the loop twice. He had learnt by that
time what it was to sideslip, and what air pockets can do to
the unwary. He had learnt the bitter consequences of coming down with the engine going strong. He had had a smash
through that all too common mistake, but not a bad smash; a
few struts and wires of the left wing were all that had gone.
A hedge and a willow tree had stopped him. He had had a
forced landing in a field of cabbages through engine stoppage,
and half an hour in a snowstorm when he had had doubts in
an upward eddy whether he might not be flying upside down.
That had been a nasty experience—his worst. He had several times taken his hands off the controls and let the old 'bus
look after herself, so badly were the snowflakes spinning
about in his mind. He dreamt a lot about flying, and few of
his dreams were pleasant dreams. And then this fantastic
old world of ours, which had so suddenly diverted his education to these things, and taught him to fly with a haste and
intensity it had never put into any teaching before, decided
that he was ripe for the air war, and packed him off to
France. . . .

§ 10

Now, seeing that Joan had at last discovered that she was in love with Peter, it would be pleasantly symmetrical to record that Peter had also discovered by this time that he was in love with Joan.

But as a matter of fact he had discovered nothing of the sort. He had been amazed and humiliated by his three days of hesitation and procrastination at Orta; the delay was altogether out of keeping with his private picture of himself; and he discovered that he was not in love with any one and that he did not intend again to be lured into any dangerous pretence that he was. He had done with Hetty, he was convinced; he did not mean to see her any more, and he led a life of exasperated Puritanism for some months, refusing to answer the occasionally very skilful and perplexing letters, with amusing and provocative illustrations, that she wrote him.

The idea of "relaxing moral fibre" obsessed him, and our genial Peter for a time abandoned both smoking and alcohol, and was only deterred from further abstinences by their impracticability. The ordinary infantry mess, for example, caters ill and resentfully for vegetarians. . . . Peter's days in the ranks were days of strained austerity. He was a terribly efficient recruit, a fierce soldier, a wonderful influence on slackers, stripes gravitated towards him, and a prophetic corporal saw sergeant-major written on his forehead. Occasionally, when his imagination got loose or after a letter from Hetty, he would indulge privately in fits of violent rage, finding great relief in the smashing of light objects and foul and outrageous language. He found what he considered a convenient privacy for this idiosyncrasy in a disused cowshed near the camp, and only realized that he had an audience when a fellow recruit asked anxiously, "And how's Miss Blurry 'Etty?" Whereupon Peter discovered a better outlet for pentup nervous energy in a square fight.

Joan saw hardly anything of him during those early and brutal days, but she thought about him mightily. She shared Oswald's opinion that he wasn't in his right place,

and she wrote to him frequently. He answered perhaps half
her letters. His answers struck her as being rather posed.
The strain showed through them. Peter was trying very
hard not to be Peter. "I'm getting down to elementals,"
was one of his experiments in the statement of his moral
struggle.

Then quite abruptly came his decision to get into the
Royal Flying Corps.

Neither Oswald nor Joan ventured any comment on this,
because both of them had a feeling that Peter had, in a
sense, climbed down by this decision to go up. . . .

In the Royal Flying Corps Peter's rather hastily conceived
theories of moral fibre came into an uncongenial atmosphere.
The Royal Flying Corps was amazingly young, swift, and
confident, and "moral fibre" based on abstinence and cold
self-control was not at all what it was after. The Royal
Flying Corps was much more inclined to scrap with soda-
water syphons and rag to the tunes of a gramophone. It
was a body that had had to improvise a tradition of conduct
in three or four swift years, and its tradition was still unstable. Mainly it was the tradition of the games and sports
side of a public school, roughly adapted to the new needs of
the service; it was an essentially boyish tradition, even men
old enough to have gone through the universities were in a
minority in it, and Peter at one-and-twenty was one of the
more elderly class of recruits. And necessarily the tradition
of the corps still varied widely with the dominant personalities and favourite heroes of each aerodrome and mess and
squadron. It was a crowd of plastic boys, left amazingly to
chance leads. Their seniors had no light for them, and they
picked up such hints as they could from Kipling and the
music-halls, from overheard conversations, and one another.

Is it not an incredible world in which old men make wars
and untutored young men have to find out how to fight them;
in which tradition and the past are mere entanglements about
the feet of the young? The flying services took the very
flower of the youth of the belligerent nations; they took the
young men who were most manifestly fitted to be politicians,
statesmen, leaders of men, masters in industry, and makers
of the new age; the boys of nerve, pluck, imagination, inven-

tion, and decision.   And there is not a sign of any realization
on the part of any one of the belligerent states of the fact that
a large proportion of this most select and valuable mass of
youth was destined to go on living after the war and was
going to matter tremendously and be the backbone of the
race after the war.   They let all these boys specialize as
jockeys specialize.   The old men and rulers wanted these
youngsters to fight and die for them; that any future lay
beyond the war was too much for these scared and unteachable ancients to apprehend.   The short way to immediate
efficiency was to back the tradition of recklessness and gallantry, and so the short way was taken; if the brave lads were
kept bold and reckless by women, wine and song, then by all
means, said their elders, let them have these helps.   "A short
life and a merry one," said the British Empire to these lads
of eighteen and nineteen encouragingly.   "A short life and
a merry one," said the Empire to its future.

If the story of the air forces is a glorious and not a shameful thing it is because of the enduring hope of the world—
the incessant gallantry of youth.   These boys took up their
great and cardinal task with the unquenchable hopefulness
of boyhood and with the impudence and humour of their race.
They brought in the irreverence and the Spartanism of their
years.   They made a language for themselves, an atrocious
slang of facetious misnomers; everything one did was a
"stunt"; everything one used was a "gadget"; the machines
were "'buses" and "camels" and "pups"; the older men
were perpetually pleading in vain for more dignity in the
official reports.   And these youngsters worked out their
moral problems according to their own generous and yet
puerile ideas.   They argued the question of drink.   Could
a man fly better or worse if he was "squiffy"?   Does funk
come to the thoughtful?   And was ever a man gallant without gallantries?   After the death of Lord Kitchener there
survived no man in Britain of the quality to speak plainly
and authoritatively and honestly about chastity and drink to
the young soldier.   The State had no mind in these matters.
In most matters indeed the State had no mind; it was a little
old silly State.   And the light side of the feminine temperament flamed up into shameless acquiescences in the heroic

presence of the flying man.   Youth instinctively sets towards romantic adventures, and the scales of chance for a considerable number of the flying men swung between mésalliance and Messalina.

The code and the atmosphere varied from mess to mess and from squadron to squadron; young men are by nature and necessity hero-worshippers and imitative.   Peter's lines fell among pleasant men of the "irresponsible" school.   The two best flyers he knew, including him of the hard blue eyes who had first instructed him, were men of a physique that defied drink and dissipation.   Vigours could smoke, drink, and dance in London, catch the last train back with three seconds to spare, and be flying with an unshaken nerve by half-past six in the morning; Vincent would only perform stunts when he was "tight," and then he seemed capable of taking any risk with impunity.   He could be funny with an aeroplane then a thousand feet up in the air.   He could make it behave as though it was drunk, as though it was artful; he could make it mope or wag its tail.   Men went out to watch him.   The mess was decorated with pictures from *La Vie Parisienne,* and the art and literature of the group was Revue.   Now seeing that Peter's sole reason for his puritanism was the preservation of efficiency, this combination of a fast life and a fine record in the air was very disconcerting to him.

If he had been naturally and easily a first-class flying man he might have stuck to his line of high austerity, but he was not.   He flew well, but he had to fly with care; like many other airmen, he always felt a shadow of funk before going up, on two or three bad mornings it was on his conscience that he had delayed for ten minutes or so, and he was more and more inclined to think that he would fly better if he flew with a less acute sense of possibilities.   It was the start and the uneventful flying that irked him most; hitherto every crisis had found him cool and able.   But the slap-dash style, combined with the exquisite accuracy of these rakes, Vigours and Vincent, filled him with envious admiration.

In the mess Peter met chiefly youths of his own age or a year or so younger; he soon became a master of slang; his style of wit won its way among them.   He ceased to write of

"getting down to elementals" to Joan, and he ceased to think
of all other girls and women as inventions of the devil. Only
they must be kept in their places. As Vigours and Vincent
kept them. Just as one kept drink in its place. One must
not, for example, lose trains on account of them. . . .

Through these months Joan maintained a strained watch
upon the development and fluctuations of Peter. He wrote
—variously; sometimes offhand duty notes and sometimes
long and brotherly letters—incurably brotherly. Every now
and then she had glimpses of him when he came to London
on leave. Manifestly he liked her company and trusted her
—as though she was a man. It was exasperating. She
dressed for Peter as she had never dressed for any one, and
he would take her out to dine at the *Rendezvous* or the *Petit
Riche* and sit beside her and glance at common scraps of
feminine humanity, at dirty little ogling bare-throated girls
in patched-up raiment and with harsh and screaming voices,
as though they were the most delicious of forbidden fruits.
And he seemed to dislike being alone with her. If she
dropped her hand to touch his on the table, he would draw
his away.

Was the invisible barrier between them invincible?

For a time during his infantry phase he had shown a
warm affection. In his early days in the flying corps it
seemed that he drew still closer to her. Then her quick,
close watch upon him detected a difference. Joan was getting to be a very shrewd observer nowadays, and she felt a
subtle change that suddenly made him a little shame-faced in
her presence. There had been some sort of spree in London
with two or three other wild spirits, and there had been
"girls" in the party. Such girls! He never told her this,
but something told her. I am inclined to think it was her
acute sense of smell detected a flavour of face powder or
cheap scent about Peter when he came along one day, half
an hour late, to take her to the Ambassadors. She was bad
company that night for him.

For a time Joan was bad company for any one.

She was worse when she realized that Hetty was somehow
reinstated in Peter's world. That, too, she knew by an al-

most incredible flash of intuition.   Miss Jepson was talking
one evening to Peter, and Peter suddenly displayed a knowledge of the work of the London Group that savoured of
studio.   This was the first art criticism he had talked since
the war began.   It was clear he had been to a couple of
shows.   Not with Joan.   Not alone.   As he spoke, he glanced
at Joan and met her eye.

It was astonishing that Miss Jepson never heard the loud
shout of ''Hetty'' that seemed to fill the room.

It was just after this realization that an elderly but still
gallant colonel, going on an expedition for the War Office
with various other technical authorities to suppress some
disturbing invention that the Ministry of Munitions was
pressing in a troublesome manner, decided to come back from
Longmore to London on the front seat beside Joan.   His
conversational intentions were honourable and agreeable, but
he shared a common error that a girl who wears khaki and
drives a car demands less respect from old gentlemen and is
altogether more playful than the Victorian good woman.
Possibly he was lured on to his own destruction.

When he descended at the Ministry, he looked pinched
and aged.   He was shaken to the pitch of confidences.   ''My
word,'' he whispered.   ''That girl drives like the devil.   But
she's a vixen . . . snaps your head off. . . . Don't know
whether this sort of thing is good for women in the long
run.

''Robs 'em of Charm,'' he said.

§ 11

It was just in this phase of wrath and darkness that Wilmington came over to London for his last leave before he
was killed, and begged Joan for all the hours she had to
spare.   She was quite willing to treat him generously.   They
dined together and went to various theatres and music-halls
and had a walk over Hampstead Heath on Sunday.   He was
a silent, persistent companion for most of the time.   He
bored her, and the more he bored her the greater her com-

punction and the more she hid it from him.   But Wilmington, if he had a slow tongue, had a penetrating eye.

The last evening they had together was at the Criterion. They dined in the grill room, a dinner that was interspersed with brooding silences.   And then Wilmington decided to make himself interesting at any cost upon this last occasion.

"Joan," he said, knocking out a half-consumed cigarette upon the edge of his plate.

"Billy?" said Joan, waking up.

"Queer, Joan, that you don't love me when I love you so much."

"I'd trust you to the end of the earth, Billy."

"I know.   But you don't love me."

"I think of you as much as I do of any one."

"No.   Except—*one.*"

"Billy," said Joan weakly, "you're the straightest man on earth."

Wilmington's tongue ran along his white lips.   He spoke with an effort.

"You've loved Peter since you were six years old.   It isn't as though—you'd treated me badly.   I can't grumble that you've had no room for me.   He's always been there."

Joan, after an interval, decided to be frank.

"It's not much good, Billy, is it, if I do?"

Wilmington said nothing for quite a long time.   He sat thinking hard.   "It's not much good pretending I don't hate Peter.   I do.   If I could kill him—and in your memory too. . . . He bars you from me.   He makes you unhappy. . . ."

His face was a white misery.   Joan glanced round at the tables about her, but no one seemed to be watching them. She looked at him again.   Pity, so great that it came near to love, wrung her. . . .

"Joan," he said at last.

"Yes?"

"It's queer. . . . I feel mean. . . . As though it wasn't right. . . . But look here, Joan."   He tapped her arm. "Something—something that I suppose I may as well point out to you.   Because in certain matters—in certain matters you are being a fool.   It's astonishing—— But absolutely —a fool."

Joan perceived he had something very important to say. She sat watching him, as with immense deliberation he got out another cigarette and lit it.

"You don't understand this Peter business, Joan. I—I do. Mostly when I'm not actually planning out or carrying out the destruction of Germans, I think of you—and Peter. And all the rest of it. I've got nothing else much to think about. And I think I see things you don't see. I know I do. . . . Oh damn it! Go to hell!"

This last was to the waiter, who was making the customary warning about liqueurs on the stroke of half-past nine.

"Sorry," said Wilmington to Joan, and leant forward over his folded arms and collected his thoughts with his eyes on the flowers before them.

"It's like this, Joan. Peter isn't where we are. I—I'm very definite and clear about my love-making. I fell in love with you, and I've never met any other woman I'd give three minutes of my life to. You've just got me. As if I were the palm of your hand. I wish I were. And—oh! what's the good of shutting my eyes?—Peter has you. You've been thinking of Peter half the time we've been together. It's true, Joan. You've grown up in love. Buh! But Peter, you've got to understand, isn't in love. He doesn't know what love means. Perhaps he never will. Love with you and me is a thing of flesh and bone. He takes it like some skin disease. He's been spoilt. He's so damned easy and good-looking. He was got hold of. I——"

Wilmington flushed for a moment. "I'm a chaste man, Joan. It's a rare thing. Among our sort. But Peter—— Loving a woman body and soul means nothing to him. He thinks love-making is a kind of amusement—— Casual amusement. Any woman who isn't repulsive. You know, Joan, that's not the natural way. The natural way is love of soul and body. He's been perverted. But in this crowded world—like a monkey's cage . . . artificially heated . . . the young men get made miscellaneous. . . . Lots of the girls even are miscellaneous. . . ."

He considered the word. "Miscellaneous? Promiscuous, I mean. . . . It hasn't happened to us. To you and me, I mean. I'm unattractive somehow. You're fastidious.

He's neither. He takes the thing that offers. To grave people sex is a sacrament, something—so solemn and beautiful——''

The tears stood in his eyes. "If I go on," he said. . . . "I can't go on. . . .''

For a time he said no more, and pulled his unconsumed cigarette to pieces over the ash-tray with trembling fingers. "That's all," he said at last.

"All this is—rather true," said Joan. "But——!''

"What does it lead up to?''

"Yes.''

"It means Peter's the ordinary male animal. Under modern conditions. Lazy. Affectionate and all that, but not a scrap of emotion or love—yet anyhow. Not what you and I know as love. You may dress it up as you like, but the fact is that the woman has to make love to him. That's all. Hetty has made love to him. He has never made love to anybody—except as a sort of cheerful way of talking, and perhaps he never, never will. . . . He respects you too much to make love to you. . . . But he'd hate the idea of any one else—making love to you. . . . It's an idea—— It's outside of his conception of you. . . He'll never think of it for himself.''

Joan sat quite still. After what seemed a long silence she looked up at him.

Wilmington was watching her face. He saw she understood his drift.

"You could cut her out like *that*," said Wilmington, with a gesture that gained an accidental emphasis by knocking his glass off the table and smashing it.

The broken glass supplied an incident, a distraction, with the waiters, to relieve the tension of the situation.

"That's all I had to say," said Wilmington when that was all settled. "There's no earthly reason why two of us should be unhappy.''

"Billy," she said, after a long pause, "if I could only love *you*——''

The face of gratitude that looked at him faded to a mask.

"You're thinking of Peter already," said Wilmington, watching her face.

It was true. She started, detected.

He speculated cheerlessly.

"You'll marry me some day perhaps. When Peter's thrown you over. . . . It's men of my sort who get things like that. . . ."

He stood up and reached for her cloak. She, too, stood up.

Then, as if to reassure her, he said: "I shall get killed, Joan. So we needn't worry about that. I shall get killed. I know it. And Peter will live. . . . I always have taken everything too seriously. Always. . . . I shall kill a lot of Germans yet, but one day they will get me. And Peter will be up there in the air, like a cheerful midge—with all the Archies missing him. . . ."

§ 12

This conversation was a cardinal event in Joan's life. Wilmington's suggestions raised out of the grave of forgetfulness and incorporated with themselves a conversation she had had long ago with Adela—one Christmas at Pelham Ford when Adela had been in love with Sopwith Greene. Adela too had maintained that it was the business of a woman to choose her man and not wait to be chosen, and that it was the woman who had to make love. "A man's in love with women in general," had been Adela's idea, "but women fall in love with men in particular." Adela had used a queer phrase, "It's for a woman to find her own man and keep him and take care of him." Men had to do their own work; they couldn't think about love as women were obliged by nature to think about love. "Love's just a trouble to a real man, like a mosquito singing in his ear, until some woman takes care of him."

All those ideas came back now to Joan's mind, and she did her best to consider them and judge them as generalizations. But indeed she judged with a packed court, and all her being clamoured warmly for her to "get" Peter, to "take care"—most admirable phrase—of Peter. Her decision was made, and still she argued with herself. Was it beneath her dignity to set out and capture her Peter?—he was her Peter. Only he didn't know it. She tried to generalize. Had it ever been dignified for a woman to wait until a man discovered her possible love? Was that at best anything more than the dignity of the mannequin?

Three-quarters at least of the art and literature of the world is concerned with the relations of the sexes, and yet here was Joan, after thirty centuries or so of human art and literature, still debating the elementary facts of her being. There is so much excitement in our art and literature and so little light. The world has still to discover the scope and vastness of its educational responsibilites. Most of its teaching in these matters hitherto has been less in the nature of enlightenment than strategic concealment; we have given the young neither knowledge nor training, we have restrained and baffled them and told them lies. And then we have inflamed them. We have abused their instinctive trust when they were children with stories of old Bogey designed to save us the bother that unrestrained youthful enterprise might cause, and with humorous mockery of their natural curiosity. Jocularities about storks and gooseberry bushes, sham indignations at any plainness of speech, fierce punishments of imperfectly realized offences, this against a background of giggles, knowing innuendo, and careless, exciting glimpses of the mystery, have constituted the ordinary initiation of the youth of the world. Right up to full age, we still fail to provide the clear elemental facts. Our young men do not know for certain whether continence is healthy or unhealthy, possible or impossible; the sex is still assured with all our power of assurance, that the only pure and proper life for it is a sexless one. Until at last the brightest of the young have been obliged to get down to the bare facts in themselves and begin again at the beginning. . . .

So Joan, co-Heiress of the Ages with Peter, found that because of her defaulting trustees, because we teachers, divines, writers and the like have shirked what was disagreeable and difficult and unpopular, she inherited nothing but debts and dangers. She had not even that touching faith in Nature which sustained the generation of Jean Jacques Rousseau. She had to set about her problem with Peter as though he and she were Eve and Adam in a garden overrun with weeds and thorns into which God had never come.

Joan was too young yet to have developed the compensating egotism of thwarted femininity. She saw Peter without delusions. He was a bigger and cleverer creature than herself; he compelled her respect. He had more strength, more invention, more initiative, and a relatively tremendous power of decision. And at the same time he was weak and blind and stupid. His flickering, unstable sensuousness, his light adventurousness and a certain dishonesty about women, filled her with a comprehensive pity and contempt. There was a real difference not merely in scale but in nature between them. It was clear to her now that the passionate and essential realities of a woman's life are only incidental to a man. But on the other hand there were passionate and essential realities for Peter that made her own seem narrow and self-centred. She knew far more of his mental life than Oswald did. She knew that he had an intense passion for clear statement, he held to scientific and political judgments with a power altogether deeper and greater than she did; he cared for them and criticized them and polished them, like weapons that had been entrusted to him. Beneath his debonair mask he was growing into a strong and purposeful social and mental personality. She perceived that he was only in the beginning of his growth—if he came on no misadventure, if he did not waste himself. And she did not believe that she herself had any great power of further growth except through him. But linked to him she could keep pace with him. She could capture his senses, keep his conscience, uphold him. . . .

She had convinced herself now that that was her chief business in life.

Her mind was remarkably free from doubts about the future if once she could get at her Peter. Mountains and forests of use and wont separated them, she knew. Peter had acquired a habit of not making love to her and of separating her from the thought of love. But if ever Peter came over these mountains, if ever he came through the forest to her—— In the heart of the forest, she would keep him. She wasn't afraid that Peter would leave her again. Wilmington had been wrong there. That he had suggested

in the bitterness of his heart.   Men like Huntley and Winter.
baum were always astray, but Peter was not "looking for
women." He was just a lost man, distracted by desire,
desire that was strong because he was energetic, desire that
was mischievous and unmeaning because he had lost his way
in these things.

"I don't care so very much how long it takes, Peter; I
don't care what it costs me," said Joan, getting her rôle
clear at last. "I don't even care—not vitally anyhow—
how you wander by the way. No. Because you're my man,
Peter, and I am your woman. Because so it was written in
the beginning. But you are coming over those mountains,
my Peter, though they go up to the sky; you are coming
through the forests though I have to make a path for you.
You are coming to my arms, Peter . . . coming to me. . . ."

So Joan framed her schemes, regardless of the swift approach of the day of battle for Peter.   She was resolved to
lose nothing by neglect or delay, but also she meant to do
nothing precipitate.   To begin with she braced herself to
the disagreeable task of really thinking—instead of just feeling—about Hetty.   She compared herself deliberately point
by point with Hetty.   Long ago at Pelham Ford she had
challenged Hetty—and Peter had come out of the old library
in spite of Hetty to watch her dancing.   She was younger,
she was fresher and cleaner, she was a ray of sunlight to
Hetty's flames.   Hetty was good company—perhaps.   But
Peter and Joan had always been good company for each
other, interested in a score of common subjects, able to play
the same games and run abreast.   But Hetty was "easy."
There was her strength.   Between her and Peter there were
no barriers, and between Joan and Peter was a blank wall,
a stern taboo upon the primary among youthful interests, a
long habit of aloofness, dating from the days when "soppy"
was the ultimate word in the gamut of human scorn.

"It's just like that," said Joan.

Those barriers had to be broken down, without a shock.
And before that problem Joan maintained a frowning, un-
successful siege.   She couldn't begin to flirt with Peter.
She couldn't make eyes at him.   Such things would be intolerable.   She couldn't devise any sort of signal.   And so

how the devil was this business ever to begin? And while
she wrestled vainly with this perplexity she remained more
boyish, more good-fellow and companion with Peter than
ever. . . .

And while she was still meditating quite fruitlessly on
this riddle of changing her relationship to Peter, he was
snatched away from her to France.

The thing happened quite unexpectedly. He came up to
see her at Hampstead late in the afternoon—it was by a
mere chance she was back early. He was full of pride at
being chosen to go so soon. He seemed brightly excited at
going, keen for the great adventure, the most lovable and
animated of Peters—and he might be going to his death.
But it was the convention of the time never to think of
death, and anyhow never to speak of it. Some engagement
held him for the evening, some final farewell spree; she did
not ask too particularly what that was. She could guess
only too well. Altogether they were about five-and-twenty
minutes together, with Miss Jepson always in the room with
them; for the most part they talked air shop; and then he
prepared to leave with all her scheming still at loose ends in
the air. "Well," he said, "good-bye, old Joan," and held
out his hand.

"No," said Joan, with a sudden resolution in her eyes.
"This time we kiss, Peter."

"Well," said Peter, astonished.

She had surprised him. He stared at her for an instant
with a half-framed question in his eyes. And then they
kissed very gravely and carefully. But she kissed him on
the mouth.

For some seconds solemnity hung about them. Then Peter
turned upon Miss Jepson. "Do *you* want a kiss?" said
Peter. . . .

Miss Jepson was all for kissing, and then with a laugh
and an effect of escape Peter had gone . . . into the outer
world . . . into the outer air. . . .

§ 13

He flew to France the next day, above the grey and shining stretches of water and two little anxious ships, and he sent Joan a cheerful message on a picture-postcard of a shell-smashed church to tell of his safe arrival.

Joan was dismayed. In war time we must not brood on death, one does not think of death if one can help it; it is the chance that wrecks all calculations; but the fear of death had fallen suddenly upon all her plans. And what was there left now of all her plans? She might write him letters.

Death is more terrible to a girl in love than to any other living thing. "If he dies," said Joan, "I am killed. I shall be worse than a widow—an Indian girl widow. Suttee; what will be left of me but ashes? . . . Some poor dregs of Joan carrying on a bankrupt life. . . . No me. . ."

There was nothing for it but to write him letters. And Joan found those letters incredibly difficult to write. All lightness had gone from her touch. After long and tiring days with her car she sat writing and tearing up and beginning again. It was so difficult now to write to him, to be easy in manner and yet insidious. She wanted still to seem his old companion, and yet to hint subtly at the new state of things. "There's a dull feeling now you've gone out of England, Peter," she wrote. "I've never had company I cared for in all the world as I care for yours." And, "I shall count the days to your leave, Peter, as soon as I know how many to count. I didn't guess before that you were a sort of necessity to me." Over such sentences, sentences that must have an edge and yet not be too bold, sentences full of tenderness and above all suspicion of "soppiness," Joan pondered like a poet writing a sonnet. . . .

But letters went slowly, and life and death hustled along together very swiftly in the days of the great war. . . .

§ 14

Joan's mind was full of love and life and the fear of losing them, but Peter was thinking but little of love and life; he was secretly preoccupied with the thought, the forbidden thought, of death, and with the strangeness of war and of this earth seen from an aeroplane ten thousand feet or so above the old battlefields of mankind. He was seeing the world in plan, and realizing what a flat and shallow thing it was. On clear days the circuit of the world he saw had a circumference of hundreds of miles, night flying was a journey amidst the stars with the little black planet far away; there was no former achievement of the race that did not seem to him now like a miniature toy set out upon the floor of an untidy nursery. He had beaten up towards the very limits of life and air, to the clear thin air of twenty-two or twenty-three thousand feet; he had been in the blinding sunlight when everything below was still asleep in the blue of dawn.

And the world of history and romance, the world in which he and all his ancestors had believed, a world seen in elevation, of towering frontages, high portals, inaccessible dignities, giddy pinnacles and frowning reputations, had now fallen as flat, it seemed, as the façade of the Cloth Hall at Ypres. (He had seen that one day from above, spread out upon the ground.) He was convinced that high above the things of the past he droned his liquid way towards a new sort of life altogether, towards a greater civilization, a world-wide life for men with no boundaries in it at all except the emptiness of outer space, a life of freedom and exaltation and tremendous achievement. But meanwhile the old things of the world were trying most desperately to kill him. Every day the enemy's anti-aircraft guns seemed to grow more accurate; and high above the little fleecy clouds lurked the braggart Markheimer and the gallant von Papen and suchlike German champions, with their decoys below, ready to swoop and strike. Never before had the world promised Peter so tremendous a spectacle as it seemed to promise now, and never before had his hope of living to see it been so insecure.

When he had enlisted, and even after he had been transferred to the Flying Corps, Peter had thought very little of death. The thought of death only became prevalent in English minds towards the second year of the war. It is a

hateful and unnatural thought in youth, easily dismissed
altogether unless circumstances press it incessantly upon the
attention.   But even before Peter went to France two of his
set had been killed under his eyes in a collision as they came
down into the aerodrome, and a third he had seen two miles
away get into a spiral nose dive, struggle out of it again, and
then go down to be utterly smashed to pieces.   In one day
on Salisbury Plain he had seen three accidents, and two, he
knew, had been fatal and one had left a legless thing to
crawl through life.   The messes in France seemed populous
with young ghosts; reminiscences of sprees, talk of flying adventures were laced with, "dear old boy! he went west last
May."   "Went west" was the common phrase.   They never
said "killed."   They hated the very name of death.   They
did their best, these dear gallant boys, to make the end
seem an easy and familiar part of life, of life with which
they were so joyously in love.   They all knew that the dice
was loaded against them, and that as the war went on the
chances against them grew.   The first day Peter was out in
France he saw a man hit and brought down by a German
Archie.   Two days after, he found himself the centre of a
sudden constellation of whoofing shells that left inky cloud-
bursts over him and under him and round about him;
he saw the fabric of his wing jump and quiver, and
dropped six hundred feet or so to shake the gunner
off.   But *whuff* . . . *whuff* . . . *whuff*, like the bark of
a monstrous dog . . . the beast was on him again within a
minute, and Peter did two or three loops and came about and
got away with almost indecent haste.   He was trembling;
he hated it.   And he hated to tremble.

In the mess that evening the talk ran on the "Pigeon
shooter."   It seemed that there was this one German gunner far quicker and more deadly than any of his fellows.
He had a knack of divining what an airman was going to do.
Peter admitted his near escape and sought counsel.

Peter's colleagues watched him narrowly and unostenta-
tiously when they advised him.   Their faces were masks and
his face was a mask, and they were keen for the faintest intonation of what was behind it.   They all hated death, they
all tried not to think of death; they all believed that there

were Paladins, other fellows, who never thought of death at all. When the tension got too great they ragged; they smashed great quantities of furniture and made incredible volumes of noise. Twice Peter got away from the aerodrome to let things rip in Amiens. But such outbreaks were usually followed by a deep depression of spirit. In the night Peter would wake up and find the thought of death sitting by his bedside.

So far Peter had never had a fight. He had gone over the enemy lines five times, he had bombed a troop train in a station and a regiment resting in a village, he believed he had killed a score or more of Germans on each occasion and he felt not the slightest compunction, but he had not yet come across a fighting Hun plane. He had very grave doubts about the issue of such a fight, a fight that was bound to come sooner or later. He knew he was not such a quick pilot as he would like to be. He thought quickly, but he thought rather too much for rapid, steady decisions. He had the balancing, scientific mind. He knew that none of his flights were perfect. Always there was a conflict of intention at some point, a hesitation. He believed he might last for weeks or months, but he knew that somewhen he would be found wanting—just for a second perhaps, just in the turn of the fight. Then he would be killed. He hid quite successfully from all his companions, and particularly from his squadron commander, this conviction, just as he had previously hidden the vague funk that had invariably invaded his being whenever he walked across the grounds towards the machine during his days of instruction, but at the back of his mind the thought that his time was limited was always present. He believed that he had to die; it might be tomorrow or next week or next month, but somewhen within the year.

When these convictions became uppermost in Peter's mind a black discontent possessed him. There are no such bitter critics of life as the young; theirs is a magnificent greed for the splendour of life. They have no patience with delays; their blunders and failures are intolerable. Peter reviewed his two-and-twenty years—it was now nearly three-and-twenty—with an intense dissatisfaction. He had wasted his time, and now he had got into a narrow way that led down and down pitilessly to where there would be no more time to waste. He had been aimless and the world had been aimless, and then it had suddenly turned upon him and caught him in this lobster-trap. He had wasted all his chances of great experience. He had never loved a woman or had been well loved because he had frittered away that possibility in a hateful sex excitement with Hetty—who did not even pretend to be faithful to him. And now things had got into this spin to death. It was exactly like a spin—like a spinning nose dive—the whole affair, his life, this war. . . .

He would lie and fret in his bed, and fret all the more because he knew his wakefulness wasted the precious nervous vigour that might save his life next day.

After a black draught of such thoughts Peter would become excessively noisy and facetious in the mess tent. He was recognized and applauded as a wit and as a devil. He was really very good at Limericks, delicately indelicate, upon the names of his fellow officers and of the villages along the front—that was no doubt heredity, the gift of his Aunt Phyllis—and his caricatures adorned the mess. It was also understood that he was a rake. . . .

Peter's evil anticipations were only too well justified. He was put down in his very first fight, which happened over Dompierre. He had bad luck; he was struck by von Papen, one of the crack German fliers on that part of the front. He was up at ten thousand feet or so, more or less covering a low-flying photographer, when he saw a German machine coming over half a mile perhaps or more away as though it was looking for trouble. Peter knew he might funk a fight, and to escape that moral disaster, headed straight down for the German, who dropped and made off southward. Peter rejoicing at this flight, pursued, his eyes upon the quarry. Then from out of the sun came von Papen, swiftly and unsuspected, upon Peter's tail, and announced his presence by a whiff of bullets. Peter glanced over his shoulder to discover that he was caught.

"Oh damn!" cried Peter, and ducked his head, and felt himself stung at the shoulder and wrist. Splinters were flying about him.

He tried a side-slip, and as he did so he had an instant's vision of yet another machine, a Frenchman this time, falling like a bolt out of the blue upon his assailant. The biter was bit.

Peter tried to come round and help, but he turned right over sideways and dropped, and suddenly found himself with the second Hun plane coming up right ahead of him. Peter blazed away, but God! how his wrist hurt him! He cursed life and death. He blazed away with his machine going over more and more, and the landscape rushing up over his head and then getting in front of him and circling round. For some seconds he did not know what was up and what was down. He continued to fire, firing earthward for a long second or so after his second enemy had disappeared from his vision.

The world was spinning round faster and faster, and everything was moving away outward, faster and faster, as if it was all hastening to get out of his way. . . .

This surely was a spinning nose dive, the spinning nose dive—from within. Round and round. Confusing and giddy! Just as he had seen poor old Gordon go down. . . . But one didn't feel at all—as Peter had supposed one must feel—like an egg in an egg-whisk! . . .

Down spun the aeroplane, as a maple fruit in autumn spins to the ground. Then this still living thing that had been Peter, all bloody and broken, made a last supreme effort. And his luck seconded his effort. The spin grew slower and flatter. Control of this lurching, eddying aeroplane seemed to come back, escaped again, mocked him. The ground was very near. *Now!* The sky swung up over the whirling propeller again and stayed above it, and again the machine obeyed a reasonable soul.

He was out of it! Out of a nose dive! Yes. Steady! It is so easy when one's head is whirling to get back into a spin again. Steady! . . .

He talked to himself. "Oh! good Peter! *Good* Peter! *Clever* Peter. Wonderful Mr. Toad! Stick it! Stick it!" But what a queer right hand it was! It was covered with blood. And it crumpled up in the middle when he clenched it! Never mind!

He was in the lowest storey of the air. The Hun and the Frenchman up there were in another world.

Down below, quite close—not five hundred feet now—were field-greys running and shooting at him. They were counting their chicken before he was hatched—no, smashed. . . . He wasn't done yet! Not by any manner of means! A wave of great cheerfulness and confidence buoyed up Peter. He felt equal to any enterprise. Should he drop and let the bawling Boche have a round or so?

And there was a Hun machine smashed upside down on the ground. Was that the second fellow?

Flick! a bullet!

Wiser counsels came to Peter. This was no place for a sick and giddy man with a smashed and bleeding wrist. He must get away.

Up! Which way was west? West? The sun rises in the east and sets in the west. But where had the sun got to? It was hidden by his wing. Shadows! The shadows would be pointing north-east, that was the tip. . . . Up! There were the Boche trenches. No, Boche reserve trenches. . . . Going west, going west. . . . Rip! Snap! Bullet through the wing, and a wire flickering about. He ducked his head. . . . He put the machine up steeply to perhaps a thousand feet. . . .

He had an extraordinary feeling that he and the machine were growing and swelling, that they were getting bigger and bigger, and the sky and the world and everything else smaller. At last he was a monstrous man in a vast aeroplane in the tiniest of universes. He was as great as God.

That wrist! And this blood! Blood! And great, glowing spots of blood that made one's sight indistinct. . . .

He coughed, and felt his mouth full of blood, and spat it out and retched. . . .

Then in an instant he was a little thing again, and the sky and the world were immense. He had a lucid interval.

One ought to go up and help that Frenchman. Where were they fighting? . . . Up, anyhow!

This must be No Man's Land. That crumpled little thing was a dead body surely. Barbed wire. More barbed wire.

The engine was missing. Ugh! *That fairly put the lid on!*

Peter was already asleep and dreaming. The great blood spots had returned and increased, but now they were getting black, they were black, huge black blotches; they blotted out the world!

Peter, Peter as we have known him, discontinued existence. . . .

It was an automaton, aided by good luck, that dropped his machine half a mile behind the French trenches. . . .

§ 15

Peter had no memory of coming to again from his faint. For a long time he must have continued to be purely automatic. His flaming wrist was the centre of his being. Then for a time consciousness resumed, as abruptly as the thread of a story one finds upon the torn page of a novel.

He found himself in the midst of a friendly group of pale blue uniforms; he was standing up and being very lively in spite of the strong taste of blood in his mouth and a feeling that his wrist was burning as a match burns, and that the left upper half of his body had been changed into a lump of raw and bleeding meat. He was talking a sort of French. *"C'est sacré bon stuff, cet eau-de-vie Française,"* he was saying gaily and rather loudly.

"Haf some more," said a friendly voice.

"Not half, old chap," said Peter, and felt at the time that this was not really good French.

He tried to slap the man on the shoulder, but he couldn't.

"Bon!" he said, "as we say in England," and felt that that remark also failed.

Some one protested softly against his being given more brandy. . . .

Then this clear fragment ended again. There was a kind of dream of rather rough but efficient surgery upon a shoulder and arm that was quite probably his own, and some genially amiable conversation. There was a very nice

Frenchman with a black beard and soft eyes, who wore a long white overall, and seemed to be looking after him as tenderly as a woman could do.

But with these things mingled the matter of delirium. At one time the Kaiser prevailed in Peter's mind, a large, foolish, pompous person with waxed moustaches and distraught eyes, who crawled up to Peter over immense piles of white and grey and green rotting corpses, and began gnawing at his shoulder almost absent-mindedly. Peter struggled and protested. What business had this beastly German to come interfering with Peter's life? He started a vast argument about that, in which all sorts of people, including the nice-looking Frenchman in the white overall, took part.

Peter was now making a formal complaint about the conduct of the universe. "No," he insisted time after time, "I will not deal with subordinates. I insist on seeing the Head," and so at last he found himself in the presence of the Lord God. . . .

But Peter's vision of the Lord God was the most delirious thing of all. He imagined him in an office, a little office in a vast building, and so out of the way that people had to ask each other which was the passage and which the staircase. Old men stood and argued at corners with Peter's girl-guide whether it was this way or that. People were being shown over the building by girl-guides; it was very like the London War Office, only more so; there were great numbers of visitors, and they all seemed to be in considerable hurry and distress, and most of them were looking for the Lord God to lodge a complaint and demand an explanation, just as Peter was. For a time all the visitors became wounded men, and nurses mixed up with the girl-guides, and Peter was being carried through fresh air to an ambulance train. His shoulder and wrist were very painful and singing, as it were, a throbbing duet together.

For a time Peter did seem to see the Lord God; he was in his office, a little brown, rather tired-looking man in a kepi, and Peter was on a stretcher, and the Lord God or some one near him was saying: *"Quel numéro?"* But that passed away, and Peter was again conducting his exploration of the corridors with a girl-guide who was sometimes like Joan and

sometimes like Hetty—and then there was a queer disposition to loiter in the passages. . . . For a time he sat in dis-
habille while Hetty tried to explain God. . . . Dreams cross
the scent of dreams.

Then it seemed to Peter's fevered brain that he was sit-
ing, and had been sitting for a long time, in the little office
of the Lord God of Heaven and Earth. And the Lord God
had the likeness of a lean, tired, intelligent-looking oldish
man, with an air of futile friendliness masking a fundamental indifference.

"My dear sir," the Lord God was saying, "do please put
that cushion behind your poor shoulder. I can't bear to see
you so uncomfortable. And tell me everything. Everything. . . ."

The office was the dingiest and untidiest little office it was
possible to imagine. The desk at which God sat was in a
terrible litter. On a side table were some grubby test tubes
and bottles at which the Lord God had apparently been trying over a new element. The windows had not been cleaned
for ages, they were dark with spiders' webs, they crawled
with a buzzing nightmare of horrible and unmeaning life.
It was a most unbusinesslike office. There were no proper
files, no card indexes; bundles of dusty papers were thrust
into open fixtures, papers littered the floors, and there were
brass-handled drawers—. Peter looked again, and blood
was oozing from these drawers and little cries came out of
them. He glanced quickly at God, and God was looking at
him. "But did you really make this world?" he asked.

"I *thought* I did," said God.

"But why did you do it? *Why?*"

"Ah, *there* you have me!" said the Lord God with bon-
homie.

"But why don't you exert yourself?" said Peter, hammering at the desk with his sound hand. "Why don't you exert
yourself?"

Could delirium have ever invented a more monstrous conception than this of Peter hammering on an untidy desk
amidst old pen nibs, bits of sealing-wax, half-sheets of notepaper, returns of nature's waste, sample bones of projected
animals, mineral samples, dirty little test tubes, and the like,

and lecturing the Almighty upon the dreadful confusion into
which the world had fallen? "Here was I, sir, and millions like me, with a clear promise of life and freedom!
And what are we now? Bruises, red bones, dead bodies!
This German Kaiser fellow—an ass, sir, a perfect ass, gnawing a great hole in my shoulder! He and his son, stuffing
themselves with a Blut-Wurst made out of all our lives and
happiness! What does it mean, sir? Has it gone entirely
out of your control? And it isn't as if the whole thing was
ridiculous, sir. It isn't. In some ways it's an extraordinarily fine world—one has to admit that. That is why it is
all so distressing, so unendurably distressing. I don't in
the least want to leave it."

"You admit that it's fine—in places," said the Lord God,
as if he valued the admission.

"But the management, sir! the management! *Yours*—
ultimately. Don't you realize, sir——? I had the greatest
trouble in finding you. Half the messengers don't know
where this den of yours is. It's *forgotten*. Practically forgotten. The Head Office! And now I'm here I can tell
you everything is going to rack and ruin, driving straight to
an absolute and final smash and break-up."

"As bad as that?" said the Lord God.

"It's the appalling waste," Peter continued. "The waste
of material, the waste of *us*, the waste of everything. A sort
of splendour in it, there is; touches of real genius about it,
that I would be the last to deny; but that only increases the
bitterness of the disorder. It's a good enough world to
lament. It's a good enough life to resent having to lose it.
There's some lovely things in it, sir; courage, endurance, and
oh! many beautiful things. But when one gets here, when
one begins to ask for you and hunt about for you, and finds
this, this muddle, sir, then one begins to understand. *Look*
at this room, consider it—as a general manager's room. No
decency. No order. Everywhere the dust of ages, muck
indescribable, bacteria! And that!"

That was a cobweb across the grimy window pane, in
which a freshly entangled bluebottle fly was buzzing fussily.
"That ought not to be here at all," said Peter. "It really
ought not to exist at all. Why does it? Look at that beastly

spider in the corner!   Why do you suffer all these cruel and
unclean things?''

"You don't like it?'' said the Lord God, without any sign
either of apology or explanation.

"No,'' said Peter .

"Then *change* it,'' said the Lord God, nodding his head
as who should say "got you there.''

"But how are we to change it?''

"If you have no will to change it, you have no right to
criticize it,'' said the Lord God, leaning back with the weari-
ness of one who has had to argue with each generation from
Job onward, precisely the same objections and precisely the
same arguments.

"After all,'' said the Lord God, giving Peter no time to
speak further; "after all, you are three-and-twenty, Mr.
Peter Stubland, and you've been pretty busy complaining
of me and everything between me and you, your masters,
pastors, teachers, and so forth, for the last half-dozen years.
Meanwhile, is your own record good?   Positive achievements,
forgive me, are still to seek.   You've been nearly drunk several times, you've soiled yourself with a lot of very cheap
and greedy love-making—I gave you something beautiful
there anyhow, and you knew that while you spoilt it—you've
been a vigorous member of the consuming class, and really,
you've got nothing clear and planned, nothing at all.   You
complain of my lack of order; where's the order in your own
mind?   If I was the hot-tempered old autocrat some of you
people pretend I am, I should have been tickling you up with
a thunderbolt long ago.   But I happen to have this democratic fad as badly as any one—Free Will is what they used
to call it—and so I leave you to work out your own salva-
tion.   And if I leave you alone then I have to leave that
other—that other Mr. Toad at Potsdam alone.   He tries me,
I admit, almost to the miracle pitch at times with the tone
of his everlasting prepaid telegrams—but one has to be fair.
What is sauce for the goose is sauce for the Kaiser.   I've got
to leave you all alone if I leave one alone.   Don't you see
that?   In spite of the mess you are in.   So don't blame me.
Don't blame me.   There isn't a thing in the whole of this
concern of mine that Man can't control if only he chooses to

control it. It's arranged like that. There's a lot more system here than you suspect, only it's too ingenious for you to
see. It's yours to command. If you want a card index
for the world—well, get a card index. I won't prevent you.
If you don't like my spiders, kill my spiders. I'm not conceited about them. If you don't like the Kaiser, hang him,
assassinate him. Why don't you abolish Kings? You could.
But it was your sort, with your cheap and quick efficiency
schemes, who set up Saul—in spite of my protests—ages ago.
. . . Humanity either makes or breeds or tolerates all its own
afflictions, great and small. Not my doing. Take Kings and
Courts. Take dungheaps and flies. It's astonishing you
people haven't killed off all the flies in the world long ago.
They do no end of mischief, and it would be perfectly easy to
do. They're purely educational. Purely. Even as you lie
in hospital, there they are buzzing within an inch of your
nose and landing on your poor forehead to remind you of
what a properly organized humanity could do for its own
comfort. But there's men in this world who want me to act
as a fly-paper, simply because they are too lazy to get one
for themselves. My dear Mr. Peter! if people haven't taught
you properly, teach yourself. If they don't know enough,
find out. It's all here. All here." He made a comprehensive gesture. "I'm not mocking you."

"You're not mocking me?" said Peter keenly. . . .

"It depends upon you," said the Lord God with an enig-
matic smile. "You asked me why I didn't exert myself.
Well—why don't *you* exert yourself?

"Why don't *you* exert yourself?" the Lord God repeated
almost rudely, driving it home.

"That pillow under your shoulder still isn't comfortable,"
said the Lord God, breaking off. . . .

The buzzing of the entangled fly changed to the drone of a
passing aeroplane, and the dingy office expanded into a hospital ward. Some one was adjusting Peter's pillows. . . .

§ 16

If his shoulder-blade was to mend, Peter could not be
moved; and for a time he remained in the French hospital

in a long, airy room that was full mostly with flying men like himself. At first he could not talk very much, but later he made some friends. He was himself very immobile, but other men came and sat by him to talk.

He talked chiefly to two Americans, who were serving at that time in the French flying corps. He found it much easier to talk English than French in his exhausted state, for though both he and Joan spoke French far above the average public school level, he found that now it came with an effort. It was as if his mind had for a time been pared down to its essentials.

These Americans amused and interested him tremendously. He had met hardly any Americans before so as to talk to them at all intimately, but they suffered from an inhibition of French perhaps more permanent than his own, and so the three were thrown into an unlimited intimacy of conversation. At first he found these Americans rather fatiguing, and then he found them very refreshing because of their explicitness of mind. Except when they broke into frothy rapids of slang they were never allusive; in serious talk they said everything. They laid a firm foundation for all their assertions. That is the last thing an Englishman does. They talked of the war and of the prospect of America coming into the war, and of England and America and again of the war, and of the French and of the French and Americans and of the war, and of Taft's League to Enforce Peace and the true character of Wilson and Teddy and of the war, and of Sam Hughes and Hughes the Australian, and whether every country has the Hughes it deserves and of the war, and of going to England after the war, and of Stratford-on-Avon and Chester and Windsor, and of the peculiarities of English people. Their ideas of England Peter discovered were strange and picturesque. They believed all Englishmen lived in a glow of personal loyalty to the Monarch, and were amazed to learn that Peter's sentiments were republican; and they thought that every Englishman dearly loved a lord. "We think that of Americans," said Peter. "That's our politeness," said they in a chorus, and started a train of profound discoveries in international relationships in Peter's mind.

"The ideas of every country about every country are necessarily a little stale. What England is, what England thinks, and what England is becoming, isn't on record. What is on record is the England of the 'eighties and 'nineties."

"Now, that's very true," said the nearer American. "And you can apply it right away, with a hundred per cent. or so added, to all your ideas of America."

As a consequence both sides in this leisurely discussion found how widely they had been out in their ideas about each other. Peter discovered America as not nearly so commercial and individualistic as he had supposed; he had been altogether ignorant of the increasing part the universities were playing in her affairs; the Americans were equally edified to find that the rampant imperialism of Cecil Rhodes and his group no longer ruled the British imagination. "If things are so," said the diplomatist in the nearer bed, "then I seem to see a lot more coming together between us than I've ever been disposed to think possible before. If you British aren't so keen over this king business——"

"*Keen!*" said Peter.

"If you don't hold you are IT and unapproachable—in the way of Empires."

"The Empire is yours for the asking," said Peter.

"Then all there is between us is the Atlantic—and that grows narrower every year. We're the same people."

"So long as we have the same languages and literature," said Peter. . . .

From these talks onward Peter may be regarded as having a Foreign Policy of his own.

§ 17

And it was in this hospital that Peter first clearly decided to become personally responsible for the reconstruction of the British Empire.

This decision was precipitated by the sudden reappearance in his world of Mir Jelalludin, the Indian whom he had once thought unsuitable company for Joan.

Peter had been dozing when Jelalludin appeared. He found him sitting beside the bed, and stared at the neat and smiling brown face, unable to place him, and still less able to account for the uniform he was wearing. For Jelalludin was wearing the uniform of the French aviator, and across his breast he wore four palms.

"I had the pleasure of knowing you at Cambridge," said Mir Jelalludin in his Indian staccato. "Cha'med I was of use to you."

An explanatory Frenchman standing beside the Indian dabbed his finger on the last of Jelalludin's decorations. "He killed von Papen after your crash," said the Frenchman.

"You were that Frenchman——?" said Peter.

"In your fight," said Mir Jelalludin.

"He'd have finished me," said Peter.

"I finished *him*," said the Indian, laughing with sheer happiness, and showing his beautiful teeth.

Peter contemplated the situation. He made a movement and was reminded of his bandages.

"I wish I could shake hands," he said.

The Indian smiled with a phantom malice in his smile.

Peter went bluntly to a question that had arisen in his mind. "Why aren't you in khaki?" he asked.

"The Brish' Gu'ment objects to Indian flyers," said Mir Jelalludin. "I tried. But Brish' Gu'ment thinks flying beyond us. And bad for Prestige. Prestige very important thing to Brish' Gu'ment. So I came to France."

Peter continued to digest the situation.

"Of course," said Jelalludin, "no commissions given in regular army to Indians. Brish' soldiers not allowed to s'lute Indian officers. Not part of the Great White Race. Otherwise hundreds of flyers could come from India, hundreds and hundreds. We play cricket—good horsemen. Many Indian gentlemen must be first-rate flying stuff. But Gu'ment says 'No.' "

He continued to smile more cheerfully than ever.

"Hundreds of juvenile Indians ready and willing to be killed for your Empire"—he rubbed it in—"but—No, Thank You. Indo-European people we are, Aryans, more consan-

guineous than Jews or Japanese. Ready to take our places
beside you. . . . Well, anyhow, I rejoice to see that you are
recovering to entire satisfaction. It was only when I descended after the fight that I perceived that it was you, and
it seemed to me then that you were very seriously injured.
I was anxious. And mem'ries of otha days. I felt I must
see you."

Peter and the young Indian looked at one another.

"Look here, Jelalludin," he said, "I must apologize."

"But why?"

"As part of the British Empire. No! don't interrupt.
I do. But, I say, do they—do we really bar you—absolutely?"

"Absolutely. Not only from the air force, but from any
commission at all. The lowest little bazaar clerk from Clap-
ham, who has got a commission, is over our Indian officers—
over our princes. It is an everlasting humiliation. Necessary for Prestige."

"The French have more sense, anyhow."

"They take us on our merits.

"If I *had* a British commission," said Jelalludin, "I should
be made very uncomfortable. It is the way with British
officers and gentlemen. The French are not so—particular."

"At present," said Peter, "I can't be moved."

"You improve."

"But when I get up this is one of the things I have to
see to. You see, Jelalludin, this Empire of ours—yours and
mine—has got into the hands of a gang of gory Old Fools.
Partly my negligence—as God said."

"God?" said Jelalludin.

"Oh, nothing! I mean we young men haven't been given
a proper grasp of the Indian situation. Or any situation.
No. This business of the commissions——! after all that
you fellows have done here in France! It's disgraceful.
You see, we don't see or learn anything about India. Even
at Cambridge——"

"You didn't see much of us there," smiled the Indian.

"I'm sorry," said Peter.

"I didn't come to talk about this," said Jelalludin, "it
came out."

"I'm glad it came out," said Peter.

A pause.

"I mustn't tire you," said Mir Jelalludin, and rose to go. Peter thanked him for coming.

"And your cha'ming sister?" asked the Indian, as if by an afterthought.

"Foster sister. She drives a big car about London," said Peter. . . .

Peter meditated profoundly upon that interview for some days.

Then he tried over the opinions of the Americans about India. But Americans are of little help to the British about India. Their simple uncriticized colour prejudice covers all "Asiatics" except the inhabitants of Siberia. They had a more than English ignorance of ethnology, and Oswald had at least imparted some fragments of that important science to his ward. Their working classification of mankind was into Anglo-Saxons, Frenchmen, Sheenies, Irishmen, Dutchmen, Dagoes, Chinks, Coloured People, and black Niggers. They esteemed Mir Jelalludin a Coloured Person. Peter had to fall back upon himself again.

§ 18

It contributed to the thoroughness of Peter's thinking that it was some time before he could be put into a position to read comfortably. And it has to be recorded in the teeth of the dictates of sentiments and the most sacred traditions of romance that the rôle played by both Joan and Hetty in these meditations was secondary and incidental. It was an attenuated and abstract Peter who lay in the French hospital, his chief link of sense with life was a growing hunger; he thought very much about fate, pain, the nature of things, and God, and very little about persons and personal incidents—and so strong an effect had his dream that God remained fixed steadfastly in his mind as that same intellectual non-interventionist whom he had visited in the fly-blown office. But about God's rankling repartee, "Why don't *you* exert yourself?" there was accumulating a new conception,

the conception of Man taking hold of the world, unassisted
by God but with the acquiescence of God, and in fulfilment
of some remote, incomprehensible planning on the part of
God. Probably Peter in thinking this was following one
of the most ancient and well-beaten of speculative paths,
but it seemed to him that it was a new way of thinking.
And he was Man. It was he who had to establish justice in
the earth, achieve unity, and rule first the world and then
the stars.

He lay staring at the ceiling, and quite happy now that
healing and habituation had freed him from positive pain,
thinking out how he was to release and co-operate with his
India, which had invariably the face of Mir Jelalludin, how
he was to reunite himself with his brothers in America, and
how the walls and divisions of mankind, which look so high
and invincible upon the ground and so trivial from twelve
thousand feet above, were to be subdued to such greater ends.

It was only as the blood corpuscles multiplied inside him
that Peter ceased to be constantly Man contemplating his
Destiny and Races and Empires, and for more and more
hours in the day shrank to the dimensions and natural
warmth of Mr. Peter Stubland contemplating convalescence
in Blighty. He became eager first for the dear old indulgent
and welcoming house at Pelham Ford, and then for prowls
and walks and gossip with Joan and Oswald, and then, then
for London and a little "fun." Life was ebbing back into
what is understood to be the lower nature, and was certainly
the most intimate and distinctive substance of Mr. Peter
Stubland. His correspondence became of very great interest to him. Certain letters from Joan, faint but pursuing,
had reached him, those letters over which Joan had sat like
a sonneteer. He read them and warmed to them. He
thought what luck it was that he had a Joan to be the best
of sisters to him, to be even more than a sister. She was the
best friend he had, and it was jolly to read so plainly that
he was her best friend. He would like to do work with Joan
better than with any man he knew. Driving a car wasn't
half good enough for her. Some day he'd be able to show
her how to fly, and he would. It would be great fun going
up with Joan on a double control and letting her take over.

There must be girls in the world who would fly as well as any man, or better.

He scribbled these ideas in his first letter to Joan, and they pleased her mightily. To fly with Peter would be surely to fly straight into heaven.

And mixed up with Joan's letters were others that he presently sorted out from hers and put apart, as though even letters might hold inconvenient communion. For the most part they came from Hetty Reinhart, and displayed the emotions of a consciously delicious female enamoured and enslaved by one of the heroes of the air. She had dreamt of him coming in through the skylight of her studio, Lord Cupid visiting his poor little Psyche—"but it was only the moonlight," and she thought of him now always with great overshadowing wings. Sometimes they were great white wings that beat above her, and sometimes they were thrillingly soft and exquisite wings, like the wings of the people in *Peter Wilkins*. She sent him a copy of *Peter Wilkins*, book beloved by Poe and all readers of the fantastic. Then came the news of his smash. She had been clever enough to link it with the death of von Papen, the Hun Matador. "Was that your fight, dear Peterkins? Did you *begin* on Goliath?" As the cordials of recovery raced through Peter's veins there were phases when the thought of visiting the yielding fair, Jovelike and triumphant in winged glory, became not simply attractive but insistent. But he wrote to Hetty modestly, "They've clipped one wing for ever."

And so in a quite artless and inevitable way Peter found his first leave, when the British hospital had done with him, mortgaged up to hilt almost equally to dear friend Joan and to Cleopatra Hetty.

The young man only realized the duplicity of his nature and the complications of his position as the hospital boat beat its homeward way across the Channel. The night was smooth and fine, with a high full moon which somehow suggested Hetty, and with a cloud scheme of great beauty and distinction that had about it a flavour of Joan. And as he meditated upon these complications that had been happening in his more personal life while his attention had been still largely occupied with divinity and politics, he was

hailed by an unfamiliar voice and addressed as "Simon
Peter." "Excuse me," said the stout young officer tucked
up warmly upon the next deck chair between a pair of
crutches, "but aren't you Simon Peter?"

Peter had heard that name somewhere before. "My
name's Stubland," he said.

"Ah! Stubland! I forgot your surname. Of High
Cross School?"

Peter peered and saw a round fair face that slowly recalled memories. "Wait a moment!" said Peter. . . .
"*Ames!*"

"Guessed it in one. Probyn and I were chums."

"What have you got?" said Peter.

"Leg below the knee off, damn it!" said Ames. "One
month at the front. Not much of a career. But they say
they do you a leg now better than reality. But I'd have liked
to have batted the pants of the unspeakable Hun a bit more
before I retired. What have you got?"

"Wrist chiefly and shoulder-blade. Air fight. After six
weeks."

"Does you out?"

"For flying, I'm afraid. But there's lots of ground jobs.
And anyhow—home's pleasant."

"Yes," said Ames. "Home's pleasant. But I'd like to
have got a scalp of some sort. Doubt if I killed a single
Hun. D'you remember Probyn at school?—a dark chap."

Peter found he still hated Probyn. "I remember him,"
he said.

"He's killed. He got the M.M. and the V.C. He
wouldn't take a commission. He was sergeant-major in my
battalion. I just saw him, but I've heard about him since.
His men worshipped him. Queer how men come out in a
new light in this war."

"How was he killed?" asked Peter.

"In a raid. He was with a bombing party, and three men
straggled up a sap and got cornered. He'd taken two machine-guns and they'd used most of the bombs, and his officer
was knocked out, so he sent the rest of his party back with
the stuff and went to fetch his other men. One had been hit
and the other two were thinking of surrendering when he

came back to them. He stood right up on the parados, they
say, and slung bombs at the Germans, a whole crowd of them,
until they went back. His two chaps got the wounded man
out and carried him back, and left him still slinging bombs.
He'd do that. He'd stand right up and bung bombs at
them until they seemed to lose their heads. Then he seems
to have spotted that this particular bunch of Germans had
gone back into a sort of blind alley. He was very quick at
spotting a situation, and he followed them up, and the sheer
blank recklessness of it seems to have put their wind up absolutely. They'd got bombs and there was an officer with
them. But they held up their hands—nine of them. Panic.
He got them right across to our trenches before the searchlights found him, and the Germans got him and two of their
own chaps with a machine-gun. That was just the last thing
he did. He'd been going about for months doing stunts
like that—sort of charmed life business. The way he slung
bombs, they say, amounted to genius.

 "They say he'd let his hair grow long—perfect golliwog.
When I saw him it certainly *was* long, but he'd got it plas-
tered down. And there's a story that he used to put white
on his face like a clown with a great red mouth reaching
from ear to ear—— Yes, painted on. It's put the Huns'
wind up something frightful. Coming suddenly on a chap
like that in the glare of a searchlight or a flare.''

"Queer end,'' said Peter.

"Queer chap altogether,'' said Ames. . . .

He thought for a time, and then went on to philosophize
about Probyn.

"Clever chap he was,'' said Ames, "but an absolute failure. Of course old High Cross wasn't anything very much
in the way of a school, but whatever there was to be learnt
there he learnt. He was the only one of us who ever got
hold of speaking French. I heard him over there—regular
fluent. And he'd got a memory like an encyclopædia. I
always said he'd do wonders. . . .''

Ames paused. "Sex was his downfall,'' said Ames.

"I saw a lot of him altogether, off and on, right up to
the time of the war,'' said Ames. "My people are furniture people, you know, in Tottenham Court Road, and his

were in the public-house fitting line—in Highbury. We went about together. I saw him make three or four good starts, but there was always some trouble. I suppose most of us were a bit—well, *keen* on sex; most of us young men. But he was ravenous. Even at school. Always on it. Always thinking about it. I could tell you stories of him. . . . Rum place that old school was, come to think of it. They left us about too much. I don't know how far you——. . . . Of course you were about the most innocent thing that ever came to High Cross School," said Ames.

"Yes," said Peter. "I suppose I was."

"Curious how it gnaws at you once it's set going," said Ames. . . .

Peter made a noise that might have been assent.

Ames remained thinking for a time, watching the swish and surge of the black Channel waters. Peter pursued their common topic in silence.

"What's the sense of it?" said Ames, plunging towards philosophy.

"It's the system on which life goes—on this planet," Peter contributed, but Ames had not had a biological training, and was unprepared to take that up.

"Too much of it," said Ames.

"Over-sexed," said Peter.

"Whether one ought to hold oneself in or let oneself go," said Ames. "But perhaps these things don't bother you?"

Peter wasn't disposed towards confidences with Ames. "I'm moderate in all things," he said.

"Lucky chap! I've worried about this business no end. One doesn't want to use up all one's life like a blessed monkey. There's other things in life—if only this everlasting want-a-girl want-a-woman would let one get at them."

His voice at Peter's shoulder ceased for a while, and then resumed. "It's the best chaps, seems to me, who get it worst. Chaps with imaginations, I mean, men of vitality. Take old Probyn. He could have done anything—anything. And he was eaten up. Like a fever. . . .''

Ames went down into a black silence for a couple of minutes or more, and came up again with an astonishing resolution. "I shall marry," he said.

"Got the lady?" asked Peter.

"Near enough," said Ames darkly.

"St. Paul's method," said Peter.

"I was talking to a fellow the other day," said Ames. "He'd got a curious idea. Something in it perhaps. He said that every one was clean-minded and romantic, that's how he put it, about sixteen or seventeen. Even if you've been a bit dirty as a schoolboy you sort of clean up then. Adolescence, in fact. And he said you ought to fall in love and pair off then. Kind of Romeo and Juliet business. First love and all that."

"Juliet wasn't exactly Romeo's first love," said Peter.

"Young beggar!" said Ames. "But, anyhow, that was only by way of illustration. His idea was that we'd sort of put off marriage and all that sort of thing later and later. Twenty-eight. Thirty. Thirty-five even. And that put us wrong. We kind of curdled and fermented. Spoilt with keeping. Larked about with girls we didn't care for. Demi-vierge stunts and all that. Got promiscuous. Let anything do. His idea was you'd got to pair off with a girl and look after her, and she look after you. And keep faith. And stop all stray mucking about. 'Settle down to a healthy sexual peace,' he said."

Ames paused. "Something in it?"

"Ever read the Life of Lord Herbert of Cherbury?" asked Peter.

"Never."

"He worked out that theory quite successfully. Married before he went up to Oxford. There's a lot in it. Sex. Delayed. Fretting. Overflowing. Getting experimental and nasty. . . . But that doesn't exhaust the question. The Old Experimenter sits there——"

"*What* experimenter?"

"The chap who started it all. There's no way yet of fitting it up perfectly. We've got to make it fit."

Peter was so interested that he forgot his aversion from confiding in Ames. The subject carried him on.

"Any healthy young man," Peter generalized, "could be happy and contented with any pretty girl, so far as love-making goes. It doesn't strike you—as a particularly recon-

dite art, eh? But you've got to be in love with each other
generally. That's more difficult. You've got to talk together and go about together. In a complicated artificial
world. The sort of woman it's easy and pleasant to make
love to, may not be the sort of woman you really think
splendid. It's easier to make love to a woman you
don't particularly respect, who's good fun, and all that.
Which is just the reason why you wouldn't be tied up with
her for ever. No."

"So we worship the angels and marry the flappers," said
Ames. . . . "I shan't do that, anyhow. The fact is, one
needs a kind of motherliness in a woman."

"By making love too serious, we've made it not serious
enough," said Peter with oracular profundity, and then in
reaction, "Oh! I don't know."

"I don't know," said Ames.

"Which doesn't in the least absolve us from the necessity
of going on living right away."

"I shall marry," said Ames, in a tone of unalterable resolve.

They lapsed into self-centred meditations. . . .

"Why! there's the coast," said Ames suddenly. "Quite
close, too. *Dark*. Do you remember, before the war, how
the lights of Folkestone used to run along the top there like
a necklace of fire?"

§ 19

The powers that were set over Peter's life played fast and
loose with him in the matter of leave. They treated him
at first as though he was a rare and precious hero—who had
to be saved from his friends. They put him to mend at
Broadstairs, and while he was at Broadstairs he had three
visits from Hetty, whose days were free, and only one hasty
Sunday glimpse of Joan, who was much in demand at the
Ministry of Munitions. And Oswald could not come to see
him because Oswald himself was a casualty mending slowly
at Pelham Ford. Hetty and Joan and returning health
fired the mind of Peter with great expectations of the leave

that was to come. These expectations were, so to speak, painted in panels. Forgetful of the plain fact that a Joan who was not available at Broadstairs would also not be available at Pelham Ford, the panels devoted to the latter place invariably included Joan as a principal figure, they represented leave as a glorious escape from war to the space, the sunshine, the endlessness of such a summer vacation as only schoolboys know. He would be climbing trees with Joan, "mucking about" in the boats with Joan, lying on the lawn just on the edge of the cedar's shadow with Joan, nibbling stems of grass. The London scenes were narrower and more intense. He wanted the glitter and fun of lunching in the Carlton grill-room or dining at the Criterion, in the company of a tremendous hat and transparent lace, and there were scenes in Hetty's studio, quite a lot of fantastic and elemental scenes in Hetty's studio.

But the Germans have wiped those days of limitless leisure out of the life of mankind. Even our schoolboys stay up in their holidays now to make munitions. Peter had scarcely clambered past the approval of a medical board before active service snatched him again. He was wanted urgently. Peter was no good as a pilot any more, it was true; his right wrist was doomed to be stiff and weak henceforth, and there were queer little limitations upon the swing of his arm, but the powers had suddenly discovered other uses for him. There was more of Peter still left than they had assumed at first. For one particular job, indeed, he was just the man they needed. They docked him a wing—it seemed in mockery of the state of his arm—and replaced the two wings that had adorned him by one attached to the letter O, and they marked him down to join "balloons" at the earliest possible moment, for just then they were developing kite balloons very fast for artillery observation, and were eager for any available men. Peter was slung out into freedom for one-and-twenty days, and then told to report himself for special instruction in the new work at Richmond Park.

One-and-twenty days! He had never been so inordinately greedy for life, free to live and go as you please, in all his days before. Something must happen, he was resolved, something bright and intense, on every one of those days. He

snatched at both sides of life. He went down to Pelham
Ford, but he had a little list of engagements in town in his
pocket. Joan was not down there, and never before had he
realized how tremendously absent Joan could be. And then
at the week-end she couldn't come. There were French and
British G.H.Q. bigwigs to take down to some experiments in
Sussex, but she couldn't even explain that, she had to send a
telegram at the eleventh hour: *"Week-end impossible."*
To Peter that seemed the most brutally offhand evasion in
the world. Peter was disappointed in Pelham Ford. It was
altogether different from those hospital dreams; even the
weather, to begin with, was chilly and unsettled. Oswald
had had a set-back with his knee, and had to keep his leg
up on a deck chair; he could only limp about on crutches.
He seemed older and more distant from Peter than he had
ever been before; Peter was obsessed by the idea that he
ought to be treated with solicitude, and a further gap was
opened between them by Peter's subaltern habit of saying
"Sir" instead of the old familiar "Nobby." Peter sat beside the deck chair through long and friendly, but very impatient hours; and he talked all the flying shop he could,
and Oswald talked of his Africans, and they went over the
war and newspapers again and again, and they reverted to
Africa and flying shop, and presently they sat through several silences, and at the end of one of them Oswald inquired:
"Have you ever played chess, Peter—or piquet?"

Now chess and piquet are very good pastimes in their way,
but not good enough for the precious afternoons of a very
animated and greedy young man keenly aware that they are
probably his last holiday afternoons on earth.

Sentiment requires that Peter should have gone to London
and devoted himself to adorning the marginal freedom of
Joan's days. He did do this once. He took her out to dinner to Jules', in Jermyn Street; he did her well there; but
she was a very tired Joan that day; she had driven a good
hundred and fifty miles, and, truth to tell, in those days
Peter did not like Joan and she did not like herself in London, and more especially in smart London restaurants.
They sat a little aloof from one another, and about them
all the young couples warmed to another and smiled. She

jarred with this atmosphere of meretricious ease and indulgence. She had had no time to get back to Hampstead and change; she was at a disadvantage in her uniform. It became a hair shirt, a Nessus shirt as the evening proceeded. It emphasized the barrier of seriousness between them cruelly. She was a policeman, a prig, the harshest thing in life; all those pretty little cocottes and flirts, with their little soft brightnesses and adornments, must be glancing at her coarse, unrevealing garments and noting her for the fool she was. She felt ugly and ungainly; she was far too much tormented by love to handle herself well. She could get no swing and forgetfulness into the talk. And about Peter, too, was a reproach for her. He talked of work and the war—as if in irony. And his eyes wandered. Naturally, his eyes wandered.

"Good-night, old Peter," she said when they parted.

She lay awake for two hours, exasperated, miserable beyond tears, because she had not said: "Good night, old Peter *dear*." She had intended to say it. It was one of her prepared effects. But she was a weary and a frozen young woman. Duty had robbed her of the energy for love. Why had she let things come to this pass? Peter was her business, and Peter alone. She damned the Woman's Legion, Woman's Part in the War, and all the rest of it, with fluency and sincerity.

And while Joan wasted the hours of sleep in this fashion Peter was also awake thinking over certain schemes he had discussed with Hetty that afternoon. They involved some careful and deliberate lying. The idea was that for the purposes of Pelham Ford he should terminate his leave on the fourteenth instead of the twenty-first, and so get a clear week free—for life in the vein of Hetty.

He lay fretting, and the hot greed of youth persuaded him, and the clean honour of youth reproached him. And though he knew the way the decision would go, he tossed about and damned as heartily as Joan.

He could not remember if at Pelham Ford he had set a positive date to his leave, but, anyhow, it would not be difficult to make out that there had been some sort of urgent call. . . . It could be done. . . . The alternative was Piquet.

Peter returned to Pelham Ford and put his little fabric of lies upon Oswald without much difficulty. Then at the week-end came Joan, rejoicing. She came into the house tumultuously; she had caught a train earlier than the one they had expected her to come by. "I've got all next week. Seven days, Petah! Never mind how, but I've got it. I've got it!"

There was a suggestion as of some desperate battle away there in London from which Joan had snatched these fruits of victory. She was so radiantly glad to have them that Peter recoiled from an immediate reply.

"I didn't seem to see you in London somehow," said Joan. "I don't think you were really there. Let's have a look at you, old Petah. Tenshun! . . . Lift the arm. . . . Rotate the arm. . . . It isn't so bad, Petah, after all. Is tennis possible?"

"I'd like to try."

"Boats certainly. No reason why we shouldn't have two or three long walks. A week's a long time nowadays."

"But I have to go back on Monday," said Peter.

Joan stood stock still.

"Pity, isn't it?" said Peter weakly.

"But why?" she asked at last in a little flat voice.

"I have to go back."

"But your leave——?"

"Ends on Monday," lied Peter.

For some moments it looked as though Joan meant to make that last week-end a black one. "That doesn't give us much time together," said Joan, and her voice which had soared now crawled the earth. . . . "I'm sorry."

Just for a moment she hung, a dark and wounded Joan, downcast and thoughtful; and then turned and put her arms akimbo, and looked at him and smiled awry. "Well, old Peter, then we've got to make the best use of our time. It's your Birf Day, sort of; it's your Bank Holiday, dear; it's every blessed thing for you—such time as we have together. Before they take you off again. I think they're greedy, but it can't be helped. Can it, Peter?"

"It can't be helped," said Peter. "No."

They paused.

"What shall we do?" said Joan. "The program's got to be cut down. Shall we still try tennis?"

"I want to. I don't see why this wrist——" He held it out and rotated it.

"Good old arm!" said Joan, and ran a hand along it.

"I'll go and change these breeches and things," said Joan. "And get myself female. Gods, Peter! the craving to get into clothes that are really flexible and translucent!"

She went to the staircase and then turned on Peter.

"Peter," she said.

"Yes."

"Go out and stand on the lawn and tighten up the net. Now."

"Why?"

"Then I can see you from my window while I'm changing. I don't want to waste a bit of you."

She went up four steps and stopped and looked at him over her shoulder.

"I want as much as I can get of you, Petah," she said.

"I wish I'd known about that week," said Peter stupidly.

"*Exactly!*" said Joan to herself, and flitted up the staircase.

§ 20

Joan, Mrs. Moxton perceived that afternoon, had a swift and angry fight with her summer wardrobe. Both the pink gingham and the white drill had been tried on and flung aside, and she had decided at last upon a rather jolly warm blue figured voile with a belt of cherry-coloured ribbon that suited her brown skin and black hair better than those weaker supports. She had evidently opened every drawer in her room in a hasty search for white silk stockings.

When she came out into the sunshine of the garden Peter's eyes told her she had guessed the right costume.

Oswald was standing up on his crutches and smiling, and Peter was throwing up a racquet and catching it again with one hand.

"Thank God for a left-handed childhood!" said Peter. "I'm going to smash you, Joan."

"I forgot about that," said Joan. "But you aren't going to smash me, old Petah."

When tea-time came they were still fighting the seventh vantage game, and Joan was up.

They came and sat at the tea-table, and Joan as she poured the tea reflected that a young man in white flannels, flushed and a little out of breath, with his white silk shirt wide open at the neck, was a more beautiful thing than the most beautiful woman alive. And her dark eyes looked at the careless and exhausted Peter, that urgent and insoluble problem, while she counted, "Twenty-four, thirty-six, forty-one— about forty-one hours. How the devil shall I do it?"

It wasn't to be done at tennis anyhow, and she lost the next three games running without apparent effort, and took Peter by the arm and walked him about the garden, discoursing on flying. "I must teach you to fly," said Peter. "Often when I've been up alone I've thought, 'Some day I'll teach old Joan.'"

"That's a promise, Petah."

"Sure," said Peter, who had not suffered next to two Americans for nothing."

"I've got it in writing," said Joan.

"I'd rather learn from you than any one," said she.

Peter discoursed of stunts. . . .

They spent a long golden time revisiting odd corners in which they had played together. They went down the village and up to the church and round the edge of the wood, and there they came upon and devoured a lot of blackberries, and then they went down to the mill pond and sat for a time in Baker's boat. Then they got at cross purposes about dressing for dinner. Joan wanted to dress very much. She wanted to remind Peter that there were prettier arms in the world than Hetty Reinhart's, and a better modelled neck and shoulders. She had a new dress of ivory silk with a broad belt of velvet that echoed the bright softness of her eyes and hair. But Peter would not let her dress. He did not want to dress himself. "And you couldn't look prettier, Joan, than you do in that blue thing. It's so *like* you."

And as Joan couldn't explain that the frock kept her a jolly girl he knew while the dress would have shown him the beautiful woman he had to discover, she lost that point in the game. And tomorrow was Sunday, when Pelham Ford after the good custom of England never dressed for dinner.

Afterwards she thought how easily she might have over-ruled him.

Joan's plans for the evening were dashed by this costume failure. She had relied altogether on the change of person-ality into something rich and strange, that the ivory dress was to have wrought. She could do nothing to develop the situation. Everything seemed to be helping to intensify her sisterliness. Oswald was rather seedy, and the three of them played Auction Bridge with a dummy. She had meant to sit up with Peter, but it didn't work out like that.

"Good night, Petah dear," she said outside her bedroom door with the candle-light shining red between the fingers of her hand.

"Good night, old Joan," he said from his door-mat, with an infinite friendliness in his voice.

You cannot kiss a man good night suddenly when he is fifteen yards away. . . .

She closed the door behind her softly, put down her can-dle, and began to walk about her room and swear in an en-tirely unladylike fashion. Then she went over to the open window, wringing her hands. "How am I to *do* it?" she said. "How am I to *do* it? The situation's preposterous. He's mine. And I might be his sister!"

"Shall I make a declaration?"

"I suppose Hetty did."

But all the cunning of Joan was unavailing against the invisble barriers to passion between herself and Peter. They spent a long Sunday of comradeship, and courage and oppor-tunity alike failed. The dawn on Monday morning found a white and haggard Joan pacing her floor, half minded to attempt a desperate explanation forthwith in Peter's bed-room with a suddenly awakened Peter. Only her fear of shocking him and failing restrained her. She raved. She indulged in absurd soliloquys and still absurder prayers. "Oh, God, give me my Peter," she prayed. "*Give me my Peter!*"

§ 21

Monday broke clear and fine, with a September freshness in the sunshine. Breakfast was an awkward meal; Peter was constrained, Oswald was worried by a sense of advice and counsels not given; Joan felt the situation slipping from her helpless grasp. It was with a sense of relief that at last she put on her khaki overcoat to drive Peter to the station. "This is the end," sang in Joan's mind. "This is the end." She glanced at the mirror in the hall and saw that the fur collar was not unfriendly to her white neck and throat. She was in despair, but she did not mean to let it become an unbecoming despair—at least until Peter had departed. The end was still incomplete. She had something stern and unpleasant to say to Peter before they parted, but she did not mean to look stern or unpleasant while she said it. Peter, she noted with a gleam of satisfaction, was in low spirits. He was sorry to go. He was ashamed of himself, but also he was sorry. That was something, at any rate, to have achieved. But he was going—nevertheless.

She brought round the little Singer to the door. She started the engine with a competent swing and got in. The maids came with Peter's portmanteau and belongings. "This is the end," said Joan to herself, touching her accelerator and with her hand ready to release the brake. "All aboard?" said Joan aloud.

Peter shook hands with Oswald over the side of the car, and glanced from him to the house and back at him. "I wish I could stay longer, sir," said Peter.

"There's many days to come yet," said Oswald. For we never mention death before death in war time; we never let ourselves think of it before it comes or after it has come.

"So long, Nobby!"

"Good luck, Peter!"

Joan put the car into gear, and steered out into the road.

"The water-splash is lower than ever I've seen it," said Peter.

They ran down the road to the station almost in silence. "These poplars have got a touch of autumn in them already," said Peter.

"It's an early year," said Joan.

"The end, the end!" sang the song in Joan's brain. "But I'll tell him all the same." . . .

But she did not tell him until they could hear the sound of the approaching train that was to cut the thread of everything for Joan. They walked together up the little platform to the end.

"I'm sorry you're going," said Joan.

"I'm infernally sorry. If I'd known you'd get this week——"

"Would that have altered it?" she said sharply.

"No. I suppose it wouldn't," he fenced, just in time to save himself.

The rattle of the approaching train grew suddenly loud. It was round the bend.

Joan spoke in a perfectly even voice. "I know you have been lying, Peter. I have known it all this week-end. I know your leave lasts until the twenty-first."

He stared at her in astonishment.

"There was a time. . . . It's to think of all this dirt upon you that hurts most. The lies, the dodges, the shuffling meanness of it. From *you*. . . . Whom *I love*."

A gap of silence came. To the old porter twelve yards off they seemed entirely well-behaved and well-disciplined young people, saying nothing in particular. The train came in with a sort of wink under the bridge, and the engine and foremost carriages ran past them up the platform.

"I wish I could explain. I didn't know—— The fact is I got entangled in a sort of promise. . . ."

"*Hetty!*" Joan jerked out, and "There's an empty first for you."

The train stopped.

Peter put his hand on the handle of the carriage door.

"You go to London—like a puppy that rolls in dirt. You go to beastliness and vulgarity. . . . You'd better get in, Peter."

"But look here, Joan!"

"*Get* in!" she scolded to his hesitation, and stamped her foot.

He got in mechanically, and she closed the door on him and turned the handle and stood holding it.

Then still speaking evenly and quietly, she said: "You're a blind fool, Peter. What sort of love can that—that—that miscellany give you, that *I* couldn't give? Have I no life? Have I no beauty? Are you afraid of me? Don't you see—don't you *see?* You go off to *that!* You trail yourself in the dirt and you trail my love in the dirt. Before a female hack! . . .

"*Look* at me!" she cried, holding her hands apart. "Think of me tonight. . . . *Yours!* Yours for the taking!"

The train was moving.

She walked along the platform to keep pace with him, and her eyes held his. "Peter," she said; and then with amazing quiet intensity: "You *damned* fool!"

She hesitated on the verge of saying something more. She came towards the carriage. It wasn't anything pleasant that she had in mind, to judge by her expression.

"Stand away please, miss!" said the old porter, hurrying up to intervene. She abandoned that last remark with an impatient gesture.

Peter sat still. The end of the station ran by like a scene in a panorama. Her Medusa face had slid away to the edge of the picture that the window framed, and vanished.

For some seconds he was too amazed to move.

Then he got up heavily and stuck his head out of the window to stare at Joan.

Joan was standing quite still with her hands in the side pockets of her khaki overcoat; she was standing straight as a rod, with her heels together, looking at the receding train. She never moved. . . .

Neither of these two young people made a sign to each other, which was the first odd thing the old porter noted about them. They just stared. By all the rules they should have waved handkerchiefs. The next odd thing was that Joan stared at the bend for half a minute perhaps after the train had altogether gone, and then tried to walk out to her car by the little white gate at the end of the platform which had been disused and nailed up for three years. . . .

§ 22

After Oswald had seen the car whisk through the gates into the road, and after he had rested on his crutches staring at the gates for a time, he had hobbled back to his study. He wanted to work, but he found it difficult to fix his attention. He was thinking of Joan and Peter, and for the first time in his life he was wondering why they had never fallen in love with each other. They seemed such good company for each other. . . .

He was still engaged upon these speculations half an hour or so later, when he heard the car return and presently saw Joan go past his window. She was flushed, and she was staring in front of her at nothing in particular. He had never seen Joan looking so unhappy. In fact, so strong was his impression that she was unhappy that he doubted it, and he went to the window and craned out after her.

She was going straight up towards the arbour. With a slight hurry in her steps. She had her fur collar half turned up on one side, her hands were deep in her pockets, and something about her dogged walk reminded him of some long-forgotten moment, years ago it must have been, when Joan, in hot water for some small offence, had been sent indoors at The Ingle-Nook.

He limped back to his chair and sat thinking her over.

"I wonder," he said at last, and turned to his work again. . . .

There was no getting on with it. Half an hour later he accepted defeat. "Peter has knocked us all crooked," he said. "There's no work for today.

He would go out and prowl round the place and look at the roses. Perhaps Joan would come and talk. But at the gates he was amazed to encounter Peter.

It was Peter, hot and dusty from a walk of three miles, and carrying his valise with an aching left arm. There was a look of defiance in the eyes that stared fiercely out from under the perspiration-matted hair upon his forehead. He seemed to find Oswald's appearance the complete confirmation of the most disagreeable anticipations. Thoughts of panic and desertion flashed upon Oswald's mind.

"Good God, Peter!" he cried. "What brings you back?"

"I've come back for another week," said Peter.

"But your leave's up!"

"I told a lie, sir. I've got another week."

Oswald stared at his ward.

"I'm sorry, sir," said Peter. "I've been making a fool of myself. I thought better of it. I got out of the train at Standon and walked back here."

"What does it mean, Peter?" said Oswald.

Peter's eyes were the most distressed eyes he had ever seen. "If you'd just not ask, sir, now——"

It is a good thing to deal with one's own blood in a crisis. Oswald, resting thoughtfully on his crutches, leapt to a kind of understanding.

"I'm going to hop down towards the village, Peter," said Oswald, becoming casual in his manner. "I want some exercise. . . . If you'll tell every one you're back."

He indicated the house behind him by a movement of his head.

Peter was badly blown with haste and emotion. "Thank you, sir," he said shortly.

Oswald stepped past him and stared down the road.

"Mrs. Moxton's in the house," he said without looking at Peter again. "Joan's up the garden. See you when I get back, Peter. . . . Glad you've got another week, anyhow. . . . So long. . . ."

He left Peter standing in the gateway.

Fear came upon Peter. He stood quite still for some moments, looking at the house and the cedars. He dropped his valise at the front door and mopped his face. Then he walked slowly across the lawn towards the terraces. He wanted to shout, and found himself hoarse. Then on the first terrace he got out: "Jo-un!" in a flat croak. He had to cry again: "Jo-un!" before it sounded at all like the old style.

Joan became visible. She had come out of the arbour at the top of the garden, and she was standing motionless, regarding him down the vista of the central path. She was white and rather dishevelled, and she stood quite still.

Peter walked up the steps towards her.

"I've come back, Joan," he said, as he drew near. "I want to talk to you . . . Come into the arbour."

He took her arm clumsily and led her back into the arbour out of sight of the house. Then he dropped her arm.

"Joan," he said, "I've been the damndest of fools . . . as you said. . . . I don't know why." . . .

He stood before her awkwardly. He was trembling violently. He thought he was going to weep.

He could not touch her again. He did not dare to touch her.

Then Joan spread out her arms straight and stood like a crucifix. Her face, which had been a dark stare, softened swiftly, became radiant, dissolved into a dusky glow of tears and triumph. "Oh! Petah my *darling*," she sobbed, and seized him and kissed him with tearsalt lips and hugged him to herself.

The magic barrier was smashed at last. Peter held her close to him and kissed her. . . .

It was the second time they had kissed since those black days at High Cross school. . . .

§ 23

Those were years of swift marryings, and Peter was a young married man when presently he was added to the number of that select company attached to sausage-shaped observation balloons who were sent up in the mornings and pulled down at nights along the British front. He had had only momentary snatches of matrimony before the front had called him back to its own destructive interests, but his experiences had banished any lingering vestiges of his theory that there is one sort of woman you respect and another sort you make love to. There was only one sort of woman to love or respect, and that was Joan. He was altogether in love with Joan, he was sure he had never been in love before, and he was now also extravagantly in love with life. He wanted to go on with it, with a passionate intensity. It seemed to him that it was not only beginning for him, but for every one. Hitherto Man had been living *down there*, down on those flats—for all the world is flat from the air,

Now, at last, men were beginning to feel how they might soar over all ancient limitations.

Occasionally he thought of such things up in his basket, sitting like a spectator in a box at a theatre, with the slow vast drama of the western front spread out like a map beneath his eyes, with half Belgium and a great circle of France in sight, the brown, ruined country on either side of No Man's Land, apparently lifeless, with its insane tangle of trenches and communicating ways below, with the crumbling heaps of ruined towns and villages scattered among canals and lakes of flood water, and passing insensibly into a green and normal-looking landscape to the west and east, where churches still had towers and houses roofs, and woods were lumps and blocks of dark green, fields manifestly cultivated patches, and roads white ribbons barred by the purple poplar shadows. But these spectacular and speculative phases were rare. They came only when a thin veil of haze made the whole spacious prospect faint, so that beyond his more immediate circle Peter could see only the broad outlines of the land. Given worse conditions of the weather and he would be too uncomfortable for philosophy; given better and he would be too busy.

He sat on a canvas seat inside the square basket with his instruments about him, or leant over the side scrutinizing the details of the eastward landscape. Upon his head, over his ears, he wore a telephone receiver, and about his body was a rope harness that linked him by a rope to the silk parachute that was packed neatly in a little swinging bucket over the side of his basket. Under his hand was his map board, repeating the shapes of wood and water and road below. The telephone wire that ran down his mooring rope abolished any effect of isolation; it linked him directly to his winch on a lorry below, to a number of battery commanders, to an ascending series of headquarters; he could always start a conversation if he had anything practical to say. He was, in fact, an eye at the end of a tentacle thread, by means of which the British army watched its enemies. Sometimes he had an illusion that he was also a kind of brain. When distant visibility was good he would find himself hovering over the war as a player hangs over a chessboard, directing fire upon road movements or train movements, suspecting and watching for undisclosed enemy batteries, or directing counter-battery fire. Above him, green and voluminous, hung the great translucent lobes of his gas bag, and the loose ropes by which it was towed and held upon the ground swayed and trailed about his basket.

It was on one of his more slack afternoons that Peter fell thinking of how acutely he now desired to live. The wide world was full of sunshine, but a ground haze made even the country immediately below him indistinct. The enemy gunners were inactive, there came no elfin voices through the telephone, only far away to the south guns butted and shivered the tranquil air. There was a faint drift in the air rather than a breeze, and the gas bag had fallen into a long, lazy rhythmic movement, so that sometimes he faced due south and sometimes south by east and so back. A great patch of flooded country to the north-east, a bright mirror with a kind of bloom upon it, seemed trying with an aimless persistency to work its way towards the centre of his field of vision and never succeeding.

For a time Peter had been preoccupied with a distant ridge far away to the east, from which a long-range gun had recently taken to shelling the kite balloons towards evening as they became clear against the bright western sky. Four times lately this new gun had got on to him, and this clear and tranquil afternoon promised just the luminous and tranquil sunset that favoured these unpleasant activities. It was five hours to sunset yet, but Peter could not keep his mind off that gun. It was a big gun; perhaps a 42 centimetre; it was beyond any counter-battery possibility, and it had got a new kind of shell that the Germans seemed to have invented for the particular discomfort of Peter and his kind. It had a distinctive report, a loud *crack*, and then the *"whuff"* of high explosive, and at every explosion it got nearer and nearer to its target, with a quite uncanny certainty. It seemed to learn more than any gun should learn from each shot. It was this steadfast approach to a hit that Peter disliked. That and the long pause after the shell had started. Far away he would see the flash of the gun amidst the ridges in the darkling east. Then would come a long, blank pause of expectation. For all he could tell this might get him. Then the whine of the shell would become audible, growing louder and louder and lower and lower in note; Phee-whoo! *Crack! WHOOF!* Then Peter would get quite voluble to the men at the winch below. He could let himself up, or go down a few hundred feet, or they could shift his lorry along the road. Until it was dark he could not come down, for a kite balloon is a terribly visible and helpless thing on the ground until it has been very carefully put to bed. To come down in the daylight meant too good a chance for the nearer German guns. So Peter, by instructing his winch to lower him or let him up or shift, had to dodge about in a most undignified way, up and down and backwards and sideways, while the big gun marked him and guessed at his next position. Flash! "Oh, damn!" said Peter. "Another already!"

Silence. Anticipations. Then: Phee—eee—eee—*whoo. Crack!* WHOOF! A rush of air would set the gas bag swinging. That was a near one!

"Where *am* I?" said Peter.

But that wasn't going to happen for hours yet. Why meet trouble half way? Why be tormented by this feeling of apprehension and danger in the still air? Why trouble because the world was quiet and seemed to be waiting? Why not think of something else? Banish this war from the mind. . . . Was he more afraid nowadays then he used to be? Peter was inclined to think that now he was more *systematically* afraid. Formerly he had funked in streaks and patches, but now he had a steady, continuous dislike to all these risks and dangers. He was getting more and more clearly an idea of the sort of life he wanted to lead and of the things he wanted to do. He was ceasing to think of existence as a rather aimless series of adventures, and coming to regard it as one large consecutive undertaking on the part of himself and Joan. This being hung up in the sky for Germans to shoot at seemed to him to be a very tiresome irrelevance indeed. He and Joan and everybody with brains —including the misguided people who had made and were now firing this big gun at him—ought to be setting to work to get this preposterous muddle of a world in order. "This sort of thing,'' said Peter, addressing the western front, his gas bag, and so much of the sky as it permitted him to see, and the universe generally, "is ridiculous. There is no sense in it at all. None whatever.''

His dream of God, as a detached and aloof personage, had taken a very strong hold upon his imagination. Or, perhaps, it would be truer to say that his fevered mind in the hospital had given a caricature personality to ideas that had grown up in his mind as a natural consequence of his training. He had gone on with that argument; he went on with it now, with a feeling that really he was just as much sitting and talking in that queer, untidy, out-of-the way office as swaying in a kite balloon, six thousand feet above Flanders, waiting to be shot at.

"It is all very well to say 'exert yourself,' '' said Peter. "But there is that chap over there exerting himself. And what he is doing with all his brains is just trying to wipe my brains out of existence. Just that. He hasn't an idea else of what he is doing. He has no notion of what he is up to or what I am up to. And he hasn't the sense or ability to come over here and talk about it to me. He's there—at that —and he can't help himself. And I'm here—and I can't help myself. But if I could only catch him within counter battery range——!

"There's no sense in it at all,'' summarized Peter, after some moments of grim reflection. "Sense hasn't got into it.''

"Is sense ever going to get into it?

"The curious thing about you,'' said Peter, addressing himself quite directly to his Deity at the desk, "is that somehow, without ever positively promising it or saying anything plain and definite about it, you yet manage to convey in an almost irresistible manner, that there *is* going to be sense in it. You seem to suggest that my poor brain up here and the brains of those chaps over there, are, in spite of all appearance to the contrary, up to something jointly that is going to come together and make good some day. You hint it. And yet I don't get a scrap of sound, trustworthy reasoning to help me to accept that; not a scrap. Why should it be so? I ask, and you just keep on not saying anything. I suppose it's a necessary thing, biologically, that one should have a kind of optimism to keep one alive, so I'm not even justified in my half conviction that I'm not being absolutely fooled by life. . . .

"I admit that taking for example Joan, there is something about Joan that almost persuades me there must be something absolutely *right* about things—for Joan to happen at all. Yet isn't that again just another biologically necessary delusion? . . . There you sit silent. You seem to say nothing, and yet you soak me with a kind of answer, a sort of shapeless courage. . . ."

Peter's mind rested on that for a time, and then began again at another point.

"I wonder," said Peter, "if that chap gets me tonight, what I shall think—in the moment—after he has got me. . . ."

§ 24

But the German gunner never got Peter, because something else got him first.

He thought he saw a Hun aeroplane coming over very high indeed to the south of him, fifteen thousand feet up or more, a mere speck in the blue blaze, and then the gas bag hid it and he dismissed it from his mind. He was thinking that the air was growing clearer, and that if this went on guns would wake up presently and little voices begin to talk to him, when he became aware of the presence and vibration of an aeroplane quite close to him. He pulled off his telephone receivers and heard the roar of an engine close at hand. It was overhead, and the gas bag still hid it. At the same moment the British anti-aircraft gunners began a belated fire. "Damn!" said Peter in a brisk perspiration, and hastened to make sure that his parachute rope was clear.

"Perhaps he's British," said Peter, with no real hope.

"*Pap, pap, pap!*" very loud overhead.

The gas bag swayed and billowed, and a wing with a black cross swept across the sky. "*Pap, pap, pap.*"

The gas bag wrinkled and crumpled more and more, and a little streak of smoke appeared beyond its edge. The German aeroplane was now visible, a hundred yards away, and banking to come round.   He had fired the balloon with tracer bullets.

The thing that Peter had to do and what he did was this. He had to step up on to a little wood step inside his basket. Then he had to put first one foot and then the other on to another little step outside his basket.   This little step was about four inches wide by nine long.   Below it was six thousand feet of emptiness, above the little trees and houses below.   As he swayed on the step Peter had to make sure that the rope attached to his body was clear of all entanglements.   Then he had to step off that little shelf, which was now swinging and slanting with the lurching basket to which it was attached, into the void, six thousand feet above the earth.

He had not to throw himself or dive headlong, because that might lead to entanglement with the rope.   He had just to step off into pellucid nothingness, holding his rope clear of himself with one hand.   This rope looped back to the little swinging bucket in which his fine silk parachute was closely packed.   He had seen it packed a week ago, and he wished now, as he stood on his step holding to his basket with one hand, that he had watched the process more meticulously. He became aware that the Hun, having disposed of the balloon, was now shooting at him.   He did not so much step off the little shelf as slip off as it heeled over with the swing of the basket.   The first instants of a leap or fall make no impression on the mind.   For some seconds he was falling swiftly, feet foremost, through the air.   He scarcely noted the faint snatch when the twine, which held his parachute in its basket, broke.   Then his consciousness began to register again.   He kept his feet tightly pressed together.   The air whistled by him, but he thought that dreams and talk had much exaggerated the sensations of falling.   He was too high as yet to feel the rush of the ground towards him.

He seemed to fall for an interminable time before anything more happened.   He was assailed by doubts—whether the twine that kept the parachute in its bucket would break, whether it would open.   His rope trailed out above him.

Still falling.   Why didn't the parachute open?   In another ten seconds it would be too late.

The parachute was not opening. It was certainly not opening. Wrong packing? He tugged and jerked his rope, and tried to shake and swing the long silken folds that were following his fall. Why? Why the devil——?

The rope seemed to tighten abruptly. The harness tightened upon his body. Peter gasped, sprawled and had the sensation of being hauled up back again into the sky. . . .

It was all right, so far. He was now swaying down earthward with a diminishing velocity beneath an open parachute. He was floating over the landscape instead of falling straight into it.

But the German had not done with Peter yet. He became visible beneath the edge of Peter's parachute, circling downward regardless of anti-aircraft and machine-guns. *"Pap, pap, pap, pap."* The bullets burst and banged about Peter.

Something kicked Peter's knee; something hit his neck; something rapped the knuckles of his wounded hand; the parachute winced and went sideways, slashed and pierced. Peter drifted down faster, helpless, his angry eyes upon his assailant, who vanished again, going out of sight as he rose up above the edge of the parachute.

A storm of pain and rage broke from Peter.

"Done in!" shouted Peter. "Oh! my leg! my leg!

"I'm shot to bits. I'm shot to bloody bits!"

The tree tops were near at hand. The parachute had acquired a rhythmic swing and was falling more rapidly.

"And I've still got to land," wailed Peter, beginning to cry like a child.

He wanted to stop just a moment, just for one *little* moment, before the ground rushed up to meet him. He wanted time to think. He didn't know what to do with this dangling leg. It became a monstrous, painful obstacle to landing. How was he to get a spring? He was bleeding. He was dying. It was cruel. Cruel.

Came the crash. Hot irons, it seemed, assailed his leg and his shoulder and neck. He crumpled up on the ground in an agony, and the parachute, with slow and elegant gestures, folded down on the top of his floundering figure. . . .

The gunners who ran to help him found him, enveloped in silk, bawling and weeping like a child of four in a passion of rage and fear, and trying repeatedly to stand up upon a blood-streaked leg that gave way as repeatedly. "Damn!" cursed Peter in a stifled voice, plunging about like a kitten in a sack. "Damn you all! I tell you I *will* use my leg. I *will* have my leg. If I bleed to death. Oh! Oh! . . . You fool—you lying old *humbug!* You!"

And then he gave a leap upward and forward, and fainted and fell, and lay still, with his head and body muffled in the silk folds of his parachute.

CHAPTER THE FOURTEENTH

OSWALD'S VALEDICTION

§ 1

IT was the third of April in 1918, the Wednesday after Easter, and the war had now lasted three years and eight months. It had become the aching habit of the whole world. Throughout the winter it had been for the most part a great and terrible boredom, but now a phase of acute anxiety was beginning. The "Kaiser's Battle" was raging in France; news came through sparingly; but it was known that General Gough had lost tens of thousands of prisoners, hundreds of guns, and vast stores of ammunition and railway material. It was rumoured that he had committed suicide. But the standards of Tory England differ from those of Japan. Through ten sanguinary days, in a vaster Inkerman, the common men of Britain, reinforced by the French, had fought and died to restore the imperilled line. It was by no means certain yet that they had succeeded. It seemed possible that the French and British armies would be broken apart, and Amiens and Paris lost. Oswald's mind was still dark with apprehension.

The particular anxieties of this crisis accentuated the general worry and inconveniences of the time, and deepened Oswald's conviction of an incredible incompetence in both the political and military leadership of his country. In spite of every reason he had to the contrary, he had continued hitherto to hope for some bright dramatic change in the course of events; he had experienced a continually recurring disappointment with each morning's paper. His intelligence told him that all the inefficiency, the confusion, the cheap and bad government by press and intrigue, were the necessary and inevitable consequences of a neglect of higher education for the past fifty years; these defects were now in

544

the nature of things, almost as much as the bleakness of an English February or the fogs of a London November, but his English temperament had refused hitherto to accept the decision of his intelligence. Now for the first time he could see the possibility of an ultimate failure in the war. To this low level of achievement, he perceived, a steadfast contempt for thought and science and organization had brought Britain; at this low level Britain had now to struggle through the war, blundering, talking, and thinking confusedly, suffering enormously—albeit so sound at heart. It was a humiliating realization. At any rate she could still hope to struggle through; the hard-won elementary education of the common people, the stout heart and sense of the common people, saved her gentlefolk from the fate of their brother inefficients in Russia. But every day he fretted afresh at the costly and toilsome continuance of an effort that a little more courage and wisdom in high places on the allied side, a little more knowledge and clear thinking, might have brought to an entirely satisfactory close in 1917.

For a man of his age, wounded, disappointed, and a chronic invalid, there was considerable affliction in the steadily increasing hardships of the Fourth Year. A number of petty deprivations at which a healthy man might have scoffed, intensified his physical discomfort. There had been a complete restriction of his supply of petrol, the automobile now hung in its shed with its tyres removed, and the railway service to London had been greatly reduced. He could not get up to London now to consult books or vary his moods without a slow and crowded and fatiguing journey; he was more and more confined to Pelham Ford. He had been used to read and work late into the night, but now his home was darkened in the evening and very cheerless; there was no carbide for the acetylene installation, and a need for economy in paraffin. For a time he had been out of coal, and unable to get much wood because of local difficulties about cartage, and for some weeks he had had to sit in his overcoat and read and write by candlelight. Now, however, that distress had been relieved by the belated delivery of a truckload of coal. And another matter that may seem trivial in history, was by no means trivial in relation to his moods. In the spring of 1918 the food supply of Great Britain was at its lowest point. Lord Rhondda was saving the situation at the eleventh hour. The rationing of meat had affected Oswald's health disagreeably. He had long ago acquired the habit of living upon chops and cutlets and suchlike concentrated nourishment, and he found it difficult to adapt himself now to the bulky insipidity of a diet that was, for a time, almost entirely vegetarian. For even fish travels by long routes to Hertfordshire villages. The frequent air raids of that winter were also an added nervous irritation. In the preceding years of the war there had been occasional Zeppelin raids, the Zeppelins had been audible at Pelham Ford on several occasions and once Hertford had suffered from their bombs; but those expeditions had ended at last in a series of disasters to the invaders, and they had never involved the uproar and tension of the Gotha raids that began in the latter half of 1917. These latter raids had to be met by an immense barrage of anti-aircraft guns round London, a barrage which rattled every window at Pelham Ford, lit the sky with star shells, and continued intermittently sometimes for four or five hours. Oswald would lie awake throughout that thudding conflict, watching the distant star shells and searchlights through the black tree boughs outside his open window, and meditating drearily upon the manifest insanity of mankind. . . .

He was now walking up and down his lawn, waiting until it should be time to start for the station with Joan to meet Peter.

For Peter, convalescent again and no longer fit for any form of active service—he was lamed now as well as winged—was to take up a minor administrative post next week at Adastral House, and he was coming down for a few days at Pelham Ford before carrying his wife off for good to a little service flat they had found in an adapted house in the Avenue Road. They had decided not to live at The Ingle-Nook, although Arthur had built it to become Peter's home, but to continue the tenancy of Aunts Phyllis and Phœbe. They did not want to disturb those two ladies, whose nervous systems, by no means stable at the best of times, were now in a very shaken condition. Aunt Phyllis was kept busy restraining Aunt Phœbe from inflicting lengthy but obscure prophetic messages upon most of the prominent people of the time. To these daily activities Aunt Phœbe added an increasing habit of sleep-walking that broke the nightly peace of Aunt Phyllis. She would wander through the moonlit living rooms gesticulating strangely, and uttering such phrases as "Blood! Blood! Seas of blood! The multitudinous seas incarnadine"; or "Murder most foul!"

She had a fixed idea that it was her business to seek out the Kaiser and either scold him or kill him—or perhaps do both. She held that it was the duty of women to assassinate. Men might fight battles, it was their stupid way; but surely women were capable of directer things. If some woman were to kill any man who declared war directly he declared war, there would be a speedy end to war. She could not, she said, understand the inactivity of German wives and mothers. She would spend hours over her old school German grammar, with a view to writing an "Open Letter to German Womankind." But her naturally rich and very allusive prose was ill adapted to that sort of translation.

Many over-sensitive people were suffering more or less as Aunt Phœbe was suffering—from a sense of cruelty, wickedness, and disaster that staggered their minds. They had lived securely in a secure world; they could not readjust. Even for so sane a mind as Oswald's, hampered as it was by the new poison his recent wound had brought into his blood, readjustment was difficult. He suffered greatly from insomnia, and from a haunting apprehension of misfortunes. His damaged knee would give him bouts of acute distress. Sometimes it would seem to be well and he would forget it. Then it would become painfully lame by day and a neuralgic pain at night. His moods seemed always exaggerated now; either he was too angry or too sorrowful or too hopeful. Sometimes he experienced phases of blank stupidity, when his mind became unaccountably sluggish and clumsy. . . .

Joan was indoors now packing up a boxful of books that were to go with her to the new home.

He was feeling acutely—more acutely than he wanted to feel—that his guardianship was at an end. Joan, who had been the mistress of his house, and the voice that sang in it,

the pretty plant that grew in it, was going now—to return, perhaps, sometimes as a visitor—but never more to be
a part of it; never more to be its habitual presence. Peter,
too, was severing the rope, a long rope it had seemed at
times during the last three years, that had tethered him to
Pelham Ford. . . .

Oswald did not want to think now of his coming loneliness. What he wanted to think about was the necessity of
rounding off their relationship properly, of ending his educational task with some sort of account rendered. He felt
he owed it to these young people and to himself to tell them
of his aims and of what he considered the whole of this business of education amounted to. He had to explain what had
helped and what had prevented him. "A Valediction," he
said. "A Valediction." But he could not plan out what
he had to say that morning. He could not arrange his
heads, and all the while that he tried to fix his thoughts upon
these topics, he was filled with uncontrollable self-pity for
the solitude ahead of him.

He was ashamed at these personal distresses that he could
not control. He disliked himself for their quality. He did
not like to think he was thinking the thoughts in his mind.
He walked up and down the lawn for a time like a man who
is being pestered by uncongenial solicitations.

In spite of his intense affection for both of them, he was
feeling a real jealousy of the happiness of these two young
lovers. He hated the thought of losing Joan much more
than he hated the loss of Peter. Once upon a time he had
loved Peter far more than Joan, but by imperceptible degrees his affection had turned over to her. In these war
years he and she had been very much together. For a time
he had been—it was grotesque, but true—actually in love
with her. He had let himself dream—. It was preposterous
to think of it. A moonlight night had made his brain
swim. . . . At any rate, thank Heaven! she had never had
a suspicion. . . .

She'd come now as a visitor—perhaps quite often. He
wasn't going to lose his Joan altogether. But each time she
would come changed, rather less his Joan and rather more
a new Joan—Peter's Joan. . . .

Some day they'd have children, these two. Joan would sit over her child and smile down at it. He knew exactly how she would smile. And at the thought of that smile Joan gave place to Dolly. Out of the past there jumped upon him the memory of Peter bubbling in a cradle on the sunny verandah of The Ingle-Nook, and how he had remarked that the very sunshine seemed made for this fortunate young man.

"It *was* made for him," Dolly had said, with that faintly mischievous smile of hers.

How far off that seemed now, and how vivid still! He could remember Dolly's shadow on the roughcast wall, and the very things he had said in reply. He had talked like a fool about the wonderful future of Peter—and of the world. How long was that ago? Five-and-twenty years? (Yes, Peter would be five-and-twenty in June.) How safe and secure the European world had seemed then! It seemed to be loitering, lazily and basely indeed, but certainly, towards a sort of materialist's millennium. And what a vast sham its security had been! He had called Peter the "Heir of the Ages." And the Heritage of the Ages had been preparing even then to take Peter away from the work he had chosen and from all the sunshine and leisure of his life and to splinter his shoulder-blade, smash his wrist, snap his leg-bones with machine-gun bullets, and fling him aside, a hobbling, stiff, broken young man to limp through the rest of life. . . .

§ 2

That was what his mind had to lay hold of, that was what he had to talk about, this process that had held out such fair hopes for Peter and had in the end crippled him and come near to killing him and wasting him altogether. He had to talk of that, of an enormous collapse and breach of faith with the young. The world which had seemed to be the glowing promise of an unprecedented education and upbringing for Peter and his generation, the world that had been, so to speak, joint guardian with himself, had defaulted. This war was an outrage by the senior things in the world upon all the hope of the future; it was the parent sending his sons through the fires to Moloch, it was the guardian gone mad, it was the lapse of all educational responsibility.

He had to keep his grasp upon that idea. By holding to that he could get away from his morbidly intense wish to be personal and intimate with these two. He loved them and they loved him, but what he wanted to say was something quite beyond that.

What he had to talk about was Education, and Education alone. He had to point out to them that their own education had been truncated, was rough ended and partial. He had to explain why that was so. And he had to show that all this vast disaster to the world was no more and no less than an educational failure. The churches and teachers and political forms had been insufficient and wrong; they had failed to establish ideas strong and complete enough and right enough to hold the wills of men. Necessarily he had to make a dissertation upon the war. To talk of life now was to talk of the war. The war now was human life. It had eaten up all free and independent living.

The war was an educational breakdown, that was his point; and in education lay whatever hope there was for mankind. He had to say that to them, and he had to point out how that idea must determine the form of their lives. He had to show the political and social and moral conclusions involved in it. And he had to say what he wanted to say in a large manner. *He had to keep his temper while he said it.*

Oswald, limping slowly up and down his lawn in the April sunshine, with a gnawing pain at his knee, had to underline, as it were, that last proviso in his thoughts. That was the extreme difficulty of these urgent and tragic times. The world was in a phase of intense, but swift, tumultuous, and distracting tragedy. The millions were not suffering and dying in stateliness and splendour but in a vast uproar, amidst mud, confusion, bickering, and incoherence indescribable. While it was manifest that only great thinking, only very clear and deliberate thinking, could give even the forms of action that would arrest the conflagration, it was nevertheless almost impossible for any one anywhere to think clearly and deliberately, so universal and various were the compulsions, confusions, and distresses of the time. And even the effect to see and state the issue largely, fevered Oswald's brain. He grew angry with the multitudinous things that robbed him of his serenity.

"Education," he said, as if he called for help; "education."

And then, collapsing into wrath: "A land of uneducated blockheads!"

No! It was not one of his good mornings. In a little while his steps had quickened and his face had flushed. His hands clenched in his pockets. "A universal dulness of mind," he whispered. "Obstinacy. . . . Inadaptability. . . . Unintelligent opposition."

Broad generalizations slipped out of his mind. He began to turn over one disastrous instance after another of the shortness of mental range, the unimaginative stupidity, the baseness and tortuousness of method, the dull suspicions, class jealousies, and foolish conceits that had crippled Britain through three and a half bitter years. With a vast fleet, with enormous armies, with limitless wealth, with the loyal enthusiasm behind them of a united people and with great allies, British admirals and generals had never once achieved any great or brilliant success, British statesmen had never once grasped and held the fluctuating situation. One huge disappointment had followed another; now at Gallipoli, now at Kut, now in the air and now beneath the seas, the British had seen their strength ill applied and their fair hopes of victory waste away. No Nelson had arisen to save the country, no Wellington; no Nelson nor Wellington could have arisen; the country had not even found an alternative to Mr. Lloyd George. In military and naval as in social and political affairs the Anglican ideal had been—to blockade. On sea and land, as in Ireland, as in India, Anglicanism was not leading but obstruction. Throughout 1917 the Allied armies upon the Western front had predominated over the German as greatly as the British fleet had predominated at sea, and the result on either element had been stagnation. The cavalry coterie who ruled upon land had demonstrated triumphantly their incapacity

to seize even so great an opportunity as the surprise of the
tanks afforded them; the Admiralty had left the Baltic to
the Germans until, after the loss of Riga, poor Kerensky's
staggering government had collapsed. British diplomacy
had completed what British naval quiescence began; in Russia as in Greece it had existed only to blunder; never had a
just cause been so mishandled; and before the end of 1917
the Russian debacle had been achieved and the German
armies, reinforced by the troops the Russian failure had released, began to concentrate for this last great effort that
was now in progress in the west. Like many another anxious and distressed Englishman during those darker days of
the German spring offensive in 1918, Oswald went about
clinging to one comfort: "Our men are tough stuff. Our
men at any rate will stick it."

In Oswald's mind there rankled a number of special cases
which he called his "sores." To think of them made him
angry and desperate, and yet he could scarcely ever think of
education without reviving the irritation of these particular
instances. They were his foreground; they blocked his
vistas, and got between him and the general prospect of the
world. For instance, there had been a failure to supply
mosquito curtains in the East African hospitals, and a number of slightly wounded men had contracted fever and died.
This fact had linked on to the rejection of the services he
had offered at the outset of the war, and became a festering
centre in his memory. Those mosquito curtains blew into
every discussion. Moreover there had been, he believed,
much delay and inefficiency in the use of African native
labour in France, and a lack of proper organization for the
special needs of the sick and injured among these tropic-bred
men. And a shipload had been sunk in a collision off the
Isle of Wight. He had got an irrational persuasion into his
head that this collision could have been prevented. After
his wound had driven him back to Pelham Ford he would
limp about the garden thinking of his "boys" shivering in
the wet of a French winter and dying on straw in cold cattle
trucks, or struggling and drowning in the grey channel
water, and he would fret and swear. "Hugger mugger,"
he would say, "hugger mugger! No care. No foresight.

No proper grasp of the problem.   And so death and torment for the men.''

While still so painful and feverish he had developed a new distress for himself by taking up the advocacy of certain novelties and devices that he became more and more convinced were of vital importance upon the Western front. He entangled himself in correspondence, interviews, committees, and complicated quarrels in connection with these ideas. . . . He would prowl about his garden, a baffled man, trying to invent some way of breaking through the system of entanglements that held back British inventiveness from the service of Great Britain.   More and more clearly did his reason assure him that no sudden blow can set aside the deep-rooted traditions, the careless, aimless education of a negligent century, but none the less he raged at individuals, at ministries, at coteries and classes.

His peculiar objection to the heads of the regular army, for example, was unjust, for much the same unimaginative resistance was evident in every branch of the public activities of Great Britain.   Already in 1915 the very half-penny journalists were pointing out the necessity of a great air offensive for the allies, were showing that in the matter of the possible supply of good air fighters the Germans were altogether inferior to their antagonists and that consequently they would be more and more at a disadvantage in the air as the air warfare was pressed.   But the British mind was trained, so far that is as one can speak of it as being trained at all, to dread ''over-pressure.''   The western allies having won a certain ascendancy in the air in 1916 became so self-satisfied that the Germans, in spite of their disadvantages, were able to recover a kind of equality in 1917, and in the spring of 1918 the British, with their leeway recovered, were going easily in mattters aerial, and the opinion that a great air offensive might yet end the war was regarded as the sign of a froward and revolutionary spirit.

The sea war had a parallel history.   Long before 1914 Dr. Conan Doyle had written a story to illustrate the dangers of an unrestricted submarine attack, but no precaution whatever against such a possibility seemed to have been undertaken by the British Admiralty before the war at all; Great

Britain was practically destitute of sea mines in the October of 1914, and even in the spring of 1918, after more than a year and a half of hostile submarine activity, after the British had lost millions of tons of shipping, after the people were on short commons and becoming very anxious about rations, the really very narrow channel of the North Sea—rarely is it more than three hundred miles wide—which was the only way out the Germans possessed, was still unfenced against the coming and going of these most vulnerable pests.

It is hard not to blame individual men and groups when the affairs of a nation go badly. It is so much easier to change men than systems. The former satisfies every instinct in the fierce, suspicious hearts of men, the latter demands the bleakest of intellectual efforts. The former justifies the healthy, wholesome relief of rioting; the latter necessitates self-control. The country was at sixes and sevens because its education by school and college, by book and speech and newspaper, was confused and superficial and incomplete, and its education was confused and superficial and incomplete because its institutions were a patched-up system of traditions, compromises, and interests, devoid of any clear and single guiding idea of a national purpose. The only wrongs that really matter to mankind are the undramatic general wrongs; but the only wrongs that appeal to the uneducated imagination are individual wrongs. It is so much more congenial to the ape in us to say that if Mr. Asquith hadn't been lazy or Mr. Lloyd George disingenuous——! Then out with the halter—and don't bother about yourself. As though the worst of individuals can be anything more than the indicating pustule of a systemic malaise. For his own part Oswald was always reviling schoolmasters, as though they, alone among men, had the power to rise triumphant over all their circumstances—and wouldn't. He had long since forgotten Mr. Mackinder's apology.

He limped and fretted to and fro across the lawn in his struggle to get out of his jungle of wrathful thoughts, about drowned negroes and rejected inventions, and about the Baltic failure and about Gough of the Curragh and St. Quentin, to general and permanent things.

"Education," he said aloud, struggling against his obsessions. "Education! I have to tell them what it ought to be, how it is more or less the task of every man, how it can unify the world, how it can save mankind. . . ."

And then after a little pause, with an apparent complete irrelevance, "*Damn* Aunt Charlotte!"

§ 4

Nowadays quite little things would suddenly assume a tremendous and devastating importance to Oswald. In his pocket, not folded but crumpled up, was an insulting letter from Lady Charlotte Sydenham, and the thought of it was rankling bitterly in his mind.

The days were long past when he could think of the old lady as of something antediluvian in quality, a queer ungainly megatherium floundering about in a new age from which her kind would presently vanish altogether. He was beginning to doubt more and more about her imminent disappearance. She had greater powers of survival than he had supposed; he was beginning to think that she might outlive him; there was much more of her in England than he had ever suspected. All through the war she, or a voice indistinguishable from hers, had bawled unchastened in the *Morning Post;* on many occasions he had seemed to see her hard blue eye and bristling whisker glaring at him through a kind of translucency in the sheets of *The Times;* once or twice in France he had recognized her, or something very like her, in red tabs and gilt lace, at G.H.Q. These were sick fancies no doubt; mere fantastic intimations of the stout resistances the Anglican culture could still offer before it loosened its cramping grip upon the future of England and the world, evidence rather of his own hypersensitized condition than of any perennial quality in her.

The old lady had played a valiant part in the early stages of the war. She had interested herself in the persecution of all Germans not related to royalty, who chanced to be in the country; and had even employed private detectives in one or two cases that had come under her notice. She had been forced most unjustly to defend a libel case

brought by a butcher named Sterne, whom she had denounced as of German origin and a probable poisoner of the
community, in the very laudable belief that his name was
spelt Stern. She felt that his indubitable British ancestry
and honesty only enhanced the deception and made the whole
thing more alarming, but the jury, being no doubt tainted
with pacifism, thought, or pretended to think, otherwise.
She had had a reconciliation with her old antagonists the
Pankhurst section of the suffragettes, and she had paid
twenty annual subscriptions to their loyal and outspoken
publication *Britannia,* directing twelve copies to be sent to
suitable recipients—Oswald was one of the favoured ones—
and herself receiving and blue-pencilling the remaining eight
before despatching them to such public characters as she
believed would be most beneficially cowed or instructed by
the articles she had marked. She also subscribed liberally to
the British Empire Union, an organization so patriotic that
it extended its hostility to Russians, Americans, Irishmen,
neutrals, President Wilson, the League of Nations, and similar infringements of the importance and dignity of Lady
Charlotte and her kind. She remained at Chastlands, where
she had laid in an ample store of provisions quite early in
the war—two sacks of mouldy flour and a side of bacon in
an advanced state of decomposition had been buried at night
by Cashel—all through the Zeppelin raids; and she played
a prominent rather than a pacifying part in the Red Cross
politics of that part of Surrey. She induced several rich
Jewesses of Swiss, Dutch, German or Austrian origin to relieve the movement of their names and, what was still better,
of the frequently quite offensively large subscriptions with
which they overshadowed those who had the right to lead in
such matters. She lectured also in the National Economy
campaign on several occasions—for like most thoughtful
women of her class and type, she was deeply shocked by the
stories she had heard of extravagance among our over-paid
munition workers. After a time the extraordinary meanness of the authorities in restricting her petrol obliged her
in self-respect to throw up this branch of her public work.
She was in London during one of the early Gotha raids, but
she conceived such a disgust at the cowardice of the lower

classes on this occasion that she left town the next day and
would not return thither.

The increasing scarcity of petrol and the onset of food
rationing, which threatened to spread all over England,
drove her to Ulster—in spite of the submarine danger that
might have deterred a less stout-hearted woman. She took
a small furnished house in a congenial district, and found
herself one of a little circle of ultra-patriotic refugees, driven
like herself from England by un-English restrictions upon
the nourishment of the upper classes and the spread of the
pacifist tendencies of Lord Lansdowne. "If the cowards
must make peace," said Lady Charlotte, "at least give *me*
leave to be out of it."

Considering everything, Ulster was at that time as comfortably and honourably out of the war as any part of the
world, and all that seemed needed to keep it safely out to the
end was a little tactful firmness in the Dublin Convention.
There was plenty of everything in the loyal province at
that time—men, meat, butter, Dublin stout, and self-right-
eousness; and Lady Charlotte expanded again like a flower
in the sun. She reverted to driving in a carriage; it was
nice to sit once more behind a stout able-bodied coachman
with a cockade, with a perfect excuse for neutrality, and
she still did her best for old England from eleven to one
and often from five to six by writing letters and dabbling
in organization. Oswald she kept in mind continually. Almost daily he would get newspaper cuttings from her detail-
ing Sinn Fein outrages, or blue-marked leading articles agi-
tating for a larger share of the munition industries for
Belfast, or good hot stuff, deeply underlined, from the
speeches of Sir Edward Carson. One dastardly Sinn
Feiner, Oswald learnt, had even starved himself to death in
gaol, a most unnatural offence to Lady Charlotte. She
warmed up tremendously over the insidious attempts of the
Prime Minister and a section of the press to get all the armies
in France and Italy under one supreme generalissimo and
end the dislocated muddling that had so long prolonged the
war. It was a change that might have involved the replacement of regular generals by competent ones, and it imperilled everything that was most dear to the old lady's heart.

It was *"an insult to the King's uniform,"* she wrote. *"A revolution. I knew that this sort of thing would begin if we let those Americans come in. We ought not to have let them come in. What good are they to us? What can they know of war? A crowd of ignorant republican renegades! British generals to be criticized and their prospects injured by French Roman Catholics and Atheists and chewing, expectorating Yankees and every sort of low foreigner. What is the world coming to? Sir Douglas Haig has been exactly where he is for two years. Surely he knows the ground better than any one else can possibly do."*

Once the theme of Lady Charlotte got loose in Oswald's poor old brain, it began a special worry of its own. He found his mind struggling with assertions and arguments. As this involved trying to remember exactly what she had said in this letter of hers, and as it was in his pocket, he presently chose the lesser of two evils and took it out to read over :—

"I suppose you have read in the papers what is happening in Clare. The people are ploughing up grass-land. It is as bad as that man Prothero. They raid gentlemen's houses to seize arms; they resist the police. That man Devil-era— so I must call him—speaks openly of a republic. Devil-era and Devil-in; is it a coincidence merely? All this comes of our illtimed leniency after the Dublin rebellion. When will England learn the lesson Cromwell taught her? He was a wicked man, he made one great mistake for which he is no doubt answering to his Maker throughout all eternity, but he certainly did know how to manage these Irish. If he could come back now he would be on our side. He would have had his lesson. Your Bolshevik friends go on murdering and cutting throats, I see, like true Republicans. Happily the White Guards seem getting the upper hand in Finland. In the end I suppose we shall be driven to a peace with the Huns as the worst of two evils. If we do, it will only be your Bolsheviks and pacifists and strikers and Bolos who will be to blame.

"The whining and cowardice of the East Enders disgusts me more and more. You read, I suppose, the account of the disgraceful panic during the air raid the other day in the

*East End, due entirely to foreigners of military age, mostly,
no doubt, your Russian Bolsheviks. I am well away from
such a rabble. I suffer from rheumatism here. I know it
is rheumatism; what you say about gout is nonsense. In
spite of its loyalty Ulster is damp. I pine more and more
for the sun and warmth of Italy. Unwin must needs make
herself very tiresome and peevish nowadays. These are not
cheerful times for me. But one must do one's bit for one's
country, I suppose, unworthy though it be.*

*"So Mr. Peter is back in England again wounded after
his flying about in the air. I suppose he is tasting the delights of matrimony, such as they are! What an affair!
Something told me long ago that it would happen. I tried
to separate them. My instincts warned me, and my instincts
were right. Breed is breed, and the servant strain came out
in her. You can't say I didn't warn you. Why you let
them marry I cannot imagine!!! I am sure the young lady
could have dispensed with that ceremony!!!! I still think
at times of that queer scene I passed on the road when I
came to Pelham Ford that Christmas. A second string,—
no doubt of it. But Peter was her great chance, of course,
thanks to your folly. Well, let us hope that in the modern
way they won't have any children, for nothing is more certain than that these inter-breeding marriages are most harm-
ful, and whether we like it or not you have to remember
they are first cousins, if not in the sight of the law at any
rate in the sight of God, which is what matters in this respect. Mr. Grimes, who has studied these things in his
leisure time, tells me that there is a very great probability
indeed that any child will be blind or malformed or con-
sumptive, let us hope the latter, if not actually still-born,
which, of course, would be the best thing that could possibly
happen. . . ."*

§ 5

At this point Oswald became aware of Joan coming out of
the house towards him.

He looked at his watch. "Much too early yet, Joan," he
said.

"Yes, but I want to be meeting him," said Mrs. Joan. . . .

So they walked down to the station and waited for a long time on the platform. And Joan said very little to Oswald because she was musing pleasantly.

When the train came in neither Joan nor Peter took much notice of Oswald after the first greeting. I do not see what else he could have expected; they were deeply in love and they had been apart for a couple of weeks, they were excited by each other and engrossed in each other. Oswald walked beside them up the road—apart. "I've got some work," he said abruptly in the hall. "See you at lunch," and went into his study and shut the door upon them, absurdly disappointed.

§ 6

Peter came on Wednesday. It was not until Friday that Oswald found an opportunity to deliver his valediction. But he had rehearsed it, or rather he had been rehearsing experimental fragments of it for most of the night before. On Thursday night the cloudy malaise of his mind broke and cleared. Things fell into their proper places in his thoughts, and he could feel that his ideas were no longer distorted and confused. The valediction appeared, an ordered discourse. If only he could hold out through a long talk he felt he would be able to make himself plain to them. . . .

He lay in the darkness putting together phrase after phrase, sentence after sentence, developing a long and elaborate argument, dipping down into parentheses, throwing off footnotes, resuming his text. For the most part Joan and Peter remained silent hearers of this discourse; now his ratiocination glowed so brightly that they were almost forgotten, now they came into the discussion, they assisted, they said helpful and understanding things, they raised simple and obvious objections that were beautifully overcome.

"What is education up to?" he would begin. "What *is* education?"

Then came a sentence that he repeated in the stillness of his mind quite a number of times. "Consider this beast we are, this thing man!'' He did not reckon with Peter's tendency to prompt replies.

He would begin in the broadest, most elementary way. ''Consider this beast we are, this thing man!'' so he framed his opening: ''a creature restlessly experimental, mischievous and destructive, as sexual as a monkey, and with no really strong social instincts, no such tolerance of his fellows as a deer has, no such instinctive self-devotion as you find in a bee or an ant. A solitary animal, a selfish animal. And yet this creature has now made for itself such conditions that it *must* be social. Must be. Or destroy itself. Continually it invents fresh means by which man may get at man to injure him or help him. That is one view of the creature, Peter, from your biological end.'' Here Peter was to nod, and remain attentively awaiting the next development. ''And at the same time, there grows upon us all a sense of a common being and a common interest. Biologically separate, we unify spiritually. More and more do men feel, 'I am not for myself! There is something in me—that belongs to a greater being than myself—of which I am a part.' . . . I won't philosophize. I won't say which may be in the nature of cause and which of effect here. You can put what I have said in a dozen different ways. We may say, 'The individual must live in the species and find his happiness there'—that is—Biologese. *Our* language, Peter. Or we can quote, 'I am the True Vine and ye are the Branches.' '' Oswald's mind rested on that for a time. ''That is not *our* language, Peter, but it is the same idea. Essentially it is the same idea. Or we can talk of the 'One and the Many.' We can say we all live in the mercy of Allah, or if you are a liberal Jew that we are all a part of Israel. It seems to me that all these formulæ are so much spluttering and variation over one idea. Doesn't it to you? Men can quarrel mortally even upon the question of how they shall say 'Brotherhood.' . . .'' Here for a time Oswald's mind paused.

He embarked upon a great and wonderful parenthesis upon religious intolerance in which at last he lost himself completely.

''I don't see that men need fall out about religion,'' was his main proposition.

"There was a time when I was against all religions. I denounced priestcraft and superstition and so on. . . . That is past. That is past. I want peace in the world. . . . Men's minds differ more about *initial* things than they do about *final* things. Some men think in images, others in words and abstract ideas—but yet the two sorts can think out the same practical conclusions. A lot of these chapels and churches only mean a difference in language. . . . Difference in dialect. . . . Often they don't mean the same things, those religious people, by the same words, but often contrariwise they mean the same things by quite different words. The deaf man says the dawn is bright and red, and the blind man says it is a sound of birds. It is the same dawn. The same dawn. . . . One man says 'God' and thinks of a person who is as much of a person as Joan is, and another says 'God' and thinks of an idea more abstract than the square root of minus one. That's a tangle in the primaries of thought and not a difference in practical intention. One can argue about such things for ever. . . . One can make a puzzle with a bit of wire that will bother and exasperate people for hours. Is it any wonder, then, if stating what is at the root of life bothers and exasperates people? . . .

"Personally, I should say now that all religions are right, and none of them very happy in the words and symbols they choose. And none of them are calm enough—not calm enough. Not peaceful enough. They are all floundering about with symbols and metaphors, and it is a pity they will not admit it. . . . Why will people never admit their intellectual limitations in these matters? . . . All the great religions have this in common, this idea is common; they profess to teach the universal brotherhood of man and the universal reign of justice. Why argue about phrases? Why not put it in this fashion?" . . .

For a long time Oswald argued about phrases before he could get back to the main thread of his argument. . . .

"Men have to be unified. They are driven to seek Unity. And they are still with the individualized instincts of a savage. . . . See then what education always has to be! The process of taking this imperfectly social, jealous, deeply

savage creature and socializing him. The development of
education and the development of human societies are one
and the same thing. Education makes the social man. So
far as schooling goes, it is quite plainly that. You teach
your solitary beast to read and write, you teach him to express himself by drawing, you teach him other languages
perhaps, and something of history and the distribution of
mankind. What is it all but making this creature who
would naturally possess only the fierce, narrow sociability of
a savage family in a cave, into a citizen in a greater community? That is how I see it. That primarily is what has been
done to you. An uneducated man is a man who can talk to a
few score familiar people with a few hundred words. You
two can talk to a quarter of mankind. With the help of a
little translation you can get to understandings with most
of mankind. . . . As a child learns the accepted language
and the accepted writing and the laws and rules of life it
learns the community. Watching the education of you two
has made me believe more and more in the idea that, over
and above the enlargement of expression and understanding,
education is the state explaining itself to and incorporating
the will of the individual. . . .

"Yes—but what state? What state? Now we come to
it. . . ."

Oswald began to sketch out a universal history. There is
no limit to these intellectual enterprises of the small hours.

"All history is the record of an effort in man to form
communities, an effort against resistance—against instinctive
resistance. There seems no natural and proper limit to a
human community. (That's my great point, that. That is
what I have to tell them.) That is the final teaching of History, Joan and Peter; the very quintessence of History; that
limitlessness of the community. As soon as men get a community of any size organized, it begins forthwith to develop
roads, wheels, writing, ship-building, and all manner of
things which presently set a fresh growth growing again.
Let that, too, go on. Presently comes steam, mechanical
traction, telegraphy, the telephone, wireless, aeroplanes; and
each means an extension of range, and each therefore demands a larger community. . . . There seems no limit to the

growth of states. I remember, Peter, a talk we had; we agreed that this hackneyed analogy people draw between the life and death of animals and the life and death of states was bad and silly. It isn't the same thing, Joan, at all. An animal, you see, has a limit of size; it develops no new organs for further growth when it has reached that limit, it breeds its successors, it ages naturally; when it dies, it dies for good and all and is cleared away. Exactly the reverse is true of a human community. Exactly? Yes, exactly. If it can develop its educational system steadily—note that—if it can keep up communications, a State can go on indefinitely, conquering, ousting, assimilating. Even an amoeba breaks up after growth, but a human community need not do so. And so far from breeding successors it kills them if it can— like Frazer's priest—where was it?—Aricia? The priest of Diana. The priest of *The Golden Bough.* . . .

Oswald picked up his thread again after a long, half dreaming excursion in Frazer-land.

"It is just this limitlessness, this potential immortality of States that makes all the confusion and bloodshed of history. What is happening in the world today? What is the essence of it all? The communities of today are developing *range,* faster than ever they did: aeroplanes, guns, swifter ships, everywhere an increasing range of action. That is the most important fact to grasp about the modern world. It is the key fact in politics. From the first dawn of the human story you see man in a kind of a puzzled way—how shall I put it? —*pursuing the boundary of his possible community.* Which always recedes. Which recedes now faster than ever. Until it brings him to a fatal war and disaster. Over and over again it is the same story. If you had a coloured historical atlas of the world, the maps would be just a series of great dabs of empire, spreading, spreading—coming against resist- ances—collapsing. Each dab tries to devour the world and fails. There is no natural limit to a human community, no limit in time or space—except one.

"Genus *Homo,* species *Sapiens,* Mankind, that is the only limit." (Peter, perhaps, might be led up to saying that.) . . .

"What has the history of education always been? A

OSWALD'S VALEDICTION

565

series of little teaching chaps trying to follow up and *fix* the fluctuating boundaries of communities''—an image came into Oswald's head that pleased him and led him on—''like an insufficient supply of upholsterers trying to overtake and tack down a carpet that was blowing away in front of a gale. An insufficient supply of upholsterers . . . And the carpet always growing as it blows. That's good. . . . They were trying to fix something they hadn't clearly defined. And you have a lot of them still hammering away at their tacks when the edge of the carpet has gone on far ahead. . . . That was really the state of education in England when I took you two young people in hand; the carpet was in the air and most of the schoolmasters, schoolmistresses, writers, teachers, journalists, and all who build up and confirm ideas were hammering in tacks where the carpet had been resting the day before yesterday. . . . But a lot were not even hammering. No. They just went easy. Yes, that is what I mean when I say that education was altogether at loose ends. . . . But Germany was different; Germany was teaching and teaching in schools, colleges, press, everywhere, this new Imperialism of hers, a sort of patriotic melodrama, with Britain as Carthage and Berlin instead of Rome. They pointed the whole population to that end. They *taught* this war. All over the world a thousand other educational systems pointed in a thousand directions. . . .

''So Germany set fire to the Phœnix. . . .

''Only one other great country had any sort of state education. Real state education that is. The United States was also teaching citizenship, on a broader if shallower basis; a wider citizenship—goodwill to all mankind. Shallower. Shallower certainly. But it was there. A republican culture. Candour . . . generosity. . . . The world has still to realize its debt to the common schools of America. . . .

''This League of Free Nations, of which all men are dreaming and talking, this World Republic, is the rediscovered outline, the proper teaching of all real education, the necessary outline now of human life. . . . There is nothing else to do, nothing else that people of our sort can do at all, nothing but baseness, grossness, vileness, and slavery unless we live now as a part of that process of a world peace. Our lives have got to be political lives. All lives have to be made political lives. We can't run about *loose* any more. This idea of a world-wide commonwealth, this ideal of an everlasting world-peace in which we are to live and move and have our being, has to be built up in every school, in every mind, in every lesson. 'You belong. You belong. And the world belongs to you.' . . .

What ought one to teach when one teaches geography, for instance, but the common estate of mankind? Here, the teacher should say, are mountains and beautiful cities you may live to see. Here are plains where we might grow half the food of mankind! Here are the highways of our common life, and here are pleasant byeways where you may go! All this is your inheritance. Your estate. To rejoice in—and serve. But is that how geography is taught? . . .

"We used to learn lists of the British possessions, with their total exports and imports in money. I remember it as if it were yesterday. . . . Old Smugs—a hot New Imperialist—new then. . . .

"Then what is history but a long struggle of men to find peace and safety, and how they have been prevented by baseness and greed and folly? Is that right? No, folly and baseness—and hate. . . . Hate certainly. . . . All history is one dramatic story, of man blundering his way from the lonely ape to the world commonwealth. All history is each man's adventure. But what teacher makes history much more than a dwarfish twaddle about boundaries and kings and wars? Dwarfish twaddle. History! It went nowhere. It did nothing. Was there ever anything more like a crowd of people getting into an omnibus without wheels than the History Schools at Oxford? Or your History Tripos?" . . . Oswald repeated his image and saw that it was good.

"What is the teaching of a language again but teaching the knowledge of another people—an exposition of the soul of another people—a work of union? . . . But you see what I mean by all this; this idea of a great world of co-operating peoples; it is not just a diplomatic scheme, not something far off that Foreign Offices are doing; it is an idea that must revolutionize the lessons of a child in the nursery and alter the maps upon every schoolroom wall. And frame our lives

altogether. Or be nothing. The World Peace. To that we
all belong. I have a fancy— As though this idea had been
hovering over the world, unsubstantial, unable to exist—until
all this blood-letting, this torment and disaster gave it a
body. . . .

"What I am saying to you the University ought to have
said to you.

"Instead of Universities"—he sought for a phrase and
produced one that against the nocturnal dark seemed brilliant
and luminous. "Instead of the University *passant re-
gardant,* we want the University militant. We want Universities all round and about the world, associated, working
to a common end, drawing together all the best minds and
the finest wills, a myriad of multi-coloured threads, into one
common web of a world civilization."

§ 7

Also that night Oswald made a discourse upon the English.

"Yours is a great inheritance, Joan and Peter," he said to
the darkness. "You are young; that is a great thing in
itself. The world cries out now for the young to enter into
possession. And also—do you ever think of it?—you are
English, Joan and Peter. . . .

"Let me say something to you before we have done, something out of my heart. Have I ever canted patriotism to
you? No! Am I an aggressive Imperialist? Am I not a
Home Ruler? For Ireland. For India. The best years of
my life have been spent in saving black men from white—
and mostly those white men were of our persuasion, men of
the buccaneer strain, on the loot. But now that we three are
here together with no one else to hear us, I will confess. I
tell you there is no race and no tradition in the whole world
that I would change for my English race and tradition. I
do not mean the brief tradition of this little Buckingham
Palace and Westminster system here that began yesterday
and will end tomorrow, I mean the great tradition of the
English that is spread all over the earth, the tradition of
Shakespeare and Milton, of Newton and Bacon, of Runnymede and Agincourt, the tradition of the men who speak

fairly and act fairly, without harshness and without fear,
who face whatever odds there are against them and take no
account of Kings. It is in Washington and New York and
Christchurch and Sydney, just as much as it is in Pelham
Ford. . . . Well, upon us more than upon any other single
people rests now for a time the burthen of human destiny.
Upon us and France. France is the spear head but we are
the shaft. If we fail, mankind may fail. We English have
made the greatest empire that the world has ever seen; across
the Atlantic we have also made the greatest republic. And
these are but phases in our task. The better part of our
work still lies before us. The weight is on us now. It was
Milton who wrote long ago that when God wanted some task
of peculiar difficulty to be done he turned to his Englishmen.
And he turns to us today. Old Milton saw English shine
clear and great for a time and then pass into the darkness.
. . . He didn't lose his faith. . . . Church and crown are no
part of the real England which we inherit. . . .

"We have no reason to be ashamed of our race and country, Joan and Peter, for all the confusion and blundering of
these last years. Our generals and politicians have missed
opportunity after opportunity. I cannot talk yet of such
things. . . . The blunderings. . . . The slackness. . . . Hanoverian England with its indolence, its dulness, its economic
uncleanness, its canting individualism, its contempt for science and system, has been an England darkened, an England
astray——. Young England has had to pay at last for all
those wasted years—and has paid. . . . My God! the men we
have expended already in fighting these Germans, the brave,
beautiful men, the jesting common men, the fresh boys, so
cheerful and kind and gallant! . . . And the happiness that
has died! And the shame of following after clumsy, mean
leadership in the sight of all the world! . . . But there rests
no stain on our blood. For our people here and for the
Americans this has been a war of honour. We did not come
into this war for sordid or narrow ends. Our politicians
when they made base treaties had to hide them from our
people. . . . Even in the face of the vilest outrages, even
now the English keep a balanced justice and will not hate

the German common men for things they have been forced
to do.   Yesterday I saw the German prisoners who work at
Stanton getting into the train and joking with their guard.
They looked well fed and healthy and uncowed.   One carried a bunch of primroses.   No one has an ill word for these
men on all the country-side. . . . Does any other people in
the world treat prisoners as we treat them? . . .

"Well, the time has come for our people now to go on from
Empire and from Monroe doctrine, great as these ideas have
been, to something still greater; the time has come for us to
hold out our hands to every man in the world who is ready
for a disciplined freedom.   The German has dreamt of setting up a Cæsar over the whole world.   Against that we now
set up a disciplined world freedom.   For ourselves and all
mankind. . . .

"Joan and Peter, that is what I have been coming to in
all this wandering discourse.   Yours is a great inheritance.
You and your generation have to renew and justify England
in a new world.   You have to link us again in a common
purpose with our kind everywhere.   You have to rescue our
destinies, the destinies of the world, from these stale quarrels; you have to take the world out of the hands of these
weary and worn men, these old and oldish men, these men who
can learn no more.   You have to reach back and touch the
England of Shakespeare, Milton, Raleigh, and Blake—and
that means you have to go forward.   You have to take up the
English tradition as it was before church and court and a
base imperialism perverted it.   You have to become political.
Now.   You have to become responsible.   Now.   You have to
create.   Now.   You, with your fresh vision, with the lessons
you have learnt still burning bright in your minds, you have
to remake the world.   Listen when the old men tell you facts,
for very often they know.   Listen when they reason, they
will teach you many twists and turns.   But when they dog-
matize, when they still want to rule unquestioned, and, above
all, when they say *'impossible,'* even when they say *'wait—
be dilatory and discreet,'* push them aside.   Their minds
squat crippled beside dead traditions. . . . That England of
the Victorian old men, and its empire and its honours and its

court and precedences, it is all a dead body now, it has died as the war has gone on, and it has to be buried out of our way lest it corrupt you and all the world again. . . .''

§ 8

We underrate the disposition of youth to think for itself. Oswald set himself to deliver this Valediction of his after dinner on Friday evening. . . .

Joan was hesitating between a game of Demon Patience with Peter—in which she always played thirteen to his eleven and usually won in spite of the handicap—and an inclination for Bach's *Passacaglia* upon the pianola in the study. Peter expressed himself ready for whatever she chose; he would play D.P. or read *Moll Flanders*—he had just discovered the delight of that greatest of all eighteenth century novels. He was sitting on the couch in the library and Joan was standing upon the hearthrug, regarding him thoughtfully, when Oswald came in. He stopped to hear what Peter was saying, with his one eye intent on Joan's pretty gravity.

"No," he interrupted. "This is my evening.

"You see," he said, coming up to the fire; "I want to talk to you young people. I want to know some things—— I want to know what you make of life. . . . I want . . . an exchange of views.''

He stood with his back to the fire and smiled at Joan's grave face close to his own. "I've got to talk to you," he said, "very seriously. It's necessary.''

Having paralysed them by this preface he sat down in his deep armchair, pulled it an inch or so towards the fire, and leaning forward, with his eye on the spitting coals, began.

"I wish I could talk better, Joan and Peter. . . . I know I've never been a good talker—it's been rather a loss between us all. And now particularly. . . . I want to talk. . . . You must let me get it out in my own way. . . .

"You see," he went on after a moment or so to rally his forces, "I've been your guardian, I've had your education and your affairs in my hands, for fifteen years. So far as

the affairs go, Sycamore, you know—— We won't go into
that. That's all plain sailing. But it's the education I want
to talk about—and your future. You are now both of age.
Well past. You're on the verge of twenty-five, Peter—in a
month or so. You're both off now—housekeeping. You're
dropping the pilot. It's high time, I suppose. . . ."

Joan glanced at Peter, and then sank noiselessly into a
crouching attitude close to Oswald's knee. He paused to
stroke her hair.

"I've been trying to get you all that I could get you. . . .
Education. . . . I've had to blunder and experiment. I
ought to tell you what I've aimed at and what I've done, take
stock with you of the world I've educated you for and the
part you're going to play in it. Take stock. . . . It's been a
badly planned undertaking, I know. But then it's such a
surprising and unexpected world. All the time I've been
learning, and most things I've learnt more or less too late
to use the knowledge properly. . . ."

He paused.

Peter looked at his guardian and said nothing. Oswald
patted the head at his knee in return for a caress. It was an
evasive, even apologetic pat, for he did not want to be distracted by affection just then.

"This war has altered the whole world," he went on.
"Life has become stark and intense, and when I took this on
—when I took up the task of educating you—our world here
seemed the most wrapped up and comfortable and secure
world you can possibly imagine. Comfortable to the pitch
of stuffiness. Most English people didn't trouble a bit about
the shape of human life; they thought it was—well, rather
like a heap of down cushions. For them it was. For most
of Europe and America. . . . They thought it was all right
and perfectly safe—if only you didn't bother. And education had lost its way. Yes. That puts the case. *Education
had lost its way.*"

Oswald paused again. He fixed his one eye firmly on a
glowing cavity in the fire, as though that contained the very
gist of his thoughts.

"What is education up to?" he asked. "What *is* education?" . . .

Thereupon of course he ought to have gone on to the passage beginning, ''Consider this beast we are, this thing man!'' as he had already rehearsed it overnight. But Peter had not learnt his part properly.

''I suppose it's fitting the square natural man into the round hole of civilized life,'' Peter threw out.

This reply greatly disconcerted Oswald. ''Exactly,'' he said, and was for some moments at a loss.

''Yes,'' he said, rallying. ''But what is civilized life?''

''Oh! . . . Creative activities in an atmosphere of helpful goodwill,'' Peter tried in the brief pause that followed.

Oswald had a disagreeable feeling that he was getting to the end of his discourse before he delivered its beginning. ''Yes,'' he said again. ''Yes. But for that you must have a political form.''

''The World State,'' said Peter.

''The League of Free Nations,'' said Oswald, ''to enforce Peace throughout the earth.''

The next remark that came from Peter was still more unexpected and embarrassing.

''Peace is nothing,'' said Peter.

Oswald turned his red eye upon his ward, in profound amazement.

Did they differ fundamentally in their idea of the human future?

''Peace, my dear Peter, is everything,'' he protested.

''But, sir, it's nothing more than the absence of war. It's a negative. In itself it's—vacuum. You can't live in a vacuum.''

''But I mean an active peace.''

''That would be something more than peace. War is an activity. Peace is not. If you take war out of the world, you must have some other activity.''

''But doesn't the organization of the World Peace in itself constitute an activity?''

''That would be a diminishing activity, sir. Like a man getting himself morphia and taking it and going to sleep. A World Peace would release energy, and as the energy was released, if the end were merely peace, there would be less need for it. Until things exploded.''

Great portions of Oswald's Valediction broke away and vanished for ever into the limbo of unspoken discourses.

"But would you have war go on, Peter?"

"Not in its present form. But struggle and unification, which is the end sought in all struggles, must go on in some form, sir," said Peter, "while life goes on. We have to get the World State and put an end to war. I agree. But the real question is what are you going to do with our Peace? What struggle is to take the place of war? What is man-kind going to *do?* Most wars have come about hitherto be-cause somebody was bored. Do you remember how bored we all were in 1914? And the rotten way we were all going on then? A World State or a League of Nations with nothing to do but to keep the peace will bore men intolerably. . . . That's what I like about the Germans."

"What you *like* about the Germans!" Oswald cried in horror.

"They *did* get a move on, sir," said Peter.

"We don't want a preventive League of Nations," Peter expanded. "It's got to be creative or nothing. Or else we shall be in a sort of perpetual Coronation year—with nothing doing on account of the processions. Horrible!"

For a little while Oswald made no reply. He could not recall a single sentence of the lost Valediction that was at all appropriate here, and he was put out and distressed beyond measure that Peter could find anything to "like" about the Germans.

"A World Peace for its own sake is impossible," Peter went on. "The Old Experimenter would certainly put a spoke into that wheel."

"Who is the Old Experimenter?" asked Oswald.

"He's a sort of God I have," said Peter. "Something between theology and a fairy tale. I dreamt about him. When I was delirious. He doesn't rule the world or any-thing of that sort, because he doesn't want to, but he keeps on dropping new things into it. To see what happens. Like a man setting himself problems to work out in his head. He lives in a little out-of-the-way office. That's the idea."

"You haven't told me about him," said Joan.

"I shall some day," said Peter. "When I feel so dis-posed. . . ."

"This is very disconcerting," said Oswald, much per-plexed. He scowled at the fire before him. "But you do realize the need there is for some form of world state and some ending of war? Unless mankind is to destroy itself altogether."

"Certainly, sir," said Peter. "But we aren't going to do that on a peace proposition simply. It's got to be a positive proposal. You know, sir——"

"I wish you'd call me Nobby," said Oswald.

"It's a vice contracted in the army, this Sir-ing," said Peter. "It's Nobby in my mind, anyhow. But you see, I've got a kind of habit, at night and odd times, of thinking over my little misadventure with that balloon and my scrap with von Papen. They are my stock dreams, with extra details worked in, nasty details some of them . . . and then I wake up and think about them. I think over the parachute affair more than the fight, because it lasted longer and I wasn't so active. I felt it more. Especially being shot in the legs. . . . That sort of dream when you float helpless. . . . But the thing that impresses me most in reflecting on those little experiences is the limitless amount of intelligence that ex-pended itself on such jobs as breaking my wrist, splintering my shoulder-blade and smashing up my leg. The amount of ingenuity and good workmanship in my instruments and the fittings of my basket, for example, was extraordinary, having regard to the fact that it was just one small item in an ar-tillery system for blowing Germans to red rags. And the stuff and intelligence they were putting up against me, that too was wonderful; the way the whole problem had been thought out, the special clock fuse and so on. Well, my point is that the chap who made that equipment wasn't particularly interested in killing me, and that the chaps who made my outfit weren't particularly keen on the slaughter of Germans. But they had nothing else to do. They were brought up in a pointless world. They were caught by a vulgar quarrel. What did they care for the Kaiser? Old ass! What they were interested in was making the things. . . ."

Peter became very earnest in his manner. "No peace, as

we have known peace hitherto, offers such opportunities for good inventive work as war does. That's my point, Nobby. There's no comparison between the excitement and the endless problems of making a real, live, efficient submarine, for example, that has to meet and escape the intensest risks, and the occupation of designing a great, big, safe, upholstered liner in which fat swindlers can cross the Atlantic without being seasick. War tempts imaginative, restless people, and a stagnant peace bores them. And you've got to reckon with intelligence and imagination in this world, Nobby, more than anything. They aren't strong enough to control perhaps, but they will certainly upset. Inventive, restless men are the particular instruments of my Old Experimenter. He prefers them now to plague, pestilence, famine, flood and earthquake. They are more delicate instruments. And more efficient. And they won't *stand* a passive peace. Under no circumstances can you hope to induce the chap who contrived the clock fuse and the chap who worked out my gas bag or the chap with a new aeroplane gadget, and me—me, too—to stop cerebrating and making our damndest just in order to sit about safely in meadows joining up daisy chains—like a beastly lot of figures by Walter Crane. The Old Experimenter finds some mischief still for idle brains to do. He insists on it. That's fundamental to the scheme of things."

"But that's no reason," interrupted Oswald, "why you and the inventors who were behind you, and the Germans who made and loaded and fired that shell, shouldn't all get together to do something that will grow and endure. Instead of killing one another."

"Ah, that's it!" said Peter. "But the word for that isn't Peace."

"Then what is the word for it?"

"I don't know," said Peter. "The Great Game, perhaps."

"And where does it take you?"

Peter threw out his hands. "It's an exploration," he said. "It will take man to the centre of the earth; it will take him to the ends of space, between the atoms and among the stars. How can we tell beforehand? You must have faith. But of one thing I am sure, that man cannot stagnate.

It is forbidden. It is the uttermost sin. Why, the Old Man will come out of his office himself to prevent it! This war and all the blood and loss of it is because the new things are entangled among old and dead things, worn-out and silly things, and we've not had the vigour to get them free. Old idiot nationality, national conceit—expanding to imperialism, nationality in a state of megalomania, has been allowed to get hold of the knife that was meant for a sane generation to carve out a new world with. Heaven send he cuts his own throat this time! Or else there may be a next time. . . . I'm all for the one world state, and the end of flags and kings and custom houses. But I have my doubts of all this talk of making the world safe—safe for democracy. I want the world made one for the adventure of mankind, which is quite another story. I have been in the world now, Nobby, for five-and-twenty years, and I am only beginning to suspect the wonder and beauty of the things we men might know and do. If only we could get our eyes and hands free of the old inheritance. What has mankind done yet to boast about? I despise human history—because I believe in God. Not the God you don't approve of, Nobby, but in my Old Experimenter, whom I confess I don't begin to understand, and in the far-off, eternal scheme he hides from us and which he means us to develop age by age. Oh! I don't understand him, I don't begin to explain him; he's just a figure for what I feel is the reality. But he is right, he is wonderful. And instead of just muddling about over the surface of his universe, we have to get into the understanding of it to the very limits of our ability, to live our utmost and do the intensest best we can.''

''Yes,'' said Oswald; ''yes.'' This was after his own heart, and yet it did not run along the lines of the Valedictory that had flowered with such Corinthian richness overnight. He had been thinking then of world peace; what Peter was driving at now was a world purpose; but weren't the two after all the same thing? He sat with his one eye reflecting the red light of the fire, and the phrases that had come in such generous abundance overnight now refused to come at all.

Peter, on the couch, continued to think aloud.

"Making the world safe for democracy," said Peter. "That isn't quite it. If democracy means that any man may help who can, that school and university will give every man and woman the fairest chance, the most generous inducement to help, to do the thing he can best do under the best conditions, then, *Yes;* but if democracy means getting up a riot and boycott among the stupid and lazy and illiterate whenever anything is doing, then I say *No!* Every human being has got to work, has got to take part. If our laws and organization don't insist upon that, the Old Experimenter will. So long as the world is ruled by stale ideas and lazy ideas, he is determined that it shall flounder from war to war. Now what does this democracy mean? Does it mean a crowd of primitive brutes howling down progress and organization? because if it does, I want to be in the machine-gun section. When you talk of education, Nobby, you think of highly educated people, of a nation instructed through and through. But what of democracy in Russia, where you have a naturally clever people in a state of peasant ignorance—who can't even read? Until the schoolmaster has talked to every one for ten or twelve years, can you have what President Wilson thinks of as democracy at all?"

"Now there you meet me," said Oswald. "That is the idea I have been trying to get at with you." And for some minutes the palatial dimensions of the lost Valedictory loomed out. Where he had said "peace" overnight, however, he now said progress.

But the young man on the couch was much too keenly interested to make a good audience. When presently Oswald propounded his theory that all the great world religions were on the side of this World Republic that he and Peter desired, Peter demurred.

"But is that true of Catholicism for instance?" said Peter.

Oswald quoted, "I am the Vine and ye are the Branches."

"Yes," said Peter. "But look at the Church itself. Don't look at the formula but at the practice and the daily teaching. Is it truly a growing Vine?" The reality of Catholicism, Peter argued, was a traditional, sacramental religion, a narrow fetish religion with a specialized priest, it was concerned primarily with another world, it set its face against any conception of a scheme of progress in this world apart from its legend of the sacrifice of the Mass.

"All good Catholics sneer at progress," said Peter. "Take Belloc and Chesterton, for example; they *hate* the idea of men working steadily for any great scheme of effort here. They hold by stagnant standards, planted deep in the rich mud of life. What's the Catholic conception of human life? —guzzle, booze, call the passion of the sexes unclean and behave accordingly, confess, get absolution, and at it again. Is there any recognition in Catholicism of the duty of keeping your body fit or your brain active? They're worse than the man who buried his talent in a clean napkin; they bury it in wheezy fat. It's a sloven's life. What have we in common with that? Always they are harking back to the thirteenth century, to the peasant life amidst dung and chickens. It's a different species of mind from ours, with the head and feet turned backward. What is the good of expecting the Pope, for instance, and his Church to help us in creating a League of Nations? His aim would be a world agreement to stop progress, and we want to release it. He wants peace in order to achieve nothing, and we want peace in order to do everything. What is the good of pretending that it is the same peace? A Catholic League of Nations would be a conspiracy of stagnation, another Holy Alliance. What real world unity can come through them? Every step on the way to the world state and the real unification of men will be fought by the stagnant men and the priests. Why blind ourselves to that? Progress is a religion in itself. Work and learning are our creed. We cannot make terms with any other creed. The priest has got his God and we seek our God for ever. The priest is finished and completed and self-satisfied, and we—we are beginning. . . ."

§ 9

There were two days yet before Peter went back to his work in London. Saturday dawned blue and fine, and Joan and he determined to spend it in a long tramp over the Hertfordshire hills and fields. He meant to stand no nonsense from his foot. "If I can't walk four miles an hour then I must do two," he said. "And if the pace is too slow for you, Joan, you must run round and round me and bark." They took a long route by field and lane through Albury and Furneaux Pelham to the little inn at Stocking Pelham, where they got some hard biscuits and cheese and shandygaff, and came home by way of Patmore Heath, and the golden oaks and the rivulet. And as they went Peter talked of Oswald.

"Naturally he wants to know what we are going to do," said Peter, and then, rather inconsequently, "He's ill.

"This war is like a wasting fever in the blood and in the mind," said Peter. "All Europe is ill. But with him it mixes with the old fever. That splinter at Fricourt was no joke for him. He oughtn't to have gone out. He's getting horribly lean, and his eye is like a garnet."

"I love him," said Joan.

But she did not want to discuss Oswald just then.

"About this new theology of yours, Peter," she said. . . .

"Well?" said Peter.

"What do you mean by this Old Experimenter of yours? Is he—*God?*"

"I don't know. I thought he was. He's—— He's a Symbol. He's just a Caricature I make to express how all *this*"—Peter swept his arm across the sunlit world—"seems to stand to me. If one can't draw the thing any better, one has to make a caricature."

Joan considered that gravely.

"I thought of him first in my dream as the God of the Universe," Peter explained.

"You couldn't love a God like that," Joan remarked.

"Heavens, *no!* He's too vast, too incomprehensible. I love you—and Oswald—and the R.F.C., Joan, and biology. But he's above and beyond that sort of thing."

"Could you pray to him?" asked Joan.

"Not to *him*," said Peter.

"I pray," said Joan. "Don't you?"

"And swear," said Peter.

"One prays to something—it isn't oneself."

"The fashion nowadays is to speak of the God in the Heart and the God in the Universe."

"Is it the same God?"

"Leave it at that," said Peter. "We don't know. All the waste and muddle in religion is due to people arguing and asserting that they are the same, that they are different but related, or that they are different but opposed. And so on, and so on. How can we know? What need is there to know? In view of the little jobs we are doing. Let us leave it at that."

Joan was silent for a while. "I suppose we must," she said.

"And what are we going to do with ourselves," asked Joan, "when the war is over?"

"They can't keep us in khaki for ever," Peter considered. "There's a Ministry of Reconstruction foozling away in London, but it's never said a word to me of the some-day that is coming. I suppose it hasn't learnt to talk yet."

"What do you think of doing?" asked Joan.

"Well, first—a good medical degree. Then I can doctor if I have to. But, if I'm good enough, I shall do research. I've a sort of feeling that along the border line of biology and chemistry I might do something useful. I've some ideas. . . . I suppose I shall go back to Cambridge for a bit. We neither of us need earn money at once. It will be queer—after being a grown-up married man—to go back to proctors and bulldogs. What are *you* going to do, Joan, when you get out of uniform?"

"Look after you first, Petah. Oh! it's worth doing. And it won't take me all my time. And then I've got my own ideas. . . ."

"Out with 'em, Joan."

"Well——"

"Well?"

"Petah, I shall learn plumbing."

"Jobbing?"

"No. And bricklaying and carpentry. All I can. And then I am going to start building houses."

"Architect?"

"As little as possible," said Joan. "No. No beastly Architecture for Art's sake for me! Do you remember how people used to knock their heads about at The Ingle-Nook?

I've got some money. Why shouldn't I be able to build houses as well as the fat builder-men with big, flat thumbs who used to build houses before the war?''

"Jerry-building?"

"High-class jerry-building, if you like. Cottages with sensible insides, real insides, and not so much waste space and scamping to make up for it. They're half a million houses short in this country already. There's something in building appeals to my sort of imagination. And I'm going to make money, Petah.''

"I love the way you carry your tail," said Peter. "Always.''

"Well, doing running repairs hardens a woman's soul.''

"You'll make more money than I shall, perhaps. But now I begin to understand all these extraordinary books you've been studying. . . . I might have guessed. . . . Why not?''

He limped along, considering it. "Why shouldn't you?" he said. "A service flat will leave your hands free. . . . I've always wondered secretly why women didn't plunge into that sort of business more.''

"It's been just diffidence," said Joan.

"*Click!*" said Peter. "That's gone, anyhow. If a lot of women do as you do and become productive for good, this old muddle of a country will sit up in no time. It doubles the output. . . . I wonder if the men will like working under you?''

"There'll be a boss in the background," said Joan. "Mr. John Debenham. Who'll never turn up. Being, in fact, no more than camouflage for Joan of that ilk. I shall be just my own messenger and agent.

"One thing I know," said Joan, "and that is, that I will make a cottage or a flat that won't turn a young woman into an old one in ten years' time. Living in that Jepson flat without a servant has brightened me up in a lot of ways. . . . And a child will grow up in my cottages without being crippled in its mind by awkwardness and ugliness. . . . This sort of thing always has been woman's work really. Only we've been so busy chittering and powdering our silly noses —and laying snares for our Peters. Who didn't know what was good for them.''

Peter laughed and was amused. He felt a pleasant assurance that Joan really was going to build houses.

"Joan," he said, "it's a bleak world before us—and I hate to think of Nobby. He's so *ill*. But the work—the good hard work—there's times when I rather like to think of that. . . . They were beastly years just before the war."

"I hated them," said Joan.

"But what a lot of stuff there was about!" said Peter. "The petrol! Given away, practically, along the roadside everywhere. And the joints of meat. Do you remember the big hams we used to have on the sideboard? For breakfast. A lot of sausages going sizzle! Eggs galore! Bacon! Haddock. Perhaps cutlets. And the way one could run off abroad!"

"To Italy," said Joan dangerously.

"God knows when those times will come back again! Not for years. Not for our lifetimes."

"If they came back all at once we'd have indigestion," said Joan.

"Orgy," said Peter. "But they won't." . . .

Presently their note became graver.

"We've got to live like fanatics. If a lot of us don't live like fanatics, this staggering old world of ours won't recover. It will stagger and then go flop. And a race of Bolshevik peasants will breed pigs among the ruins. We owe it to ourselves, we owe it to the world to prevent that."

"And we owe it to the ones who have died," said Joan.

She hesitated, and then she began to tell him something of the part Wilmington had played in their lives.

They went through field after field, through gates and over stiles and by a coppice spangled with primroses, while she told him of the part that Wilmington had played in bringing them together; Wilmington who was now no more than grey soil where the battle still raged in France. Many were the young people who talked so of dead friends in those days. Their voices became grave and faintly deferential, as though they had invoked a third presence to mingle with their duologue. They were very careful to say nothing and to think as little as possible that might hurt Wilmington's self-love.

Presently they found themselves speculating again about

the kind of world that lay ahead of them—whether it would
be a wholly poor world or a poverty-struck world infested
and devastated by a few hundred millionaires and their fol-
lowings. Poor we were certain to be. We should either
be sternly poor or meanly poor. But Peter was disposed to
doubt whether the war millionaires would "get away with
the swag."

"There's too much thinking and reading nowadays for
that," said Peter. "They won't get away with it. This is
a new age, Joan. If they try that game they won't have five
years' run."

No, it would be a world generally poor, a tired but chast-
ened world getting itself into order again. . . . Would
there be much music in the years ahead? Much writing or
art? Would there be a new theatre and the excitement of
first nights again? Should we presently travel by aeroplane,
and find all the world within a few days' journey? They
were both prepared to resign themselves to ten years' of work
and scarcity, but they both clung to the hope of returning
prosperity and freedom after that.

"Well, well, Joan," said Peter, "these times teach us to
love. I'm crippled. We've got to work hard. But I'm not
unhappy. I'm happier than I was when I had no idea of
what I wanted in life, when I lusted for everything and
was content with nothing, in the days before the war. I'm
a wise old man now with my stiff wrist and my game leg.
You change everything, Joan. You make everything worth
while."

"I'd like to think it was me," said Joan idiomatically.

"It's you. . . .

"After all there must be some snatches of holiday. I shall
walk with you through beautiful days—as we are doing today—days that would only be like empty silk purses if it
wasn't that they held you in them. Scenery and flowers and
sunshine mean nothing to me—until you come in. I'm blind
until you give me eyes. Joan, do you know how beautiful
you are? When you smile? When you stop to think?
Frowning a little. When you look—yes, just like that."

"*No!*" said Joan, but very cheerfully.

"But you are—you are endlessly beautiful. Endlessly.

Making love to Joan—it's the intensest of joys. Every time—— As if one had just discovered her.''

''There's a certain wild charm about Petah,'' Joan admitted, ''for a coarse taste.''

''After all, whether it's set in poverty or plenty,'' said Peter; ''whether it's rational or irrational, making love is still at the heart of us humans.'' . . .

For a time they exulted shamelessly in themselves. They talked of the good times they had had together in the past. They revived memories of Bungo Peter and the Sagas that had slumbered in silence since the first dawn of adolescence. She recalled a score of wonderful stories and adventures that he had altogether forgotten. She had a far clearer and better memory for such things than he. ''D'you remember lightning slick, Petah? And how the days went faster? D'you remember how he put lightning slick on his bicycle?'' . . .

But Peter had forgotten that.

''And when we fought for that picshua you made of Adela,'' Joan said. ''When I bit you. . . . It was my first taste of you, Petah. You tasted dusty. . . .''

''I suppose we've always had a blind love for each other,'' said Peter, ''always.''

''I hated you to care for any one but myself,'' said Joan, ''since ever I can remember. I hated even Billy.''

''It's well we found out in time,'' said Peter.

''*I* found out,'' said Joan.

''Ever since we stopped being boy and girl together,'' said Peter, ''I've never been at peace in my nerves and temper till now. . . . Now I feel as though I swung free in life, safe, sure, content.''

''*Content*,'' weighed Joan suspiciously. ''But you're still in love with me, Petah?''

''Not particularly *in* love,'' said Peter. ''No. But I'm loving you—as the June sun loves an open meadow, shining all over it. I shall always love you, Joan, because there is no one like you in all the world. No one at all. Making love happens, but love endures. How can there be companionship and equality except between the like?—who can keep step, who can climb together, joke broad and shameless, and never struggle for the upper hand? And where in all the world shall I find that, Joan, but in you? Listen to wisdom, Joan! There are two sorts of love between men and women, and only two—love like the love of big carnivores who know their mates and stick to them, or love like some man who follows a woman home because he's never seen anything like her before. I've done with that sort of love for ever. There's men who like to exaggerate every difference in women. They pretend women are mysterious and dangerous and wonderful. They like sex served up with lies and lingerie. . . . Where's the love in that? Give me my old brown Joan.''

"Not so beastly brown," said Joan.

"Joan *nature.*"

"Tut, tut!" said Joan.

"There's people who scent themselves to make love," said Peter.

"Experienced Petah," said Joan.

"I've read of it," said Peter, and a little pause fell between them. . . .

"Every one ought to be like us," said Joan sagely, with the spring sunshine on her dear face.

"It takes all sorts to make a world," said Peter.

"Everybody ought to have a lover," said Joan. "Everybody. There's no clean life without it." . . .

"We've been through some beastly times, Joan. We've run some beastly risks. . . . We've just scrambled through, Joan, to love—as I scrambled through to life. After being put down and shot at." . . .

Presently Joan suspected a drag in Peter's paces and decided at the sight of a fallen tree in a little grass lane to profess fatigue. They sat down upon the scaly trunk, just opposite to where a gate pierced a budding hedge and gave a view of a long, curved ridge of sunlit blue, shooting corn with red budding and green-powdered trees beyond, and far away a woldy upland rising out of an intervening hidden valley. And Peter admitted that he, too, felt a little tired. But each was making a pretence for the sake of the other.

"We've rediscovered a lot of the old things, Joan," said

Peter. "The war has knocked sense into us. There wasn't anything to work for, there wasn't much to be loyal to in the days of the Marconi scandals and the Coronation Durbar. Slack times, more despair in them by far than in these red days. Rotten, aimless times. . . . Oh! the world's not done for. . . .

"I don't grudge my wrist or my leg," said Peter. "I can hop. I've still got five and forty years, fifty years, perhaps, to spend. In this new world." . . .

He said no more for a time. There were schemes in his head, so immature as yet that he could not even sketch them out to her.

He sat with his eyes dreaming, and Joan watched him. There was much of the noble beast in this Peter of hers. In the end now, she was convinced, he was going to be an altogether noble beast. Through her. He was hers to cherish, to help, to see grow. . . . He was her chosen man. . . . Depths that were only beginning to awaken in Joan were stirred. She would sustain Peter, and also presently she would renew Peter. A time would come when this dear spirit would be born again within her being, when the blood in her arteries and all the grace of her body would be given to a new life—to new lives, that would be beautiful variations of this dearest tune in the music of the world. . . . They would have courage; they would have minds like bright, sharp swords. They would lift their chins as Peter did. . . . It became inconceivable to Joan that women could give their bodies to bear the children of unloved men. *"Dear* Petah," her lips said silently. Her heart swelled; her hands tightened. She wanted to kiss him. . . .

Then in a whim of reaction she was moved to mockery.

"Do you feel so *very* stern and strong, dear Petah?" she whispered close to his shoulder.

He started, surprised, stared at her for a moment, and smiled into her eyes.

"Old Joan," he said and kissed her. . . .

§ 10

When he returned to the house on Monday morning after he had seen the two young people off, a burthen of desolation came upon Oswald.

It was a loneliness as acute as a physical pain. It was misery. If they had been dead, he could not have been more unhappy. The work that had been the warm and living substance of fifteen years was now finished· and done. The nest was empty. The road and the stream, the gates and the garden, the house and the hall, seemed to ache with emptiness and desertion. He went into their old study, from which they had already taken a number of their intimate treasures, and which was now as disordered as a room after a sale. Most of their remaining personal possessions were stacked ready for removal; discarded magazines and books and torn paper made an untidy heap beside the fireplace. "I could not feel a greater pain if I had lost a son," he thought, staring at these untidy vestiges.

He went to his own study and sat down at his desk, though he knew there was no power of attention in him sufficient to begin work.

Mrs. Moxton, for reasons best known to herself, was interested in his movements that morning. She saw him presently wander into the garden and then return to the hall. He took his cap and stick and touched the bell. "I'll not be back to lunch, Mrs. Moxton," he called.

"Very well, sir," said Mrs. Moxton, unseen upon the landing above, nodding her head approvingly.

At first the world outside was as lonely as his study.

He went up the valley along the high road for half a mile, and then took a winding lane under almost overhanging boughs—the hawthorn leaves now were nearly out and the elder quite—up over the hill and thence across fields and through a wood until he came to where the steep lane runs down to Braughing. And by that time, although the spring-time world was still immensely lonely and comfortless, he no longer felt that despairful sense of fresh and irremediable loss with which he started. He was beginning to real-

ize now that he had always been a solitary being; that all
men, even in crowds, carry a certain solitude with them; and
loneliness thus lifted to the level of a sustained and general
experience ceased to feel like a dagger turning in his heart.

Down the middle of Braughing village, among spaces of
grass, runs the little Quin, now a race of crystalline water
over pebbly shallows and now a brown purposefulness
flecked with foam, in which reeds bend and recover as if
they kept their footing by perpetual feats of dexterity.
There are two fords, and midway between them a little
bridge with a handrail on which Oswald stayed for a time,
watching the lives and adventures of an endless stream of
bubbles that were begotten thirty feet away where the eddy
from the depths beneath a willow root dashed against a
bough that bobbed and dipped in the water. He found a
great distraction and relief in following their adventures. On they came, large and small, in strings, in spinning groups, busy bubbles, quiet bubbles, dignified solitary
bubbles, and passed a dangerous headland of watercress
and ran the gauntlet between two big stones and then, if
they survived, came with a hopeful rush for the shadow under the bridge and vanished utterly. . . .

For all the rest of the day those streaming bubbles glittered and raced and jostled before Oswald's eyes, and made
a veil across his personal desolation. His mind swung like a
pendulum between two ideas; those bubbles were like human
life; they were not like human life. . . .

Philosophy is the greatest of anodynes.

"Why is a man's life different from a bubble? Like a
bubble he is born of the swirl of matter, like a bubble he re-
flects the universe, he is driven and whirled about by forces
he does not comprehend, he shines here and is darkened
there and is elated or depressed he knows not why, and at
last passes suddenly out into the darkness. . . ."

In the evening Oswald sat musing by his study fire, his
lamp unlit. He sat in an attitude that had long become
habitual to him, with the scarred side of his face resting upon
and ·hidden by his hand. His walk had wearied him, but
not unpleasantly, his knee was surprisingly free from pain,
and he was no longer acutely unhappy. The idea, a very

engaging idea, had come into his head that it was not really the education of Joan and Peter that had come to an end, but his own. They were still learners—how much they had still to learn! At Peter's age he had not yet gone to Africa. They had finished with school and college perhaps, but they were but beginning in the university of life. Neither of them had yet experienced a great disillusionment, neither of them had been shamed or bitterly disappointed; they had each other. They had seen the great war indeed, and Peter knew now what wounds and death were like—but he himself had been through that at one-and-twenty. Neither had had any such dark tragedy as, for example, if one of them had been killed, or if one of them had betrayed and injured the other. Perhaps they would always have fortunate lives.

But he himself had had to learn the lesson to the end. His life had been a darkened one. He had loved intensely and lost. He had had to abandon his chosen life work when it was barely half done. He had a present sense of the great needs of the world, and he was bodily weak and mentally uncertain. He would spend days now of fretting futility, unable to achieve anything. He loved these dear youngsters, but the young cannot give love to the old because they do not yet understand. He was alone. And yet, it was strange, he kept on. With such strength as he had he pursued his ends. Those two would go on, full of hope, helping one another, thinking together, succeeding. The lesson he had learnt was that without much love, without much vitality, with little hope of seeing a single end achieved for which he worked, he could still go on.

He drifted through his memories, seeking for the motives that had driven him on from experience to experience. But while he could remember the experiences it was very hard now to recover any inkling of his motives. He remembered himself at school as a violent egotist, working hard, openly and fairly, for his ascendancy in the school games, working hard secretly for his school position. It seemed now as though all that time he had been no more than a greed and a vanity. . . . Was that fair to himself? Or had he forgotten the redeeming dreams of youth? . . .

The scene shifted to the wardroom of his first battleship,

and then to his first battle. He saw again the long low line
of the Egyptian coast, and the batteries of Alexandria and
Ramleh spitting fire and the *Condor* standing in. He recalled the tense excitement of that morning, the boats rowing to land, but strangely enough the incident that had won
him the Victoria Cross had been blotted completely from his
mind by his injury. He could not recover even the facts,
much less the feel of that act. . . . Why had he done what
he had done? Did he himself really do it? . . . Then very
vividly came the memory of his first sight of his smashed,
disfigured face. That had been horrible at the time—in a
way it was horrible still—but after that it seemed as though
for the first time he had ceased then to be an egotism, a
vanity. After that the memories of impersonal interests
began. He thought of his attendance at Huxley's lectures
at South Kensington and the wonder of making his first dis-
sections. About that time he met Dolly, but here again was
a queer gap; he could not remember anything very distinctly
about his early meetings with Dolly except that she wore
white and that they happened in a garden.

Yet, in a little while, all his being had been hungry for
Dolly!

With his first journey into Africa all his memories became
brighter and clearer and as if a hotter sun shone upon them.
Everything before that time was part of the story of a young
man long vanished from the world, young Oswald, a personality at least as remote as Peter—very like Peter. But
with the change of scene to Africa Oswald became himself.
The man in the story was the man who sat musing in the
study chair, moved by the same motives and altogether un-
derstandable. Already in Nyasaland he was working consciously for "civilization" even as he worked today. Everything in that period lived still, with all its accompanying
feelings alive. He fought again in his first fight in Nyasaland, and recalled with complete vividness how he had loaded
and fired and reloaded and fired time after time at the
rushes of the Yao spearmen; he had fought leaning against
the stockade because he was too weary to stand upright, and
with his head and every limb aching. One man he had hit
had wriggled for a long time in the grass, and that memory

still distressed him. It trailed another memory of horror with it. In his campaign about Lake Kioga, years later, in a fight amidst some ant hills he had come upon a wounded Sudanese being eaten alive by swarms of ants. The poor devil had died with the ants still upon him. . . . Oswald could still recall the sick anguish with which he had tried in vain to save or relieve this man.

The affair was in the exact quality of his present feelings; the picture was painted from the same palette. He remembered that then, as now, he felt the same helpless perplexity at apparently needless and unprofitable human agony. And then, as now, he had not despaired. He had been able to see no reason in this suffering and no excuse for it; he could see none now, and yet he did not despair. Why did not that and a hundred other horrors overwhelm him with despair? Why had he been able to go on with life after that? And after another exquisite humiliation and disappointment? He had loved Dolly intensely, and here again came a third but less absolutely obliterated gap in his recollections. For years he had been resolutely keeping his mind off the sufferings of that time, and now they were indistinct. His memory was particularly blank now about Arthur; he was registered merely as a blonde sort of ass with a tenor voice who punched copper. That faint hostile caricature was all his mind had tolerated. But still sharp and clear, as though it had been photographed but yesterday upon his memory, was the afternoon when he had realized that Dolly was dead. That scene was life-size and intense; how in a shady place under great trees, he had leant forwards upon his little folding table and wept aloud.

What had carried him through all those things? Why had he desired so intensely? Why had he worked so industriously? Why did he possess this passion for order that had inspired his administrative work? Why had he given his best years to Uganda? Why had he been so concerned for the welfare and wisdom of Joan and Peter? Why did he work now to the very breaking-point, until sleeplessness and fever forced him to rest, for this dream of a great federation in the world—a world state he would certainly never live to see established? If he was indeed only a bubble, then

surely he was the most obstinately opinionated of bubbles.
But he was not merely a bubble. The essential self of him
was not this thing that spun about in life, that felt and
reflected the world, that missed so acutely the two dear other
bubbles that had circled about him so long and that had now
left him to eddy in his backwater while they hurried off
into the midstream of life. His essential self, the self that
mused now, that had struggled up through the egotisms of
youth to this present predominance, was something deeper
and tougher and more real than desire, than excitement, than
pleasure or pain. That was the lesson he had been learning.
There was something deeper in him to which he had been
getting down more and more as life had gone on, something
to which all the stuff of experience was incidental, something
in which there was endless fortitude and an undying resolution to do. There was something in him profounder than
the stream of accidents. . . .

He sat now with his distresses allayed, his mind playing
with fancies and metaphors and analogies. Was this profounder contentment beneath his pains and discontents the
consciousness of the bubble giving way to the underlying
consciousness of the stream? That was ingenious, but it
was not true. Men are not bubbles carried blindly on a
stream; they are rather like bubbles, but that is all. They
are wills and parts of a will that is neither the slave of the
stream of matter nor a thing indifferent to it, that is para-
doxically free and bound. They are parts of a will, but what
this great will was that had him in its grasp, that compelled
him to work, that saved him from drowning in his individual
sorrows and cares, he could not say. It was easy to draw
the analogy that a man is an atom in the life of the species
as a cell is an atom in the life of a man. But this again
was not the complete truth. Where was this alleged will
of the species? If there was indeed such a will in the species, why was there this war? And yet, whatever it might
be, assuredly there was *something* greater than himself sustaining his life. . . . To him it felt like a universal thing,
but was it indeed a universal thing? It was strangely bound
up with preferences. Why did he love and choose certain
things passionately? Why was he indifferent to others?

Why were Dolly and Joan more beautiful to him than any other women; why did he so love the sound of their voices, their movements, and the subtle lines of their faces; why did he love Peter, standing upright and when enthusiasm lit him; and why did he love the lights on polished steel. and the darknesses of deep waters, the movements of flames, and of supple, feline animals, so intensely? Why did he love these things more than the sheen on painted wood, or the graces of blonde women, or the movements of horses? And why did he love justice and the revelation of scientific laws, and the setting right of disordered things? Why did this idea of a League of Nations come to him with the effect of a personal and preferential call? All these lights and matters and aspects and personal traits were somehow connected in his mind, and had a compelling power over him. They could make him forget his safety or comfort or happiness. They had something in common among themselves, he felt, and he could not tell what it was they had in common. But whatever it was, it was the intimation of the power that sustained him. It was as if they were all reflections or resemblances of some overruling spirit, some Genius, some great ruler of the values that stood over his existence and his world. Yet that again was but a fancy—a plagiarism from Socrates. . . .

There was a light upon his life, and the truth was that he could not discover the source of the light nor define its nature; there was a presence in the world about him that made all life worth while, and yet it was Nameless and Incomprehensible. It was the Essence beyond Reality; it was the Heart of All Things. . . . Metaphors! Words! Perhaps some men have meant this when they talked of Love, but he himself had loved because of this, and so he held it must be something greater than Love. Perhaps some men have intended it in their use of the word Beauty, but it seemed to him that rather it made and determined Beauty for him. And others again have known it as the living presence of God, but the name of God was to Oswald a name battered out of all value and meaning. And yet it was by this, by this Nameless, this Incomprehensible, that he lived and was upheld. It did so uphold him that he could go on, he knew, though happiness were denied him ; though defeat and death stared him in the face. . . .

§ 11

At last he sighed and rose. He lit his reading lamp by means of a newspaper rolled up into one long spill—for there was a famine in matches just then—and sat down to the work on his desk.

THE END

Printed in the United States of America.

www.ingramcontent.com/pod-product-compliance
Lightning Source LLC
Chambersburg PA
CBHW030740030726
47497CB00001B/65